SUMMARY

Book XIV in the Vampire Queen Series

Loss left them only rage.
Until they found each other...

Cai doesn't want a servant, he doesn't want to be associated with damn vampires. Rand just wants to forget his human side, stay in his wolf form and find a violent, bloody way to bring it all to an end.

But when a young female vampire's life is at stake, the Vampire Council drafts Cai to enter a dark world he never wanted to visit again. Rand is too honorable to let him go alone, and the only way that can work is if the wolf shifter is Cai's fully marked servant, bound to the vampire for all eternity.

So fate decides these two lost souls need each other. Even if they have to tear each other apart to figure it out.

VAMPIRE'S SOUL

A Vampire Queen Series Novel

JOEY W HILL

Vampire's Soul

A Vampire Queen Series Novel - Book #14

Copyright © 2017-2019 Joey W. Hill

ALL RIGHTS RESERVED

Cover design by W. Scott Hill

SWP Digital & Print Edition publication September 2017 by Story Witch Press, 452 Mattamushkeet Dr., Little River, South Carolina 29566, USA

The following material contains graphic sexual content meant for mature readers. Reader discretion is advised.

Digital ISBN: 978-1-942122-63-0

Print ISBN: 978-1-942122-64-7

ACKNOWLEDGMENTS

As usual, I can't express enough how my critique partners' suggestions improve a book, every single time. The occasional random typo, timeline or continuity error might drive me crazy when I catch it post-publishing (despite multiple and laborious editing rounds). However, a far bigger issue to me is when the story or characters don't reach their potential because I missed a way to make them stronger, more exciting or thought-provoking.

Without my critique partners, I would miss a lot of those opportunities. Sometimes the writing process very much reflects the saying, "She missed the forest for the trees."

So thank you, Vampire Soul editing and inspiration team: Judy, Lauren, Debi, Sheri, Angela, Shi and Donna. The same way vital touches make a house a home, you all helped make Cai and Rand's book into a story. And an extra thanks to those who kept after me for a story with a wolf shifter hero. Here it is – at last!

Author Note: Cai and Rand were introduced in *Night's Templar*. While at that time it was clear they intended to have their own book, unfortunately when characters appear earlier than their own story, an author can box herself into things the muse wishes to take in a different direction. Therefore, apologies in advance for any discrepancies between their presentation in *Night's Templar* and here. We tried to reconcile the two versions and stay out of those troublesome waters, so I hope the attempts to do so will amuse, please, or pass unnoticed – but not disrupt your enjoyment of the story.

CHAPTER ONE

*S*omething was wrong.

Cai paused. No stars in the sky tonight, no moon. Heavy cloud cover and he could smell the weight of a storm brewing within it. He hoped it was a violent one, with thunder that vibrated through the ground, as lightning split the sky and rain lashed the earth. The forest creatures would take shelter while he would stand in its fury, defy heaven or hell to show their fucking selves and bring the fight to him. There was no stillness or peace in pain. Only the din of violence drowned out everything else.

Yeah, I'm in a bitch of a mood. Which only happened on days that ended in y. He frowned. What the hell day *was* it? Wednesday? What did it matter? In the wilds he preferred, time was about day or night, winter or summer.

It wasn't like he had a dinner date or a dentist appointment. *Hey doc, polish up the fangs for me. Come close, let me hear that bass drum beat in your throat.* His eyes half shut as the thought bumped up his hunger.

About time to feed again. Last time, he'd swallowed his distaste for more human-populated areas to forage in the nearest town, about twenty-five miles away. That had been nearly a month ago. Within the past several weeks, no hiker or hunter had unwisely yet conveniently chosen to be out this deep alone when he needed blood. Another meal was due.

He drew in a deep breath, taking in the heat. In the mountains of

1

West Virginia, it was closing in on fall, but summer's heat was lingering. The day's warmth still lay heavy on everything. A storm might cool things off. In a couple of ways.

He turned, his brow creasing. It was more than the impending storm, within and without. Something really was off. Wrong. Someone else's pain, a vibration of it so strong it thrummed through his nerves, tightened his gut. Empathy wasn't big on his list of personality traits, but curiosity was another matter. Paying attention often brought opportunity.

Following instinct, he cut off the deer path and moved, silent and swift, through the thick woods, emerging onto a more beaten track. Hunters used it most often, scouting out deer and other game, depending on the season. Dropping to his heels, Cai cocked his head, his senses open and sharp. He worried the rough sides and steel point of his one prosthetic fang with his tongue, an unconscious habit.

Then he scented human, and the still attached and very real fang on the other side of his mouth lengthened.

One, alone. His lips curved in a grim smile. Dinner had delivered itself.

He rose and moved without sound through the woods. While hunting, nothing would escape his notice, from the shift of a squirrel in her nest twenty feet above his head, to the rasp of a snake moving over the earth before it glided into creek water, splitting the water currents with its twisting body.

It didn't take long. With his speed, he closed in on his prey fast. He normally didn't prolong the stalking phase of things. He had no interest in playing that game. But as he perched in the crotch of a tree and studied his meal, he realized the hunter, his rifle at the ready and with night vision goggles in place, was following something.

A blood trail. It came to Cai with the wind shift and explained why the hunter was still out after dark. It was illegal for him to hunt then, but apparently what he'd shot had gotten away and he was willing to bend the law to ensure he hadn't left something injured. Cai could respect that. When he got ready to kill this guy, he'd give him the same consideration.

That didn't say anything about his own respectability. He made all his kills fast. While he knew vampires who liked toying with their prey, because they claimed the fear and suffering gave the blood an extra kick, he guessed he had a blander palate. He had no more interest in tormenting his prey than a human would his Domino's pizza.

To stay within the bounds of hunting regs, the hunter had to have made his shot by a certain time before sundown. The target had led him on a good chase. It wasn't like Cai needed to be up on West Virginia hunting regulations, but the last time he'd taken a hunter, the man had had a copy of the manual in his pack. Cai had whiled away some time reading. It would have been nicer if the guy had had a thriller or mystery tucked in the multiple pockets, but you took what you could get out here. And he'd been carrying some Skittles, which had been a tasty dessert.

The hunter Cai was following stopped. He raised the rifle, not to shoot, but to look through the scope. Abandoning stealth, he whistled and straightened. "Fucking hell. You're not a bear. Holy shit." His deep voice was tinged with excitement. "Can't fucking believe it. A wolf in West Virginia. Look at the size of you, you beautiful son of a bitch."

The wind picked up, and Cai stiffened. That wrongness, a wall of it, impacted him like a baseball bat trying to hit a home run with his jaw. The blood he was smelling wasn't human. Nor vampire. Wolf smell for certain. But he'd smelled wolf before and this had something else to it.

Something he couldn't identify, which meant it had to be something the human hunter would consider myth, and Cai had never encountered.

Cai eased forward until he could see the small clearing where the man had emerged, and what had caused his anticipation. He was no more than five feet from the man, but the human's attention was riveted on his prey. Cai didn't blame him. His gaze went there, too.

The dark form was as large as a fully grown black bear, which explained why the hunter had mistaken him for one. Now, though, the creature's head was arched back, so the triangular shape of the ears and the long nose were visible, as well as the bushy tail, limply curved along the bumpy earth. The wolf was black with only a spare peppering of silver and brown strands around his face and ruff. He was a piece of the night himself.

But Cai could see in darkness as well as he could in light. Better, in

3

some ways, because the body's energy was more distinguishable to him. The animal throbbed with a miasma of pain. When life was about to end, a being projected fear, pain. Adrenaline. Sometimes a brief flash of anger. Or resignation.

What he felt from this creature was different. There was pain, yes, but no fear. Only rage. The hunter thought the wolf was dead because he wasn't moving. But his chest wasn't rising and falling because the wolf was taking measured, shallow breaths, to fool his tracker.

The hunter was about to become the hunted, and he didn't even know it.

Cai settled back into the foliage to watch. Who passed up dinner and a show for the same price?

The hunter approached cautiously, proving he knew his trade, and poked the wolf sharply with the muzzle of the gun, still holding it in a ready position. The body gave limply, no movement.

"The guys aren't going to freaking believe this. A wolf. Where'd you come from, buddy? Think if I take you to the wildlife cops, they'd let me keep your pelt? Yeah, right." He snorted to himself. "Well, far as they and everyone else knew, wolves are extinct in these parts. My guess is you escaped from a roadside zoo. But you look too damn healthy for that."

The hunter straightened and considered the motionless creature. "Man, you are a beauty. I'll stretch my girl out on your fur in front of a fire this winter and she'll love the way it feels against all her pretty skin. Going to be a bitch to get you back to the truck, though. I'll have to use my Boy Scout training and make a litter."

Yeah, keep talking. The more he talked, the more motionless the wolf became. Humans couldn't see how dense energy became with a self-imposed stillness, that waiting to strike. But a vampire could. It was as clear to Cai as if the wolf was tying a napkin around his neck and picking up a fork and spoon, like Sylvester getting ready to dine on Tweety.

Wolves were smart, but not that smart. And they weren't this large either, particularly in a state where the species was thought to be gone, hunted to extinction decades ago.

Since vampires were so much faster and stronger than humans, an ignorant mortal would consider them magical beings. However, aside from varying levels of hypnotic compulsion skills, which suggested they were distant cousins to the python genus, most vampires didn't have any more ability to manipulate and command energy than the average human did.

Cai had a few more tools in his arsenal than the typical vampire—something he wasn't about to share with anyone other than himself—but he didn't need them for this. Vampires might not be able to do magic, but because they left their senses far more open to other world energies than Joe Human, their sharp senses wouldn't miss the wave of it Cai sensed now.

Cai wasn't sure what the wolf's deal was, but it posed no immediate challenge to him, so he'd hang around and satisfy his curiosity. Plus, the wolf could do the work of taking down his meal, before Cai embraced the challenge of taking it from him.

The hunter set his rifle aside, leaning it against a tree, and started to scout for branches to put the litter together. That was when the wolf lunged from the ground.

He sprang like a mountain lion from his resting position, impressing Cai with the power of the move. But the concussion of energy that rippled outward from the wolf told Cai how much effort it took. Magic or not, the beast was wounded. Blood had matted and soaked the fur on his haunch, leaving a muddy puddle beneath him. The bullet wound was a serious injury. Perhaps fatal out here.

It wasn't stopping him.

He was large enough that his paws landed on the hunter's shoulders as he slammed into his back, throwing him to the ground. The hunter let out a surprised shout, but he was no lightweight. He'd drawn a knife to cut branches, and he had his arm up to take the brunt of the wolf's first bite as he managed to flip and sought the wolf's unprotected side with the knife. The first strike hit the ribs and glanced off, though it tore flesh. The wolf took his own trophy, eliciting a scream as his powerful jaws snapped the bone and ripped out a chunk of flesh. He pulled back, shoved his great head under the male's now useless arm, and went for the throat.

Cai had seen wolf packs bring down deer. It was a remarkable, coordinated effort, but it wasn't pretty, because the dance to stay clear of thrashing hoofs and antlers, combined with the use of teeth as the only killing weapon, didn't make a fast, clean kill possible.

This was an ugly struggle of mere seconds. The wolf laid open the throat all the way to the cervical column. The man's death throes were short, his soul light blinking out like a popped bulb.

Well, hell. Cai preferred the carotid because the blood taste there was best. He couldn't have that now, obviously, but he was going to have to move fast if he wanted the benefit of any of it. The guy was oozing blood like a boat with a bucket-sized hole. Plus, if Cai was feeding from a corpse, it wasn't going to be over ten minutes dead. After that, the blood was like consuming days-old rotted food.

Cai emerged from his cover. The wolf sprang up and around, standing over the body, teeth bared and eyes glowing like gold embers. Blood spray from the hunter zigzagged over his face and ruff, but plenty of blood elsewhere wasn't the hunter's. The man's blade had found a couple new entry points, because blood was dripping onto the ground with the animal's movements. The wolf was also favoring the injured back leg, clawed toes curled and barely brushing the ground.

Cai obligingly bared his own fangs at the display of aggression. "That's my dinner, bitch. You're probably going to die anyway, so get the hell away from it. Go find a place to lick your wounds. I don't want to hurt you."

The wolf's lip lifted as the rumble in his throat became full-volume thunder. His expression was clear. *You and what army, motherfucker?*

The wolf was badly enough injured he probably wasn't hungry. It was the principle of the thing. His kill, no one else's. Cai could respect that opinion. What could he say? He respected the hunter, he respected the wolf. He was a respectful kind of guy. But he had no intention of being denied what he wanted.

The wolf's rage was cocked and ready to go, and Cai also understood that feeling. He didn't usually find it in an animal, because animals didn't waste time on manifesting their baggage the way humanoids did. Attack was all about prey or fear. Sometimes play.

This wolf wasn't in a playful mood. He'd let a hunter believe he was tracking him, and he'd set him up. Now he was ready to take on Cai over rights to feed that he wasn't likely to live long enough to enjoy. Even now, he was starting to sway.

That groundswell of energy hit Cai again. Natural magic, what Cai considered just a fancy word for energy use beyond the physical limits of the body. It put him on guard, though, because he still couldn't identify it. His gaze darted around the clearing while he kept the bulk of his attention on the wolf, in case he decided to spring at Cai as he had with the hunter.

Instead, the wolf sank to an elbow, slowly, visibly fighting the compulsion. Then he was literally knocked to his side by those forces Cai couldn't see. His head arched back and a strangled howl tore from his throat. He was struggling against something, with a determined ferocity that told Cai it might be harder to take his dinner from the wolf than he'd anticipated.

Cai drew closer, and the wolf's eyes focused on him, crazed, despairing. Furious. Cai stopped. One of the two golden eyes was now blue. Cobalt blue, with a dark ring around it that enhanced the size of the pupil. The other iris stayed sunlight gold. Then both eyes closed and the animal convulsed, body rippling as if water moved under the skin. Cai heard the crack of bone and the wolf snarled, pain and frustration.

Holy shit... It couldn't be. A fucking shifter.

There were rumors of their existence, so unsubstantiated they could be called fairy tales. Yet being a vampire, and knowing that a lot of what humans called imaginary creatures *could* exist, Cai wasn't in the habit of asserting something couldn't, just because *he* hadn't seen it. Even so, he'd never heard of anyone who'd seen a wolf shifter.

He was seeing one now.

The transformation energy cocooned the wolf like rope, tightening, pulling his body in multiple directions. If every shift was this brutal, Cai had no idea why any wolf shifter would do so voluntarily, and maybe they didn't. But he had to wonder if the wolf's obvious resistance to the transition was making it even more excruciating.

Maybe he thought he was more vulnerable to Cai in that form. He probably was, but...

Cai drew closer. The wolf seemed almost insensible to him now, so he dropped to his heels next to him and laid a hand on his fur. The covering felt much thinner, like a silk scarf instead of a thick pelt. That scarf was about to tear.

The magic coiled around the shifter snapped away, striking Cai with stinging heat before it dis-apparated the wolf. The shift had seemed gradual, torturous, but then, in a final blink, there he was. Cai was staring at a man lying against the corpse of another, their blood mixed together and soaking the earth beneath them.

Fuck.

Cai's gaze traveled over the shifter. As a wolf, he'd been as big as a black bear. As a human, he kept the same impressive build. Long brown hair tangled over broad shoulders, his wide chest covered with a temptingly thick mat of gleaming chestnut hair that arrowed down to cock and balls, tree trunk thighs. In the naked male's position, sprawled on one hip, Cai had a good view of his ass.

An ass worth saving, noted his dick.

Why hadn't the wolf just shifted to human when he was out of range of the hunter's sight? When the hunter stumbled on the wolf in wounded human form, he might have been curious about why the shifter was naked, but guilt over thinking one of his bullets might have missed his supposed bear and hit a camper would have made him set questions aside, and aid the wounded male.

Maybe shifters considered hospitals and doctors pretty much out of the question. Like vampires, their anatomy probably didn't exactly line up with humans.

But reviewing the evidence of the past few moments, Cai decided that wasn't why the shifter had let things play out the way they had. He'd wanted the hunter to catch up to him. He'd wanted to take him out. Cai remembered the look in the wolf's eyes as he'd sprung. He'd wanted the fight.

"Take my blood, vampire," the male growled. His voice was rough, broken. "Take all of it. I'm dying. Might as well finish it."

Well, vampires might not have realized wolf shifters existed, but this one knew enough about vampires to identify one. Cai had no idea what shifter blood would do to a vampire, but it smelled just as appetizing as the human's. More so. Cai didn't spend a lot of time worrying over those things. If he died from drinking it, he died. No great loss, as long as it was his choice.

That was the philosophy he saw in the shifter's eyes now. He knew he was dying, and he wanted it to happen according to his own terms. He'd taken out the predator who'd gotten him first, and he'd given the vampire permission to drink from him, despite knowing he could do little to stop Cai. It was another point of pride, like defending his prey against Cai when he could barely stand on his four feet.

A lot of balls on this one. Literally. Cocking his head, Cai gave them a leisurely look.

The shifter noticed him noticing. Cai stiffened as a hand that could probably palm a cantaloupe reached for his face, but there was no harm in it. The male brushed bloodstained fingers over Cai's lips and his own mouth curved in a humorless smile. Even bloody and dirty, those lips were appealingly firm, enhanced by the layer of biker-guy-sexy stubble on the strong jaw. He wound his fingers in Cai's hair, nowhere near as long as the wolfman's, but long enough to take a good grip, and he put pressure there.

"There's nothing else once the dark closes in. We both know it. Give me something good before there's nothing."

Under the rusty quality, his voice had a melodic, deep woods hillbilly kind of sound, and Cai's ears reacted to it like his taste buds did to fresh, heated blood. Cai was pretty sure he knew what the male meant, but the shifter removed all doubt when somehow he lifted his dying, bleeding body enough to wrap his arm around Cai's shoulders and bring his mouth close. Cai caught up, cupping the back of his head, tangling his fingers in brown hair as thick and soft as the wolf's pelt. He tightened his grip.

"Hold still, and I will," he ordered, meeting his gaze. As a human, both the shifter's eyes were blue, with gold flecks and a gold ring around them. Extraordinary and mesmerizing. Full of dull pain and raging need. The pain wasn't from his wounds. Cai knew that kind of pain, the empty agony of a loneliness well beyond fixing.

However, in response to Cai's order to be still, the shifter's lips curled in an appealing sneer which teased Cai's dominant instincts to bust-your-ass level. Even so, he wasn't going to deny a dying man. Not when the request served his own interests.

He brought his mouth to the other man's, stopped just short and stared into those feral eyes. "What's your name?" Cai didn't question why he wanted to know, but when the guy died, he wanted to remember him. Wanted to think of him with a name attached.

"Rand."

"Easy enough. Cai."

No need to be tentative or gentle about it, and that wasn't what the wolf wanted anyway. When Cai brought his mouth against those appealing lips, strong fingers dug into Cai's shoulders. The sound the male made in Cai's mouth was so split between human and animal, Cai's cock hardened to lead pipe from the first touch.

Hellfire... Yeah, there might not be anything after, but that was because somebody had tipped divine flame out of the heavens and given it all to this male's mouth. Cai's blood hunger disappeared, swallowed by a far different kind of greed. He didn't give a damn what was offered willingly beyond the kiss. He was going to have it all.

Heat. A slick agile tongue that played with Cai's fangs in a provocative way no dying man should have been cognizant enough to do. But hell, if the guy was dying, what better thing was there to spend his energy toward? His hands slid over Cai's hair, his neck, his shoulders, down to his biceps and gripped him as if he wouldn't ever let go. Cai broke that grip and pushed him to his back, away from the hunter and against the brown earth. He stretched over him so he could clasp his rough jaw and throat and kiss him as deep and long as he desired. He allowed the male to latch onto his upper arm and side with either hand, but the position made it clear Cai was the one in control.

He saw the flame of need and lust in Rand's blue eyes. As well as a hopeless surrender that tore into Cai's chest and opened wounds he kept closed with the help of solitude and regular doses of violence.

Sex could be violent.

It was only when he clutched the male's hip with possessive demand, and the shifter stiffened, that Cai remembered. Hell, he was mortally wounded.

Well, fuck that. This bastard was living, even if Cai had to turn him into a vampire to do it. He adjusted his hold to the male's cock, fingers wrapping around it. Despite his injuries, hell, it was semi-erect. Even at half-mast, there was way more than a handful to play with. The blue eyes darkened, a flash of surprise among the simmering ferocity. "You aren't dying," Cai said. "Your ass belongs to me."

Sparks of rebellion delivered a straightforward *fuck-you* message, and then the wolf shifter lost consciousness.

CHAPTER TWO

*T*he heat of the day had finally been swallowed by the night. Rand felt the touch of Dylef's hand. They would shift and run together tonight. Hunt for Sheba and their pups.

No. No, they wouldn't. Dylef was dead. They were dead. He imagined the young ones' fear. It had all happened so fast, they hadn't totally understood. He hoped. But when he was human, it was on constant replay in his mind, a never-ending torture session. It was why he'd stayed a wolf for so long. But not long enough. He was still alive, goddamn it.

Why the hell was he still alive?

Because I wanted you to be. It's your own fault.

Rand stiffened. He was used to the endless monologue of his own internal voice, an unwelcome intruder that never shut the hell up except when he was in wolf form. Which...he wasn't. It felt strange, his human body like ill-fitting clothing. He needed to shift, wanted to shift.

"Oh no you don't." It was a rebuke and command, and reinforced by a firm caress along his abdomen. That unexpected sensation, a humanoid touch on his humanoid flesh, effectively pulled his attention away from his unwelcome state like fresh raw meat did when he was ravenous.

"Yeah, blood's like that, too. Yours is potent, wolf. But I want something else right now."

A strong hand, more powerful than twenty of the brawny hunter he'd fought, clasped his throat. It tightened just enough to shoot his attention to his cock and make him realize it was stiffening, despite his weakened state. The vampire put his mouth over his.

Rand remembered this. Just before he thought he was going to die. Demanding, uncompromising, unsympathetic. The vampire hadn't given a damn about his condition. He'd taken what was offered and given back. Enough that Rand grudgingly remembered a fleeting spark in his soul, a reaction to finding one damn thing to regret about leaving this life behind.

The vampire's tongue was teasing his, the fangs scraping his lip. Rand growled and tried to pull him down on top of him. He wanted to feel his body against him. But as he did, pain seared through him, like an iron shoved through his thigh and side. He clutched the vampire's bare shoulder, and a growl became a low snarl.

"Yeah, ease back. Might be a little soon to get that aggressive. But you're healing good. The second mark isn't as strong for self-healing as the third, but it gave you the edge you needed to put off death for another day. And I wasn't in the mood to link our souls for all eternity, no matter how great an ass you have."

Rand opened his eyes. They were still in the forest, though a sufficient enough distance from where he'd killed the hunter that anyone coming to look for the man wouldn't stumble on this camp. Not that he suspected that posed a danger to either of them. Between vampire and wolf senses, nothing human had a chance of sneaking up on them.

He vaguely remembered the vampire over him before. Jeans and hiking shoes, a dark-colored T-shirt. The smell of cotton and denim, the leather of his belt, faint soap smells over skin and hair. Earth scent was embedded in the fanged creature, telling Rand he was also a forest-dweller. Most vampires he'd heard about, or sensed when he'd been in the city, preferred to be a shadowy part of the human world to take advantage of the comforts of that civilization. Not this one.

Rand could paint a picture with scent alone, but in his human form he added to it with sight. It wasn't a chore. As he swiveled his gaze in that direction, he saw the vampire wore nothing, making Rand's already dry throat drier, particularly as the male rose and moved to the small fire.

He was tall, tall as Rand. Since all vampires were reputedly a seduction to the senses, it was no surprise to see he was pleasing to look upon. But the sharp need that jammed itself through Rand's balls and up into his cock like a railroad spike didn't want to argue about how much of the desire came from Rand, and how much from the vampire's effect on any humanoid that could feel lust.

He should be near death, with no thoughts to spare on sex. Yet he couldn't take his eyes from calves, thighs, ass, back and shoulders. The muscle groups were a twisting, flowing, rippling sculpture that made Rand want to dig into the clay. Mark it. There was a scar on the vampire's shoulder, an unusual thing, since their self-healing powers were absolute, as far as Rand knew. But it was as if a grenade had been shoved into an open wound and allowed to detonate. The scarring formed a splattering over his shoulders, circling that one deep, oblong scar. It looked like a sun throwing off scattered rays.

The vampire's clothes hung from a tree branch close to a small fire. The T-shirt was a darker shade than Rand remembered. Dampness. Since the vampire had moved Rand, he'd likely stained his clothes with blood, and they'd needed washing. Rand vaguely remembered the digging probe and fiery burn of a knife blade, and suspected the vampire had cauterized the bullet wound after removing the projectile.

He also remembered something odd... It was probably fever, but when the vampire had removed the bullet, he'd cupped his palm over the wound and there'd been something...an energy. Rand knew the touch of what others might call healing magic. This had been sort of like that, but not. He couldn't grasp it. He was still far too fuzzy.

No vampire he'd ever heard about had healing powers, or any magical powers at all. Not like a witch or sorcerer. Vampires seemed too arrogant a race to believe in the power of magic. They believed in their hunting skills; speed, strength, and some ability to entrance their prey, through seduction or other hypnotic means. And—referring back to the arrogance—they believed they were at the top of the food chain in the mortal realms. No argument from Rand...if that conversation didn't involve shifters.

The male turned away from checking the clothes. One glittering eye was visible under a fall of dark hair. It wasn't long, not even quite to his shoulders, but it had an unruliness to it that tempted touch. Rand remembered clutching it to draw him close.

"Mark me, hmm?" the vampire murmured. "So it's that way. Alpha of your pack, aren't you? Making everyone toe the line."

Dylef. Sheba. The pups. Maple, Cira, Teague...Shy.

The pain that stabbed him this time was ten times worse than the throb in his leg and side. A bullet and a knife couldn't compete with the loss.

"Thank..." He cleared his throat. The words were strange in his mouth. He didn't want them to sound human. But there was no other way to communicate what was needed.

"Good now. You can move on."

"Maybe you should say it the way you wanted to say it. 'Go the fuck away.' Right?"

The male came and squatted over him. With Rand on his back, it was a dominant position he didn't particularly care for. A human wouldn't know, not consciously. But from the flicker in this vampire's gaze as Rand stared up at him, the bloodsucker sure as hell understood the cues, and likely demanded submission from anyone that wasn't him. Yeah, that wasn't happening, even if he was wounded.

"Okay. Go the fuck away." He stumbled over the unfamiliar exercise of human speech, but he managed enough to be understood.

Fangs bared in a grim smile. One of them wasn't a fang. Well, it was shaped like one, but it was metal, a sharp, curved point, crudely but effectively wired to the adjacent ones. His inability to retract it was probably what gave his bottom lip the faint scar. It never had the chance to heal before it was cut again, and it had given up and callused over. Rand remembered the sense of it when it was upon his own mouth, an intriguingly different texture.

The vampire had daylight clear blue eyes. They were a striking contrast with the coal color of his brows and hair, dark as the forces behind those eyes, like the storm that had been closing in on them before the hunter came for his supposed prey. That was another reason the vampire might be drying out his clothes. Rand smelled the lingering scent of fallen rain.

His face had the same sculpted quality as his body. Strong, well-formed. All of it had persuaded Rand to touch, to stroke, do what he'd thought was going to be his last act on this cursed earth.

"That's why I said it was your fault you're alive. If you'd just puked up your guts and lost your bowels, like most dying bastards, I would have let you have your merciful end. But you decided to show me just how worthwhile it would be to keep you around."

"You're not keeping me at all," Rand said. He glanced down at himself. "I don't see any chains."

He was as naked as the other male, something that made his brainless cock even more eager, hardening against his abdomen. What the hell? In his current state, the damn thing was going to make him pass out.

The vampire's gaze slid to it. Vampires were known for their ambivalence about sexual preference, the sex itself the driving factor, not the gender with whom it was indulged.

Rand would have preferred that, because it could be another step toward treating the male's interest as purely physical, opportunistic. Easier to dismiss. But this vampire looked at him and kissed as if he had a distinct preference for his own sex. Just as Rand did.

"Chains are an intriguing idea," the irritating male commented. "Not out here, though."

Rand narrowed his gaze. "Am I your prisoner, vampire?"

"Not at all." He rose and returned to the fire. For the first time—proving how disoriented he still was—Rand noticed a pair of rabbits spitted and cooking over it.

"Know you prefer it fresh and raw as a wolf, but in your human form I suspected it was best not to take the chance of you getting sick off raw meat. Especially with you already running a fever from those wounds. Like I said, the second mark called you back from death, but it won't heal you without normal bumps in the road for mortal flesh. Though I don't know much about shifter healing ability; if it's any better than human."

"Faster. And our bodies can bounce back from a lot more punishment."

That intrigued look swept him again, and Rand felt more than fever warm him. "I'll keep that in mind," the male said.

At times, his voice was like the wind when it was strong enough to reach the forest floor, moving and twisting through the trees and foliage. At that deeper level, it passed over the fur and through the body, bringing all sorts of messages in its scent.

"You're not my prisoner," he continued. "You can drag yourself off into the woods, make things worse. I'll give you time to do it, prove to yourself how stupid you're being, before I catch up, re-treat your injuries and make you eat something."

"You could just let me die."

"We covered that," the male said shortly. "No one but yourself to blame." His gaze slid up to Rand's face, lingered. "You and that made-for-sin mouth. It lost you your window. I expect you wanted to die in a fight. Now your choice is to die of your wounds. Far less satisfying, right? So get better, and you can live to fight and die another day."

"Don't you have better things to do than nurse an injured wolf?"

"Tons. But not right now. If that changes, you'll be the first to know." The vampire removed the spit and brought the rabbit to him, dropping to his heels again to offer a piece he tore off. "Here. Eat. Your growling stomach is scaring me."

Rand's lips twisted, but the proximity of the cooked meat made it impossible for him to refuse. He reached up to take the morsel, and found his hands were shaking. Bloody hell, he felt like shit. The fever had coated his muscles in a light sweat, and suddenly the meat made him queasy, even as his stomach rumbled in a demanding way. The instinct of the wolf told him to gulp down whatever food was available, while his human anatomy warned him against eating anything.

"Here." The small portion was brought to Rand's mouth. "You won't be able to eat as much as usual and keep it down, but you can take the edge off and give your body some fuel to help heal itself. If that doesn't stay down, I'll boil some broth out of this rabbit."

"If I shift, it will help." It was a lie, but he didn't like this form. He felt too exposed, too vulnerable.

"If you shift, you may become a lot less cooperative. Not that you're winning any awards on that now. And I won't do this."

Rand's shaking hands were too slow to prevent the vampire from curling his fingers around his dick. He sucked in a breath as the vampire showed he knew his way around another male's body. As he stroked him, Rand's traitorous hips pushed his cock into the vampire's grip. He clamped his hand on the male's thigh for an anchor point.

The vampire's gaze shifted to the contact, but he didn't remove it. He merely watched Rand as he pumped his shaft, rubbing his thumb along the bottom, over the slit. Fuck, it hurt like fire to move, and he still felt queasy, but he couldn't resist the urge. It was as if his libido was operating in a whole different area of his brain than his broken body.

The vampire released him, squeezing Rand's hip. "Yeah, sex drive increases with every mark. Rumor is, third marks want to fuck even on death's door. Take the food."

He wasn't sure what the vampire meant, but Rand had bigger concerns. He wouldn't allow himself to be fed. He had that much pride.

The other male gave him a long look, then nudged the food against Rand's curled fingers, lying loosely against his chest. Rand managed the transfer from that more stable position and brought the food to his lips. Despite the surge of nausea, he got it into his mouth and swallowed.

"Good. So you said your name is Rand. Is that short for something? Randall, Randy?"

Rand's brow furrowed, parsing the meaning of the question. He noticed the vampire was scrutinizing him, and before he could answer, the fanged annoyance had another question.

"How long has it been since you shifted back to human?"

Long enough. He'd lost track of days, seasons...no, he remembered the seasons. They'd died in the late spring, when it was just giving way to summer. He'd remembered the nearly one-year mark when the summer flowers started cropping up among the sunlit rocks in open spaces. He'd grieved anew and been glad when summer passed into another fall. But by wintertime, it had all proved too much. The last time he'd been human, the despair had overcome him and...

He pushed that away. Over two years. Except for surfacing that one futile time in the second winter, he'd stayed a wolf over two years. He'd felt it taking more and more of his human side away, and he'd let it go with no desire to ever take it back. But imminent death at the hunter's hand had forced a shift back to human. When a shifter lost control of his faculties, deepest instinct took over and ensured he was in the form most likely to ensure his survival.

Instinct wasn't always a friend.

No brainer on why he'd shifted to human this time. The vampire wouldn't have tried to save him if he'd thought Rand was merely a wolf.

He hadn't answered the male's question. None of his damn business. Rand kept taking bits of food from his fingers, though. The grease made the contact a slick passage that in turn made him think of other slick things. The vampire's nakedness showed he'd responded to Rand's arousal in kind. His cock was as frustratingly perfect as the rest of him, big and thick enough to make a male lose his train of thought, flesh stretching out into heated smoothness as the shaft lengthened and curved toward his flat abdomen.

Rand wanted to clasp his greased fingers over it and see how the vampire responded to being worked as he'd worked Rand.

Or work that grease over his own cock and then fuck the high, muscular ass, show him exactly why he shouldn't have messed with a wolf. But the strength in the vampire's hand said that it wouldn't be as easy as Rand fantasized it would be. Whereas the vampire taking his ass? Right this second, it would be as easy as it had been for the vampire to skewer the dead rabbit.

The vampire kept watching him with those eyes, that contradiction of water-clear blue irises with an abyss of darkness behind them. It was as if he could read his mind. But if he could, he didn't speak to Rand's thoughts. Not directly.

"So Rand isn't a nickname?"

"No," he managed at the additional prompt. "Just Rand."

"Hmm." A grunt in reply. "I'm Cai. You may not remember me telling you that. Mordecai Wallace originally, some two hundred years ago. Made vampire. If you know anything about my kind, you know that makes me blue-collar class among the fanged bipeds."

Rand had to recall what blue collar meant. When he figured it out, he wasn't sure how that applied to vampires, but he repeated the name. "Cai."

The vampire wiped Rand's mouth with a caressing thumb, startling him. "Terrible table manners. Don't talk with your mouth full. Someone would think you'd been raised by wolves."

Wolf jokes. Great. A few days of this and dying of his wounds instead of in battle wouldn't look so bad. Maybe a few hours.

Cai's lips curved again and this time there was no mistaking the timing. Or the food was helping to clear Rand's mind. Suddenly, the incomprehensible comments about *marks* sank in. He also remembered Cai's voice in his head when he woke. A startled panic rippled through him, agitating the wounds anew as he started back, an involuntarily reaction.

You can read my thoughts?

"Yeah. That's part of what second mark means." Cai gave him an odd look. "My blood can also spur your healing, somewhat. Thanks to the first mark that's part of the second, I can locate you wherever you are, within a few thousand miles. As I said already, the marks also give you some additional healing properties, and not just from drinking my blood. Though I gave you some when you were out, just to be sure and help you along."

"I didn't consent to that."

Cai's brow rose, a silken dark curve. "I didn't ask your permission, wolf. For one thing, you were dying and out of it. For the other, what makes you think I had to ask?"

"Decency. Moral code. Respect for another will."

"Yeah. Vampires don't really go for that kind of stuff. Where's your pack, alpha wolf?"

As he spoke, Cai removed the rabbit from the spit and laid it on a flat rock beside where Rand was lying. When the vampire used his sharp knife to cut more uniform pieces off the rabbit, Rand noted it was a knife more than capable of gutting prey. Or using lethal force to repel an attack.

Rand closed his hand on the discarded, conveniently sharpened stick.

Summoning a reserve that came purely from will, not from physical strength, he propelled himself up, seized the vampire by the back of the neck for leverage and thrust the stick toward his chest. He shoved himself against the vampire to turn him in the necessary direction.

Because he was injured, he didn't expect to match the vampire's speed and strength, even with the element of surprise.

But if they managed to take one another out, Rand wouldn't have any problems with killing the vampire, rather than simply pissing him off to initiate the mortal combat he craved. Cai had goaded Rand twice, the intelligence in his gaze saying he knew the likely reason an alpha would be a loner. He was right. Decency wasn't part of him, and that supported what little Rand knew of vampires, leaving him no regrets for his ungrateful act. But he hadn't asked to be saved.

Cai deflected the blow, but it made good contact, jamming up under his ribs hard enough to produce a grunt and result in a puncture that broke skin, but that was as far as it got. He knocked the weapon out of Rand's hand and seized his arm, wrenching it back. The pain drove Rand in a different direction and he took it at a full mental run. He contorted, the cry that broke from his lips becoming a howl. The shift was agonizing with his wounds, should have killed him, but maybe that would happen in the aftermath.

The important thing was he'd escaped to his sanctuary. If he was going to die, he was dying as a wolf.

The vampire jumped back, his eyes hard and glittering as Rand finished the transformation and made it to his feet, panting hard, swaying but standing. His ears went flat on either side of his head as he bared his teeth and crouched, prepared to spring. The effort to think like a human was discarded, intent narrowed back to the simplest terms.

Run. Leave. Fight if he tries to stop me.

He charged.

The vampire stepped aside and let him go. Deep inside, what was already desolate became even more barren. The wolf had a disturbing, confusing image in his mind. A hand reaching out, the sensation of touch, the first he'd felt in a long while that meant more than nothing.

But it wasn't enough. He wouldn't let it be.

Cai let him run. Restraining a wild animal when he was already injured would only stress him out further, particularly when he was in a fighting mood. He suspected Rand had been in a fighting mood for a while now.

But holy fuck. Even injured, the guy had damn near made the killing blow. Only the speed of Cai's reaction had saved him, and he wasn't sure it would have, if the shifter was at full strength. Go figure. He supposed most vampires went through life assuming they were the biggest, baddest things ever. Which just showed they hadn't had the shit kicked out of them enough. Didn't take long to lose that sense of superiority.

Unfortunately, it meant the wolf had done it again. Despite the male's intriguing physical attributes, Cai doubted he would have broken camp to chase after the surly *canis lupus* if Rand had no more to offer than the novelty of watching him shift—check that off the list—and being a hot alpha male human—double check. Cai had already invested more time in him than he'd expected, hauling Rand's two hundred plus pound body far enough away from the hunter kill site.

But thinking the shifter might be a match for him physically? Well that made the challenge of having his ass all the more irresistible. Definitely a departure from the usual same-day, different-shit mantra Cai carried inside him.

Even so, for form's sake, Cai grumbled at the need to pack up camp, including the cooked rabbits, but he completed the necessary tasks, pulled his damp clothes back on, and went back on the hunt.

Based on Rand's fever, how he'd been shaking and the severity of his injuries, Cai estimated the wolf might make it a mile before his wounds dropped him. He made it three, winning a grudging smile from Cai, and something else.

When Rand had gone after him with the spit, trying his best to get Cai to kill him, the up-close-and-personal depth of his agony had penetrated Cai's cynicism, something he admittedly maintained to a hard-as-rock exterior.

Part of it was how the wolf hadn't been entirely self-sacrificing about the matter. He would have been happy to take Cai down with him, a convenient perk to his suicide wish. The shifter was hurting, grieving, and yet pissed as hell. A worthy opponent. He wanted to die, supposedly, yeah, but he wanted to go down in a struggle to the death with an adversary, someone he could fight to deal with that grief.

The loss of his pack. His family.

Yeah, that part wasn't hard to decipher. Everyone had pain and loss. Big fucking deal. The shifter had lost his family. Boo-hoo. Yet the look in his eyes when he'd spat out those words, *decency, morality*, had made Cai feel...less. That intrigued him.

Anyone who could get him to feel anything intrigued him.

As he dropped to his heels next to the wolf, Cai probed with all his senses to be sure he was unconscious, not wanting a replay of the hunter's mistake. This time he hadn't shifted back to human. Since the guy obviously preferred his quadruped body, Cai guessed there were states in which the shift was involuntary, like when he'd become human in front of Cai, despite an obvious desire not to do so.

His gaze coursed over the wolf. When Rand was standing on all four feet, his lifted head would damn near reach Cai's shoulder. Cai revised his opinion on the weight issue. Given the bone structure of both man and wolf, he expected Rand was probably two hundred and fifty pounds or more in full health, and the wolf wasn't far from the same. The guy had looked a little on the lean side, like he hadn't been eating as much as he should to feed all those muscles.

At least Rand had fallen out near a fresh water source, a gurgling creek. Spreading out his bedroll, Cai considered moving Rand's bulk onto it, but decided on something else first. Dropping back to one knee, he laid his palm on Rand's rising and falling chest. His breath was shallower than it had been before. The dumbass had pushed himself.

"You're not dying." He wasn't taking any more shit on this from the Grim Reaper. This wolf was going to live, at least long enough for Cai to enjoy a good, thorough fuck with him.

Creation was a multi-faceted tool, even when staying clear of the darker side of its coin. It could reach out and feel so much, translate different kinds of languages, all unspoken.

Cai closed his eyes, connecting to it, and to what was beneath his palm. Rand's energy...it was earth and blood, wind against his face. And pain. The wolf and the man had experienced the grief and loss together, but the wolf was less self-destructive than the human side... and more protective.

Could he have done it if Rand was awake, in control of his faculties? Probably not without a hell of an ugly fight, but it was a path Cai was able to follow right now, probably because it served both his interests and that of the wolf's.

He let the energy unwind and then broke the contact as whatever was inside Rand took over, triggered by Cai's push and the shifter's unconscious will to survive. Literally.

The shift was smoother this time, more like watching sculpting clay shape itself on a spinning wheel. A few breaths later, the man lay there, not even a tuft of wolf hair remaining.

"Nifty." Cai grunted. He cleaned the wounds again, ripping up one of the shirts in his pack to bind them. Because vampires healed instantly from anything but death blows, he didn't carry a first aid kit. A quick trip to town might eventually be needed. He really was investing an unreasonable level of effort in this guy.

But the hunter's vehicle was a few miles off. He could use the SUV to save him some running time. Leaving it even farther away from the kill site wouldn't be a bad thing.

With some antibiotics and other supplies to keep the wounds clean and dressed, Cai suspected the shifter's own healing ability, and his second mark upon Rand, would do the trick.

Teasing the male's lips open with the neck of his water bottle, Cai massaged his throat to get him to swallow. Small amounts at a consistent pace to keep him hydrated. Cai also dampened a piece of the ripped shirt and ran it along Rand's face, neck and groin area to help cool him down. It was a pleasure to touch his body, to handle his inert cock and heavy testicles, the tender crevices, pale lengths of inner thighs. He had a nice crisp layering of hair on his legs that Cai stroked with his fingertips as he rubbed the soaked cloth over his feet, bemused by the long arches and surprisingly smooth soles.

"Why not...let me die?" A strained whisper.

"Because I'm pissed at the world, too," Cai said shortly. "It isn't a good enough reason to check out. You're right, there's nothing after, so how the hell can you make everyone else miserable if you're not around?"

At the resulting silence, he looked up. Rand's eyes had closed tighter, as did his mouth, reflecting a pain that had nothing to do with his wounds. "Can't fight what you can't change," the male said. "Hurts. Just want to stop...hurting."

Abandoning the cloth, Cai poured some of the water over his hand and used the flesh-on-flesh contact to cool the flaming skin. "You're less vindictive than me, wolf. If I'm hurting, I want everyone else to suffer with me."

"Love...not like that. Only...assholes."

Rand's eyes opened to mere slits, the gold-flecked blue. His fingers reached out, questing, and Cai looked down as the male touched his chest, the place through which Rand had almost succeeded in shoving the stake. The shallow puncture had already healed, though with his current state of hunger, Cai could still feel the throb beneath the skin. He'd had some of Rand's blood when he'd given him the second mark, but he hadn't taken more than a swallow or two, not wanting to drain the injured male's strength.

"You're delirious," Cai informed him. "Which makes you very attractive, but not very credible."

Rand's fingers coiled and dropped limply to Cai's denim-covered thigh. The wolf was out again.

Cai passed the time keeping him cool, listening to the forest sounds, getting more water into him. On a usual night, he'd enjoy a run through the forest, covering miles and miles. Climb trees to the topmost branches that could bear his weight, and stare out at the view. Chase down deer or smaller game to hone his reflexes and speed. Keep his senses tuned for any human activity that could result in a meal, when it was time for him to feed.

But after all those things were done, often his night didn't look much different from this. Sitting and listening, not doing much thinking. Just experiencing freedom. Solitude. Things that had been so absent during the first century of his life that he hadn't caught up with the unquantifiable need for them, even after hitting his two hundredth birthday.

As he returned to his patient's side, a touch told Cai the fever was turning to chills. The male was mumbling, talking to someone, nothing intelligible. Delirium was taking hold.

If he had to do it, he'd give Rand the third mark. Unless a third mark didn't lock into a shifter the way it did a human, it would save Rand's life. Nothing could kill him then, short of a metal stake through the heart or something irreversible, like a decapitation.

Cai wasn't sure if he believed the eternal soul-binding bullshit about vampires and fully marked servants, but there was enough about it out there he'd shied from doing it. Yeah, the wolf might not intrude on his solitude the way a human did, but hooking up souls for all eternity? Cai couldn't tolerate anyone more than a few hours, so a third mark might not prolong the wolf's life.

His lips twisted wryly, but then Rand called out hoarsely, hands reaching, grasping at something he seemed to miss catching, because they clutched and all his muscles spasmed. He arched his head back and let loose a chillingly real wolf howl, a cry of pain and need whose haunting poignancy and roller coaster volume made Cai back up a few paces.

"Okay, no," he said decidedly. "We're not doing that."

He dropped to his heels beside Rand, intending to stroke, soothe, do a few things like that to calm him down. Or shake him awake with a sharp command if necessary. Yet his skin was like ice. Rand's eyes opened, but they were seeing something beyond Cai and the camp. They were filled with an anguish that speared Cai through the chest.

"No...no..." Light died out of them and Cai's gut clutched. His one fang started to lengthen, instinctive response to his decision to third mark the guy if he came too close to that edge. But then he realized the dullness of Rand's gaze was an emotional response.

The shifter was doing something with his hands. Looking down, Cai noticed he was rubbing one hand in a scraping motion against the wrist of the other arm. Closer inspection showed it was a deliberate motion, not a convulsive tic, and the hand was curled as if holding something. Something that could cut.

Cai's eyes narrowed. He'd cleaned the male's wounds, but he was still in need of a bath to get all the blood and dirt off him the night's efforts had incurred. As a result, Cai hadn't catalogued the older scars the wolf shifter had. Suddenly, two were far more noticeable.

He gripped the male's wrists, tugging the moving hand with firm insistence away from the other arm. He stared at the thin vertical scar. Lifting the other captured wrist, he saw there was a matching one there, beneath the curl of his fingers.

Like most things, it pissed him off. But this bugged him more than usual, and he wasn't entirely sure why. People couldn't hack it and offed themselves. It happened. Life could suck too much sometimes and they didn't have it in them to push past it, strike out instead of self-destruct.

"Didn't let me." Rand's sudden coherent words and harsh chuckle startled Cai. Looking up, he met the shifter's eyes. Fever made the already vibrant color deeper, the gold like sparks of sunlight in the ocean. "Wolf took over...shifted. Somehow...pinched off the arteries. Wouldn't let me bleed out."

"So your wolf isn't the pussy that you are."

Rand didn't acknowledge the caustic comment. His muscles were all tight, sheened with sweat again even though he was shaking from cold. Yet his fingers were reaching, touching Cai's face, tracing it. Cai gripped his wrist, holding him. Feeling the ridge of the scar beneath his palm, he wondered if the scars would disappear if Rand was third marked. He didn't have a lot of experience with servants, but he'd heard that some old scars didn't go away, and no one knew why. Or maybe they did know why, and they just didn't want to talk about it.

Their clasped hands fell on Cai's chest and Rand's fingers curled against it. He'd removed his shirt again, giving the heavy weight cotton more time to dry from the earlier rain. Vampires didn't have hair below the neck, so Cai's chest was smooth, a contrast to Rand's, with its gleaming brown curls that Cai had been threading his fingers through as often as he pleased.

Another shudder passed through Rand and his eyes rolled up into his head. His jaw was twitching, teeth chattering. "Fuck it," Cai muttered.

Stretching out beside the shifter on the blanket, he wrapped it up around the two of them. He put his body flush against Rand's, arms around his massive frame, adjusting Rand so his head was tucked under Cai's jaw. It bemused him when the male's unconscious reaction was to wind his powerful arms tight around Cai, one around his waist and the other over his hips.

"Hang in there," he found himself murmuring. "Don't die. Soon as you're all right, I'm going to kick your ass for even trying."

He didn't know the guy. If he died, he died. But he still said it, meant it. Maybe because with his arms around Cai it was impossible to ignore that touch was the most basic of needs for almost every species on the planet. A need sometimes more important than any other.

Rand grunted, but it wasn't an acknowledgment. He kept muttering, saying very little that was understandable. Some of it sounded like wolf speak, coming rough and awkward out of human lips. He'd stayed in that form over two years. That was what Cai had read from the male's mind. Was that normal for a wolf shifter? He expected it wasn't. From how much Rand seemed to want to flee back into his animal self, Cai also suspected it wasn't the best thing for his long-term recuperation.

He had a couple ideas of how to handle that. But for now, he stroked the male's snarled hair, flattening his palm against the broad back and tracing his shoulder blades. When Rand pressed his bare hip into Cai's groin, his cock responded with a healthy push back under the denim, his ass tightening to help it along.

"Fuck you," Rand muttered.

Cai had no idea if it was a plea or a curse, and if it was aimed toward him, the universe or an unknown enemy, but he'd take it as a raincheck invitation. He cupped his hand over the male's jaw and face, his warm palm against clammy flesh as Rand shook some more. "It's okay," Cai said. "I've got you. You're all right."

No idea where the hell that came from, because he didn't do the nurture thing, but he kept saying it. It seemed to help the wolf shifter settle deeper into his embrace, his breath evening out, his turbulent energy easier.

"There you go. We can fight or fuck later. Just get better."

Cai had been alone a long time. He'd be alone again. But maybe, for just a little while, he'd enjoy what not being alone felt like, even if it was with someone who wished Cai had never come into his life.

Well, that wouldn't make Rand different from almost anyone else who'd ever known Cai, would it?

His lips twisted, but Cai found himself brushing them against Rand's brow. When the male tipped his face up, Cai thought *what the hell*, and kissed him again, a long, slow swim in fevered waters, where Rand's hands wandered over his body in unconscious response. He dug into Cai's back when Cai deepened the kiss, so Cai cupped Rand's muscular ass, holding him tighter against his groin.

Rand groaned into his mouth, his shuddering increasing, such that Cai made himself ease back. No good if he pushed the guy into the Reaper's hands by overtaxing him. But even injured, unconscious, the shifter's response was mesmerizing. Cai wanted him now. Only the desire to have him more than once reined him back. He wasn't above fucking his prey before they expired, sending them to the other side with a last good memory, heavily helped by the pheromones vampires could release with their bite. But he wanted more than a single memory with this one.

Yeah, Rand had admonished him about consent. The guy seemed to know more specifics about vampires than Cai would have expected, but that rebuke told Cai the shifter's knowledge was surface stuff. Because anyone inside the vampire circle knew the word "consent" wasn't in their vocabulary.

Cai had learned that the hard way.

CHAPTER THREE

"*O*pen up. Here you go."

Rand tried to avert his face, but the hand and cup followed, and the broth was pushed up against his nose. Realizing what it was, he followed it down to the ground and drank greedily. He needed meat. Not just meat-flavored water. His wish was granted, half a rabbit dropped next to the cup. It was cooked, not fresh and bloody, but he tore into it.

"Take it slow so you don't make yourself sick. I thought you were getting better today. You've been in and out on me for three days." The vampire's voice sounded pleased. "Wounds are closed, no infection. No fever." His hand passed over Rand's head and shoulder.

Rand twitched away. Not pack. No touch. He showed his teeth, warning the male away from his food, never mind that he'd given it to him.

"It's intriguing to listen to your thoughts in this form. Far more basic, but understandable. Yeah, it's another reason I knew you were getting better. You shifted in your damn sleep, and were strong enough, even in that state, to keep me from overriding you. But the man's still in there. Which I think will turn out to be useful."

Rand listened with half an ear, not really caring what the vampire was talking about as long as he kept his distance. He focused on the food. Then, as his first hunger abated, Rand realized something else. He was chained.

He lunged against the collar, realized it was too snug to slip, and it pulled him up short. Whirling around, whimpering a little at the sudden twinge of pain in his side and leg, he saw the chain running to the nearby tree. No. He wasn't going to tolerate being bound. Typical vampire, thinking a chain could hold him.

He was still healing, but he knew he was strong enough to free himself. Rand dropped, rolled and got the chain wrapped around his chest, under his leg. Enough of a harness that when he lunged again, the chain met his formidable strength, propelled through his shoulders.

One or more of the links should have busted. At the very least, stretched. He could compete with a tow truck in top form. Instead, the chain tightened around him, dug into his chest and shoulders, and held, though it didn't cut into his flesh, as he would have expected. As pain bloomed in his side, he did it two times, three, the panic of an animal trying to surface. Recognizing that for the trap it was, Rand stopped and forced himself to calm down. Panting, he rolled his eyes toward Cai.

"Been doing a little reading," the vampire said conversationally, though his gaze was on Rand, tracking his every movement. He squatted on his heels a short distance away, forearms loosely braced on his knees, thumb and middle finger of one hand flicking in idle, unconscious movement. Rand changed position, four feet braced as he faced off with the vampire.

"Went into town to snag the chain and collar, and raided the local library for the shifter stuff. Figured a lot of it was going to be complete bullshit, same as it is for vampires, though they do get some things right, like the darkness and blood." Cai lifted a book that was on the ground by his side. Rand flattened his ears in response, not sure of the intent of the movement until Cai laid it down again.

It's a damn book. Think. He could shift his mind to think like a human while in wolf form, if he focused. He just usually preferred not to do so. He'd done it that night with the hunter, tricking him into thinking he was dead, but he'd been particularly motivated.

"A few stories say if a shifter stays in his animal form for too long, he'll be stuck that way forever," Cai continued in that same annoying, persistent tone. "I expect most shifters would consider that a warning, something to be avoided. For someone who seeks oblivion and to forget the human side of things, I expect it would be really damn appealing. So I was thinking..."

Cai rose, and sauntered over to a nearby tree, taking a seat beneath it. "The best way to combat that kind of urge is to remind the shifter what's appealing about the human form. And I don't know a male in the world who won't act in the best interest of his dick."

With deceptive casualness, he unbuckled his belt, left it dangling as he pulled open the top button of his jeans. Working the zipper down with the pressure of his fist, he curled it around the cock he revealed, since he wore no underwear under the garment. "I think you're up to the reminder, and I'm done waiting. I'll be gentle, but I want that ass."

Rand fought his human side, tried to push it back, but his eyes locked onto the vampire's movements as he settled in to jack himself off. One knee was bent, the other rocked out wide as he slowly pumped his member and considered Rand. He wasn't wearing a shirt, and Rand's attention was all over him, the vampire's scent filling his nose, fueling his hunger. The vampire was right. His body was healed enough for his cock to be stupid.

"Yeah. I expect your shifter healing abilities and that second mark finally started to work in the same direction. You're not a hundred percent, but probably in about the eighty-percentile range. So you can have this as a reward." Cai tightened his fist around his stiff cock, with its scimitar shape and appealing thickness. "Or maybe it's my reward. Doesn't matter. I think by the time I'm done, you'll consider it a win-win."

Vampire arrogance was even farther off the charts than he'd heard. Rand told himself that, even as his eyes clung to what Cai's hand was doing, and his body trembled on that precipice, the human male inside the wolf wanting, and wanting badly. It had been so long...

"All you have to do to get it, and to get out of that collar, is come back to human form." Cai lifted his free hand and waggled the thumb. "Useful for unfastening buckles. Or unhooking chains, if you like the feel of the collar I put on you enough to keep wearing it."

That outrageous statement came with an infuriating, quick grin. It showed the tip of the vampire's fangs, both the real and the metal one. Rand had never heard of a vampire missing one fang. He didn't want to be curious. Didn't want to care.

Cai's gaze slid down as he fingered his belt with his free hand. "If you shift to human, I could strip this off and use it on your fine ass, punish you for causing me so much work."

Rand backed up, moved sideways, fought the chain again. He let the rage have him. The chain creaked enough to have the vampire's brow rising, which was gratifying, but it still held. He'd embrace it until he passed out, taking him away from a decision he couldn't afford. He didn't want to feel. Why wouldn't the vampire leave it alone?

The pain in his side built to fire, and he snarled as the vampire was suddenly on his feet and behind him, arms banded around his throat and the barrel of Rand's chest, holding him up on his hind legs.

"You aggravate that wound again, and I will fucking tie all your feet together," Cai breathed against his ear. The threat sent a shiver of sensation through Rand's body. "I'm glad I assumed you were at least as strong as I am. I've reinforced that chain with something you can't fight. It's cheating, yeah, but I want a level playing field. Come fight me, man to man. Shift."

Rand snapped at him, but the vampire stayed out of reach, his hold tightening. "If you don't," the vampire promised, "I'll prove how little of a moral code I've got. I'll shove my dick up your wolf's ass."

The idea was so repellent to Rand, he almost shifted then and there, but he pushed back the reaction for another few minutes to prove the vampire couldn't order him around or threaten him into doing his will. The problem was his human part wanted what the vampire was offering. The lust, strong and heated, surprised him, but the vampire had kept that need kindled over these past few days, hadn't he? Rand recalled it in quick flashes; a hand passing over his face, his chest, a wet cloth bathing his genitals...

He shifted, fur becoming flesh. The vampire moved with him, more smoothly than seemed possible with the quick, snapping convulsions that accompanied a swift shift. However, when Rand was done, he was still securely in the vampire's hold. He fought him to be free and this time he won, twisting out of the vampire's grip and backpedaling away, catching himself before he tripped. He had a momentary impression of the vampire's hands slipping away, and realized the male had had one palm molded over the wound in Rand's side to protect it.

The collar was loose on his neck now, but as Rand reached for it, he hit a field he couldn't get through. He couldn't even curl his fingers over the darn thing and try to pull it over his head, which he should have been able to do, since the wolf's neck and ruff was far thicker than his own.

Magic. He couldn't read the shape of it, but it was obvious that was what it was. He hadn't imagined that healing wash of heat after all. The damn male was a magic user *and* a vampire. Something Rand had never heard of, but his knowledge of vampires was far from complete.

Regardless, it made the vampire double the trouble and annoyance.

Cai's fangs flashed in a grim smile. But as he moved in on Rand, Rand closed his hand over the chain, and realized he *could* touch that, even if he couldn't unhook it from the collar. The flash of *oh shit* in the vampire's eyes was mildly gratifying as Rand dodged past him and employed the chain as a weapon.

He just about clotheslined him. Cai ducked under the chain. He'd had the presence of mind to refasten his jeans so vulnerable things weren't hanging in the breeze, but Rand's body was still torqued by the erotic display of rippling muscle and grace as the vampire entered a warrior's dance with him, up and forward, around. Near pins, missed punches. Twisting, grappling, the chain clanking and the vampire dodging away and out of range before Rand could get Cai tangled in it. Then he closed back in again.

They were like a mirror, anticipating one another too well. Twisting. It occurred to Rand that Cai was in his head, and if he could follow his thoughts that fast, he'd stay ahead of Rand, get the advantage. Except Rand used instinct, not thought, and that leveled the playing field.

Then Cai got him pinned against a tree. Rand plunged a fist into his gut that knocked him back. It made the vampire swear, and emit an odd half chuckle. Then the fight got serious.

Damn it, Rand was tiring out. That eighty percent was working against him. But he wasn't going to stop fighting. Maybe the vampire figured that out, because suddenly he was outside the ring of combat, just beyond the chain's length. He stood there, studying Rand, arms crossed over his bare chest.

"Fucking hell," he murmured. "That was fun."

It had been...stimulating. Rand's hands closed into fists. He didn't want to feel that way. Didn't want to think about his cock being hard and stiff against his belly, and the vampire noticing it with avid eyes. Cai was just as worked up under his jeans, ready to go.

"Let me go," Rand growled.

Cai considered, then dipped his head, a short nod. He walked toward Rand, easy, casual, as if they hadn't just been grappling like enemy combatants. His clear blue eyes were intent on Rand's, yet seeming to cover every inch of skin at the same time, lingering on Rand's mouth as he arrived toe-to-toe with him.

"Promise not to run. Let yourself have this, wolf. You want me, I want you. It can be that simple."

Rand closed his eyes. He wasn't promising anything, but he wasn't moving, either. As he stood there for several dozen heartbeats, everything seemed to move in the forest except the air around them, a silent cocoon.

The vampire's palm rested on his chest, molded over his pectoral, stroked his biceps, the taut nipple. Rand drew in a breath. It had been so damn long...

Cai lifted his touch to the collar. Rand felt a tingle, a release of energy that he recognized as the light coating of heat he'd felt over his shoulders and upper chest when he roused to eat. He'd thought it was a lingering symptom of his injuries.

As the magic dissipated, Cai's hands closed over the collar. He unbuckled it, the attached chain clinking, his fingertips whispering over Rand's throat. The leather smell, the stroke of the strap leaving his flesh and replaced by the vampire's fingers, made Rand's body tighten. The collar and chain dropped to the ground with a louder clank. Cai's palm covered the healing scar on his side, one of the knife wounds.

"If you'd stayed human more than a minute at a time," the vampire said, "I could have kept a bandage on your wounds with some topical that would have helped them heal faster."

"Didn't need a nurse." Rand opened his eyes and flashed an angry look at him. "Unless you're going to put on one of those cute outfits."

It was a stupid thing to say, but Cai was too close, the silken tangle of hair over his forehead only enhancing the intensity of his gaze, so near to Rand's.

Cai chuckled, a dark sound. "Yeah, convince me you like pussy. The last one you touched was your mother's when you were coming out of the womb."

"Females are okay." The vampire was wrong, technically, because Rand *had* managed to mate with Sheba.

He pushed that thought away fast. Fortunately, Cai proved a good distraction. The vampire slid a rough palm down the center of his back, slow, exploring. Rand closed his eyes again. Fine. Cai wasn't Dylef, but Rand wasn't that maudlin. He wasn't betraying Dylef. It was sex. Just sex, and he could enjoy it without giving it more significance than that. The vampire sure as hell wouldn't.

"Sex done right doesn't need a lot of sentiment attached to it, wolf," Cai said. "The value of a thing for what it is, not what we think it should be."

Or wish it could be. Rand let out a sigh that was half wolf, half man. He couldn't do anything about the vampire being in his mind, either. Might as well enjoy pure sensation. The vampire was good at this. Creatures of the night, seductive and mesmerizing. He caressed, stroked, learned the lines of Rand's body, brought every inch of flesh to life. Doing no more than stroking Rand's shoulders, back, hips. When he reached Rand's ass, Cai turned his hand over so his knuckles glided over his buttocks, the seam between them.

"You could bounce rocks off this work of art. All that running, I expect. Do you like to run, Rand? It's an animal thing, stretching out over the ground, going faster and faster, connecting to the elements as you do it. Feeling the wind, the earth beneath you, the sky above."

He wanted to do it right now, merely from the images Cai was planting, but Cai's hand closed over his buttock, a hard grip that snagged Rand's attention fully again.

"Stay with me. I'll give you a different way to feel like you're flying."

He didn't say it like a boast. A simple assertion of fact. Cai nudged his knee. "Spread these apart."

It was a command, which raised Rand's hackles, but as Cai's hand slid down between his legs from behind, he complied, and swallowed a growl as the vampire captured his testicles in a strong, kneading grip. His fingertips whispered over the base of Rand's hardening cock.

"There you are. Fuck, you are a treasure." Cai clasped Rand's hip with the other hand. The vampire's possessive hold on his balls resulted in a surge of further desire.

"Do you like pain and restraint, wolf? Are shifters more conservative and vanilla, or do you like taking that animal dominance and submission into darker waters, same as vampires do?"

Whereas vampires stayed in the shadows, wolf shifters *were* the shadows. But they kept tabs on their non-human brethren, like vampires. Wolves learned about their competitors in the predator world as much as they could. In addition to the information about their speed and strength had come other rumors. How deep and brutal their sexual tastes ran.

And that they were insatiable.

"No," Rand said, to cover all angles of the question. But he needn't have said anything, since he suspected his mind revealed some of it. He hadn't thought of such things, and it hadn't been part of his life before. Well, not beyond how they manifested in a wolf's normal makeup, as Cai had pointed out. But the things that woke to life when the vampire threatened to mark his ass, or drove him to his knees, were confusing but undeniable. Darker, deeper parts of what was already in Rand's mind. A desire for pain, punishment and pleasure, so strong everything else would be swept away. Every agony of the heart too great too bear.

He pushed that away, too, put it back on a physical footing. It was likely the vampire allure, opening their prey's minds to possibilities they wouldn't normally entertain.

"No, you don't do pain and restraints, and no, wolves aren't more conservative." Cai chuckled, a sound that cinched around Rand's cock like a leash, jerking it to attention. "Or simply no, to tell me we're not having that conversation."

"Wolves don't talk this much during fucking."

"No, I don't expect they do." Cai gripped Rand's buttocks, spreading them, and rubbed his cock in the channel. Rand's muscles tightened, a ripple going through his arms and shoulders. He was standing there, rigid, but like a tree, he was starting to sway.

"You're tiring, and I don't want to wear you out," the vampire said mildly. "So how about we make this one straightforward. But I like all the directions your mind goes when I touch you, wolf. We'll have to explore that."

"I'm not hanging around long enough for a guided tour."

Cai made a noncommittal noise, and then his grip tightened, his body pressed flush against Rand's, shoulders to cock to knees. "Go down for me, wolf. All fours. Your favorite position."

Rand would have locked his knees, but Cai didn't force it. He nudged, with one knee and the temptation of his cock teasing against Rand's ass, and another quiet whisper. The words were almost unintelligible, but the meaning clear enough, especially since he let Rand hear it in his head.

I'll make it feel good. Simple and easy.

Rand let his knees give, and when he was on them, dropping to his palms, the vampire delivered. He used his saliva to lube Rand's opening and his cock, too, he expected, since he felt the vampire working his shaft in his hand as he rubbed against Rand's ass.

I'll bet you have something else to ease my way, coming out of that hard cock of yours. Let me have it.

Rand gripped himself, slipping his curled fist over his cockhead and finding the pre-come there that Cai had anticipated. His erection was substantial, so he didn't know why his own response surprised him. Mixed emotions held him as he reached back, palm open and up, and Cai's strong grip closed over his wrist.

He held Rand's palm steady as he rubbed his cock over Rand's damp palm and fingers. It really didn't add a lot, but it shoved the arousal factor up another two or three notches. Then Cai released him to guide his cock, slippery enough from the combined lubrication, into Rand's opening. He nudged, playing, teasing, until Rand was pushing back against Cai, frustrated.

"Be still, wolf," Cai said mildly. "Or I'll put you on your elbows and show you who's boss."

Rand snorted, and Cai answered with one of those sensual chuckles. But the moment of humor disappeared, swallowed by darker, needier things. *Do it. Just do it.* Cai's hands were all over him, kneading and squeezing his ass, running along his back, his sides, learning him, appreciating him. Enjoying more than just his cock.

Too close to intimacy. Things were growing too hard to manage inside of Rand, making it hard to breathe. He was about to throw the vampire off, start that battle once again...

Cai thrust through both sets of ass muscles, seating himself with a hum of satisfaction. Rand bit back a groan at his traitorous cock's leap of satisfaction. Maybe because of that eighty percent, maybe because the vampire put pressure on him he didn't recognize until it happened, Rand found himself on his elbows. But as they dug into the ground, the anchor and angle took the other male deeper, filling him up. Cai set both hands to his hips.

"Nice," he purred. He bent close over Rand's back, his breath caressing Rand's spine, and fangs scraped over his flesh. The wound in Rand's side was starting to burn, as was the healing bullet hole in his thigh, and Cai noticed.

"Does it hurt, wolf? Hurt too much?"

From the rumors Rand had heard, that would only turn the vampire on more. Cai chuckled.

"Sometimes," the vampire acknowledged. "But that's not the right kind. That's the type that causes me more work and makes you a one-time fuck, and I want far more out of this fine ass than that."

Rand snarled and pushed back against him, a message itself. Cai chuckled. "Long as I don't take too long about things, you don't care, right? You won't get to shorten things between us in the future, wolf. But today, I'll be merciful."

Mercy had a different definition to vampires, apparently. Cai started thrusting again, but he paced himself, making Rand ride that edge of pain from his injuries while building him up to a mind-boggling arousal. Cai was taking Rand toward orgasm, but at his own pace, until Rand was held away from it by little more than a breath. If this was shortening things, an actual full health fuck with a vampire might be life-threatening.

Cai teased him, spoke to him in that low, sensual voice, saying things that Rand should have ignored, shouldn't have affected him at all. But his body responded to the words as much as he did to the fucking. The male had a way with words, and a substantial cock, and he knew what to do with both. He could wield the latter like a damn blunt instrument or a precision tool. A power tool, for damn sure.

Cai's additional chuckle made Rand's ears burn. Fuck, he needed to remember the vampire was in his head.

"Think any thought you wish, wolf," Cai said, covering his body, dropping his hand on the ground behind Rand's braced elbow. "It makes me want you more. I want to feel you come, take me over by squeezing me with that incredible ass of yours."

Sure, he could just do it on command. Right. Cai's long fingers wrapped around Rand's cock, his breath hot on Rand's nape. "When I give you an order, wolf, you better listen."

Before Rand could retaliate for that, he was shoved off the edge. In three deft strokes, Rand's body convulsed, no matter that he tried to suppress the reaction. Cai was relentless, driving him, fucking him, uttering a grunt of male satisfaction as Rand spurted, his seed bathing his belly and chest.

It had been so long for a reason...it was incredible, so incredible, that feeling of pure physical pleasure. He could ride it; he wouldn't fall off as long as he focused on that, and not on what rode parallel to it, things of the broken heart and shattered soul. If it intersected, if they touched, he might be lost forever in that abyss.

You stay right here with me, wolf. Just a good fuck. Simple and straight forward. Cai's mind voice was strained, telling Rand how close he was, too. *No different than taking down a good meal, feeding on blood or flesh well-earned...*

He could do that. He could. Yet he shuddered when Cai released inside him, his quiet groans and the clutch of his hands on Rand's hips reminding him of how deep a pleasure it was, taking a lover over that cliff, sharing that ride together.

Yet when they finished, Rand remembered that wasn't what they were. "Just sex" could be a great ride, but it was also a poisoned double-edged sword in the aftermath.

As he got his breath back, Rand felt that deep-seated physical need and anxiety to be wolf return. He needed to get away from the surge of feelings trying to break loose inside him. He wasn't a coward. He could face the flood, but he didn't want to face it in front of a stranger.

"Try to stay on two legs for a bit," Cai advised, sliding free and running a hand down his back, nonplusing Rand when he considerately eased him to his side, steadying him. "It really will help you get to a hundred percent faster. Think of it this way. Your hope to be rid of me can happen that much more quickly."

He'd overlooked Rand's more personal, desperate thoughts. Rand wasn't naïve. The vampire wasn't being kind. He just didn't want to be bogged down in Rand's baggage. Rand told himself he preferred Cai to be apathetic, but it didn't help him feel better about it. Or himself, for letting the sex overwhelm him, sweep him away.

"I could be rid of you now," Rand said, more tartly than intended. He rolled away and stood up. "There's no reason for you to nurse me. I'm in no danger of dying from my wounds now."

Damn it, he'd been close enough to see the light at the end of the tunnel, and he was totally fine with it being a train, obliterating him. Why had the vampire interfered with that?

"You've had your fuck. Why do you care if I live or die?"

Cai shrugged, seemingly unoffended. "Because I've only begun to tap your fine ass, and it's a long trip to the nearest town for that. There's wooing and courtship, buying drinks and pretending to be human to get close to my prey. I'm lazy. You're here and available."

Rand wanted to snap at him, but he realized he was swaying on his feet. Cai was up and at his side. Before Rand could shove him away, the vampire had maneuvered him over to a tree and eased him to a seated position against it.

"Okay, you're maybe eighty or ninety percent, except for right after sex. But in all fairness, sex with me can take a lot out of someone. And that was nowhere near my best work."

Cai squatted next to him and stroked a lock of Rand's hair back from his face. Rand twitched back, but the vampire merely followed, continuing the caress. The guy really didn't take a hint. Baring his teeth, Rand knocked away his hand with his forearm.

"If you want a fuck toy for a couple days, I can live with that. We can scratch the mutual itch. But you won't touch me as a lover would. You'll have to tie me up to do that kind of shit."

Cai's gaze gleamed. "Terms accepted."

Rand looked away. Cai's hand rested on his arm, and this time he didn't have the strength to push him away, especially when he could close his eyes and imagine Dylef's hand. *The stroke of it over his face, his hair, his chest. Dylef, his beta wolf, curled under his arm, his limbs sprawled over Rand as they slept. "You take up so much of the bed, you're like a one-man litter of puppies."*

In the morning, Dylef had often woken first, bringing Rand coffee, and stroking him awake. Sometimes with mouth and hands, enjoying Rand's morning erection and leading to pleasure for both of them.

But sometimes he did it just like this, touching Rand's face, his hair. Dylef had loved his hair. He brushed it for Rand some days, braided it when Rand was going to work in the fields of their small farm. Or was headed out to supplement their income by mowing highway right-of-way.

A thickness was in Rand's throat. He pressed into the touch, curled his hand around Dylef's wrist to hold his palm there against his face, absorbing it, wishing, wishing so damn hard...

He jerked back, letting Cai go. Cai opened his hand in a simple "peace" type gesture, though his expression was unreadable. Sure, the bastard could jump in his head and read his thoughts, but he wasn't as closed to Rand as he might think he was. To the wolf side, the vampire smelled...curious. The mix of emotions there were odd, a hard-to-decipher reaction to Rand's thoughts.

"You need to eat some more. And sleep." The vampire rose and moved back toward the camp supplies, returning with another cup of broth and more of the rabbit, which he'd ripped into chunks and put on a plate. He set both by Rand.

Rand lifted his head. Cai had relocated their camp during Rand's phasing in and out of consciousness. They were closer to some of the trails used by deep woods hikers, though still far enough from them that any such travelers posed no concerns. But the wind now brought Rand the scent of a human on those trails, alone. A lone hiker, probably.

It was of passing interest to him, but catching it from his mind, Cai's eyes lit. "Seems my dinner is also ready. You're good luck. Haven't had one of those in a few weeks. I'll be back. Don't run off. It will just piss me off."

Rand grunted, swallowing a mouthful of rabbit. "If I prove to be too much trouble, you'll just give up and go into town to get what you need."

"Don't underestimate my stubbornness. Vampires don't like to be defied and we'll pretty much go to the ends of the earth to prove that point."

"Did someone knock out one of your fangs for being such a bastard? Is that why one's fake?"

"They felt threatened by my overabundance of charm and good looks. Jealousy is an ugly thing."

Rand rolled his eyes. But he was arguing to be contrary. He didn't intend to leave the camp while Cai was gone. The sex and the struggle had taken a lot out of him. The vampire was right. He needed to give the wounds time to heal.

"That a boy. Live to self-destruct another day."

"You call me *boy*, ever, and that will happen sooner than later. I'll stake you, and get it right this time."

"It's an expression, wolf." Cai chuckled. "You really need to get back out in the human world."

"Yeah. I'll put that on my list right after having my testicles gnawed off by a badger."

Cai's lips curved, showing appreciation. "Humans aren't my favorite company, either. But fortunately, my food doesn't talk long." He picked up his shirt and pulled it on. Buckled the belt he'd left loose, though he'd fastened and zipped the jeans. It was an appealing view that Rand didn't deny himself, but a thought tickled his mind, an uneasy one.

"You compel them to silence when you feed off them?"

"That's one way of looking at it." Cai was moving away. Rand shoved himself to a straighter position.

"You're going to kill the hiker?"

"Yeah. He won't feel anything bad." Cai stopped and lifted a brow. "No different than me killing that rabbit for you. Don't be a hypocrite."

"The rabbit can't donate his meat to my hunger and walk away. Vampires don't have to kill to feed."

"No, but if they don't, they have to feed every few days. Couple of weeks, tops, is how long the oldest ones can hold out. A lethal amount from one human will last someone my age a month. I couldn't take much from you while you were at your worst. My last meal's run out. And you get your panties in a twist about me playing with your hair. Can't imagine you'd like to donate meals to me, which is a far more intimate thing."

Cai cocked his head. "You're puzzling me, wolf. You just said you don't care much for human company."

"Not caring about them, and being okay with killing them when their deaths aren't necessary, are two different things."

"Oh, an eco-wolf. How refreshing. I must have missed your Greenpeace card. If carrying a wallet is problematic on four legs, get yourself a man purse you can sling over your neck." Cai turned away again.

"Back soon. I'll miss you, too."

"Don't." Rand made it to his feet. He was not going to make this point sitting on his ass. "You're not going to kill that hiker."

"Really?" Cai turned, squaring off with him. "Who's going to stop me?"

"You'll have to kill me first."

Cai swept him a scornful look. "You might be able to outrun me in another day or two. But not today."

Despite the vampire's mocking tone, there was a look in his eyes that had become cold and settled. Up until now, because of Rand's self-absorption with his own situation, Rand hadn't focused much past the snark. Now, from the set of his jaw, the coolness of his gaze, his stance—neither offensive nor defensive, simply prepared to handle any attack—Cai was clearly a predator about to go on the hunt, and was merely curious, not offended or swayed, by his opposition.

Like wolves, vampires liked taking down prey, and it was hard to rein that back. Rand knew there was a rule among vampire kind that they could kill as many as a dozen humans in a year, including what they called the annual kill, one essential life-taking that maintained their overall strength. That baker's dozen was okay, if they didn't attract human notice, the guiding tenet of all those the clueless humans called fantasy.

Most vampires seemed content with that limitation. Born vampires understood the need to keep a low profile in the human world, and made vampires...well, they'd been human. Enough said.

Cai was a made vampire, yet he seemed chillingly detached from his former species, as if killing humans was something he did all the time, like picking up a burger at a drive-thru. All Rand scented from him was uncomplicated hunger.

Though Rand always thanked the spirit of the animal he caught, a common-sense spirituality, he didn't suspect that thought even crossed Cai's mind. But there were layers below that attitude that smelled like the damp, murky muck of a swamp.

No time to get out a shovel and dig, and Rand wasn't sure he wanted to do so anyway. But he'd address the problem in the way he could.

"Feed from me," he said.

Cai had started toward the edge of the clearing again. Now he pivoted, studying Rand head to toe.

"You need all your blood until you're fully healed."

"Maybe. But if I drag my ass after you to stop you from killing that hiker, I might relapse. Ruin all your efforts to keep me healthy enough to screw for the next few days."

Cai's expression suggested he didn't care for how crudely Rand had put that, but it was what it was. Why dress it up?

"Perhaps it's your hypocrisy that pisses me off," the vampire retorted. "I can't read your soul with a second mark, but I can read your mind, and I'm smart enough to connect the dots between the emotions I pick up from you. You may want to die, but it's been a long time since you've been touched or taken, Rand. The pull of that, for the moment, is stronger than the pull of death. Admit that, and I'll feed from you."

"Fine. I admit it. Here's my vein." Rand extended both arms, so he could have his choice. Cai swept a gaze over them. He lifted his attention back to Rand's face and dwelled there, his intensity as palpable as a touch.

He was moving, but no longer toward the forest. Rand couldn't help looking at the play of muscle under Cai's T-shirt, the swing of his arms and movement of his shoulders and hips. The thin line of his firm lips as he stopped before Rand. He'd just fucked Rand, but with one sexy swagger, he could get him thinking about it again.

"It's interesting to me how you know so much about vampires," Cai observed. "Your brain's like an encyclopedia of Vampire 101."

"My cousin is a servant to a vampire. Distant cousin," Rand added. "No wolf genes."

"Pity. I was about to have some serious threesome fantasies." Cai's serious expression didn't change, despite the dry comment. His tone sharpened. "Put your arms down. Clasp your hands behind your back."

Rand's brow creased. "Why—"

"Do it."

Rand could say fuck off, but the vampire would kill the hiker. So yeah, he'd backed himself into the corner of being an obedient dog. For the moment.

Cai's gaze glinted. "Not a definition I would apply to you, especially with that dangerous look on your face, wolf. Where are your hands?"

Rand heaved a sigh and clasped them behind him. Despite his studied indifference, a swirl of reaction tightened into a knot in his stomach as he restrained himself that way, lifting and exposing his chest to the vampire's heated gaze. Suddenly he was far more aware of how naked he was, and how the vampire was fully clothed. Cai moved a step closer, so Rand's pectorals brushed the soft cotton fabric of his shirt. His nipples tightened at the contact.

The vampire leaned in, lifting a hand to brush Rand's hair back over one broad shoulder. He coiled his hand in the hair, so Rand lifted his chin at the implied demand. His pulse elevated as he realized the vampire's intent, and Cai confirmed it, meeting his gaze.

"Blood from the throat is sweetest. And the most intimate. Even more than the femoral, though that puts a vampire close to a nice dessert. This hurts at first, but the pain goes away quickly."

"Just do it," Rand bit out, though his voice sounded hoarse. The vampire chuckled.

"You like to rush. I don't. You're going to have to learn patience."

He breathed on Rand's neck, used the tip of tongue to trace and taste. Rand swayed, his hands tightening into a knot against his ass. Cai slid an arm around him, holding him steady, holding him up, making it clear he had the strength to do it. It was an odd feeling, since Rand didn't have the kind of physique that suggested it was possible for one person to hold him on his feet.

I could carry you like a fainting girl, wolf. But it's not the image that comes to mind when I hold you like this. You're all male, a fighter, and I want to take a few tasty bites out of you, from the places of my choosing. Starting right here.

Rand stiffened as the vampire's fangs sank into his throat. His immediate, animal reaction was to yank away, to fight for his life, but Cai's grip on his hair increased, reminding him of the here and now and the purpose for all this.

Cai swallowed, making a pleased noise, apparently at the taste and richness of his blood. When his thigh shifted so it was pressed against Rand's groin as he held him by the hair, Rand leaned into him, his hands in that same knot. As Cai drank, a heat ran through Rand, a heady surge of desire that had him pushing against Cai. He'd just come. What the hell...

Pheromones released from my fangs. Lovely effect on prey, Cai offered. *See what you selfishly took from the hiker? He'd have died, but quite happily.*

Rand's cock bumped against the rough texture of Cai's jeans. Cai dropped his other hand to clasp him, work him in casual, teasing pulls as Rand rocked against him, damn near humping his leg as the pheromone effect increased. Cai wasn't unaffected himself. His clutch on Rand's hair became an insistent pull on his scalp. The smell of blood misted between them, goading two predators' instincts to life.

Cai was backing him toward the tree, a good option since Rand was pretty sure his knees were going to buckle. He reacted, but not fast enough, when Cai released his throat and picked up the discarded chain, whipping it around the tree and looping it over the bend of Rand's elbows and across his chest. He had to drop his grip on Rand's cock to make that happen, but seeing the vampire's fingers wrapped tight around the chain to hold Rand, still pulling on it enough for him to feel the dig of the metal links into his flesh, had a similarly stimulating effect.

"What..."

"Don't fight me, wolf. Just feel."

Then he bit Rand again, on the other side of his throat.

As the vampire drank and Rand's cock throbbed, his buttocks flexed against rough bark and his hips thrust, fucking the air. Cai lifted his head enough to tuck in the chain end and reclaim the collar that had been clipped to it.

Though Rand tried to jerk away, Cai had the collar around Rand's throat.

Their eyes met as Cai slipped the tongue into the buckle. "Let me," he said, a silky, sensual tone. *Let me show you how this can feel.*

He didn't say the words; Rand felt them. Still holding his gaze, Cai tightened the strap. One hole, two, three...all the way to the place where it could snugly hold a thick human male throat, instead of a wolf's.

Rand hadn't ever done any overt BDSM stuff, but feeling the vampire tightening the collar, hearing the feral sounds of hunger Cai made as he brought his lips to Rand's throat again, only seemed to spur the power of his own arousal. Which spiked even more as Cai's fangs sank back into his flesh below the collar's hold and he swallowed more of Rand's blood. The pressure seemed to make his flesh more sensitive, not just above the strap, but everywhere else.

Rand closed his eyes. The scent of Cai's body, his heat, the blood, combined with other sensory input to goad his desire and take away any other thought. The chain clinked as the links dug deeper into Rand's chest and arms, because he was straining against it. He liked the way that felt, and strained harder, not to bust free, but to feel the binding, feel the discomfort, the proof that he was bound, could submit and let go. Let all of it go for this moment.

You please me, wolf. Come.

For the second time in less than an hour, Rand obeyed with no ability to stop himself, his come splashing on the dried remnants of his previous climax. Good thing he wasn't wearing any clothes, because at this rate he'd be a fucking mess in no time.

I like that thought. You always naked around me, collared and serving my pleasure. Your body marked by your seed and mine until I allowed you a bath, no more than once a day. Maybe every other day.

Rand finished his climax, with a deep groan and a few more involuntary jerks of his hips. His mind was scrambled, but he still managed a fragmented thought.

Can't control me. I control myself.

Cai drew back, his one fang retracting. Rand noticed dazedly he tucked the prosthetic one back under his lip with a brief flick of his tongue, an act of apparent long practice to keep from appearing snaggle-toothed. He watched Rand wind down with avid enjoyment, reaching out to caress his cock, his eyes glittering as Rand twitched at the contact on his hyper sensitive glans.

He kept doing it, until Rand gritted his teeth and held still, let him stroke. He told himself to do it because the rule about bullies was not to give them the satisfaction of a response, but when Cai's gaze lifted to his face and nodded in approval, it gave Rand strange, different feelings.

"Very good, wolf. You're learning."

You could fight me for control, over and over, but you didn't just now. Not hard enough to get free, just hard enough to tell me you won't be pushed around. I like that. Look where it took you. Both of us.

Cai withdrew his hand and gave the steel bar beneath his jeans a hard stroke that made Rand's mouth dry. Hell, he wouldn't be acting so stupid about this if sometime over the past couple years he'd gone into a town for an occasional hookup.

"If I could trust your teeth," the vampire observed, "I'd feed my cock between your lips and let you serve me to my finish."

"I think I've given you more than you deserve already," Rand retorted, though the idea of sucking Cai off was far too appealing an image in his mind. "I want loose."

"Give it a minute." The vampire wiped his own lips with the back of his hand. "Take a rest; you've earned it. A few days ago, I rescued a fellow fanged creature from a hunter. Now you've paid it forward for an oblivious human. Good for you."

Rand stared at him as Cai stepped back. The vampire's erection wasn't abating, noticeable under his jeans. He ignored that, best as he could. "Does everything you say have to be marinated in sarcasm?"

"No. I prefer to spice things up with jaded cynicism and outrageous acts of selfishness."

The chains clinked from the expansion of his chest as Rand sighed. A glint of humor and appreciation went through the vampire's gaze. But Rand capitulated for now, dropping his head back against the tree and gazing down his nose with a neutral expression for the vampire. He could get loose. He could feel it in the give of the chains, and the end was just tucked under the loops across his body. That helped.

He told himself he shouldn't be playing the vampire's game, that doing it after the heat of the moment had passed took it into some odd territory. Yet the way the vampire's gaze consumed him, the arousal still vibrating off him, had Rand staying where he was. But he wasn't going to let the vampire control everything.

"Where did you get the scar on your back? The one shaped like the sun."

Cai had moved away, but only to sit down against another tree a few feet away. He cocked his head, and let his hand drift down over his own chest. Not to titillate Rand. It appeared he was enjoying touching himself as he looked at the wolf, or imagining Rand's touch upon him without being close enough to allow that contact. Which produced another indescribable knot of feelings in Rand's gut.

He wasn't sure if Cai had heard him. The vampire kept up that distracting, idle caress of his own body, over muscular abs, the smooth pectorals, the inside of an elbow and back down again, to cup himself over his jeans. Rand couldn't take his eyes away, though he wanted to know the answer to his question.

"Another vampire," the vampire said at last. "He went after me with a knife. Threatened to skin me, but couldn't get me to hold still for that. Go figure. Instead we had a sporting wrestling match where he cut my shoulders up pretty good before he drove the blade into that center 'sun' spot and twisted it like a maid churning butter." Cai's teeth flashed in a humorless smile. Rand noted his eyes had that cold look again.

"I fought him, reached back, dug into his neck. Managed to rip his head off. First time I'd done that. Kind of cool to realize you have that kind of strength in your fingers." The vampire paused. "Me killing him was a milestone of sorts, so the vampires I was with, they held me down and used my blood to burn the scars he left on me. Makes them permanent. Ironic, right? A vampire with a scar shaped like the sun."

Cai opened his jeans, reached in and took a grip on his cock. He handled himself with practiced ease and a total lack of self-consciousness. He settled his shoulders, a contented sigh coming from him. "A good meal and jacking off; nothing better than that. Especially with a view like this."

Rand's legs were splayed out, showing his replete cock and testicles. The collar rubbed against the fang marks that Cai had somehow sealed to keep them from bleeding, but the snug hold of the strap increased their dull throbbing, a hammer reminder in his brain that he'd just fed a vampire. And was being held somewhat pinned by one as he jacked off, studying Rand with keen desire.

"Fuck, you'd make a hell of a guard dog, wolf. Chained up in my yard, ready for my cock anytime I wanted to take you. If I had a home and a yard. But the fantasy..."

Cai's eyes drifted half closed, and he kept stroking his cock. Though Rand's cock couldn't revive that fast, the strong ripple of reaction in his upper thighs and deep in his loins said he'd remember this vividly when he was ready. He could fight against the chains, get loose.

"Try, wolf. I like to watch you try."

He felt that cloak of heat, this time over his arms and chest where the chains dug in. The vampire had done that binding thing, but it didn't feel as...immovable. Rand tried to get loose. He didn't succeed, but there was enough give that he kept trying. Or maybe he kept trying because of the way the vampire's desire grew, the more he watched Rand's muscles bunch, the more he struggled...

He was *not* getting hard again. It was impossible, but there it was. The more Cai worked himself, the more logic and anything human in Rand took a backseat, leaving him to a hot, simmering feeling somewhere between anger, lust and need.

"There you are. Let me have that. It's like nectar from your mind. Fuck..."

Cai's head tipped back and he came, his seed fountaining over his fist. Rand wet his lips. A flash of images went through his mind, and he hoped they came from the vampire, because the alternative was unthinkable.

Cai putting him on the ground, chained and collared, forcing his cock into Rand's mouth, hand on his hair as he demanded that Rand take him, suck him off.

He turned his face away, closing his eyes. That was not something he fantasized about. Not ever. He'd fantasied about doing it to Dylef, and they'd done something similar a couple times, but not quite that... forceful.

"But you wanted to, didn't you? Just like you kind of want me to try and force you to it, because a fighter likes to fight, on either side of the equation."

Cai's eyes went to slits as Rand's attention returned to him. The vampire rose, jeans still open, and moved to the nearby creek, squatting to wash his hands. "Time to let you go so you can finish your dinner. Then I think it's time to drink some Jack. I've been carrying a bottle for a couple weeks and I'm tired of toting it around. We can share. It'll help you sleep and forget about me for a while. Promise."

He smiled, an easy, uncomplicated gesture that took Rand off guard. Rising, Cai fastened his jeans before coming to him and loosening the chains. When he unbuckled the collar, his fingers caressed Rand's throat. The feeling was different from earlier. Quieter, but no less intense. Rand felt a tightness in his chest he didn't understand.

Cai nodded. "A collar isn't always about subjugation, taming. Sometimes it just means belonging. You're a pack animal, Rand. Everything to you is about belonging."

"Vampires aren't like that?"

Cai scoffed. "Alone is better for us. We're vicious killers, Rand." His mouth tightened, though he kept the same light, I-don't-give-a-damn tone. "Some of the vampires pretend to be civilized so they can live in the human world. Then they get surprised when they try to tear one another apart. But maybe all of us humanoids have that problem." Cai studied him. "Except one like you."

He retrieved the meat and broth, bringing it back to Rand. "There. Put this away. Then we'll talk about our lives and feelings, the way self-respecting males do it. With a stranger and copious amounts of alcohol."

CHAPTER FOUR

"So how did you lose your pack, wolf?" Cai gestured with the half-empty bottle of Jack and Rand took it, indulging another long, generous swig that helped the swirling, pleasant numbness along.

"You can finish it," the vampire said. "Had all I need."

Rand nodded. He'd eaten the rest of the rabbit and, as the night deepened, Cai had brought out the Jack Daniels. They didn't talk about too much of import at first. Cai asked him some more about what Rand knew of vampires and servants. At first, Rand thought Cai was testing him, determining the extent of his knowledge, but the vampire's follow up questions and curiosity suggested he wasn't aware of a lot of stuff about the relationship between vampires and servants. Curious.

The firelight got even more wavy. Rand was feeling sleepy. He could ignore the vampire's latest question, about the loss of his pack. Answering it would hurt too much. Thanks to the alcohol, maybe not quite as much as it usually did, but still. If he had to choose between a rusty knife excising his organs, or a truck running over him, backing up and doing it again, he'd tried to avoid either. He asked his own question instead.

"Tell me why you're not hanging out with your own kind."

"Vampires aren't pack animals." The vamp made it sound like an insult, but Rand ignored the goad.

"Yeah, but you still usually have a servant or belong to a territory. Network or that type of thing, with others of your kind."

"Network." Cai let out a short laugh, amused but ugly. "Your vocabulary wasn't entirely lost while you were four-legged. That's a hell of a word to describe vampire social skills. But okay. You tell me your touchy-feely sob story and I'll tell you whatever closely approximates it from my sad, wasted life. But you have to go first or no deal."

"You"—Rand pointed at him, squinting a little—"are a miserable bastard."

"Yeah. But I'm good at fucking. Admit it."

Rand snorted. "So's a deodorant bottle, you lube it up enough."

Cai chuckled, leaning back on his palms on the other side of the fire. He had his legs stretched out and ankles crossed in a far-too-appealing way. He seemed to like the jeans-only, no-shirt look. Maybe because he knew that it kept drawing Rand's attention. His laughter was genuine, though, inspiring Rand to grin at him. "Now I get it," Cai said. "You hadn't had a good deodorant bottle in months. I happened along..."

"And I couldn't control myself." Rand nodded vigorously and drained the last of the Jack.

"Need to take you to a sex toy store, wolf. They've made some serious improvements on that bottle idea."

When Rand's cheeks warmed, Cai's brows lifted. "You've never?"

"Of course not. I don't...we didn't..."

"Ever been to a strip club?"

"No." Sheba would have taken a strip off their hides. But it was more than that. "The noise and scents...they're unpleasant. A co-worker who didn't know what I was tried to take me once. Dirty place at an old truck stop. No windows. Closed in."

"Ah. They've made a lot of improvements on the venue, too." Cai's gaze glittered behind the leaping flames. He was looking at Rand as if he'd told the vampire he was a virgin, but thankfully, Cai moved on. "While I nurse my bruised feelings about being equated to a toiletry item, tell me more about shifters. Beyond the fact they avoid human vices. Except for drinking."

Rand studied the bottle. When it had been half full, the reflected firelight had danced through the remaining liquid. Becoming a wolf was where he went when he needed to grieve, so he hadn't indulged the bottle much, hadn't used that crutch. He wasn't much of a drinker, so he guessed he didn't have a good tolerance for it. The vampire was having no problems. Oh, he was acting friendly and mellow, but those sharp eyes were just as sharp. Maybe vampires didn't get drunk; they just used alcohol to take the edge off. Well, no argument with that. He kind of wished Cai had another bottle, but refused to ask.

Start with the easier stuff, he thought to himself. He didn't have to start at all. But maybe it was the intimacy-of-strangers stuff, the alcohol, the fucking. Cai saving his life and knowing so much about him already, so fast. He knew he was going to talk. So might as well do it. He'd likely regret it.

"Pack leaders are hetero." Rand moved his attention from the bottle to the flame. Trying to keep the images in his head to a minimum. "Just the way it is. You have to produce pups to keep the pack strong, right? And wolves just aren't... There aren't many of them like me. But I found one. Dylef. That's probably getting ahead of things, though. You don't know much about shifters."

"Only what I know from the one I found in the forest. Clever and violent. They bleed. Stubborn as hell. Made-for-sex body when the fur goes away." Cai's gaze slid over Rand's chest and down to his genitals. "Well, when most of it goes away. I like the pelt that remains. Start with the general stuff," he added quietly, uncomfortably reinforcing Rand's own thought. "Work up to the other."

"Not going to tell you the other." Rand lifted the bottle, remembered it was empty, set it down again. "Shifters are kind of like vampires. Most of us are born shifters. Bitten people don't shift unless they consent, are approved by a pack and are brought in to do the ritual for it. And it doesn't always take."

Cai pursed his lips. He had a good mouth. A distracting one. "Does a born shifter come out in a litter of puppies or as a human baby?"

"A litter." Rand nodded at his expression of surprise. "Once the female conceives, she can stay in human form for a little while, but eventually she has to shift. She'll stay a wolf through their birth and weaning. The pack remains close, in either form, during that time, because she's unable to defend herself without risking the pregnancy. Maybe because of the mix of anatomy, it's hard to carry a shifter litter to full term. About one out of every five conceptions results in a litter, and most often it's the alpha male and female in a pack who manage it."

He shrugged at Cai's curious look. "No idea why, but wolf wolves—"

"Is that the official term for wolves that aren't shifters?"

"Not officially." Rand ignored Cai's smirk. "Shut up if you want me to tell you. Non-shifter wolves usually only have one breeding pair per pack, and it's the alpha male and female. They lose about sixty percent of their litters to starvation or predators."

Not being able to supply food for his family. That was a problem he hadn't had. Before...everything that had happened, he'd thought about the non-shifter wolves, and how awful it would be to have a pup die merely because you weren't fast enough, couldn't find enough game...

"I guess that's part of why shifters have been able to stay so invisible. Low population." Cai's voice drew him away from that darkness. Rand focused on the vampire, saw the blue eyes watching him, watching him deep. But not in a mean way.

"Yeah." Rand resumed his explanation. "When she shifts back to human is when the pups shift to human for the first time."

At Cai's fascinated expression, the corner of Rand's mouth tugged up. "You know how some mothers don't want to give up on breast feeding? Well, the wolf version of that is the mother wolf who holds off on that first shift as long as possible. Part of it is because it's hugely stressful. The babies have no control over it. It's a compulsion that hits them when the mother shifts that first time. One moment they're a wolf puppy, the next, they're a human baby, a few months old. If the pups are healthy, it's rarely fatal, but for the first couple days they're pretty freaked out and need a lot of attention."

"I'd think it would be the mother who would be freaked out, suddenly having a volleyball team of human babies."

Rand chuckled. "We don't have more than three or four in a litter, but that's still a lot. It's why having pack members is critical at that time. When she does the shift, the event is planned. All hands are on deck to help with the transition. There's a celebration. Like a birthday party for the pups, an accolade to the mother and her mate. The pups are communally raised. Which is good. It means everyone gets a chance to be parents, even if they can't conceive or bring a litter to term."

"So when do they shift back to wolves again?" Cai asked. His questions about less personal aspects of Rand's life was giving Rand more space to breathe. Maybe he didn't have to talk about the other stuff. He laid his spinning head back on the tree behind him.

"About five years old. They shift back and forth with no control, which means they're closely monitored until they get a handle on it. That happens around puberty. Most pups are home schooled until they reach their teens. Until then, stress or unpleasant emotion can flip the switch." Rand pushed that thought away, again avoiding the dark chasm that waited beyond it.

"Once they learn control, what's to stop them from doing it to impress their human friends? They're still teenagers."

"Yes, but far more mature than kids at that age. If you think about it, a non-shifter wolf lives to be somewhere between ten and eighteen, depending on how tough life is on them. While we have a human's longevity, there's a certain level of accelerated maturation for pups. A thirteen-year-old shifter is about a decade ahead of their human counterparts, at least in impulse control. The bond with the parents is also extremely strong. They defer to them on all decisions until they're old enough to establish an adult role in the pack."

"Ah." Cai shifted, lacing his fingers behind his head. Bare-chested and bathed by firelight, it increased the distraction effect. Things probably weren't helped by Rand's nakedness, where every reaction he had to the vampire was all the more noticeable. But Cai hadn't offered him clothes, and seemed to prefer him like this, another unsettling message.

Rand's mouth was dryer than it should be. Cai must be hearing Rand's thoughts, but his expression gave nothing away. Holding the upper hand. The vampire was just dominant by nature. He didn't really understand the significance of it, the gravity that attended such dominance. Which was why Rand resented his own reaction to it, the craving it opened in him. He was craving an illusion, and his brain was too fogged by grief and alcohol to care.

"Want to come sit over here?" Cai asked.

Rand shook his head. "Time for you to tell your sob story."

"Let me get a few more details of yours. Mine's boring."

"You're avoiding."

"Maybe. But I find you far more interesting than me. Where were you born?"

Rand gave him a look, but relented. It was an easier question. "Colorado. Lost my parents early, car crash. But the new alpha of the pack, my father's beta Sylvan, did okay for a while. He had Sheba, his alpha female, and she was tough as nails. Dylef was accepted into the pack soon after that. He had left a pack in Washington state when there was a change of leadership. I met him one night on a run in the forest."

Rand paused, remembering it. He liked to run on his own at times, and that had been one of them. When the unfamiliar scent crossed his path, he tracked it. Dylef had shifted to human, and was bathing in a deep-water creek, the noise and wind direction masking Rand's approach.

Dylef had a wolf tattoo that stretched across the broadest part of his back. If Rand closed his eyes, he could almost reach out, trail his fingers along it like he had then, for he'd shifted, too. Come slowly into the water, the two of them staring at one another, knowing. As rare as shifters were, what they were—male wolves who preferred males—was even rarer. It didn't make Rand desperate. He had had hookups with human males to take the edge off, but inhaling the scent of a fellow wolf who looked at him with sexual interest, the way he looked right back at him...

His instincts had led him. He'd drawn closer, stood before Dylef, met his gaze. Dylef had not spoken, but after some long, weighted moments, punctuated by the sounds of the creek, the wind and the birdsong, he'd averted his gray eyes just enough, dipped his head. Rand had leaned in, pressed his nose to his crown, inhaled. Dylef had dark blond hair, a little long, and it tickled Rand's nose. He liked everything he smelled, and he let his mouth drift to his ear, nipped there, nipped the neck. Nudged him so he turned, so Rand could trail his fingers down his back. Over the tattoo.

Then, with a tilt of his head and playful flash of his eye, Dylef bolted from the water, shifting beautifully into a silver and white wolf. Rand had leaped after him, and the chase, the beginning...had begun.

He'd been quiet for a while, he realized. The crickets were chirping, the fire making its soft crackling, popping noise. It had been warm for a fire tonight, but the vampire seemed to like having one and Rand didn't object to the ambient light.

"Then Grey came in." He should have left it there, but something brought forth the words.

"Grey? His parents stretched themselves on that name. I guess Wolfgang was taken."

"Yeah." But Rand didn't smile. He turned the bottle in his hands, watching the firelight get captured and released by the glass.

"Grey came from an urban pack. They're a different, harder breed, less connected to the land, stronger footholds in human culture. He'd been run out of there by a stronger alpha. Well, a stronger alpha and a team of betas that knew he was bad news. He was tossed out with three or four male wolves who became his betas. Big, mean. Street smart. If they were the weaker members of the pack, I'd never want to meet the alpha, though I applaud his decision to kick Grey's ass out. Just wish he'd killed him instead, but I guess even the urbans have a strong code on that. There aren't enough of us to be killing one another over anything less than the gravest offenses. At that time, I guess Grey hadn't crossed that line."

"Too bad you can't kill someone for future crimes, right?"

Rand's gaze shifted to Cai. He wasn't surprised the vampire was already putting it together. It wasn't a hard story to follow, or even all that unique of one. Didn't make the pain any less.

"Grey challenged Sylvan. When he beat him, he didn't accept Sylvan's capitulation." Rand shook his head. "We didn't see it coming. We'd let ourselves become too complacent, expecting all wolves to respect our pack rules, no matter where they came from. He killed Sylvan, and then ordered his betas to take out Sylvan's pups. Four six-year-old kids."

Rand's jaw hardened. "In the wild, wolves, lions, certain pack animals like that, will kill the pups of the dominant female to put her back into heat, after they run off or take out the male. Don't know if he was so messed up he thought that was what he was doing, but nobody was going to stand for that.

"We all fought them, including Sheba. Others in the pack formed a rear guard, helped Sheba and her pups get away. Because of the age of the kids, she needed at least a couple of pack members to escape with her, provide ongoing protection. That ended up being me and Dylef.

It was a brutal fight, but we got lucky. None of the pups were harmed, though several of the pack were badly wounded, helping us get free. We heard later the rest of them scattered."

He looked into the darkness of the forest. He could shift and run. Just run and leave all this behind. He didn't know what the alcohol would do in his wolf's system, but he didn't really care.

"Hey." He turned his head. How had the vampire moved next to him without him noticing? Cai slid Rand's hair over his shoulder, his strong hand stroking tense muscles. He nudged beneath Rand's chin, his mouth landing on Rand's pulse to suck and nip. Rand's hand on the empty bottle tightened, his head dropping all the way back. Too late, he realized it would be interpreted as an act of submission. Rand wanted to shove him away, but Cai caught his hand, interlacing their fingers. "Tell the rest of it," the vampire murmured.

"Not like this. Let this...just be this." Rand closed his eyes as Cai's tongue teased him, down to his collar bone. He let go of the bottle to lift his hand, stroke it over the vampire's short hair. His touch drifted to the top point of Cai's spine, his back, over that sunburst set of scars, as Cai worked his way down his chest, his abdomen. Rand eased back to a reclining position, resting his upper body on his elbows.

"Your propensity for being naked when you shift is very useful. And yes, fucking distracting," Cai noted, before his mouth closed over Rand's cock, and went all the way to the root. It was an impressive accomplishment, since Rand was on the way to being fully hard. The vampire's grip moved, one hand resting on the base of Rand's throat, a touch to admonish him to stillness. The other wrapped around his cock as Cai went after it with a singular intensity that had Rand shoving up into his hold, strangling on a gasp.

No time for the thoughts of loss to completely flee before they were drowning in sexual desire, an unsettling mix that tore things open in his chest. "Stop...Cai."

Did the vampire think that it would help, that somehow sex could shove the other out of the way? The loss of love and family, of connection. The only way someone could think that was if that someone had never actually had those things. The thought flitted through Rand's mind, a revelation about the vampire, but too much of his own personal crap was swamping him to hold onto it.

So long, too long since he'd been worked over like this. And Dylef, blessed Dylef, it'd been more of a give and take between them, though Rand was top most of the time.

Cai lifted his head and brushed lips that smelled and tasted like Rand's musk against him. He settled back on an elbow, too, but he was leaning over Rand so he could keep his hand on Rand's chest, playing in the gleaming hair there. Rand guessed Cai liked it so much because vampires were hairless below the neck. The contrast seemed to please him. "So keep going," Cai said, though his eyes slid to Rand's cock, hard and high on his belly. "Tell me all of it and I'll finish what I started."

The arousal had been goaded by Cai's touch, by his looks, by the experience they'd had earlier. But at those words, desire left Rand. The hard fist already squeezing him below the ribs increased its reach, bringing his heart into it. Rand rolled away and rose, staring down at Cai.

What lay behind the vampire's eyes? They were so flat, someone without Rand's senses would have thought there was nothing beneath. But he sensed more to Cai than that. Which just pissed Rand off worse.

"I'm not going to give you any more of my story. I really can't. You can use my dick for a distraction, but not my family. I get that you think it's in the past and done with, who the hell cares, the wolf's story a fun diversion between hard-ons, but it's not like that for me."

For him it was two seconds ago, right now, all of it flashing through his head two, three, ten times a day. Except when he shifted. God, he wanted to shift. He was starting to feel wrong in his skin.

"Stay with me," Cai said quietly, a command but also something else. He rose and stepped back into Rand's personal space. When he caressed Rand's jaw with his knuckles, Rand clasped his wrist, but he didn't push away. Just increased the pressure. A warning.

"Why? Except for wanting to screw me as a human, why do you care?"

The vampire's gaze revealed something that surprised Rand, especially when he reversed their grips so he was holding Rand's forearm, bringing his wrist up to eye level between them. When Rand tried to wrest away, the vampire set his feet, meeting him with equal strength.

"*This* bugs me," the vampire said shortly.

The direction of his glance, the tightening of his grip just below it, told Rand what he meant. The vertical scar on his right wrist, remnants of a razor-sharp cut that had opened the vein, matching the one on his left.

"Well, don't let it." It took a hard yank, but Rand pulled his wrist away and stepped back. The churning emotions surged up out of the clogged drain, ready to drown everything. "That's my business, and it's done here. I didn't need you to save me, hunt for me or take care of me, but you did, all for a good fuck. Well, payment delivered. I'm done."

The vampire's jaw hardened and Rand tensed, ready for the fight he was sure was about to erupt. Instead, Cai's expression shuttered again, and he stepped back. "Fine. Take off, wolf."

As Cai spoke, Rand was already letting the shift have him, reaching for it as eagerly as a meth addict. The comparison didn't please him, but he couldn't think of an analogy to replace it. That was fine. Only his human part worried about that kind of thing. His wolf didn't do metaphors, analogies or self-analysis of any kind.

He plunged into the forest at a run, leaving the vampire behind, his addictive touch and toxic personality. But eventually the burn in his side and hitch in his gait, evidence of the healing still needed, forced him to slow. He kept moving forward, wanting to put as much distance as he could between him and the vampire. Rand tried to keep aware of game, but a search for food he didn't really need couldn't prevent the rest of the story from unfolding in his mind. Images that neither wolf nor human could escape brought him to a halt, and he stood, quivering, his mind caught up in what could never be left behind, no matter how fast he ran.

He, Dylef, Sheba and her pups had settled on a rural piece of land in the foothills of Tennessee. Rand didn't have a lot of funds, but Sheba and Dylef did, so they'd purchased a big rambling farm house with plenty of rooms. They were close enough to a town that Sylvan's pups, when they were old enough, would be able to attend the local school, learn about human society, develop human friends. Even preferring woods and wild spaces, most shifters knew familiarity and comfort with human society was critical to blend and have more resources to protect them.

Rand had never developed that comfort, though he was familiar enough. Dylef loved the human world, with its movie theaters, cocktail theme bars and art museums. Rand teased him about it, but Dylef had talked him into a few trips to indulge his interest. Rand hadn't found it as odious as he expected, but he still mostly did it because making Dylef happy made Rand happy.

To pull his weight financially, Rand did highway roadside mowing through a contractor. Dylef was a forest ranger with the National Park Service. He never failed to stir Rand's libido when he donned the park uniform. One night, Dylef had called him a badge bunny, joking that if he'd chosen to be a cop, Rand never would let him out of bed. In response, Rand had fucked him within an inch of his life.

Yeah, sometimes that give-and-take resulted in an outright taking. Dylef had been surprised at the roughness, but his response had said he wanted more of that from his alpha wolf. Way more. Rand wondered if they might have eventually ended up at one of those toy stores Cai had flustered him by mentioning.

They'd settled into that life for several years, and it was a nice life. Dylef and he had a wing of the house with a lockout door that was never locked, except when he and Dylef needed privacy. They didn't want Sylvan's young to stumble on them, since they were becoming way too curious about such things. Then one day, Sheba came to have a heart-to-heart talk with him.

"You were meant to be a pack leader, Rand. What happened that day with Grey..."

~

Sheba had dark eyes and shiny ebony hair. She was tall and slender, and her wolf was likewise light-bodied, long-legged and sleek, her fur a dark brown. When she and Sylvan had hunted with the pack, she'd been the fleetest, the one most likely to get in front of a deer, dart in and clamp down on the nose to help bring the meal down.

She was gentle with her pups, and a loving and firm matriarch to their family, small and unorthodox as it was. But Rand would never forget the brutal savagery she'd showed when they fought Grey. She had the heart of a warrior. She and Sylvan had been life mates. Rand had no doubt she'd shed a waterfall of tears for him, but except for right after they'd gotten away, she shared them with no one. She was the strongest female he'd ever met.

"*You* were meant to be a pack leader," he told her in amused response, but it was true. She could have been, if not for the simple fact that alpha male wolves were physically stronger than alpha females. No matter how much their human sides embraced tolerance and diversity, wolves were guided by practical animal instinct toward black and white decisions.

"You jumped into the fight the moment Grey...the moment he didn't accept Sylvan's capitulation. Same as I did." A shadow moved behind her gaze. "If you hadn't responded so quickly, the full pack might not have gotten involved, and we might have lost...more."

She removed her light wrapper against the evening's chill. He sat on the bed, so she surprised him by kneeling on the floor, tilting her head up toward him in a submissive gesture. "I know you haven't pursued a pack because you are too honest, and you don't want to put a female into the position of being your mate, when you couldn't love her as you believe you should."

Rand's brow furrowed and he took her hand, resting on his knee. "Come sit with me, Sheba. What's this about?"

She shook her head, remaining on her knees. "I'm petitioning you as my pack leader, Rand, because that's how I see you, and how I defer to you." A light smile touched her lips. "You may not recognize it when I'm scolding you about wiping your feet before you come into the house, but there it is. We're not mated, but you're the alpha now, to me and to Dylef. I won't love another again like I loved my Sylvan."

Her fingers closed into a fist on his thigh, her face becoming resolute. "I will be your mate. You, Dylef, my pups, and whomever we conceive together, will be our pack. Your pack. We need to form a strong family here, one that someone like Grey will never be able to threaten again."

~

He and Dylef had talked it over, and yeah, it made sense. He loved her and Dylef, as well as Sylvan's children. Yet he hadn't understood how much, or how such a love could etch grief on one's face and heart in permanent grooves.

After she'd lost Sylvan and they left Colorado, those lines had appeared on Sheba's face. Like a painting that had been redone over the original, so subtly that only someone who understood it would notice. But when they did, when they recognized it because they'd been there themselves, there was nothing subtle about it.

Rand broke back into a run, no matter the burning in his side or the pain in his leg. Maybe it would help. But the memories kept coming.

She'd become pregnant almost immediately, and Dylef had teased him about his virility. He'd offered Dylef the honors before it happened, but Dylef had only rolled his eyes. "You're the alpha," Dylef said dryly. "That's truth and instinct. I lay a paw on that female and she will rip off my dick with her teeth." He'd sobered then, nudging Rand. "It's you. You're our leader."

As Rand looked back at himself through that lens, he saw how young they'd all been. How fucking stupid. But none of them wanted to be at anyone's mercy again, and it had seemed like the smartest way to do it. They had time. Right? Wrong.

His children had been born the spring after she had that discussion with him. Four pups. It had been a remarkable blessing, her carrying Rand's first litter to term. She'd had three miscarries with Sylvan before it took.

Five years later, Grey found them again.

Through various communications with old pack members over the years, they knew that Grey had tried to pull the Colorado pack back together. He'd succeeded somewhat, through sheer brutality, and built the pack up, but his methods caused ripples of reaction from other packs. To most wolves, a pack was about family. To Grey, it was about conquest. Dylef had once called him Napoleon with fur, with grim humor. Given that a pack's territory was usually large, his ability to run afoul of trouble with other packs exceeded all expectations. When the area packs banded together and gave him the choice of execution or exile, he chose exile.

What they didn't know was that, in his frustration, Grey decided that all his problems had started with Sheba's snub and Dylef and

Rand's defiance. With nothing to hold them in Colorado, he and his betas had started tracking them down.

Rand had underestimated Grey's hatred, how it fueled his willingness to travel all the way across the country to express it. While he already knew that Grey followed no protocols but his own, this time he broke almost every rule, using resources no honorable wolf would to resolve a dispute.

The only rule he didn't break, the one that allowed Rand to take him out, came far too late.

Rand couldn't outrun it. He skidded to a halt, swung his head and hit it against a tree trunk, hard enough to knock himself insensible. He didn't want to see it again, couldn't. The pups. God. His young. Sheba's. Dylef.

He was whimpering as he struck himself again. He couldn't do it hard enough. If there was a cliff nearby, he would have flung himself from it.

Rand, don't. Sshh...Easy.

The voice helped, but he couldn't identify it. There was a sense of someone nearby, coming closer. A comfort, though he told himself that was an illusion.

He dropped to the ground, panting, his body quitting on him, overcome by too many different types of pain. Too much.

Make it stop.

They set the house on fire. Grey and his males had shifted to human, something wolves didn't do during a challenge. There was a ritual. Grey had challenged Sylvan and fought wolf to wolf. Not this time.

Grey's wolves had come in downwind. They used the guns they brought to shoot Sheba as she was coming out of the front door. That was where Rand had found her. She'd been distracted, Rand guessed. His four offspring, now shifting randomly between human and wolf, were a lot to handle. Everyone helped, including Sheba and Sylvan's children, the three now in high school, but Sheba was most involved in their care.

Dylef apparently burst from his woodworking shed when he heard the gunfire. They shot him in the chest. Rand had imagined the blood blooming there as he fell to his knees, his eyes confused, hazy. Then vacant. Gone in a blink, no time for good-byes, last words. Nothing. The last thing he'd said to Rand had been something ridiculously innocuous like, "I'll be out to help you after I put a coat of finish on the table." The scent of the finish had also masked the approach of Grey and his pack.

Rand was out in the back field, working on the tractor they used, because they sold crops on the side to supplement their income. The engine was running, so he didn't hear the gunfire, but an uneasy feeling had him cutting off the tractor to listen, scent the wind. That was when he smelled smoke.

Running; he was running, hearing more gun fire. They were torching the house when he got there. Two of Grey's betas came out of the kitchen door. They carried bats. Bloodstained bats, the baseball bats he'd bought for Sylvan's boys, who were on the team at their high school. They practiced in the backyard with Dylef and Rand some nights while Sheba made dinner and watched with a smile out the spacious kitchen window.

"Not worth wasting a bullet. Easy as taking out water balloons," one of the betas had laughed.

Rand hadn't realized the soul could be destroyed by laughter. Sometimes the heart didn't have the strength to comprehend—or survive—the cruelty of the soulless.

His children. Maple, Teague, Cira. Shy. His little girl, frailer than the rest, but gaining strength every day. She should have grown up to be teased by her brothers and sisters about being the runt of the litter.

But realizing they were gone, putting together those bloodstained bats with the unthinkable, had come later. At that second, Silas and Slate, Sylvan's boys, exploded out of the attic windows with a shower of glass. In wolf form, they ran across the roof line and launched themselves onto the shoulders of the two males.

The attic was their hangout, where they listened to music and did their homework after they finished their chores. Sheba usually gave them a couple uninterrupted hours to do that before she had them take over babysitting, while she and Mischa prepared dinner.

They'd probably had the music up so loud, and hadn't realized the intruders were in the house until it was too late. The young males came out of the windows with the single-minded ferocity of their parents, not hesitating to launch themselves at the men armed with guns.

Rand redoubled his efforts to get to them, but even with his speed, it wasn't enough. Still, Sylvan would have been so proud of his children. Slate and Silas killed those murdering bastards before Grey's other followers shot them, cowards that they were.

Later, Rand would learn they'd already killed Mischa, on the basketball court they'd poured for the kids behind the barn. She was trying out for the school team.

All the teens had been so athletic. So strong and beautiful, every one of them. When he shifted, Slate's wolf form looked so much like his father. Gray and white with shimmering threads of brown that gave his coat the salt and pepper look.

Rand had one goal, and nothing stopped him. The bullets fired at him missed as he shifted in mid-run, clothes torn away. He charged through their ranks and landed on Grey with a roar of rage and pain that should have echoed through the forest a mile around.

Though his men had their dishonorable weapons and were in human form, once the alpha was directly engaged in challenge, no other wolf would interfere. The one single, fucking law they refused to break. Tragic and laughable. All he had in that second was rage. They hadn't been able to stop him from getting to Grey. Now the coward had to face him, fight him.

And they fought. How long, Rand didn't know. Later he would recall he took Grey out in a matter of seconds. It didn't matter. His heart was broken, his soul shredded, and every moment since then had felt like an eternity.

He pinned him down, ripped out his throat, broke his back, dug into his chest cavity and ate his heart. Then he stood over Grey's mangled body, his muzzle soaked with blood, and snarled like a hellhound. Every one of the other males backed up, dropped to a knee, guns lowered. A couple of them he scared so bad they turned wolf in their clothes and groveled on their bellies while tangled in the garments.

There was no victory to it. Sheba had been right. He was meant to lead a pack. But he'd been so busy trying to lead a simple, quiet life, he'd made the same fucking mistake, leaving his guard down. Only this time, he'd lost everything worth living for.

~

Rand was up and running again. Running. Pain was such a small matter, even when the closed wounds broke and bled.

He ran until he stumbled and fell to the ground, too exhausted, hazy with alcohol and blood loss, to think anymore. Mission accomplished.

Yet when he came to that forced halt and collapsed, he had enough turmoil left inside to put his head back and howl his agony. Long, haunting rolls of sound that echoed through the forest, stilled every other voice, because all souls understood that song.

He'd given Cai the rest of the story. He'd always turned into the wolf to mute the picture and sound of those memories, but this time his human side had refused to cooperate, his mind refusing to shift all the way to animal. The thoughts had unrolled in his mind like a map the vampire could use to dig deeper into him. And he probably would, for no reason other than curiosity.

He could do it at a distance. This time Rand was going to go even deeper into the forest, as far from human habitation as his feet could take him. When he could get up.

It wasn't really a surprise when the vampire sat down next to him. Rand smelled him coming, and Cai could run as fast as he could. Not that Rand had been setting any speed records.

He was so not in the mood for his shit. But the vampire said nothing. He checked the wound, and put pressure on it with a folded-up bandage he had brought with him in a small pack. He ignored Rand's half-hearted growl, uttering a mild murmur of rebuke. Rand wouldn't have minded the fight, but he was just too tired.

Then the vampire did something peculiar, which reminded Rand of that brief voice in his head earlier, soothing him.

He stretched out behind Rand, who was lying on his side, panting. Cai put a hand on his head, stroking, then rested it on his ruff and shoulder. He brought his body closer, spooning it around Rand's wolf form.

"Rest," the vampire murmured. "I'm sorry, Rand. Sorry I'm a bastard, and so sorry that happened to you."

A breath shuddered out of Rand. He didn't want to shift, but he was doing so. Why? Because he wanted to feel Cai's body spooning against his in the way humans did, the way Dylef had slept with him, and sometimes Sheba, especially if they all piled into the one king-sized bed together.

Cai made a warm sound of approval that felt better than it should have. He clucked over the mess it made of the bandage, but rose to re-dress it while Rand lay there, eyes staring into the forest. He wanted to be somewhere else, and yet here, too. He didn't know why until Cai lay behind him again. He tugged Rand's hair, winding it around his fist. Rand was learning that hold could be oddly distracting, tightening things in his chest and lower abdomen.

"Sorry, I'm still hard," the vampire said, without sounding particularly apologetic. "It's a vampire thing. Ignore it. I don't want that from you right now."

Or translation: He wasn't so much of a bastard that he would try to take it in this moment.

Rand closed his eyes. He could feel the vampire's cock against his lower back, and it reminded him of how this had all started, the vampire's hand on him, his mouth. He hadn't been ready for that, too much else pushing down on him, but now it had all drained away, the plug pulled. Why not focus on the temptation, take another type of drug, before the sadness filled him up again?

Rand hated himself for thinking it. Why couldn't his pain make him immune to that type of need? It should.

But what did it matter? There was no right way to deal with loss. If turning into a wolf or lying with a vampire gave him a moment's distraction, who was he to be high and mighty and pretend he wasn't truly an animal at heart, resorting to physical gestures to minimize mental pain? Maybe sex could push things away. Even if it made him simultaneously feel horrible.

"Something you want, wolf?" Cai said. His tone was quiet, neutral.

Not taunting or even seductive. "You quivered against me just then. If you want something, ask for it."

Rand shook his head. *If you want sex, do it. I need it, want it, but I'm never going to beg for it.*

"That's why the promise of tomorrow is so sweet, wolf,' Cai muttered. "All the nevers that can be toppled."

Cai didn't fuck him, though. He pressed his cock against Rand's ass, and Rand moved back against him. Cai's hips moved just enough, Rand's counter push rocking them in a sweet, delicious roll of feeling. The vampire was being slow, gentle, easy. His hand slid around Rand's hip, and he cupped Rand's balls and cock, covering as much of them as he could, and pressing tight, using that intimate but stationary hold to keep Rand where he was, just as close.

It was arousing but also enough on its own. The contact, a possession of sorts, brought a sense of relief Rand didn't want to examine too closely. He let out a breath, and the vampire shifted his grip up to his chest, their fingers interlacing like a net, drawing them closer together.

Rand pressed his face into the ground, making a despairing noise as Cai's mouth found his throat. He gripped Rand's jaw and tried to turn his face back toward him for a kiss. Rand shook his head and kept his face pressed down. No kissing, nothing that intimate. Just simple fucking, nothing complicated.

The vampire paused. Cai could push it, Rand knew, force the issue. But in the end he didn't, holding them in that spooned, finger-interlaced embrace, rocking them. Rand got lost in the movement, which kept him a hand span above the memories of blood and death. It was a tenuous thread that could be snapped, but for this, he would stay human a little longer.

Just a little longer. But he was still leaving.

CHAPTER FIVE

*C*ai beat him to it. In a manner of speaking.

Daylight found the vampire gone. Last night, he'd reminded Rand he went to ground during sunlight, since over the past few days Rand had been mostly unconscious during the daylight hours.

Right. Vampires and sun didn't mix.

"Go wherever you want to go, wolf," Cai had added. "If I have the desire to track you, I'll catch up. With the first and second mark, it's a waste of energy to hide or run from me. But I'd suggest you find a place nearby to take it easy. Another full day of rest, and you should be good to go. So to speak."

Rand had made it clear, rather nastily, that if he chose to leave the vampire's company, that was not to be interpreted as running or hiding from him. It merely showed Cai was too thickheaded to get the hint. Cai had flashed his annoyingly devastating grin and said nothing more. His hand had whispered down Rand's flank, clamped on it hard and given his ass a bruising pinch. The fingerprints were still visible on Rand's human flesh in the morning light, so he shifted pretty fast back to wolf.

Rand wondered if the vampire had found a cave, but his scent ended right at the camp boundary. Must be another vampire skill, and a damn annoying one. Rand didn't like not knowing where Cai was.

Not because he gave a damn, but to respect the wisdom of "keep your friends close, but your enemies closer."

He wasn't sure Cai was an enemy, but he couldn't think of him as a friend, no matter the confusing signals the male sent. When he'd found Rand in the woods last night, he could have pushed the sex, and Rand would have gone along with it. But he hadn't. It made it harder to categorize his interest in Rand as merely a new diversion.

That would be easier, though. Rand wasn't opposed to fucking as human. Humans savored and explored the act at levels far different from the rest of the animal world. Cai had reminded him of that, vividly. Everyone knew vampires were seductive and gorgeous, and so sexually driven that even a fledgling became an experienced lover in no time. So why shouldn't Rand enjoy the vampire's skill?

It wasn't like empty sex with a promise of nothing else could suck any more life out of his soul. Couldn't get any marrow from a dry bone.

That's what he told himself, but when Rand had the thought, it came with the hope the vampire woke up with no desire to track him and moved on. Then Rand wouldn't have to deal with a decision or choice. Truth, if Rand had less pride, he would have spent the entire day running to put as much distance between them as possible, in the hopes of being too inconvenient to bother with.

But Cai had said it would take a few thousand miles to be out of mind-touch range. If Rand couldn't shut the vampire out of his head, he *would* find a more effective way to kill himself. Or the vampire.

Rand paused in a patch of sunlight, sure he felt a frisson of humor run through his mind in a way he hadn't initiated. As if the vampire was listening to him and was...amused. Bastard.

I need something to take into my dreams with me, wolf. I showed admirable restraint last night. Put your hand on your cock and stroke yourself to release.

What? No. Good grief, was the vampire never sated? Though with that damn second mark, his body responded to the suggestion with an annoying twitch of interest in his lower parts.

I can see it in my mind. Cai was continuing his annoying fantasizing. *You, stretched out on the grass, your fingers wrapped over yourself, ass pressing into the earth as you thrust and retreat, thrust and retreat. And then you roll onto your knees as you get close, and spill your seed, holding yourself up on one arm, hard muscles rippling like water over your back and shoulders, your hair falling forward. If you get your come in it, you could bathe in a creek, and I could feel you doing that, the cool water on your heated flesh, you sliding your fingers through your hair to comb it back from your face...*

No. He was in wolf form. He didn't want to become human. But the vampire was too good at this.

Maybe if you have time between self-destructive urges today, you'll think about what we could do tonight when I rise. How I'll want you with such fierce hunger, I won't leave you any choices, no room for guilt or sorrow in your mind. I'll call your hunger to mine.

Rand dropped into a seated position and irritably scratched his ear with one back foot. *Boy toys in city,* he thought in abbreviated wolf speak. *Go. Too needy for me.*

I like it out here in the wild, where I have you all to myself. Do it, Rand. Or I'll bug the shit out of you for the next three hours. I can hold out that long before I have to sleep. Though it takes a lot out of me, which means I'm likely to wake cranky and rape your fine ass rather than finesse it.

Rip your dick off with teeth first.

He'd rather have the vampire's savagery than the finesse that messed with his head, so Cai being cranky wasn't a great threat. But three hours of incessant talking? Christ.

The male was proving it, rattling on about something...McDonald's hamburgers? How he preferred them without the onions, and then there were the new drink machines, the ones that mixed flavors with one button, and totally sucked because they didn't taste right or as sharp as the other way of preparing the sodas...

Shut up if...I do? Rand once again ignored the eager leap of his loins which suggested it had different reasons for wanting to comply, other than his grudging agreement under the threat of chatty blackmail.

I know every Sesame Street song by heart.

With a sigh that nearly heaved him back onto his feet, Rand shifted into his human form, ending up on his hands and knees. "Not if you want my cock hard," he said with a scowl.

Then get to it.

Rand didn't like the hard lust that shot through his balls at the clear command. He thought longingly of how he would shift back to wolf, soon as he did this for the vampire.

He settled at the base of a tree, a convenient arrangement of roots forming a vee-shaped notch for his ass and a prop for his calf as he stretched one leg out and left the other bent, knee hooked over the exposed root. His legs were spread, yet he was in a comfortable sprawl.

Nice. He could almost hear the husky heat in Cai's mind voice.

Putting his head back against the tree's broad trunk, Rand slid his hand down his abdomen and curled his fingers around his dick.

Cup your balls first. Squeeze and stroke them. Let your thumb tease the base of your cock as you do it. The way I'd do it. Only I'd tighten my hand on you when you least expect it, holding you fast, pulling so you arched up to follow my hold...

The vampire could paint pictures in his head. Telling himself he was doing it to get it over with, Rand followed his direction, his lower belly coiling up tight as he squeezed and caressed himself. It sort of felt like the vampire was doing it, having him in his mind like this. The wind moved through the branches, touching his face.

Rand closed his eyes, losing himself to sensation, with the result being the bad tightness in his lower gut gave way to a different tightness.

Don't push into your hand. Not until I say. Let's draw this out, make you hotter.

Rand moistened his lips, and thought he felt a ripple of reaction to the gesture. "Can you...see me?"

Yes and no. I'm in your mind, so I see through your eyes somewhat, but mostly I feel your reactions and thoughts, which are even more of a turn on. I want to suck on your mouth, Rand. You have a beautiful mouth. I want it serving my cock.

Rand growled and received a dark chuckle in answer. But he remembered the shape of Cai's cock, the thickness of it. He wet his lips again, as if he could feel it there, the vampire's hand on his nape, holding him fast, shoving his cock between his lips, even if Rand fought him. He remembered what Cai had said. *A fighter likes to fight, on either side of the equation.*

His fingers worked up and down his length, a slow pump that quickly became hard to resist, meeting the movement of his hips.

Hold off. Let it build. Grow stronger.

Piss off.

Don't screw with me, wolf. I'll make you suffer for it if you do.

"Like you aren't already doing that." Rand squeezed his eyes tighter. "I don't want to feel this. Don't want to do this."

No one's forcing you, wolf. Are they? You're such a gorgeous big bastard. The vampire's mind voice had a sensual purr to it that Rand liked hearing, he couldn't deny it. *"You need a man's desire, his hold upon you, to help you power through the pain. That's what you're reaching for, even if you won't admit it.*

Shut up. Say the other stuff.

That infuriatingly sexy chuckle came in his mind again, laced with a darkness that told him Cai was right, that he was offering something twisted that Rand craved.

Work yourself, wolf. Fuck, you're beautiful. Tell me when you think you're going to come.

He could be contrary and not do it. But he got harder at the sound the vampire made in his head when Rand looked down at his hand holding his cock, the flex of his thigh muscles as he pushed his organ into the loose, slick circle his fist made, since he'd used his thumb in the slit to spread that moisture.

Fuck...yeah. Wish I was fucking you right now. Not going to be slow or gentle about it at twilight. Will do it again later, two or three times, be slower and more thorough, then. But those first few minutes, wolf, your ass will be all mine. It will be all about you getting me off, serving me entirely.

"In your dreams," Rand muttered.

Oh, you'll be front and center in those today, I promise you that. I keep thinking about how still you got when I was putting the collar on you. Hold yourself tighter. Thrust now. Show me how strong you are, even when you're healing.

He did it, because he could feel the vampire's desire surging through him, mixing with his own, one hot, wet tide carrying them both toward the inevitable conclusion.

He'd fleetingly thought he might have to summon an image of Dylef to make this work, but from the first moment the vampire had invaded his mind, Cai had driven this journey.

Yeah, I don't share. You try to get your rocks off visualizing some other male, that's not going to turn out well for you.

Defiantly Rand imagined Dylef, but he couldn't see him. He was just a shadow with a faint smile, a tall man standing in a field, taking off his bill cap to wipe the sweat off his brow with his forearm. *Ah, God...*

Stay with me, wolf. It's okay. The vampire's voice was easier, friendly. *Come back this way. Lust is easy. Right?*

Nothing is easy anymore.

I know. Which is why, if I was there, I'd put you on your stomach. I'd tie your arms and legs to the trees. You could tear loose if you wanted, but maybe for just a while you'd lie still, see how it felt to let someone have all the control. I'd put my mouth all over your shoulders and back, your ass. I'd grip both those muscular cheeks, part them, and tongue fuck you until you plowed the earth with your cock, and begged for release, for oblivion.

"God," Rand breathed. Arousal building, he was pistoning into his grip, strong and sure.

I could give you that kind of oblivion; same kind I'm going to give you in a different measure now. Look at you, fisting yourself, getting hotter from the thoughts I'm feeding you. I'd keep you tied until I touched every inch of you with mouth and hands. I'd jack myself off over your back, mark you good. I'd work myself back up again with nothing more than the sound of your groans, your need to release denied you until I allowed it, all your muscles tight and flexing. I'd drive back into you, plunge deep, and we'd both spill... Fuck, look at you. Move your hips. Thrust hard and deep. Keep doing it.

Rand was doing it. He wanted to howl, to run, to let go of all of it. To just let go.

Come for me, Rand.

His cock convulsed and spurted thick, white fluid over his knuckles, his body spasming with the reaction, his head tilting back. The bark of the tree bit into his back, and he embraced the discomfort, using it to goad the climax, drive it farther, deeper.

A long pause later, all was quiet. Well, inside. The birds were singing, the wind was moving through the trees, and life was as noisy, chaotic and unstoppable as it always was in the woods during daylight hours. Rand would have thought the vampire had succumbed to sleep, but there was an odd current of feeling running through Rand, like a stroke to his heart and mind, a humming calm, helping his breath to even out.

"Did I save myself from Sesame Street?"

You did. I'm a little disappointed. There were some Bert and Ernie duets I thought the two of us could do together.

Rand coughed over an unexpected chuckle, his lips curving in a gesture that felt strange and unfamiliar. "You really are kind of a jerk."

Only kind of? You're more tolerant after getting off. Hold onto the feeling, wolf. Don't overdo today, but enjoy the sun and wind for us both. Good morning. And in case you're as confused as most are, that's Good night in vampire. I leave you to your thoughts, but I'm not leaving you alone. Keep that in mind.

When Rand felt a slow withdrawal, a drifting away of that sense of *other* pervading his senses, he knew the vampire had given himself to sleep.

If the vampire offered any recognizable clue that he gave a damn about anyone other than himself, Rand might have concluded the whole scenario was designed to keep him from steeping himself in too much melancholy. Or keep him connected to his human form so he didn't completely lose that link.

Sheba and Dylef had both warned him about that, coaxed him to stay human more often than he would have done if he was alone. Sheba said he didn't like being human, and he ran alone more often than most wolves, maybe because he'd lost his parents young. But even before then, he'd been a more solitary wolf than most. For a pack animal.

When he was with Sheba and Dylef, staying connected between the two worlds had been important. It wasn't so important now. And if it wasn't that important to him, it made no sense why it would matter to the vampire. Yeah, Rand was imagining things. The guy just liked fucking him, which was fine. He was good at it.

So one less puzzle he didn't have to solve. He felt better, which would have discomfited him if he didn't attribute it to endorphin release from the sex. Time to go catch himself some breakfast. He didn't want the vampire having to feed him, claiming Rand was dependent on his presence.

Yeah, that was never going to happen. Yet even as he had the thought, Cai's mocking retort from last night came back to him.

That's why the promise of tomorrow is so sweet, wolf. All the nevers that can be toppled.

∼

Rand caught and devoured several rabbits, getting more confident with his speed and strength with each kill. He was supposed to eat about ten pounds of meat per day to stay at full strength. He'd been getting by on about five to seven, the amount a non-shifter wolf might eat, but he knew it had put him on the lean side. That didn't matter to him, so he wasn't sure why it mattered now, except he was hungry. Something new for him.

After consuming all that meat, he wasn't in the mood to travel far. When he woke at twilight and stretched, he was surprised not to sense the vampire close by, but maybe Cai had slept in.

He wasn't going to make it easy for him. Rand told himself that, but remembering the vampire's provocative words, the fantasy he'd painted, Rand found his feet headed toward their last campsite. Though Cai's belongings had been gone, Rand assumed it was the most logical rendezvous point for them, and it had the creek. Vampire or no vampire, he liked the idea of a bath and accessible fresh, running water.

However, some distance from it, he stilled, lifting his nose to scent the wind. Someone else was there, and whoever it was incited a deep uneasiness in him. As Rand fell into track and hunt mode, he kept his mind shifted enough to grasp all his human faculties. He also maintained his hold on his wolf's instincts and tracking abilities, so he had that plus the type of complicated reasoning that most animals didn't need in their daily lives.

It took several decades of maturity to handle that mental straddle without strain. He had that, but it still took more effort than usual. The skill was rusty, since he hadn't needed to use it much until recently, first with the hunter and then with Cai.

He'd drawn close enough to the campsite to realize what had set off his alarm bells. Vampires. Three of them. Great. With three humans. He surmised they were servants because there was a different quality to their human smell that carried their blood link with the vampires. He bore some of that scent himself with Cai's two marks, but these servants had stronger scents. Maybe because of the third mark.

As he closed in on the group with stealth and started picking up snippets of conversation, he realized two key things. They were looking for Cai. And they didn't sound like they were friends. Maybe that was why there was no sign of Cai.

Cai, you awake? You have visitors.

Rand didn't know if vampires were like humans. Some bouncing right out of their coffins perky and alert; others definitely not "morning" people, dragging their asses out way past full dark. If he had to guess, he'd say Cai was the latter.

Without any evidence of where the vampire had gone, it was possible Cai had left and was miles away. Rand could clear out of here himself, shrugging off the whole thing. But Rand wasn't certain. If Cai was somewhere nearby, holed up and vulnerable...

He thought of earlier today, the vampire's voice whispering in his mind's ear. Whether Rand had wanted to live or not, the vampire had saved his life. He had a code, which had more to do with his respect for karma than a desire to protect Cai. The guy was an asshole, but if Rand left him at the mercy of enemies when he could help, well, fate would figure out a way to zap *him* in the ass.

But exactly what could fate do worse to him? He had no one left but himself.

Just shut up, he told himself.

"He's close. I can sense it."

"You said that earlier, and we ended up going another bloody ten miles." A male voice sighed. "There's something here, though. Some... vibration of energy. The sorcerer said the amulet would help, and it's as red as it's been thus far."

Rand, on his belly in the leaves and well-concealed by foliage, saw one of the vampires hold up a red-stone pendant on a black cord. He was tall, with long golden hair plaited back to show a sharp-featured face, his slate eyes in concentrated slits. The other male had short, choppy dark hair and a Goth fashion sense, an absurd choice for hiking, though his thick tread silver-buckled boots looked decent enough for the terrain. If he hadn't been a vampire, he would have lacked any menace, a skinny male who looked barely out of college. But physical age was an unreliable measure with vampires. Cai looked about thirty, though he was over two hundred.

Scent always told Rand more about someone than they'd ever want to reveal. Gold Hair smelled older, way older than Cai. Maybe around four centuries. The Goth was about three hundred. The final member of their group fell somewhere in between.

She was a dark-haired woman wearing jeans, T-shirt and hiking shoes, the only vampire properly dressed for the environment. Her expression was steady, set. Determined. She was the hunter, probably the biggest threat of the three.

In comparison, Gold Hair was wearing freaking Armani and a Rolex. But he also appeared to be in charge and not unsettled by his surroundings. Not by so much as an out-of-place hair, and he looked coldly intent upon their goal.

The servants with them were one female and two males, properly deferential and quiet, unremarkable except they were dressed in adequate hiking gear and looked capable of handling any physical threat launched by a mere mortal.

Twilight grew deeper, darkness taking full hold. Rand wondered where the vampires had stayed out of the sun, this deep in the woods, then surmised they or their servants had scouted out one of the narrow caves that creatures of stealth and good observation skills could find throughout the mountains. Still, their being up and about this close to dusk probably reinforced their greater age, since Rand did know that older vampires had more tolerance for the approaching dawn, or being out sooner after sunset, than their younger counterparts.

Cai was outgunned, if they meant him harm. But why come to harm him? *Who have you pissed off, vampire? Other than me?*

Can't keep all this charm exclusive to you.

Rand let out a held breath. He was awake.

Stay hidden, Cai advised. *If they haul me off somewhere, you don't need to worry about it. It's been a pleasure, wolf. Maybe our paths will cross again sometime.*

What? But why would they—

When Cai had told him he would go to ground during daylight hours, Rand had taken it as an expression. He couldn't imagine anyone, even a vampire, willingly burying himself in the earth. Apparently, Cai was just such a vampire.

He emerged from beneath a covering of soil and dead leaves less than forty feet away from the cluster of vampires and their servants, startling them as well as flushing a covey of birds. The depth he'd chosen explained why his scent had ended at the edge of the campsite. Rand had to assume he used his magic to smooth the earth, rake the debris over him so that the living grave didn't stand out from the rest of the forest floor.

He wore a long-sleeved shirt and an old faded pair of jeans. His version of pajamas, Rand supposed, preserving his other clothes from soil stains. Though he looked remarkably clean as he brushed earth off himself and gazed at the assembled vampires with cool eyes.

"I hear you're looking for me."

The golden-haired vampire recovered his aplomb first, giving him a sneer. "Burying yourself like the grub you are, Trad? No self-respecting vampire would do such a thing, except as a desperate measure."

Trad? Rand frowned. The term was unfamiliar, but Cai's reaction to it was telling. A flash went through his eyes, deep and sharp as a killing rage. While it was gone in a blink, it sent a dangerous ripple of energy through the clearing. The servants exchanged uneasy glances.

"Maybe you just haven't learned to appreciate a good dirt nap. Or the irony of the undead taking one." Cai's gaze glinted. "Who are you, and what do you want? I assume you didn't come traipsing up here in your city shoes to trade insults. I'm no Trad."

"Save it. We're here to take you to Lord Greenwald and a Council delegation."

"I don't know Lord Greenwald and could give less than two fucks about the Vampire Council. None of their business is mine."

"We'll take you by force if necessary. We brought the means to do it." The woman stepped forward, unlooping a chain over her hands. Cai scoffed at her.

"If you think that will—"

Cai. Rand barked it in his head as the Goth male moved. Before Cai could whip around, he'd tossed a handful of what looked like innocuous pebbles at the vampire.

Cai's expression was appropriately baffled, just a flash. Energy shimmered and the pebbles erupted into something very different. The rocks became the sharp points on a coil of barbed wire that whipped around Cai as if he were a magnet, holding him from shoulders to knees. When he fought the binding, it constricted around his calves, toppling him to the ground. As he struggled, the lines cut into flesh, causing blood.

Stay back, Rand. Don't...let them see you.

Rand crouched in the forest undergrowth, lip curled back, animal body trembling with anger and nerves. Indecision. These weren't his people. His fight. But the vampire was obviously in pain, and yet he was taking the time to warn Rand to stay out of sight.

"Amazing how often a woman can cause a man's attention to wander at just the right moment," the female said. "Nicely done, Chavez. And the pain element is a bonus. Did the sorcerer throw that in for free?"

"Hell no." The Goth scoffed, as if he didn't think much of what the sorcerer had offered them. "That's a little gift from a blood source of mine who dabbles in the dark arts. She said it would save time, skip the negotiation step. Don't care what they told us; everyone knows a Trad's going to kill, not talk."

"It only hurts if you struggle, vampire. Which should make this an entertaining trip." Gold Hair aimed a kick at Cai that flipped him over and tightened the barbs as a result.

Pain...cruelty. Chavez's eyes glittered with a look Rand knew all too well.

Go, Rand. Leave. Goddamn it...

The barbs cut into Cai's throat and arms and made Chavez grin. The woman's gaze remained impassive, disinterested in the games.

"Lord Greenwald told us to make sure you arrive in a condition conducive to instant cooperation," Gold Hair added.

"Say...that...three times...fast," Cai spat, his eyes alive with hate despite the quip. "Still not getting shit out of me."

The Goth aimed another kick, and Rand sprang.

No!

Rand hit Chavez like a battering ram, the two of them rolling in a flailing, cursing tangle a few feet away from Cai. Chavez screamed as Rand clamped down on his shoulder, punching through skin and muscle to bone. The collar bone shattered under the power of his jaw.

Chavez managed to heave him off only because Rand saw the female moving in the corner of his eye. He sprang away from the Goth and back, landing in a hovering position over Cai's body. His hackles were raised, increasing his already formidable size, and a menacing sound came from deep in his chest, a message loud and clear.

"What the fuck... *Shoot it.*" Gold Hair had pulled Chavez back out of range and three sets of wide vampire eyes were now on them. Gold Hair's barked command was to the three servants. Two drew handguns from the shoulder holsters they wore.

Shift, Rand. Damn you, shift, or they'll kill you right there. You're outnumbered.

Trying to take out three vampires and their servants. Rand couldn't think of a better way to go.

You and your fucking death wish.

"Goddamn it, don't harm him," Cai snapped. "Or whatever the hell you want, the chance you have of getting it from me goes from slim to not-in-this-fucking lifetime."

The servants hesitated. Since their gazes didn't leave Rand, Rand expected that was because they'd received a message from their vampires to hold. The female studied Rand and tossed an amused look at Gold Hair. "Who would have thought a Trad would have a pet? They sneer on having human servants, but this one'll have a dog. Priceless."

I will rip out her throat. The urge to do it consumed Rand's gut, and translated to his saliva glands.

She'd gut you before you have a chance. I appreciate the thought, but I'm not worth it. You know I'm not. You were a fun fuck. Run along and maybe we'll hook up next time a hunter tries to shoot you.

If he didn't know the vampire was trying to get him gone for his own well-being, Rand would have torn a strip off him for the patronizing tone. Most everything the vampire said was true or meshed with Rand's own rational thinking. These were not his people, and he had no idea if Cai had done something to deserve whatever these vampires were doing to him. But Cai was outnumbered, which seemed unfair. And Rand couldn't forget those couple of instances over the past few days where the vampire could have been consistently selfish and unkind...and instead he'd behaved the way a friend would.

The deciding vote came from a whole different line of thinking, though. The wolf said they weren't going anywhere, and Rand was never disregarding that instinct-driven side of his soul again. His wolf had said they hadn't seen the last of Grey; that Rand should have gotten Dylef and Sheba settled with an established pack, and then hunted Grey down to avenge Sylvan's death. He hadn't listened.

So it was the wolf who answered Cai. Rand adjusted so his back feet were against Cai's bound side. He laid down, ears still flat and his warning growing in volume and ferocity, while all gleaming sharp teeth were on full display. He wasn't going anywhere.

The female vampire drew her own gun and fired.

The three vampires had been considering their options, and Cai had been sure none of them would be good. The only thing working in their favor right now was a few minutes of time. The vampires were more than a match for one wolf, but no one liked getting dog-bit. Anyone who watched reality cop shows, where badass criminals reacted to K-9 units like scared babies, knew that.

Then the female vampire used her weapon.

No, goddamn it. Fucking hell.

Rand's mind dissolved into gibberish, and his heavy furred body sank down on Cai. Adding weight to the barbed wire, not that Cai could even feel the pain. Adrenaline and horror rushed in together. She'd killed the wolf. Just killed him.

"Good timing, Tyra," Gold Hair said.

She sniffed and leveled a look at Chavez. He was sitting on the ground but feeding off the wrist of one of the servants, which would provide a swift patch to the wound Rand had inflicted upon him. Unless the wolf's saliva contained some kind of flesh-eating parasite. Too fucking much to hope for.

"You weren't the only one to bring reinforcements," Tyra told the Goth. "Lord Brian said these tranquilizers would slow a vampire down, but not kill him. I figure it should work on a big-ass wolf."

Okay, so there was a chance he was okay. Cai calmed enough to register that yes, Rand was breathing. He was alive, and wasn't giving off the signals Cai would be receiving, both through direct contact and the second mark, if he was badly injured.

Had Rand been trapped in some crazy loop of dog-loyalty thing? It was the only thing that made sense, because Cai hadn't done anything to deserve the male's championing like this.

Seeing how pale Chavez was felt good, though. The Goth hadn't expected a wolf to be such a match for him. Even now he was probably convincing himself Rand wasn't as strong as he'd seemed. Whereas Cai had no doubt, when Rand took the male down, he could have killed him. He wished he had. Only his defensive move to put himself between Tyra and Cai had likely stopped it.

Not the biggest and baddest things in the universe, are you, shitheads?

But much as he would have liked to see Chavez turned into wolf food, it was probably good Rand hadn't done it. If he'd killed the vampire, that would have suggested he was something other than just a supersized wolf. Hopefully, though these three didn't seem shy about using magical tools, they had no actual aptitude or sensitivity to the type of energy Cai could feel around Rand full time, suggesting he was something more than "just a wolf."

Chavez had struggled to his feet, weak but obviously determined to appear strong in front of his two companions. Not surprising, since Cai's experience was that vampires were more into cutthroat competition with one another than into becoming beer buddies.

Chavez approached and gave Rand a kick. It was his still healing side, and Rand made a whimpering noise, even while only partially conscious. Cai was going to rip the Goth's fucking nose rings out, puncture his anus with them, and watch him bleed out. "Good, he's out. We can leave him behind, Voltaire."

"No," Voltaire said. He was apparently Gold Hair. Cai had picked up on Rand's mental nickname for him. "He's more cooperative with him, so the beast may provide us leverage."

Voltaire dropped to his heels by Cai. "But leverage or not, Greenwald will get everything he wants out of you, Trad. Or you will suffer ten times what you'll suffer on the trip to him. We know what you and your people have done. There's no mercy for your kind. Not today, tomorrow or any other day. Pray your information wins you a quick death. That's your best hope now."

"I don't pray to gods," Cai managed. "Gods are just another set of pretentious bastards like you who think it's okay to fuck with other people's lives."

That earned him a kick. Then they were dragging Rand off of him, binding the wolf in a bunch of ropes. He and the shifter were put on separate, crudely put together litters that the servants dragged along through the forest until they reached one of those hiking trails wide enough for an ATV. Several of the vehicles were waiting. The litters were hooked to two of them, and they were pulled through the forest.

Every bump, every twitch of his body made the barbs gouge deeper into his wounds and fuck, it bloody hurt. Cai figured out they had a hold and release cycle. If he stayed still through the worst of the pain, the wires would ease up after about fifteen very long seconds.

He understood and could handle pain. So getting an occasional glimpse of Rand's inert body bouncing behind another ATV was the only distraction helping Cai keep his mind away from a different issue. But it was a fight he was starting to lose, against an enemy within.

Being restrained, being taken against his will somewhere, experiencing total loss of control, was a problem. He was helpless, and that feeling was what became a full-blown crisis, harder and harder to manage.

When they reached a deserted parking lot cloaked in full darkness and containing two vehicles, including a van, he reached overload. All that was holding him to the litter were ropes. They were letting the barbed wire do all the work. Voltaire's back was to him as he opened the van side door.

Okay. I'm fine. Okay. Not okay. So totally not okay. Not going to make me do anything, treat me like this. No one. No fucking one, never again. Okay, you want to die, let's die together, Rand. I'm cool with that. Ready, set, go.

He let out an abrupt roar and rolled, splitting the ropes with a snap. Bouncing off the litter, he landed against Voltaire. The golden-haired bastard fell, and Cai had the satisfaction of tearing his pretty Armani shirt with the barbed wire.

Then Chavez hit him with what felt like a hot stick, sending electrical current through the metal barbed wire bindings. Everything seized up; brain cells, vision. Voltaire snarled, since Chavez hadn't waited until he thrust Cai off of him to do it. It would make Cai snicker, when he could figure out how to align his top and bottom row of electrified teeth again.

He was kicking at Voltaire, best as he could with his legs bound, and screaming incoherently at Chavez. From the Goth's wide eyes, Cai was confirming all their theories about Trads, the crazed, live-in-the-woods vampires who refused all trappings of civility, who didn't take servants, who killed their human prey rather than sipping on them like wine at one of their fancy fucking dinners.

You're not better than me, fucker. And you're going to be dead, really soon.

They hit him, hard enough to break bones. No problem. He was a vampire, they'd heal. He could handle this, but he had to get loose. He had to. He couldn't be helpless again or he would just fucking lose it.

Tyra was getting up and dusting off her taut ass, so he must have taken her down while rolling around with Voltaire.

Then, amid all that, Rand's mind reached out to him, and it was... calm.

Calm like quiet meadows and dark, starry nights. Cool breezes through thick fur, the soft call of an owl in the distance. He was in hunter mode. Still. Waiting. In control, even when that deadly ferocity waited, just below the surface.

Which reminded Cai he was a goddamned hunter, too. He wasn't a scared kid, or a frightened victim. His gaze darted to the wolf's body. It was still inert on the litter, Rand seemingly unconscious. *Pull your shit together*, he told himself. *You're embarrassing yourself in front of the wolf.*

My eyes are closed. Some grim humor, and a touch of seriousness, not just because of their situation but probably because Rand's wolf senses could tell how thin that layer of calm actually was for Cai. He couldn't get his mind off the bonds. He had to struggle, fight...

Breathe with me in that world, vampire. The bindings on you don't mean anything there.

Cai was going to tell him he didn't go for that New Age meditation bullshit, but truth, he was so spun up over feeling trapped, some part of him grabbed that calm voice and imagery like a life line. Even if Rand's tranquility were caused by groovy tranquilizer effects, Cai found himself trying to sync his breathing with Rand's as the male kept thinking that same mantra. *Breathe with me. Bindings mean nothing.*

It gave him the room he needed. Cai struggled for control and calm. He'd had to contain all of it for so long, so many years, he could find it again. He just needed loose from these bonds, he just...

Breathe. In time they'll release you. You know they will. Or we'll figure out a way to escape.

Or you break loose from your bonds, I roll over them like a barbed log, and we go down in a blaze of glory.

I think we should give Plan A a chance first.

"Why do you assume that's not Plan A? I give you a great chance to end it all, and you wimp out on me now?

Though wimp was not the word that came to mind, remembering Rand standing over him, a fully pissed wolf with death gleaming in his eyes and off his bared teeth.

Cai *could* calm down. The wolf made it possible. But before he could prove it to anyone other than himself, he lifted his head to see Chavez holding Tyra's tranquilizer gun. He shot the rest of the load pointblank into Cai.

They apparently mistook a tranquilizer for truth serum. After he and Cai were loaded into the van and on their way, the vampires took turns kicking and beating on Cai, asking him questions he never answered. Partly because he was in and out of consciousness, and partly because he had far more clever observations.

Like about Chavez's nose rings, the hair product Voltaire used, or why Tyra shouldn't wear a push-up bra. No reason to pump up Mount Rushmore, right?

Since Rand still felt like he was swimming in a fog soup, he admired the vampire's unrelenting smart-assery. He did use the gradual clearing of his mind to do some thinking about their situation, because it kept his mind off what they were doing to Cai that he couldn't stop. If he dwelled on that, his wolf would start struggling, which would help nothing.

He reminded himself that Cai could handle the chance to talk trash with his captors, better than the vampire could handle the reality of his bindings. The male's panic and anger had been curious. He'd seemed to do better once they'd started beating on him in the van, as if the distraction kept him from focusing on what seemed to bother him more than the torment—being trapped and unable to call the shots.

So though his human side was no less thrilled with what was happening to Cai, Rand forced himself to consider what options they had. He was sure Cai would have a smartass response to *that*.

Cai obviously had a gift for pissing others off, but this seemed more than that. He pissed off Rand, but not to the point Rand wanted to tie him up, torture and drag him off to see a top guy who was probably going to do more and worse to him. He'd picked up the gist of that during the first part of the beatings.

Holy God, could they get where they were going soon?

They'd bound Rand in ropes, tying his legs and muzzle, and dumped him toward the rear of the roomy van. They'd run ropes from his bonds to handles embedded in the sides and back so he couldn't turn over or see what they were doing, which sucked. He had the strength to rip those handles loose, he was sure, but it would serve no purpose right now except maybe getting him darted again.

If he shifted, it was likely he could get free even faster and do some damage. Still, it wouldn't be enough to give him good odds against three vampires in close quarters and their human servants, two of whom were following in another vehicle while the third one drove this van. Plus, at this point, they thought he was just a wolf. Cai could have told them he was a shifter, and he hadn't. Maybe because most vampires didn't believe shifters existed and Cai wanted to keep it that way. Or to leave it as an ace in the hole if it would come in handy for escape. Hard to know.

At some later time, Rand would puzzle over why the vampire had stuck his neck out for him and given him repeated attempts to take off, no help requested.

As for Rand being here, he'd already answered that. The good thing about his wolf side was it didn't analyze the crap out of things. Instinct had told him not to abandon Cai, so he hadn't. End of story. No great meaning, no need to analyze his feelings or his relationship with the vampire—and, er, fuckbuddy did not equal relationship. It was what it was. He didn't care if he himself lived or died, so why not tag along and see what was up with this? And yeah, maybe some of it was guilt, because when he'd gone after the Goth vampire, Cai had agreed to go along reasonably quietly if they didn't kill Rand.

Rand figured out they'd driven out of the West Virginia mountains, bypassed a few smaller towns and ended up in horse country Virginia. Though his being tied down kept him from seeing anything out the windows except what was straight up—the dark sky—they were cracked and brought him the tempting scent of well-fed horses. He imagined they were traveling through an area filled with nice brick mansions on multi-acre spreads, the glossy horses grazing on lawns enclosed by wide white picket fences.

At last, the sleek dark van bumped up the long driveway of one of the properties that didn't have horses. The lingering scent was there, but very old. When the van was brought to a halt, Chavez stepped over him and went out the back, leaving the double doors open. Rand saw a barn, which looked like it had been converted to living space, maybe guest quarters.

He heard a muffled grunt as Cai was jerked out of the van and dumped unceremoniously on the asphalt. They did the same to Rand, leaving his legs and muzzle tied, Voltaire shoving his bruised ribs with his foot to flip him over. That was when Rand finally saw Cai.

Ah, hell.

The vampire was a bloody mess. They'd struck his face and body repeatedly, with fists or blunt objects. Pain was a raw, red throbbing heat coming off him. Bastards.

It's all right. I'm a vampire. We're the best kind of punching bag. A blood meal and I'll heal right up. You okay?

Except for tranquilizing and tying him up, they hadn't done much of anything to Rand. He wanted to say *Yeah, good*, but he couldn't verbalize, even in his mind. So he did it in wolf speak. He stretched out his bound muzzle and brushed it briefly against Cai's upper arm. The vampire turned his gaze to him, lingered there briefly.

You're pretty impressive in that form, wolf. Try to tone down the gleam, so no one starts thinking about you as a fur coat.

"I told you to get Lord Greenwald," Voltaire said sharply as Chavez returned from the house. The Goth was still favoring the shoulder and wearing the bloody, torn shirt, but he looked even paler than when Rand had attacked him. He jerked his head like he had a nervous tic, though it apparently was an indication someone was coming behind him.

"The Council delegation arrived," he hissed in a whisper. "It's—"

"Lady Lyssa," Tyra said in a tight tone of fear and respect. She dropped to one knee.

Cai had laid back his head and closed bloody, swollen eyes, as if uncaring who was coming to look at him. But since Rand felt her even before he angled his face to see her, he looked.

Vampires had a certain scent. So did Fae and shifters. She had some of all three scents, which was intriguing enough. But there was also a solid wall of power around this vampire. Chavez's panic, Tyra's reaction and Voltaire's sudden tension telegraphed it.

All vampires were beautiful, and she was no exception. Long, straight dark hair, slightly Asian features, jade green eyes. Deceptively petite and slim-boned. Her head might reach Rand's chest. He wouldn't underestimate her based on her size. Not a chance with that power beating against his senses like a "realize she can kick your ass twelve ways to Sunday" wake up call.

She was wearing a fitted skirt that stopped a couple inches above her knees, a silky blouse that clung attractively to small curves, and toothpick heels. She navigated the paved drive in them with as much grace and ease as a basketball player in athletic shoes.

She had a male with her that Rand guessed was her servant. He had midnight blue eyes, russet-brown hair to his broad shoulders, and a muscular physique. He emanated the calm readiness of a veteran fighter.

Two other vampires, one male and one female, accompanied Lady Lyssa. The male had cool, amber eyes and long copper-colored hair tied back. Compared to Lyssa and the other vampire, he seemed to project an old-world style, though his clothes were modern enough. Khakis, dress shirt, shiny shoes. The third vampire, the other female, had German features, a voluptuous body well-displayed in a classy outfit of slacks and blouse, and an equally steady brown gaze. Her blond hair was in a thick twist on top of her head.

Servants accompanied them, too. The woman's was a big Viking-looking guy in a kilt. The copper-haired vampire's servant was a female with brown hair, delicate features, but who projected a strong will. She also seemed very interested and concerned about Rand, her lovely gray gaze resting on him, her brow furrowed. She had a kind heart and didn't like to see him bound this way, though she spared very little attention for Cai, seeming to avoid looking at him.

It wasn't that she didn't care, Rand realized, taking a deeper scent. Violence and blood distressed her, stirred up some bad things. The copper-haired vampire's gaze had gone to her, picking it up, but she tightened her jaw and resolutely nodded. An *I'm okay* message. His expression softened slightly, but when he turned his attention back to their group, it was flat and unreadable.

Like most fully mature adult vampires, all of them looked around thirty years old, but Lyssa felt ancient, and the other two vampires weren't far behind. None of these were fledglings. Neither were the three who had caught them, but now that Rand had a comparison, he knew Voltaire, Tyra and Chavez were much younger.

Another vampire arrived then, one who didn't look cool and steady at all. He wore a white shirt, black jacket, and slacks. Despite the tailored elegance, he seemed disheveled. Maybe vampires couldn't do physically rumpled, so it only manifested internally. The outside said GQ. The inside vibrations said a guy in tatters, likely ripped by his own fists.

At the sight of Cai, he leaped forward, hands curling into claws he set upon Cai to jerk him off the ground. Rand peeled back a lip. He'd kept his wolf contained, but under all the current stresses, that grip was getting more tenuous. Seeing yet another person hurting the vampire, his inner beast said it'd had enough.

And then he got a break. Literally. One of the ropes snapped.

It loosened the hold of the others. Rand thrashed his way out of the bonds, quick as a twisting snake, too fast for the others to react. The helpless anger and banked ferocity of the past few hours boiled forth, his wolf ready to tear something apart.

While normally those tasty horses would take top billing, something else loomed larger in his mind. He had one goal, and he got right to it. He didn't have to think or plan. That was the beauty of being a wolf fueled up on a hundred percent high octane pissed-off.

He hurled himself at the male vampire attacking Cai.

CHAPTER SIX

"*N*o...fuck..." Cai spat out. He was trying to get words past the choke hold the berserker vampire had on him when Rand landed on them both and sank his teeth into the attacking vampire's shoulder, same as he'd done with Chavez.

Since the fucking wolf was a tank and pure muscle, Cai could only imagine the pressure of his jaws. The other male communicated the information graphically.

This vampire was stronger than Chavez. He managed to throw Rand, but Rand was back on him like the duck on the proverbial June bug. Necessity had the vampire releasing Cai to grapple with the wolf. Their three captors moved in, shouting in alarm, eyes wide and worried. Cai would have been grimly satisfied by their troubles, but Rand was all wolf now, his mind in full attack, offense and defense mode. Both eyes were that lava gold color. Cai couldn't reach him with normal modes of logic. Fuck, they really were going to kill him this time.

The idea filled him with such helpless rage, things connected to old pains, that he couldn't fucking bear it. He didn't care that the barbed wire had his nerve endings screaming in agony, and his head hurt from landing on it twice now—once when he was thrown from the van and second when this guy dropped him. He summoned all his energy and thundered out his reminder, because he was pretty sure it hadn't been memo'ed out to the Council delegation standing here.

"Hurt the goddamn wolf, and you get nothing from me, you psychotic, bloodsucking, arrogant, shit-for-brains, assholes." He ran out of air to fuel the words, but not descriptive expletives. He finished them up in his head and took another breath. "Stop it. Stop hurting him. He doesn't understand, goddamn it."

He'll keep fighting you, because the closer to death he is, the better he feels. Cai didn't question the tight feeling in his gut that came with the thought, but if they did irreparable harm to the wolf, he was going to take his own pound of flesh in retribution. If he could get out of this damned wire.

He'd succeeded in drawing attention to himself. An order was barked and miraculously, Tyra, Voltaire and Chavez jumped back as if that hot stick had been used on them. They were replaced by the Viking-servant and the one with Lady Lyssa, the broad-shouldered male who'd been standing by Lady Lyssa.

The Lady Lyssa. Even Trads and vampires who lived in the remote corners of the world knew who she was. If they didn't, her power signature alone would warn she was top of the psycho vampire pyramid. Last of the royal line of the Far East clan, over a thousand years old. Reputedly carrying Fae blood as well as vampire.

He'd expected her to be taller. But even at five-foot nothing, the slim, elegant woman emanated power like a convoy of Mac trucks screaming down an interstate at a hundred miles per hour.

Her servant was no lightweight, either. However, he and the other servant were having a hell of a time containing Rand. They'd thrown some of the rope back and forth to each other and used it to snug his head down, tie his feet. Unlike Voltaire and his two cronies, however, their entire goal seemed to be quelling the wolf's attack, not to harm or enrage him to the point the fight became uglier. Lady Lyssa's servant was even speaking quietly to Rand, as if to soothe him.

That wouldn't work. Cai's lips twisted in grim satisfaction when the wolf snapped at the male's hand, latching on and tearing out a hunk of flesh. Cai tensed as the male swore creatively. But he didn't retaliate, instead muttering, "Yeah, if I didn't see that coming, I deserved it."

The other servant shot him a grin which he quickly lost as Rand almost nailed his forearm. The men left off their banter and concentrated harder on keeping the big wolf pinned down. Even tied, he was fighting like Godzilla taking Tokyo. Admiration surged inside Cai for his determination, but he'd better not let it get too far. Or the wolf might kill the two servants and they'd be back into execution-by-vampire territory. But Rand was still in there, because he seemed to recognize the difference between psychos like Chavez and the manage-and-contain strategies of the two servants. He was fighting, but not necessarily with lethal force.

Which suggested though Rand had retreated back into his wolf, the second mark bond might have some pull. A leash the wolf might heed.

Easy, Rand. They're not hurting me anymore. It's okay. Just relax. I have a feeling this is about to become a more manageable situation.

"If you'll take this fucking thing off me and let me stand up, he'll be much better," Cai grated, tossing the comment to the vampire queen. "What, I'm going to bolt and cleverly conceal myself in acres of open field and horse shit? Or single-handedly attack your army of vampire thugs?"

"Your wolf seems to embrace the idea," she observed. She had a voice that put sultry tags on every syllable. There was no apparent urgency to her, but she was an emotional wall. She could be having a panic attack and no one would be the wiser.

"Yeah, well. Dumb animal. What can I say? He's all about foolhardy acts of honor. I'm about living to stab you in the back another day when the odds are all in my favor."

He heard gasps from Tyra and a couple of the others, but really? He had anything to gain from sucking up when they were already kicking the shit out of him?

"Take off the wire," Lady Lyssa instructed Chavez.

She'd given Cai's thrown-out threat the weight he knew it carried. He could come on that female in bright daylight, with her in a full vampire sleep, and she'd still kill him before he was within ten feet of her. With or without the help of her servant, who was doing a pretty damn good job of sparring with the shifter.

Lyssa's gaze went frigid when it was pointed toward Tyra and Voltaire. "This was not how the sorcerer's tool was to be utilized. He will not be pleased to hear the power was abused. And I do not know how you've bound our guest, but I won't repeat myself again. Free him."

Chavez scampered to Cai's side to do as he'd been bidden. His obvious terror of the female vampire was delightful, but Cai would have an easier time reveling in it once the fucking barbed wire was off. Staving off another of those stupid panic spurts about that, he tried to focus on what was happening around them. Knowledge was power, yeah. But he'd still prefer an Uzi and a bolt-action wooden stake launcher.

Lady Lyssa turned her attention to the vampire who'd attacked Cai. He was currently being held by the other two Council vampires. He'd struggled at first, but was now limp, seemingly dazed.

She moved to him, laying a hand on his arm to command his attention. "Lord Greenwald, I understand the pain you are feeling right now, but you must control yourself so we can make the most of this opportunity. If you can't, I will have you taken back to your bedroom and held there until we can formulate a plan of action. I suspect you'd much rather be part of those plans. Correct?"

The male nodded, though his gaze on Cai was still feral and desperate. It held so much rage, if he could have taken Cai down with it alone, he would have. That didn't really bug Cai. It was the uncontrolled look behind it which gave him an uneasy feeling. Not that the whole situation wasn't fucked, but there was a wrongness to the male that made him wonder about Lyssa placing that hand on him. It was as if she thought simple words wouldn't be enough.

"I swear, I didn't know my latest kill was your tailor." Cai swept a scornful gaze over the male. "But I expect you can find someone else to measure your inseams for you."

With a scream of pure, killing wrath, Greenwald tried to burst out of the vampires' hold. Which set off Rand again, such that the Viking and Lyssa's servant had to renew their efforts to keep the wolf from breaking his bonds.

Fuck it. Cai shut his mouth while Chavez started to remove the barbed wire. Lyssa had freaked the Goth out. He was muttering a chant to help with the removal, but he went too fast, because he cursed and had to start over, taking the words more slowly.

In the meantime, with a chastising look at Cai, Lady Lyssa moved toward Rand. Cai stiffened, but she knelt gracefully and put her hand on his broad, dark head. She'd smoothed the skirt modestly beneath her as she dropped to her heels, and it only made her look sexier. Her servant began to speak, probably to warn her, but she shook her head. Her small, slim fingers curled into the thick fur.

The power-radiating vampire queen and the large black wolf gazing up at her, created the type of picture displayed on glossy fantasy novel covers. Cai noted that Rand must have heard him and started to settle some, for though his gaze was hostile, the hellfire gold had retreated, so he had one blue and one gold eye again.

Rand was huffing through the hold of the ropes on his muzzle. He needed to breathe, to pant, damn them. Cai glared at Chavez, as if that would speed him up.

"You are more than you seem, beautiful wolf," Lyssa murmured. Her gaze lifted and met Cai's. "Is he what I believe he is?"

"A pain in my ass? A noble idiot? Yes, on both counts."

She kept looking at him with that eerie-ass, unblinking stare. Cai swallowed.

Stop being a fucking smartass and answer the lady's question before she rips Rand's head off to prove she can, he told himself.

"Yes."

Her eyes widened slightly, her servant's face reflecting the same surprise. Cai should have lied. He wasn't sure why he hadn't. He had a terrible vision of them tossing his ass on the street and keeping Rand imprisoned as a circus act for the rest of his life. *Why didn't you just run, damn you?*

He received a mixed bag of response, all in wolf speak. He thought of how Rand had touched his muzzle to his arm, an unexpected intimacy. Yeah, it was just the way wolves talked, no need to get mushy over it, but it had been a steadying connection. A new experience for Cai when he was in a jam. Usually his allies numbered one—the guy he looked at in the mirror but couldn't see.

"Demons," Lord Greenwald said, his voice cracking. "Demons come to take my girl. Kill them, and they will release her. Make them feel pain. My pain."

Cai noted a significant look pass between Lady Lyssa and the other two Council members. He also observed a less-hard-to-decipher communication happening between Voltaire, Chavez and Tyra. Anticipation, competition, and something unpleasantly on the edge of bloodlust. There was more happening here than the guy's daughter being gone. Lord Greenwald wasn't well.

He'd seen it happen to at least a couple of vampires, though there hadn't been a lot of time to register the symptoms, since where Cai grew up, such weakness resulted in an immediate death sentence. *Ennui.* The only hundred percent incurable disease that seemed to affect vampires, usually those over five hundred, which Greenwald clearly was.

From the cues being dropped all over the place like marbles, Cai concluded that Greenwald was probably an overlord. Lyssa calling him Lord Greenwald wasn't a guarantee of that, since born vampires immediately earned the title by birth. But Chavez, Tyra and Voltaire were acting like underlings vying to take his spot. When they didn't immediately correct their lord, it suggested they weren't averse to letting him believe his daughter had been taken by demons, which would goad his unstable impulses.

All just speculation, but Cai was good at putting together a puzzle with only a handful of pieces.

Lady Lyssa's gaze had passed over Greenwald's people, and though she was still as readable as a blank page, Cai figured she knew the lay of the land. He just couldn't tell whether she was for or against their machinations.

She stroked Rand once more and rose to her feet, gesturing to the Viking and her own servant. "Torrence, return to Lady Helga's side. Jacob, let Cai release the wolf from his bonds. I believe it will work better that way."

"There's no time for this," Lord Greenwald snapped.

"You're correct," she said, and her tone cooled. "If your vampires had brought him to us as instructed, instead of torturing him and working his wolf into this state, I expect we would right now be sitting down to discuss how Mr. Mordecai Wallace can assist us. But since—"

"He's a demon," Greenwald raged. "He's—"

"Georg." Lyssa spoke firmly, but with an uncontestable authority that apparently penetrated the fog capturing Greenwald's mind. She stepped to his side again so she dominated his field of vision. "We are not dealing with demons. You collected valuable intel that there was a Trad who had left their ranks within the last hundred years, who was unsympathetic to their ways. Our sorcerer helped you pinpoint his location. You sent three of your people to retrieve him and bring him here to help us."

"I'm not a fucking Trad," Cai said sharply. Lyssa lifted an imperious and quelling hand without looking his way. Her servant, the one she'd called Jacob, shifted to Cai's side.

"Let her talk him down," he murmured. "So you can get to your wolf."

Cai glanced at him, surprised. Jacob was the first to speak to him as if he was more ally than enemy. The queen's servant was neither to him, but there was a self-preservation benefit to acknowledging courtesy. He just wasn't usually smart enough to do it.

"Okay," he muttered. "But the next person who calls me a Trad is going to get fucked up the ass by my steel-toed hiking shoe."

Jacob's lips quirked, but he nodded gravely. "I might just tell Torrence to call you that, so you can carry out that threat. It would be endlessly entertaining."

Cai was glad the servant was amused, because he fucking wanted out of these bindings now, and he wanted to be at the wolf's side even sooner. Jacob hadn't sounded mocking, though. His eyes remained serious, his gaze sweeping over everyone as if gauging what would happen next so he could get ahead of it.

His legs were free. Cai was instantly on his feet, quivering with impatience as the Goth finished releasing him from the barbed wire. The relief from the pain and suppressed panic of being immobilized was so immediate and overwhelming he wanted to bolt. Or tear out Chavez's abundance of nose rings.

Cai did neither. He did stiffen when Jacob reached out courteously to steady him. The servant took the hint, abandoning the gesture in mid-motion. Lyssa gave Cai a slight nod, communicating that Greenwald had settled enough for him to approach and release Rand. Not that he'd been waiting for that. Soon as he was steady on his feet, he was headed toward the wolf.

When he knelt by Rand's side, Cai saw the wolf's gaze sweep him, all the blood and torn clothes. His panting increased. Cai felt his anger, the desire to bite and tear flesh. His patience at being held down was at an end.

He laid his hand on the wolf's shoulder and began to loosen the bonds, starting with the muzzle. *Stay with me there, wolf. Easy. They've released me. We'll figure this out together. Don't run off, okay? The local horse farmers will freak the fuck out if they see a wolf the size of a cow running around. You with me? Give me something so I know you're on an even keel again. I don't want you to die here. Let's calm down and figure it out together.*

Rand's gaze slid up to his, held. Cai pressed his lips together, his hand resting briefly on Rand's head after he removed the snug tie that had pulled it down and attached it to his front feet. He wasn't sure why he took a second to do that, but he did.

When he lifted his palm, Rand stretched his head back, loosening the neck muscles. Cai automatically moved his hand there to massage. While Rand didn't reply in his mind, he arched under Cai's touch, accepting the cosseting. His bi-colored gaze focused on Cai's upper body. Abruptly, he shifted into an upright position, extended his long nose and began to lick the blood off Cai's chest, where the shirt was torn open. He was tending him, the sleek fur on his head rubbing Cai's jaw.

Some weird emotional reaction set up camp in Cai's chest, making him want to tighten both hands in the wolf's ruff and...do what? He had no idea except holding on. And this was so not the moment to explore that reaction.

He murmured to the wolf, nothing coherent, just a reassurance, and rose. He rested his hand on Rand's shoulder to hopefully keep him at his side. No such luck. The wolf apparently recalled himself, whatever wolf-insanity that had made him be so affectionate probably replaced by more human-Rand sanity. He stalked away, flattening his ears and baring his teeth at the vampires, but he took an alert stance about fifteen feet away from all of them, staying watchful.

It was a smart idea, since it gave him a vantage of anything coming up behind Cai, but Cai didn't know if that was why Rand had done it. He couldn't parse Rand's thoughts from the wolf's, and the wolf's were still sometimes a little too cryptic for him to translate perfectly, especially when Rand was worked up.

Have back. Want horse meat.

Okay, clear enough. Hopefully he'd sit on that last urge, at least right now.

"Good." Lyssa had been watching the two of them shed their respective bonds and make it to their feet. Now she turned at the appearance of another human, this one a slim male whose wary look toward Lord Greenwald suggested he was a house servant used to his Master's erratic nature. But Lyssa took charge of things. "Giles, escort Mordecai and..." she glanced at Cai, then significantly to Rand.

"Just Wolf," Cai said. "I'm not sentimental enough to name him."

A lie, but he couldn't believe he'd confirmed what he thought he'd confirmed to her. Maybe if he played dumb she'd think he'd meant something else. No need to make it worse.

Her gaze flickered. "In a moment, Giles, I wish you to escort Mordecai and his wolf to a room where they can clean up. Provide a change of clothes in the appropriate sizes. Mordecai is here as a Council guest."

Her attention cut to Greenwald's underlings, and then to Greenwald himself. "From this moment forward, any who treat either him or his wolf otherwise will answer personally to me. Do you understand, Georg? You are an overlord. Do you doubt my ability to handle this situation properly?"

Greenwald seemed to be regaining control of his faculties. He rubbed a hand over his face, a brief gesture of vulnerability and helpless fury that had Lyssa's hand resting on him in comfort this time, instead of to admonish restraint.

"It's all right," she said. "I know stress makes it worse. But you're all right. You're with us again. Just try to stay as calm as you can. That's what Dovia needs right now, isn't it?"

His gaze lifted to her. He had light brown eyes, a bisque complexion and a short crop of black hair. He was tall and lean, a male who, when he straightened and took a breath, showed the command that had landed him the role of overlord, before the illness had taken him. "Yes, my lady. I'll... I'll go check on Leona."

Clearing his throat, he strode back up onto the front stoop and disappeared into the house. Lyssa leveled her gaze on Voltaire. The jade green eyes were abruptly as sharp as Rand's teeth. "Overlords are appointed by Region Masters and confirmed by Council members. Keep that in mind, Voltaire. To some, taking advantage of your lord's illness might seem like initiative. To others, it seems cruelly opportunistic, especially if your actions are designed to take advantage of a terrible situation, and push him further toward the inevitable conclusion of his state."

She took a step forward. Whatever Voltaire saw in her expression had him stepping back, Tyra and Chavez likewise shrinking away.

Cai noticed that Jacob had gone from the casual stance he'd adopted during their conversation to a far more alert and hard-eyed look, as had Torrence and the female vampire Lyssa had called Lady Helga. Ditto on the death-look from the copper-haired vampire. His servant managed somber well enough, but unlike the others, she fell short of menacing. From the glint in her eye and set of her chin, she could be tough, though.

"If you wish to explore the depths of cruelty and how far it can take you in this world," Lady Lyssa continued, "I am happy to show you that personally, until you will beg for Hell. Re-evaluate your tactics."

"Yes, my lady," Voltaire said, wisely not choosing to argue the point. He bowed, his eyes lowered, his jaw tight.

"Good. Be gone from my sight. You'd do best to stay that way awhile."

The three vanished like smoke. Cai didn't blame them. He cleared his throat.

"If I'm a guest, does that mean I can say *thanks but no thanks* and hitch a ride out of here?"

When Lyssa's frosty eyes landed on him, he knew for sure he was an idiot. But what else was new? "Do you go by Mordecai?" she said, after a moment heavy with tension.

"Cai," he said.

"Cai, then. There is a reason you've been brought here. A very important one. We're hoping you will be able to advise us on the best course of action. Lord Greenwald's daughter is twenty-two years old and she has been taken by an Appalachian sect of Trads. I expect you're familiar with them, since you grew up among them. Yes?"

The world grew black for a second. Black, dark, and it turned upside down. Cai fought out of that mental oaken barrel ride, swearing if he did something mortifying like faint he'd just kill himself when he woke up. He shoved back a million images, most of them populated with screams, blood and other things that belonged to horror shows, and blinked once, twice, three times. Slow. Then he spoke.

"Yes, my lady."

He didn't know how she knew his origins, let alone how they'd decided he was a "Trad unsympathetic to their ways," but he wondered how much else she knew.

Rand's gaze snapped to him when he made the honorific.

Yeah, I do know how to be polite. Don't die of shock.

Lyssa was continuing. "While he had you brought here in a brutal and unsanctioned manner, Lord Greenwald loves his daughter and is not thinking quite clearly. I'm sure he might tender an apology to you, especially if you have information that can help us."

"Don't know how much help I'll be, and don't want an apology from him." Cai couldn't inject too much venom into the comment, though. Now that the puzzle pieces were in place, he saw the desperate, enraged father beneath the savagery. Not that he wouldn't punch him in the mouth if he got the chance. "I'll tell you what I can. Like to be headed back the way I came before the night gets too late."

"Good. Go with Giles and refresh yourself, clean up. Join us in the study as quickly as possible." She nodded in a noncommittal way and gestured to Giles. The servant took the lead and Cai followed, though he paused at the front stoop. Waiting for Rand.

With another baleful stare around him, the wolf trotted through their ranks and joined Cai, so they mounted the stairs together.

Under far too many prying, expectant and overly curious eyes.

The house was what Cai expected. Reeking of money and comfort. From a couple quick questions to Giles, he learned Lord Greenwald had been overlord of the territory for nearly twenty years.

When they reached the underground level, they passed an open door where a small shape was curled on a king-sized bed, covers pulled up high. The room looked like it belonged to a young woman. A girly teenage décor, including a graduation cap, stuffed animals and a couple posters of beefcake, were mixed with touches brought to it by the older version of the same female. Vase of flowers, a few pictures. College school books rested on the desk.

A worried look crossed Giles' face and he drew the door to a small crack. "Leona, Lord Greenwald's full servant," he said quietly. "Dovia's mother."

In Dovia's room, no doubt. When they moved on, Cai realized Rand wasn't following. Looking back, he saw him nudge open the cracked door to stare inside. Giles came to a full halt when he realized it, his expression tightening in a way that said he knew he couldn't protect the woman, but he wasn't going to do nothing. Cai appreciated the guy's protectiveness enough to give him a heads up.

"Believe me, the last thing that wolf will ever do is harm an innocent. Or a grieving mother. He's cool."

Giles studied the wolf's quiet posture. After a moment, Rand turned and padded toward them. Cai resumed their trek, Giles breaking into a trot to take the lead again. He showed them to a guest room and turned on the bathroom light. "Towels, soap and other toiletries. If you tell me your sizes and preferences, I'll find you some clothes."

Cai glanced at Rand. *You want him to bring some in your size?*

Rand blinked, flattened his ears.

That'd be a no. Regardless, Cai told Giles to bring two sets of clothes, and ignored the servant's puzzled look when he provided two different sets of sizes. He and Rand wouldn't be completely off on pants length, but otherwise, yeah, it needed to be two sizes. As broad-shouldered as Cai was, Rand had him beat by another hand span, and his chest...

"If you have anyone in the house with the upper body build of a male gorilla, you'll be in the right ballpark," he instructed Giles.

On that issue Giles didn't miss a beat. "Torrence, Lady Helga's servant, should have something. Um...do you have a servant that will be joining you? Is that why you want the second set of clothes?"

"Yeah, that's a good way to put it. He might or might not need them. So Helga's the blond vampire with the monster-sized servant. Which means the vampire with the fashion-model hair is..."

Giles blinked, obviously nonplused. "That would be Lord Mason. His servant is Jessica."

"Great. Not a lot of time for introductions when I was being kicked in the teeth. If you're wanting to feel useful, a bowl of water and a good raw steak wouldn't be amiss for him." Cai nodded to Rand. "I'd be happy with ice water and a stiff tumbler of Gentleman Jack."

A variety of expressions crossed Giles's face. Cai was sure he didn't fit the mold of anything with fangs that had crossed the servant's path before, but he provided a courteous response. "I'll attend to it."

The servant headed toward the door, but came up short at the threshold, turning as if he might say something. His dark brown eyes under an unruly mop of blond hair revealed a sudden depth of worry that even world leaders didn't carry.

Then all that was swiftly squelched. Giles did another pivot, apparently changing his mind and executing a nice three-sixty twirl to head back toward the hallway.

"What?" Cai asked before he could get away.

Giles stopped as if yanked to a halt with a fish hook. "I'm so sorry, sir," he stammered. He didn't look toward Cai. "It's not my place to speed you along, sir. Or even to suggest it. But...Dovia is a beloved member of this household, sir. And Lord Georg and his servant are sick with worry."

He hadn't suggested anything, so it took Cai a second to catch up, but then he realized Giles was concerned about Cai kicking back with his Jack and taking his sweet time about showing his ass topside again. Like Lyssa would tolerate that.

"That's why I want you to get me the stuff, so we can eat it here while we're getting cleaned up. Makes us ready that much faster."

Giles was surprised enough at the reasonable response that his gaze snapped up and met Cai's. Cai should probably remind him that not all vampires were as touchy-feely as him.

Hearing the wolf equivalent of a snort in his mind, he sent Rand a look, then spoke. "How long have you been here, Giles?"

"Six months, sir."

"Six whole months?" Poor bastard, stepping into all this shit where Georg's power was being contested and his daughter taken. "I'm sure you've been told not to question vampires. Or, in your case, even cryptically hint that you're about to."

"Yes sir." The male's expression whitened. Kid wasn't much older than Georg's daughter, which made Cai put together another few pieces.

"You her full servant?"

Giles shook his head. "Second marked to her father, but here for her blood needs. And to tutor her in languages."

"She doesn't have a second mark or full servant?"

Giles expression tightened. "No full servant. Her second mark, Petra, was killed when she was taken." Another flash, this of grief. They'd obviously been friends.

Would have been too helpful to have someone who was in her head, Cai thought with a mental sigh. Her father would be linked to her mind, but with the advanced Ennui, he likely wasn't able to get through the way he would normally. Adding to his rage and frustration. Her mother's connection would be through the vampire parent's mind. Same issue. Another reason Cai was here. He wondered if the kidnappers had figured out how to block that connection, or if they'd known about Greenwald's state. Or some of both.

"Okay. Just remember you're lucky I'm not interested in proving how goddamn superior I am by ripping your tongue out of your throat and watching it flop on the ground like a trout. You might not get so lucky with the next vampire. Now go grab me some clothes."

"Yes. Yes, sir." Giles disappeared out the door

Cai ran a hand over his face. Just because he'd been brought here to provide information, didn't mean he would actually be of any assistance. Any hopes Giles had for him might be wasted.

Cai didn't give it much further thought, though, since he was used to falling far below expectations. But a shower followed by a drink was going to feel hellishly good.

Cai moved toward the bathroom, already stripping off his ruined shirt and the bloody jeans. Next came footwear.

Rand had accurately realized his faded old clothing was Cai's version of pajamas. But thank the stars Cai had learned to keep his shoes on when resting in the earth. Picking his way daintily across Greenwald's asphalt driveway because Cai had tender soles would have been demoralizing. He was pissed at the loss of his pack, even though he didn't ever carry much, and nothing that he couldn't replace. It was the principle of the thing.

He was most annoyed at the state of his clothing. He'd had the T-shirt and jeans broken in to the right level of slumber softness. Thanks to those barbs, pretty much everything but his hiking shoes were a loss, and they had some rusty brown blood stains on them, damn it.

Cai stepped into the shower, letting the water stream over him. He moved his palms with brisk precision over his bruises and gashes, ignoring the tenderness. Soon as he had some blood, they'd disappear entirely.

Hearing the clicking of toenails, he saw the dark wolf lie down on the tile outside the wavy texture of the shower door. He thought about Rand earlier in the evening, and the different ways the wolf had acted since then. If this was quid pro quo, you scratch my back and I'll scratch yours, then it was damn appreciated. When he'd licked the blood off Cai's chest, it was the first time in quite a while that Cai had been anyone's random act of kindness.

Stepping out of the shower, he saw Giles was as good as his word. There were two sets of folded clothes on the king-sized bed, and a nearly empty water bowl. Water had been slopped over the sides, leaving dark drops on the carpet. A licked clean second metal bowl still smelled faintly of steak.

"Messy eater. Didn't leave me a bite, did you?" He grinned and tossed the towel over the wolf's head. Rand dodged it, showing teeth. "Shift for me, Rand. It's just you and me alone, and I need to talk to you."

He didn't respond immediately. Cai repeated it, a couple times. Unease touched him when he realized Rand wasn't ignoring him. He'd gone somewhere so deep in his wolf that human speech sounded like gibberish. Cai sharpened his tone and Rand's head came up. Using intuition, since he didn't have a how-to-talk-to-your-second-mark-when-he-shifts-into-a-wolf manual, Cai tugged on that bond. What do you know? Rand felt it. His eyes darted back and forth, muscles tightening as he fought an internal battle.

There. He'd started to shift. As before, Cai was amazed at what an amazingly clean process it was. Not even a thread of hair left on the white tile, not even what Rand might have shed when he lay down outside the shower. A nifty bit of forensic magic.

The male pushed himself up and onto his heels, all grace and no self-consciousness in his magnificent nudity. As they regarded one another, Rand was the one who broke the silence. And amusingly to Cai, he skipped over everything that had happened in the past few hours and went right back to twilight, before Cai had woken to meet the Three Stooges. Interesting, since his own mind was dwelling on the same timeframe.

"If I'd known you buried yourself in the earth," Rand said, "I'd have dug you up at noon so you could get some sun on that pasty skin of yours. Would have saved us all the road trip."

Cai grinned. "A very good point. But only one of us is allowed to have suicidal urges at a time. And you've used up your quota, by the way. Come into the bedroom. I need to eat so I can be as badass as usual."

Cai moved to the nightstand, exploring what was in the top drawer. Yeah, it was a vampire household, all right. He turned his attention to the bed and the stacks of clothes there. Lifting a T-shirt obviously in Rand's size, with a good amount of stretch in the cotton to accommodate his shoulder span, Cai pursed his lips. "Nice response time. But then, they want something from us. It makes all the difference."

Rand shook his head, probably at Cai's cynicism, and reached for the clothes. That was when Cai moved.

He sprang, caught Rand about the waist and shoved him to the bed. He had the element of surprise, but it lasted him about a second. He told himself it was thanks to blood loss that Rand unhorsed him with a counter wrestling move and they hit the floor next to the bed with a jarring thump that probably vibrated through the mansion's foundations. Shit, he felt that through every bruise.

Rand sat on top of him. He had his hands on Cai's wrists, his fine, muscular ass on Cai's cock. With his body canted over Cai, his loose brown hair fell forward and shadowed his frowning face.

Cai pushed against his grip. Rand's fingers tightened and Cai let a slow smile cross his face. "You want to play rough, wolf? I can do that."

"You yelped when you hit the ground," Rand pointed out. "You're in pain. What are you doing? You heard what they said. There's a female at risk."

"I did not yelp. And she's a female vampire," Cai reminded him. "So why do you care? More of the decency and morality thing?"

"A remarkable number of people possess some version of it. You don't care what happens to her?"

"Didn't say that." Cai didn't let his head go there. He'd much rather focus on what was in front of him, the intriguing pleasure of the shifter's strong grip on his wrists, the weight of his body.

But at Rand's penetrating stare, he sighed. "I think if she's been taken by this particular group of Trads, she's as good as dead. Because they'll destroy her trying to get what they want and, even if her father gets her back, this crowd won't want her because she'll be too broken. Vampires don't respect weakness in their own kind. Be torn apart there, torn apart here, what does it matter?"

"Her father loves her."

"Yeah, sorry. Couldn't appreciate his loving nature while his minions were whaling on me."

"Cai." Rand gave him a severe look and released his wrists, sitting up to cross his arms over his broad chest. "There's no point lying to a wolf. I can sense your emotions, you know. Her fate does matter to you."

"Okay, say it does. Get on your hands and knees on the bed so I can fuck you senseless. That way I can give them the benefit of my infinite wisdom about saving the girl sooner rather than later."

Rand narrowed his gaze. The male was...so adorably stern. Cai found a reserve of energy to prove who was in charge and managed to heave him off. Another few minutes of serious wrestling, and he had Rand beneath him again on the bed, Rand face down, Cai on top, his hand wrapped firmly around Rand's cock, sandwiched between the press of Rand's body and the mattress.

Cai wasn't entirely sure the shifter hadn't held back because he was more worried than Cai about property damage...or Cai's physical state. Well, to hell with that. To hell with everything but this very second and what he needed. Or wanted, rather, he corrected himself.

"Don't stress over it, wolf. I have to feed, and I can do this at the same time, so neither you nor Giles has to get your shorts in a twist." He leaned down, so he could speak in Rand's ear, brush his lips against the curve.

"What did I say I was going to do, the first opportunity I had you to myself?" Cai whispered it. "To keep you remembering there's a reason worth not hiding in your wolf."

"Can't believe you remembered that after a three-hour beating," Rand muttered.

"You remembered," Cai pointed out, his grip constricting. "I can tell."

Rand struggled and tried to buck him off. It rubbed his rim against

Cai's cock, where the head of it nestled in between his buttocks. Rand bit back a groan.

"Tell me what I said. There you are." Cai's clever fingers had Rand's cock springing to further attention, though he suspected it was his words as much as anything else that accomplished it.

"You were going to fuck me." Rand growled.

"Fast and hard. We got interrupted. Didn't mean I forgot, sweetheart."

Rand elbowed him, and made solid contact with Cai's jaw, enough to shoot a few stars through his already aching skull. "Don't call me sweetheart. Ever. Got it?"

Cai cursed but emitted a harsh half-laugh at the same time. "Bastard. But that's more like it. I like a fair fight, wolf. Don't pull your punches. But right now, I want this. And your blood, if you'll lend me some."

"I didn't think vampires ask," Rand retorted. "They just take."

"We take. But we also give." Cai stroked and Rand's hips quivered. He was fighting the arousal rising in his body that Cai wanted. Rand probably didn't realize it would be the best soothing balm for any injuries Cai sustained. Or maybe he did, and that was why he wasn't fighting harder.

"You're very single minded," the shifter complained, though there was a satisfying hitch in his voice.

"On the contrary, I can multi-task with the best of them. I just haven't forgotten what my top priority was at the beginning of my evening. I'll have that before the day can get any more abysmal and the chance slips away entirely. *Carpe diem*, and all that shit."

"Today could get worse than it's already been?" Rand tossed it off, a barbed response, but Cai felt the almost immediate mental pause in the shifter's mind.

Yeah, it could. Guess we both know that, right? It can always get worse.

Rand's head tilted. *You never did tell me your sob story.*

"No, I didn't. And not going to right now. Talk about a mood-killer." Cai reached over him and pulled out the lube he'd found in the drawer of the night table.

He used it, resting his free hand on Rand's back, sitting on his thighs. The shifter crossed his hands under his cheek, forming a pillow of his overlaid knuckles and giving Cai an even more superlative view, thanks to the shift of back and shoulder muscles, the bunching of his biceps. His lashes swept down, telling Cai the male was pulling a glimpse of Cai working the lube over his cock. Cai's shaft jumped in his hand as Rand moistened his lips.

"Getting harder, wolf?"

"I'm not the only one," Rand grunted.

"Damn right." Cai slid his greased hand under Rand's body. Rand's hips lifted. Not much, but even the slight accommodation sent a jolt of pleasure through Cai, the physical evidence that the wolf wasn't merely putting up with him.

He tangled the other non-greased hand in Rand's hair. "This mane needs combing and a trim. Maybe we'll take care of that while we're in civilization."

"Cai..." Rand's voice sounded strained, maybe because Cai was working him in his fist. Slow, the skin sliding up the shaft to the ridged head, then back down again, Cai's thumb stroking the sensitive line beneath.

"Yeah?"

In answer, Rand adjusted, Cai moving with him as the male got onto his knees, using his elbows to balance on all fours on the mattress. When Rand dropped his head against his crossed forearms, Cai folded over him to brush a kiss between his shoulder blades. He felt tired suddenly, beat up, but glad to be skin-to-heated-skin with this particular male. Gratitude. It was an unsettling feeling. "You're a good guy, Rand. You really should have run."

"Yeah, maybe." Rand's body rippled in response as Cai guided himself into his tight backside, working his way through the muscles, loving the slick glide.

"Nothing like a quality lube. Makes enjoying the ride all the easier. Right?"

"God..."

"Yeah." Cai went deep, all the way to the balls, and stayed there a good, pushing, grinding, plowing moment before withdrawing and doing it again. Harder, deeper, if that was possible. Fuck, the male's muscles squeezed down on him as he came out, pushed in, like he was resisting. Or gripping, so Cai couldn't leave.

He moved a hand to Rand's broad shoulder, the other coiled in his hair. Yeah, a trim, but not a cut. He loved wrapping his hands in the stuff. He yanked the male's head up as he brought him off his hands and Cai slid his arm over his chest. He held him that way as he rocked and slammed into his ass, balancing them both on their knees on the bed despite the force. He might be somewhat under his normal strength, but he was still capable of being light as a cat on his feet and twice as agile. He pulled the hair to Rand's right shoulder and grazed his bared neck with sharp fangs.

"Want to taste you. Nourish myself from your blood, wolf."

Tension rippled through Rand. He didn't say no, but Cai wanted to hear an answer, from the firm, sensual lips, the deep voice. "Say yes."

Rand's mind was surprisingly hard to read, as if he'd left the rooms of human reason in favor of animal instinct, so the former didn't invade and cause problems. At least that was how Cai preferred to see it. A long pause, but then the broad shoulders shifted against him as Rand drew in a deep breath. "Yes."

Cai struck, biting deep, almost moaning at the taste that flooded onto his tongue. There was a rumor among vampires about the legendary shifters. That a vampire-shifter servant pairing would be a match made in heaven, because their blood was supposed to be richer and more potent to a vampire than three humans at once.

He thought of how quickly Chavez had healed, merely from a fully marked human donor. The shifter blood might be all bullshit wives' tales, but there was no denying the compatibility factor was off the charts. Cai wasn't sure he'd ever want to drink another human's blood again. Anyone's blood but his wolf's.

Not your wolf. Just a guy who unfortunately got dragged into your shit. He reminded himself of that, and turned his mind to what mattered. Feeling pleasure, and there was a lot of it to go around.

As he drank what was needed, Cai reached around Rand's hip and stroked his thick, hard cock again. He reveled in the sounds the shifter made. The dip of his head and shoulder, as Rand leaned more on one elbow to brace himself against Cai's thrusts. His thoughts, swirling and hard-to-pin-down though they were, were equally plea-surable. Rand liked how Cai yanked on his hair as he thrust.

Cai retracted his fangs and sealed the wounds when he'd had all the blood that he needed, but he wasn't sure he'd ever get enough of the male's beautiful body.

The part of him that loved to deny, to wait until the gratification was overwhelming, wanted to keep things going another hour, but he hadn't lied to Giles. Or Rand. He knew time was ticking away, and, if nothing else, the sooner he gave Lady Lyssa whatever pointless info she needed, the sooner they could leave and they could spend hours at this. Well, if the wolf didn't say *so long* and that was the end of it.

Cai released, jetting seed into the tight, gorgeous ass. Rand climaxed at the same time, hips jerking in a way that made Cai see bliss and stars and every damn version of Heaven there was.

This was just a quick, casual fuck on some nice linens. They'd made a hell of a mess. Well, Rand had. It pleased Cai to see it. He wanted to take the shifter all over again.

Stroking the male's back slow, he laid another kiss on the middle of it. Cai felt an unsettling urge to stay there, press his face into heated flesh, sink into the male's strength. Let the clock tick away so he didn't have to face whatever was outside this door.

Yeah, like that ever worked. Annoyed that the thought had unfurled anxiety and urgency in him, Cai straightened and took hold of his emotions. As he eased out of Rand's ass, he gave it a satisfying swat that left a handprint and earned him a startled and delightfully dangerous look.

"Grab clothes or fur, your preference, wolf. We have to go rap with the queen."

CHAPTER SEVEN

*W*hen they were ready to leave the room, it was once again as vampire and wolf, for Rand had shifted by the time Cai put on his clothes. The garments did fit reasonably well, a black button-down shirt over stressed designer jeans that made him look a step above homeless vagrant in this crowd. Fortunately, he still had his scarred and bloodstained hiking shoes to keep anyone from thinking he was too civilized.

When he made that observation to Rand, the wolf's expression suggested there was no risk of that. Rand gave him an odd look as Cai took the armload of clothes Giles had brought for Rand and tucked them into a pillow case in the closet. "They're too nice to leave behind," Cai explained. "I'll make an excuse to come back up here before we leave and toss it out the window, pick it up on our way out."

At Rand's disapproving look, Cai snorted. "Lady Helga's on the Council. Torrence probably has new clothes for every day of the year. Man, he was a big son of a bitch. Probably no more than a nickel's difference in your dimensions. Maybe he's from your same litter and just didn't get the shifting bug."

As they stepped into the hallway, Rand chuffed a response which Cai assumed equated a snort. "You know, that stern look you did while sitting on my junk, your arms crossed over your sexy chest?" Cai tapped the wolf's head with a finger and grinned at the show of teeth. "Maybe we'll play 'student takes ruler away from school master and

114

paddles *his* ass.' And see there? Who knew wolves could roll their eyes? It's a miraculous world."

They moved down the hall toward the staircase. However, at the cracked door to the missing girl's room, Rand slowed and came to a halt.

Peering in discreetly, Cai saw Leona was still that same motionless lump beneath the covers. Well, not so motionless this time. Her shoulders were quivering and Cai could detect the muffled weeping.

"Rand..." Cai hissed, but the wolf had already pushed open the door with his shoulder and moved into the room. He went to the bed, jumped on it with surprisingly light-footed grace, turned a circle and lay down, resting his heavy head on Leona's hip. Giving comfort.

Cai braced for screaming, but the figure became very still. Slowly, the covers were pulled down enough to show a silken fall of chestnut hair and a slim shoulder. She was wearing what scent and appearance suggested was one of Lord Greenwald's shirts. Her hand slid out of the linens, reaching back to rest on Rand's head. Then the fingers convulsed, slipping down to clutch his ruff as a harder shudder went through her. Cai studied the tableau and nodded.

Catch up when you're ready.

Rand didn't feel happy about Cai going on without him, but he looked even more reluctant to leave her. Cai was good with that. It bothered him, the woman lying here all alone. Because she really was alone, wasn't she? Greenwald's episodes of Ennui meant he was accelerating down the slope toward losing his mind. There was no good end to the disease. His term as overlord would end soon and, not long after that, he'd walk into the sun or be taken down by other vampires. Though from Lyssa's surprising patience toward him, Cai thought the vampire queen might provide him more protection than Cai would have expected.

But Leona lying there crying, while her vampire master stomped around and had tantrums and delusions that sent his cronies to beat people up and look for demons? Greenwald had said he was going to check on Leona, but when Cai and Rand had come down here, not more than a couple minutes later, he'd been nowhere in sight. It kind of sucked that Greenwald hadn't even thought to post another servant like Giles to watch over her fulltime.

Most times, Cai didn't think of humans beyond their purpose as food. He had no particular liking for them as a species. He'd lost the empathy a long time ago, no matter his own human origins. But he didn't torture his food and, when he took a life for his monthly blood needs, he made it pleasurable or quick, depending on the circumstances. He had no desire to make them afraid or suffer.

This was the problem with being social. You thought about shit you didn't normally consider. It was hard to stay dispassionate, seeing those quivering shoulders and her fragile fist curled in Rand's fur. In the vampire world, twenty-two was pretty much a baby. Dovia was a fledgling whose wings were still wet. Was Leona blaming herself? Probably. Every parent did when they had a child taken, right?

An image came to his mind, so quickly and viciously tamped down that Rand's ears twitched, as if feeling the concussion from the slammed door in Cai's head.

If anyone should be blaming himself, it was Greenwald. He was the overlord, the guy in charge, who kept everyone in line. Yet Trads had stolen his daughter right out from under his nose.

Having been beaten by his minions, Cai experienced some petty satisfaction about that, but it was short-lived. This was his child, to protect against every possible harm. And he'd failed.

Thinking of it that way made it hard to get any mileage out of the gloat. Cai worked hard to be a soulless monster, but today he was falling short. If Leona was blaming herself, a servant who was subordinate to her Master, where important decisions were his, not hers, to make, how much more of that was Lord Georg experiencing? Cai could understand the guy letting the disease take over more of his mind, if it gave him respite from the agony he must be feeling.

When he felt a glimmer of reaction from Rand's mind, Cai realized he didn't have to look further than the shifter to know how the loss of a kid could eat someone from the inside. But making that connection still took Cai into not-fucking-going-there territory for himself.

He was still leaning in the door. Cai told himself his unwillingness to leave had to do with the distasteful task of meeting with the contingent upstairs, but that wasn't all of it. Rand lifted his head, gold and blue eyes focused on him.

Maybe he did have some information that would help them find the girl. Cai wouldn't hold back on that. But he gave himself one more second to step away from the uncomfortable blowback of feelings about the situation and remember just an hour ago. Rand beneath him, the strong body flexing as they wrestled. The tilt of his head as Cai stroked his back. He didn't have to think when he was around the wolf. Crazy thought, right? They'd known each other like two minutes. But maybe that wasn't a relationship thing. That was Rand's animal nature, making it as easy to be around him as if he truly was all animal.

It suggested Cai enjoyed fucking a wolf more than a human or vampire, which *so* didn't sound right to say. At least not at cocktail parties. A real problem, because he went to tons of those. Not.

Suppressing a sigh, he pushed off the doorframe. Feeling Rand's attention upon him as Cai left sent a weird spike through his chest. Pushing that away, too, he headed up the stairs, following voices to a spacious ground level sun porch. It provided a nighttime view of a pond with a lit fountain in the middle of it.

Greenwald, Lyssa, Mason and Helga were sitting on the porch. An in-depth discussion of some kind was happening, but Cai wondered if Greenwald was hearing any of it. His bloodshot eyes lifted at Cai's appearance and filled with malevolence. Yeah, if the Council hadn't been here, the torture fest would have continued. Cai had no doubt of that. Took care of his empathy, that was for damn sure. Dried that well right up.

"Where's the wolf?" Voltaire demanded. He was standing behind his lord's chair. Lyssa's admonition may have toned down his behavior, but he was keeping himself front and center. A reminder he was the one who should be considered as a replacement when Greenwald faltered just enough. It made Cai want to see his limbs tied to a four-some of tractors. Their slow amble away from one another would make his dismemberment a satisfying spectator sport.

"He's with the girl's mother. She needed comfort. Being a big goofy dog lying next to her was more desirable to him than sharing your company," Cai said.

Greenwald gestured to Voltaire and the younger vampire headed for the door. Cai stepped in front of him, bringing Voltaire to a halt.

"If you're checking on her wellbeing in his care, I've no objection to that," Cai said, and meant it. The overlord's quick dispatching of his minion to her side was the first evidence he'd had that her state of mind mattered to Greenwald. "But you fuck with him in any way, and I will rip your fucking head off. We clear?"

Voltaire's fangs showed. Cai didn't give a shit. He stood his ground. Voltaire wanted to throw down with him, but with the Council here and Greenwald, he was hampered. Cai wasn't.

"If all is as you say it is, Voltaire will cause no harm to the wolf," Lyssa said. "I've stated you are a guest, and your beast belongs to you, Cai. He's safe."

Yeah, as long as circumstances didn't change, which they could in an instant. But it was as good as he was going to get. Giving Voltaire another hard look that was answered with barely veiled contempt, Cai made a mocking gesture of courtesy toward the double doors. He also sent a message to Rand that the vampire was coming and his intent, and received a push of acknowledgement.

Greenwald rose. "I've waited long enough. Tell me everything you know, Trad. Or nobody here will be able to save you."

"You're going to have to narrow that down. I know lots of things. Like how to navigate by the stars, fix a great PB&J, get blood out of clothing so your fabrics last longer..."

He could have tried to move out of range, but Greenwald had him by a few hundred years and they were only a handful of feet apart. Avoiding the blow would have been pointless, so Cai merely braced himself.

Even so, the face punch sent him to the floor, hard enough his elbow cracked the tile. Son of a bitch, the guy could hit. But it confirmed Rand's blood had done a good job for him. He didn't feel any residual twinges from his previous injuries. No yelping.

Rolling to his back, Cai propped himself on his elbows. As he ran a thumb along his split lip and considered the blood, he angled a look up at the furious overlord. Deliberately, Cai crossed his ankles, squinting through the throbbing pain to blink at Greenwald.

"Should I stay down so you can do some kicking? Will that get her back faster? Make me talk sooner?"

Mason was up. For as fast as Greenwald had moved, the copper-haired vampire made him look like a snail. Which meant he could stomp Cai like a bug. Fortunately, Mason had more impulse control than Greenwald.

Greenwald struggled against Mason's hold, but the Council

vampire held fast. "Easy, my lord. His behavior may deserve your ire, but he's correct. This is solving nothing."

"I cannot tolerate this despicable...thing, in my home," Greenwald said through gritted teeth to Lady Lyssa. Cai noted she sat quietly, with regal straightness, but her eyes were missing nothing of the interchange. "Pain is the only way to break Trads, my lady. We are wasting time."

"Hey. Georg."

The overlord's head swiveled around, his eyes widening. "You disrespectful—"

"Georg's your name, right?"

"Get to the point and do not goad him needlessly," Mason said. The vampire's gaze was cold, but it wasn't the implied threat that reached Cai as much as the look behind it. While the vampire might understand the reason for Cai's behavior, the even tone was a clear admonishment for Cai to grow up and be the bigger vampire.

Else Mason would rip his arm off to reinforce the point.

It wasn't threats that brought Cai back to his feet, but he did try to tone his abrasive nature down. Somewhat. He squared off with the overlord. "Georg Greenwald? Did you escape from a Harry Potter book? Torture me all you wish, vamp. You can carve every inch of skin off my body and cut off my balls, and you'll still get squat. But here's what *will* work. How about some fucking courtesy? Instead of saying I'm your guest, actually treat me like one."

Cai turned his attention to Lady Lyssa. She was five feet nothing and should have seemed diminutive compared to the males, and even the voluptuous Helga. Yet she was the only one he felt compelled to address by her title, even if only in his mind. That told him how he wanted to do this.

"I'll provide the information you seek," Cai said. "But I'll tell you. Alone."

Mason's amber eyes glinted. Yeah, he was a scary bastard. So the fuck what? "You do not demand a solo audience with the Council head," the vampire said.

"Why? Is a thousand-year-old queen afraid of being alone with a two-hundred-year-old vamp?" Cai tossed a look at Lord Georg. "It's sure as hell not going to be here, with him interrupting every other word. She can share with him what she wants to tell him. Then I'm out of here, and fuck the lot of you."

As the Council members stiffened and Cai thought he might truly be in danger of being limbless, clicking toenails brought everyone's attention to the door. Rand shouldered open the cracked door and entered the room.

Without a word, he moved to stand at Cai's side.

～

Leona had fallen asleep again, so when his ears, nose, and the mind linked to Cai had detected the blow, the blood and pain, Rand had left the room, run up the hall and bounded to the top of the stairs, passing a surprised Voltaire on the way.

It had been a kneejerk, protective response. He should have remembered Cai's nature. Now inside the sunroom, Rand could tell the vampire father was quivering with a rage so overwhelming that the one called Lord Mason was staying close, as if anticipating having to restrain him once more.

Stop being asshole, he thought hard at Cai, but met only a silent wall. He was going to pummel the vampire himself.

The other vampires had broken off their conversation as he entered, and Rand was uncomfortably aware all eyes were on him. Evaluating, assessing... Lady Helga's gaze coursed over him from head to toe, so thoroughly it might have been her hands. It suggested Lyssa had shared what she'd guessed he was with the other Council members. He didn't think Georg knew, however, for the way his gaze passed over Rand, dismissing him, suggested he only saw a pet.

"Based on how I was brought here, and what you're all so eager to know, I've earned the right to demand the terms for the information," Cai said, continuing the conversation.

"Oh?" Lyssa's brow lifted, her expression tightening. Rand noticed the room dropped by about twenty degrees. Everyone else registered it with uneasy looks. Could all vampires do that?

You think I'd be sweating my ass off in the summer if I could? She's supposedly part Fae.

"What terms are those, Mordecai?" Lyssa asked.

Cai blinked. "Exactly what I just said. A solo audience." His expression cleared, and he let out another harsh laugh. "You thought I was going to demand something for the information? Money, power? A position?" He snorted in derision. "You all have nothing I fucking want. Except an exit door."

Lamb and pork chops in kitchen. To-go bag nice.

Where his earlier comment hadn't penetrated, he saw an easing to Cai's shoulders at that one, and a deprecating side glance from the vampire. *Figures, a wolf would think with his stomach.*

Better than dick. Live longer.

Blah blah blah.

Voltaire had slipped back in the room, taking his position behind Greenwald with another baleful look at Cai.

"Very well." Lyssa drew Rand's attention as she rose, stopping his internal dialogue with Cai. "You and I will retire to the study." She paused, her head tilting as her servant, Jacob, who'd been standing attentively behind her chair, took a step from the wall. Her lips curved, her eyes reflecting mild reproof, but also something else. Deep regard. Rand sensed Cai's surprise at seeing it.

Rand's cousin had strong feelings for his female vampire, which were acceptable, but he'd told Rand that if a vampire had reciprocating feelings for a servant, they kept them hidden. It was pretty taboo, vampires being in love with their servants. But the connection between Lyssa and Jacob was impossible to miss, even without wolf senses.

"My servant will accompany us," Lyssa said.

"Then so will he." Cai jerked his head at Rand.

She nodded. "I'll meet you there. Third door on the left down the hallway, once you exit these chambers." Her gaze slid to the others. "We will return shortly."

Mason looked the least thrilled by her decision, though no one looked overjoyed. However, they all held their comments, respecting the queen's command. As she disappeared through an alternative exit Jacob opened behind her, Cai turned on his heel and strode out of the chamber, not giving anyone a further look. Rand followed.

Once in the hall, the heavy double doors closed behind them, though Cai caught a last glimpse of Voltaire's sneering face. He was probably planning how to dissect Cai with the help of his buddies, Tyra and Chavez.

Rand bumped Cai's leg, hard enough to knock him off track, and moved in front of him. He brought Cai to a halt with his body and an unexpectedly angry stare.

His daughter in danger. You play games.

Cai knew Rand's emotions were running high, having just come from Leona's side. But Cai was dealing with his own shit, and the accusation in Rand's eyes knocked some of it loose. Maybe that was for the best. Letting it lead him, Cai shoved him out of his way. The wolf moved back, his eyes flickering with annoyance.

"Did I ask your opinion?" Cai bared his fangs, ignoring the wolf's startled look. "If you can't follow me like a good dog—the way they like their servants to act—then stay here."

Rand laid back his ears. *Cold-hearted bastard. Playing with heads. Hearts.*

Cai curled a lip over the steel fang, the rough edges of it a familiar reminder against his callused lip. "Go away, wolf. I don't need you. Take off. This isn't your world or your problem. Stop acting like it is. If you're going to pretend to be something you're not, do it with your own kind. Find yourself a happy little picket fence pack, if you can get another female wolf to be your beard."

If not for the situation with Georg and his daughter, Rand would have taken the vampire down, right then and there. Cai saw it, that derisive sneer crossing his face, another taunt, before he pivoted, walking away.

"Anytime you feel lucky, wolf. You might spill a few drops of my blood on her carpets. She won't think twice about putting you down for something like that."

Cai headed down the hall. Rand stayed in place, trying to contain the red haze of temper. It would feel good to let the animal take over, go after him, wreak havoc. But he was no pup with impulse control issues, no matter that Cai seemed to have a unique ability to trigger them.

No, he hadn't known the vampire long, and Cai didn't act like he cared overly much for anyone or anything, but it didn't seem his style to be deliberately cruel.

As the vampire reached the study door, he did something curious. Putting his hand on the door latch, he paused. A deep breath, then his shoulders squared, and he turned the latch, pushing the door open.

Oh, hell. Rand's anger dissipated. He really had been away from human society too long if he'd fallen for the *go away dog, I don't want you* routine they did in countless children's movies.

Cai didn't want Rand in that room. Rand just didn't know why.

So Rand followed him. If Cai had closed the door, he'd knock the damn thing down, though the oak looked solid as a brick wall. Fortunately, the door was only pushed closed, not latched. Rand nudged it open and slid into the room.

Cai's head turned just enough to show his profile, then he returned his attention to Lyssa. She was sitting at a desk, Jacob nearby, leaning against a bookcase, arms crossed over his broad chest.

Rand was surprised when the servant nodded to him. He would have been equally surprised if he'd given him that courteous nod while Rand was in human form. Maybe servants cut each other some slack, knowing that an asshole vampire didn't necessarily make for an asshole servant. The servant might even deserve some sympathy for putting up with said asshole. And a stiff drink. Or a raw steak.

"So I am here," Lyssa said. "Speak your words, Cai." Her jade-colored eyes frosted. "If your reason for an audience is simply to wield power you have not earned, and not to give me useful information that will help Lord Georg's daughter, you will sorely regret testing my patience. Be courteous and speak swiftly. I will not warn you to mind your manners again."

"Yeah." Cai sat down in the chair across from her. The one word wasn't spoken as a sarcastic challenge, however. More as an absent-minded acknowledgement as he focused on other things.

"There's only one enclave of Trads in the Appalachians. You're sure they're the ones that have her?"

Jacob nodded.

"How?" Cai asked bluntly. "And how did you know about my connection to them?"

Jacob glanced at Lyssa, and the queen spoke. "We petitioned the help of a sorcerer and his wife, who is a powerful witch with even more powerful friends. One of them performed a divination spell to determine how best to locate Dovia before it was too late. Your name and a few particulars came up. Not too many about you or the Appalachian group, unfortunately. Just that you had been with them, but were no longer, and if we found you, the chances were high you would have information and resources to help our purpose."

"Oh, thanks. That explains everything." Cai nodded sagely. "You went to a fortune teller and she told you a mysterious stranger would put you on the path to success."

Rand winced at the caustic tone. He sincerely hoped the vampire queen wouldn't kill Cai. If anyone was going to kill that annoying son of a bitch, it was going to be him.

Lyssa didn't bat an eye lash. "Thanks to that sorcerer and his wife," she said, "you were found within twenty-four hours. In the middle of thousands of acres of national forest, with the aid of an enchanted necklace."

Cai blinked and a moment of silence reigned. Then he shrugged. "Okay. Fair point."

Leaning forward, he laced his fingers between spread knees. Rand noticed a sudden tension in the way his hands were locked together, in the set of his shoulders.

"The ones who took her are a hardcore purist Trad sect," Cai said. "Originally all born vamps. But Trads go through cycles when their numbers decrease and they realize they have to dirty their purist beliefs with a certain amount of made ones. They have a lot of protocol and ritual to it, both the choosing and the indoctrination process, which makes them feel better. They've had more applicants to choose from in recent years. Made vamps coming into their ranks from the outside, the ones who are disillusioned with your way of doing things."

Lyssa's expression remained flat. "We are aware of that trend."

"They've only added to the existing hard-on that run-of-the-mill Trads possess to snag a born female vampire. That's the ultimate prize for all of them. But for this Appalachian group, it's the holy fucking grail. Doesn't matter how slim the chances of conception are; to have a Trad born from that union would prop up their purist manifesto for centuries. They've got a whole chosen ones' thing, about being the only ones smart enough to make it happen, and elevate the Trad race. Psycho and stupid, but that's their crazy-assed MO."

He took a breath. "They won't waste time. They want her to

conceive as soon as possible, and they'll set aside hierarchy. Normally, it's might is right and the strongest can take and keep what he wants, even more so than in your society. However, in the interest of having her conceive as quickly as possible, the guy in charge will share her with the rest of his select group of hangers-on."

His voice became wooden. "They won't be gentle about it, but they won't be physically brutal, either. They don't want the vessel or the potential conception to be at risk. They'll feed her, see to her basic needs. Far better than they do for the human women they've taken and tried to breed with. They're not as careful with them, because human women can be replaced more quickly and easily."

Rand felt ill. Jacob's face had hardened with unmistakable anger. Lyssa's countenance still revealed nothing, but the room temperature was a different matter. Rand wouldn't have been surprised to see icicles form a border on the front of the large desk. When she leaned forward, her gaze fixed on Cai like it could spear him. His wolf wanted to start backing up. "So, they have likely already begun this...process," she said.

"Yeah. Kind of what I meant by 'they won't waste any time,'" Cai confirmed.

Those jade eyes sharpened in warning. "You know where this sect is."

"Approximately, yeah. They like a particular stomping ground, but it covers a wide area. One of the most human-remote parts of West Virginia, deep-assed mountains, not much human activity. I can draw you a map."

As Cai described some of the landmarks, Rand sat up taller, ears twitching. Cai glanced toward him. Rand hadn't meant to draw attention, but if the location Cai was describing was where Rand thought it was, there might be at least one shifter pack nearby. Additional eyes and ears.

Not that he'd want that shared with the vampires. Hell, he kept forgetting about the mind reading thing.

Cai cocked his head, his firm lips quirking, but the worry Rand felt was quickly alleviated. Cai finished his explanation without revealing Rand's thoughts. A cue they'd discuss it later, just the two of them.

Lyssa templed her fingers. "You're a made vampire, Cai. A Trad."

His lips tightened. "Yes to the first. No to the second."

"How are you not? To validate your information and use that to help us retrieve Dovia, I need to establish your history with them."

"Trust is your problem. You don't need shit. I tell you what I want to tell you and—"

Cai stopped abruptly. Lyssa hadn't moved, but something had changed about the energy around her. Rand felt a note of distress strangled from Cai's mind, which was suddenly eerily open to Rand, yet obscured in a fog.

"Stop," Cai managed in a choked snarl.

Rand didn't think. Simply surged forward, gathering himself to leap, ready to land all four feet on her desk, his snapping jaws inches from her face. Why, he didn't know, because he'd been ready to tear Cai apart himself. Maybe this second mark shit made his pack instinct override everything else.

Jacob met him halfway. Rand was startled that the servant could move that fast, but they came toe to toe and Jacob risked his fingers by throwing up an admonishing hand.

"Wait and watch," he murmured. "She knows what she's doing. Your Master will come to no harm unless he deserves it."

Oh, he deserves it. That's not the point. And not my Master, Rand added for good measure, though pointless since he was only talking to himself.

"You demanded this meeting out of courtesy," Lyssa said quietly. "I demand the same from you, Mordecai."

She did something that released him, for abruptly Cai's body slumped as if cut from a gallows arm. He sprang up just as quickly, moving behind the chair and taking a defensive stance, fists up and face laced with fury. She didn't move. Jacob stepped back, though he stayed close, in Rand's peripheral vision.

"Don't do that," Cai gritted. "Ever again."

"An improvement. You didn't curse, though you didn't say please." Lyssa gestured to the chair. "Shall we try again? Explain to me why you're not Trad, but you know so much of them."

Cai stared at her. The vampire seemed conflicted about what to do next, but it surprised Rand when he returned to the chair. He sat on the edge of the seat, though, his body reflecting his tension.

If I throw that rock now, will you go?

No.

Cai coughed over a harsh half-chuckle that had no humor in it. *Stubborn-ass shifter.*

Lyssa had given him a curious look at the laugh. Cai subsided, falling silent and staring a hole in the side of the desk. The vampire queen clasped her hands in a loose knot on the desk.

"You are correct," she said abruptly. "You were brought here against your will, Mordecai. While that isn't always an inappropriate thing in the vampire world, I'll offer you something for your total honesty. Whatever things you wish protected about yourself will not leave this room. I won't tell the others how you come by the knowledge you have, unless it is pertinent to finding her."

Now Cai looked surprised. Lyssa's expression didn't change. Rand thought she must practice being a statue, but whatever Cai read from her face seemed to work. Rand tended to use senses other than vision to pick up what was really happening. Even as human, his sense of smell was far more developed. What he detected from Lyssa, after exercising whatever power had allowed her to manacle Cai's mind that brief moment, was a sliver of sympathy. She'd seen something in Cai's reaction that had made her realize a different tactic was needed, a different type of sincerity. Rand had no idea what it was until Cai spoke.

"I was taken by a Trad from that Appalachian group when I was fifteen. And human."

Rand's gaze snapped to Cai. He was standing where he could see the male's profile, and Cai's expression looked brittle as glass.

"Why would the Trads take a young male?" Jacob asked.

Cai's voice took on a bitter edge. "I met the choosing guidelines. I had some abilities they thought would be useful."

"Which would be?" Lyssa asked.

Cai said nothing for a long moment. Then he reached toward the desk and the potted plant there, which had a variety of purple blooms. Plucking one off its stem, he closed it in his hand. After another pause, he lifted his gaze and met Lyssa's eyes.

Magic warmed the air around Cai. Different from what he'd used to reinforce the chains or heal Rand, but similar. Closer to this.

Perhaps twenty seconds had ticked by when Cai opened his hand. Rand and Jacob pressed forward to see what he had revealed to Lyssa.

A newborn flower was breaking through the seed that had been fertilized inside the cup of the blossom. Before their eyes, it kept growing until it bloomed, a newer, vibrant version of the mature flower. The threadlike roots overlapped the split sides of the seed and spread out over the lines of Cai's palm.

Creation magic. That was why it hadn't felt exactly like healing energy to Rand. Creation magic could be used to heal, though in a different way from healing magic itself. Creation magic could not only spawn life, but it could change the nature of things, accelerate their process, like healing a wound, or making chain far stronger than expected.

Rand hadn't expected a vampire like Cai to possess the talent for it, or the head of the Vampire Council to recognize it. But the flicker in Lyssa's eyes said she did. Cai had said she was part-Fae, after all.

Sorcerers, the Fae, shifters. While all of those knew of creation magic, few could use it as Cai had just done. And he was implying he'd had the ability as a young human, perhaps even since birth. But to what extent?

The exercise or presence of such magic would leave a detectable signature to a shifter, and possibly even other vampires. Though Rand had detected those traces of power from the vampire, when not in use, their presence was so faint as to be overlooked or mistaken for the latent power Cai had as a vampire. Was that natural or practiced? Had Cai intentionally learned to mask it so completely? If so, why?

Lyssa and Jacob had their gazes locked on the vampire, and Rand could only imagine the ricochet of thoughts passing between them. With an odd self-consciousness, Cai worked the new flower into the plant's soil, tamping it down around the roots with gentle fingers before he sat back. "I expect you understand why the Trads would be interested in a guy who could make a seed germinate."

"Any seed." Lyssa said it as a statement.

"Yeah, that's what they thought." Cai's lips twisted. "I'd be king of the world if we ever get hit by famine, because it only works on plants. Fortunately, I have the survival skills of a cockroach, so when they realized I couldn't make a human woman fertile from their seed, those skills helped me figure out how to stay alive. They never caught a female vampire while I was with them, but eventually they believed I couldn't do it with any type of female mammal. By that time, I was making my mark as a useful member of their fucked-up little society.

Another vampire in the group turned me. Not the one who took me from my family."

He lifted a shoulder. "A made vamp can leave if he kills at least one other member of the clan, proving he's no longer the bottom of the totem pole. It took a hundred years, but I did it."

"That's an extraordinary amount of determination," Lyssa said.

"I don't like anyone to take choices out of my hands." He met her gaze. "Don't do what you just did to me, ever again."

Her lips curved. "Can you stop me?"

"No. Not right now. But I figured out how to kill a Trad after a hundred years. I'm willing to put in the time to figure out how to set you back on your heels if you fuck with me."

Jacob shifted and Lyssa's gaze slid to him. He stilled, a muscle flexing in his jaw. Rand had moved with him, though, and the midnight blue eyes cut to him. "Going to take us both on?" the servant asked the wolf, with deceptive mildness.

"He gets stupidly protective in that form," Cai advised. "Logic won't have anything to do with it."

"Hard to figure out how to stop me if you're dead," Lyssa pointed out to Cai, ignoring Rand and Jacob as if the servants' exchange hadn't happened.

"Trads tried their best to kill me. If you succeed where they failed, then that's that. But otherwise...just don't."

Rand's gaze slid back to Cai. The note in his voice was unclassifiable, but it came out close to a proper petition to a vampire queen. Well, as close as someone like Cai could manage. But the emotion behind it was one soul speaking to another.

Cai liked this queen, Rand realized. Respected her, as much as the vampire could respect anyone. He had obviously picked up in a short time what Rand had drawn from her, too. She wasn't set against him, against anyone. She would act in the best interest of the vampire girl, and of the vampires as a whole.

Before Rand could get used to Cai's shift in attitude, he went right back to being confrontational.

"Some years after I was taken, I found out my human mother went above and beyond to try to find me. When she started babbling crazy shit about vampires, my father was afraid for the rest of my siblings and had her put in an asylum." Cai stared at Lyssa.

"You know how awful most of those were in the early 1800s? But before that happened, she discovered who the local vampire in charge was and went, a lowly human, to seek an audience. Graham. Think he's an overlord in California now. Not that I give a flying fuck about your attempt at a government, but I've tried to keep track of him."

Cai's jaw tightened. "He told her that the fate of humans fallen into vampire hands, particularly Trads, was not their concern. Unless she had something to trade worth having, she wouldn't leave an audience with him alive. So she was shared with him and several other visiting vampires for a couple days. She would have died there, but his servant risked Graham's wrath, and dropped her off at a city hospital during daylight hours. That was when the babbling about vampires landed her in an institution. Her mind was probably broken from those few days with them, so she couldn't pretend not to know about vampires. She died a few years later."

He rose. Jacob drew closer, but Lyssa lifted a hand, stilling him. "Let him say his peace," she said quietly.

"Yeah, let me say my peace." Cai's lip curled. "So, when you want me to care about fucking vampires, you are barking up the wrong fucking tree. I owe no one my allegiance, and any one of you can do your best to kill me, but it won't change that. I'll be dead and gone before I'll pay a tithe, bow down, suck the dick or follow whatever the hell protocols that overlords, Region Masters or the head of the goddamn Vampire Council lay out."

He took a breath, and Rand heard that unsettling note in his voice, felt the intensity of it. "I'm a vampire now, and I'm cool with that. Thanks to the seed magic stuff, I was already something different from most humans. That was why I was taken. But she was my mother. I remembered her."

Cai paused, realizing he was letting his need to strike out take over his emotions. But God, he did remember her. Two hundred years, and he still remembered her smell, the touch of her hand, her eyes. Her smile. "I remember enough of her that, one day, when I'm strong enough, Graham will die at my hands. I've already taken two of the others who were at that audience. It's not my main reason for eating and sleeping, but I know our paths will cross when the time is right."

Silence ruled the room. When Lyssa did speak, it was in an unexpectedly mild tone. "Since you don't walk in our circles, you may not be aware. This Council bears no love for Graham. Because he has violated our restrictions one too many times, he was recently stripped of his overlord title and is on a probation that will end in his death if one more violation reaches our ears."

She unlaced her hands and placed the palms flat on the desk. "If that happens, his servant will be separated from him, if she doesn't wish to follow him into death."

Cai blinked. "You can do that? Separate a fully marked servant from the vampire?"

"We have had some limited success, for special situations." Lyssa waved a hand, indicating she wasn't going to be deviated from the topic. "She's not responsible for her Master's crimes. However, she is not the same one who helped your mother, I am certain, for he goes through servants at a distasteful rate. He's a disgrace to our society. But Lord Georg is not. He has been a good overlord before this happened."

"Before the Ennui got to him?"

Her expression closed. "You are aware of the condition."

"I know a few things about your world. It's also affected some Trads."

"Then you have shown more discretion and kindness than I anticipated from your attitude." She inclined her head. "Georg is an overwrought father and vampire seeking a target for his helpless rage, his fear for his daughter. But I expect you know that, which is why you requested a private audience, isn't it? So you could speak frankly without causing him more distress."

Rand's gaze slid to Cai, surprised when his face shuttered. Thanks to Cai's explanation of his background, most the ire he'd felt at the vampire's callousness had evaporated. He was still acting like an asshole, but Rand now understood better why. Though, because he could be an asshole, Rand wasn't entirely sure why Cai hadn't wanted him here.

Did he think finding out he'd been a victim would change—

Not a fucking victim.

Jacob started, and even Lyssa stiffened in surprise as Cai erupted from the chair, so violently it thudded to its side. In one step, he was facing off with Rand like he intended to attack. His fists were clenched, eyes like living flame.

It happened so fast, Rand reacted exactly as a wolf would. Flat ears, curled lip, hackles raised, tail out straight and feet braced. Ready for a fight, knowing he was standing right on the threshold on one. Cai met his gaze in unmistakable challenge, his mouth set in a flat line.

If that's what you think, then I mean it. Get the fuck out of here and don't you fucking come back.

He wanted Rand to attack. Rand had pressed the trigger that would let Cai act out, wreak havoc. Anything but having to sit here, talking in this absurdly civilized study about something wild and hellish unearthed from a place deep inside of him he didn't touch.

Rand had told Cai a shifter was a virtually foolproof lie detector. He hadn't explained that an extension of that was the ability to use animal intuition and human insight together to translate a language just as illuminating. His emotions.

Slowly, Rand's flattened ears lifted to a pricked-up position, his tail lowering from the pre-battle stiffness. He moved forward, watching the vampire's expression turn confused as Rand stopped next to him. Rand lowered his haunches to the carpet, the rest of him following as he settled into an alert, heads-up but lying-down pose on the carpet. His shoulder was against Cai's leg.

The vampire was facing away from Lyssa and Jacob, so they didn't see what Rand did, the easing of tension from his features, the bitterly rueful look. Cai closed his eyes, and his fist opened, his fingertips brushing Rand's face as Rand dipped his head to the contact, a dignified acknowledgment.

You're in my personal space, wolf.

Have your back. You piss off all.

It's my superpower.

Cai's shoulders lifted in a sigh, and Rand watched his face rearrange into a more neutral expression before he turned to face the desk again. "Sorry about that," Cai said politely. "Domestic issue. Where were we?"

Lyssa studied him. Rand could feel the current of tension through Cai. He wanted to get this done. Really wanted to be out of here.

Fortunately, Lyssa seemed to understand and didn't linger on the unexpected episode. "So you can lead us to where these Trads are," Lyssa said. "Do you think a single assassin could do an extraction? Or would an armed party have better success?"

Cai shook his head.

"I said I could draw you a map. But it won't help, whether you send one or a hundred. They'll hear you coming a mile off, because you don't move in their world. They'll take off with her as soon as they detect you're in the area tracking them. Which they will. If by some miracle, you corner them, they'll kill her just to spite you. Unless she's already conceived, which isn't likely unless some miracle happens that hasn't been pulled off to date. And when they kill her, they'll do it in the ugliest way possible, so her father gets back only a pile of meat, bone and blood."

As Lyssa's expression tightened, Cai tipped his head toward Rand. "If you want tactful, talk to him. Even when he's in the drool and fur state, he's subtler than I am."

"No doubt," Lyssa said. "I expect him to curb his drooling. Hard to clean out of the carpets."

See? Told you about the carpets.

"Would they trust you, Mordecai?" Lyssa continued. "To infiltrate their ranks and retrieve her, get her to safety and give us time to send you backup for the extraction?"

He blinked at her. "Don't know, because there's no way in hell I'm doing that."

She tapped a nail on the desk. "It has been my experience there is always something someone wants, enough to compel them to attempt something unwise or impossible."

"Both apply to that scenario."

"I can't compel you to do it," she said. "But I will ask you, is it possible?"

"No. Not if you're asking an amoral bastard like me to do it. Now, if you had someone who'd lived with the Trads who had his moral sensibilities," he jerked his thumb at Rand, "you might get a needle through that hell-tight sphincter."

"So if both of you went—"

"No." Cai's voice went flat with menace, right on the brink of the fury he'd displayed moments earlier. Rand noted Jacob tracking that aggression, but he stayed where he was. From Lyssa's still gaze, her deceptive relaxed state, she had things in hand, even if Cai came over the desk at her, which Rand sincerely hoped didn't happen.

"If I had an insane inclination to drop in on the colony that has her, he wouldn't be part of that. He's not my full servant, Lady Lyssa. He's second marked, but that was to help him heal from serious injury. He has no commitment to me and I place no bond on him. He's not human, so he's not going to out the damn vampire secrecy code."

"Indeed." She pursed her attractive lips. "Well, since you have no bond on him, I can ask him directly what his feelings about it are." She turned her gaze to Rand. Cai moved in front of him, just as fast.

"I said fucking no. You supposedly know a dozen languages. You have trouble understanding that word, bitch?"

Aw, hell. Rand was glad his wolf expression concealed his inner cringe. *Damn it, Cai...*

Lyssa had proven she'd tolerate a certain lack of manners from someone unused to her world. The wave of coldness, all amiability wiped from her expression, said she'd reached her threshold. Cai had just stepped in it.

But from the set of his shoulders, Rand expected Cai knew that. Fuck, had he done it to protect Rand, just like he'd done before? But whatever the reason, a distraction was needed. Now.

Going to need those clothes.

He could shift in a matter of seconds when needed, though fluidity had to be sacrificed to speed. Fortunately, he managed it without it becoming too much of a bone-breaking, skin-splitting horror show.

Jacob's set expression, reflecting his lady's displeasure with Cai, transformed to fascination, and then a slow smile. It was the reaction shifters appreciated the most, somewhere between a kid realizing dragons did exist and always knowing they had been there, just out of sight. Lyssa, on the other hand...

Rand guessed he should have anticipated a vampire's reaction would be well-flavored by strong sexual interest. He was alive because of Cai's, after all.

The vampire queen's appraisal started at the feet and went up with lingering thoroughness. When she reached Rand's face, he thought he might be blushing.

"If all shifters looked like you, Rand, I expect vampires would have dug them out of the mountains long ago."

Cai was looking between them like he wasn't sure if he needed to fight the vampire queen or smack Rand in the head. Putting his hand on Cai's shoulder to hopefully prevent either option, Rand executed a short bow.

"My lady," he said courteously, "Cai was trying to protect me. I expect you have those in your life you'd take similar, inadvisable steps to shield."

Lyssa blinked. "It has been said."

As Jacob coughed over a chuckle, she sent him an admonishing look.

"My servant has clothes up in the room," Cai said shortly. *Fancy words work better if your junk isn't hanging out there, being a distraction.*

Without distraction, you'd probably be a greasy spot on the carpet.

She likes me. I can tell.

Lyssa glanced at Jacob. "Send Giles to retrieve Rand's clothes. He need not be too hasty about it."

It was Jacob's turn to give her a narrow look, but he crossed the room and stepped to the door. He kept it cracked so the house servant couldn't peer within. While his voice stayed low, Rand detected the last words. "Make haste."

The glint in Lyssa's eyes became like that of a faceted jewel. Jacob returned to her side only a couple moments later, clothes in hand. She gave him an openly amused look. "I was unaware Giles was an Olympic sprinter."

Jacob offered an ambivalent grunt.

As Rand took the clothes and stepped aside to pull them on, she turned her attention back to Cai. "Your convictions need not be brayed like a mule to be truth. I've lived long enough to experience loss, betrayal, and know how terribly unfair life can be. It can also be glorious, when the essential elements needed as a balm to those feelings are discovered. I hope your tongue allows you long enough to find them."

She switched back to the original topic, ignoring Cai's bemused reaction. "Are you still accepted as one of them?" Lyssa asked.

"I said I won't—"

"Indulge me in a hypothetical. Are you still accepted as one of them?"

Cai scowled. "Probably. Yes. No. Maybe. The one who leads them now is the vampire who stole me when I was a kid. Goddard."

∼

He should just stop talking, but he'd promised honesty. It was no big deal. Cai could say it out loud. It didn't mean anything and he'd be out of here soon.

But saying the male's name was harder than it should be. He wanted to spit it out a few more times, just to prove it had no hold on him, maybe scream it and add a few expletives to embellish it...but that might make him seem a bit unhinged. Right? More than he'd already proven he was.

He could feel Rand's gaze on him. *He's alive, why?*

Cai appreciated the male's wave of homicidal support. Just as he'd appreciated his reaction of a few moments ago when he'd lost it like a fledgling. It should have made Cai even more unsettled, but the wolf sitting down next to him, leaning against his leg had been...calming. Fuck.

Rand had donned the jeans and shirt. Rand and Torrence were almost an exact match in size and breadth, though Rand had a slightly narrower ass. Or Torrence preferred to wear his jeans looser. Cai was guessing servant preferences didn't usually dictate their clothing choices; their Master or Mistress did. Helga would want her servant's ass to be as nicely defined as possible in his clothes, so Rand's muscular butt being narrower was likely the correct conclusion.

"You have a sorcerer who could find me among millions of square miles of parkland," Cai reminded the vampire queen. "Why don't you just have him poof her out of there?"

"Unfortunately, there are strict limits to how he may help us, and we have reached those." She lifted a shoulder and frowned. "Particularly since Greenwald's retrieval team used his help inappropriately. But we have a support member of this Council, Lord Brian, who is our scientific research director. He is on his way here and has said he has additional resources for any rescue attempt we are framing."

Cai set his jaw. "And I'm the picture you want to put in that frame. Doesn't matter what ideas he has, we're still talking slim-to-none chances."

"True. But according to your information, our slim window of chance rests on having someone who can get in there without raising alarm. That person would have the resources we could provide. And our gratitude. Which, in our world, goes a very long way. You may not want us to give you anything, Cai, but how very pleasing would it be for us to owe you?"

Before he could formulate a response to that, Lyssa cocked her head.

"Why do you have one steel fang?"

Cai blinked at the sudden change of topic. "Because Trads are elitist assholes," he said flatly. "A vampire made from one of their captured humans is considered inferior. Citizens of their fucked-up world, yes, but second-class ones."

Cai bared his fangs and pointed to the steel one. "They break one off and dig it out from the root, then cauterize it with your blood so it won't grow back. The 'one fang' designation says you were made within the Trad clan, but you're not a pure vampire. You were once one of their slaves."

He could feel Rand's gaze on him again. Not that it had ever left, but sometimes it felt as if the guy was staring inside his head. The second mark wasn't an open two-way street, but with Rand, it felt like it was. Cai really should have done a better job of pissing him off so the shifter would have stayed out of this pointless meeting.

"On the other hand, for all their faults, Trads are pretty self-sufficient." Cai swept his gaze over the room. "Those made vampires I talked about? I'm betting most leave within a short time, because they're not prepared for the rustic realities of Trad life, the lack of comforts. A true Trad wouldn't be caught dead here."

Lyssa watched him another unsettling moment. "You're an interesting mix, Cai. So full of hate for both sides, but you will favor one over the other when it suits your purpose to sneer at the one before you."

Cai shrugged. "I'm an asshole. It's the best thing I know to be."

"Hmm. I think that suit of armor has been purposefully dinged and tarnished. I don't think you want that young female to be harmed, or to die."

"I don't want a lot of things," Cai said harshly. "But my wants have never meant a damn to anyone but me. So can we get this over with? Go ahead and torture me under the illusion that it will get me to agree to a suicide mission, or kill me."

"Neither at the moment, I think." She ran a fingertip over the surface of the desk, back and forth, a meditative gesture. "I wish to give this matter some thought and talk to the rest of the delegation. Georg exceeded his authority in how he brought you here, but don't leave until I grant you permission. We may need further information from you. If you exercise patience, you'll be released without further harm. You have my word."

"Patience isn't my strong suit. Nor trust."

"I wouldn't have guessed." That faint smile again. Her gaze slid to Rand. "I've told no one but the Council delegation what Rand is, and it won't leave that circle at this time. It's your decision whether to expose his human side to anyone else here."

Rand nodded, a courteous albeit cautious appreciation. Cai was less impressed. He lifted a brow.

"That a threat? I behave or else you'll tell everyone shifters exist?"

Lyssa blinked. "You told me very specifically what your terms were for this audience, and chastised me for believing you were angling yourself for greater spoils. I believe you can take my response at similar face value."

Well, he hadn't expected that. Expected to believe her, that is. Unsettled, Cai looked toward Rand. *Up to you. You can shift back to wolf before we leave the room. Or, since the only ones we have to fool are Greenwald and his staff, we can build on what Giles has likely already spread around. That you're my servant, and you just arrived. I'll tell anyone who asks that the wolf is out hunting in the forest.*

Rand accepted that with an interesting push of agreement that was wordless, much as he'd communicate it in wolf form. Cai managed an awkward half-bow to Lyssa that made him feel like an idiot, but she inclined her head. Probably laughing her ass off behind that neutral expression. Or maybe not. What had been discussed these past few minutes, and what had brought Cai here, weren't really laughing matters.

When he left the room, Rand stayed close enough on his heels Cai felt the heat of his presence. Yet he didn't draw a deep breath until he heard the double doors close behind them. Even then, it felt as if something was constricting his chest. Holding him back, holding him tied to the words in that room.

Goddamn it.

~

Jacob crossed his arms as he watched the two depart. Rand had followed Cai, but paused at the door, looking back at Lyssa with a hard-to-read expression on his face. Then he left.

A shifter. I wish Kane could have seen that.

Yes. Lyssa offered an absent smile as he referred to their son. She meant it, but Jacob knew a lot of far more troubling things were turning over in her head.

To ensure their privacy, Jacob continued to speak in his Mistress's mind. *You won't convince him, my lady. His mind and heart are set. The trauma they did to him runs deep. You're asking a man not just to confront his nightmares, but wade into them up to his neck and risk drowning.*

She lifted a shoulder and turned the desk chair to face him. *If there's any chance of convincing him, it won't be me who does it. It will be his wolf.*

Jacob lifted a brow. *He just said the bond between them is recent and functional. They're not a true vampire-servant pairing.*

That's not what I see. Lyssa met his eyes, her own warming as he drew closer. When she rose in his arm span, he put his hands to her waist and dipped his head to kiss her, letting his lips linger on hers. He needed no reason to want to touch her. It simply was there, like breathing.

Like all vampires, Cai has the Dominant's drive, but Rand is more like my servant. Service-oriented but not submissive. And I expect in most all his other relationships, Rand has taken the Dominant role.

Her eyes were half-closed and body relaxed into his, telling him she was fully enjoying the contact, but her clever mind was still calculating. *Their bond is new, and they are still working it out. But I sense it has the potential to open something inside Cai, locked beneath all the tarnished armor.*

From your mind to God's ear, my lady. Because our alternative is sending in an extraction team, and I believe Cai when he says they'll kill her without a thought if they're spooked.

So do I. The humor disappeared from her face. She reached out over the miles, Jacob riding on that pathway, and they touched the soul of their young son, currently safely fortressed at Lyssa's Atlanta estate.

If someone took Kane from me as the Trads took Dovia, I would burn down that mountain range in retribution for giving him a moment's fear, for daring to put their hands upon him. A goddess's rage flashed through her, and Jacob didn't doubt it. He'd be right at her side, adding to her destruction.

And Mason, she added. *He thinks of Farida, his own daughter.* Who was also in Atlanta, in the same protected surroundings.

I know, my lady. We'll get Dovia back. Jacob was troubled by the seemingly insurmountable challenge, but believing it couldn't be done and they had no options wasn't going to help them discover a strategy that might work. He hoped Lyssa was right about Rand. There was no doubt the shifter was an honorable male who'd throw himself into the situation without hesitation. But for the slimmest chance of success, they needed Cai.

They needed him to have a change of heart, risk what no one had a right to ask him to risk. But perhaps, if his conscience was already overburdened with regrets and things he couldn't change—not an unusual state for a two-hundred-year lifespan—a miracle might happen. Cai would decide he didn't want one more straw on that camel's back.

CHAPTER EIGHT

$\mathcal{T}$he house was the size of a mountain, but inside it, Cai felt trapped. Too many fucking people everywhere. Like damn bees in a hive, their energy a damn buzzing along his fucking nerves. He exited out the back and found a landscaped garden area and wide lawn that backed up to the forest. As least he could breathe in the night air.

He sat down on a bench and studied an assortment of concrete deer arrayed around a shallow gazing pool. Strange, the things people did to adorn their stationary worlds. His feet were already itching to move, cover miles. In two hundred years, how many times had he circled the globe, left to right, top to bottom?

"When I got free, I decided I was going to explore every square," he said abruptly. "You know, the longitude/latitude blocks? For a long time, I carried a map, and colored them in as I went. Have hit pretty much all the land masses. Ocean's a little tougher. I get seasick out of sight of land."

Rand sat down next to him. The bench was a decorative thing, though sturdy, so it held their combined weights but required Rand to be close enough to brush shoulders with him.

"Shifter territories are pretty big, just like non-shifter wolves," Rand answered. "But we're still homebodies. I've never left the States. Haven't even explored much of that."

"There are a lot of places to see. Maybe you could come on a couple trips with me. If you want." Cai said it casually. "I was thinking I'd do something desert-like next. There's this area in Syria that's cool, and I have contacts there. A real live sorceress. One time I hung out with a special forces guy, tracking WMDs smuggled across the border by the Russians and French before the Iraqi war. Well, he didn't know we were hanging out, but I saved his ass a few times. He never saw me, but we still made a good hunting team, him for his job, me for my dinner. He carried a couple good paperbacks. Robert Ludlum fan."

Rand blinked. "Yeah, because a barren desert in a politically unstable country is everyone's idea of a tourist hotspot."

"I don't go as a tourist. I live there. Adapt to the environment. It's a good way to stay on my toes. And stay out of the way of permanent connections, civilization, all that shit."

"Yeah, you're right." Rand pursed his lips. "That hot shower and steak was the worst. Don't get me started on the Egyptian cotton towels."

"See how easy it is to succumb? A cushy prison is still a prison. Would you want to be chained to a doghouse just because it's comfortable and safe? Or do you want to be able to run?"

"I want to be able to run," Rand said. "And at the end of the day, I want to be able to come home."

Cai shifted his attention to Rand's profile, which was quiet and contemplative as he considered the garden features. Something with large white blooms climbed up the trellis arched over their bench. Cai reached out and touched one. "Wonder what these trumpet things are?"

"Trumpet flowers."

He glanced at the shifter, assuming he was being a wiseass, but saw Rand was serious. "Hmm. Something with a name that actually reflects what it is. Unique."

"Sometimes the answer's pretty obvious, even if we don't want to hear it. I might be interested in going to Syria with you. After we go get the girl."

Cai blinked. "Come again?"

Rand turned his head, met him squarely eye to eye. "You know you need to do it. Lady Lyssa's right. You're the only one that can. You've been where she's been."

Cai suppressed the urge to get up, move. He wasn't going to lose it again. He had this shit locked down and it was staying down.

"The Trads have had a lot of victims," he said. "They're not exactly forming an army of retaliation. Probably because ninety-nine-point-nine-nine-nine percent of them are dead. And why the hell would you want to come with me to do something like that?"

"Because I owe you a debt for my life. And because it's another chance to get myself killed in an honorable way."

Cai curled his lip. "Yeah, because once you're worm food, how you died really mattered."

"It reflects how you lived," Rand said calmly. "Or wished you'd lived, if it's an act of redemption for past shortcomings."

Deciding to leave that alone, Cai raised a brow. "You didn't want me to save your life. Cursed me repeatedly for it. And now you think you owe me?"

"Doesn't change the code. A wolf owes a favor to the one who saved his life, even if he didn't want it saved. If I'm going to my death, which it happily sounds like I am, I don't want any debts left unpaid when I cross over. Don't want to be saddled with your ass forever."

"Good thing I didn't give you the third mark, then," Cai said.

"So that part is really true? That the vampire and servant are eternally connected, and the servant has to follow the vampire not only into death, but into the afterlife?"

"It's absolutely true. Countless vampires and servants have returned from the dead to verify it." Cai surged up off the bench. "It's bullshit. All of it. I'm not doing it, Rand. Yeah, my conscience will grow thorns like a damn rose bush for a while and keep me up at night, but it took me a hundred years to get free, and fifty after that to completely cut those ties, which was part of what all the traveling was about. It took a hell of a lot of distance and keeping as far away from wherever Trads were holed up to make it work."

Cai shook his head. "Staying clear of Goddard I could do, but I was considered part of the Trad world. Took me years before I could come back to West Virginia without worrying about them messing with me."

"That's where your family was from, wasn't it?"

"A different part of it. It's a big state."

"That's why you're there, instead of Syria or some far away longitude/latitude block," Rand realized. "It's home."

"It's not home. No place is home. It's just a familiar stomping ground." Cai made a slicing motion with his hand. "Get back on topic. I'm sorry about it, but I can't change a damn thing for her."

"Even if you get her out of there? You got out."

"Did you miss the hundred years part?" He leveled a hard gaze on Rand. Why wasn't he walking away, telling the guy to give him some fucking space? Why was he still talking? "And yeah, I got out. Look what a waste of cell matter I am. I go where I want, do what I want, take what I want. I don't feel, I don't connect, I don't get close. I choose to be a shallow pond rather than a deep ocean, even if it's a muddy, nasty bog that nobody wants to be around. I prefer it that way."

"Yeah. Except you don't." Rand's attention remained on him, too close, too personal. "You could have gone into town to get a good fuck anytime. You didn't have to hang onto me. You could say it's the freak factor, getting the chance to fuck or feed from something like me, but I'm not buying that, either. You can't connect to humans, you can't connect to vampires. But I'm something else, and you connect with me."

Cai turned away again, but the wolf wasn't finished. He continued, in that matter-of-fact deep timbre that stroked his nerves in the right way, while disturbing him at the bottom of the muddy, nasty bog that was his soul.

"Can't really say I like you much yet," the wolf mused, "but we're still hanging out together. Maybe because we're both pissed at what the world's taken from us and we haven't figured out how to work that out. Waiting together for that knowledge to come is a hell of a lot less lonely than doing it alone. So, in the meantime, here's this do-or-die situation that's fallen into our laps. Maybe someone's trying to throw us a bone."

Cai sighed and tossed him a look. "You really didn't just use a canine metaphor."

Rand's mouth quirked. "It happens. Those lamb chops smelled really good. I was wondering if they kept any bones."

"Well, before you get yelled at for going through the trash, let me ask you this." Cai pivoted and crossed his arms over his chest. "Have you lost your fucking mind? Fate doesn't throw anything at anyone. Life just sucks for some, doesn't for others, and the wind changes direction for fuck-knows-why. That's life. You start reading signs and meaning into things and—"

"Life might just start to have more meaning again."

"Ugh." Cai spat in disgust. "Fine, okay, I get it. You lost your family and you're trying to deal with that pain. But sorry, getting me killed isn't going to make *me* feel better."

"What about having the vampire queen owe you a favor?" Rand suggested shrewdly. "The whole Council? She knew how to aim that arrow."

"Yeah, she did. Doesn't mean I have to prove her right. I prefer to be contrary even if it's against my own best interests."

"You don't say," Rand said dryly. He glanced at the bench next to him. "Why don't you come sit next to me again? I want to show you something."

"Saw that earlier. Wouldn't mind seeing it again, but timing's a little off, wolf."

"Bite me. That's one that works for wolves or vampires. Come sit down."

"Careful. That almost sounded like an order. I'm the only one who gives those around here."

"In your dreams." Rand's gaze had stilled, become steadier. Cai sighed and grimaced.

"Fine." He sat down next to the wolf. He couldn't deny that the press of the broad shoulder and hip against his own was welcome, but he stilled as Rand ran a caressing hand along his back to his waist, hooking his thumb in the waistband of the jeans to tug.

Affection. Wolves were into physical affection. With no other motive than that, Cai could relax into it, even though most of his body felt rigid as a tent pole. Rand kept his gaze on the flowers, rather than looking at the vampire. But after a moment, he bumped Cai with his elbow.

"Tell you what. If you do this, I'll keep having all the sex with you that you could want. And provide you meals."

"You're a terrific lay, wolf, and your blood's incomparable. But getting my appetites met doesn't balance with happily walking back into the bowels of hell."

"What would? Killing this Lord Graham asshole? Taking out the Trad that took you from your family?"

"Yeah to the first, no to the second."

He felt Rand's puzzlement. "Why are you dead set to take out Graham, but not the Trad that took you?"

Cai shifted his attention back to the gazing pool. "Goddard was too powerful. I didn't stand a chance against him. Maybe one day."

It was more than that. It was a deep-seated feeling of revulsion, a terribly strong and overwhelming need to avoid the world that had held him for so long. That compulsion was far stronger than needing to take out Goddard. So Cai had told himself, for years and years and years. But Graham...Graham had hurt his mother.

"Besides, none of it would change anything."

"Exactly." Rand's tone of satisfaction suggested Cai had made his point. Rand's gold-flecked blue ones met his. "Nothing will change any of it. Because nothing can give you back what you really wanted. Your life, before it all happened. The only thing you can do is try to help her."

Rand dug into the back pocket of the jeans. "I snagged this from a small stack of them on the hallway table. Leona was holding one. She's way messed up. If Sheba had lived, she would have been the same. No way she would have survived losing two litters like she did."

He handed the small portrait to Cai. Vampires couldn't be photographed or reflect in a mirror, so those who wished to have their image captured did it the way that it was done prior to the invention of the camera. A painting. Only modern technology could now turn the portrait into prints, so proud vampire-servant parents like Georg and Leona could be just as annoying as the family who went to the mall portrait studio. Provide the picture to all friends, family members and Christmas card recipients in handy-dandy wallet size. Christ.

Cai guessed the stack of them was to spread hardcopies to other vampires and servants in the area, in case they'd seen something help-ful. Vampires watched crime shows too, apparently.

Yet when Rand placed the picture in his hand, and Cai looked upon it, his iron-clad hold on his cynicism slipped a notch. He'd have to be heartless not to feel something as he looked at the young female. Dovia had red hair, a soft smile and the glowing beauty of a young vampire. But her eyes were what caught Cai's attention. Direct and intelligent, with a hint of laughter in them, as if the portrait painter had said something to amuse her.

The smile possessed that genuine quality that occurred when laughter and smiles didn't have to be manufactured by cynical bullshit and one-liner comebacks designed specifically to keep actual emotion at bay. Her expression also reflected a trace of poignancy. Since this was a recent picture, Cai guessed that had taken root while watching her father's illness advance.

He handed the photo back to Rand. "How strong do you think she is?"

Kudos to the shifter, he picked up on what Cai was asking immediately. "I see what you see in that picture. I also got some further hints from Leona. She talked to herself while I was with her."

Or she talked to the wolf, Cai surmised. An animal who required nothing from her and was a nonjudgmental, listening ear.

"Growing up, Dovia wouldn't play with female servants or vampires. She always wanted to play with the boys. Even now, she competes with them in sparring, running, strength. A bit of a tomboy, in vampire terms. But one who still likes all the perks of being a girl."

"Okay."

"Okay?" Rand raised a brow. "Meaning?"

Cai leaned forward, clasping his hands loosely between his knees. "Do that thing to my back again. What you were doing before."

"Petting you?"

"Not if you're going to call it that. Fucking asshole." But as Cai rubbed his hand hard over his face and the back of his neck, fighting a hundred different things inside him, Rand complied. His strong hand swept over the curve of his spine, palm pressed firmly against Cai, so he felt the warmth through his shirt. Rand hooked his fingers in Cai's waistband again, stroking and teasing the top of Cai's buttocks, thumb sweeping over the dip in his spine just above.

Maybe if Rand hadn't been here to ask the questions that unlocked that memory box, Cai could have kept it closed and moved on, just as he'd described. But he had a full list in his head of the despicable things he was and wasn't, and coward wasn't one of them. He'd put aside personal vengeance for the same reason anyone stayed away from the most horrible nightmare of their life; to try and keep their head above it, not be sucked into who and what they'd been in that nightmare. As long as he could keep Goddard a figment of his past, he could move along in his life without going back there.

But now Dovia was in that nightmare. Cai had no reflection in a mirror, but he wasn't sure he'd be able to look someone like Rand or Lyssa, or even the earnest Giles, in the face and see the reflection of what he'd be if he didn't do something. Something he had no chance of surviving.

Well, fuck. Two hundred years was a good run, right? Way more than he would have had as a human.

"I have a condition," he said abruptly. "You become my third mark servant."

When he turned his head toward Rand, the male's blue eyes were puzzled, wary. "You want to link our souls."

"I don't believe that shit. The only verifiable thing about the third mark is that it links your life to mine. They kill me, you die."

Rand blinked. "That's kind of you."

"Yeah. It is." Cai set his jaw. "I won't go in there knowing if they kill me, which is a pretty damn certainty, that you'll be left to their mercy. A fucking shifter? Might as well call it Christmas. There are legends about your blood, and what it can do for a vampire's strength and mental acuity. It's probably just mythical bullshit, but I don't deny it's like a high-octane energy drink next to human blood. However, the guy that leads this little sect of Trads has pursued every damn wives' tale, no matter how unlikely, to figure out how to conceive upon vampire females."

Cai put his hand on Rand's thigh, gripped. "Apart from being staked through the heart with steel or the obvious stuff, like decapitation, you're also pretty indestructible. My blood and our bond can bring you back from almost anything."

Rand considered that. "So we succeed or fail together."

"Pretty much."

Rand still had his thumb hooked in Cai's waistband, and his fingers curled over the denim on the outside, an absent caress. Cai's shoulder was pressed to his chest, and he realized they'd somehow eased into a fairly intimate position with one another. If that was a wolf thing, he didn't mind it so much. But vampires had a little edgier way of showing affection.

Rand was thinking, so Cai slid his hair back from his shoulder and put his mouth to his throat, taking a nip and then holding it there, letting the fangs press inward. Not breaking skin, just a clamp, his tongue lazily tasting the caught flesh. Rand's fingers tightened and his deep voice came out satisfyingly more throaty. "What are you doing?"

"You did say whenever, and however much I liked. Just enjoying the flavor of you, wolf." But Cai lifted his head so their faces were close. "So, do we do something stupid, or do we go to Syria?"

"You're letting me make the call?"

"No," Cai said decisively. "But if you prefer Syria, it's going to be way easier for me to talk myself out of the stupidity you just talked me into."

"So I am making the call."

"No. Aren't you listening? I'm the vampire, you're the servant. I'm always in charge."

Rand's lips curved. "Sounds like you've decided we're going to do something stupid."

"And you're good with that."

Rand shrugged. "It's a chance to go out doing something worth doing."

Cai shook his head. "Just like that. 'Hey, let's do a third mark soul-binding, hike into the Appalachians, and find a bunch of psychotic fuckheads. They'll probably torture us to death in ways so creative, Lucifer will award said fuckheads an Exceeds Expectations trophy. Whaddya say?'"

"Anything that turns out better than that will be gravy." Rand shrugged again.

Cai grimaced. "Forgot to add the worst part of it. Being saddled with a cheery optimist with dog breath. Kill me now and spare me undue suffering."

Rand snorted, but he became serious once more. "Why do you kill them?"

Despite the jump in topics, Cai didn't have to ask what he meant, but he thought he'd covered the ground back when they'd had their last argument about it. Rand didn't seem to agree, though, since he pressed onward.

"You were human. You were taken from your family. You

remember what it is to be human. You know who Harry Potter is, so you spend enough time in their company to connect with them."

"I like to read," Cai argued. Rand pressed on, ignoring him.

"You abhor Trads, but your feeding habits are theirs. You kill humans rather than take what you need and leave them alive. I need to understand why."

"Why?" Cai could feel himself locking up, and told himself not to do it. For one thing, the wolf could sense it, and if it didn't matter much to Cai as he claimed, he wouldn't get defensive about it, would he? "If I give you the wrong answer for your comfort zone, will you let me off the hook for this whole save-the-girl shit?"

"You made the choice yourself, remember?" Rand arched a brow. "You're the vampire, I'm the servant. All choices and decisions are yours." His expression softened. "I'm just trying to understand."

"Well don't," Cai said shortly. "Don't try to figure me out like you're going to get to the bottom of it, and find out I'm a nice guy who got permanently mindfucked somewhere along the way. I mean, yeah, that's the story, but who the fuck cares? Not my prey, right? Rabbits don't sit around and try to understand why a wolf decides to chow down on them instead of a rat or a deer."

"It's a little different. If you can survive without taking a life, but you choose to do so..."

"It started out as survival, proving I was as much of a psycho as those around me," Cai snapped. "Like smoking to be cool with your so-called friends and then getting hooked. Simple enough."

Rand's brow furrowed. "I'm pretty sure that's a stupid analogy for what we're discussing."

"Doesn't make it less true. Just makes it more appalling. Go back to square one. I'm a fucked-up asshole. It's easier." Cai sighed, and turned his gaze to the forest. "Somewhere along the way, Rand, I lost whatever compass guides someone like you. No, not lost it. I smashed it myself. It was a desensitizing thing. They treated me like I was nothing because I was human. Then, when I became a vampire and finally had a measure of power, that was how Lodell, my sire, taught me to feed. He told me I was no longer human, and that was the best way to remember it. He was right. I couldn't go back and, in some weird way, I wanted to make sure of that. Make sure I didn't even look, didn't think of what kind of human I'd be, if things had been different.

"So I fed the way he fed. Unlike some of them, he was never cruel about it. Said we were actually more honest about it than people who sit down to a hamburger but could never in a million years handle killing the animal themselves."

Cai shook his head. "One-on-one, sure, there are humans I've connected with, but when it comes to food, going on the hunt, something else entirely happens. Maybe because we don't shift to fur, your kind doesn't see it in a vampire, but it's no different. When you were sitting out on your porch as a human with Dylef or Sheba, how many times did you see a deer come out of the woods and get tickled by it, that I'm-all-connected-to-nature-harmony shit?"

Cai locked gazes with Rand. The dangerous hardness in his eyes raised the small hairs on Rand's neck. "But later, when you're a wolf, and you're hungry, that deer crosses your path again. When she runs, something else rises in you. Something real and undeniable, and linked to the deeper, darker pulse of nature. The Trads made me a vampire, and there's no going back from that. I don't spend a lot of time bullshitting myself about it, and taking my prey the way I was taught is part of that."

Rand's thumb slipped over the valley of his spine, a caress of flesh. "Would it hurt too much to try to change?"

"Change for what? And for who? The only one I have is the one in the mirror and oh, hey, I have no reflection."

Cai rose, moving away from that distracting touch, and repeated his earlier mantra.

"Don't make the mistake of thinking there's something better here than what you see, Rand. Some vestiges of that fifteen-year-old kid. I learned a long time ago that soul is long dead."

Cai left Rand after that. In his usual smartass way, he told Rand to occupy himself for an hour, maybe by begging the kitchen help for those bones. He said he'd rejoin Rand shortly.

As Rand watched him stride off, he suspected the vampire would leave the grounds entirely. Walk the quiet roads and trails amid horse country, until he could work out in his head whatever he was thinking. Maybe strategy. Maybe trying to talk himself out of this. Maybe taking off entirely. Rand wouldn't realize he'd gone until hours had passed, but he didn't expect that.

The vampire was a solitary creature. Rand had been surprised the male had responded to physical affection earlier. It had moved him, twisted something in his heart, remembering how easily he and Dylef gave that to one another. He was in no danger of thinking Cai was like Dylef, but it had been welcome, that response to touch that didn't have an immediate sexual drive behind it. But Cai putting his mouth to his throat had reminded Rand vividly of the differences between his relationship with his former mate and...whatever he and the vampire were.

Even Cai shied from calling Rand his servant, except to goad or tease. Their bond at this juncture was unclassifiable, but if they did this, they would be brothers-in-arms, relying on one another in a situation where having each other's back was necessary. Vital.

Rand didn't know if Cai could be trusted for that, though his death wish took care of making it a top concern. But there was more at stake here than Cai's trustworthiness or Rand's careless attitude toward his own life. Dovia. It was one thing to go on a suicide mission to exorcise one's demons once and for all; another, when an innocent's life hung in the balance. He and Rand might be her best hope of survival, slim though Cai seemed to think that was.

It was only about an hour from dawn when Cai reached out to Rand in his mind and told him that he'd given Lyssa his decision. The queen had instructed everyone to go to ground and rise at dusk, with the intent of finishing up the planning phase, getting Cai and Rand on their way as soon as possible.

Cai didn't ask for company, but Rand chose to meet him at the top of the steps to the lower level. He wanted to see Cai arrive. The male smelled of the outdoors, wet grass, gravel, asphalt, night. Pastureland and horses. His hair was damp, for a drizzle had started about an hour ago and hadn't yet abated, giving the air that autumn rain smell. His shirt clung lightly to his upper body, his jeans freckled with the rain drops.

Cai met his gaze but didn't say anything. Just jerked his head at him and headed down the stairs. Rand followed the unusually quiet vampire back down the hallway, but when he slowed at Leona's room, Rand stopped with him.

Lord Greenwald was with Leona, sitting on her bed. He held her hand, had his forehead resting on it, the rest of his powerful body sheltered over it as her other hand rested on his head, an unbroken circle for two broken parents.

Like Cai, Rand had not been as kindly disposed toward the father as the mother, since until now he hadn't seen evidence of a connection between them, of a fair exchange of comfort. This eased some of his concern about Leona's support from her Master, no matter his ailing state of mind. The slight lessening of tension in Cai's shoulders suggested he felt the same.

Georg lifted his head at the quiet noise of their passing. The haunted look in his eyes was instantly replaced by guarded aggression, but it was tempered by the unavoidable truth of the evening's events.

His daughter's fate rested squarely in the hands of the male he'd treated as a surrogate for those who'd taken her. There would be no apology for that. All of Rand's knowledge of vampires before Cai had been secondhand, but it had only taken a short time to realize that their arrogance, sexual volatility, and creative brutality were innate to them. Yet in Greenwald's gaze there was a painful pleading mixed in with those things. Rand wasn't surprised to see Cai turn away from it and continue up the hall. Rand nodded to the vampire and followed.

Third mark. Cai had said he wanted to do that before they embarked. The soul binding part was a bit disquieting, even if Cai didn't believe in it. If they did survive this, Rand's life would be bound to the vampire's, but Cai wasn't the type who'd turn that into indentured servitude. They'd see where they were at when this was over. He might still join the cantankerous male in Syria.

The past few days, Rand had had far less time to think about death and the pain of his losses. Cai was a good diversion, if nothing else.

Rand expected the vampire to counter such thoughts with sarcasm, but he seemed deep in his own head. When he reached the room, Cai stripped off his clothes without any erotic intent and washed his face in the bathroom. He stayed curved over the sink for several long minutes, running dampened hands over his neck, then braced his long, muscular arms against the sink.

When he lifted his head and stared at the mirror, Rand wondered if that held any pain to a vampire, never being able to see his reflection. Not knowing what his face looked like, except when some artist gave him an interpretation of it.

It took him back to a morning that seemed no more than a minute ago. He'd woken to find Dylef leaning over him, tracing his face with his long, capable fingers. When Rand opened his eyes and smiled, Dylef had smiled back, but there'd been something deep and full in his gaze. *"I don't need a mirror around you. I see everything I need to know about myself in your eyes."*

A quiver went through Cai's shoulders. The sudden wave of distress from him made Rand move into the bathroom, stand behind him. Before he could reach out, Cai shrugged him off and pulled a towel from the rack to mop his face and hair. Tossing it aside, he clipped off the light, leaving Rand standing in darkness, and headed for the king-sized bed.

"Get in with me and get some sleep. We'll only be able to travel by vehicle to a certain point, then it'll be a deep hike into the mountains. As I said, I know their vicinity, but not their exact location. We might have to talk to some locals who could tip Goddard off we're looking for him."

Which reminded Rand they still hadn't talked about the shifter pack that might be in the area. He held off on it for now, though, since the vampire didn't look in the mood for conversation. He did ask one question, however. "Won't they ghost if that happens, like you said?"

"Not if they know it's me looking for Goddard, and not some Council vampire extraction team. If needed, my cover story will be that I need a favor from Goddard. I've pissed off some Region Master who's reported me to Council, so I need a place to lie low. Which will make him laugh his ass off, but he might agree to it." Cai pulled back the covers. "That is, if I agree to lop off a limb to prove my renewed loyalty to him, or some such shit. We'll figure it out. If you don't want to sleep right now, then take a hike and let me get some shut-eye."

"The third mark thing—"

"Yeah. In a bit. Not right now." Getting into the bed, Cai turned his back to Rand. He shut off the bedside lamp, putting them in more darkness.

A curt way to treat someone who'd decided to go to hell with him and watch his back, but Rand didn't take offense. He was starting to understand Cai's patterns. Even if Cai had told the Council to go fuck themselves and left, in several days Rand would have expected to find him on the same path. There was something down deep inside the vampire...

Indigestion. Shut up or I will fuck you into exhaustion and suck out a couple gallons of your blood to make you unconscious.

Rand could have taken the spot next to him, but he'd expected Cai to do the third mark first and the thought had him keyed up. He'd shift and take a hard run around the grounds to burn off some energy, then grab a shower and come to bed. The house servants would think the wolf had returned from his hunt, supporting Cai's cover story.

However, at the door, Rand turned back, studying the motionless vampire. Unease flitted through him about leaving the vampire by himself, but he couldn't figure out why. That thought was derailed, somewhat, by imagining the vampire carrying out the first part of the threat. Hell, they were both males, and it was what it was. They might not see eye to eye on much else, but their sexual compatibility was off the charts.

Or maybe that was a vampire with anyone he chose, since they were so practiced at sexual arts. Rand didn't particularly care for that thought. Cai with others, exercising those skills without discrimination.

Damn wolf nature. No matter how unrealistic it was, Rand couldn't keep himself from thinking of sex as a mating act. Shifters didn't take it lightly, couldn't. Fortunately, his human side saved him from being stupid about it. He forced himself to leave the room.

Things were getting way quiet in the house as the sun crested and hit the front windows on the upper level. He came through the kitchen and found a far more informal atmosphere, where house servants were laying out food for the visiting Council vampire servants who would be coming up soon.

"Got to tuck in their vampires," the cook observed with a mischievous grin. He was a burly male who looked like he could have been a cook on a naval vessel, the service tattoos on his arms supporting Rand's theory. He wondered how he'd come into the aristocratic Greenwald's service, but with how long they lived, every vampire had to have a colorful past. "Feed them good," the cook continued, "then come here to replenish themselves and let us all catch up on the gossip."

"Jacob will be the last one up. He's very thorough about feeding his Mistress." That came from one of the maids, punctuated by a giggle as she sampled some of the frosting on a newly made cake. She accepted a swat from the cook's wooden spoon with a saucy swing of her hips, though she danced out of range before he could follow up. He gave her a stern look, though his lips were twitching.

"Show some respect, girl. Vampires and servants have long ears." The cook glanced toward Rand. While his expression was courteous, Rand was aware that most in the kitchen were studying him with avid curiosity, as would be expected toward the "servant" of the vampire reputed to be a Trad.

"You're welcome to sit and join us," the cook said. "If you're new to our world, no better way than the breakfast gatherings between servants to figure out how things are done."

The cook meant it kindly, Rand could tell. While Rand agreed it seemed a great way for a new servant to come up to speed, Cai and he were a different kind of pairing, with way too many secrets. Not the least of which was what their relationship actually was. Most the time, it seemed as much a mystery to the two of them as anyone else.

Plus, he really needed to run. His decision was made when the first two servants to arrive were Tyra and Chavez's. They might not be as bad as their vampires, but their scrutiny was far too close, and it made him uneasy. He'd spent plenty of quality time with them already.

Shifters were a clannish species and, unlike the vampires, they didn't have a head Council that imposed rules about secrecy on all their members. Shifters just followed pack rules and good common sense when it came to discretion. Cai's serious warning about shifter blood and vampires had also made an impact. So though Rand lingered enough to eat some bacon and eggs, he ate swiftly and kept his answers vague before he excused himself.

"Speaking of the wolf, I told Cai I'd find him on my usual morning run. When I send him back here, if you could give him a plate of the sausage, I'm sure he'd appreciate it."

He directed that toward the maid, and she dimpled at him. "For you, I'll save him a whole plateful, honey. He's a beauty. Just like you."

He offered a smile, but hastily made his getaway before he could be drawn into her flirting. He was surprised, though, when she turned it up to full wattage on Tyra's servant, indicating they'd been intimate in the past.

Maybe vampires were okay with their servants having sex with other servants, as long as they were available to them when needed. Cai seemed unfettered in his own sexual preferences. Rand recalled his earlier thought about wolf mating rituals, where sex was supposed to mean something, be done with someone who mattered.

With Cai, he wouldn't say it was meaningless—that felt wrong— but he knew the vampire hardly considered it heart-and-flowers commitment. Yet how did Rand himself feel about it?

Conflicted. Confused. And wanting to do way the hell more of it, enough he'd played with the idea of annoying the vampire into carrying out his threat. With the additional hope maybe it would make Cai feel better. Because now that the decision to rescue Dovia had been made, it had stirred up some bad debris in the vampire's subconscious. Rand could feel it, scent it.

He considered how he would feel if someone said: "Hey, let's go back to the night your family was murdered. No, nothing will change. They'll still be dead, and all that horror will still be there, but maybe you can save one pup. Just one, mind you. And not one of yours. Or Sylvan's."

If Rand had been given the opportunity to snatch even a stranger's pup away from that brutal death, he'd have taken the opportunity. Earth and stone, why was he even going down that road?

Because he'd put Cai on this track toward his past, and he was concerned about Cai's state of mind.

Rand ran a few miles under the cover of mist-filled patches of forest backing up to the farms. It kept him out of view of the early morning risers caring for their horses. But then he cut the run short and circled back. He bypassed the chance to catch a couple rabbits he flushed, deciding he'd get the second helping of meat from the servant. He just wanted to be back. Every stride was fueled by more urgency, until he was at a full run, favoring the lingering ache of his injuries as little as possible.

As Rand closed in on that last mile, images swam into his mind that weren't his own. A darkness came with them, with a power so thick and heavy it was like a smothering blanket. Words erupted in his mind, screamed into a void. He startled, an animal fight-or-flight instinct that knocked him off his path. But he recovered fast, leaped forward, his stride covering over three times his length with every bound.

No. Stop... Mama...

If he'd been human, the hairs would have risen on the back of his neck, because the last word was screamed in the voice of a teenage boy whose voice was just beginning to break toward manhood. It held all the desolation and desperation of a mind pushed toward an edge where the fall would break it irreparably. In the blink between one terrified heartbeat and the next, the boy had become a broken, scarred man.

Rand barged through the kitchen door as a maid was coming out of it. He ignored her shriek of surprise, his nails scrabbling for purchase on the tile floor. He hit the butcher block island hard enough to jar his shoulder and tip the fruit bowl on it, sending oranges and apples over the edge. He ignored that, too, and the startled looks of more servants, as he shot past them and ran through the house.

When he reached the top of the stairs to the lower bedrooms, there were a couple servants set as a posted watch. However, they could hear a muffled version of what he'd heard in his mind, echoing up the stairs, and let him through.

By the time he reached their guest room door, he'd shifted to human and turned the latch without a pause. To hell with who saw him, though fortunately the hall seemed deserted and all doors firmly shut. He'd forgotten his clothes, where he'd hidden them on the periphery of the garden.

When he lunged into the room, he realized what was causing the smothering sensation. Cai was used to sleeping beneath the loosely packed earth where he could move as needed. He'd somehow wrapped himself in the blankets so tightly it was almost like he'd been shrouded, the covers over his head.

Rand shoved him out of the bed, unrolling and shaking him loose rather than trying to touch or hold him. Cai exploded into a standing position, chest heaving, fangs bared, fists clenched. Rand backed into the corner, dropping to his heels. He was breathing hard himself, a combination of his long-distance run and the sudden sprint to get here. He spoke aloud and in his mind, hoping one or both methods would get through. He said what came to mind, no analyzing the meaning of the words. That didn't matter.

"You're here, vampire. With your wolf. Not with them. Take a breath. Be easy."

During the short time Rand had known Cai, the vampire had handled both Rand's dangerous animal and pissed-off human side with a sort of unflappable control. Even when the vampires had been beating on him, his attitude had been virtually unassailable. But that initial panic attack when bound, and the explosion of rage in the study, had opened the vampire up to Rand's ability to reach far deeper into him.

Lyssa had called it right. Cai's behavior was a full, adhered-to-the-skin armor, containing what was within as much as it was to defend himself from what was without.

As Cai stood there, swaying, fangs bared, eyes wild but unfocused, part of him was in the here and now, while another part was still in the dream. Rand saw a two-hundred-year old male who looked far younger, and yet ancient beyond the expression of time. The look the young had in the middle of war zones.

Maybe the primary reason he was still here didn't have to do with a kidnapped female, though that was important enough. Since Dylef, Sheba and the pups, no one had needed him. Or rather, Rand hadn't let himself be put in a position to be needed, because he couldn't handle the responsibility without getting the shakes, just thinking about the chance of losing someone again.

But this situation, this male, had saved his life and linked their paths. Cai was strong and capable, a good fighter and a dangerous vampire. He wasn't helpless, but that didn't mean he didn't need help.

This was where Rand was meant to be. Cai needed Rand, and so did a young female vampire. If the danger to her had not been evident before, seeing it drive Cai out of this bed and stand, ready to fight, with a look of terror and desperation on his face, was a full broadcast of it.

Rand shifted back to wolf and left his corner, padding across the floor. He pressed his body against the side of Cai's, giving him a literal reminder of his presence that backed up his words. It startled him when the vampire's knees buckled. He adjusted fast so he broke Cai's fall. Cai clutched his thick ruff, his face buried there, the rest of him shaking. He was ice cold.

Rand made as much of his body available to him as possible, to share warmth. Cai was gasping, and vampires didn't have to breathe, not like that. But the vampire was trying to slow it down, reassuring Rand that he was heading in the right direction. He just needed to be here, quiet and patient. He'd shifted for the same reason he'd gone to Leona as a wolf. Sometimes there was nothing so comforting as a dumb beast, something living, warm and affectionate who required no exchange of words, merely the physical contact that could offer so much more.

Rand's heart lurched at the words he heard murmured into his fur.

"So fucking scared...hate it. Just fucking hate it."

Be with you. Scared...together.

It took a while, but at length a sigh lifted Cai's shoulders. His chest flattened against Rand's massive torso.

"Okay," the vampire murmured at last. "Okay."

He rose. Rand stayed close to his side. When Cai slid back into the bed, Rand leaped onto it. Cai tugged on him so Rand lay down before him, and the vampire laid an arm over his barrel chest, his face pressed into Rand's thickly furred nape.

"This is nice," the vampire murmured. "But when I wake up with a hard-on, you better be the human version of you."

Rand dropped his head back to bump Cai's nose with the flat of his skull and earned a muttered oath. "Asshole."

As things settled, Rand felt the male's body temperature returning to a more normal heat level, his occasional shudders getting further apart. Finally, Cai's breath evened out and stilled as he trusted himself to fall back into dreams. Or the pull of the daylight sun above became too strong. But he continued to hold onto Rand as if the wolf could keep him from sliding into nightmares. Rand hoped so.

But as he thought of what Cai had said, he made a mental note to shift before he fully fell asleep. When the vampire woke, that armor would be back in place, with the attendant barbed sense of humor. Rand didn't put it past him to try and stick himself up Rand's wolf ass just to piss him off. And then Rand would bite his dick off.

What does it matter? Cai's thoughts were slurred, sleepy. *It's still you in there, right?*

Yes, but the wolf...it's a sanctuary, of sorts. A haven from everything. That feels like an invasion. Using a battering ram on a door that hasn't been opened to you.

Cai snickered against his back. "You compared my dick to a battering ram. I feel so virile and manly."

Rand let out an exasperated huff. And bit back a mental smile.

Armor it might be, but damned entertaining armor.

～

Twilight closed in. As a shifter, Rand was more nocturnal, often sleeping during the day and hunting at night, so his sleep patterns worked well with a vampire's. Though as he woke, he found himself wondering about the servants in the kitchen who'd obviously anticipated a busy few hours taking care of business for their Masters and Mistresses while the vampires slept. Maybe third marked servants had less need for sleep. What other changes would he notice? Would all of them be the same for a shifter, someone not fully human?

I know precious little about servants, so couldn't tell you. Guess we'll find out. But it's the best protection I can give you for where we're going.

The vampire's arm slid further around his chest. He muffled a warm chuckle against Rand's back as he threaded his fingers through his chest hair. "Even as human, you're still furry." His hips crowded up against Rand's bare ass, testing. "Keep yourself lubed up around me, wolf. Saves us both some time."

"Or maybe you should let me handle your needs a different way." Rand turned and pushed Cai to his back, earning a heavy-lidded look hard to interpret. The vampire stretched, a distracting work of art as his arms, legs and torso rippled, arched and spread, then he was back to a resting pose, his fingers laced behind his head.

Rand turned his gaze to his target, the heavy wakeup erection resting on Cai's belly, his testicles an appealing cushion for the thick base. His body had the smooth perfection of a Grecian statue, a marked contrast to Rand's thick pelt of chest hair, the layer of dark threads on legs and arms, the thatch between his legs. It didn't seem to bother the vampire, though.

"Why would it?" Cai unlaced one hand to reach up and coil it in Rand's loose, long hair, stroking and gripping at once. Bringing him down with a tug. "I love all your hair. I want your mouth, wolf. I want it now."

Rand resisted. He'd always been the one in charge, even with Dylef. Being treated as the bottom, it wasn't that he disliked it; it unsettled him how easy it was for him to embrace it with Cai. As if he deferred to him as the alpha of their two-man pack, which was usually something that had to be earned. Not taken, as Grey had tried to do it.

Cai's gaze drifted to Rand's mouth. "I dreamed of that mouth on my cock. My hand in your hair like this, tightening, pushing you down, watching all those muscles in your ass and back flex as you were bent over me. I was dreaming how I'd take you afterward. Just fuck you good and hard, so when we go upstairs and start this circus, my come will be in your ass, my scent all over your body."

He propped himself up on his elbows, his expression becoming something more serious.

"I don't have your need to belong," he said abruptly. "Grief's kept you a lone wolf, not your nature. You've just been alone too long, Rand. You need a pack, and I'm pretty much what you've got. I stumbled across your path. That's all."

Rand frowned, but Cai shook his head before he could say anything. "Sorry as hell for that and, if we both don't end up dead, I hope something better comes along for you. But I can make some parts of it not so bad. Like this. So put your fucking mouth on me. Don't make me get rough."

Rand was caught between lust, humor and annoyance, all of which came with a surge of adrenaline at the vampire's deliberate challenge to turn things in a different direction.

He wouldn't mind fighting it out with the vampire, see who ended up with top dibs, but maybe not this morning. For one thing, the furniture in this room looked expensive. For another, Cai had already pissed Greenwald off a couple times, and Lyssa at least once. He'd been lucky to leave his audience with her with both testicles.

"Yeah, she's one scary bitch," Cai noted. "Hot as hell, too. Jacob's one lucky blood bank. *Rand.*"

The one word wasn't like a command. It *was* one, and Rand obeyed, because his mouth was begging for the taste of the handsome male, particularly after that unconsciously provocative stretch. He closed his mouth around the broad head and worked his way down the shaft. He might not have a wolf's tongue in this form, but he'd learned a lot about its versatility, and some of that could be translated to a human mouth. Cai approved, if his sucked-in breath and sudden thrust were any indication. It was a different kind of full body stretching, giving himself to pleasure, and he took Rand with him.

His hand flexed in Rand's hair, pushing him down deeper on him, as he'd warned. Rand relaxed his throat, let it happen, taking him all, and kept working his tongue over him. He liked the taste of the vampire, salt and earth. Heat. He spread his hands over Cai's abdomen and chest, the narrow line of his hips. Reaching between his legs, nudging them further apart with his knuckles, he cupped and rolled his testicles, stroked and probed at his ass, and earned a muttered, reverent curse. He dampened his fingertips on Cai's precome and played between his cheeks at the rim, adding to the sensations.

"Going to fuck you through this mattress," Cai growled. "Suck me."

Rand complied with a thorough enjoyment. It was nice, having regular access to another male, to satisfy his need to give and take. This felt like both. Cai had initially tensed when he was caressing his chest and stomach, his hips, but as Rand kept doing it, he relaxed into the stroking, gravitating toward it. The male was very sexually adept, but he acted as if all those skills had been honed toward driving the pleasure of his chosen partner, not seeking any intimacy in return during sex. Just sexual gratification centered on his cock and ass.

Which was a waste, because exploring the male's body, watching how it responded to the lightest tough, was a gift.

Rand didn't think Cai was in his head right now; he was riding too high on the physical wave of lust. But confirming Rand's thoughts, Cai brushed his hands away too soon, guiding them back to his cock and balls.

It deflated some of his own desire, but not enough he couldn't give Cai what he'd promised. Rand sucked him all the way to the edge and drew satisfaction from the anticipation of bringing the vampire release.

Cai had different plans. Before Rand could forestall him, he'd moved with vampire speed, exercising brutal strength to switch their positions. He put Rand on his stomach on the bed, thrust his hand between his thighs and took a firm grip on his balls. He used that hold to make Rand lift his hips off the mattress. Using the lubrication that Rand's mouth had left on him, Cai drove in. It wasn't quite enough lubrication, so the thrust wasn't entirely pleasurable, but he realized Cai intended that.

He covered Rand, pushing him down flat on the bed when he was all the way in, his lips at Rand's ear. "Next time I tell you to keep yourself lubed for me, you'll remember. And if I wake up and want to fuck you, that's not a negotiation where you get to suck me off instead of giving me your ass. Got it?"

Rand's first instinct was to fight him. Something had Cai's ire up and was making him drill in the point, literally and figuratively, and Rand bristled at it.

But despite his ability to remind the vampire he wasn't with a human he could overpower, Rand found his feet knocked out from beneath him by something he didn't expect. An overpowering wave of physical and emotional response from Cai.

The vampire had a body meant for sex, and knew how to use it. But beneath that, what had driven the nightmare, the rage in the study, and that moment at the sink, when the vampire had stared sightlessly at the mirror, reached out with hard, edgy need. It found an answer in Rand, deep down where his own aggressive, erotic cravings recognized something in Cai's approach that could coat past wounds and losses, paint the way to a different level of connection between their bodies.

And what a connection. When he was forceful, intending to underscore who was on top here, Cai could be damn well irresistible. Plus, he knew what he was doing on the mechanical end of things, hitting just the right rhythm, friction and placement with that capable dick of his. Rand's balls were tingling from the impact of Cai's slapping against them. The vampire knocked Rand's legs out wider, leaving his hips only inches off the bed, just enough to achieve the right angle. It rubbed Rand's cock against the bed linens and oh hell, that friction.

"You want to come, don't you? Prove who your ass belongs to."

He'd wrap a rubber band around his cock rather than confirm that statement. Cai chuckled darkly and reached between them to caress

Rand's balls. Taking a firm grip on Rand's dick, he tugged it as Rand bucked beneath him.

Okay, now was the time the wolf needed to come out. Rand shoved himself up, one hand clamping on the head board. Cai moved with him, wrapping his hand around Rand's throat. He sank his fangs into the pumping artery, sealing his lips over the spot. The vampire slid his arm around Rand's chest to hold him up, his cock buried deep in Rand's ass as he fed.

No, not just fed. Rand stiffened as Cai released something into his blood. Something that charged and burned, sizzled. It reached out to all four limbs, but it was when it hit his brain that the real fireworks began. It unleashed a wave of emotions, formless, as if waiting for something to bring them clarity, something that made him crave blood. Cai's blood.

The third mark. He was giving him the third mark.

Cai eased them both to the covers, lying full upon Rand. His breath caressed Rand's neck as he held his mouth there another few moments for a gentler sucking. When he withdrew his fangs, he lifted enough to do something that jostled their coupled bodies. He held out his wrist before Rand's face, and Rand saw the movement had been caused by the force of Cai's strike on his own wrist. Blood oozed out of the two puncture wounds.

"Drink. That will close the third mark loop and link us."

Rand didn't have to stop and think. He'd made his decision. Though the vampire would deny he'd said it exactly that way, Rand knew it would maximize their chances to help Dovia against already impossible odds, so there was nothing left to debate. Rand closed his mouth over the vampire's wrist, gripping it with his own hand to steady the connection.

Three swallows of blood, and the whole world changed.

CHAPTER NINE

*C*ai had seemed so matter-of-fact about it. Because of that, Rand hadn't expected anything much different from the second mark. This was...

He'd gone rigid in Cai's arms, no matter that his cock was still throbbing with impending climax, and having Cai deep in his ass was a burning pleasure. This overruled that. It was as if his cells were being remade, every one of them bound to a matching one with the male flush against his back, bearing him down against the mattress.

The second mark had put Cai's thoughts in his mind, an adjustment to mental privacy, but wolf communication was as much intuition and body language as it was speaking, so it hadn't been a big leap. This was way beyond that.

Rand could actually feel the vampire descending through all the levels of his mind, deeper, even deeper, penetrating everything. Beyond the mind, and way into the heart and soul. He was walking straight into those rooms, able to throw any door open without Rand's say-so. He'd told Cai that being fucked as a wolf would be like invading a sanctuary? This nowhere-to-hide, child-like but undeniable fear, caused the type of panic Rand didn't experience too often.

Cai's arm had tightened around him, making it worse. Rand withdrew on every level. Or tried. He was thrashing. "Let me go...can't breathe."

Cai fortunately listened, pulling out and moving back, giving Rand room to scramble free of the bed. He was disoriented, having trouble making sense of anything. His mind was split in two. Nothing sacred or private any more. He was like a cut open fish, still flopping on a bank, in agony. He hit something, maybe a side table, sent it crashing, and knocked over something else that shattered. A vague burning, like glass cutting into his feet. He didn't care. He was trying to escape, and he knew one sure way to do that.

No, Rand, don't...

He shifted, but the disarray of his mind made it one of the worst shifts of his life, as if his bones were being broken and remade. A cry became a howl of agony and he was writhing, thrashing on the floor, caught between human and wolf. Fuck, it was a Split, increasing his terror. It happened sometimes, to wolves caught up in a trauma where they were unable to keep their wits about them. It could become permanent.

Permanent and fatal, because there was no way to exist with a foot physically in each plane.

Help...

∾

"Rand, I'm here. Calm down. Breathe. You're not stuck, goddamn it. You're just worked up. Just breathe." Cai scrambled to his side, his own mind in chaos, still trying to manage all the images and connections with the shifter, while simultaneously trying to figure out what had gone wrong. Well, to do that, he'd need to know what the fuck he was doing, right? And obviously, he hadn't. Some of this stuff, like opening and closing his mind to the shifter to communicate, had been easy as falling asleep, no instructions needed, making him believe the vampire-servant thing was ninety-nine percent common sense and instinct. But this...

Oh, God, the shifter was...he was part man, part animal, a macabre, monstrous mess of human and wolf body parts writhing on the floor. Fuck, what could he do? Cai didn't know who he could trust here, and he'd...what the hell had he been thinking?

He whirled at a knock, but the one knocking didn't bother to wait before he entered. It was Jacob, Lady Lyssa's servant. He took in the scene at a glance and came swiftly across the room, though was sensible enough to stop a few feet back when Rand threw his head back and snarled. Rand's mind was being swallowed by his wolf, the human part still caught up in the marking change, trying to sort it out.

"How can I help?" Jacob asked. He wasn't deferential the way most servants Cai had met were, but he was honest and direct, which Cai appreciated. Rand didn't have time for him to weigh trust pros and cons.

"I'm not sure. I was third marking him. Least, I think I was. I've never done it before, and I don't know much about human servants, making them, having them..." Cai broke off at Jacob's startled look. "I never witnessed...I was just told the basics. Take blood, release serum, give blood. He's a shifter, I don't know... There was something in his mind about Splitting, this in-between state. He's frightened. I don't know how to help."

"Okay." Jacob moved to the upended side table, found the house phone where it had fallen behind the bed, and picked it up, punching in a number. "Debra, Jacob here. Are you in? Just landed? Good. We've got an emergency. Not sure what we'll be needing, but Brian's probably the best bet to figure it out."

He gave the unseen woman details based on some of what Cai had told him, and added info that Cai hadn't. "Think it might have been an unprepped third marking. Going to have my lady come help talk him through it, but it'd be good to have you as backup in case I'm wrong." He paused. "Tell Brian not to wet himself, but the servant is a wolf shifter. Yeah, they really exist. We're keeping that knowledge classified."

At a later time, Cai would be impressed by how calm the servant remained, with a thrashing half-man, half-wolf on the floor in obvious distress. But Cai was going to lose his fucking mind if someone didn't do something. Now.

Jacob hung up and returned to Cai's side. "My lady's on her way."

"What? I..." Cai had shot his mouth off to her earlier. That was different, when he'd been making a point driven by his emotions and what-the-fuck attitude toward almost everything. In a heartbeat, he positioned himself over Rand. The mutated male was tearing Cai's heart out. He'd subsided into a painful whimpering, eyes glassy. He had three wolf legs and one human one, and the jerking of human and animal limbs in a mindless mimic of attempted flight was killing Cai. He'd done this.

"If she's coming here to take a stripe off my ass or do something terrible to him, she'll have to take me apart piece by piece to do it."

"I believe something terrible was already done to him," Lyssa said coolly, stepping inside the door and closing it behind her. "By an inexperienced vampire who should have asked questions rather than hiding behind his ego and pride."

Cai swallowed, his fists half clenched. Jacob straightened, his expression saying he was about to warn Cai to stand down, but Lyssa took care of that herself. She crossed the room, wearing a hunter green dress that flowed over her curves and moved with the same rippling appeal as her dark hair, loose on her shoulders. Unbound, it reached her waist. She was barefoot and dropped to her heels next to Rand, so close to Cai her shoulder pressed against his knee. He noticed Jacob shift closer, a protective gesture. He wanted Cai to move back, but Cai wasn't doing it. Yeah, he'd fucked this up, but that didn't mean he'd abandon Rand.

"Your shifter is not going to come to harm from me," Lyssa said. "Put your hand where mine is."

She laid it on Rand's chest, a curious patchwork of wolf fur and human chest hair. The ribs on the right side were spread in a strange, unsettling way, as if about to split from the skin. He understood why Rand's mind was a red haze of spiraling chaos and pain. His was in danger of going the same way if he couldn't fucking help him. Lyssa's calmness helped, he couldn't deny it, but the tightness around her mouth, and close way she was studying what was happening to Rand, didn't assure a good outcome.

"A third marking is different from a second marking," she said in that mesmerizing voice, drawing Cai's gaze to her face, though his hand remained over Rand's rapidly beating heart. "It is more than releasing the serum and the two of you exchanging blood. The first third marking for a young vampire like yourself is often mentored and guided by an older vampire, when necessary. I expect you dismissed the soul connection as spiritual nonsense."

"Save the lecture for later. Fix him, help him."

"It's not a lecture," she said in reproof. "Only his Master, the one who marked him, can fix him. You. So listen, if you truly care for his welfare. Because if you can't, you will have to end his suffering by taking his life."

Cai's startled glance shot to her. Her face was stern, uncompromising, but not without compassion. The last surprised him, as did the gentleness of her touch when she gripped his other hand and moved it to Rand's abdomen, so one palm was on his chest, one there. Then she moved behind Cai, laying one hand over his heart, behind his shoulder blade, the other to his lower back.

"Close your eyes. Don't look at his outer form. Look inside. Breathe with me. Slow. We need to slow it all down, detach from his physical suffering so you can reach past it, end it. You've been in his mind as a second mark. Go there first. Go where it's familiar. A third marking is a soul-to-soul binding, Cai. Heart to heart. You can be everywhere inside him, to the deepest, darkest, most hidden areas of his soul, the uncharted pathways of his heart, and anywhere in his mind. You essentially become total Master of this soul, responsible for its care and existence, even as it becomes your bound servant through eternity."

"I didn't...I didn't realize it was all that."

"No. And now you regret, and wish you could take it back, because that type of commitment scares you."

"I also didn't warn him. He didn't know."

"Which is also a big part of the problem. First things first. Focus. As you relax and focus, you'll be able to see those pathways inside him. You'll see where your marking has rushed in like floodwater, taking up too much room. Too much, too fast. Too deep. Drowning him. Imagine instead your binding with him is a mist like fog, light as air. Draw back slowly, give him room to be Rand, to find himself and all the things he knows about himself. No, do not withdraw all the way or too fast. Get past your guilt and fear."

Her tone was a gentle reproach, but effective. Cai wondered how the hell she was sensing all this through her palms. She had no access into his mind, but it was as if she did.

"You're his Master. You must help him. He must know you're there, that you're linked and bound, yes, but he isn't imprisoned. There's no need for him to be hurt and afraid. You are there, and you will care for him. Help him make sense of this. Speak to him in his mind, because you are his lifeline back."

He doubted her at first, but as he followed her direction, breathed, focused, Cai was startled to see exactly what she described. Pathways opened, winding, twisting together, forming amazing tapestries made up of life threads that ran from the core of Rand's soul, connected intimately to his heart. Then, his mind, a control center for it all, thrown into chaos like an engine with a wrench in it. Cai could pull out that wrench. He identified his own presence, a shifting energy that he started to reel in, how the fuck he didn't know, but suddenly he did, even if he couldn't describe it.

Rand made a noise somewhere between a growl and a question, and Cai pressed his palms harder against his chest and stomach, firm reassurance. *I'm here.* He remembered the wolf's words as he came out of his nightmare and rephrased them. *I'm your vampire, and it's all right. Just relax. Become man or wolf, whichever is easiest. You have the space. You know how. I just knocked you off your axis because I didn't know what the hell I was doing and wrecked the car, turned us upside down.*

"Just back away from the wreckage and settle down. You've done it a million times. Go forward or back. Just don't stay like this, because they'll sell you to a freak show to pay for the damage we did in here."

He wasn't sure if the humor would help but hell, it helped settle his nerves, so he threw it in. Cai realized he'd said it aloud when he felt Lyssa's fingers flex against his back. He wasn't sure what she was doing, but a cool, steady energy flowed through him from her contact. It had an unnervingly calming effect.

He felt the shift grind back to life again, though he winced as the initial jolt of it pulled a sound of pain from Rand's lips. Cai held onto him, talked to him, watched the human leg give way and disappear before the introduction of the fourth and final wolf leg. His torso twisted, rocked, and that amazing melting effect happened, things blurring. Suddenly, the human was gone.

As Rand finished the full transition to wolf, Cai let out a relieved breath so strong it rocked him on his heels. The wolf lay there, panting, and he was stroking his fur. "It's all right. We'll figure it out." *I'm sorry, Rand. I fucked up bad. I get it if you want out of this gig. I won't hold you to it.*

In answer, two gold eyes focused on him, telling Cai that Rand was deep inside the animal, beyond the reach of his humanity, unless Cai wanted to push it. He didn't need Lyssa to tell him how bad an idea that would be. The wolf staggered to his feet and swayed. Cai stood up and moved back, Lady Lyssa at his side. Jacob was on the other side of the wolf, a faint frown creasing his brow as he watched Rand, all of them waiting to see what the wolf would do.

The large black head lifted and Rand's eyes swung back to Cai again, taking the measure of them all. With a quick snap of teeth and flattened ears, the wolf sprang. But not toward them. He went for the door and was gone, the sound of his toenails hitting the stairs reaching them briefly before there was nothing.

"I'll make sure he gets out," Jacob said, heading toward the door. He glanced over his shoulder at Cai. "If that's the best thing?"

"Yeah. Letting him out is the best thing." Cai pushed away the sudden heaviness inside him. It was like a gift had been handed back to him, weighing ten times more than it had when he gifted it.

Turning to Lyssa, he hesitated but sketched an awkward bow. Another first for him. "Thank you, Lady Lyssa."

In answer, she moved to a guest chair that hadn't been upended by the mayhem and gestured imperiously to another. "Sit, and tell me how much you know of having a human servant. The truth this time. Caginess has its place, but hiding your ignorance about this provides you no advantage, Mordecai. Obviously."

He couldn't even bristle at the rebuke. "Doesn't really matter. That was probably my first and last experience. If he has any sense, he's running his ass off toward the nearest forest." It would have been nice to say good-bye face-to-face, but Cai guessed he could do it mind-to-mind. And receive a big Fuck-You silence in return.

"Servants, when they are meant to be ours, can surprise you. I think it's best you be prepared. Even if he doesn't return, you have third marked him, Cai. His life is forever linked to yours now. You will know when he is afraid, hurting...dying." She folded her hands in her lap and crossed her legs, regal in the velvet dress even with her bare feet. Her toenails were painted the same hunter green. She wore no jewelry.

Jacob returned. "He's out. He headed straight for the woods." The servant's gaze shifted to Lyssa, a curious look passing between them. She nodded.

"I will find him if necessary," she said.

"He'll stay out of sight," Cai assured her. The idea of Lady Lyssa traipsing through the woods wolf-hunting was something he couldn't imagine, though he didn't doubt she would do it. "The wolf's cautious about being seen by humans. He won't cause you any problems."

"No, I don't expect he will. You, on the other hand, interrupted my usual wake-up ritual." She glanced down pointedly at her feet.

"Well, you have a really nice pedicure. You should show that off." Cai bit his tongue and put his head in his hands, his elbows propped on his knees. He sighed. "Being a wiseass is just what I am, my lady. Not going to fucking apologize for it every second. But fuck, I didn't mean to screw him up like this."

He straightened. "I don't know a lot about servants. Trads don't keep humans as servants, except as breeding stock. And he's not fully human, so I don't even know how much of any of it applies. But hell, what you just did worked pretty well."

"I am glad for that. Because of his different physiology, I had no idea if it would."

He looked at her, surprised. "You acted like you knew exactly what you were doing."

She smiled, though her gaze remained serious. "Calm assurance was what you both needed. I provided it to you, so you could provide it to him."

"Damn. You are one unflappable bitch. Lady. Queen." He closed his eyes. "Sorry. Again."

"Perhaps it's best if you listen and I talk. Your chances of survival will increase exponentially."

"Like I haven't heard that before." But he did his best to look respectful and attentive. As well as tamp down an unsettlingly strong desire to take off and find Rand, make sure he was okay. He was, he knew it. He just needed space.

"Rand seems to have many of the best qualities, human and wolf, that contribute to being an excellent servant," she observed.

"I'm not so sure of that. He's an alpha," Cai said. "I mean that literally, in the wolf sense."

"How delightful. An alpha male servant is a gift to be prized, Mordecai. Even when their will poses some difficult challenges." Her eyes warmed on Jacob, before her attention came back to Cai. "I wish you well on the exploration of it."

Cai stared down at his hands, loose on his knees, his planted feet below. "Is there anything else, like this marking, that I should know about?"

When his head lifted, her cool eyes had warmed. "That's a far better track to follow than self-flagellation. And the answer is yes. Navigating that soul-link without pushing too hard upon it, is important to protecting his well-being and strengthening the connection between you. I'll give you the information you need to avoid causing your beautiful wolf further, unintended distress." Her eyes gleamed. "Because it goes far better for you both, when punishments and pain are planned."

After a thorough and eye-opening introduction to the vampire-servant relationship, Cai's brain was almost as overloaded as it had been when he'd so rashly inflicted the third mark upon Rand. Lord Brian had arrived at the tail end of the conversation, announced by one of the house maids via phone. Jacob had thanked her, told her to take Brian and his servant to a guest room and get them what they needed to settle in, as there was no longer an emergency requiring Brian's immediate presence.

"No, the wolf's not here right now," Jacob said, in answer to a question Brian had apparently posed. "Don't worry; he'll be back."

"Lord Brian is likely disappointed he can't rush right down to see your wolf," Lyssa said with amusement. "He's not our typical vampire. His energy and passion are devoted to science, particularly issues related to vampire kind. Fertility, vampire-servant bonds, and Ennui."

That meant Lord Brian likely also was here to evaluate Greenwald's current condition, and treat it however they best could under the present stress load. But hearing the scientist might have a specific interest in Rand made Cai uneasy. He probably wasn't the only vampire who'd heard the legends about shifter blood.

"His servant, Debra," Lyssa continued, "is his equal in running our Council research facilities. Her interest in Rand will be no less than his."

At Cai's look, she shook her head. "No one will do anything to him against his will. You were invited as a guest, no matter how you arrived," her gaze sparked, "and your hospitality will not be further abused."

"Unless Rand counts the million questions Brian will ask if he can corner him," Jacob observed dryly.

If he comes back, Cai thought.

Lyssa seemed sure of it. Cai wished he had her confidence. She rose. "It will take Lord Brian a few moments to get settled, but I expect he'll head straight from the guest room to the study to set up his mobile lab. Your first priority is to meet with him and go over the suggestions he has to help you with your mission. We all understand time is of the essence. I'll expect you to join him there in the next fifteen minutes."

"Yeah." Cai said. It wasn't top of his mind right this second, but he'd said he'd go and he would. If he had to do it without Rand, well, he'd still do it. Safer for Rand that way, anyhow.

Lyssa gave him a searching look, but nodded to Jacob and took her leave, a faint trail of floral scent and a swirl of energy left in her wake. Jacob turned to Cai. "Anything you need before I go?"

A wolf to get his ass back here. But Cai shook his head. "This Brian guy. He's really a scientist?"

"Him and Debra. Both brilliant. Ever seen any of the Bond films?" Jacob asked. "Think of Lord Brian as the vampire version of Q. You remember how to get to the study?"

"Yeah."

"Good. If you have need of me again, just hit zero on the house phone. As the Council head's servant, anything major regarding household operations goes through me, even if it's not my house, as long as my lady and I are in residence. If it's minor, hit 1, and you'll get the staff. They'll take care of you right away. You might have them make up a ton of food for Rand for when he comes back. I remember shortly after I was third marked, I felt like I could eat an entire cow."

Jacob moved toward the door. He carried himself with a warrior's self-possession, even in the casual wear of jeans and a Wolverine X-Men T-shirt. Cai told himself not to ask, but he did anyway.

"Why does Lady Lyssa think he'll return?"

Jacob turned. "A sense of something between you two. New, but it's a bond. Plus, he cares what happens to Dovia."

"He figures if he rescues her, it will make him feel better about losing his family."

"Can't make him feel worse, right?" Jacob pointed out.

"Yeah, maybe." Cai really wasn't up to arguing about anything right now. He was drained. "Um...your lady, she's all right. I didn't expect that. I've hated Trads so long, and the things they told me about non-Trads didn't seem much better. Particularly Council. Made them sound like a bunch of heartless tyrants more concerned with lording it over everyone than doing anything worthwhile for anyone."

"Vampires aren't likely to win any humanitarian awards, and not only because they're not human." Jacob flashed a smile. "She can be brutal, but she's fair. She's overlooked your rough edges because she doesn't look at only the surface of things. But now that you've seen that, I suggest you do show her respect. Or she *will* rip out your lungs."

"If I had a dime for every time I've heard that," Cai muttered as Jacob closed the door behind him, leaving Cai alone.

He felt like crap. He knew Rand hadn't become bionic or been beamed thousands of miles away by aliens, because he could thankfully still touch the connection between them. If he closed his eyes, ghosted through those pathways Lyssa had shown him, he could hear the male's heartbeat, the rush of his blood, the turmoil of his thoughts. He was there, agitated. Cai could push deeper, but he didn't. He withdrew, and chose the considerate way. For once.

Rand, just tell me you're okay, or I'm going to run your ass down. You know I will.

Silence. Shit. *I didn't fucking know. I didn't realize it was like that.* Cai cut off that line of thinking, at least on an open channel to Rand. As Lyssa had said, he didn't need an audience for self-pity. But that part when Lyssa guided him in Rand's heart, mind and soul... Even though he was focused on helping Rand get through the shift and not losing his own mind, now that Cai was thinking it through again, he remembered the way it felt, being heart to heart, soul to soul with the guy. It was like standing in the same space in the universe, never feeling alone. Maybe the way twins talked about feeling, times a hundred. Only in that case, they remained separate people, affected by one another but neither controlling the other. Vampires and servants were different.

Darker shadows closed around his mind as he remembered Lyssa's further explanation about the third mark. *You are his Master, responsible for his care, capable of tearing him open or putting him back together.* Fuck, he should have known. Vampires had always had a Masters-of-the-Universe thing going on. He just hadn't realized how literally true it was in the vampire-servant relationship. But he couldn't deny it was part of his makeup. How many times when he'd taken Rand had that "mine" feeling surged, wanting to take over the wolf completely?

And it wasn't all about physical strength. Hell, since he was all alone in his own head, he'd admit it. The couple times he and Rand had tangled had left Cai thinking he and the shifter were on a level playing field as combatants. Rand just wasn't immortal. Cai recalled that intriguing exchange, which seemed a lifetime ago.

I don't know much about shifter healing ability; if it's any better than human.

Faster. And our bodies can bounce back from a lot more punishment.

Cai thought of Lyssa's sensual tease, about punishments and pain being more enjoyable if they were planned. Cai didn't know if he would have been a sexual Dominant as a human adult. Hell, he was fifteen when he was taken, and sex with anything willing was of interest, no need to specialize into BDSM, gay, straight or otherwise. The Trads twisted him, fucked him up, and it took him decades of self-therapy to work it out. Even now, he wasn't always sure if he had the four-lane-highway-wide, sexually dominant streak of a typical vampire, or if he needed to be a celibate in the forest who didn't deal with that craving.

Well, okay, he could answer the latter. Since the first time he'd seen Rand in his human form, every thought of celibacy was laughed over a cliff, falling so far he never heard the splat. Probably because he was too busy exploring the other male's long, muscular body and wresting moans from his corded throat. Fuck, that ass. Cai wanted it right now. Wanted to caress the broad, endless chest, tease the tiny buds of his nipples with flicks of his fingernails and watch Rand stiffen, blue eyes flash with desire and a predator's aggressive response. He wanted to take as much as Cai did. Maybe that was the key to why the wolf intrigued him.

Rand didn't always have to win. He didn't always need to be on top. But he relished fighting for it.

Sighing, Cai cleaned himself up and headed for the study, telling Rand in his mind where he was going in case he wanted to circle back and join in. He hoped Lyssa was right. Rand might not come back for him, but the plight of this female vampire had snagged his attention, and he had the rescuer complex. One would think finding his children clubbed to death would have cured him of thinking anyone could be saved.

Cai stopped, leaning against the hallway wall, and rubbed an impatient hand over his face. Fuck, he was glad he'd blocked that thought. He really was a shit most of the time. Maybe that was why he was doing this impossible thing, rescuing a female vampire from the Trads. Rand had convinced him it was the right thing to do, and Cai wanted that to matter to him again. Even if it was likely the last thing that ever did.

If he was one of these vampires like Voltaire or Tyra, he'd look around this place and see how good and comfortable life could be. He could have figured out a job, settled somewhere, right? But it was no wonder everyone kept accusing him of being a Trad. He'd lived with Trads for a hundred years and, though he claimed to hate everything about them, their ways had become his ways. Walls were a prison. Vampires weren't supposed to live like humans. Yet why not?

He'd stayed in cities, knew all about running water and delivery pizza. He grudgingly understood both the "civilized" vampire and shifter viewpoint that, when one looked human, but wasn't, it was important not to give up the camouflage that passing as human could provide.

So, as Rand had pointed out, he'd read Harry Potter and caught the occasional movie. When he needed money, he stole it in small quantities, or stole the item he needed. He didn't need much, so none of that tripped his guilt meter.

But he always returned to the wild spaces. Maybe because there the noise wasn't so loud. The towns triggered things in him the silence of the wood couldn't. There, he could find the closest thing there was to peace. In towns, he saw humans doing things that made them far more than his food.

Yet even the forest was no longer enough. He didn't know what would be. Or if anything could be. Maybe this was the answer to that. Go down for something, rather than living for nothing.

He found the study had been swiftly converted into a work space, just as Lyssa had said. Three computers were set up, along with a couple handcarts of file boxes and a large trunk of items that appeared half unpacked. Clothes, yes, but it looked as if the clothes had been carelessly tossed aside to get to other items. Things that belonged in labs, like test tubes and a microscope. Two giant stacks of printouts, heavily tabbed with sticky notes.

A young male vampire with sand-colored hair was studying some of the sheets in the notebook, flipping through them at a quick pace. "Damn it, Debra, where—"

A slim woman, her dark blond hair in a loose coil on her neck, her body clad in a modest linen dress that classily showed off an appealing figure, came to his side. Reaching over him, she picked another tab and flipped to it, putting her finger on what the male was seeking.

"Oh." He snorted. "Of course."

She bit back a smile and turned toward Cai. She didn't seem surprised to see him, but vampires and servants had heightened senses. She and the young male would have heard him when he entered the hallway leading to this room.

"Mordecai?" she asked.

"Just Cai is fine. Only Lady Lyssa uses Mordecai."

"I expect she's fully aware of your nickname and prefers to use the proper one. She's formal like that."

"I noticed. Probably why I haven't spent any effort on repeated correction. That, and she'd probably freeze my dick off." Cai slid his hands into his jeans pockets at her startled glance. "Sorry. Yeah. So, they tell me Lord Brian might have some stuff to help me on my suicide mission. You or this other lab geek know where I can find him?"

The young male straightened and turned, his hazel eyes showing some amusement. "I'm Lord Brian."

The guy couldn't be more than eighty, and vampires optimally stayed close to their sires or parents until age fifty. Guy was practically the human version of a college student. He was supposed to give Cai tools to help him deal with Trads?

Brian obviously read his skepticism, for his lips curved in a grim smile. Taking a closer look, Cai noted a seriousness in the male's direct gaze that suggested he might be far more mature than his years. Hopefully.

"You think any vampire over the age of two hundred would be on the leading edge of vampire science?" Brian asked pleasantly. "Most of them don't even know what a phone app is."

"Lord Belizar has made some excellent progress," Debra pointed out. "He sent that last text to you without incident. And he's far older than two hundred."

"Yes." Brian snorted. "He spelled out every word. It was eleven pages long."

"I'm not seeing any centuries-old vampire, let alone one with 'lord' tacked to the front of his name, getting into the whole LOL, OMG and BFF lingo," Cai said, his feet back under him. "Let alone emojis. Though I could be wrong about that. Everyone likes using cute pictures."

Debra hid a chuckle behind her hand. She had some of the delicate-beauty quality that Lord Mason's servant Jessica had. But as Cai took the same kind of closer look he had with Brian, he noted the razor-sharp intelligence in her brown, long-lashed eyes. This was the human servant to whom both Lyssa and Jacob gave equal props as Brian's partner in the lab.

Cai's brain power might be seriously outmatched here. Didn't stop him from making quips, though. Fortunately, it appeared Lord Brian had a sense of humor.

"Indeed. I shudder at the miscommunications which could happen if they even tried. Jacob brought me up to speed on where you're going, and I've a couple things that might aid you. I also want to ask you some additional questions in case I've overlooked anything."

His scrutiny increased as his gaze swept Cai, but his manner became even more polite, putting Cai on alert. "And later, when you return, I'd like to ask you further questions about the Trads. We know precious little about them from a sociological standpoint, and the more information I have about vampires as a whole, the more it contributes to the different divisions of work we do at our lab facilities."

"The returning part is a big if, but sure, maybe." Cai shrugged. "I wouldn't give me anything that's a prototype you want back, because my chances of succeeding are right up there with launching an arrow from the roof of this building and hitting the moon."

"Yet you're still going," Debra said. "That's very brave, to risk your life for a female you don't know."

"Not really. Just going to do it. Don't care to think about the why, because if I did, I'd realize it's monumentally fucking stupid, and I won't do it. So let's move on."

She blinked. Lord Brian gave him another hefty scrutiny, but he turned to rummage through a plastic box of vials. After studying the labels on several, he handed one to Cai. "This doesn't require refrigeration and its potency lasts about two weeks. Put it in something they're all drinking, wine, whatever. No more than a few drops will knock a vampire out in a matter of minutes. Five tops, and it dulls the brain's warning system so they feel like a drunk passing out and won't fight it. At night, they'll remain solidly unconscious for a couple hours, give or take a few minutes, depending on their age and will. If administered near dawn, the effects last longer. When they wake at twilight, they'll have a short hangover period that can slow their wits."

The scientist went to his stores, returning with a pack of gum.

Cai shook his head. "I really don't chew gum."

Brian smiled. "Chew a piece of the red gum if a vampire has forcibly taken your blood. The binding effects, their ability to track you, will be neutralized."

"Okay." Most of it was probably bullshit, but the guy seemed to think it would work, so Cai pocketed the vial and the gum. He looked curiously at the other things overflowing the trunk. "You don't travel light."

"I'll be setting up a temporary lab here for a few days. It will keep me closer, in case Dovia needs care. I have several degrees, one of which is in internal medicine. Doesn't apply to everything about vampires, but it can point me in the right direction."

Since the multi-degreed guy was being professional and impressive, Cai realized he should make an effort to appear like he was thinking stuff through, too, planning ahead. "Okay. What will she need, if she's in bad shape and we're not close enough to get to you right away?" *If we find her at all, if we rescue her, if we don't all end up dead.*

"Blood's the obvious thing. From your servant ideally, depending on her state." He paused and Cai tensed, anticipating a question about Rand's blood, its potency, but Brian moved on. "Keep her warm, reassure her, and get her as far away from them as possible."

"Thanks. Definitely needed a few medical degrees to figure that out."

Brian gave him a humorless smile, but produced one more vial. "This will help her sleep. Only two doses at a time, though. She can't overdose, but the mix can put her in a prolonged sleep that could turn on her. She could get caught in her dreams and feel trapped there."

It reminded Cai uncomfortably of his nightmare earlier, that smothering feeling. He took the vial without any further snark and added it to his pockets.

"I'd like to be as prepared as possible," the scientist said. "What do you think her condition will be?"

"Depends on her will. We're different from humans, aren't we?" Cai said. His tone had gone flat, but he didn't know how to change that and answer Brian's question. "She's an object to them, a means to an end. They'll have no empathy for her, and the longer she's with them, the more she'll question if she has any identity at all, if she's become an 'it,' because that's how they see anyone not part of their circle."

He'd been there himself. But they hadn't broken him, had they? Maybe it was the vampire strength Lodell had given him that had turned that tide, or something else, but Cai had to wonder. How many human women had he seen the Trads break? Captives who eventually could be left unbound during daylight hours, because it didn't occur to them they had any choices that were their own to make.

Debra looked startled by the concise summary, but there really wasn't a way to fucking soften it, was there?

"Thank you." Brian spoke the words neutrally, but his hazel eyes had gone cold, his jaw tightening. "We will prepare for it."

"How?" Cai asked abruptly. "How does anyone prepare for that? Make that easier?" He lifted the bottle. "Except with this. Total oblivion. Even that, if you take too much, it puts you right back in the middle of it."

"We take a couple things with us that'll tie her back to this life, to the comfort and love of her parents. To remind her that broken isn't dead."

Cai turned. Rand was leaning in the doorway. It was hard to sneak up on a vampire, but Rand had managed to do it. Maybe because Cai had convinced himself the shifter wasn't coming back.

He'd been wrong.

CHAPTER TEN

*R*and had a teddy bear tucked in the crook of one elbow, both hands in his jeans pockets. His expression was unreadable, and his mind likewise oddly free of thought. He only noted simple, random things, like the rosemary and lavender smell of Debra's soap and shampoo, and Brian's chemical and male scents, a mix of lab and man.

"Concept's good," Cai said with forced casualness. "We just have to accomplish it another way. The bear carries her scent, and they'd wonder why we have it."

Cai moved to the doorway and stood before Rand. The male looked put together, but what was beneath the surface was untamed, raw. Their eyes met and held. Even with all the stuff unresolved between them, Cai couldn't help taking the wolf shifter in through all his senses. And feeling guilty for how much he meant the next words. "Glad you came back."

When the male said nothing, Cai plucked the bear out of his hold and lifted it. "Fortunately, *you* can convert to a fuzzy cuddle toy if she needs it."

Rand's gaze sparked. Yeah, now wasn't really the time for Cai to be a wiseass, but that always seemed to be the time he found it impossible not to do it.

Rand had talked about being able to shift his brain to mostly human while in wolf form. Apparently, he could also do the reverse.

Cai realized the shifter was keeping his mind in a passive state by letting the animal side hold onto as much of it as possible. Intriguing.

"You still coming with me?"

"I wouldn't have returned if the answer to that was no."

"Not true. Because you're not like me. You like closure and being polite and noble. I like things rude, messy and left dangling like a dick in the wind."

Brian cleared his throat, drawing the two men's attention back to him. "The gum works for neutralizing the tracer on a vampire or a human servant. But I don't have enough information about shifters to say for certain it will work on him."

"Nobody's putting their mouth on him but me unless they want to experience a full fang extraction." Cai lifted his lip to display both of his.

Brian's gaze sharpened and he came closer, peering at Cai's mouth in an alarmingly intent way, as if he might stick his hands in there. "Why do you have an artificial fang? The original should have regenerated."

Cai drew back, bumping into Rand, an involuntary white coat reaction to the scientist's unexpected eagerness to touch, probe. Reminding himself he was a grown-up who could set this guy on his ass, Cai planted his feet.

"Fire and blood. It was cauterized with my blood. Not going into the whys. None of your damn business." He'd told Lyssa, but that was different. He was getting antsy. He wanted to be alone with Rand, resolve some of this shit. Get on his way. Get out of here.

Fortunately for the scientist's long, elegant fingers, Brian didn't attempt a dental exam, but his attention remained on Cai's mouth. "If you'll let me take some quick dimensions before you go, I can have a replacement one made that fits better, without the wiring, and has retraction ability. We had to do something similar for another vampire, one caught in a house fire."

Brian's turned back to Rand. The gleam in the young vampire's gaze reminded Cai of Jacob's veiled warning about a full interrogation. "I recognize your quest is urgent," the scientist said, "but I'd also like to request a blood and hair sample from your servant for study, and about fifteen minutes to ask him some questions."

"You can ask all day long," Rand said. "But I'm standing right here and saying no."

Brian's expression cooled. "You're his servant."

"We're blood bound due to circumstances and to up our chances of survival," Cai said. "That's all."

"Oh." Brian sent Cai an odd look. "You truly aren't very well versed in our ways."

"The first hundred years of my life I was with Trads, and the rest has been as far away from vampires as I can put myself. So yeah, that's accurate." Cai's brow furrowed. "What, because he's my servant he has to do everything I say?"

Lyssa had pretty much said the same, but hearing it reinforced under practical circumstances made it more unsettling.

"Yes," Brian said simply. "In the eyes of our society, he's your property. You've third marked him. We've only recently been able to unmark servants from vampires who feel the relationship was not what they intended it to be, but permission for that is being granted on a case-by-case basis. Some vampires...are not patient."

"They kill their servant, because that's allowed," Cai guessed.

"Yes." The male vampire looked uncomfortable. "Not advised, and not officially sanctioned by Council."

"But not punished, either."

Brian said nothing. Cai noted Debra's expression had become flat as a still pond. He wondered if that was how she covered disapproval, or if she simply didn't have an opinion on it.

Rand's mind *was* a still pond, giving away nothing. Though the look in his eyes, trained on the younger vampire, suggested more of the wolf than the man. Despite Debra's reaction to her Master's words, she'd noticed it too. Cai saw her studying Rand as intently as Brian had been studying Cai's mouth.

Cai shifted partly into the field of view between the shifter and the scientists, commanding the attention of the latter. "We're different," Cai said. "I'm not a Trad, but that doesn't make me part of your world, either. We'll do this job, and then I'll cut Rand loose."

He'd invited him to go to Syria, but since Rand didn't say anything to contradict him, Cai guessed being future travel buddies was off the table.

"That's not permitted," Brian said. "Simply cutting him loose."

"He's not a human. He's no threat to exposing our world. All due respect, how are they going to stop me?"

"They could track him down and kill him," Brian said in a neutral tone. "He would be safer if you could discuss it with Lady Lyssa, when the time comes. If it comes."

Cai bristled at having to discuss any decision with anyone other than his own damn self, but if it would keep Rand safer, he might be okay with another chat with the queen. And maybe getting that new fang wouldn't be bad. Least they could do if he brought them back their vampire girl.

While he allowed the scientist to take some fang replacement measurements, Cai took his mind off the guy having his hands in his mouth by watching Rand. The shifter moved out of the doorway and took a seat in a cushiony chair. He stretched out his legs and crossed them at the ankles, a deceptively easy pose. The watchfulness behind his gaze remained the wolf, scrutinizing everything with those glittering eyes.

Tell me you're okay, Rand. You know I didn't know any of this shit. We won't let them dictate to us. I won't let them. Okay?

Rand met his eyes. Cai saw a slight softening of his mouth and he inclined his head, a bare nod. Not exactly a vote of resounding trust and confidence, but at least it was direct communication.

Brian was finished and typing in some notes on his computer to wind things up. Cai pivoted as he sensed another human coming down the hallway. The place was crawling with house servants, so he should have ignored it, but there was something familiar about this one.

A blink later, the hairs on the back of his neck prickled, and something with jagged edges gouged his gut from the inside. When the male stepped into view, entering from the second door to the study, Cai already knew who it was.

This was no human servant. There could be no reason this male was here, except to deceive and kill vampires.

Cai was in motion before his brain had to order it. The human was as good as dead.

Instead, the male managed to twist and duck at the last second, despite Cai's speed. It was as if he anticipated the movements of a vampire and was ready to counter them, even if he had no chance of repelling them in close quarters.

No more than what Cai would expect from a fucking vampire hunter, a human who made his kills through cowardly deception, not hand-to-hand combat. He was going to learn what it was like to be torn limb from fucking limb.

Cai caught him, seizing him by the throat and shirt front. The thundering in his ears was like the white noise after an explosion, muting sound and leaving only a faint ringing, like a toneless bell. It deafened him to everything but the need to do what he was trying his best to do. Kill this human, make this moment his very last.

Cai swung the male into the wall like a sack of bricks, savagely pleased with the thud, the grunt of pain. He absorbed the hit to the face, the kick, noting the strength was considerable. Guy was built solid, all six feet of muscle. But it wasn't enough to deter Cai or make him let go. He rammed his fist below the rib cage. Fueled by fury and vampire strength, it punched through flesh, and his lips peeled back in a victorious grimace. Cai was going to rip his fucking heart out. So easy and so quick. Guy wasn't so tough now, when he didn't have the element of surprise.

He saw the flash in the hunter's midnight blue eyes. He knew he was fucked. No fear, but a great deal of pissed-off. Didn't matter to Cai. Dead was dead, however you got there, but some fear would have been gratifying.

Lord Brian grabbed his arm, trying to pull him off the human. Not going to work, since Cai had over a hundred years of strength and speed on him. Rand joined the fray with a snarl that told Cai he'd shifted. Damn it. Brian cursed as the big wolf latched onto his arm.

Brian fell back, taking Rand with him. Cai had a brief impression of Debra's wide and startled gaze. Brian shouted an order at her to stay clear of the scuffle, but she was already looking for a weapon to drive Rand back, get him to release her Master.

Cai knew the wolf was acting in his defense, rather than with an intent to maim or kill. No way in hell he was releasing his death grip on the hunter, but he didn't want Rand hurt.

Before he could spare a thought through his killing rage to get Rand to ease off, another barked order penetrated that white noise, powerful enough to vibrate a house on its foundations.

"*Stand clear.*"

Smart fucking idea. He didn't know who had the thunder god

voice, but it would defuse Rand, and Cai didn't want Brian hurt, either. But nothing was going to stop him...

White hot pain shot through his core, like something had detonated in his gut and spread up through his diaphragm and chest. Suddenly his lungs were pumping madly, heart jumping.

More rage filled him, because the pain was so overwhelming it drained his strength and loosened his grip on the vampire hunter's throat. Looking down, Cai blinked, startled to see a sharp blade sticking out of his stomach and curving up close before his ribs and chest. Someone had jammed a long, curved sword into his lower back and let it emerge from his upper abdomen.

That would explain why it fucking hurt so much, though if the blade hadn't been so wicked sharp, he expected it would be hurting like a hundred sons of bitches, instead of ten. Maybe twenty. And it hadn't severed his spine, because otherwise he would have lost feeling in his legs and crumpled to the floor.

All sorts of unlikely plans to twist free of that blade shot through his mind, but his assailant was faster even than them.

A palm clamped onto his shoulder, thumb against his neck, and a hard body, thigh to chest, pressed to his right side, so close it was lover intimate. The menace in the deadly voice that spoke against his ear wasn't pillow talk, though.

"Let him go."

Cai had his wrist deep in body cavity, his forearm running with blood. The human's heart was so close to his fingertips he could feel the thud. The vampire hunter should be focused on bleeding out. Instead, his mouth was twisted into a matching sneer, adrenaline and anger overriding pain. With the least opportunity, he'd keep fighting.

Both of them pinned and wanting to fight; neither able to do so. Life was a bitch.

"Withdraw your fist from my servant's chest, slow and easy, or you die right here."

That came from the one who'd skewered him, making it clear why the vampire hunter wasn't well on his way to dying.

"He's no servant," Cai spat. "He's a vampire hunter. A killer."

"He was at one time. Now he serves me. I will not tell you again." The voice did something with the blade that sent more indescribable pain vibrating through Cai, wresting a cry from his lips. He heard a growl and realized that growl had been growing in volume and strength while he'd been distracted by his impalement.

A slight movement from the male vampire who held him said he might have spared a glance to his right. "Your wolf is close to attacking again. If he does, my *cher* and Lord Brian will be forced to break him into pieces. Pick your battles. This isn't one of them, unless you wish to die, here and now. Do it."

Cai curled his lip, but he'd lost his chance to accomplish what he wished. If he twitched his fingers anywhere closer to the heart, the vampire would know because he was there, wasn't he? Deep in the head, heart and soul of his servant. He'd slice and dice Cai before he got anywhere close, and then Rand...fuck, he'd third marked Rand.

Shit. Slowly, he pulled his hand out of the vampire hunter. He gave him credit; the human's eyes never wavered. His face was tight with agony, but he still looked like he'd be happy to go a couple more rounds with Cai, as soon as either one of them was capable.

But as Cai withdrew, a female vampire with sable brown hair and blue-green eyes was there, easing the human down the side of the wall. She refused to back off even when he seemed to want her to move back from the fray.

He was protective of her, that was obvious. It was also quite necessary, because the female was even younger than Brian, and a made vampire on top of that. Maybe only a few years as a vampire under her belt, which meant Cai could crush her even more easily than he could have Brian.

The one at his back was a different matter. He smelled...ancient. He held the power of centuries. Not as old as Lyssa, but raw power and something else made Cai think this vampire would be a match for her, regardless of the difference in ages.

"Be still. I don't want to sever your spine," the male said in a cool, even tone. "You'd heal, but it would take a very unpleasant day or two, and I understand there is a need for your services. I've not harmed anything that can't be sufficiently healed within a couple hours, with some of your servant's blood. But you must remain still."

Cai decided not to tell the vampire what he could do with his instruction. He hated that when the blade slid free, he hissed out another sharp cry. Fuck, that hurt. He didn't expect Rand to be there to catch him as the beautiful female had his opponent, so he was surprised when Rand was indeed there, in human form, easing him down to the floor.

The older vampire wiped his sword across Cai's shirt front in a ritual cross movement. It was probably some crazy samurai sign of *yeah, I kicked your ass*. Rand shot a notably hostile glance his way. The male seemed unaffected by it, but he did straighten and step back, sheathing the katana in a scabbard harnessed to his back.

He was tall, lean, with unnaturally dark eyes and a loose fall of black hair around his sculpted face. He wore a *gi*, as if he'd been working out with that deadly blade before joining them in the study.

He moved to the side of the female vampire and the injured human. Cai's bloody hand closed into a fist again, feeling how close that beating heart had been.

"I should have done it," he muttered. "Why the hell did I mark you like that?"

"That isn't what stopped you. Who is he?" Rand asked. He'd pulled on his jeans but he knelt by Cai shirtless, his hand over the sword wound, stanching the blood with his balled-up shirt. Cai swallowed over the sudden wave of weakness, the inevitable result of an injury that severe.

"He's a vampire hunter. He killed someone I know...a while back. A friend."

Rand glanced over at the other wounded male. "I thought you had no friends or family."

"I don't. Not anymore. There was just the one."

"Oh. Just one...ever?"

"Yeah, I don't make friends easily. Shocker, I know."

Rand pressed his lips together and lifted his wrist toward Cai's mouth, offering. Cai shoved it away, ungraciously. "Not here. I won't fucking be nursed like a baby in front of him."

Rand laid a hand on the side of his throat. He seemed remarkably unconcerned about anything else happening in the room. "If you're too stubborn to feed here," he said steadily, "then we go back to our room where you will. You're very pale. More corpse-white than usual."

"Nice. I can't die."

"Yes. But you also can't leave until you're strong enough to do so, and we both wish to leave here sooner than later, correct?"

Calm logic. Whatever had kept Rand so deep in his head when he first arrived seemed to have been put aside to handle the immediate crisis. That semblance of his normal self relieved Cai, though he felt like a shit for everything suddenly being about him, when Rand had had the far more stressful past few hours.

"Yeah, yeah," Cai said gruffly. "You just want to be the hero who saves the girl."

Rand gave him a patient look. Cai would have shot off a couple more stupid things, but Lord Brian, who had been examining the injured hunter, now came to Cai's side. As he squatted next to him, Cai saw he'd shed the lab coat that Rand had bitten through. The sleeve off his dress shirt had likely been punctured, but he had that rolled up high on his arm. The area above the elbow was bound up in a torn piece of the coat, a temporary dressing to handle the blood until the wound knitted.

"I'm sorry," Rand said. "My wolf doesn't always reason the way I do."

"I expect you and your wolf are very much on the same page most times. Your Master was under attack. That's all that matters to a servant, when the bond is true." Lord Brian slanted him a benign glance. "And a small price to pay to see you shift twice."

He turned a more serious gaze back to Cai, pulling the torn shirt up to examine the sword wound. Cai would have protested and shoved him away, but he was taking a break from belligerence in favor of recuperation.

True to vampire healing abilities, the run-through was already closing, though he would need blood to accelerate the internal healing process, as Rand had pointed out.

Brian's expression was far less amiable when he met Cai's eyes. "You're alive right now only because you are of use," he murmured. "And because Lord Daegan was aware of that and would not kill you indiscriminately. You understand?"

"You understand how little I give a shit?" Cai closed his eyes at Rand's look. "Did you give us everything you need to give us, so we can get the hell out of here?"

Brian shot him an inscrutable look when Cai opened his eyes, but offered a tight nod. "Almost. Lord Daegan and his servant, Gideon, were going to discuss other tactical considerations with you."

"Gideon Green." Cai bared his teeth. He'd already known it, but hearing it confirmed, said aloud, provoked his bloodlust once more. "What the fuck is a vampire hunter doing here, bound to a vampire?"

"Bound to two, actually. Anwyn and Daegan." Brian glanced toward Daegan and the female bending over Gideon. He'd been coaxed or compelled to stretch out on the floor. Cai noticed Anwyn had opened her wrist and put it to his mouth. Her other hand was on his face, and her profile was worried. Angry.

"He's pretty much the most notorious vampire killer there is from the human race, and he's just part of the gang now?"

"It is a complicated story, and not mine to tell," Brian said firmly. "But it's why he and his lord are here. They have a vast repository of knowledge about confronting vampires in less than ideal circumstances. After you get blood, I suggest you talk to them."

"I won't be talking to Gideon Green, ever," Cai said bluntly. Lord Daegan, sitting on his heels, cocked his head and looked his way. Yeah, with vampire hearing, nothing of this conversation was going unnoted. Fuck, he was a creepy-looking bastard. Those dark eyes that had seemed almost too dark to be real now had crimson sparks in them and way too little whites.

Cai blinked, and they were simply dark eyes again, steady and cold upon him. Yeah, he'd resume his slice and dice routine if Cai kept shooting his mouth off. Which changed nothing. "He killed the only friend I ever had. If he comes near me again, I'll finish the job."

"Good luck with that. Bigger dicks than you have tried."

With those words and a rasping cough, Gideon struggled to a sitting position, no matter Anwyn's sharp word to him. The painfilled, midnight dark blue eyes were deep set in a strong face...and familiar. Which was odd, because Cai knew the male by scent more than sight. He'd only ever seen him at a distance, never close enough to recognize eye color.

The male had dark hair, a lot of muscle and concentrated energy, a honed hunter, thanks to the additional powers being a servant gave him. A servant marked by two vampires, one of them being centuries old.

"Without your Master, you'd be dead," Cai sneered at him.

"I'm alive because you announced yourself with that buffalo charge of yours. You would have done better to get a little closer, give me a friendly handshake instead of going berserker." Gideon's gaze locked with his. "Which I expect is the type of thing Brian wanted us to go over with you. Subtlety when strength isn't enough."

Cai laughed. He didn't care that it hurt, or that it sounded like the bark of a wounded moose. There were things in his gut that hurt worse. With a grunt, he started to get to his feet. Goddamn it, he was going to stand.

Though Rand had to help, he managed it, and pushed a pace away so he could stand on his own. Rand stayed close enough to be a prop, if Cai needed it. He didn't. Not for this.

"I lived a hundred years among Trads, vampire hunter," he told Gideon. "Every fucking day I spent with them as a human, I had to convince them why they shouldn't gut me, drain me. I spent my first couple decades being tortured in ways you wouldn't have survived, as a mortal or a servant. I know, because I saw the humans they brought to the camp die, while I continued to survive. Do you really think there's anything you can tell me about that environment I don't already know?"

He was aware a silence had fallen on the room, but he kept going, didn't look anywhere but in that male's face. If he couldn't kill this asshole, he'd see if there was a scrap of conscience in him that Cai could shred.

"And when I reached the end of what I could bear, there was only one thing that kept me going. Lodell. He patched me up, taught me how to survive. Eventually, he turned me. I hated him for it, hated his guts for the longest time."

He'd accused Lodell of figuring out the worst way yet to torture him. Making him more indestructible only gave Goddard and his crew a bigger range of ways to hurt him. Lodell had told him, *I've given you the way to survive, and win. You've proven you're too goddamn stubborn and mean to die. You were meant to be a vampire. We're both going to win this fight, boy."*

"He left the Trads before I did. When I was finally free, I saw him a few times. We had our different paths. But then, not too long ago, I went looking for him again. I was told he'd been decapitated in an alley. He died next to a Dumpster, thanks to you. Sunlight made his ash part of the garbage."

Cai paused, his jaw flexing. "I tracked you, got almost close enough to take you. But then you disappeared. Otherwise, you would have been dead. I never thought to look for you here."

Gideon was another, like Graham, on his list to kill. Cai's voice was hoarse, his body shaking. He really needed to time his dramatic monologues better. "He was...a friend, in a place where no one offered friendship, because it would expose you to weakness. But he did. He cared for me. And you killed him like he was an enemy."

Some distant part of him understood all the conflicts and hypocrisy in his little speech. He himself hated Trads; would kill them all for what a small group of them had done to him. He didn't feel much more warmly toward the type of vampires in this room, for the reasons he'd told Lyssa. If he'd somehow found a way to be human again, he might have joined the ranks of those like Gideon Green, to destroy as many of them as he could.

But he'd met Lodell. And Lodell had showed him that not all vampires, not all Trads, were the same.

Gideon's expression had turned to stone. Not in rejection of Cai's words, but as if he'd needed to hold himself still to absorb the impact of the words. "I'm sorry about your friend," he said at last in a rough voice. "I became a hunter, because a vampire killed my high school sweetheart right in front of me. I got over it and figured out one vampire didn't make all of them bad. But it took me years to get there, and I didn't get over it until I met her. And him."

He glanced toward Anwyn and Daegan. Anwyn might have appreciated the sentiment, but she was occupied, leveling a murderous glare at Cai. If he twitched wrong, he was pretty sure she'd do her best to disembowel him. Daegan looked a little less murderous. He was far more capable of killing Cai, but vampires who'd been around a long time tended to get past shit like this faster. Probably because they had a lot of the same experiences to weigh them against.

Cai wasn't there yet. He still felt as homicidal as Anwyn looked.

"Perhaps I should have stated that not killing other guests is a house rule."

Lyssa stood in the doorway with Jacob. The displeasure in her tone was obvious. Jacob touched his lady's arm and moved past her to drop to Gideon's side. As he did, Cai realized why Gideon's eyes had seemed so familiar.

"Fuck, they're related," Cai muttered. "Great."

Jacob glanced toward him, but brought his attention back to Gideon. "Here I was, thinking you'd make it a whole week without someone trying to kill you, brother," he said lightly.

Gideon grunted. Jacob put his hand on his shoulder, his other moving to cover Anwyn's on Gideon's chest, a gesture obviously intended to reassure the female vampire.

"He's taken some of my blood," Anwyn said. "But he needs to lie down awhile and have some of Daegan's. His is more potent."

"Don't be making him fuller of himself than he already is," Gideon advised, looking toward the impassive Daegan. Then he looked back up at her, a faint teasing expression on his face. "See? This is why I told you I always conceal-carry wooden stakes."

Anwyn shook her head. "Which you didn't have time or opportunity to use."

"I had time and opportunity," Gideon rejoined. "I showed self-restraint, something you never give me credit for doing. Daegan had a dagger strapped to his calf, but did he use that? No, he whipped out the big-ass sword. He sleeps with that thing more often than with us. He's going to slice off his dick one night."

Gideon's words were laced with tiredness, though. He was no vampire and Cai had done him some damage. But when Daegan's eerily empty gaze remained on Cai, an unspoken but undeniable threat, Gideon put his hand on Daegan's arm and squeezed, drawing the male's attention. "If someone had killed one of my friends, I'd feel the same way," Gideon said.

The sardonic humor dropped, his tone weighted with the kind of memory Cai knew too well. "I did, right? For a long time. And every vampire I've killed was probably someone's friend or family member. It is what it is. Take it as another check on my long list of karma debts."

Daegan's jaw flexed. Cai suspected he was still debating whether to sever him into three pieces. But at last his attention shifted back to his servant. "I think you will need the nine lives of a cat to survive that list."

"Good thing I'm so indestructible."

"Not indestructible enough," his Master replied. Then he and Jacob were helping Gideon up, supporting his considerable bulk.

Rand closed the gap between him and Cai, and this time Cai had to accept the prop or let his knees buckle. Cai was impressed he didn't whimper like one of the wolf's pups. Fuck, that sword had hurt. Worse, it had messed up the expensive shirt he'd been given to wear. That sucked.

Anwyn stepped forward, meeting Cai's gaze with her own hostile one, drawing his mind from fashion regrets.

"You will not touch him again." Despite her youth, the steel in her countenance was impressively intimidating. "He's ours. You have a problem with him, you bring it to us. That's what a vampire does."

He was going to say something unwise like "oh, so I can ask you to kill him for me?" But the pressure of Rand's hand on his arm kept the snappy and stupid retort between his lips.

That, and the truth of the hunter's words, were something Cai couldn't ignore. Gideon had become a hunter because of someone who'd killed his girl. Cai had killed a lot of humans while with the Trads and even beyond. So how many family members felt the same way about him? He wanted to care, but often didn't, as if somehow the Trads had managed to excise his human conscience.

Moments like this suggested maybe, just maybe, it was still there. It could be restored. He just wasn't sure he wanted it to be, because he couldn't handle hurting, regretting, missing, wanting, and needing something else in his life.

Now Lady Lyssa was looking his way. Great. He knew when he was about to be raked over the coals. He braced for it, but she merely asked a question.

"Are the terms of our agreement still in place? Do you intend to honor them? If you do not, I need to know now, for we'll have to send someone else after her."

There was an uncomfortable pause in the room, or maybe it was just uncomfortable for him, feeling all those eyes on him. Most of them probably expecting he was going to bail. Well, he didn't give a fuck what they thought.

"I'll bring her back if it's possible."

It was that simple. No embellishment, no grand, noble speeches, just he'd do it. Damn if he knew why.

She blinked once. Those eyes were like a green vale, containing too much for him to decipher. "Very well." She shifted her gaze to Rand. "Take your Master to your room and tend to him. Then, if Lord Brian is done with you, and you don't wish to avail yourself of the knowledge Gideon and Daegan can offer, I expect you can be on your way."

Translation: You've overstayed your welcome. Or she wanted him gone before he fucked up something else and/or got himself killed. Fine by him. He didn't want to spend another moment in this mindfuck hole than he had to.

"Blessings on your journey, Cai," she said, that unsettling look resting on him once more. "We'll all pray your efforts are successful. Jacob will give you further details on transportation."

She turned and left the room. She was big on silent departures. Cai couldn't even detect her footfalls once she left his view. It wasn't exactly a pep talk, but it also hadn't been a vote of no-confidence. Good that someone had confidence in this trip, because he wasn't feeling much of that himself.

Jacob stepped closer. Cai knew he should be on guard in case Gideon's brother wanted to retaliate in some way, but Jacob's expression was neutral.

"The van that brought you here is yours to use as far as it will take you," he said. "It has a false floor and is reinforced with certain materials to allow you to handle sunrise. Not comfortably, but it'll provide protection and speed your journey. And speed is important," he added, as if anticipating Cai rejecting Greenwald's vehicle.

"Fine." Cai didn't assume a thank you would be expected. "Since my blood's already been shed in it, it'll feel like home sweet home."

Jacob nodded, another stoic response. Cai realized he really wasn't feeling any ill will from Lyssa's servant. Tapping into Rand's instinct-driven mind, Cai found the wolf wasn't, either. Maybe it was as simple and straightforward as Gideon had stated it. A warrior understood every life he took came with a cost to bear.

Even shining that same light on himself, Cai wasn't sure he could control himself if he had to look at the vampire hunter much longer. Fortunately, Jacob had turned to the other three and they were moving toward the door, Daegan and Anwyn still supporting Gideon.

Cai stared after them, but his mind was in the past.

Lodell. He'd been a skinny vampire, tough as three-hundred-year-old beef jerky. Bright eyes the color of red clay, long, lanky dark hair he kept wrapped in strips of leather made from human skin. He wore bracelets he claimed were strung with human baby finger bones.

Though he'd told Cai later they were from the carcasses of a few racoons he'd found after predators were done with them.

It's all about appearing badass and being willing to back it up, boy. Don't matter how scared you are. How much pain you have to take. Make them believe you're tougher than they are. Don't show them any weakness...

But Lodell had shown him mercy. Sometimes in the daylight hours, he'd take Cai to bed with him in the tunnels where they'd had the Trad camp. He'd wrap his arms around Cai as he shook, sure he couldn't survive another day. But as a result of Lodell, he had.

The male had never touched him sexually, but every touch was intimate, a connection Cai hadn't had since Lodell had turned him. Because following that, Lodell was exiled to a nearby Trad camp where Cai saw him rarely. Well, he was exiled after Goddard had the male's leg cut off, making it permanent the same way they'd done Cai's missing fang. Fire and blood.

Lodell had fucking survived that, had eventually gotten away. But then died in an alley at the hands of the male Cai had just done his best to kill. A fucking human had brought down Lodell.

"We don't belong here," he said aloud, his voice strange to his own ears. "Go. We need to just go."

"All right." Rand tucked himself under Cai's arm, his own around his waist. "You'll feed and we'll go. Okay?"

"Yeah, fine." Cai didn't want anyone's help to walk, but right now he needed it. Fortunately, Rand didn't make a big deal of it, but before they passed through the door, Cai looked back into the study. Brian had stripped off his shirt and was sitting on a stool, studying his closing wound as if he was cataloging data even faster than the healing rate. Debra was setting aside the cleaning solution and cloth she'd used to clear off the blood. Her fingertips lingered on Brian's bare shoulder, and it was a nice shoulder. Cai had been right about the scientist's physique. He had a good-looking upper torso, layered with toned muscle.

"Very efficient and powerful," the scientist observed. Lifting his gaze from the wound to focus on Rand, he added, "I suspect your jaw pressure is significantly more than that of a standard wolf."

"A wolf can crush an elk's leg bone," Rand said thoughtfully. "I've never hunted anything bigger than that, so I couldn't say. Sorry, though, for using any of that pressure on you."

Brian shook his head, a light smile crossing his features. "Such things are part of our world. A day without blood and violence is a rarity. At least this time it was educational."

Yeah. Fucking educational. Cai didn't feel in the mood for conversation, so he was good with letting Rand make the good-byes.

They traversed the hall and stairway to the lower level without meeting anyone. With it being nighttime, all the vampires might be upstairs. Even Daegan, Gideon and Anwyn might have chosen an upstairs room to help the hunter recuperate.

When they reached the bedroom, Rand found a towel in the bathroom, spread it on the bed, then eased Cai down on it to protect the linens. Cai wouldn't have thought of it. The wolf was more civilized than he was. Though Cai *had* picked up the night table and chairs, set them where he thought they had been, before he left to meet Brian.

"I still want to kill him. Don't think I could stay here and see him, and not do that."

"I get that. That's why we'll go, soon as you're ready." Rand slid onto the bed next to him, over him, curling his arm around Cai's shoulders to lift him more securely into the cradle of his burly arms. It put Cai's head on his chest, an unsettlingly nurturing pose, but Rand acted matter-of-fact about it. At Cai's look, Rand shrugged. "Throat's the strongest source, close to the heart, right? Better than the wrist?"

"That's not what I'm concerned about. Far as I know, the side effect of a fucked-up third marking is not warm and fuzzy feelings toward the vampire. Unless you're one of those whacked personality types that gets all forgiving and gooey when the guy you're pissed at is suddenly weak and needy. Not that that's what I am at the moment. But it might appear that way..."

He trailed off at the light in Rand's eye. "You're laughing at me. I'm going to punch you in the nuts."

"No." Rand shook his head, and that light disappeared, but it settled into a rueful twist of his firm lips. "It's not that. And if you punch me in the nuts, I'll twist yours off."

"Yeah, right." But Cai gave him a closer scrutiny. Rand was still holding him, the hand curved around Cai's back moving in an absent up and down caress of his upper arm. Well, hell. He could just reach into Rand's head, right? Figure out what was happening. Was he too chickenshit to do that?

Lyssa had told him a vampire could tear a servant's soul in half by delving too deep, in the wrong way. Rape Rand's soul, strip his mind. So yeah, maybe after the fucked marking, Cai was a little gun shy.

He didn't want to hurt Rand, more than life already had. As Rand stayed lost in his own thoughts, Cai's attention dropped to Rand's other forearm, lying loosely on Cai's abdomen. Cai reached for it, gripped and turned it over to look at the scar on Rand's wrist.

He'd intended to use it as a validation of his own thoughts. Instead he stilled, staring down at an indelible mark that had changed.

Well, not exactly. The disturbing scar the shifter carried was still present—the third mark hadn't made it disappear as Cai had wondered if it would—but now there was something over it. Something that looked a lot like a figure eight brand, a raised, precise design.

"There's one here, too." Rand lifted the other hand from Cai's arm so he could see Rand's left wrist. The new mark was also over the old scar, and looked like a tongue of flame, with some discoloration of the skin that enhanced the effect.

"Son of a bitch. That's the third mark." At Rand's quizzical look, Cai explained. "Along with the internal effects of the third mark, there's a permanent mark that comes up on the servant's skin. Never fades." He colored a little under Rand's amused look, realizing he sounded like he was reading from a book. "Lyssa gave me some Servant 101. She said it usually has some symbolism to it. The number eight have any meaning to you? Or something that looks like fire?"

Rand's brow furrowed, but he shook his head.

"It could be bullshit," Cai said. "Just a mark that doesn't mean anything."

But it did odd things to him, seeing evidence that the third mark was true...and permanent. He needed blood. He was getting weird and maudlin.

"Drink," Rand said.

Cai's head lifted. He and the wolf were nearly eye to eye. "That's what it is," he said abruptly, stiffening. He pushed up straight, made himself sit up and face Rand. "You're in my head. You can read my mind, same as I can read yours."

He was sure of it, even though all his vampire senses said his mind was closed to Rand, that he was only letting him hear what he wanted him to hear. And the expression on Rand's face confirmed it.

"Yes and no," Rand said. "You're not reading mine right now. You think you'll do something wrong again and break my brain."

Cai blinked. Rand's lips twitched, and the shifter lifted a shoulder. "Shifters read emotions, body language…energy. We can pull it together and pretty closely translate it into what someone's thinking. Almost as accurate as having a link to someone's mind. So I'm not in your mind," he corrected Cai. "I'm reading everything about you, basically, and translating it into thought. Difference between your mark and my abilities is I have to be close to you to do it. Have to have your scent first and foremost, and then sight and hearing help feed the intuition sensors, so to speak."

"Ah." Cai digested that. "How does that factor into you being okay with me now, instead of pissed off?"

"I wasn't angry with you. I was freaked out. I had to run, to clear my head. I did. And I heard everything you thought at me. That's a nice perk to your ability. I can't telegraph to you with mine." Rand sighed. "I realized it's all just a kick in the ass from fate, you know. Losing my family, getting shot by the hunter, you and me crossing paths, this girl needing us. I realized I can't figure any of it out. I can only follow what I know is right. And trying to get Dovia back to her family is right. Might not fix anything inside me, but it's better than running around the forest by myself, wallowing in self-pity. Sheba and Dylef would have been ashamed of me."

"No." Cai's reaction to that was instantaneous. "I mean, okay, fuck it, what do I know about family? But my guess is they loved you, much as you loved them. You're allowed to grieve."

"Maybe." Rand shrugged, and there were shadows in his gaze, that grief still there, but mixed with other things. "But I think you were my wakeup call to do something better with my life."

"Wow. Pretty sure I've never inspired anyone to that. Think I was just hitching a ride on your bitch slap wakeup call."

Rand's brow quirked and he looked down. Cai realized he'd reached out, rested his hand on Rand's thigh. He'd wanted some kind of contact, apparently, and his mind hadn't even asked what he thought about it. Just done it.

Cai took his hand away. "Break your brain? It's already broken. Dumbass wolf."

Rand smiled, and it was a sweet gesture, irresistible because the shifter had no idea how it made Cai feel, seeing him smile with ease again. It also made Cai want to be in the shifter's head, see what was happening.

"Then do it. You're not going to break me, vampire. I'm way tougher than your kind."

"I'm sorry; who found who, shot by a hunter?"

"Who practically carried you to this bed?"

"You did not carry me," Cai contested, but they were both grinning like loons. "Ah fuck it."

It was like taking a jump into a swimming hole on a hot day, something he wanted to do, but there was that hesitation for fuck-knew-why reason, before you committed yourself to gravity.

There. He was in Rand's mind, and all the words that Rand had spoken, they were there. Truths, a mix of shadows and light, so many pathways, and all of them ones Cai could follow, explore. Bound. They were soul bound.

Maybe other vampires would have reacted differently to what Cai had figured out and Rand had revealed, but Cai didn't think it was such a bad deal for Rand to be able to read him almost as accurately as Cai could do the same, even if they were going at it different ways. He didn't mind having a level playing field with the shifter. In certain ways.

Rand didn't respond to that. Not with words. He was still reclined on the bed the way he'd been when Cai had been in the curve of his arm. All that brawn was propped on one elbow, denim cupping and stretching over his lower body the right way. The shifter considered him, then slowly flattened his palm on the mattress, moved it forward and back, a short, inviting stroke.

I liked holding you when you were about to drink from my throat. Liked the way you felt there.

Rand didn't have two centuries of carefully cultivated emotional suppression that would make him pretend like he didn't want something he did. Something that shot an arrow straight into someone else's heart.

Cai was wrapped up in Rand's thoughts. Did the wolf realize he had no context for the softer side of sex? Intimacy and caring...

"Then don't get bogged down in that," Rand said quietly. "Just come and take the blood your servant is offering."

The words rippled through nerves, over his skin. Cai reached forward, touching Rand's face, sliding fingertips along his jaw. When Rand started to lift his hand, Cai shook his head. The shifter paused, then put it down, remaining still as Cai slid his touch down, using the pressure of his thumb to tell Rand what he wanted.

Rand tipped his head up, his body sinking back onto the bed. Cai could play hard to get, though it really wasn't his style. But taking charge of things...that was a different matter.

Stretching out beside him, Cai put his hand up against the other side of Rand's throat, his fingers curling into his broad shoulder.

He'd liked it when Rand was holding him. He wouldn't go that route now, because he was feeling too exposed, but as he closed his eyes, Cai remembered Rand leaning over him, a welcome shelter of heat and blood, his long brown hair brushing Cai's face and neck.

Cai knew blood was blood, but vampires did seem to get more... emotional sustenance taking from the throat. He'd leave it to nerds like Brian to figure out why. He didn't care to question it. All that mattered was Rand's scent, the taste of him so temptingly close in that beating artery.

No other conversation was needed. He bit, and Rand slid an arm all the way around him, holding Cai tight as he drank deep. He admonished himself not to take more than he needed, but God, the male's blood was like vanilla-scented sex. Rand wasn't immune to the effect, either. His hand slid down Cai's back, pressed into the small of it, large fingers curling over the top of his buttocks. Just that light caress sent tingles of sensation right to Cai's balls. Cai made an approving noise in his throat. He wouldn't mind grabbing Rand's ass with both hands, but his fingers were occupied tangling in the male's hair, and feeling heated skin and the pulse of his blood in Rand's shoulder and throat.

Rand adjusted again, this time moving them onto their sides, and then, yes, Cai let the wolf move them so he was on his back and Rand was over him, his hair brushing Cai's face and shoulder as Cai drank from his throat and explored his broad shoulder and back, dug his fingers into his waist, through the T-shirt Rand was wearing.

When he realized he was seeking the intimacy over the lust, it should have freaked Cai the fuck out, but he ignored that and took the gift. He'd been stabbed by a katana. He was allowed one weak moment.

After a time, he closed the wound and lay back, gazing up at the wolf. Rand stayed canted over him, hand resting on Cai's hip bone. Cai's shoulder was tucked in under Rand's propped elbow and wall of chest.

"I'm sorry, Rand. About the third mark thing. I really am an ass."

"Yeah, you are." Rand didn't sound all that bothered about it, and his furrowed brow said he'd moved on to other things. "I think one of us should talk to Daegan and Gideon about strategy. If their experiences would give us an advantage with the girl, I think that's worth it. I can go see them. If the information isn't useful, we've only lost a few moments. If it is, it's more we have in our arsenal."

Cai sighed. "Yeah. Why don't you go do that and I'll rest up here? I should be good to go in about an hour."

Rand rose. "Don't leave without me. I'll just track you down."

It was an intentional regurgitation of the threat Cai had used against him when Rand was recovering from the hunter's bullet wound. Cai was absurdly reassured by the attempt at teasing, and gave him back some of the same in his head.

Yeah, good luck with that, your four feet against a V6 engine.

It felt good to talk inside his head, and there was an even easier quality to it than he'd experienced with the second mark. Rand recognized it, too.

Cai wouldn't leave him here, but that tiny corner of his soul that wasn't a selfish bastard wished he could keep Rand from going with him into the bowels of the Trad world. And bowels was exactly the right word. They'd be neck deep in shit, with nothing but their wits and bare hands to survive it. Let alone rescue a girl who was likely already dead.

He was a complete dumbass for agreeing to do this.

CHAPTER ELEVEN

*T*hey took their leave with little fanfare. Cai had no interest in a tearful parental admonition from Leona, and veiled threats from Georg would just piss him off. Rand had returned from his meet with Gideon and Daegan with tactical information about approaches and exit strategies that were unexpectedly helpful to the plan Cai was formulating in his mind. They'd given Rand a burner phone he or Cai could use to report location updates. Daegan and Gideon would be following behind them, staying near as possible without spooking the Trad enclave.

"They get that they can't be too close," Rand had told Cai. "But they'd rather be twenty-five miles away instead of a few hundred, if we need backup."

It made sound sense, though Cai avoided admitting it. "Okay," he said. "Long as they understand we have a far better chance getting her out if Goddard and his bunch have no fucking clue anyone's in the area looking for her."

"They do."

Cai didn't want Gideon involved in any of this, but a human who could hunt vampires effectively would know the meaning of the word stealth. Cai couldn't deny that. And he expected Daegan was like a shadow himself.

He and Rand left out the kitchen entrance, because it was the quickest way to the van that had been pulled up to the house. Cai noted someone had courteously cleaned the interior, so not even a whiff of his blood was detectable. "You know, if being Voltaire's muscle-brained bitch doesn't work out, you have a promising career in cleaning crime scenes," he told Chavez, who handed over the keys.

"Fuck you. Just bring her back," Chavez said. "Or we'll hunt you down and what I did to you will feel like the best day of your life.'

"More threats. How original. Do me a favor and stand directly behind the van as we're pulling out."

Chavez sneered. "Georg's desperate if he's asking some scumbag Trad for help. You can say you aren't one all you want." His nostrils flared. "Smells like one, acts like one, is one."

"Better that than a bunch of sycophants pretending to care about his daughter being rescued, when what you really hope is she isn't. Then you can fight over his job when he falls to pieces."

Chavez's jaw clenched, along with his fists, and Cai braced himself for another match. He was fortified with Rand's blood and he wanted some payback. He also wouldn't mind spilling off some of the tension that was building up in him. If Chavez had had to face the things Cai had faced with Goddard, he'd shit himself three different ways, curl up in a ball and call for his mommy. Cai had been down that road, so he knew it was true.

He took a step forward, encouraging Chavez. But Chavez's gaze shifted past him, toward the kitchen door, and he backed off. Cai could feel her there, Lady Lyssa, but he pretended not to see her. Rand could handle the niceties.

Cai really didn't want to talk to anyone, feel the weight of anyone else's expectations. This would either work or it wouldn't. A bunch of words wouldn't change anything.

He handed the keys to Rand and climbed into the back. He wasn't completely recovered from the wound in his chest so, even though it was still a few hours from dawn, he'd probably take a nap in the back seat for the full re-charge while Rand handled the driving.

Despite all the other possible drawbacks to this evening, one thing pleased Cai. The third mark had given Rand the extra boost needed. There was no evidence, inside or out, of Rand's previous injuries from the hunter.

On the down side of things, Cai saw the queen coming toward the van and stifled a muttered curse. Figuring Rand wouldn't obey him if he told him to peel out before she could get there, Cai slouched down in the seat behind him. Jacob was with her and offered Rand a zipped tote through the driver's open window. "Some food for the trip," he said. "To help keep you both fortified."

Rand nodded his thanks. Jacob turned and rolled back the passenger side door of the van for Lyssa. Cai stayed in the same position, pretending to be half asleep. He could feel Rand's wincing disapproval. Yeah, some part of Cai might want to straighten and assume a more respectful pose, but he seemed to have a contrary side that refused to let him do things the easy way.

"There's no need for a send-off," Cai said gruffly. "My chances of failure are astronomical. I'll send your girl back to you if I can get her. But I don't expect to cross your path again."

"Pity. I was planning a ticker tape parade down Madison Avenue if you succeeded." Lyssa's gaze held a touch of dangerous humor. "Give me your hand."

She put her own out, palm up. Cai paused, but then shrugged and complied. Her fingers were slim and strong. She wore a small ring on one, a whimsical trinket, rather than the expensive heirloom he'd expect. It was pewter, with a small fairy design.

"Creation magic is a powerful thing," she said. "You've experimented with it some, but because the Trads wished to exploit it, you've done your best to explore it as little as possible. Am I correct?"

Cai lifted a noncommittal shoulder and she made an equally neutral noise. "Don't overlook its use as a weapon or ally where needed. Such magic is hard to quantify and often opens your path to other abilities you didn't know you had."

There was a noticeable energy in her palm, that met a similar energy in his own. As she lifted her hand, Cai blinked at the sight of a small rosebud clasped between them, still glowing with the combined energies that had created it. Lyssa smiled at his startled look, and she released him, leaving the rose in his hand.

"You are an angry person, Cai," she said softly. "With many dark spaces and things to resolve. But I believe you're also a good and honorable male."

"No offense, but if you think that, you're a rotten judge of character."

"It's not your behavior which has told me this, but his." She nodded to Rand. "He wouldn't follow one not worthy of it."

He snorted. "He's even more of a dysfunctional mess than I am. I wouldn't trust his judgment, either."

That touch of humor came and went again, and she stepped back. "Do your best, Mordecai, and you'll have my gratitude. As well as Lord Greenwald's. You may not seek friends, but we often need them in the world. Goddess keep you."

Jacob moved to close the door, but Cai straightened and handed the rose back to Lyssa. "For safe keeping," he said. "Nothing beautiful should be going where we're going."

She sobered. "I'll keep it safe and growing until your return, and we'll put it by Dovia's bedside together."

Cai had no reply to that. He practically sighed in relief when Jacob closed the door. Taking that as his cue, Rand turned over the engine and put the van in gear.

A glance in the rear-view mirror showed the wolf looking...optimistic. The little magic show had apparently given Rand a needed spike of hope. Cai wished it was possible to borrow the feeling.

Though it was a couple hours to daylight, a pre-dawn mist cloaked the asphalt drive up to the house. It was peaceful and quiet here, the air flavored by the nearby active horse farms; grass, glossy flanks and the oddly not unpleasant faint odor of manure.

"So where should we drop off the van?" Rand ventured when they reached the turnoff to the highway.

Cai gave him a mental map of the national park he had in mind. "Once we reach that part of West Virginia, that's where we'll hit the hiking trails, then leave those behind. If humans have seen Goddard's group and lived to tell the tale, they'll be classified as some kind of anti-government, off-the-grid types. Which, multiply that by a crazy power of three, and you have Trads. Throw in a few doses of total psycho serial killer mentality and that's Goddard. He's a warm and fuzzy guy. We should bring him some Girl Scout cookies as a peace offering. Or just Girl Scouts. Even better. Now, tell me about this shifter pack you think is nearby."

Rand glanced up at him in the mirror. "Good memory."

"Hey, I'm the guy who remembered fucking you was on my to do list, even when I was interrupted by a several hour beating." Cai tapped his forehead. "Mind like a steel trap."

"More like a lump of iron," Rand scoffed, but he answered Cai's question. "Several years ago, a family I knew lived in that area. We lost contact, but if they're still there, it's possible they could help us locate Goddard faster. They tend to keep track of human or humanoid movement."

"Why didn't you go looking for them after you lost your own pack?"

"It doesn't work that way." Rand shook his head. "You have to observe the proper protocols, be invited. I wasn't ready for any of that."

"Huh." Cai watched him in the mirror. Rand switched lanes, passing a farm truck. The passing margin was narrow enough that, less than a blink later, an oncoming semi passed them, rocking the van with its concussion. "You know," Cai observed, "I forgot to ask how long it's been since you've driven a vehicle. This is a little different from a commercial mower."

"The concept is the same," Rand said, unruffled. "Just faster."

Cai grunted. His eyelids were drooping, but he forced them to stay open a little longer.

"End-of-the-earth West Virginia is a big area. Why do you think that pack will have crossed paths with our merry band of Trads?"

"Fane had traveled there in his younger years, taken pictures. He and Lynn showed them to us when they visited us in Colorado. Some of the geographical features you discussed looked like what was in those pictures. He also described the area, in case they did get their wish to live there and we tried to find them."

"You were close with them," Cai noted.

"Yes. A long time ago." Rand lifted an uncomfortable shoulder. "But after Grey...I think Dylef, Sheba and I were afraid to make old contacts, bring trouble to anyone's door. Plus, once we settled in a more human-inhabited area, there were the pups to consider...just the daily demands, and then Dylef and my relationship wasn't something we felt like hiding, and we weren't sure how Fane and Lynn would feel about it. The years stretched out. We should have gone to see them."

The reasons not to have done so seemed ridiculous now. Rand

pushed away the too-familiar surge of guilt and continued. "Most shifters do live primarily as humans, though on the fringes of towns and cities, so they can let their wolves run. This pack that might be near where these Trads are...I guess you could say Fane and Lynn are the wolf version of Trads, in their preference to be more wolf than human, though they do maintain connections in the human world. Their children have sought professions in those worlds, while the parents have stayed in the forest. Fane runs a home-building company that specializes in mountain get-aways, vacation homes, which lets him stay on the fringes of the deeper forest he prefers."

"Sounds like the perfect fit for you," Cai persisted. "You prefer to be more wolf than human, and I expect he could find a place for you on one of his building crews."

"It's not that simple," Rand repeated, with a touch of impatience. "Even beyond protocols, there's a probationary period. Some are immediately rejected as a threat."

No matter that he looked as if he was half-asleep, the vampire proved his brain was sharp and alert as he put it together. "There's room for only one alpha, and you're definitely an alpha."

"A sterile one, for all intents and purposes," Rand said, though it hurt to say it that way.

"One that won't snake in on another alpha's territory."

"No. And what I am, who I am...it's confusing to the way a wolf pack works. Wolves like continuity, consistency. Things that make sense. When a leader is already in place, but pack members begin to defer to me, it causes problems, even if I'm not making a play for the leadership. Because..."

"Because one of the main roles of the alpha male is mating with the alpha female. You did it with Sheba. You can't fake it enough to find yourself a place?"

Rand kept his eyes on the road. "You should rest. You're not at full strength yet and the sun will rise in a couple hours."

"None of my business. Got it." But Rand could feel Cai's eyes resting on him before he stretched out behind the second set of seats. A rattling, and the sound of the floor trapdoor opening, told Rand the vampire had decided to avail himself of the space between the actual and false floors. Earth packed in the walls around the cramped space made it possible for a mature vampire to travel during sunlight. While

Jacob had warned that it wouldn't be incredibly comfortable, at least Cai was used to digging himself into the earth, so the familiar scent might make it less uncomfortable for him than for most vampires.

Rand turned his mind to the pack he'd discussed with Cai. The last time they'd crossed paths had been out in Colorado, before Sylvan had died. Lynn's aging mother was in West Virginia, so Fane and she had decided to move back there. They'd been part of a California pack, but the dynamic in that was changing, growing too large, and they were ready to split off with their offspring and form their own. Lynn had sent Sheba a postcard shortly before Grey's invasion, noting that her mother had passed and they were going to move deeper into the woods. Go off grid, as she and Fane had longed to do for some time. Their two litters were growing up strong and healthy, the foundation to a good family pack.

When he, Dylef and Sheba had to cut and run, they'd played with the idea of tracking Fane and Lynn down, but they'd detoured to Tennessee when Dylef had the good job opportunity there with the Park Service. Since Sheba and Dylef both gravitated toward the human world, Rand had followed their wishes because he loved them.

If he'd tried harder to get them to join Fane, they'd have had more protection. So many pointless what ifs. It was what it was. To Cai it was all about practical considerations. Go join this pack. Do this, do that. Yet when Rand was close to another wolf shifter, the memories of Dylef, Sheba and the pups crowded in, so hard he could barely breathe. Seeing another pack play and touch, rub against one another, run together...

If the hunter had shot him in the chest three times, it could not hurt worse than how Rand felt when he remembered those things.

Cai's initial reluctance to get back into Rand's head meant that he'd missed why Rand had been able to accept the third mark so readily—after they got past the Split part, that is. It was a way to be in a pack a different way, bonded to the vampire. It helped ease that ache in Rand's chest, without taking him too close to the jagged grief that made him worry he wasn't ever going to be strong enough to get that close to his own kind again.

Cai was right. Lone wolves didn't exist except where one was too injured or broken to be part of the pack. Or, in the case of a shifter, one who had no idea where he belonged anymore. Or if Rand could bring himself to want to belong.

He started as an arm slid over his chest. Cai rested his chin on the seat back. Rand had been so deep in his head, he hadn't heard the vampire emerge again. Cai's fingers tunneled inside his shirt, caressing his chest. He didn't say anything. Didn't indicate whether he'd heard Rand's thoughts. Just sat there and stroked while Rand drove. He stayed that way until the sun started to threaten the horizon with glimmers of rose and gold light. Then Cai squeezed his pectoral lightly, offered a teasing caress of his nipple, and withdrew, putting himself beneath the false floor again.

Rand drew a steadying breath and decided to fish around in the bag for food. It was better than thinking about what it all meant. He found a pack of homemade cookies and several ham sandwiches, and ate them all, which also helped. Food always did, but the quiet solidarity of a very unpredictable and hard to understand vampire had as well.

By late afternoon, Rand had reached their destination, a national park where the hiking trails would start leading them deep into the mountains and beyond the touch of human civilization. He parked in a corner of the lot and laid the seat back, intending to catch some sleep before twilight. He used the burner phone to text Gideon where the van would be and their current location. Greenwald's cronies would probably come and pick it up.

As Rand drifted toward a doze, he thought about his earlier conversation with Daegan and Gideon. Both of them were hunters, in every sense of the word. Despite the earlier confrontation with Cai, Rand had felt comfortable in their presence. He thought Gideon would have made a pretty good wolf. He'd also been honest with Cai about his understanding of Cai's actions, for when Gideon opened the door for Rand at their quarters, Rand had scented no lingering antipathy toward the absent vampire.

Anwyn was curled up on the couch in their suite, a glass of wine close to hand and a book on her lap. She wore a light robe that clung to her curves and suggested that the two vampires had found other ways to restore Gideon's strength.

Gideon was putting on a fresh shirt when Rand arrived; he'd opened the door with it unbuttoned and open. He'd already changed into a non-bloodstained pair of jeans and, though the wound was still angry and red, it was knitting and Gideon looked steady on his feet. Daegan's blood had restored him quickly.

The female vampire appeared wary of Rand, but didn't show the open hostility she had toward Cai. "Is your Master healing?" she asked politely, surprising him.

"He's not my Master, but yes." Despite the assertion, Rand felt an unmistakable satisfaction, knowing his own blood had provided equal benefit to Cai.

"Good. Means he'll be leaving sooner than later," she said.

"You're always saying I need to be taken down a peg or two," Gideon pointed out to her. "Some vamp has the *cojones* to do it; excellent fast strike, by the way"—Gideon tossed that to Rand—"and you get mad at him."

"Call it the capriciousness of women," she said, an edge to her voice.

"The craziness, you mean." He snorted, but his expression upon her was fond. Daegan sat in another chair, cleaning and sharpening that sword. He nodded to Rand without speaking.

It put Rand in an odd place. Cai wouldn't want him making apologies or excuses for him, and it wasn't Rand's place to do so. Yet this world had so many unfamiliar protocols for vampires and servants. He didn't know if showing up like this to get the information they'd been invited to have would be considered rude, since it was the servant who had come for it, instead of the vampire.

Gideon's relaxed behavior helped ease Rand's mind on it, particularly as he spoke again. "When I wasn't worrying about my heart getting ripped out of my chest, I noticed you're a good fighting team. You slid in there almost seamlessly to take on Brian. Good thing you didn't crush his arm. Lyssa's almost as fond of that geek as she is of Jacob.

"You should do some of that," Gideon continued thoughtfully. "Spar with a pair like me and Daegan so you can coordinate moves and tactics. It's done wonders for my fighting style when I'm with him."

He nodded to Daegan. The vampire had sheathed the sword, the scabbard balanced on his knees as he watched the conversation with an unreadable expression.

Rand remembered hunting with Dylef, moving together as one, cornering a deer, bringing down the creature with the help of Sylvan's offspring, to feed Sheba when she was pregnant. "I'll keep it in mind. Is that some of the information you want to share with me?"

"Yeah. We'll go over some other stuff. If Cai's as well-versed with the Trads as he said, he's right. He doesn't need a lot of direction from us on that part, but I suspect this is the first time he's going in with backup, so most of our suggestions will have to do with different extraction scenarios and working as a team. I get the feeling that's not been his forte in the past."

Rand was out of practice himself. Except for the disastrous fight with Grey and his betas to help Sheba and her pups escape in Colorado, he and Dylef had never refined their team hunting skills for combat. Though if they had, and had later drawn the teenagers into that training, maybe they would have held their own better against Grey.

Earth and stone, his guilt was a festering wound that never healed. Ignoring it to give full attention to what might be beneficial for Dovia's rescue, he listened intently to Daegan and Gideon for the next half hour. He kept part of his mind open to Cai during that time, sensing his presence and proximity, and verifying he was still resting. Rand didn't want the vampire to take off without him. That was why he kept touching that connection.

That was what he told himself.

Returning to the present, Rand realized he'd drifted off. It was twilight. As he let himself come fully awake, he stretched, then ate the last of the cookies. Vending machines were placed by the restrooms, and they advertised coffee. Probably didn't taste all that good, but it was coffee. He left the vehicle to get himself and Cai some. After he returned, he sat and sipped from his cup, watching the last few hikers and dogwalkers emerge from the woods and head off for the night. It wasn't long before he heard the rasp of the trapdoor opening.

He handed the full and still steaming cup over his shoulder without looking, smiling a little as it was taken from his hand.

"You know," a grumpy voice said, "technically caffeine has no proven effect on vampires."

"I saw that study in the latest Scientific American," Rand said. "But I figured you might like the taste."

He handed back several sugar packets and one cream. A pause, then those were also removed from his grip, the vampire's fingers brushing his.

"Okay, that's creepy damn specific mind reading, wolf."

"Now you know how I feel, having you crawling around in my head."

"Wise ass." A rattle of paper as Cai added the condiments. "For all we know, Lord Brian has submitted articles to Scientific American. Vampire scientists. Next thing, there will be vampire lawyers, a redundant term in so many ways."

The pause drew out as they drank coffee and watched the night darken.

"You want to kill him, but you don't hate him, do you?" Rand asked. "Gideon. Because you get it."

Silence. Rand wisely said nothing for a few minutes, letting Cai sip his coffee.

"Yeah," the vampire said. "But you said you have a code. It's like that, right? I may get why he did it, but he still killed someone whose death I feel like I should avenge, because Lodell did me a solid."

Rand glanced back. The vampire's hair was tousled from his sleep, his blue eyes annoyed, his mouth set in a line. The line of questioning was bugging him. On a whim, Rand leaned back and brushed his mouth over his, tasting coffee and Cai. He used his thumb to remove some of the coffee residue from his lip. The blue eyes flickered in surprise.

"You have a strange sense of honor," Rand observed. "You kill humans to feed, but you avenge your sire because of the kindness he showed you, and we're here, going after a female vampire you feel certain is dead or wishes she was."

"That's because you're considering it from your human side. Think like a wolf," Cai advised. "Have you ever seen a rabbit in a meadow, nibbling on a tasty flower, enjoying a sunny day? That's a happy creature. He could die in a second, has probably seen lots of his family and fellow rabbits caught and killed, so he enjoys that moment. Versus humanoids, so caught up in baggage, they can't feel the sun shine on their faces. Even if it was half the distance it is to earth and fried them like an egg."

"You're a vampire. You don't feel the sun."

"Okay, go with moonlight, or a fucking sun lamp. You know what I'm trying to say. Don't worry about my contradictions. Humans will stop being annoying before you can figure those out. Focus on that meadow. Sunny pep talk over."

Cai exited the car, crumpling up the cup and tossing it in the trash as he shouldered the pack Jacob had also provided them. It was stocked with changes of clothing and other supplies, like Lord Brian's vials and gum.

Rand shook his head, but followed his lead. He thought about offering to carry the pack, but after his nap, Cai looked as if he was suffering no residual effects from the katana. Vampires really did have spectacular healing powers. Or Cai was right about shifter blood. Or both.

They locked the van and left it behind. Within a few miles, Cai stopped, checked his compass, and left the trail to head into the unmarked terrain. It was full dark now, their eyes gleaming in the moonlight. Rand began to unbutton his shirt. "Mind carrying these clothes in the pack, in case I end up needing them?"

Cai squatted to his heels, back against a tree, gazing upon him as if he had hours to watch Rand strip. "Nope."

Rand eyed him. "Don't you ever get tired of sex?"

"Vampires have to be dead to be tired of sex. Even then, they're probably checking out the available action in the line to the Pearly Gates." The vampire tossed him a bland look that concealed none of the sensual intent behind his steady gaze.

Snorting, Rand stripped off shirt, jeans, shoes, socks and underwear, folded them neatly and brought them to put in the pack. Cai accommodated that, then his gaze slid up Rand's tall, bare form. "What if I did want sex?" the vampire asked pleasantly. "If I demanded it?"

Rand shook his head. "I don't take orders from you."

"Only a pack leader, hmm?"

Rand nodded. "That's the way it works." He knew Cai was thinking about the thoughts Rand had had a few hours ago, about the third mark and its appeal as a substitute pack. Then it had made the vampire come to him, stroke him, share a silent companionship. Which was nice. But he was going down another road now, making Rand respond a different way. Provocation had several meanings, after all.

Cai glanced around. "I don't see a pack here. Didn't see any at Greenwald's house, either. Just a lot of vampires circling one another like suspicious dogs."

"Some of them seemed pretty well bonded with their servants."

Cai shook his head. "Vampires can't have relationships with their servants. You heard Brian. Want to be my property, able to do only what I say?"

Neither Jacob, Gideon nor Debra had seemed like slaves, though it was undeniably a far more extreme form of Dominant and submissive relationship than humans sometimes embraced. It had a stronger echo in the structure of a wolf pack; however, except for packs led by those like Grey, anyone could leave at any time, if they didn't agree with the structure. Like Fane and Lynn. So maybe it was different.

But there was an odd look in the vampire's gaze. Something was going on in Cai's head, and for once Rand couldn't quite work it out. Which meant it was something beyond his understanding, no point of reference.

"We should get going," Rand said mildly, and moved away, preparing to shift. He'd ponder it while they traveled.

The vampire leaped for him, an elegant, powerful move, like a dragon exploding into flight. He tackled Rand and they rolled across the ground, with Cai ending up on top, Rand on his stomach in a pin.

"What the—" Rand turned, fought, and they rolled further down the slope, collecting leaves and dirt as they went. Rand cursed as sticks poked him in tender, unclothed places.

The vampire had an edge on him tonight, because Rand had been driving while Cai had been sleeping. Rand threw an elbow and slipped a headlock, only to find himself back on his stomach again, Cai's hands locked on his wrists, the vampire's weight sitting on his ass.

Rand huffed out a breath and eyed him, his cheek on the forest floor. The vampire looked a little too appealing, his eyes glittering in the dark, mouth in a firm line. He was like a live wire on Rand's back, energy vibrating from him.

"Thought you didn't believe in the owned-soul stuff." Rand decided to address his last statement, and underscored it by fanning out and wiggling his fingers above Cai's manacled grip.

Cai's eyes registered the motion, but he brought his attention back to Rand's face. "I never said that. I said that's what vampires believe about their servants. I've never had a servant, so it's all new to me." He leaned down and whispered against Rand's ear. His breath rasped, heated and rough. "Truth is, I'm starting to appreciate the idea more and more."

He straightened, stripped off his shirt and tossed it over a branch. Then Rand heard his belt clink as he removed it. Cai leaned down over him, wearing only the jeans.

"I want to fuck a beast, but only the kind with two legs, lots of hair and muscles, and tan, tan skin." Cai's lips moved over his shoulder, his back. The vampire wasn't going right for the ass or cock. Which made the sensations sliding along Rand's skin even more potent.

A fang slid over Rand's flesh, the tip a sharp prick on his shoulder blade. Cai paused, lifting his head. "While you're with me, *we* are a pack. I *am* your alpha, Rand. You decide it's done, you leave, that's the way you wolves are. But in my world, it's done when I say it's done. When the alpha says it's done. Kind of interesting, the way you and I straddle that line."

The vampire could do things with his hands and mouth that only demons could do, Rand was sure. It was the touch of his lips and the whisper of his breath at the right moment, along the column of his spine, his nape, his jaw. He'd never particularly thought of that as an erogenous zone until a fang with its threat of delicious penetration scraped against it. Cai was good at taking decisions away, making it impossible for Rand to do anything but what the vampire desired. That they both desired. Two sides of the same coin.

As Cai slid his cheek alongside Rand's, Rand turned the tables. He put his mouth over Cai's, not so much like a kiss, but as if he was covering Cai's mouth so he could bite his lips gently, above, below. In wolf form, he would do such playful nips when feeling like mating, or expressing affection. He'd put his leg over the neck of the wolf to reinforce it.

"What are you doing?" Rand murmured against Cai's flesh.

"We're in the forest and you were going to shift to wolf. Figured it would be too long before I'd get another chance at your ass."

Rand nuzzled his cheek, the bridge of Cai's nose, pleased when the vampire dipped his head to allow it. "I think you underestimate how good you are at this," Rand said quietly. "And how long it's been since I've been touched."

Cai's head came up, their eyes locking. The heat that gripped the vampire's gaze met a matching surge of need in Rand, so immediate and fierce, Rand knew it had to reflect on his face. "Take your pleasure now *and* later, vampire. I'll serve you."

There. He could actually feel it, every time he re-affirmed that thread of connection with Cai, a vibration between the two of them like a chord echoing in a vast, endless canyon of wants and needs. He wanted to test it, pluck it again, to see if he was right.

"I heard it said a lot at Greenwald's house. But in a moment like this, if I call you Master..." Rand paused and an inexplicable satisfaction expanded inside him, enjoying the truth. "Yeah. Your fingers grip me a little tighter, your body bumps mine, and your eyes, that blue gets even bluer. It's more than just what vampires are. It's what they need. Scary predators with no pack skills, but if they can own a heart, maybe they can drop some walls and open theirs."

It's not about the ownership, Rand thought. *It's about someone willingly saying they belong to you.*

Cai went even more still, yet Rand sensed the fire beneath, the furnace of emotions. The vampire stayed in that stasis for a few more heartbeats. The heat between their two bodies seemed to only increase, as did Rand's awareness of the angles and hardness of limbs, flesh and muscle, the straining need, held barely in check. The pleasure of being so close to the edge of decision.

Cai drew back, his hand sliding along Rand's shoulder, his side, to his hip, his fingers curling in. Rand could feel him teetering between withdrawal and doing what Rand had suggested. Taking what he wanted. Rand met those blue eyes again.

"Don't be a chickenshit," he said softly.

Cai grimaced, but rueful amusement was there. Then his face reflected another type of emotion. Determination.

"Stay still," he said roughly. "Don't you move."

Rand didn't, dropping his cheek back to the ground and closing his eyes. But he listened with all his senses, as Cai open his jeans and lubed himself up with his saliva, keeping one hand on Rand's hip almost the entire time, fingers gripping as he stroked himself. He brought Rand up onto his hands and knees, and rubbed his cock between Rand's ass cheeks as he played. He kept doing it, teasing Rand, making him wait, making him feel those rhythmic movements as he worked himself against him.

Rand's arm muscles quivered, his ass and thighs tight, his balls drawn up and cock aching steel. But Cai had told him not to move and Rand obeyed.

The truth was, it turned him on. The way Cai needed to take him over, and how Rand, powerful as he was, could prove that he was a match for the vampire, yet give him that gift. Both their natures taking them to this moment.

He sensed the vampire's arousal spiking even higher, merely from feeling Rand's struggle not to push against him, insist, turn the tables and demand. In another moment, Rand *was* going to turn and roll the male, because he didn't want to wait any longer. That was part of the charge for them. Knowing that line was there, and either one of them might cross it.

Cai slid the head of his organ down between Rand's cheeks and Rand forced himself not to lift.

"Think you're having some trouble with self-control, wolf. Let me help."

The vampire reached beneath him, gripped his cock in a firm fist, and used that hold to keep him still as he began to slowly push in, stretching him.

"Try to take me, hmm? Another day, that might be an interesting fight. Not today, though. Today this tight ass is all fucking mine."

Rand let out a groan as Cai finally pushed through, sinking deep. But he did more than that. He wrapped both arms around Rand, held tight. He didn't object to Rand putting one hand over his, clasping to hold on as they moved together, an endless rhythm that built and built until they were both gasping, groaning, straining together. Cai took it up another level, sinking his fangs into his shoulder. As desire coiled around the spear of pain, Cai's tongue slid over Rand's skin, his fangs withdrawing as he licked and soothed the way a wolf might.

"Come," he muttered against Rand's flesh, his fingers tight on his cock. "I can feel how much you want to. I want you to come while I'm hard as a fucking pipe inside you, feel your ass clutch me like you'll never let go."

Rand obliged with another deep groan, hips working underneath Cai's, the two of them as tight together as spoons. The friction was unbearably erotic but the closeness even more so, such that the movements were small but the reaction all encompassing. Rand exploded, spurting over Cai's hand, against his own belly and chest. As he smelled his own musk, and sensed Cai's need reaching the same precipice, Rand went with his gut and spoke in the vampire's mind.

Now, Master. I've got you.

Cai slammed into him, a convulsive, almost involuntary movement that got faster, a jackhammer style of fucking that took the climax Rand just had to a whole other level, his cock milking out another spurt of white cream and wresting a growl from his lips. He wanted to feel Cai's muscular body moving against his, sliding and demanding, for hours and hours. He didn't want their bodies to separate, because he wanted that internal connection to continue. It had expanded beyond a single tie to a full, thick ribbon that unfurled between the two of them, inside hearts and souls, covering and holding every pain and regret in stasis.

He hadn't been so overwhelmed by sex since he was a teenager. Rand still had his fist knotted over Cai's on his chest, and was down on one elbow, reminding himself to breathe. Cai's mouth was on the back of his neck, his heart thundering.

"We can't..." Cai drew a shuddering breath. "We can't do that when we meet the Trads."

Rand managed a half chuckle. "I wasn't planning on seducing you while we were in the middle of a rescue."

Cai shook his head, and held Rand a little tighter. His face dropped, pressing between Rand's shoulder blades. Rand felt him draw an even deeper breath, a different kind of shudder going through him. A different wave of emotions starting to invade upon what they'd just done.

"I'm going in there pretending to be allies with them," Cai said, muffled. "Which means I have to act like a Trad. If you're with me as human, that means you're slave-bound to me. You hate me. I'd have to have sex with you in front of them, and you'd have to be detached... like I was forcing you. I would be forcing you."

He slid from Rand and sat back against a tree, stretching out his legs and adjusting so he could hitch the jeans back up. Rand turned on his hip. The vampire looked like he wished he hadn't said anything, that he'd let this moment be exactly what it was. But now Rand knew what had really driven the vampire. A need to be with Rand in a way that wasn't tainted by where they were going.

"So I go in with you as a wolf."

"No." Cai shook his head. "You don't go in with me at all. You stay hidden, keep an eye on what's happening, and be ready. If I can get them to trust me, we might get a window of opportunity to make a run for it, far enough to meet up with that backup before the Trads can catch up to us."

"I'm not letting you go alone."

"You aren't." Cai showed his teeth in a grim smile. "But it makes a hell of a lot more sense for you to be some wolf lurking in the trees around their camp, watching what's going on, than coming in as my abused slave, where both of us could get jammed up so neither of us could go for help."

"Will he go for your story? That you need safe haven from a Region Master?" Rand moved to sit shoulder to shoulder with him, drawing up his knees.

"Maybe." Cai reached down and plucked off a leaf stuck to Rand's hip. "Sorry about the sneak attack."

"I'm not complaining." Rand linked his arms loosely over his knees and propped his chin on one so he could look at the vampire. "What kind of reception are you expecting to get?"

"Oh, they'll throw a party, I'm sure." Cai grimaced. "I didn't tell Lyssa everything. Goddard had a female vampire. Not a captive; a masochistic made chick, one of the few willingly among the Trads. I planted a seed in her belly, because he told me to do it. I told him it wouldn't work, that I could only do it with plants. He didn't believe me. So a jungle grew up inside her, split her from the inside out."

Rand blinked. "It staked her?"

"Well, it was a woody plant," Cai said dryly. "Couldn't happen to a nicer vampire, promise. An army of harpies would be preferable."

Even so, his expression had darkened at the telling. Whatever his feelings about Goddard's mate, seeing her death had not been pretty, or brought much vindication before being replaced with a far more horror-stricken reaction.

Then the mask fell back in place and Cai spoke casually again. "I've said before this is a suicide mission. While I know you dig those, it will take both of us to get her out of there. Suicide-by-Trad is off the table until we save the girl. And if you die while saving her, then no one will ever know you got your heart's fondest wish."

Rand shook his head. "You like mocking the pain of others, vampire."

"Nope. I find my own pain just as hilarious. I'm equal opportunity." Cai sighed, then nudged him. "Go ahead and be a wolf. We'll get some more miles covered and see if we can stumble into the territory of your pack friend."

"Okay." Rand watched the vampire get to his feet. He could still feel Cai against him, hear the rough whisper against his ear. He curled his fingers around Cai's calf as he straightened.

"What?" the vampire asked, though his hand fell to Rand's hair, his shoulder, fingers curling in a brief stroke.

Rand shook his head. He expected the vampire could see what was in his head, the mix of emotions from what they'd just shared and what lay ahead. He'd simply wanted the contact, that one brief moment, to even things out.

And to remind Cai they stood at the starting line together.

It took several more hours, but then, between Rand's nose and Cai's night vision, they started to recognize some of the geographical features they'd discussed. Shortly thereafter, Rand came across familiar—and fresh—wolf markings. Fane.

Rand stopped, lifting his nose to scent the air. He yipped, a query. Cai heard nothing but silence in return, but like Rand, he sensed it when, a few minutes later, Rand registered that they were under scrutiny.

The big black wolf stopped again, only this time his body posture became stiffer, warier. Not openly aggressive, but prepared.

What's happening, wolf?

Not sure. Fane...feels different. Stay back.

Cai was tempted to toss out a comeback like *who's afraid of the big, bad wolf?* but from the wheels turning in Rand's head, Cai realized Rand wasn't worried about Fane hurting Cai. He believed the other wolf's wariness might be because Rand was in the company of a vampire, and Rand thought Cai hanging back might help the situation.

When Fane finally emerged, Cai wasn't as sure.

Fane was a gray and brown wolf. Not as big as Rand, but still a comparable size. He appeared when they reached a small open area of ground, where the wind moved the grasses so they threw finger-like shadows under the crescent moon. The same wind rippled over Fane's ruff, but otherwise, he remained stock-still. Though wolves used their noses more than their eyes, both senses seemed focused solely on Rand, not on Cai, despite Cai being visible across the clearing.

Cai squatted down next to a tree, attempting to look non-threatening. However, he watched the new wolf as closely as Fane was watching Rand. Rand's reputed friend was not projecting friendly vibes.

Rand moved forward a couple steps, ears pricked forward. Fane's tail and ears were straight up like a ramrod, and as Rand moved, Fane's lip curled, exposing glittering teeth. A rumble started in his chest.

All right, wolf. I'm being unobtrusive, but I'm not liking where this is going.

Handling this. Stay quiet.

I'm going to attribute that bossy attitude to your minimalist wolf speak and not you looking for an ass kicking.

Shut. Need focus.

Cai snorted mentally but subsided. For now.

Rand moved forward another few steps. His tail was lowered to a more horizontal position, his ears up but in more of an attitude of inquisitiveness.

Fane's growling increased, and his ears got flatter.

Rand wasn't a pussy, Cai gave him that. He curled his lip in return, offered a matching vocalization, though if Cai hazarded an interpretation, Rand's was more *what the fuck*, whereas Fane's was *get the hell off my lawn.*

Confirming it, Rand didn't press an attack, but instead sat down, then stretched out on his stomach. Though his head and shoulders were up, it was obviously a pose intended to telegraph that he wasn't here to challenge Fane's dominance. Cai recalled how Rand had done that with him in the study, and the feelings it had set off inside him.

Given the current circumstances, he didn't expect the other male to have the same reaction Cai had experienced. Fane remained wary and combative, but Rand taking the lower position seemed to reduce his aggression. He took another step into the clearing. Cai's muscles tightened, preparation if the male leaped onto Rand. He didn't think he'd moved at all, but Fane's gaze went to him, and that lip curled back again.

Yeah, you show me yours, I'll show you mine, and you can run back into the woods with your tail tucked between your legs.

Cai. Spread hands. Sit all way down.

The fuck I will.

Cai.

Cai did it. He'd already proven to Rand how quickly he could leap up from that position, so it was more the principle of the thing than giving up a strategic advantage. Fane watched him a long minute, then his gaze returned to Rand.

Rand moved forward a few inches on his belly, and made another of those yip noises. Fane stalked over to him, and Rand cocked his head. When Fane stood over him, Rand touched his muzzle to the male's, a little nip at his chin, and then drew back. He couldn't pull off submissive, but Cai admitted he did a pretty good job of communicating non-threatening and *hey, let's chat.*

Then Rand bowed his head, a ripple moving over his body, that energy wave that preceded his shifting. Fane retreated a few feet, giving him the room, and Rand was there on the ground in his human form. He rolled to a one-knee position. "Come on, Fane. Talk to me. We need your help."

Fane backed up. For a second, Cai thought he'd just take off into the woods. He saw another shiver of energy go through Rand, and knew if that happened, Rand would shift, that blur of speed where flesh became fur, to give pursuit. But it turned out that wasn't needed.

Fane shifted, and now the two men faced one another.

Cai already liked Rand being naked so much of the time. Seeing two handsome shifters wearing only a wary, we-might-have-to-fight tense posture, was double the perk.

The other male was dark-skinned. He had thin dreadlocks and piercing dark eyes. His body was sculpted muscle, tight ass, semi-erect cock, probably from the mutual show of testosterone. He had long scars across his back, five score marks like a big cat had swiped at him. Perhaps a mountain lion.

Though they could converse as humans, it seemed a silent pissing contest was still in progress. Fane's brown eyes were sharp and aggressive, body angling as if he might shift again, for offense or defense.

"What's going on, Fane?" Rand said quietly. "I come as a friend."

"That remains to be seen."

CHAPTER TWELVE

*T*hough Rand knew it had triggered Cai's battle instincts, the brief confrontation, for the most part, was standard for shifters who hadn't crossed paths in some time. A way to confirm, "Okay, I'm still the guy you knew." Fane had a pack to protect, so unlike a human, he wouldn't accept Rand unconditionally on past experiences. Not after a two-year-plus disappearance from contact with any other shifter. A lot could change a wolf during that time period.

So Rand had expected some posturing, some wariness from the pack leader. But even before Fane's cryptic comment, he could tell more was going on.

When Rand invited Fane to take a seat on a fallen log so they could talk, the shifter looked as if he might refuse. His body language remained exceptionally rigid. Since Fane kept Cai upwind and in his view, Rand might have attributed it to suspicion of another species, but Fane seemed even more suspicious of Rand.

Since Fane wasn't being forthcoming on the conversation side of things, Rand decided to start with why they were here and see if that broke anything loose in Fane's attitude. As Rand briefly explained their mission, Cai stayed sitting against the tree. Picking up a branch, he began to whittle on it with his gleaming knife, probably his attempt to look as harmless as possible.

Though the vampire could choose to shoot his mouth off at the most inauspicious times, apparently vampire authority figures triggered that trait quicker than a potential wolf ally. Rand counted it as a surprising blessing with a limited shelf life. He had no doubt, despite his disinterested façade, that Cai was listening to their exchange intently.

All that was fine. What wasn't fine was how often the vampire's gaze strayed over Fane's body with lingering appreciation as the shifter rested his elbows on his splayed knees, head bowed in concentration over Rand's words. Fane's long ropes of hair slid forward over his brown shoulders.

Cut it out, Cai. He's already acting twitchy. If he figures out you're eyeing him, he could get aggressive and less cooperative. Most wolves aren't that tolerant of males who prefer their own gender.

Sure you're not just jealous?

He suspected the vampire could tell exactly what Rand's reactions were. He couldn't help his wolf's possessiveness; it was that mating instinct again, which could be tripped even after a casual coupling. Rand knew how to recognize it, and manage it for what it was. He just wasn't used to someone being able to pick up on it. He turned his attention back to Fane.

"We've no intent of pulling your pack into this. I'm just asking if you've seen them. Cai says they're likely a small group, three to five vampires, because Trads don't like to congregate much. Especially not this group. They'd have a female vampire with them."

Fane lifted his head. For the first time, he seemed to really focus on Rand, see him, though his dark gaze shifted from Rand to Cai, and back to Rand again. When he spoke, he went a different direction, as if Rand's information had been addressing other, far more important questions he had. And he wasn't satisfied with the answers.

"Why aren't you with a pack, Rand? News travels. There was talk. It's said that you killed Grey." Fane's jaw set. "And a litter of his pups."

"What?"

Aggression and affront came quickly. Rand was off the log and taking a step toward the other shifter in mindless reaction. Fane came to his feet and Rand felt Cai tense. *I've got this.*

Then calm him down or calm yourself down, because if he goes for you, I'm not sitting out.

That was unexpected, but maybe vampires had their own streak of possessiveness. Or maybe it was just as simple as no one got to mangle a vampire's toys while he was still playing with them.

Cute. Asshole. But he could feel Cai's affront on his behalf, reinforced by the vampire's next thought. *But killing kids? Does this fucking guy know anything about you?*

It echoed Rand's sentiments, but he tried to contain his temper. "How long have you known me, Fane?" he asked, quiet and cold. "In what universe would I ever harm a pup?"

"I've known you," the male said evenly, not backing away or breaking eye contact. "But no one has seen you for over two years. I haven't seen or heard from you in longer than that. Now you show up traveling with a vampire. One whose scent is all over you." His gaze grew equally cool. "Word is, you got angry when Dylef mated with Sheba. You killed them and their litter of pups, as well as Sylvan's, and torched their house. That's why you dropped out of sight."

Rand's mind stopped for a full second, struggling with the idea that anyone could think...but then, realistically, how could they not? The house had been on fire, and, remote as they were, that would attract attention. He'd only had time to put the bodies killed outside the house into the flames before he'd had to shift and leave.

He'd hated throwing Grey's in with them, since it was the only burial site his family had, but without dental records or other ways to identify the bodies, there needed to be a body that could pass as his. Grey's followers had run with their tails between their legs, but he should have anticipated they would spread lies. Lies that had only grown, without him appearing in any shifter's territory to provide a different story and defend himself.

The Colorado shifters might have doubted the story, being more familiar with Grey and his betas, but shifters on this side of the country wouldn't have that background. The betas could easily make up stories about their own origins, so they became strangers merely relaying local shifter news they'd "heard."

Vindictive bastards, trying to make sure you couldn't find a place for yourself if you surfaced. After we get done here, we'll run their asses down and set them on fire. We'll skip the killing-them-first step. More fun the other way.

Cai sounded like he meant it, though Rand couldn't answer, his brain spinning.

Fane was studying the reactions on Rand's face. "There are wolves out there who have said, if and when you ever surfaced again, we should kill you on sight. Put you down like a rabid dog."

Cai rose, sheathing the blade. He didn't move away from the tree, but by standing and leaning against it, he made his readiness clear. "I would reevaluate that idea," he said mildly.

Rand didn't bother to tell the vampire to back down this time. It didn't feel bad, with the ground turned to quicksand beneath his paws —or rather, feet—to have someone who could see the full truth of all of it in his mind.

"The male I knew would not have done such a thing," Fane continued. "But I need to hear what the story is and decide for myself."

The urge to tell him to piss off if he was going to believe such bullshit was kneejerk testosterone. But Rand reminded himself if he were in Fane's position, he would have the same need to verify.

Rand sat back down on the log and gestured, inviting Fane to do the same. Fane warily complied as Rand prepared himself to say the terrible words. "You probably heard Sylvan was killed during a challenge?"

Fane nodded, his expression getting more serious. "It was a grievous loss to all of us. I wondered why the challenger took it so far."

"Because Grey was a sadistic bastard. He tried to kill Sheba and Sylvan's pups. Some of the pack, including Dylef and me, fought him. We got Sheba and Sylvan's pups out of harm's way before he could kill them. Over time, we decided to form our own pack. I mated with Sheba."

Fane's dark brows lifted in surprise, but Rand pressed forward. "We relocated in Tennessee. We talked about finding you, about reaching out, so many times over those several years. I wish to God we had. I knew you'd gone mostly off grid and we wanted to respect your reasons for doing that, not interfere with it. Dylef and Sheba... they wanted to be closer to human civilization. And I guess maybe, somewhere in the backs of our minds, we knew that...we weren't entirely safe. But we weren't wary enough."

He paused, then pushed onward. "We figured as long as we put a good distance between us and Grey, he'd let things lie. We were wrong. He was obsessed with having Sheba as his own. He came after us. He didn't observe the rituals."

Rand swallowed and shifted his gaze to the forest. He could never say it without seeing it in his mind, but maybe it was good that Fane could see his reaction. All he knew was he wanted to reach some point in his life he never had to say it again.

"He and his betas killed Dylef and Sheba. And all the pups. I killed him, and Sylvan's boys took out a couple of his followers, but all too late."

Rand's voice had gone flat, but over by his tree, Cai felt what it took out of his soul, every time he had to say the words, opening a wound that never fully closed. He wanted to get up, get in Fane's face and tell him to fuck off. Rand's honesty, guilt, and ironclad honor emanated off him like a cloud of Boy Scout cologne mixed with Superman and choir boy aftershave. It was damned annoying, but impossible to miss, even by the completely clueless.

Rand cleared his throat. "From your version of the tale, I'm assuming some of Grey's surviving betas have spread the lies to have me ostracized, if I sought another pack."

Fane's expression relaxed into sadness and anger. "I can smell the grief upon you," the male said softly, reaching out to touch Rand's stiff shoulder. "I'm so very sorry." He dipped his head, a gesture that was both human and oddly wolfish.

"You are the male I once knew," he said formally. "Your strength as a hunter and a protector is welcome at our table and under our roof."

"Thank you, Fane." Rand bowed his head in the same gratitude and deference. "I am honored."

Vampires were duplicitous and intensely political, so Cai was surprised that the resolution was that simple between them, but then he remembered what Rand had said. Wolves had instinct and highly developed scent skills that were better than polygraph tests. They knew what was truth and bullshit, simply by asking for the answer to their questions. Lie detectors. Plus, Fane had known Rand before, so there was history there.

"Is it only your grief that has kept you from seeking a pack?" Fane asked. From his direct expression, he revealed the question wasn't an idle follow up. Which made Cai guess he already knew the answer. He just wanted to hear Rand say it.

"Yes, and no." Rand's gaze reflected the same awareness. "I prefer males exclusively, Fane. That's why you smell the vampire...all over me. From your look of surprise when I mentioned mating with Sheba, I expect this isn't news to you. You suspected."

"Your open confirmation of it is more surprising than the news itself," Fane admitted.

"I am honor bound to see this through," Rand told Fane. "But I would enjoy spending time with your family again, when time allows it."

"He's not honor bound," Cai said. "He can go run off with you anytime. I can handle the situation with the Trads. Just point me in the right direction."

Fane cut a glance at him that suggested his contribution to the conversation—hell, the reminder he was still here—wasn't enormously welcome. Rand spoke before Cai said something nasty, however.

"You can't release me from a bond of honor I've imposed upon myself," Rand said.

"But he has a point," Fane said. "What is a female vampire to you? Most of the vampires don't believe we exist, and that's preferable. They're savage, codeless." His gaze passed over Cai as if he were a particularly repugnant mold on the forest floor. "Not pack oriented at all."

No, vampires weren't. And Cai still didn't care much for his own kind, either. But the shifter's blanket judgment rubbed him the wrong way. He hadn't known Lodell. Or seen Georg sitting with Leona; the trace of compassion in Lyssa's eyes when she touched Georg's arm. The coldness she'd inflicted upon his underlings, trying to take advantage of him. Vampires weren't overly sentimental and they built their society on power—who had it, who didn't—and crafted the rules accordingly in the favor of those with power, but that wasn't the whole story. Those with power weren't necessarily amoral.

He was here to rescue a vampire girl he didn't know shit about and whose father had tortured him, right? By vampire standards, he should be nominated for sainthood.

"This male saved my life," Rand said.

You wanted to die. I was just being contrary.

Shut up if you want his help.

"The female vampire is a fledgling," Rand explained to Fane. "What humans would deem a teenager, or us as a young hunter, still in need of guidance and maturity before being out on her own. I've seen good in their kind. And even if I hadn't, the code is clear."

He nodded toward Cai. "I owe him an act of equal weight. If he has no backup, his chances of surviving this are slim. They are slim even with help."

Fane seemed as if he might argue further, but after another glance at Cai, he merely said, "Very well. There's a group of vampires like you describe. Four males. We give them a wide berth. We haven't been within scent distance in the past several weeks, because they set up what appears to be a permanent base camp. Which is unusual, because before that, they moved every several weeks, rotating in and out of our territory."

Fane spread out his hands. "We didn't detect a female vampire with them back then, but at the distance we maintain, the males' stench is strong enough to mask it. I forbid any of our pack to come close enough to determine more specifics. Even my first beta and oldest son, Stalker. I am the only one who has seen them with my own eyes."

Cai stepped forward. "If I described a member of the group to you, would you be able to recognize him?"

For a minute, Cai wasn't sure if he'd address him directly or not, but then Fane did, his deep brown eyes unblinking. "Yes. Do you intend to kill them?"

"If they have her, we intend to rescue the girl. If we're able to knock out one or two in the process, I won't be losing any tears over it, but we're an extraction team, not a staking squad. With four vampires, I'm outgunned in the killing department. And no, before you get uptight about it, that wasn't a request for reinforcements. Fast as they'd kill me, you and yours would barely be an afterthought."

Fane bristled, but Rand put out a calming hand. "He's not insulting your bravery or strength, brother. Merely commenting on their lack of regard for life."

And saying he's not you. I expect you're more kick-ass than the average shifter.

You'd be surprised, vampire. Rand sent him an even look and Cai shrugged, not conceding the point, but not arguing it, either.

Fane settled back, mollified. "Describe your target."

"The leader of this group would be tall and rangy, like a stripped oak tree," Cai said. "He likes to wear camouflage because he has delusions that he's some great military leader. His hair is dirt brown, kept really short. Sometimes completely shaved. Cold eyes, a mix of gray and green, some brown. That hazel color people talk about."

Fane nodded. "He always smells of old blood and decaying earth. He is the oldest and strongest among them."

"Yeah, that would be him." Cai shifted his glance to Rand. "That's Goddard." He ignored the cold ball in his stomach that had suddenly twisted his intestines.

Not that he'd had much doubt who it was. Goddard never had played well with others, and he liked this section of the Appalachians. Which was why Cai had always kept a wide berth around it when he was in a mountain-man frame of mind. Good thing West Virginia, Virginia and Tennessee offered plenty of deep wood elbow room for the reclusive, psychotic and furry.

Fane spoke to Rand again. "If you confirm she is with them, will you attempt your extraction tonight?"

Half the night was already gone. Cai knew Rand hated the idea as much as he did, leaving Dovia at their mercy yet another full day, but rushing it wasn't going to increase their miniscule chances of success. Hell, he just wanted to get it over with and done with, but the plan would likely work best if he thought through all angles of it. And one extra night meant Rand could spend some time with his own kind. With old friends.

Cai ignored the sour feeling that gave him. Yeah, his baggage was practically written on his forehead. No reason to be an ass and deny Rand a good night before they walked into a den of psychos.

"Rand, have him get you close enough to verify if she's there. Then go home with him, relax, eat, hang with his family. We'll head out at twilight tomorrow."

"Come with us," Rand said. Fane made a noise that drew Rand's attention.

"He's not welcome, Rand," he said, low. "I don't wish to be inhospitable, but I won't bring him to my family."

"Vampires have enhanced hearing," Cai noted. "No reason to whisper."

Fane had the grace to look discomfited, but his countenance set. "I'm sorry," he told Cai. "But I can't risk them."

"They'll come to no harm from him, I swear it on my life," Rand said. "I'm third marked, Fane. He can follow me anywhere, hear my thoughts. If your reason for excluding him is to keep your home base protected, then you can't trust either of us there. Now or in the future."

Rand spoke the words in a firm and courteous way, but Cai felt his reaction. A noticeable part of him hungered to go join that pack, be with them tonight, have that deep-in-his-soul need for family connection met. While another part of him warred against it, knowing it wouldn't be what he truly wanted.

What he wanted was Dylef's warm body against him, Sheba's laughter in the kitchen, her mock threats against the pups as they swarmed around the table for dinner. Cai saw them, the young faces, the teenagers competing for an audience as they told their parents about their day at school. A small boy leaned against Rand's hip, and an even smaller girl, one with Rand's smile, was cradled in the crook of his elbow.

"Your mother says if I keep carrying you everywhere, I'll have to carry you on my back when we hunt."

As he spoke to the child, there was an easy laughter in Rand's voice that Cai had yet to experience. Would never experience, because what could he offer Rand even close to that?

Not that he'd want to. That wasn't him. Family man and joiner would not be on his tombstone if he had one. Bastard prick, however; *that* would probably be hammered out in nice bold letters, by whoever felt any kind of affection for him.

Cai stepped forward. "I have no interest in being under your roof," he told Fane. "Rand is free to go with you, free to stay with you, and I won't use whatever comes to his mind in your company against you. You don't have to trust me when I tell you that, if you trust his word. If he believes me, then it's so. Give him the night with your family. He deserves it."

Rand opened his mouth to speak, but Cai cut across him. "While no, I can't release him from his honor bond, I'm the last person who'd hold him to it. I'd rather him live. Maybe you can talk him out of being so damn noble and he'll stay with you as he should." He ignored Fane's look of surprise and moved his attention back to Rand. "I'll be traveling swift and far tonight to hunt, so I'll touch base with you at dusk tomorrow on where to meet."

"Cai," Rand began, his expression ominous, but Cai was already moving into the wood. He was aware when Rand shifted, to try and chase after him, but he defeated that with the clear message sent by a blast of vampire swiftness. *Leave it alone for tonight.*

He'd only intended it to be a sprint, but as Cai ran, he lengthened his stride and kept running. Accumulating more and more speed, and he didn't question why it felt so damn good, like ripping off a scab and letting the blood run. He stretched out, ran as hard and fast as he could, taxing every part of his system.

From a practical standpoint, it was a good thing to do, to make sure the skill sets he might need over the next couple days were in order. When he at last slowed, he'd covered at least twenty miles. The nearest town was another ten miles, but there was a sufficient dotting of scattered cabins and family homes populated by generations of those who'd grown up in the rural area. They were loath to part with their independent lifestyle, even if members of the family had to drive into town to work to supplement the income.

Cai sat in the woods, listened, waited and watched, deciding on his quarry. A full measure of human blood could carry him for several weeks, as long as he wasn't injured. That way he wouldn't be dependent on Rand or anyone else, if Fane successfully talked Rand out of joining Cai.

He didn't want to think about doing this without Rand. But if he didn't have to take the shifter down with him, that would be a check on the good karma side of his scorecard. If he believed in that shit.

There. Three sons lived in the sprawling farmhouse with the parents. Adult sons, strapping boys with strong muscles and blood that would practically fizz with health. As Cai closed in on the site and watched his quarry move toward the barn, Cai regretted that this one emanated straight vibes, because being served by all those nice manual labor farm muscles, the chapped mouth and probably nicely shaped cock, would have been a good pre-dinner appetizer.

A strong shot of pheromones in his bite, plus some serious seduction skills, would undoubtedly overcome those inhibitions, but Cai wasn't in the mood to work that hard.

The young man's hair was short, not long. The hair on his arms and chest, visible through the neck of his shirt, was a light covering. No dark fur on him, no bulked muscles that would smell of earth and wolf...

Cai put that aside and thought through the best approach to take his quarry down with minimal fuss and noise. He glided along, stealthy as a snake. The male unconcernedly whistled his way out to his predawn chores, probably intending to milk the cows Cai could hear lowing in the barn.

Yet as he closed in, Cai found himself hesitating. He thought of Rand, and the vision of his boy against his hip. That male could have grown up to be a young man like this, his father proud simply to look upon him. A young version of Rand.

Fuck. Do not let that fucking wolf fuck with your head and your meal. He needed the blood strength if he was going to stay sharp for Dovia.

Cai took the male when he had circled to the back of the barn to retrieve a couple buckets. Cai was an efficient hunter, no wasted movement, no chance for the quarry to make a sound. Usually in this kind of circumstance, he snapped the neck and fed swiftly before the blood could get that death tang to it he disliked.

This time he went with pressure on the windpipe, rendering his prey unconscious. As the man slumped in his arms, Cai pulled him into the shelter of the woods and ripped open the shirt, fanning his palms out on nice farm boy flesh. Tight nipple buds, but yeah, only a baby fine covering of hair on the chest. Plus, his scent was wrong. No, not wrong. It was fine enough, apples and pine wood. Just not wolf.

He struck at the male's throat. He drank and drank, taking that nourishment, but found himself stopping short of the fatal amount. Just. When he sat back on his heels, wiping his mouth with his hand, he studied the unconscious man. He could finish it, drink the rest. But he wouldn't.

He carried the male back to the barn and left him there. Before he took off, he fired a rock through the front window of the house. It made a large crash, and resulted in lights popping on in three windows. Then he disappeared into the woods. They'd get him medical help, a blood transfusion, and he'd be fine. He'd taken as much as he could without killing him, and he'd make do with that. Didn't know why the hell he hadn't taken the amount he normally would. Not efficient.

But he felt better for it, when he thought of Rand and his kids. For about a minute, before he called himself an idiot. Then he simply missed Rand.

~

When Fane and Lynn had come through Colorado years before, their two litters were aged nine and sixteen, a total of seven pups. Now the first litter was in their twenties and the others in their teens. Lynn could still bear children, and since shifter females had a stronger constitution for later pregnancies than human women, it was possible she and Fane might decide to have one more litter to further strengthen the pack. Or, since they also had a handful of daughters, the honor might go to one or more of them.

However, it was fortunate no one was currently pregnant, because if that had been the case, Rand knew Fane wouldn't have invited him home, no matter how much he believed Rand's story about Grey. Male shifters became more aggressively protective when one of the pack females was pregnant, and even more so when it was the alpha female. When she was no longer able to hunt, the male alpha would bring back and present the day's kill to her. Once she accepted it, it would be prepared and eaten by all, but the male alpha would bring her plate to her, not allowing anyone else the honor.

During her pregnancy was also the one time when she would take lead role in the pack, calling the shots on hunting schedule, location, and where they'd "den," so to speak, when it was time to have the pups.

Even when not pregnant, Lynn was still a strong-willed woman and wolf, though the bond between her and Fane was a loving one. She respected him as the head of their pack, a lead the others followed both from her example and because he'd earned it.

Because Fane's birthday had been mid-week, Rand had the pleasure of meeting pretty much the whole family, who'd come to stay for the weekend and celebrate their alpha's birth date. The young adult shifters—Stalker, Sangra, Todd and Cilya—viewed Rand with some wariness, but when his welcome was confirmed by Fane, that was all it took for them to relax. The teenagers—Darcy, Windrunner and Chad —were even more accepting, despite the odd vampire scent upon him.

Fane told Rand he'd wait to explain that after dinner, along with the reason for him being in their area.

No matter the late hour, wolf hospitality demanded that a guest be fed a meal. In a house of wolves, especially growing teenaged ones, there was no lack of enthusiasm for a "second dinner." Rand was amused by the mix of pajamas and daily wear he saw around the table. Pajamas for the teens, mostly day wear for the adults.

They had a spacious two-level cabin. It had been built by the hands of everyone at the table, and they were excited to share what each had contributed to their home, laughing and speaking over one another, but in that amicable way that siblings did. The energy of it soaked into Rand's body, putting him at ease.

There were several at the table who were not Fane and Lynn's offspring. Idris was the mate of their daughter, Sangra. They'd met while she was away at school. Sangra was a nurse, which complemented her brother Todd's specialty of veterinarian medicine. He was part of a practice in the town fifty miles away and had an apartment there, though he came to the woods to be with his family most weekends. His wife was human, something that obviously concerned Lynn, though she was friendly enough to Zelda.

Mated to a shifter, Zelda could apply to be bitten according to ritual, and become one of the pack. Perhaps Lynn's concern was that Zelda didn't want to do that.

It wasn't unusual for shifters to choose human professions and blend into that life. It was what had kept them mostly invisible to the world for so long, not just vampires. And yes, some did mate with humans, though the relationships often didn't work out long term. Partly because shifters were as paranoid as vampires about hiding their existence from humans. Which meant many shifters who mated humans never told them, instead figuring out how to live a double life.

Fane's other adult daughter, Cilya, was divorced. Though the reasons for that weren't discussed, Rand wondered if that was part of the cause. She had only arrived an hour before he had, having had a work commitment in the city that had run late.

While Todd had revealed his identity to his wife, the other challenge to a shifter-human relationship was children. As difficult as healthy births were for shifters who were born wolves, the percentages were even lower for a transformed human female. And a human female who didn't want to become a shifter couldn't conceive with one.

That issue didn't seem to concern Todd and Zelda presently. The two were obviously still in a honeymoon phase. And Todd seemed comfortable with the human life he led.

Whereas during his grieving period Rand had rarely wanted to shift out of being a wolf, there were shifters who stayed in human form most of the time. Some eventually embraced their human side and only ran as wolves...well, once in a blue moon.

Unlike the wolf shifting side, there seemed to be no permanent effects to a shifter staying human for long periods of time. They could become wolf anytime they wished, though Todd joked that, when he did have time to shift and run in some of the more wooded parks near his home, sometimes his joints felt like they needed WD-40.

Wolf shifters didn't have many of the limitations vampires did to blending into society, Rand realized. They could be out night or day; when they were human, they looked human. No oddness to their eyes, or a preternatural stillness or deliberation to their movements like Cai had. That eerie yet compelling scrutiny that made someone want to get closer to him.

On that note, he'd noticed Cilya watching him more closely than the others. She was attractive and well put together, with straight hair to her shoulders in a soft bob, large dark eyes that seemed to miss little, and a pleasant mouth. Because she'd run late from work, she still wore her work clothes; slacks and a sleeveless blouse that complimented her curves. A pretty necklace of thin wire and sparkling stones was tucked into the V-neckline.

Polite conversation revealed she was a dean at a middle school. There was an insightful intelligence and firm directness to her that reminded Rand of Sheba. None of the pups had been able to get a lie past her, or would even try. She valued integrity and had instilled that in them. Cilya seemed to exercise the same code toward her charges. Rand liked the entertaining stories she told about mentoring her at-risk kids, and when he chuckled a couple times, she looked his way and seemed pleased that she'd made him laugh.

She sat beside him at the table, and the relaxed contact of wolves, her hand touching his when the food was passed, or the brush of her hip, was not unwelcome or overly forward. Just wolfish.

She and Lynn were the cooks in the family, and Rand appreciated their efforts, especially at the late hour. Dinner was generous platters of venison, with cornbread muffins and collards, the latter dutifully eaten under Lynn's sharp eye. She firmly reminded everyone that human health had to be tended as much as wolf health. When Darcy pointed out impishly Cilya had put an artery-clogging amount of butter into the greens to make them go down better, Cilya swatted her head with a smile, admonishing her not to be a tattletale.

Rand commented on the crops they had growing to supplement income and asked if the milking cows had ever seemed spooked by the underlying wolf scent that other animals could detect, even when a shifter was in human form.

That set off a rash of anecdotes about mishaps the younger ones had had when they were learning to control their shifting.

"Though Darcy did it deliberately once," Todd said, shooting a teasing look at his younger sister. The girl, with a vibrant, dyed-red mop of corkscrew hair, and twinkling brown eyes amid a scattering of freckles, gave a mock scowl.

"There was a storm coming and I needed them to get into the barn. They were being stubborn, so I shifted and chased them all in."

"She was as good as a border collie," Chad added. "I said we should enter her in a competition so she could bring home blue ribbons to compete with my track trophies."

As the banter continued, Rand tried hard not to let it happen, but the scene blurred, and it was another family sitting around him, the give and take of conversation between those who knew and loved one another. Family. Those with hopes and dreams for futures that would never come.

Even a five-year-old could have strong opinions. Maple wanted to be an astronaut. Teague was like Fane's Stalker. He just wanted to be a wolf and a farmer, never going anywhere near a human city. Cira, she'd been undecided, changing her mind from day to day, depending on what book they read together at bedtime.

And Shy... She'd curled in her father's arms and said she wanted to be his little girl forever. Something only a little girl would say.

At a touch on his arm, Rand tuned back in to realize, mortified, that every eye was upon him, and he had tears rolling down his face. It was Cilya's hand upon him, her dark eyes filled with kindness. Fane was on the other side, his palm molded over Rand's shoulder.

"It's all right," Lynn said softly. She was across the table, and had moved her foot to press it against Rand's. "We understand, Rand. How could we not? I'm so very sorry."

He nodded. "I'm uh...going to..."

He struggled to get up, free himself from the confines of the picnic table style seating of the big dining table. Fane rose to give him room, which made Rand feel more self-conscious. Once he managed it, aware of the hands reaching out to steady him, he mumbled something he hoped was polite and appropriate and left the kitchen. He and Fane were supposed to go check out the Trad camp after dinner, but he could come back later for that.

Rand kept going until he reached the front door, the porch, the steps, and he was out into the night, away from the house. He needed to breathe.

Fortunately, Fane understood, for no one followed him. Rand took deep gulps of air. He wondered what Cai was doing, where he was.

But then he wished he hadn't thought about it. A cold knot formed in his belly. Cai thought he might be alone tomorrow night, that Rand would change his mind about backing him up. The vampire didn't count on anyone to stay true to their word, even himself. And, assuming he'd be alone, Cai would want to be well fortified with blood. He'd gone to kill.

No. Not tonight. But I did get myself a big meal. And I didn't doubt you'd keep your word. I just hoped you'd think better of it.

There was a momentary silence, where Rand felt like Cai was even deeper inside him than he was himself, seeing things Rand couldn't face. Like Cilya and her ability to intuit the needs of the young, only Cai's insightfulness was targeted right at the man, and what they knew about each other.

I'm about a mile away, if you want to come to me, wolf. I'm here. I'm sure you can pick up my vampire stench.

Rand took off his clothes, left them folded under a tree, and shifted. He took off, not dwelling on why he went away from that warm cheerful light and happy family, toward a surly vampire who wouldn't know what a pack and family meant if his life had depended on it.

Well, his life had depended on never counting on anyone, right? So that made sense. Yet when Cai told Rand where he was, Rand heard two things in the information. Not just an acknowledgement of where Rand's head was, what he might need, but what Cai himself might be wanting.

He found the vampire lying on his stomach in a moonlit meadow, hands stacked and pillowing the side of his face. He had his eyes closed as he apparently digested his meal. Rand sat down next to him, pressing furred warmth against his cold side. Cai didn't act cold, but Rand was glad to give him warmth and he wanted the contact. He laid down, resting his big head on Cai's back, between his shoulder blades.

"Good boy," Cai murmured. No biting sarcasm to it, no teasing. It made Rand feel odd, but not unpleasant, so he kept lying there. The male had no shirt or shoes on, just his jeans.

"I've hung out at a bunch of libraries afterhours," Cai said. "Books say grief heals after a while. And it helps when you're around people who actively help with the healing process. Rather than those who live their own miserable, solitary existence."

Rand rubbed his face against Cai's back.

"Do not get your drool on me." The male's shoulders lifted in a sigh. "Not talking to me tonight, hmm? Staying deep in that wolf head of yours."

Rand rolled to his side, putting the aforementioned head on the small of Cai's back and rise of his ass. He stretched his paws out before him. He didn't want to feel sad. He just wanted to feel like a wolf.

"Okay. Don't let me sleep through sunrise. That would suck."

Cai didn't say anything else but that. They both slept for a time, though Rand thought they alternated staying semi-alert to their surroundings, so he was aware when Fane approached. Cai's eyes opened, but Rand rose to handle it.

When he padded to the edge of the clearing, Fane met him there. The male was in his human form.

If he was offended that Rand had left his hospitality to be here, with Cai, he didn't show it. But he could understand, couldn't he? They had seven children, and every parent thought about the nightmare of losing them.

"Stalker and I checked out the Trad camp." He shook his head at

Rand's laid-back ears. "We risked nothing but the vampires scenting a couple wolves, and we were well out of range of their vision. But a female vampire is there. Young, like you described." Fane hesitated, his jaw tightening. "I also thought I detected human female, but the life signs were faint, masked somehow. Perhaps old prey. It was hard to tell."

So Cai's instincts had been right. Goddard had her. Rand just wished it wasn't so close to dawn, so that they could go now.

The Trads have to sleep through daylight as well, Cai reminded him. *And before you think it, no, you trying to take her after sunrise won't work. She's too young to survive being transported during daylight hours, since we don't exactly have a road to bring in a fancy vehicle like that van. Goddard's also old enough that, below ground, he could still wake up and fight you, even in the middle of the day. And I couldn't help you until the sun went down.*

It was logical, but knowing she was so close was maddening. Rand wondered if Fane had known that and tried to ease the burden on him by doing the verification reconnaissance with Stalker instead.

Rand communicated his thanks with a wolfish rub against Fane's leg and hip. When Fane brushed his body against him in response, dropping to a squat to affectionately butt heads, Rand tried not to let his heart twist into knots at the double-edged sword of welcome, long-overdue contact, the rich body language of another wolf.

"When your task is done, you come and run with us, Rand," Fane murmured. "You have had your grieving period. You now need to heal fully, and for that, you need your own kind."

Fane paused, his hand resting on Rand's back. Human eyes met wolf ones. "Lynn remembers Sheba's strength and kindness," he said. "She told my mate that you were one of the strongest and most noble wolves she'd ever met. If you get into trouble, you may turn to us for help. I don't know what response I'll be able to muster, but I don't wish you to come to harm."

Rand was moved, and transmitted it with another head butt that had Fane chuckling, though his expression remained serious. But as Fane himself had pointed out, this wasn't about wolf kind, nor wolf kind's fight. Rand wouldn't risk a single member of Fane's family, no matter that he, Stalker and Idris were all formidable-looking men, which usually translated into a similar-sized wolf. Todd and Chad had a slimmer build, but that didn't mean they couldn't fight just as well.

Same for Cilya and Sangra. Fane was a good fighter and he'd have taught those skills to all his young.

Rand's response was easy enough for Fane to read. The male set his jaw. "You call for aid if needed. Grey's pack spread their lies and, in your absence, I didn't trust what Lynn and I knew of you. I owe you a debt for that. Cilya's already taken me to task. She told me that your integrity was as obvious to her as one of her students declaring he hadn't eaten candy, while chocolate was still on his face."

Rand cocked a head, his eyes glinting, and Fane smiled. "She doesn't mince words." Putting his hand on Rand's massive shoulder, he rubbed his jaw along Rand's muzzle, a quick solidarity. "Though I have no love or trust of vampires, I respect your regard for him. But the vampire can't give you what a wolf's heart and soul needs. I think you know that. You're a strong, valuable pack member. Don't take that away from all of us."

Fane nodded at Rand's sudden, intent look. "Yes, I'm offering what you think I'm offering. We all agreed. If you want to be part of our pack, we will find a place for you."

To be wanted, included. Yes, he'd gone out of his way to avoid it, but in the perverse, self-destructive nature of grief, he'd also longed for that feeling again. Rand swallowed, struggling with his emotions. He would think on it. But regardless of his decision, he rubbed himself once more against Fane, knocking him back with his enthusiasm and winning a smile. He wanted to be sure the male knew his gratitude. Fane was the first to offer Rand acceptance and kindness since he'd lost his family. Well, the first wolf to do so.

Despite what Cai said to the contrary, he'd been the first.

Fane straightened and stepped back. As if reading Rand's thoughts, he added, "Perhaps, one day, we'll allow your vampire friend to join us at dinner. If only for the company, since I expect what we offer won't be his preference."

Depends on if a certain wolf I know is sitting at the table. Cai distracted Rand considerably with follow up images to that. Rand wondered what Cai thought of the other things Fane had said, but the vampire was silent on that issue.

Rand bid Fane farewell. He didn't immediately return to Cai, but instead decided to go hunting. Not so much because he was hungry; Lynn had fed them exceptionally well. Too well. He probably needed to run some of it off so he was fight-ready. He needed to hunt, stalk, trap. Exercise his full range of skills in his wolf form, since that was how Cai needed his backup.

He disappeared in the woods with just a brief mind touch that Cai answered with a neutral acknowledgment. Maybe the vampire was going to sleep some more.

Rand was able to use his skills, several times. He pinned a rabbit, releasing her before her fragile heart could hammer its way through her chest. Soon after, he caught a fat quail mid-air as he flushed him from the bushes.

Then he came upon a true challenge. The four-point stag foraging on his own detected him immediately and bolted, but Rand was already in motion. He ran a zig zag track through the trees after the deer, exulting in high leaps over logs and roots. As they emerged into a clearing, the deer leveled out.

Here was another way a shifter differed from a non-shifter wolf. One-on-one, a healthy deer like this one could outrun a wolf on open ground. Whereas Rand closed the distance between them.

If he'd been with a pack, the females, lighter and quicker when it came to darting maneuvers, would have been snapping at the deer's legs, weaving in front of him. They'd stay a safe distance from the dangerous antlers or hooves, but cause as much panic and confusion as possible to slow him down.

Hunting in a pack had an energy he had always relished, but it wasn't necessary for him to make the kill. The power of the chase fueled every powerful muscle as he gathered himself to leap.

The stag dodged but Rand twisted in mid-air and landed where he intended, on his back, teeth set to the neck. He could end it there. Instead he avoided being bucked off and gored by launching himself, hitting the ground in a roll and letting the stag continue its flight. Standing there panting, Rand watched him disappear into the woods on the far side of the meadow. A noble opponent, free to live and run another day. As a lone wolf, he chased deer regularly to stay in practice for hunting them, but he rarely took one down. Far more meat than needed for one wolf.

Then he saw Cai.

The vampire had been running with him, he realized, a shadow on his peripheral vision. Cai opened his mind to him, purely in pictures and feeling, letting him see how he'd watched Rand leap onto the stag's back, the gleaming fur over rippling muscle, the sharp teeth that could take life...but hadn't.

The vampire moved forward, dropped to his heels, and bared his fangs. A challenge. *You need a work out before we go into the lion's den? I feel like doing a bit of hunting myself before dawn, wolf. And you're who I'm after.*

Rand stalked forward, and Cai's feral smile widened. They circled one another, and then Rand charged. Cai braced, and Rand sailed over him, landing on the opposite side and bulleting into the woods. He knew forest terrain, but so did Cai. In and out of trees, over branches and roots, fallen logs, rocks. Through a creek, water splashing up, birds sending alarm calls from their nighttime roosts as the two of them wound through the woods in a chase that was part hunt, part mating ritual, part something else that had Rand's heart hammering in his chest.

He wanted to turn and fight. He wanted to run and see if Cai could catch him. He wanted to run Cai to ground himself. He wanted to run with the male for miles, because running with a pack was a place of peace for the mind, even as the body was strained to its maximum limits.

Cai got close enough to leap, and managed it with power and grace, landing on Rand's back and rolling them both across the forest floor. Rand snapped at him and Cai wrapped his arms around Rand's chest and the narrow part of stomach and hips. His four legs thrashed as Rand writhed, tossing his head back into Cai's with a resounding thwack. Cai let out an oath and loosened his hold. Rand flipped, making a getaway. Cai tackled him again, burying his face in Rand's fur over his ribs, his arms once again wrapped around him, holding them both sprawled on the ground, the vampire lying against Rand's scrabbling back legs.

Shift for me, wolf. I want my mouth on your skin. Cai nuzzled the thick fur, and the heat of his breath teased the flesh beneath, penetrating the four-legged animal's instincts to the two-legged one.

Rand resisted it, as he always did, but as Cai's fingertips stroked his fur deep, firm, letting him feel the commanding touch, his body listened. He shifted in the vampire's arms. Cai adjusted to accommodate him so that when the shift was complete, he was lying upon

Rand, arms around hips and waist, body sprawled between his spread thighs.

Cai was as good as his word. He began to press his mouth against the valley between Rand's pectorals, over them, tongue flicking his nipples, teeth nipping at his shoulders. His hands stroked the arrow of hair down Rand's abdomen, fanning out to tease every muscle until he gripped Rand's hips. Cai's chest pressed Rand's aroused cock hard into his pelvis.

Rand's hands fell naturally on Cai's head and shoulder, fingers digging, curling...caressing. He explored that sunburst scar, all the different textures of uneven skin. He thought of how Cai had killed another vampire to win his freedom from the Trads. Into how many pieces had Cai broken to survive? Was the cynical, hard-to-understand male simply a patchwork of all those pieces, stitched together? Did he remember his mother? His father? His life, before his life was stolen?

Cai didn't pause in his ministrations, and Rand didn't know if that was because he didn't wish to acknowledge the thoughts, or if he was completely immersing himself in what he was doing. The latter was an overwhelming thought.

Cai moved down, his intent clear, and he wrapped his hand around Rand's wrist, holding it to his thigh in a firm pin when he moved to put his mouth over Rand's cock. He slid down, sucked on it, from root to tip. Up and down, slow glides that had Rand gasping and pushing up into his mouth. Cai took his balls one by one into that same heated cavern, playing, teasing, making Rand curse and writhe, before Cai lifted his head to flash him a quick grin and went down on him again, occasionally letting Rand feel the slide of a fang.

Stay still, wolf, or you'll get punctured. Feel everything I'm doing to you. Did I take you down because I caught you and overpowered you, or because you wanted to be taken down? Which idea turns you on more?

He had no words as Cai did something else with his tongue and God...he slid slickened fingers into Rand's ass, probing deep, playing, stroking. Rand groaned, and tugged on him with his one free hand. Cai's grip only tightened on the other wrist.

Watching you run...fuck, I had this perverse desire to chain you up, keep you in a cage and only let you run on my command, so I could see it, every moment of it, every time. You'd have to rely on me to let you do that. I'd be the gateway to get what you want and need. I wouldn't let you feel sad or lonely, or grieve. You can be the animal with me, Rand. It's okay. I don't ask for more than that.

Rand's hand trembled in the grip of his. Cai meant business now, his mouth and fingers insistent.

Want to feel you release in my mouth. Do it now. Do it hard.

That he could do. Rand's hips jacked up and his groan deepened as the release started jetting, bathing the back of Cai's throat. Cai gave him the full measure of satisfaction, even as he worked Rand's seed over his palm and clasped it around his own cock, lubing himself up with Rand's release. He lifted himself up between Rand's thighs, gazing down at him.

Rand pressed his lips together, knowing how Cai was about to take him. Face to face. No, too intimate. His mind was too full of the past tonight, the touch of—

Cai moved so quickly, it startled Rand, froze thought and word. He had his fingers wrapped around Rand's throat, his knee pressed against his cock, still semi-hard. "This," the vampire squeezed his hand around his neck, hard enough for Rand to feel the constriction, "tells you who has you right now. You even *think* another male's name, and I will make you very, very sorry. Who are you with right now?"

"You," Rand whispered. The things in the vampire's expression, in his mind, held him. Made him want to touch and take, too. Possessiveness, dominance, sexual heat, yes. Rand was feeling all of that. Also a fierce, deep well of emotions that hit him straight in the heart and found an answer.

He knew what Cai was feeling, because all those feelings were as close to him as breathing. Loneliness, a need so sharp it could cut, and being lost in a dark wood with nothing to grasp but this, the heat and warmth of another. But the craving was more specific than that. Specific to a someone, not a something.

Cai nodded, his eyes dark and intent, and echoed Rand's answer. "You're with me. You bet your fine, accessible ass you are." He began to guide himself in, pressing Rand's thighs up, knees to his chest, and settling in lower, bringing their faces closer as he slid in deep, deeper, all the way. He adjusted, cupping Rand's ass in both hands to keep him at the right angle and still stay in intimate proximity to his face. Chests almost touching as Cai's body curved to accommodate the position, then his mouth was on Rand's throat. An approving sound came from the vampire as Rand automatically tipped his head to the side, offering him the vein if he wanted it.

In wolf speak, showing the belly or throat was a concession to another's dominance. Rand was giving Cai that, at least in this moment. Whereas in a pack, such a sign of submission was to serve function and order, here it was about that deeper, darker thing inside the vampire, that found an answer inside a lone wolf.

"You don't close your eyes," Cai ordered, his voice harsh, eyes glittering.

Rand reached up to him, not surprised when Cai intercepted the motion and grasped his wrist in a restraining hand. "You either," Rand murmured.

Cai stroked, pressed, thrust. Rand met him, motion for motion. What started as an impact point, a testosterone match to see who could come together with greater force, evolved into something different. The wind whispered around them, but otherwise the two predators commanded silence from the night except for what came from their own voices, the friction of their flesh moving against one another and the earth. Cai's touch on Rand's wrist became less of a hold, more of a caress, slipping up so their fingers ultimately were twined together.

Their bodies moved in rhythm, and Rand drank in Cai's aroused expression. The vampire's other hand was threaded in Rand's hair, spread on the ground, tangling, tugging. Rand slid his free arm up under Cai's, around, palm to his lower back and then to his buttock to bring him closer, deeper.

Cai adjusted, rolling Rand's hips up some more and sliding his own arm under Rand's shoulders, taking advantage of their preternatural flexibility to curl Rand up into more of U-shape and bring his mouth to his. A hot, deep, yet slow kiss as they rocked together, gripping one another to maintain the connection.

Cai came first, groaning against Rand's mouth, breaking the kiss in involuntary reaction. His mouth brushed the side of Rand's jaw, landing on his shoulder. Cai put his face there and Rand curled his arm over the vampire's head as both of Cai's arms wrapped around him, holding him even tighter in that folded position as he released, knees driving furrows into the ground.

Having come so soon before, Rand didn't expect to come, and

especially without some additional friction, but he did, Cai's jet of seed inside him hitting just the right place. Though Rand thought it might be the whole situation itself, the emotional as well as physical stimulation, tipping him over that cliff. He dropped his head back and let it have him, savoring the scrape of Cai's fangs as he made the move.

He started as Cai sank them into his flesh, not because he was surprised the vampire had bitten him at the height of his climax, but because of where. Cai had bitten his pectoral, right over his heart, his fangs driven deep in the flesh above where that organ beat with a strong and sure rhythm, pumping fast as a result of their mutual pleasure. His tongue played over Rand's nipple, circled the heated skin, and Rand's cock jumped, a small spurt of additional response.

Cai apparently registered it, because he put his hand down between them, rubbing his fingertips over the sensitive tip. He brought what he collected back to his own mouth, smearing it on Rand's skin where he was biting him and adding it to the blood he was sampling.

I could stay inside you like this for days.

Rand pressed his forehead to Cai's crown. He didn't have words for that. He could just be in this moment, which worked, since he was pretty sure that meshed with Cai's thought.

At length, the vampire eased back, licking the wound until it closed, and released his hold enough to let Rand uncurl, lay back on the ground. The vampire had to pull out, but he didn't go away. He lay full upon Rand, damp cocks pressed into still heated skin, the give and take of flesh and muscle as Rand recovered his breath and their fingertips glided over each other. It reinforced the intimacy Cai had demanded earlier.

Rand felt an answering clutch in his gut and loins that said he wasn't entirely against it. Just not sure what any of it meant.

"It means it's a nice feeling until Goddard figures out a way to dismember or disembowel me," Cai said. "Then you can move on and look elsewhere in the afterlife. Or in your next life."

A wolf's howl, not too far distant, split the air. Rand lifted his head from the ground, listening, and a deep surge of pleasure went through him.

Fane's family were out running. He hadn't even thought to ask if they'd already run tonight, though it was a favored evening pastime for most wolf packs. Maybe Fane had been dropping a hint earlier about coming to run with them. Or maybe after he'd returned home, they'd decided to give Rand a taste of what he was missing. It sounded like something the savvy Lynn would think to do. Or maybe even her daughter Cilya, with her knowing eyes and intuition that shepherded so many young souls. Rand wasn't a young soul, but the needs of the heart didn't change all that much from childhood, did they? They just gained different shape and forms of expression.

With a smile, Rand turned his attention to Cai, parting his lips to explain. Cai's expression had done that shuttering thing, and when Rand reached up to touch his shoulder, the vampire was already up on his knees and then standing, pulling his jeans back up.

The contrast was a little too symbolic. Rand, completely naked and lying before the vampire, exposed, while Cai hadn't taken off all his clothes or even his shoes for their coupling.

It didn't fit with what they'd just shared and experienced together, but neither did Cai's closed expression now. It wasn't unfriendly. Just... removed. Cai squatted before him, putting a hand on his calf. "You going to run some more?"

"Maybe." Rand stared at him. There were a lot of things he could say, but he realized none of them felt right. They shared intense things, intense feelings, but, especially facing what they were facing, there was no room for permanence, growth...

Rand couldn't help thinking how easy it had been tonight, the emotions and affection displayed around Fane's table, compared to how mercurial and sometimes combative Cai could be. He completely understood why Cai was like that, he did, but...he wished Cai would come with him. Could run with them.

"But I can't." A muscle twitched in Cai's jaw. He backed up a few steps. "Go, wolf. I mean it."

"I'll find you at dusk."

"Do what you got to do." Cai pivoted and strode away, disappearing in the shadows of the forest.

Damn it. He hadn't handled that well. Rand sat up, rubbing a hand over his face. He wanted to fix it, but he wasn't exactly sure how. More of that aforementioned mercurial shit.

More howls split the air. They were calling him. Cai might not accept anything else from him tonight, but they would. And maybe Rand could find some answers to the confusion of feelings he had about the vampire, the loss of his family, and the way things were changing inside him.

Actions would speak louder than words. At twilight, Rand *would* find the vampire, no matter that Cai thought Rand was abandoning his ass. But in the meantime, Rand would give himself this, the perfect ending note to an evening with great meal and mind-blowing sex.

~

Rand shifted. When he came to a raised berm over a ravine, he lifted his head, scenting the air. On a whim, he put his nose to the sky and howled, long and deep.

He was answered by an enthusiastic chorus that hit him like a shot of pure adrenaline. He ran through the forest, letting the wolf have him once more, though he had to moderate his pace since the climax had drained some of his stamina. The vampire knew how to work a man over, that was for sure.

Rand followed the howls, the inviting yips, and caught up with them. They were running through the forest purely for the joy of it. Cilya nipped his shoulder flirtatiously as he joined the pack. He rolled her in playful answer and they were all up and moving together, running, stopping briefly to sniff and take a different direction. Flushing out a mole, Todd gulped it down in one swallow, an after-dinner snack.

If they'd been hungry, if they'd been with him when he ran down the stag, they would have hunted as a pack. They would feed in order of hierarchy, unless there were new pups just starting to eat raw meat who needed to feed first, to ensure their strength. Then the alphas, Fane and Lynn, then the beta, Stalker. Then the others.

Rand, if he was part of their pack, might be recognized as a beta ranked over Stalker, because Fane would acknowledge his contribution to protecting and caring for the family, and offer his respect to Rand for not challenging Fane's domination of the group.

Though they identified strongly with wolves, there were key differences between wolf shifters and actual wolves. Like most wolf packs only had the one female, the alpha female. And she'd be the only one to get pregnant. In contrast, Rand suspected Lynn was hoping rather strenuously for grand-pups from Sangra and Idris. Todd and Zelda might or might not ever have children, but Rand didn't see Fane or Lynn discouraging the couple from being together. Sometimes you just had to let things happen. And hope for the best.

It'd been awhile since he'd let himself have that kind of optimism about families. Attributing it to the pleasure of running with a pack, he left it at that.

When they ran themselves to near exhaustion, he flopped down next to Cilya. She rubbed against him affectionately, the two of them mouthing one another's muzzles in play, though it stopped there. Rand saw the speculation in Lynn's dark eyes, but he knew Fane would tell her. It was different when he was a wolf; he could flirt and play, and enjoy that, but actual consummation outside wolf form...not so much.

He and Sheba had consummated as wolves because it was easier for him that way. Perhaps for her too, with her memories of Sylvan as a human male, holding her in their bed, touching and kissing her. Her heart had still belonged to her dead mate, all the way to the moment she joined him in that afterlife.

He envied her that, far too much. He thought of Dylef, every intimacy shared, even daily irritations, the grind of work, farm life, dealing with the pups, and those blissful moments at the end of the day when they could lie in bed together and wake the same way. It had been a life, a good life. And it was gone.

He thought of Cai, warning him about thinking of another male while they were together. The idea of being wanted, needed...claimed, wasn't bad. But that could be fleeting, if the other part wasn't there, if there was no potential for it. Intimacy, companionship, sharing the daily stuff.

He heaved a sigh and closed his eyes as Cilya propped herself against his side and started fencing muzzles with Chad over him. It was as Cai had said. They'd both likely be dead soon, so rather than wish for what once had been, Rand would enjoy what he had right now. That would have to be enough.

CHAPTER THIRTEEN

*A*fter a time, Fane's family returned home for the night. Rand stayed out through sunrise. He prowled the woods, doing some advance scouting around the area Fane had showed him. He didn't go too close to the Trad camp, however. He was well-aware both his human and wolf form might not be able to restrain himself if he saw the girl in distress, and then their plan would be blown before it even started. This was a fight one wolf could not win.

Restless and dissatisfied, he went to find Cai. The vampire had gone to ground before the sun rose, but now that he knew what he was looking for, Rand tracked him to a mound of earth artfully concealed by debris and a stand of saplings. Their shadows provided some additional cover but didn't have a deep root system to inhibit digging a man-sized hole. Rand curled up on top of the mound of earth, deciding to spend the first part of the day sleeping. It was going to be a long night.

When twilight came, Rand felt the vampire stir. He padded a few feet away from his resting spot to lie down again. Cai rose and stretched, eyeing him without comment, and moved to the nearby spring to wash up. Rand realized he must have petitioned Giles for replacement "pajamas," similar to what Cai had had, since he was wearing a worn T-shirt and jeans so faded they were almost white. Rand cocked his head, curious, as Cai changed into his daywear.

Bugs don't get you?

"Nope." Cai grunted as he pulled on his heavier weight cotton T-shirt. "They crawl around me but seem to avoid contact. And yeah, yeah, I know what you're thinking, but it's not my repulsive personality. Most vampires are bug repellants."

Rand sneezed, and Cai gave him a narrow look. Thankfully any lingering tension or unspoken words from when they'd parted hours before seemed to be gone, for both of them. Now there was only one task ahead, one focus.

Done dressing, Cai finger-combed his damp hair, a partly rakish, partly boyish gesture that appealed to Rand more than expected. The vampire didn't seem to notice the reaction, thankfully.

"Why don't you take the lead?" Cai asked. "We both know where we're going, but your nose has a better memory of the best way to get there than my brain. We'll split up the way we planned when we get closer."

In answer, Rand rose and took off. After shouldering their backpack of belongings, Cai followed with an easy jog. Rand wondered if he was concerned about Goddard taking the backpack from him, causing them to lose the chance to use Brian's tools. However, the only thing the vampire unloaded as they drew closer to their destination was the gum that would eliminate a blood tracer on a vampire, and the sedatives for Dovia.

Cai took a couple of the pea-sized gumballs from the tin, but put the rest of it in a sealed plastic bag, which he buried and marked with a trio of flat rocks.

"Will you be able to find it again, even in the bag?"

Rand gave him a mental nod and Cai rose. Rand understood Cai's intent. If they both had access to the substance, whichever one of them managed to get her out of there could give her the gum, and then the sedatives, when she was safe. She was the priority.

They resumed their journey in silence. Maybe because they saved their energy that way, or because they had an extra dose of nerves for the coming challenge, neither was winded after they covered the last couple miles. Rand slowed and dropped into a silent stalk. The vampire adjusted off to his right, a shadow slipping through the woods.

When they were close enough to the camp, in mutual accord, Cai circled around to scout one side, Rand the other.

As Rand peered through the trees, screened to invisibility by their cover, he examined the Trad camp. A sturdy cabin, a couple nearby outbuildings. A well. Surprisingly tidy and clean, but he remembered what Cai had said about Goddard's military illusions. He ran his camp organized, the way a commander would. With one notable exception.

Rand quelled the rumble in his throat. There were two humans here, the shift of the wind bringing their unwashed, sickly odor to his nose and fueling his anger.

Two women. They were chained by their throats and wrists to the well, one on either side so they couldn't reach one another or easily communicate. They were naked, huddled against the sides of the rock to gain what meager warmth they could from the shelter as the mountain evening cooled.

He lifted his head and met Cai's eyes on the other side of the clearing. *Goddard likes to keep a human female or two for menial labor,* the vampire supplied, *and on the off chance they can impregnate one. They usually give up on that after a week or so. They don't believe in fucking humans for pleasure, and they refuse to mark them; against their extreme purist principles. Don't look for any kind of help from them. Their minds are likely broken.*

Rand squelched his anger with effort. *If Fane had scented them, I'm sure he would have tried to free them.*

And he or others in his family would have died. Doesn't matter, Cai thought, cutting him off. *There's a lot of bad shit in this world you can't do a damn thing about. Shit is what it is.*

~

Cai could tell the wolf was dissatisfied with that answer, but there was no good answer for that kind of thing. Plus, Cai had to have a different focus now. An unwavering one. There was only one ball that could matter in this game.

Showtime. He cracked his neck and his fingers, drew a couple deep breaths, and let it all go quiet. No fear, no feeling, no nothing. He heard Lodell's voice in his head, as if the skinny bastard had popped up at his elbow.

To get free, you become nothing. Nothing to notice, nothing to fear...until the day you are. To do that, you have to learn to be nothing 99% of the time. That left-over 1% stays buried down so deep inside, the whetting stone for the blade, waiting until the right moment for the killing stroke. All while that 99% plays the dumb slave, the helpless idiot.

Let the fear show. That helps you. Bury the rest. Let it rot in the ground, and every night you emerge from the earth, don't bring it up with you. That fear's not going to help you. 'Nothing' is what helps you.

"Nothing helps you." Lodell had repeated it as a play on words, with a chuckle.

At that point, Cai hadn't even remembered what laughter was. He'd quelled the urge to touch the man's mouth, explore the gesture. He'd wanted to understand what laughter was again, but he'd been afraid understanding would bring more pain.

Cai opened his eyes, and let it settle over him. Nothingness. He vaguely remembered the wolf and sent him a message. *Going in. Watch my back, but everything is mind-to-mind. Stay clear, no matter what, because you're the best chance to pull her out. They don't know about you.*

Just like that. It took Rand by surprise, not just the suddenness of it, but Cai's abrupt mental distance. Their gazes locked over the expanse of the clearing, but Rand could have been looking at a brick wall. Cai had gone somewhere else in his head to deal with this. Rand wasn't sure if that was good or bad.

Cai going ahead, no further discussion, made an unsettling kind of sense. They were as prepared as they were going to be, so there was no real reason to wait. The plan was fairly straightforward, while any contingencies would be unpredictable, resolved on the fly.

Cai, do you think...

It's best not to, when dealing with Trads. Just go by instinct. You're good at that. If things go bad and the numbers are too great, leave me. I mean it. There's nothing you can do for me or her at that point. Just go back to your woods and to Fane's family. You'll do well with them. You felt happy...when you were with them.

What the hell? But Cai was done with talk. He rose, and that adrenaline pumped through Rand as the vampire made himself as visible as a neon sign against a dark sky. Cai moved down the short bank, jumping lithely over the wide creek and landing easy as a panther on the other side.

Downwind, Rand could inhale every nuance of the vampire's scent. Beneath all of it, there was densely packed strata of emotion that might have contained fear, loathing, hatred. As well as the desire to be as far away from this as possible, but not even a trace of it was visible in the upper layers. On the outside, Cai looked as relaxed as if he were walking into a McDonald's to order a burger.

It occurred to Rand then that, despite the tragedy in his life, the loss, he'd always been where he could express it. He could grieve, rage, pine. There were those like Fane and his family to whom he could have reached out. Cai, on other hand, had not had those options with the Trads. He'd tailored his emotions to what would allow him to survive, thrive, overcome and ultimately free himself from them. Which meant the way he expressed his emotions might be totally fucked...but it made them no less genuine.

Rand didn't regret what had happened last night, but he did wish he'd figured out a way to keep Cai close. The vampire had pushed him away pretty decisively, yes, and maybe he'd needed his alone time to prep himself for this, but still...

Ah hell. It was something to think about and revisit when they made it out of here. If they did. Cai seemed pretty sure that was wishful thinking, but the emotion that surged in Rand, watching the vampire walk willingly into a world he abhorred, made him determined to succeed against those impossible odds. That trip to Syria was sounding more and more appealing. Hell, compared to this, it was going to be the Disneyland.

The two captive humans didn't stir, but the women's eyes were open. If they'd been second marked, they'd just warned the vampires they had company. But Cai had seemed sure they weren't. Beyond that, he wasn't trying for stealth.

"Goddard, you there?" Cai called out. "Half the night's already been pissed away. You still in your coffin?"

Noises inside the main cabin and the two outbuildings, movement. Rand's sharp ears calculated perhaps three or four occupants. When the door to the main cabin opened, he saw Cai's description had been spot on. Goddard was a tall rangy vampire who reminded Rand of a bent oak tree stripped of bark and leaves. He wore camouflage pants and a tight dark green T-shirt over a compact, powerful frame. He was fastening his pants and tucking in his shirt. Rand's senses went on full alert when he heard a small sound escape from the inside before he shut the door.

A stifled sob. A female one. A second later her scent hit him. Dovia.

The doors to the outbuildings opened, producing two other male vampires. They wore camouflage outfits like Goddard's, and matching unfriendly demeanors. Rand's nose received an information dump. Guns, explosives, old blood. Rancid body odor. They didn't bathe or, if they did, they didn't do it often.

Female fear, a sharp wave of it. It was coming from the two women chained to the well area. Cold anger shot through him.

You can't do anything for them. Try to rescue them now, and you'll die here. One of them's too far gone already.

Not too far gone to feel fear. Rand was surprised Cai had spared time to send him the thought, for his attention appeared absolute on the vampires circling him. They projected a menace comparable to an army of wolves a breath away from attack. Even as Rand tensed, prepared to jump into the fray if needed, his human side heeded Cai's warning and stayed on top of the wolf instincts, so he wouldn't act precipitously and lose their advantage.

The wind shifted, and Rand's attention snapped away from the clearing. Too late. Something hard struck his head, eliciting a painful whimper, and then there was darkness.

He woke, bound up in rope. He was still in wolf form. From the throbbing, he suspected his head had a serious dent in it. He was inside a building, the main cabin. Outside, the Trads' odor had been offensive. Inside, it was overwhelming.

"It's awake." A toe prodded him and he snapped, a thwarted reflex, since he was muzzled with more rope. "You never were very clever, Cai."

It was Goddard talking, standing near Rand's head. "Voltaire wants to be overlord of Greenwald's pathetic little kingdom," the Trad said. "What better way to make sure Greenwald completely loses his mind to Ennui than to help Trads kidnap his daughter and ensure their one rescue attempt fails? Easy enough when Voltaire gave us the heads up about the idiot being sent to snatch her back. And his pet wolf."

Rand couldn't move his head enough to see him, but he could smell Cai's blood. Seemed to be Cai's week for getting the shit kicked out of him. He was awake, though, and Rand detected so many compressed volatile emotions from the vampire, there was no separating them. His wolf wanted to tear flesh, to protect what was his, form a barrier of teeth and fur between Cai and this situation, but he kept a lid on it.

"Now, who's the idiot?" Cai scoffed. He might be in pain, but his refusal to appear cowed by anything was in working order, reassuring Rand. "They snatched me, beat the fuck out of me, threatened my life and said 'hey, we'll let you go if you rescue this vampire bitch for us.' Of course I said I'd do it. Why do you think I came here? To tell you that, so you could move camp before they send anyone else after you. Could have saved myself the goddamn trip if I'd known Voltaire was behind it all. Why in the fuck would I help Council vampires?"

Goddard prowled the cabin. With the limited range his bonds provided him, Rand noted his males were a trio of sinister figures lurking in the shadows, sitting on rough-hewn benches and tables.

"Why bother coming to warn us at all?" Goddard said. "Why not simply bolt when they cut you loose, put a few thousand miles between you?"

"Because I survive by not burning bridges. By coming to you, I can at least convince them I made the attempt. By coming to you, I have your protection from them, rather than making a run for it and getting caught."

Goddard laughed. "You think I would protect you from them?"

"If it's in your best interest. I go back and say she's dead, that I found the ash pile where you left her in the sun. Game over. Sure, they might spend some time trying to track you down to kill you, but you're Trads. You know these mountains like the squirrels do. They're fucking Council vampires, silver spoons stuck up their asses. They have to have GPS in their fancy SUVs to find a QuikMart."

There was a nasty chuckle or two at that from the other vampires. It didn't signal a warming to Cai, but he'd effectively reminded them of the background they shared, and their mutual contempt for non-Trads.

Goddard appeared to be thinking. After several weighted moments of silence, he crossed the floor to Rand. Rand felt it coming, braced for it, but still snarled when Goddard kicked him in the side. "What about this one? Voltaire said there's something different about him. He thinks he's a shifter. I've never seen a wolf this big, and there is an...otherness to him."

Despite the spike of *oh shit*, Rand noted the key words, "thinks he's a shifter." Voltaire hadn't seen him shift.

Cai had picked up on it, too. "Voltaire has a vivid imagination," he scoffed. "I saved the wolf's life from a hunter. We bonded. He's a pet, and blissfully silent. We both like the woods, we're both loners."

"Not so much. Voltaire also said you had a servant. He thinks the wolf and the man are the same. If it's not true, where is he? This... servant."

Goddard said the words with revulsion, as if accusing Cai of betraying all of vampire kind.

"I knew you'd damage or kill him, so I didn't let him come along. Wasn't going to waste a good resource. He's my blood supply so I don't have to go into towns as often. It's practical. What do you care? I'm not part of your Kool-Aid drinking anti-servant cult anymore, and I've found having a servant to be damn useful. I can be a lot lazier with one around."

"Hmm."

Rand could feel Goddard's eyes on him. Though he knew it wasn't a sensible thing to do, he struggled to look up, snarl at him again. Like all vampires, Goddard was disturbingly handsome and virile, but his eyes took care of any appreciation Rand's brainless cock would have had for it. Goddard had dead eyes, same as every soulless bastard who thought this kind of behavior was okay. He and Grey were spawned from the same hell demon.

The vampire's lips curved in a very distasteful and unsettling way. His reaction to Rand's aggressive behavior was no different from an indifferent stranger's to a child's tantrum. The dead eyes shifted back behind Rand to Cai. Though his nose was a better sensor than his eyes, Rand still wanted to see the vampire. The blood and the tension in his voice said they'd taken him down hard. Why? Why hadn't he just let them take him down, if he was going to pretend to be an ally?

Because he was Cai. He didn't do anything the easy way.

Now that his concussion was clearing, Rand could sort through more of the data coming to his nose. It said volumes about the Trads' elevated disrespect for personal hygiene, why Rand hadn't picked up one particular scent immediately.

Dovia.

She was curled in the far corner, naked. A collar around her throat connected to chains bolted to the logs forming the cabin walls. Her arms were bound behind her back. The chains were so short she couldn't sit on the ground, nor completely stand up. Having her hands behind her meant her balance was precarious whenever she tried to shift position.

His receptors were sensitive enough to know what blood came from surface wounds and what came from other invasions. *They won't be gentle about it, but they won't be physically brutal, either.* There was no way a woman being forced, her body unprepped and unwilling, could ever *not* be physically brutal. But it told Rand what Cai had suffered as a teenager at Goddard's hands, that he could rate unimaginable violence that way.

Rage hazed his vision. Fucking bastards; they all deserved to die. The faces of all their children flashed before him—his own, Fane and Lynn's, Sheba and Sylvan's. Rand wanted to give in to the animal, who was certain that righteous ferocity would be enough to tear them all apart. It didn't make it easier, knowing he had the strength to break those ropes. But Cai had reminded him, several times. They wouldn't win a toe-to-toe fight against four vampires. They had to wait for the right moment. For Dovia.

Her eyes turned to him, dull and hopeless, so young. He wouldn't have recognized her from Leona's portrait, except for the red hair. But as he gazed at her, he saw the brown eyes like her father's. She had her mother's sweet bow mouth, pale skin. It appeared they'd hacked at her hair with a knife, burned some of it away.

She looked at him, too. As they continued to stare at one another, he looked deeper, and saw more than hopelessness. There was a spark there, life. If given the opportunity, she would fight for her freedom, to get away. She was biding her time. The greatest battle she was fighting—and it was formidable—was against the despair, terror and pain, that could numb her mind to opportunities for escape.

Things were not looking good, but if she could keep it together after what she'd been through, she'd get no less of an effort from him. They weren't leaving without her. He would get her out of here or die trying.

"I've never liked you, Cai," Goddard said abruptly. "You may be here for exactly the reasons you say, but it doesn't really matter. I'm tired of your existence. Your belief that you don't have to account to us or anyone else. You aren't powerful, a vampire strong enough to fight off other vampires. You care for no one but yourself. You don't want to be part of the Trads, so you contribute nothing to our society."

"Society?" Cai barked a harsh laugh. "Hate to break it to you, Goddard, but living like a bunch of survivalist wackos in the woods, kidnapping helpless girls to rape, and believing indoor plumbing is the road to hell hardly qualifies you guys for a NatGeo documentary. Even other Trads think you all are the looney fringe. Don't be throwing stones in glass houses."

Goddard ignored him. He faced the trio of waiting vampires. Their appearance continued the tree theme. With identical round bowl haircuts, dark eyes, swarthy skin, knotted muscles and varying heights, they looked like an assortment of cypress knees. Rand wondered if they'd all been made by Goddard, and he'd chosen them for their similar features.

"Take Cai out and stake him," Goddard ordered, snapping Rand's attention back to him. "You can amuse yourself with him until sunrise. Then he can become the pile of ash we send back to Voltaire to show his master and claim it's his daughter. Thank you for that idea, Cai."

"Anytime," Cai said dryly, and spat. Goddard was rolling something back and forth in his palm as he spoke. Rand realized it was the metal prosthetic fang Cai wore. Goddard or one of his minions had ripped it from his mouth.

"Let that piece-of-shit traitor think we've helped him in his grand plan," Goddard mused. "He may prove useful later, if he succeeds and doesn't want it exposed that he helped Trads depose his overlord. But you know what I think, Cai? Voltaire is many things that wear on my nerves, but he is also observant."

Goddard moved behind Rand. From the difference in pitch and direction, Rand suspected Goddard had squatted next to Cai. The intensity of his next words suggested he had his full attention fixed on the vampire.

"I think Voltaire may be right. That your servant and this wolf are one and the same. We hear rumors of them in these parts, often enough I've begun to question if shifters are truly the myth we believe them to be." Goddard's voice settled into a disturbing mildness. "A human brain locked in a wolf's body as he is taken by each of us. That would be interesting."

Cai spoke in a flat voice. "Bestiality, Goddard? Really? I know Trads are backwards mouth-breathers, but that seems barbaric and crude, even for you."

A grunt as Cai was kicked, probably by one of Goddard's men. Rand's lip curled.

"Is it bestiality, if there's a man trapped in an animal's body?" Goddard asked. "It's merely a costume."

He rose. "Take Cai out of here, take care of him. Then we can return our attention to the female. And while we may not care to test Voltaire or Cai's honesty about this beast, there are other ways we can amuse ourselves. I've never skinned something alive before."

The men started to rise, the boards vibrating under their feet. The wave of cruel anticipation, a sharp, volatile smell mixed with their other revolting odors, would have made Rand's human form gag.

"You kill me, she never conceives."

Cai's tone was colder than a blast of displeasure from Lady Lyssa.

A weighted stillness, then Goddard's heavy boots crossed the floor. The cabin shuddered as he apparently picked Cai up and slammed him against the wall.

Rand's growl was deep as fire inside the earth, but he was drowned out, the thudding impact echoing as Goddard did it several times, until Rand was sure blood from Cai's skull was splattering the logs. Rand howled over Cai's grunt of pain. The vampire nearest him kicked him. Rand tried to bite him, despite the ropes holding his muzzle. The vampire seized his nape and punched the flat of his nose with a blow hard enough to break cartilage. He released his grip and stood over Rand, with a look that dared him to do anything else.

The violence saturating the room drove out any rational thought or logic. Rand was strangling himself, trying to get free of his bonds. But then a movement caught his eye.

Dovia's lips moving, silently, her eyes appealing to him. Her body twitched as if her fingers were curling and uncurling behind her back, wanting to reach out. Other reactions penetrated; her heart hammering inside her chest.

It upset her that they were hurting them. Despite what had been done to her, she wanted to help, to make it stop.

They were her only chance. Her only hope. Rand fought his nature, fought to calm himself, no matter that it felt like they were in a maelstrom.

Goddard was shouting. "You dare? You dare bring that up? You said you could make it happen, and a fucking plant split out of Megan's belly, staked her through the heart."

Cai's words were garbled, until Goddard apparently eased up enough his response could be heard. It was dripping with contempt. "What do you care? You hated that bitch. She was more Timmon's, anyhow. Least until you killed him and drank his blood with her, your sick little mating ceremony. And it went bad not because I intended to turn her into garden fertilizer, but because I didn't know what the hell I was doing. I told you that and you didn't listen."

Cai took a breath. "But I know what the hell I'm doing now."

Another sudden silence descended on the cabin, while the tension and anticipation increased tenfold. The other three vampires exchanged glances. Rand had managed to flip over when the vampire dropped him, so now his eyes went to the corner where Goddard and Cai were.

Aw, Christ. When they'd ripped the fang from his mouth, it looked like they'd used it to slice open Cai's face. The cut was healing, from ear to corner of the mouth. However, based on the other places he was bleeding, he'd need some serious blood to regain strength. They had his wrists bound with thick rope. Something a vampire could remove, as a shifter could, but not with their four adversaries standing over them.

Goddard dropped him, and Cai crumpled to the ground, his legs unable to hold him. He still managed a bloody grin and spat more of the red stuff on the floor. The vampire's blue eyes were hot with vindication. "Got your attention, didn't I? You're right. I'm lying about why I'm here. I could have just bolted after they let me go, but I'm sick of being on my own. And I don't want to be part of the Council vampires. You kidnapped me, made me a Trad, and I hated you for it, but after a couple fucking centuries it's clear that's what I am. I needed a gate pass, and so I spent time working on it. I didn't plan it this way, but Greenwald's daughter was the best excuse possible for me to come back, put my foot in the door."

He jerked his head toward Dovia. "I can prove it with her, if someone's had her in the past few hours."

Goddard snorted. "I was pulling out of her cunt when you started braying like a mule outside our camp. Each of us had her once so far tonight."

"Great. Eager little bunnies, all of you."

Cai's voice was dry, cynical. Rand didn't know how he did it, shutting down all evidence of empathy for the girl. He felt sick, for so many reasons, on so many levels.

He thought of Fane's neutrality, his wonder that Rand would help a vampire, but if Fane was here, Rand was sure he'd feel no differently from Rand. Yes, she was a vampire, but all he saw was a female in pain, afraid. And so young. Like Sylvan's adolescent wolves had been, on the cusp of adulthood, not quite there, but brimming with the energy and impatience for it, as youth often was. She would have had that, only a few days before. He could still see the embers of it in the depths of her eyes, but that light was dying. The Trads would stomp it out completely.

So it didn't matter what they were. Wolf, human, vampire. Beneath all the rest, the soul was what it was. Hers was worth saving. He just didn't know how strongly Cai felt about it. Yes, he'd decided to do this, against very personal and vocal reservations, but how long would that resolve last?

"So, for this to work, you're going to have to untie me and stop acting like I'm here to launch a freaking futile rescue attempt," Cai continued. "Do I look that stupid? Okay, correction, you already think I'm stupid, but do you think I'm that kind of stupid?"

Goddard studied him a long moment. "No, I don't. But I want to test this dubious loyalty of yours. Brutus, Malvin and Hector are going to take you outside. They're going to tie you down next to the storehouse. It keeps two feet of shade on the northern side this time of year, even at the sun's height. As long as you don't lose consciousness from the pain of being above ground during the heat of the sun, and roll fully into its path, you'll survive until nightfall."

"No deal," Cai said. "I show you that she can conceive right here, right now. Or I don't do it at all. You know how fucking spiteful I am, Goddard. I don't have a problem burning to ash just to deny you and Meeny, Miny and Mo here what you've always wanted, a pregnant fucking vampire female."

The one Goddard called Brutus had dropped to his heels next to Rand and was prodding him with a fire poker. When Rand showed his teeth, best as he could with rope around his muzzle, the vampire sneered at him, poked harder, a quick jab in the ribs that hit bone and tender flesh. Goddard shot them an annoyed look when Rand couldn't bite back the yelp. The vampire desisted.

"You care nothing about your own life?" Goddard asked Cai. "I find that very unlikely."

"Oh, I'm very fond of saving my own skin. Ask my complete lack of friends. But I have one reason to sacrifice it that trumps even my inflated self-interest. Pissing you off. I prove she can conceive, and you untie my wolf, treat us as close to guests as you barbaric hillbillies know how to do it. In return, we'll contribute extra hands to your little camp here, as long as I think I need to stay to avoid the wrath of the Council or help you repel any incursions by them. That's the deal."

Goddard's lip curled, but Rand sensed the frustration brewing under the surface. If Cai was bluffing, he was doing a hell of a job with it. Goddard's attention shifted to Rand. "Perhaps you care nothing for yourself, but what about your companion, who I sense is far more than wolf? Other than your squeamishness for bestiality, it means nothing to you if we violate him in whatever ways we please?"

Cai rolled his eyes. "Even if he was my servant and not just a wolf, servants are used to being violated by whoever, whenever. It's what being a slave means. So big fucking deal to either of us."

Goddard's expression tightened. "I've heard that many of these humans come to vampires willingly. Because of a bond with them. That does not arise without reciprocation. It takes two ends of rope to tie a knot."

"Don't give up your day job to write love poetry," Cai advised. "A lot of them come in with romantic notions and, when those notions are destroyed, they're already caught. You know how weak the human mind is. It doesn't take long to turn them servile. They want someone to own them, most of them. They crave the subjugation. If they're not food, they're pets, no different from my wolf, only way more fuckable. I figure you know some of that; else you wouldn't have those two females chained out there."

"They're breeding stock."

"Maybe at one time, but as usual you've abused them to the point their chances of conception are nil. They're just dying plants you're ignoring. Only reason they're still here is you've set aside your distaste for milk cow style feeding and are using them for a blood source, so you can stay close to camp and the vampire girl."

Goddard's expression hardened, but Cai sighed. With blood smeared on his face and clothing, his body heeled to one side, favoring whatever was broken or bruised, he shouldn't have been able to look bored and irritated, but he did.

"Hell, Goddard, are we going to talk about this until dawn? Fucking let me go so I can give you a bouncy baby psycho on the vampire bitch. Then we can all make up and be friends before we call it a night. Or has your need to be a sadist outgrown your need to be a daddy?"

Goddard stared at him another long moment. Then he gestured to his thugs. "Untie him."

Malvin cut Cai's bonds. Hector released Dovia from her bonds, including the collar, but grasped her by a handful of snarled hair and dragged her unceremoniously across the cabin. The lack of reaction to her muffled gasp and yelp verified that none of Goddard's cronies had a scrap of empathy for her. Hector could have been dragging a chair across the floor.

But Goddard...Cai didn't have to look to know the vamp was getting off on it. Many Trads truly had no emotional connection to any but their own kind. Dice up a human in front of them, and they'd react as if watching someone cut up carrots for a salad.

Goddard's heightened connection to other life forms was motivated by one thing only—sadism. He got off on inflicting pain upon anything weaker than himself. Which was likely why he'd never had the patience to try and impregnate his human females. If it didn't happen after a week, the sadism won out.

After being at his mercy for decades, Cai was pretty well-versed with all the nuances of his psychotic fuckery, and he could use them now. Everything was an advantage. He was going to keep telling himself that, at least until he was being burned to ash outside.

He knew Rand was wondering what was happening in his head. He could hardly blame him for wondering if Cai would abandon the girl to save his own skin. But it was better for things to seem hopeless right now. Cai kept his blue eyes as reflective and flat as mirrors under Goddard's relentless stare.

When Hector deposited Dovia practically in Cai's lap, Cai caught her before she could topple. She sucked in another breath. Pain. Since she was naked, every bruise and cut showed. She wasn't healing, which meant she was hungry. Really hungry.

"Christ, Goddard. Have you not let her feed since she got here?"

"She refused to feed from any of us, or the humans out in the yard. Said she'd rather die. Until she conceives, her life or death is of no consequence to us, and if she conceives, we will force blood into her, by injection if necessary."

She'd automatically flinched from his touch, and Cai loosened his grip enough to hopefully help her feel a little less trapped. "I'm not going to hurt you," he said gruffly. "All you have to do is be still."

He had to say it in a neutral, I-don't-really-give-a-shit tone, but he couldn't imagine she would have felt any better or more trusting if he said it in a tone as soothing and nurturing as her own mother would have used. She stared up at him. No matter how wretched and beaten down she seemed, how frightened she was, he saw the stubbornness in the chin that explained why she'd refused their blood. She was a fighter.

But she was also young, scared, in pain, and her soul was quivering, screaming at the violation to her body and mind that had been visited upon her, over and over.

"Okay," he said. "If this works, they won't touch you again. Understand?"

"What?" Goddard said. "Her cunt isn't—"

"For the first couple weeks the rooting, for lack of a better word, is fragile. No stress, no abuse, and regular infusions of blood daily. If she won't take it direct—and I can't blame her, because I wouldn't put my mouth on a single one of you filthy bastards—put it in a cup." Cai met her gaze. "You'd drink it then, wouldn't you? To stay alive."

She stared at him, so hard it was as if she was trying to see words on a blank surface. But at length she nodded.

"Yes."

She was hoarse. He didn't know if that was from screaming or other things he didn't want to think about. Fuck. She needed blood. Really good, energized blood.

He looked across the room at Rand. They were about to lose one hell of an advantage in favor of the slim possibility of another. But Cai would let it be Rand's call. Not that he doubted his decision, the noble bastard. Fuck.

Hell, Goddard already suspected. And maybe there'd be another way to deal with this where Rand being in human form would be advantageous, much as Cai despised the idea of him being made more vulnerable. He couldn't think about what they might do to Rand as human. He had to hope everything came together before that happened. Or else Cai would have incurred yet another reason to hate himself.

He gestured toward Rand. "Let him go so he can shift to human. What I'm going to do has a better chance if she's fed, and the best blood for her to drink is his."

"So he is a shifter," Goddard said, vicious satisfaction in his voice. "And your servant."

"Yeah, yeah. You're really smart. I'm so impressed. Untie him."

Malvin grunted. "Leave him tied. He can shift a portion of his body, like his arm. Right?"

Cai sent Malvin a censorious look. "Seriously? Are you in charge of the stupidest question division of this conglomeration of fuck ups?"

He swiftly curled his arm around Dovia, tucking her upper body into a ball against his chest. He took Hector's punch to the face without defending himself. Spitting blood, he glared at him, then at Goddard. "You want this to happen or not? For the next half hour, let's all work on our anger management skills so I can get this the fuck done."

"You better be able to do this, Cai, or it will go far worse for you," Goddard said, eyes glittering.

"Yeah, because right now it's all peaches and honey. Untie the wolf," he repeated. "Let him come to me. I need to keep my hands on her, monitor the changes in her temperature and temperament."

Goddard frowned, but he jerked a short nod at Brutus. "Do it. Guard the door."

Brutus bent and untied the ropes, shoving Rand back so he was off balance as they fell away. Rand leaped to his feet, hackles raised like a porcupine and feet braced. His bared teeth looked three feet long. If their situation wasn't so fucked, Cai would have gotten a serious hard-on from how dangerous the male looked. The vampires tensed.

Rand, shift to human. Remember, I need you to act reluctant toward me, like you hate me. But we need to feed her. She's starving and afraid, and I know how your blood rejuvenated me. She's not down and out, and more strength will help her keep fighting.

The wolf's head turned in his direction. Cai kept his gaze trained on Rand's, not allowing anything to interfere with the connection. The wolf's mind was a violent thicket, but Rand was in there. Suspicion emanated from those bi-colored eyes.

I'm not going to sell either of you out. But if I don't remind these assholes I'm as much of a selfish bastard as they are, they won't let up and give us any opportunities to turn the tide. You're going to have to trust me, when I know we haven't known each other long enough for that. But really, what other fabulous options are presenting themselves? Trust a soulless bastard who might be on your side or...?

CHAPTER FOURTEEN

*R*and's hackles slowly lowered. Cai bit back a sigh of relief, because Goddard was already getting antsy. If they suspected a long conversation happening between them, things could get worse quickly.

Rand shifted with a reluctance that was convincing because it wasn't feigned. Cai didn't blame him. The vampires murmured, their eyes widening, the universal reaction to watching animal turn human or vice versa. Rand did it smoothly, ending up in a crouch on his heels, his gaze shifting balefully around the room. When they landed on Cai, they were filled with resentment. Hate. Cai wondered what he was channeling and decided not to look inside his mind to find out.

"Magnificent," Goddard breathed, in a way that made Cai want to rip out his lungs and pitch them into a meat grinder. Rand ignored him, which Cai found even more magnificent. But he made his tone sharp, impatient.

"Get your ass over here, or you'll be sorry."

Rand's lip curled, but he obeyed and moved to their side. The shifter dropped to a squat again next to Dovia. Whereas his expression toward Cai remained hostile, he put a hand on the girl's back. She'd stayed curled against Cai's chest after Hector hit him, her fingers dug into his shirt and chest. Cai found it difficult not to put his arms around her in a gesture of comfort. But he could do it now, under the guise of something else, and with a surrogate.

"We're going to change positions," he told Rand. "Put her in your lap, your back against the wall. I need to be where I can put one palm on her stomach, another on her lower back."

Rand held out his arms. Dovia resisted being moved at first, but then her senses took in Rand. Heat, and that special something he had. After what she'd been through, a large naked male should have been the last thing she wanted near her. Yet suddenly she was moving, reaching for him.

Rand adjusted into the position Cai had dictated, settling Dovia into his lap, holding her secure in his arms. Since both of them were naked, when her ass pressed into his lap, she tensed, but Rand murmured a reassurance to her. Fortunately, he integrated it with a hostile look toward Cai that said he held him as much to blame for their situation as the Trads, which nicely reinforced the idea that the wolf had no love for his Master. Truth was the easiest lie to pass off, right?

Yet Cai caught a fleeting thought from him, unexpected. Rand had to quell an urge to reach up and wipe the blood from Cai's mouth. Cai kept his gaze on the girl, focused on what he was doing, so he wouldn't betray any reaction to that. In this environment, an act of kindness might completely unravel him. He made his mind-voice brusque.

See if you can seem kind of thick, more animal than human. That shouldn't be too tough.

Cai almost grinned at the colorful response to that, devoid of any unsettling tenderness from his wolf. Cai laid a palm gently on Dovia's bare stomach, his other on her lower and upper back. His hand was large, and she was a little thing, so the coverage worked. Her gaze shot to him, wary.

"Feed from Rand," he said. "Let him nourish you. What I'm going to do, as I said, it won't hurt." And it would offer her the only protection she'd get in this place.

He didn't think she'd put together what he was doing, or perhaps the idea was so ludicrous and her mind so exhausted from fear and stress, she had nothing to lend to resist it. Rand was stroking her hair. When Cai reached up to put his fingers against Rand's jaw, expose his neck to her, Rand curled his lip back again, his eyes flashing.

Cai seized his hair in a harsh grip, and banged his head none too gently against the cabin wall. It made Dovia cringe, which he hated, but he kept his gaze locked on Rand's. "We've been round and round on this, wolf. I'll touch you however and whenever the fuck I want. You're bound to me. You can't run from me, and every time you try, I leave scars on you that take days to heal. You resist me one more time, I'm going to break the same leg every night for a week until it refuses to heal up. Tone down the attitude."

Rand's eyes were blue and gold fire, but as Cai held the gaze with a threatening one of his own, the fire died back. His wolf's expression became sullen rather than defiant. He turned his attention to the girl in his arms, though the rest of his body where Cai brushed it remained rigid.

"You'll have to tell us how you captured a shifter, Cai," Goddard said. "It appears there is a story to be told."

"Pretty much what I already told you. Saved him from a hunter, marked him, and it's been a battle of wills ever since. He's more wild animal than man most days. Easier to handle as a wolf." Cai tossed out a harsh chuckle. "He's actually protective of me in that form, like any dog is of his Master, which pisses him off. I'd sleep with one eye open if I couldn't kick his ass any day of the week. He's a little stronger than your average human, but not by much."

Rand's body stiffened further at the insult, but he kept his head down. If they lived through this, Cai expected he'd have a serious ass-kicking coming.

Count on it.

Fuck, he really couldn't afford the repartee, because it did something to him, knowing he wasn't in this all by himself. Rand's life depended on his hardness, so Cai pushed away all the soft feelings and went radio silent.

When he heard the scraping of a chair, he saw that Goddard had taken a seat only a few feet away. The others were positioned in a half circle, though on their feet. He guessed that was in case he or Rand tried some foolish attempt to bolt.

"I liked your fur," Dovia whispered shyly against Rand's chest. "It's pretty."

Rand dipped his head and blinked. The quiet comment surprised Cai as well. Perhaps the girl's mind was already broken, or in the first instance of safety she'd had, deceptive though it was, she'd simply spoken what came to mind.

Rand's most recent experience with vampires had been those at Greenwald's, their sexual sophistication out front and overwhelming. Even a twenty-two-year-old vampire, being a sexually mature young woman, would have some level of it, when healthy and not terrified for her life. But vampires her age could be innocents in other ways. Impulse control for bloodlust was so poor that they could kill a human if not taught and monitored by someone. She seemed to have been taught well, for her fangs unsheathed instantly at proximity to Rand's throat, but she didn't leap on him like a mountain lion on fresh game.

"Would you prefer a cup, my lady?" Cai asked quietly.

"There's none of that *my lady, my lord* bullshit here," Goddard said irritably. Dovia flinched. As Cai kept his back to him, ignoring him, she met his eyes and shook her head.

Putting her slim fingers on Rand's throat, she stretched up slowly, brought her fangs to his artery. A tiny growl came from her, a desperate noise, and a shudder went through her. It was as if she was fighting her own urges, maybe because her body was sending a lot of conflicting messages about male contact. *No fucking kidding.* But Rand's arm tightened around her, a gentle encouragement, not a restraint, and she bit. The relief from her was palpable as blood flooded her mouth, feeding her hunger.

Cai was startled by an unexpected reaction. For an absurd second, he wanted to growl himself, pull her away from Rand's throat. Rand was his servant, and no other vampire had the right to touch him, feed from him. Feeding wasn't functional for vampires. It was intimate, sexual...

Yeah, he'd lost his fucking mind. For Dovia, it *was* functional and all about survival, and he was being an idiot. Hell, if the intimacy, the involuntary sexual response all vampires felt from feeding, brought her the fleeting illusion of safety or control, he wasn't begrudging it to her. Plus, he had other things to handle.

There were a lot of things wrong about what he was going to do. And dangerous. And part of the reason he'd stayed so fucking far away from vampires for as long as he could. He hadn't told Lyssa the whole truth. No one knew the whole truth.

He'd never actually successfully done it to a female vampire. But that wasn't because he couldn't do it. It was because he'd never tried.

The bitch he'd killed by turning her into a hydroponic, he'd done that deliberately. He'd no more have tried to plant a baby in Megan's belly than he would have dropped a toddler into a vat of acid.

Yet the ability had been in him for so long. To create life, in many different forms. Not just plants. The first time he'd felt it, Cai had known he could do it the way a baby knew it would be able to walk even before he did, which was why the child tried.

But this ability was different from that. Not unnatural, not exactly. It was creation magic, after all. It was simply wrong on a fundamental level. Because he had the power didn't necessarily mean he should use it. Power without judgment was just a fuck-up waiting to happen. If he knew one thing for certain about himself, it was that he and good judgment were not on the same page, book, or planet.

Here he was, ready to prove it. Right or wrong, her life would depend on the life he could put inside her, a life that wouldn't be something she'd want or was meant to be.

He'd indulge in moral mastication later when their lives weren't in the balance. He started slowing everything down in his mind. He had to open everything within him, get a full energy flow going, and he knew that opened his mind to Rand. That wasn't necessarily a bad thing. Maybe his subconscious could reassure the wolf in a way Cai couldn't afford to do otherwise.

Rand was holding her, stroking her, his gaze fixed on Cai, eyes widening as he started getting the feed.

Cai couldn't describe it. He'd figured out a long time ago that saying God works in mysterious ways wasn't a copout; there simply weren't words for how Creation worked. It was a feeling, a force. The flow of water and wind, the breaking open of a seedpod, the stem pushing up through the earth toward sunlight. It was a spark. It pulled from something inside him he didn't understand, that he'd never known where it came from.

Hell, his father had been a farmer; his mother the baker's daughter he married. Faithful and loyal to one another. Though he'd heard stories about changelings, Cai was pretty sure he wasn't Fae, especially when Lodell was able to turn him into a vampire.

People like Lyssa's sorcerer were human, but drew their talent for magic from something inside them, right? So maybe he was someone like that, born with the gift.

He didn't linger on the theories, and especially not on the images of his parents. Nothing could exist when he was doing this, except this. Trads disappeared, the girl's distress, the slim-to-none chance they would survive. Everything disappeared.

Everything but Rand, curiously. His presence was still there, like a heartbeat inside Cai. He inhaled his warmth and, though he was in human form, Cai could smell the wolf, the sun-drenched fur, the musky oil of him. The moonlight when he ran at night, forming lightning bolts of gleaming color on his coat. He was creation, too, in a sense. Every time he shifted.

There it was. The energy was like being lowered into heated water, everything silent, slow moving, rich and powerful. The first time it had happened, he'd been four or five. He might have even done it before then and not remembered.

His mother had been sharing a cup of tea with her friend Olive, who was crying because she couldn't conceive. She was afraid her husband, a merchant, would get a bastard on a mistress so he could have a son to take over his business. She talked in a low voice to Cai's mother about having "tried again" last night, hoping against hope.

Cai laid down his toys and went to her. His mother was about to shoo him away when he reached out with both small hands and laid them on Olive's stomach. He felt it quicken within him, that energy. In the simple terms of a child, he took two ends of rope, her husband's seed still in her body, and one of her eggs, and brought them together in that dark, safe triangle of space in her body. There was something not quite right, but he fixed it, with a thought, a good wish, a little flare of heat from his palms. They were planted together, snug in that soft bed of tissue. And the light was there, and it was good.

He'd pulled back, smiled a child's smile and said "baby."

Olive had tried to answer the smile through her tears. She thought he'd heard their talk of a child and assumed she was pregnant. Hugging him, she said, "I hope so, Mordecai. I really hope so."

Shortly thereafter, she skipped her courses. Even though the early nineteenth century was mostly past the witch hunt days, it was probably a good thing that the timing didn't point to him causing it. But his mother had given him some odd looks, that day and then when Olive rushed in to give the good news several weeks later.

But mothers kind of guessed when there was something freaky about their sons, even if they didn't want to acknowledge it.

There it was. Cai found those tendrils of magic, pushed away the thought of whose hated seed he was marrying to that innocent, unknowing egg, and put the two together. Vampire biology was different when it came to fertility, so things were not as welcoming as when he'd done it for Olive, but his will could overcome physiology.

He wove the right conditions to make it happen, even if her womb wouldn't have sustained it for whatever reason so many vampire females didn't conceive. Cai was able to replace that with his magic and make it work, even as he felt his strength decrease exponentially, exacerbated by his physical condition.

Olive had delivered a beautiful baby girl, healthy as a horse, screaming her lungs out. Her husband had wanted a boy, so soon as Olive was back on her feet, he started beating his wife again for her shortcomings. Cai had been too young to know the difference between desperation and hope. He just felt her desire for a baby, which, under his mother's abundance of love, Cai assumed was always a good thing.

Olive took the blows to protect her child, but it wasn't enough. One night, her husband tossed the kid down the ladder from the hayloft, pissed off when she hid from him. The child died.

He'd told himself shit like that happened all the time, so there was no verifiable proof that God was any better at deciding who should have a baby than Cai, with his random act of misguided kindness. But lesson learned. He'd never used it toward another human again, but as he grew older, that power in him increased. He was smart enough to learn how to use it, even if he didn't extend his practical applications beyond plants and goats. He liked baby goats.

It felt almost too easy, too natural, which disturbed him. It was as if there was even more power waiting behind it, if he delved too deep. The thought brought an uncomfortable flash to Lyssa's parting words to him. *Such magic is hard to quantify and often opens your path to other abilities you didn't know you had.*

That ease-of-use was part of why he rarely used it. That, and it was the reason he'd been taken from his family, which had made him pissed off at it for a long time. But then he'd realized that was like a guy being mad at his own money because someone stole it and left him penniless.

Cai had no idea what the future of this baby would be. But he felt the seed take, knew when the rooting was sound and had the right start.

As he surfaced, slowly bringing himself back, he found Rand was as pale as a vampire himself, his gaze caught between incredulity and something darker. He'd taken that journey with him, Cai realized, following him in his mind.

"Holy God," the wolf murmured.

Dovia had finished her meal, and was half conscious against Rand's chest, him still holding her. From the feel of the night, Cai guessed maybe an hour had passed. He'd given her an hour respite, hopefully more, if he could prove to Goddard what had transpired.

I don't think you'll have a problem with that. There was an energy around you, Cai. It was almost...visible, like air with weight. They know something happened.

"Good." He turned his head and looked at Goddard. "If you'll come here, I can prove to you she's pregnant."

Dovia's gaze flew open, her expression shocked. Rand murmured to her when she started to struggle. The sight of Goddard rising to his full height froze her. If she could have folded herself into a tenth of her size and hidden in Rand's hand, she would have. But she seemed to recall herself as Goddard approached. Her backbone stiffened, her face going blank.

Inside she was a turmoil of emotions. Cai had felt it, waded through that jungle, had to mute it to do what needed to be done. He admired her control, even as he knew it wouldn't hold long. She was about as physically and mentally exhausted as it was possible to be. She'd been half-asleep before his words had startled her awake.

Goddard squatted next to him. God, Cai hated that smell, that unwashed odor that so many Trads thought was a badge of honor. Because of it, even when Cai stayed in the woods for weeks at a time, he bathed daily. He gestured. "Give me your hand."

When the Trad hesitated, Cai scoffed. "Believe me, I have as much desire to touch you as a leprous snake. Give me your damn hand."

Goddard complied with a threatening look, and Cai met Dovia's gaze. "It's all right," he said.

He laid Goddard's hand on her lower abdomen, molded it there. Dovia recoiled, but Rand held her steady, speaking to her in a low, soothing tone. The energy Goddard would be feeling mostly came from Cai's hand, but it connected to the magic he'd done, like an electric current passing through Goddard's palm. It won a startled expression, then a cruel flash of triumph. Even vampires could identify creation magic.

"Fuck, I think he did it."

The other vampires surged up with a scraping of chairs and thumping of boots. Dovia shrank back, and Rand showed his teeth, human self notwithstanding. Cai gave him a warning look and a calming thought.

If they confirm it for themselves, they'll leave her be. Treat her far better than they have been. Give us some more options.

Rand managed to settle himself, with visible effort, but when Brutus looked as if he was going to yank her from Rand's arms forcibly to paw at her, Cai was the one to intervene. He stood up and shoved at the male, startling him.

"Remember what I said. The first two weeks, she'll be very fragile. The seed has taken, but the roots are new, tenuous. Regular blood, in a cup so she'll drink it. A clean bed and a private corner of this shit-hole that's hospitable enough for a woman to be comfortable. Let her walk around at night. Fresh air. No more chains."

Goddard threw up a hand when Brutus seemed as if he was going to punch Cai through a wall and yank the girl away from Rand anyway. "Indulge him," he said shortly.

He turned a wondering gaze to Cai, his usual malevolence warring with the unknown. It gave his face a macabre harlequin look.

"It's a kick in the ass, isn't it?" Cai said sardonically. "The slave you tried your best to kill because I couldn't do what you wanted then, ends up being the road to the survival of your oh-so-special Trad purist bullshit. So here are my terms. You treat me as your guest. No more of the abuse and threats. In return, I'll become her personal nanny, keeping her safe and well through her pregnancy, making sure you get a bouncing baby boy."

"It's a boy?"

"Yeah, I figured that's what you wanted. Sorry I didn't check with you to see if you'd already picked out pink for the nursery."

"You can choose?"

"If I can create it in her, I can choose what sex it is." Cai snorted. "That's the easy part."

No, I totally can't do that, he told Rand. *But I want him deliriously happy, and this misogynist crowd is all about the penis factor.*

To Rand's credit, he didn't react to that by so much as a blink. But deep in Cai's head, he thought he heard a grim chuckle. A nice moment of solidarity in a totally not-good situation. This time he could handle it without cracking.

"Hmm." Goddard stared down at Dovia. She had tears running down her face, and had gone tense as a board in Rand's arms. Her look, when it fell on Cai, was one of revulsion. Cai tried not to let it affect him. *Stupid kid. I'm trying to help get you out of here, so stow the attitude.* He avoided Rand's eyes, not wanting to see the same issues there he saw in the disquieting abyss of her dark gaze.

Goddard frowned. "I admit...I am impressed."

"That means so much nothing to me."

Goddard snorted. Moving away, his head down and expression almost meditative, he stopped by the table, which held a variety of weapons ready to hand. Passing his fingers over them, he hovered over a set of brass knuckles, picked them up and slipped them over his fingers. Then he turned toward Cai.

The light in his eyes was one Cai recognized all too well. It brought a surge of childhood terror, desperation and hopelessness, which rose like a wave to overcome the man he was now. A man who yeah, you could fuck with him, but you couldn't own him. Not now, not ever.

He told himself that, even as he braced for the worst Goddard could bring. Because he could tell it was coming.

Somewhere during their back and forth, Rand had closed his eyes. Now they opened, for he felt the danger, the hairs lifting on his neck. Cai and Goddard's mutual contempt was obvious, but beneath that, he felt something far deeper and more sinister.

Absolute hatred for one another.

Goddard returned to Cai, facing him. There was a significant pause, and then things went bad. Really bad.

Fast as the clichéd snake, but Rand could think of no other comparison that fit, Goddard struck Cai in the face three times. Breaking things. His nose, more of his teeth. Maybe his jaw. Rand's protective instincts went into full forward gear, but even through the phenomenal pain, Cai's mind roared at him.

No! You don't care about me. Her. Protect her.

Rand scrambled out of the way, taking Dovia with him. He retreated to the farthest corner, holding her close, keeping them clear, though it was the last place he wanted to be. Fuck, he would have preferred to be bound head to foot, rather than be unable to go to the vampire's aid. It was too much like that helpless feeling all over again, the day his family had died.

Cai had fallen against the wall and slumped down to the floor. Dropping to his heels and bracing his hand next to the vampire's head, Goddard spoke in a reasonable tone that sent chills up Rand's spine. "That will take some time to heal without blood. More, with the sun draining your energy while you're tied in that narrow shade spot outside. You will suffer greatly, Cai. And when I bring you in tomorrow night, you'll do what you said you'll do, yet you'll do it not as a demand, but to survive."

Goddard's gaze shifted to Rand, eyes empty as a hell pit. "Today, your wolf will not be touched, because I want to emphasize to you that I respect a servant, a piece of shit fuck toy and blood bag, more than I respect you. You are not my equal, you are nothing. You were not born a vampire. You were human chattel brought here because we thought you would be useful. When you weren't, you somehow clawed yourself to a level of acceptance that was tolerated by all but me. Your return is a dream come true. I did hate Megan, but you destroyed her, an act far above your station. You must pay the price for that."

He rose and jerked his head at Brutus. "Put the girl on the cot. Chain one wrist to keep her there, but that's all. Treat her as Cai said."

The male vampire came and plucked Dovia out of Rand's arms. Dovia clung to Rand, and Rand wanted to hold onto her, but he saw Brutus was following Cai's direction. His grip was firm but not cruel. Rand still didn't like it, but he relinquished her.

"Now," Goddard said pleasantly, turning back to Cai. "Should you come back tomorrow night and still be stubborn and putting on airs, I will not only fuck your wolf, but while I'm doing so, I will tell Hector to start skinning him, whatever form he takes. His pain and suffering means nothing to me. And as much as he detests you, I know that feeling is not mutual. You've always been a liar, and you are lying when you say he means nothing to you. You will give me yet one more way to hurt you, Cai, and that brings me immeasurable satisfaction."

He straightened, slipping the brass knuckles off and tossing them on the table with a clank that made Dovia jump. Brutus had put her on the cot as instructed. It had a drawstring curtain around it, but it was pushed back so Rand could see her as she curled on the bed, arms wrapped around herself. She was shaking.

"On the brighter side," Goddard continued, "since it seems you have made seed quicken in her womb, I will give you sanctuary from the Council until I tire of you. But you will do so on your knees, lower than that human dung out there, and you will suck my cock every day and do whatever shit jobs need to be done. You're my slave, Cai. Should that baby not survive, your life will become far worse."

Cai coughed up more blood, but the look he shot Goddard was glittering with hate, and he bared his one fang. "That's your problem, Goddard. You're a fucking hypocrite. You aren't a Trad wanting to promote your race. You're just a fucking psychopath. I think you want the baby to fail."

He looked toward the other three vampires. "Watch her close. Because if anyone's going to try and sabotage that pregnancy, it will be him."

That set off another round of pummeling from Goddard. Rand leaped at him, shifting in mid-air to wolf again, blood lust taking over everything else. Goddard ducked the charge and Rand hit the unguarded door hard, rolling out into the yard. He was on his feet, prepared to leap back in to Cai's defense, but Brutus reactively slammed the door, locking him out. Rand threw himself against the door, but it wouldn't yield. He backed off but started to circle the cabin, letting out short howls of frustration.

Fortunately or unfortunately, with Cai's mind available to him, Rand could hear the conversation inside clearly.

"You're right." Goddard chuckled. "The wolf within him protects you, even as the man hates you. Perhaps you enjoy the more complex levels of torture better than you let on, Cai."

"Careful. You sound like a proud daddy, Goddard. Fucking lunatic."

Cai grunted as Goddard kicked him in the side. Hector glanced out of a slit between two of the logs. "He's still circling. Dumbass bitch doesn't know he could run away right now."

"You weren't listening," Cai rasped. "He's bound to me. Even when he goes to hunt, he comes back. Man knows I can track him; wolf responds to the marking. Loyal. Dogs. Bet you wish you had someone who felt like that about you, asshole."

More beating, this time with Hector's participation. Dovia's cry of distress at being a front row witness made Rand howl louder. He circled the cabin again, pawed at the ground, but somewhere amid the distress, his human side picked up the need to further Cai's ruse. Rand backed off to the edge of the clearing, taking a seat. Panting and distressed, but to all appearances, he looked like a wolf who wouldn't be going anywhere without his Master. If they would just stop hitting him. Goddamn them.

At length, they did, and he heard Goddard give the order to Hector and Malvin. "Take him out and stake him by the shed."

"Don't mess with my fucking stuff," Cai said, and Rand knew he was looking toward the tote that had been tossed in the corner, probably when the vampire was first hauled into the cabin. "Got a bottle of wine in there I've been saving for a special occasion. Baby shower, you know…"

So much for human logic. As they dragged Cai out, his face a bloody mess, his psyche laden with unimaginable pain, physical and emotional, Rand charged. He was going to fucking kill every one of the sadistic bastards. He was—

Malvin kicked him in the face and Hector followed up with more of the same, driving him toward the door of the main cabin.

Let them get you back inside. Even overcome by stress, Cai was adamant.

Rand made that as difficult as possible for Goddard's vampires, within reason. He felt Cai's alarm with how close he cut it, dodging, weaving, snapping. He caught flesh a couple times. Which meant he took some hard hits of his own, but at least it looked real.

Yeah. They snap your spine, it'll look real...authentic. Backpack. Go...sit on it. Make them take it from you.

The direction, the hint of a plan, distracted Rand from the vampire's obvious pain and his own desire to tear the Trads apart. At one last kick from Hector that lifted Rand over the threshold and had him thudding onto the floor of the cabin, he whimpered and staggered to his feet, but slunk toward the backpack. When he crouched over it, Malvin bared his fangs in an ugly smile.

"Oh no, mate. That's ours now."

More kicking, growling, snapping. When they finally drove Rand from it, he ended up next to Dovia's cot. Dovia reached out to him to hold him back. She didn't fear him.

Stay with her. Protect her. That's it...for now. Brian's serum...in the wine. Let's see how stupid they are. Stay wolf.

It was a miracle that Cai's voice remained so clear in his head, even though agony haloed the words.

He could protect her. Stay a wolf. Those things he could do. Rand planted himself before Dovia, her fingers adjusting but still curled in his fur. He wouldn't deal with these males in a human form. He didn't want to engage in conversation, and this was the way he could fight best if fighting was needed. Though he knew four vampires could overpower him in a heartbeat, the wolf side of him obviously made them warier of him. What was it Cai had said? No one liked getting dog bit.

Rand remembered how his wolf had brought Leona comfort. Now her daughter gripped him the same way, stroking him. She burrowed her fingers in even more deeply, as if she could feel her mother's touch, and was trying to bridge that distance by putting her hands where Leona had.

As Hector tossed the backpack on the table with a hard clunk from the wine bottle, the others took a seat around it. They cast only cursory glances his way, mainly to be sure the fight had gone out of him. Then their attention shifted to Dovia.

"We clean up the cellar before dawn," Goddard said shortly. "Put the cot down there, some other things for her comfort. If the spoiled little cunt needs that to carry the babe to full term, that's what she'll get. One of us will stay with her during daylight, but hands off, just as he said." He pulled the pack over to him and rummaged through it, bringing forth the wine. His brow crinkled, and he gave a sour smile. "Decent label. Wonder what he was really saving it for."

He pulled it out of reach when Brutus extended a hand. "We prep things for her, then we split it to celebrate." His lips split in a thin smile. "We're going to be daddies, boys."

Rand...

As the vampires moved to make the arrangements, the impending dawn making their movements more hurried, Rand heard Cai's whisper in his mind. He could feel the dawn, too, and he was out there in it, so close to the heat.

You have to get away. Cai's voice was strained.

Not leaving you. Or her.

Mostly her. Cai's acid chuckle bugged him, but the vampire continued without pause. *I'm not being noble, you idiot wolf. If they drink that wine, they'll be out for a while. And remember Brian said their reflexes will be slower, at least for a short time, when they wake at twilight. Get out of here, activate Plan B. Bring Daegan up to speed. Soon as you can make it work, start sniffing around like you're looking for a place to piss. Don't let them lock you in when they go to ground. Don't know what kind of security measures they put in place on the door. We've bought the girl some time. Let's not waste it.*

Rand didn't think about how Cai had bought Dovia time, mainly because he still wasn't sure what to think about the amazing, terrible thing Cai had been able to do. What it meant, what the vampire thought about it, how it would impact...all of this.

Instead, he sat with Dovia for the next half hour while the vampires acted with surprising efficiency, ferrying down a cot, linens, and even a couple old magazines they'd dug up from somewhere. Though Rand wasn't sure how much she'd enjoy Guns & Ammo and Survival Daily. They didn't speak to her, and the looks they cast her way were far from kind, but they left her alone. It was the best she could hope for among their company.

Rand knew he needed to do what Cai had said, but every protective instinct in him raged against leaving her. The worst part was he couldn't tell Dovia what he was doing. Or why.

Cai had become progressively quieter, not responding to Rand's last couple of thoughts. The approaching sun added to Rand's uneasiness and sense of urgency. Though Cai had asked for no aid, Rand knew in a few moments he would need his help even more than Dovia did. The vampires would be coming for her soon to take her down-stairs, and Rand couldn't risk them locking him in with her.

Rand nudged her face. Her gaze rose and held his. He gave her a long, long look, and then he moved away from her clutching fingers. His heart cracked at her stifled sound of panic, but with feigned indif-ference, he began to amble through the cabin, sniffing at this or that. When he was sure Hector had noticed him, he started to lift his leg.

"Hey, no, don't do that. Fucking hell."

He jumped just like a dog would at the snapped curse. However, like a wolf—and letting some of his true self through—he laid back his ears and growled menacingly, a rumble that vibrated through the boards of the cabin. Malvin laughed.

"He'll rip your face off, Hector. Open the door and let him out. Hell, with that bond Cai talked about, he might go lay next to the bastard. He'll keep him warm if he's feeling cold, right?"

There was some ugly laughter about that, but when they looked toward Goddard for confirmation, the Trad shrugged. "Cai's right. This place is filthy, but I don't want it smelling like wolf piss and shit."

Regardless, Rand felt the head vampire's eyes on him, assessing, so he made damn sure that when the door was open he slunk warily along the edges of the cabin, taking his time about it, rather than charging straight for it.

"Though..."

Rand almost paused, as he would if someone had spoken to him, but thank all the gods, he caught himself. He kept moving toward the door without hesitation, the vampire's words nothing to a wolf but nonsense, though his ear stayed swept toward him to gauge threat.

"If you are more sentient than your Master claims, wolf, or your human side has more care for him than you act like you do, I will tell you this. You leave him here, I will do so many unspeakable things to him, you won't recognize him if you meet again. His soul itself will be in shreds."

"Fuck, who cares, Goddard?" Brutus asked. "Cai's the one with the ability to care for the girl."

"If he has a servant, we don't have to find blood for him," Goddard said shortly. "And the wolf hunts for himself. A win-win."

There was more to it than that. Even if he hadn't received it loud and clear from Cai, Rand understood that Goddard was the broken one of this group. The others were probably mostly interested in their autonomy from Council vampires and adding to the Trad idea of a pure vampire race. They exercised brutality toward anyone as a matter of pecking order. But Goddard was addicted to the cruelty. He liked how the wolf seemed slave-bound to Cai and would enjoy the benefits that could provide.

Yeah, that wasn't going to happen. Rand had cleared the door, and received a follow-up from Cai.

Go. Soon as you can get to the edge of the clearing. Go.

Rand ignored him. He found a place at the edge of the clearing, screened by foliage, but he didn't leave. He waited. They were minutes from sunrise. Alert and tense, he stayed on the periphery of the camp, an agitated whine caught in his throat. It turned into a growl when his sharp ears and nose detected Dovia's movements. As they took her down to the cellar, she was struggling and crying. She was terrified again, thought she was abandoned, wasn't sure if Cai and Rand would bolt on her.

Would Goddard torment her in ways he felt wouldn't endanger what she was carrying? Rand hated hearing and feeling her desolation. For a brief few precious seconds, he'd been an ally. It tore his heart out of his chest to hear her cry. Putting his nose down on his paws, he closed his eyes tight, and counted the minutes.

He was relieved to see Goddard and Hector leave the cabin, and go to the outbuildings. The vampires didn't apparently prefer to share sleeping quarters. Goddard was carrying the bottle of wine, and it was half-empty. Hector had a canteen cup in hand, probably his share.

That left Malvin and Brutus guarding Dovia in the cellar. While Rand wished she could be completely left alone, Goddard was the one Rand had been most concerned would stay with her. Evil had a smell, and the Trad stunk of it. But maybe Goddard understood his own weaknesses, and that was why he left his other men in charge of her.

Things got quiet. The sun crested the horizon. Vampire safe zone. Somewhat. Rand was willing to bet the cellar of the main cabin connected to underground bunkers in the other outbuildings, so all the vampires could respond to a threat. Unless they were unconscious from the wine, they still had the advantage, because she was too fragile for Cai and Rand to risk a fight in close quarters. If the Trads thought they were at risk of losing their prize, they would kill her. Scorched earth policy.

Why are you still here?

For you.

Now that there was no risk of vampire interference, Rand left the bushes. He had no way of knowing if they were studying any underground surveillance, so he stayed in character, circling the cabins, sniffing, marking, but made his way steadily to where he knew they had left Cai. Based on how Cai had described his protective instincts, it wouldn't be out of character for the wolf to seek out his Master.

He was starting to form a list of things he wished he could un-see, and Cai's appearance made the top of the list. They had him practically mummified in chains. They'd forced one length into his mouth like a horse's bit, tightening it enough it cut into the corners. They'd also stripped him naked, his clothes folded in a neat pile a few feet away.

All Trads horrible? Rand asked in wolf speak.

No. You won't find any of them at a PTA meeting, but Goddard and his clan are the serious crazy end of the spectrum in the Trad world.

Cai didn't open his eyes. He was coated with a sickly-smelling sweat, and Rand could feel his pain, already a dull roar, increasing to a full-fledged cacophony with the strength of the sun. He would have shade here, but as Goddard had said, at the sun's height, it would narrow precipitously. They'd laid Cai up against the side of the shed like a log.

You need to fucking go, Cai insisted.

Stay short while. You said I'd stay close. Because of bond.

That part is actually kind of true. Though I can't make any fucking sense of it. Dumbass dog loyalty. Cai's eyes stayed closed. He was shaking harder than Dovia, but Rand didn't want to point that out.

Dig hole. I can do that.

Cai shook his head, a sharp jerk. *They're likely still watching. Best you just seem distressed and take off. Best for both of us. This is going to get real ugly, real fast. Vampires Lyssa's age can be above ground as long as they're in a nice brick mansion, or a dirt coffin hidden in a van, but their strength is sapped by it. For those like me, made vampire, and two hundred years old, I'm going to be a fried egg for the next few hours. And extra crispy on the edges.*

His brow creased, lines deepening on his face. *There may be some screaming, a lullaby to put Goddard to sleep. As distractions go for you to get away, couldn't have come up with any better. That Goddard. What an idiot genius.*

Rand moved his head so it rested on Cai's chest. He knew the vampire was on fire, but that shaking was more than physical. It went down to Cai's soul, and he knew the vampire needed the contact. Cai's eyes briefly opened, rested on him.

Goofy dog. His mind voice was an intimate murmur, despite the pain stressing it. *Didn't like her drinking from you, you know. How stupid is that?*

Can't leave you. As his emotions swelled, the wolf's mind took over even more of his speech patterns. *Her. Dovia. Tearing guts out. Crying. Thinks abandoned.*

She'll forgive you in a New York minute if you come back here with some kickass cavalry. Your other choice is playing Nana during her pregnancy until Goddard has his hell spawn. Then he'll let his cronies rape her to death to put her and all other Council vampires symbolically in their place. Your choice, but I'm leaning real strongly toward the cavalry.

Never take anything...serious.

Take it serious and realize how fucked up all of this is? How fucked up I am? Facing reality is pressing the red button and going up in a mushroom cloud.

Cai's eyes met his. For a flash, Rand saw it, saw that maelstrom. Then it was locked behind a door again. *But hey, you get back, manage to rescue us, I might consider couples' therapy, honey. Long as the therapist has a nice tight ass and includes going down on me as part of the service.*

Rand nipped him lightly and Cai strangled on a laugh, one filled with such agony it made Rand immediately chagrined. But it hadn't been the bite. It was the impending dawn.

Go, damn you. His fevered gaze locked on Rand. *Only you can save our lives and, if you fail, well, fuck, no guilt, you hear me? You did your best. Don't make me haunt your ass. Go.*

Rand felt as if he was being ripped apart by ropes tied to all his limbs, his heart, his soul, his mind. He had to act like a wolf. Had to act like a wolf. He blocked out Dovia's crying, detectable to his sharp ears, the rasping of Cai's breath, the shock waves of pain coming off the vampire. He made himself circle the camp once more, sniffing.

Even though the vampires couldn't go out in the sun, their age made it possible for them to be up longer below ground, monitor things, get suspicious. The wine would hopefully take care of that, but nothing was certain. It was best to take the time to maintain the ruse that he wasn't smart enough to be a real threat.

He passed close by the human females; silent, motionless women with virtually no spirit left to them, no interest in him. Cai had been right. One was too close to death's door. He could smell it upon her.

Rand thought of Lady Lyssa and Jacob, and all the things he'd seen and felt when at Lord Greenwald's home. Yes, Cai had been mistreated, because Greenwald thought he might be part of the same group that had taken his daughter, and Greenwald was obviously not thinking straight. And Voltaire...

Rand's teeth showed briefly as he thought about the traitor. Dovia was the most important thing, but if they lived to see Voltaire brought to justice, that would be gravy on the bone.

But this horrible brutality...he could understand Cai's lack of good feeling toward any vampires, but if a choice had to be made, Rand would gravitate toward the Council vampires. They at least seemed to have a recognizable code of behavior.

He circled and pawed Cai, whined. Cai made a noise as if warding him off, cursing him. After a few more moments of agitation, Rand lifted his head, scenting the air, seeking game. Then he headed into the trees as if he'd caught a trail. Once out of sight of the camp, he started to run, letting the hunter take over.

But not for food. His eyes went cold, teeth sharp and gleaming, ears laid back as he stretched out. He flew straight as an arrow and twice as fast.

Yet when the sun began to climb in the sky, he heard Cai's first screams. Because there was no outrunning what Rand could hear in his head.

CHAPTER FIFTEEN

*R*and exceeded the fastest speed he'd ever run, his wake flushing deer, rabbits and birds that normally would have caught his attention. Before they'd left Fane's, Rand had called Gideon, told them where the Trads were with Dovia, and that they were going in. The Council's warrior had indicated they would find a discreet approach that would put them near Fane, and use Fane as a communications relay. Fane had been amenable to that.

So Daegan wasn't very far away, hopefully, with reinforcements, but he couldn't come out in the daylight any more than the others. Rand hoped he had a good idea about extracting Dovia. Or maybe Cai did. Cai seemed to do his best thinking on the fly.

Rand skidded to a halt. Things had gone completely silent in his head. Over time, the screaming had become hoarse, then broken, then fallen to groans, but it had still been there, a terrible proof of life in Rand's head.

No. Cai wasn't dead. If he was dead, Rand would be dead. With a stab of feeling, Rand realized what had happened.

Cai had blocked his mind, used up precious energy so Rand wouldn't have to hear him, suffer from that sound. If the vampire would be consistently an asshole, it would be so much easier to know how to feel about him.

Rand resumed his course at the same breakneck pace, but his mind was whirling just as fast. He thought about the magic he'd seen

Cai do. Creation magic. While shifters weren't like Fae or other magic users, they had a rudimentary awareness of it, and there was no stronger energy.

Everyone who knew about vampires knew that the biggest challenge to the strength of their race was the fertility problem. Their population was decreasing, and there'd never been many of them. Born vampires were stronger than made ones, for the most part. When they had children, the children were of sturdier stuff than made ones. If it was learned a vampire could help female vampires conceive...

Cai had serious reservations about using that magic, about the right and wrong applications for it. Rand had caught a glimpse of something, about a woman he'd helped conceive, but that had been cloaked in forbidding shadows, as if Cai hadn't wanted to think further about it.

He hadn't wanted vampires to know he could do it for anything but plants. But he'd used it to protect Dovia.

Hell, he was so confusing. Maybe the key was in that nuclear comment he'd made. *Facing reality is pressing the red button and going up in a mushroom cloud.* Rand had felt dark things from the vampire. Yes, dark as in sad and tragic, brutal and frightening, shadows of his past. But also...darkness. Like a tunnel deep in the earth that led nowhere but to an absence of light. All the treasures were there, but hidden, never to be seen, because it was better that way.

He was getting close to his destination. Exercising an abundance of caution, he hadn't used howling to signal ahead. He redoubled his pace, though his lungs were already burning, muscles aching. He could tell down to the boot size every place he'd been kicked.

Fane was working in the back fields with Stalker and Chad. All three males came to full alert as Rand leaped the furrows of turned earth and slid to a stop in front of them, almost bowling over Fane. He couldn't breathe, had to drop his head, take long, gasping breaths. But he shifted at the same time, since he wouldn't be able to tell Fane what he needed in wolf form. It was time he contributed his own ideas to this half-baked, desperate and doomed-to-fail rescue plan.

"Help," he said. "I need help. And a phone."

~

London broiling. Londontown, falling down. My fair lady. Hot, hot, hot... Song on the radio. Cai watched the one human woman die. Laying there, her eyes on him, and suddenly, she wasn't there. Life gone. The other woman called her name, weakly, desperately, the first show of life she'd had. Now she'd be alone. Amazing, how anything could still matter when someone had been through so much, and what mattered was usually the connection to someone else.

Lodell, his mother, his father. Rand. Those were his connections in life, over two hundred years. What a pathetically short list. Oh, there'd been a kid...that kid, the one who thought Cai was a shut-in but would play near Cai's cabin. That had been back when Cai had tried having a house in the Tennessee mountains. Seeing what it was like to stay in one place. Had his place been like Rand's home, decades later, with the oh-so-perfect Dylef?

That was a crappy thought, but he was being tortured. He was allowed to be petty. He focused on the kid again. Just a waif, with a mop of greasy hair and brown eyes like a raccoon's. Kid was poor as dirt, with nine brothers and sisters. Parents didn't even notice him being gone. Cai found him things to eat he didn't normally get, stealing them from the general store at night. Kid liked candy. What kid didn't?

When Cai abandoned the idea of being a homeowner, he left the kid the house. That had been, what? Fifty years ago? Probably married with a bunch of kids and had left that place long ago. Time took everything away. No bonds lasted.

Servants, though...that was a bond that was supposed to last into eternity. Nice wishful thinking. Unless you were bonded to someone who drove you crazy, and then that was like a sentence to Purgatory. But Rand...

Everything hurt, was on fire, screaming, blinding pain. He was in the shade, but it didn't matter. It was like being in an oven, slowly being roasted. His skin blistering and peeling, his throat closing, making him feel like he was suffocating. He knew he wasn't, but he supposed it was the vampire form of waterboarding. The brain was on five-alarm fire alert, screaming for water, air, all engines to report to the scene...nothing, though. No one would come. Not for him. Maybe for Dovia. She deserved it. Nice kid. Didn't deserve this.

Rand. Cai didn't have any particular thoughts associated with that one word. It merely brought him comfort to say it, feel it. Rand had put his head on his chest before he went. Maybe that was just a wolf thing. They did a lot of communicating by rubbing faces, bodies, bumping one another. It could have been a *so long, asshole, it's been fun.*

Yeah, but no. Dovia. Rand would do whatever he could to rescue Dovia, and that was fine. Dovia deserved that kind of knight in shining armor shit. God, this hurt. Would it never end?

But he'd been through worse, survived worse. It was just getting harder to do it, over and over again. Hell, he was pissed at that human woman for dying. Give up, bitch? Hell, you only knew the tip end of this kind of suffering. Lightweight.

But she'd died staring at him, and that look had crawled into his burning soul. *Stop looking at me. Stop.*

What time was it? Mid-afternoon, maybe. A few more hours to go. Then Goddard would have proved his point and things would get better. He'd let Cai take care of Dovia, and Cai would wait on his chance, if Rand couldn't find anyone to help. No. Daegan was coming. If they could trust Council vampires, that terrifying son of a bitch with his big-ass sword or the equally terrifying thousand-year-old queen would make something happen. Just a matter of biding time.

Worst case, Goddard rabbited with Dovia, Cai, and his cronies, and escaped being caught. Disappeared deep into these mountains, deeper than any humanoid knew, the way Trads could. People thought the oceans were uncharted. There were places no one went except Trads, Fae. Dinosaurs that people thought were extinct. Or shifters that vampires thought no longer existed. So yeah, maybe Rand could track him there. He wouldn't give up.

If that worst-case scenario happened, then Cai would have to help Dovia, be there, protect her as much as he could, look for other chances. And hope it wouldn't take until the baby was full term. But if it came to that, maybe he could manipulate Goddard enough to let Dovia and Cai go after she had the baby, get her away from him.

They had no nurturing qualities. Without its mother, the infant would die, which was the best thing that could happen to it in this crowd. Woohoo, kid, you win a first-class ticket right back to the Hall of Souls, jump on the train and leave Psycho Fuckhead Town behind... But only after the kid suffered, and that didn't sit well with Cai. He remembered the spark in Dovia's eyes, the tightening of her chin, a mirror of the look in her mother's face. Leona. Leona had seemed broken, overwhelmed, but he'd seen her through Rand's eyes and knew broken wasn't helpless. Hell yeah, Cai knew that firsthand.

Dovia wouldn't leave the baby behind. But it wouldn't matter. Unless they could get Cai to turn her into a baby machine again, they'd kill her soon after she gave them what they wanted.

Or she'd kill herself if they did try to make her into a baby machine. But she wouldn't have to do that. Cai would become a one-hit wonder, only able to make it happen that once, by sheer dumb luck and desperation for sanctuary from the Council vampires. That'd be his story.

Shadows. Shadows falling upon him, increasing the shade, but it didn't help. God, he wished it did.

"Cai." It was Rand, in human form, beautifully naked, wrapping him up in blankets. "This is going to hurt. I'm sorry."

He almost laughed, and it came out as a hysterical gurgle that tasted like blood. Then he was in the full sun, he could feel it through the blanket. He would have done some more screaming if his throat hadn't given out long before. He was going to turn to ash. But Rand moved faster than he knew Rand could move. They were in the forest, the deep forest, and Rand laid him down inside a pit of cool, cool earth. A wonderfully deep one.

The wolf had dug him a hole. It was the nicest thing anyone had ever done for Cai.

They left one blanket on him, probably thinking it was best to keep the dirt away from his wounds, but he struggled weakly against it, and Rand understood. They took it off him, put him bare into the ground. Wolves were shoveling the dirt back over him with fast trundling paws. Soft, cakelike crumbles, mixed with dried leaves and debris that abraded his skin where they made contact, but then they had his lower body covered and it was okay. They blanketed him all the way to his neck, his head comfortably nested in cushiony soil, like a mother's breast and twice as welcome. A wolf stood at Rand's shoulder and Rand offered his wrist to him. The wolf obliged, snapping down on it to create an open wound.

Cai would have snarled at the wolf for biting what was his, but what Rand was doing penetrated his fogged brain. Cai only had one functioning fang, and he was weak as something embarrassing, like a kitten. Rand brought his bleeding wrist to his lips and let a few drops of blood fall there, igniting his even weaker hunger.

"Drink, vampire. We'll need you for the fight to come. Unless you've given up on me."

He never gave up. Because giving up meant the bastards had won, and they were never getting that goddamn satisfaction. He was gifted with a flash of Rand's tight smile, but it didn't reach the male's eyes. He cupped a gentle hand under Cai's skull. Cai freed his arms from the loosely packed earth enough to grip Rand's wrist with both hands. They were trembling so hard, he could barely get his mouth on the flesh. Rand steadied him.

Good thing he'd already made that cut, because Cai was pretty sure, once his hunger roused, he would have almost torn Rand's wrist in half to get to that blood. He was like a fledgling, his body so stressed and wounded, the blood it needed limitless. More than Rand had. He couldn't stop himself though. Couldn't...

Rand, don't let me drink too much. Get...lightheaded, stop me. I will drain you. You'll be the one laying out of this fight.

Rand had an answer to that, too. Fane had shifted to human and was next to him. When Rand extricated his wrist, Fane had already cut his own with a pocket knife and replaced the food source at Cai's mouth. The male didn't actively engage Cai's gaze. Cai could feel his reluctance, borderline revulsion, at being a vampire's food. However, the way he looked toward Rand said his regard for the other wolf was what made him do it.

Him and Rand, yin and yang. Sweet and sour. Timmy and Lassie. Everyone had found Timmy intensely annoying and wouldn't have minded if he stayed down in that well while Lassie hooked up with some hot supermodel as his Mistress, since the actor dog Lassie had been male. Following her adventures every week...

Shut up, vampire. Drink. Be easy. Rand stroked Cai's hair back from his burned forehead as he fed. His long fingers gathered more earth around Cai, his jaw and ears, framing his face. The wolves had mounded more dirt on him below the neck, so only his hands and a portion of his forearms were visible where he held onto Fane. Cai noticed a bunch of wolves milling in the shadows of the forest. Laying down, sniffing the air, waiting. They had a fierceness to them, an edginess. A war party. They were ready to kick some vampire ass. Glory hallelujah, except if they did it after dusk, they'd all be killed. Because when he and Dovia would be ready to move, so would Goddard and his idiots.

"Typical vampire. Thinking you're the biggest, baddest thing out there. Don't worry about that right now. We've figured it out." Rand continued to caress his hair, lightly touching his face. "Here I thought you were as devoted to males as I am, and you fantasize about Dominatrix supermodels."

The skin seemed less raw now, so the contact felt good. Cai's tongue still wasn't working for talking, partly because it was occupied with blood. He was drinking from Fane's son Stalker, donor number three. But he rallied enough to respond, at least in his mind.

I'm very eclectic. I sometimes fantasize about tree knotholes, particularly if they're shaped just right. Is Daegan...

"Yes. His servant is transporting him as we speak, to put him as close to us by nightfall as possible."

Cai let go and nodded his thanks to Stalker, who withdrew with Fane to join the rest of the pack. Apparently, their communication would be with Rand alone. Cai didn't rate direct conversation.

They don't want to be here.

"They see little reason to fight for vampires," Rand acknowledged. "But they'll fight because I asked. Because I told them an innocent is an innocent, whether vampire, human or wolf. And because Fane didn't realize the vampires had human captives." Shadows crossed Rand's gaze. "He said the distance they maintained and the vampire scent masked it. When they caught a whiff of human, they simply assumed it was the remains of their feedings. If he had known, he would have done more."

One died this afternoon.

Rand's mouth tightened. "Blessings upon her soul," he murmured.

He said it like he meant it. Like he thought there was something out there that could take care of a soul after death, make everything all right. Crazy dog.

"Wolf," Rand corrected. "Don't insult me, vampire. I can kick your ass right now without hardly trying."

It almost made Cai smile, but his mind was starting to engage. *We need more of a plan, don't we?*

"Some diversionary tactics would be useful. With your knowledge of the Trads, we thought you might have an idea or two."

"Here I was, thinking you were feeding me because you liked having me around." They were the first words Cai had attempted. Though they came out rasping and broken, like a bad cell signal, he was pleased to see Rand's eyes crease with humor.

"You know far better than that, vampire." Then Rand sobered. "Any ideas?"

Cai sighed. "No. Yeah. Hell, I don't know. I'm used to doing this by the seat of my pants."

"You don't say." The quick flash of humor on Rand's face made Cai want to lift a hand to it, touch the male's strong jaw.

He tried, and noticed that his arm, while still weak and trembling, didn't look as burned, though he could sure as fuck still feel the sun, even if it was screened by the forest canopy. He needed to get all the way under.

The skin was sloughing off like a snake's. While a good sign, it also put him at the bottom of the barrel when it came to being an appealing fuck.

"Yes, rolling you over and having my way with your ass is uppermost in my mind."

Hell, he wasn't blocking his thoughts from Rand. But he guessed that was okay. It might be easier for Rand to ladle ideas out of the soup in his brain than for Cai to form coherent sentences. But then Cai got something. A pleasant surprise, proof that his brain *was* working.

Okay, I've got an idea. If it works, your wolves won't have to fight, at least until Daegan gets here. It's just Daegan?

"His servant asked me how many vampires we were facing. I told him four, and he said Daegan was all that would be needed." Rand lifted a shoulder. "I don't doubt him. Hunting vampires...I think it's what Daegan does for the Council."

He stuck a sword in my back when I was distracted. You're easily impressed.

Cai ignored Rand's who-are-you-kidding look. But he'd come to a similar conclusion at Greenwald's. A vampire who was a vampire hunter. With a vampire hunter for a servant. It made sense. A lot of things made sense right now, because he was too brain-fried to question them.

"Let's hope he's not overestimating the size of his dick. Or sword. My idea is going to rely on me being in full health and walking out of this hole in the ground at twilight, and you and your wolves staying out of sight until I signal for you. Doable?"

Rand nodded, but his brow furrowed. "I'm only getting part of what you're thinking..."

Good. It meant Cai's brain was scrambled enough to hold some things in reserve. He didn't necessarily want Rand anticipating him on part of his plan.

"It's all right. You'll recognize the cues. You're pretty sharp for a quadruped."

At twilight, Cai walked out of the forest as planned. Thank God for shifter blood. If he'd only had access to human blood, he suspected he would have still felt a bit woozy, but after a total of four shifter donors, including Idris, Cai assured a dubious Rand he was glowing with health. The only residual symptom was the emotional wobbles that happened after being tortured, and hell, dealing with those was home territory for him.

Since late afternoon was the most likely time for a vampire of any age to be completely out, it had been decided a couple hours ago to take the risk and free the human woman. Cilya and Chad had cut her loose and taken her with them, headed back to Fane's place, where she'd be turned over to Sangra's care and transported to a hospital.

The human had insisted that the other woman's body be taken too, stretching out her hands toward her in mute appeal. They'd agreed, never mind that it put them down an additional wolf for what was coming. No one was going to argue it, even Cai. He wondered if the two women had known one another before they'd been brought here, but that didn't matter. They were bonded now.

Returning to the present and his semblance of a plan, Cai strode into the clearing, much as he had little more than a day before, though this time he carried a branch about three feet in length. Since he'd been stripped of his knife and didn't know where it was, he picked up a hunting knife someone had left stuck in the picnic table near the well. It had the odor of human blood on it. Fuck only knew why, and he wasn't going to spare it thought. Taking a seat on the top of the picnic table, he broke the branch in half and started whittling upon the two pieces. Waiting.

Malvin came out first. His eyes narrowed at the sight of Cai, which told him they either didn't have the monitoring equipment Cai had assumed, or Brian's serum had kept them out of it during the key footage of Cai's release. Malvin did look nicely groggy. Rand had told him he'd mounded up some dirt and debris so if the camera feed was as grainy as it typically was for a security camera, a passing glance would have made it look like he was still there.

Malvin's mouth tightened in disappointment. He'd probably been anticipating being the first to stand over Cai and gloat over his horrific condition. Subsequent to the short nap he took after his feeding—completely, blissfully buried under the earth—Cai had risen and found a creek to finish the skin sloughing process. It had been on the screaming side of painful, but it looked better. He was a little pinkish and mottled, like a kid too long in the sun at the beach, but he'd assured Rand he'd have his milky-white corpse complexion again in no time.

"You were chained," Malvin said. "Even if your wolf had shifted, he could not have freed you. How did you..."

"Kind of boggles the mind, doesn't it? Makes you think I have more tricks up my sleeve than you first imagined." Fane had broken the padlock and chains with the bolt cutters they'd brought from the farm. Cai cast a glance over himself. Since he'd only donned the jeans from the clothes Brutus had so courteously left folded up next to his block of shade, he added, "Well, since I'm not wearing a shirt, I guess that would be tricks up my ass, but you get the gist."

He waved the knife generally before taking another peel off the ever-sharpening stick. "The lying aboveground screeching thing was boring, so I got loose, went and hung out in the forest. Freed your blood sources, since that's twisted and sick, and it nauseated me to see it. What respectable Trad keeps a human for blood rather than hunting for it? You guys have gone downhill since I saw you last."

Hector's lip curled in a pre-battle sneer, his fists starting to curl, but Cai pointed at him with the knife. "Hold your ground. I'm done dicking with minions." He raised his voice. "Goddard, unless you think you need four vampires to deal with one, why don't you bring your ass out here?"

He heard Rand's voice in his head, quizzical. This was the part he hadn't let him see fully because Cai wasn't in the mood to turn it into a debate. He didn't bother to respond, since his plan was about to be obvious. He was betting his normally conservative wolf would come up with some creative swear words. Cai was looking forward to it.

Goddard emerged, zipping up his pants. Cai's gut clutched, remembering earlier, but sick as Goddard was, he wanted that baby. And he was coming out of the outbuilding he and Hector had shared, not the cabin where Dovia was. While Cai didn't doubt there was a tunnel between the two, from the scent that hit his nostrils and reflected off Hector, he confirmed that Goddard had expended his insatiable needs on Hector. That was a mental picture Cai wished he didn't have to have, but it was better than one involving Dovia.

Goddard had never been particular about the gender of the orifice he used, and his earlier threats suggested even species barriers didn't bother him. He really would have screwed Rand as a wolf. Cai was even more certain he would have skinned him the way he described. Which might be a big part of why Cai was doing what he was about to do.

Rand had told him his wolf form was his sanctuary, but even if he hadn't, the feelings Cai had picked up from the male would have made it crystal clear. Rape was rape, and all of it was awful, but if Goddard had carried out that threat upon Rand, it might have broken something in the wolf's mind that could never be repaired.

Cai had seen the scars on Rand's wrists, in Rand's heart and soul. He'd been broken enough for one life. And Goddard was going to pay for even thinking about adding to it.

Goddard looked toward Malvin and Malvin shrugged. "He was like that when I came out. No idea how he got free."

Goddard scoffed at Cai. "You've learned to be more resourceful. It changes nothing."

"Yeah, nothing's changed, that's for damn sure. Trads are all brutal assholes, but most of them have a code. It's about staying pure predators. Their interpretation of what that means is still pretty fucked, but it's consistent. My wolf is a natural predator, and he doesn't have a sadistic bone in his body."

Cai rose from the picnic table and squared off with Goddard. "You're sick of me? I'm sick of you. Sick of knowing you exist. We're going to fight, just you and me. You claim to be better than me, stronger? You claim I'm nothing? You're going to have to back that shit up. We throw down right here, you and me, to the death."

He tossed the two stakes he'd carved on the ground, his aim decent enough that the pointed ends lodged into the earth halfway between them.

Cai? Even back in wolf form, Rand's consternation came through. *Goddard older. Stronger. Faster.*

Yep. Let's hope Daegan and Gideon didn't stop at Cracker Barrel to eat dinner. You wanted a good distraction for their approach, you got it. When it's in play, circle to the back of the main cabin. When they had me chained over at storage, I noticed the bottom two logs are rotting, water damage. A couple of you should be able to knock them out, go through and pull Dovia out of the cellar. Use the gum on her first thing, in case they did a blood tracker on her.

He spoke over Rand's protests. *If things go wrong...I'm sorry. I don't want to take you down with me, but worst-case scenario, you'll get to be with your family, the way you want to be.*

Cai...

Busy now. Shut up.

He received a searing blast of feeling, so articulate he almost grinned. He was right. Rand had a creative way of swearing. Better than words.

Goddard stepped forward. Cai matched him, pace for pace, and the vampire stopped.

"This is foolishness. I'll kill you. You know it."

"Hmm. Big talk." Cai lifted a hand and, right on cue, a nice dramatic touch, the wolves started to materialize from the woods, ringing the clearing around the cabin and grounds. Hell, more had arrived. Cai had been so focused on his plan, he hadn't sensed them. Fortunately, so distracted by Cai and how he'd gotten free, neither had Goddard and his cronies.

Rand had a lot of loyal friends. About fifty wolves, enough to give even four vampires pause. It was a lot of teeth and glowing eyes. What was even more unexpected was about half of them weren't shifters. They were actual wolves.

We are both wolf and human, vampire. Is it unusual we have bonds with those who are all one or the other?

No, come to think of it. But it was pretty damn cool. Cai nodded in the general direction of the wolves. "They're here to make sure this stays between you and me. If Brutus, Malvin and Hector want to be up to their armpits in pissed-off wolves, all they have to do is help you in any way. Though if that happens, I'll be disappointed. You make yourself out to be such a badass, it's going to be surprising if you scream like a little bitch for their help. But on the plus side, it'll be extremely gratifying to me if you do."

Goddard was measuring him and the wolves, his brain doing a lot of calculations, Cai was sure. Cai didn't see Rand, and expected he and a couple of the other wolves were circling to the back as he'd suggested. Fane had taken lead position for the pack. He looked damn intimidating, glittering eyes leveled on the vampires, teeth bared, a low growl rumbling from his throat and matched by that of all the other wolves and shifters. Good as the beating of drums and yelling by an invading army.

Goddard was holding the same frozen, I-will-kill-you-all expression, but his boys were looking a little nervous.

Cai dropped to his heels, tenting his fingers on the ground, his gaze leveling on Goddard. Yeah, this was about a distraction, on the surface, but as things narrowed down to this moment, another part of him opened up. Cai wasn't leaving this field until Goddard was dead. Every inch of his hated face stomped into the ground, every finger broken that had ever taken from Cai's flesh. His tongue ripped out to destroy any more words he could say to rip apart a soul.

Cai wanted him dead, and he wanted to personally be the one who sent him to hell. He didn't care that Goddard was faster and stronger, that a two-hundred-year-old vampire was no match for a four-hundred-year-old one. Cai had enough hate built up in him to balance the scales. He was fucking sure of it.

Goddard opened his mouth to say something more, but Cai was done with dramatic monologues. He surged up from the ground and went for the stakes, moving at a speed only vampires and astronauts knew was possible.

~

Cai's idea might buy them time, but it didn't make Rand feel any better about it. The vampire was risking a hell of a lot on factors that might or might not pan out. But when the cache of pent-up pissed-off broke loose inside Cai, Rand recognized that rage.

When hurt beyond what you could bear, and something broke and had to be remade from what was left over, it would never be as good or whole as what had been before. That spawned a festering anger that got buried so deep, a soul often didn't realize how strong it was, until a moment like this one happened. Then it took over like the wrath of a god.

Rand could hear the wolves moving, circling, feinting an occasionally snap at the other vampires to keep them mindful of the threat if they interfered with the fight. He wasn't going to get a better shot at Dovia.

He had Stalker and Windrunner with him. The teenage girl was devoted to her older brother, and had refused to be left behind, even when Fane brought all his pack authority to bear on her, mandating she and Darcy would remain at home with Lynn and Sangra.

Windrunner had insisted she would follow them, if they left her behind. Rand was sure Fane's children didn't often defy him, but Windrunner, even cowed down to a submissive position from her father's anger, had a look that said she wasn't letting Stalker go without her.

She was a wolf, but she was also a teenager. After a long look between Fane and Lynn, Fane had allowed it, if she promised to stay at the back and out of any direct confrontation. It was part of why Rand chose her to accompany him now.

When they found the rotted wood, he and Stalker shifted to human, using feet to kick and break it, and those helpful opposable thumbs to pull it loose. Windrunner stayed wolf, but pitched in with some enthusiastic digging. Thanks to her smaller size, she was able to fit through the opening pretty quickly. Kid had a lot of guts.

The wind direction kept them apprised of the vampires, but Stalker shifted back to wolf and went to the corner to keep a visual on the three. As Cai had predicted, all the vampires seemed to be caught up watching the fight, but Stalker's tense body posture suggested things weren't going well.

Rand didn't dwell on what would happen if Cai were killed, if he would feel whatever mortal wound Cai took the same way, or if he would simply drop. All that mattered was Dovia.

He heard Windrunner's whine, and she was there again, nosing and nudging Dovia. The girl's eyes were wide in her delicate face, but at the sight of Rand, she reached through the opening without hesitation so he could pull her out. Windrunner squirmed out behind her. Dovia was still naked, since they'd only provided her a "blanket" for her comfort, but they'd figure that out. In his earlier exploration of the cabin, Rand had found no clothes for her. Bastards.

Cai, got her.

He wasn't expecting a response, so he jumped when the emphatic reply blasted through him like a shout. The staccato-fast syllables told him Cai was fighting for his life.

Get her to Daegan. Run. Gum.

Shit, he had almost forgotten. Windrunner pressed up next to him and he felt for the slim collar Lynn had fashioned for her daughter to wear, buried in her ruff. They'd fixed the small container of gum to it. He pulled it off, opened the tin and dumped the handful of gumballs into it, no bigger than peas. "Chew this now," he told Dovia. "It erases any blood tracer they put on you."

She was lucid enough to obey immediately. He turned to Stalker. Thank God male shifters were bigger than even the largest breed of wolves, and Dovia was a petite thing. He put her on Stalker's back, closing her hands on his ruff. "Just hold on tight with your knees and hands," he told her. "Can you do that? Are you strong enough?"

She nodded. He squeezed her hand and met Stalker's gaze. "Head southwest. Daegan's coming for her from that direction. He can't be far now, and he won't be difficult to scent. He's very, very old. He carries a sword, a lot of weapons, he and his servant. Find a safe place to hole up until we come for you. Don't take her to your home or anywhere they could track her by other means and cause harm to your family."

Dovia reached out and clung to his arm. "You have to come, too."

"He and Windrunner will take good care of you," Rand said firmly, putting her hand on Stalker again. "I have to stay. Cai is here." He hesitated at Stalker's look, but then he said it, because he couldn't not say it. "I'm his servant. I won't leave him."

Understanding crossed her face. That was good, because he wasn't sure he understood it himself. He just knew it was true. "Pull a couple of the others as a rear guard, in case," he told Stalker. "Don't let their absence be noticed. Go."

Stalker nodded and bounded off, Dovia clinging to him, Windrunner on his heels. A couple yips to signal, and Rand knew that another pair would be joining them from those surrounding the clearing. He shifted again, fast, and used the cover of the forest to return to the camp outskirts. He stayed screened by foliage so a sudden appearance by a wolf familiar to the vampires wouldn't be noted. Or, more importantly, make them question why he'd been absent until now.

It was all he could do to keep position, though, when he saw what was happening.

Cai was losing.

Hell, the vampire was giving it all he had. It wasn't enough. And yet...

Maybe someone not blood-bound to the vampire couldn't pick it up, because Rand didn't see any reaction to it from the watching vampires or shifters. But energy was starting to build, an energy with one magnetic hub.

Amid that fierce, determined storm inside Cai, a weapon was shaping itself. Something Goddard wouldn't expect to be facing; something Cai himself might not realize was just waiting to be called. Sooner would be better than later. A shiver went through Rand, a need to jump into the fray, do something to alert the vampire, remind him of it...but any distraction could prove fatal.

It was a wonder, to be so closely linked to the male's mind, feel all those emotions, the waves of violence, fight strategy made and remade in split second decisions. Cai was using every scrap of energy, including any emotional defenses, to fight Goddard.

Rand hated watching him fight without helping, but at least he could hold that line, that connection. Some intuitive—or foolish— part of him thought it helped, closing his mental fist around that rope, keeping it steady. Unbroken.

While that wave of energy kept building like a tsunami.

Now the wolves felt it. Some of the ones closest to him shifted uneasily, ears twitching and eyes flashing. Rand's lips curled back from his fangs. This was about to get ugly.

But hopefully in the right way.

～

Cai snarled as Goddard put him down on the ground once more, with a blow like an anvil slamming into his torso. He even folded over it, like the proverbial cartoon character. When Goddard fell upon him, trying to drive the stake he clasped into Cai's chest, he rolled with a flash of desperate speed.

The older male had thought he'd play with Cai, emphasize his superiority, but he was finding it was a hell of a job to spear a cockroach with a toothpick. Especially if the cockroach had had about a hundred years to study every fight tactic and cue his opponent had. Cai couldn't match him in strength or speed, but he could out fucking think him. Which would work until Cai got too tired to think.

He was up again, holding his side. Hell, that was probably a cracked rib. Hopefully the next blow wouldn't shatter it and puncture his lung. Some levels of pain were too damn distracting. Blood ran into his left eye and he knuckled it away before dodging another lunge. Time for some offense.

He charged and hit Goddard full body, rolling them over and over in the dirt, squirming and punching, trying to avoid being caught in a lock with the stronger male. He'd prefer not to have his head ripped off the way Cai had done to Goddard's minion all those decades ago. He rather his own karma have some variety, some note of surprise.

His knuckles rapped a rock half buried into the dirt. Ripping it free, he hammered it into Goddard's face, driving the vampire back, making him scramble away.

They were back on their feet, facing one another, both getting tired. He noticed the other three vampires had edged closer. But the wolves had noticed, too, and had closed their own circle. Cai didn't want any of the wolves hurt. This wasn't their fight. They were here for Rand, who was...what the hell?

His wolf was supposed to be gone, carrying Dovia as far from danger as possible. Instead, he'd taken the lead position from Fane.

He looked like the tip of a lethal spear, jaw snapping, his growling like the thunder of a fast approaching storm. His eyes were glowing with that hellfire light. His one gold and one blue eye. They hadn't gone full gold because Rand, human *and* wolf side, were channeling all that fury equally.

Cai had thought Fane looked intimidating, but that was until Rand had stepped into those paws. If Goddard made any more forward progress on harpooning Cai, the wolf was going to leap into the fight.

They'd put effort into covering Rand's strengths to help Dovia, but now, the way Rand looked, like he could hold his own with Lucifer's own hellhounds, was enough to have Goddard giving the wolf a second, uncertain glance.

You're not touching my wolf. Cai leaped for Goddard, grappling, striking him in the ribs with his one empty fist. Hell, holding onto the stake was just hampering him. Cai tossed it away and went after him with both hands. He'd plow through Gideon's rib cage like match sticks, but unfortunately a vampire's bone structure was a bit more resistant, especially if the vampire in question could twist away fast as a snake. Goddard flipped over and brought the heel of his boot down on Cai's stomach. If he'd had anything in there, it would have come up. He swallowed back a grunt of pain.

He knew how to do that, didn't he? Not make a sound, no matter his agony?

His first year as a vampire, Goddard had broken both his legs, hog-tied him in that position for hours. *"Every time you make a noise of pain, you'll stay that way another hour."*

It had been Goddard's punishment for Cai not moving fast enough, thinking fast enough, not being what he wanted, or being exactly what he wanted. His fucktoy, punching bag, and receptacle for Goddard's insatiable need to cause pain.

It was an ill-timed flashback...or maybe not.

Enough. Fucking enough.

The energy was there. Had been there since the start of the fight. He could use it. Should have used it at the beginning, because now, fueled by this level of rage, Cai wasn't sure how to stop it. It was an encounter between an oil spill and a bonfire.

He hurt, he was tired of all this bullshit. Yeah, he could just die, but Rand would die, too. And Rand hadn't figured out that life still had some pretty good stuff for him. Probably not for Cai, seeing as he was such an annoying prick, but he could ride his coattails. Or his ass. It was a damn fine ass. And it was bound to him for all eternity. That meant he had to take care of it. Lyssa had said so.

Fuck it. *Move them back, Rand. Move them* back.

Just like when he helped life take root inside of Dovia, Cai shut everything out, focused on his breathing, let the energy inside him grow. A force of creation could also be a force for destruction, couldn't it?

Goddard charged. This time, when he was nearly upon him, Cai thrust out both fists, a battering ram move. And he put all that energy of creation—and destruction—into it.

It was like watching a fireworks display explode at ground level. Leastwise, that's what Rand would tell him later. His fists went through Goddard's chest and came out the other side, blood and bone blurred by a shower of green and gold energy, a blaze of firelight that roared up and over, consuming them both. Cai felt the heat run up his arms, across his back. Him and Goddard, a pyre that would blaze to the gates of hell, leaving a trail of ash, and—

He was jerked back by human hands, a move that made all the things hurting in his body hurt worse. He cursed whoever the rude bastard was who'd done it. He was freed from Goddard and rolled to put out the flame as the other vampire stumbled back, screaming, trying to figure out what was happening to him. Then his eyes lighted on Cai and he ran at him again, unholy fury in his face and flame whipping around him. Goddard was a determined fucker when he was pissed.

Rand laid Cai on the ground, snatched up the dropped stake and ran at him. He was going to meet that charge. Cai shouted a weak protest, but he couldn't grab onto him.

The truce, if that was the best word for a nuclear deterrent, ended. The other three vampires leaped forward, the wolves springing to intercept, the full storm of violence erupting.

Cai tried to struggle to his feet. *Rand, goddamn it.* He saw Goddard's eyes light on the wolf, and the vampire's fangs lengthened. Even with the magical fire engulfing him, he was dangerous, he could—

Rand didn't hesitate. He ran into the grip of those flames, and was engulfed with Goddard. Cai caught the flash of shock on Goddard's face when Rand knocked his blocking arm out of the way as if it was nothing and shoved the stake into Goddard's chest.

His wolf was thorough. Clamping one big hand on Goddard's nape to give him extra leverage, Rand slammed the stake home so the point came out the other side.

But Goddard had one more fuck-you in him. As he struggled in Rand's lethal embrace, he turned, twisted like a pinned cobra. It made Rand stumble.

Shit. Rand!

Goddard brought his boot down on Rand's leg, right above the knee. Even through all the other noise happening, Cai heard the horrifying sound of snapping bone and Rand's hoarse cry.

Wolves could heal. Servants could heal. But Cai's magic was a wild card that could change everything. The oil and match combination had ignited and was starting to mushroom. And Rand was caught in the middle of it. His cry elevated to a scream as that green-gold fire rushed into the wound caused by the split bone punching through flesh.

Cai forced away rational argument that his body couldn't contain another blow, another wound, another injury, and focused on saving his wolf. As that pending explosion took its deep breath, ready to burst Goddard into a million teeny tiny satisfying pieces, level the forest and everything living in it for a mile around, Cai caught the edge of it and held on.

You're my power. My fucking power, and you listen to me, goddamn it. The power of creation, turned in a wrong direction, but he could yank it back.

He would learn later the scream that ripped from his throat was something even more unsettling than Rand's, a primal noise that raised the hackles on every wolf's neck. He was jerked up off his knees, arched back in an impossible way, almost levitated off the ground. Emerald and sun beam arcs of power spun around him, Goddard, and Rand.

Dorothy in the tornado, no house to protect her. That's what he was, but he wouldn't let the tornado call the shots. As Cai grimly hung on, channeling the power into the ground, the sky, the buildings, and even through his own body from whence it had come, he had brief flashes of things.

Fire, making macabre silhouettes of the trees, bending back from the force of a lashing wind. Wolves, running against that backdrop. Taking down Brutus. No stakes, but no problem for the shifters. Tearing a vampire apart worked as effectively as a stake. Surreal.

A yell of warning and the wolves scattered. The fire reflected against steel, a flash, and Malvin's face showed an almost childlike expression of surprise. His head toppled from his shoulders. Before his body even hit the ground, Hector had likewise been decapitated, in a gruesome spray of blood. So quick and effortless, it was almost annoying.

Daegan apparently *did* live up to assessment of both dick and sword. Though, in all fairness, Cai had provided one hell of a distraction. He doubted anyone would remember that. He wouldn't, because while he hadn't been staked or decapitated, he felt one step away from worm food.

It was sometime later when he had that cohesive thought. Then he realized the wind had died, and there was no more flame. Just little flickers on the ground here and there. A few of the wolves had shifted to human and were stomping out anything that could leave a threat of forest fire.

There were no buildings left in the clearing. Goddard's camp had been reduced to smoking piles of ash. Occasionally something that looked like an electric charge, a quick, ground-covering bolt of lightning, rippled over those mounds. Cool.

Cai blinked. He was on his back, head turned to stare at the main cabin, the biggest pile of electric ash. He didn't want to look at that. His eyes moved to a body. Goddard, dead eyes, stake in his chest, rest of him mostly burnt up. That was a good feeling. But it still wasn't what he wanted to look at. He had one important thing to see before he decided if he needed to puke up some internal organs.

Yeah, there he was. Rand. Pretty much wallpapered with smoke and ash, but still naked enough to give Cai prurient imaginings. Well, if he wasn't worried about why he was lying on the ground. Fane was over him, along with Todd. They were doing something...

Cai winced, feeling a sympathetic stab through his leg as Todd and

Fane splinted Rand's. Rand white-knuckled Todd's biceps, another of those harsh cries coming from him, but then it was quiet.

Didn't matter. It still hurt worse than the million pains of his own that Cai knew were hovering just beyond that cloud of limited awareness. He should be over there, his arm the one that Rand should be bruising. He wanted Rand to be up and walking, not hurt. Only guy he knew who could walk with his dick swinging free and make it look sexy, not foolish.

"You're in too bad of shape to think about anyone's dick right now, let alone mine."

Cai opened his eyes. What the fuck? Apparently, he'd zoned out again and woken up like a defenseless baby. Trying to orient himself by the position of the moon above, he realized probably another hour had passed.

"Given the day you've had, you can be forgiven for taking a cat nap."

Cai's lips tried to stretch into a smile, but it just hurt too damn much. *Do wolves chase cats like dogs do?*

"No, we eat them. Though the meat isn't great. Carnivores don't taste that good."

Rand had a big stick acting as a crutch under his arm, though it was stretched out alongside his leg, because he was sitting on a propped-up stump someone had brought from somewhere so he could sit right next to Cai's recumbent body. The shifter's leg was swollen and he was in obvious pain, but he had a tight, feral grin on his face. Anyone else would have been screaming, but Cai expected the wolf was temporarily anesthetized by adrenaline, like all of them.

"I'd have to be dead not to think about your dick," Cai said, recalling the earlier comment, which he hoped was a few minutes ago, instead of a couple hours. Nothing was clear. He wasn't even sure if the words came out. His throat just didn't seem to be functioning. But he was alive.

Todd was there, helping him up. Rand got up at the same time. As he did, he reached for Cai with his one free arm, a gesture that said he wanted Todd to turn Cai over to him. Todd glanced at Rand's leg, but Rand just gave him an intent look, and Fane's son acquiesced, though he let go of Cai gradually in case Rand was overestimating himself.

He wasn't. As Rand slid an arm around Cai, Cai had an odd

compulsion he followed, pressing his face briefly against the male's jaw and temple. He inhaled the scent of smoke and lingering magic from Rand's snarled hair, and found his voice again. "Don't ever do something like that again. If he was strong enough to break me, he could have done worse to you."

"He was not strong enough to break you," Rand said.

There was a lot of weight to those words, and they made things inside Cai even harder to manage, so he ignored them.

"Yeah, he was. He just got distracted by the green fire shooting out of his ass and every other orifice."

He thought of Rand running toward Goddard, stake in clenched fist, that killing light in his eyes, the sheer power of him, as strong as those flames. Yeah, maybe that kind of strength was far easier to break than most realized. But Cai was never underestimating the wolf again. Even as he'd still bust his ass later for doing something that stupid, no matter how capably he'd done it.

He blinked, clearing another hazy recommendation for unconsciousness out of his eyes. "We should find a place to sit for a really long time."

"We will. In a minute. Gideon is coming."

Cai focused enough to see what Rand was seeing. Gideon was striding toward them. Daegan was nearby, too. Sitting on another log, he appeared to be cleaning his sword or sending thanks to the decapitation gods. Cai figured Gideon was his emissary to check on how they were doing.

"Don't be mad at him," Gideon advised, showing he'd heard what Cai had said. "For one thing, that was a truly stellar staking. Second, it's what we servants like to do."

"Stake vampires? How reassuring." Cai realized his voice was really fucked. It was like a frog with smoker's cough.

Gideon grinned. "Help our vampires. Save their asses on occasion." He glanced toward Goddard, the remains of Brutus and all the piles of ash. "We were on our way, you know."

"Yeah, but you were taking such a damn long time about it. I figured you'd stopped off at the general store to get yourself a Coke and a Moon Pie."

Daegan joined them, the sword disappearing into the folds of that movie-prop style duster he wore. It should have seemed melodramatic, but he seemed to live up to the coolness of the coat. Not that Cai was going to tell him that.

Gideon tossed his vampire master an amused look. "Hell, we should have done that. These two and the wolf pack had everything in control. Those double-decker Moon Pies are awesome."

"If you don't annoy me on the way back, maybe we'll stop and get you one," Daegan said.

"Dovia," Cai rasped.

"We came upon Lady Dovia and the shifters protecting her, just before we arrived at this location," Daegan said. "I told them to take her on to a safe place and wait for a signal that all was clear."

"Good," Cai said. How had he gotten back on the ground? Rand was there with him, sitting propped up against the stump, Cai pretty much lying in his wolf's arms. He should do something about that, but it didn't bug him enough, looking up at everything from that vantage point. Whenever he tried to move his head, the world tilted in the wrong direction.

Cai tightened his hand on Rand's, lying loosely on his bare chest. "Danger's past. She can go to Fane's for the night. No reason to bring her back here."

"Except to see he's dead," Gideon said. "Sometimes, that can be important."

Cai met the male's midnight blue gaze. Lot of blue eyes going around—his, Rand's, Gideon's—but all of them different shades.

"Yeah. It is." He shifted his attention to Rand. "Let it be her decision.

"Of course." Rand drew a female shifter over and spoke to her in a low tone. In human form, she was slim as a willow, her curves small but appealing. She had long, dark hair and looked like a Native American. At Rand's direction, she shifted back to a wolf, her coat an interesting-looking golden color. She moved out of the clearing, likely to get a good acoustic point to send up a relay signal. Confirming it, a series of howls and yips kicked off a few minutes later, thankfully from only one or two wolves, because Cai didn't think he was up to a full victory serenade.

Time to be manly and get on his own feet. He struggled up, with Daegan's help. The vampire courteously stepped back once he was vertical. Gideon had assisted Rand, mainly because the splinted leg wouldn't make rising easy, but Cai was mortified that Rand looked steadier, even with his crutch and messed-up knee. Cai swayed alarmingly.

Rand shifted closer, though Cai mostly tried not to prop with his full weight. "Hell." He looked down, blinking to focus. "My legs are still attached, right?"

"All of you is in one piece, but you look like Sybil at the prom." Gideon slid a critical look over him. "A lot of blood on you, and I think most of it's yours."

"A feeding would be in order. For both of you." Daegan was studying him as closely. "What happened there, at the end? The fire."

"Explosives," Rand said. "Gas lines between the cabins. Fane and his boys figured out how to turn it to our advantage. They're handy that way. Respectfully, we need a moment."

Rand said it courteously enough, but was already moving Cai away from the two vampire hunters.

He is totally not going to buy that shit.

"Have him prove differently. Here." Rand kept a bracing arm around his waist and back. "Use me to lean. Where are we going?"

How had he known what Cai was wanting, needing? Was his mind that open? Emanating feelings that he couldn't even figure out himself, Cai stopped again, swaying this time from an even more alarming rush of...everything. Rand's arm tightened around him, that strong, muscular arm and big, stable body. Cai had never leaned on anyone, let alone someone he felt he could lean on forever and who wouldn't give an inch.

"You need to lean on me as much as I do you," he said defensively, pretending not to see Rand's knowing look.

"Whatever you say, vampire. This was an incredibly stupid plan, you know," Rand said, studying the carnage.

"That's what usually works. I'm going that way."

"I know."

They limped together to where Goddard lay. Dead eyes staring. Dead. Actually dead. Cai's lips pursed and then the world tilted again as something shifted in his chest, so large, powerful and fierce. He wished he was like Rand and could howl. Howl out all of it.

"Goddard took me from my family." Rand knew it, and Cai could have thought it, but somehow it was important to say it, even in that crazy frog-voice. "All these years, the others are gone, because his freaky-assed sect of Trads have a way of turning on each other and ending up dead, big surprise. All these years..."

Cai's lips firmed. He was wrong. He did feel like he'd been staked, or that the fire he'd used to immolate Goddard was still burning in his own chest. "I need you to step back."

"You'll fall."

"Maybe."

Rand gave him a searching look. He stepped back, but he stayed close.

Cai made one very unsteady step toward Goddard, standing over him. "For every time you did it to me, asshole."

Maybe it was because he'd been hanging around wolves too much, but it was the one thing that made sense to him right now. He unzipped his pants and, heedless of the wolves milling, the silent regard of Daegan or his servant, he pissed all over the dead vampire's body.

He managed to get his pants fastened and done up, and was able to step back a couple paces before his knees buckled. Rand caught him around the chest, and Cai found his face back in that same welcoming broad shoulder. How in the hell was the guy still standing? He had a sturdy-assed crutch. That's what it was.

"Thank God I don't have a shy bladder; else that would have come off far less cool," Cai muttered.

"You're assuming it was cool to begin with. I merely assumed it was your way of acknowledging he beat the piss out of you." But there was a gentle note to Rand's voice that eased some of that pressure off Cai's chest.

He moved Cai toward the edge of the clearing. Cai could see a nice patch of ground he thought might be a good place to lie down and peacefully die.

"No dying. There are enough deer trails close to this place that an ATV can get through. One's being brought to us from Fane's."

Cai's gaze shifted to Rand's broken leg. "You need a lift, too. And my blood, to help that heal." He hoped. He thought of that magic, turned into a destructive force, the way it had tangled around the break like barbed wire. It gave him an uneasy feeling. He didn't know shit about the magic, had just given it free rein. If he'd crippled Rand...

"Stop borrowing trouble. I didn't know vampires did that. Piss."

Cai's mind stumbled over the segue, the innocuous question, but he felt a weak smile tilt his lips at the wolf's mild chastising. "Sometimes you're like a wife, you know that? One of those sitcom ones."

"Blow me."

"Maybe in a bit." Cai's brow furrowed, grasping at the question. "Born ones don't, I think. Pee. Have to ask that one to be sure." He nodded toward Daegan, conferring with Gideon. "Make sure he's in a good mood before you ask him if he has to pee like the rest of us non-gods. Oh, wait; better idea. Ask Lady Lyssa instead. I'm sure she wouldn't construe a question like that as disrespectful."

Rand snorted. *Yank my chain, and I'll tell Dovia's father you impregnated her. Since I won't share how, he'll assume the normal way and chew off your dick.*

Eww. That may be how a wolf father would retaliate, but not *a vampire. Just saying.*

Cai didn't want to think about the issues Rand's comment had raised, issues that had been set aside for higher priority ones of survival, until just now. Rand's gaze darkened with regret. He hadn't intended to treat the subject flippantly, Cai saw, but it was okay. It had been a rough day. There was room for some social faux pas.

Rand lifted his head at a distant howl, followed by another series of yips. He met Cai's gaze. "She doesn't want to come."

"Yeah, that's what I figured." Cai let his gaze pass over the clearing. He thought of the spacious home with the fences and forest around it, Leona's loving arms and Greenwald's devotion, even if muddled by Ennui. "It may take a while, but she has what she needs to reclaim her life. She doesn't need to come back to the nightmare to get past it. She's a tough female."

Rand made a noncommittal noise, but cocked his head as further communications came. "She doesn't want to go to Fane's home yet, either. She wants me and you to meet her where she is. Stalker took her somewhere pretty. Good lad."

Fane had approached Daegan and Gideon, apparently to communicate what his son had relayed. Nodding, Daegan moved toward Cai and Rand, Gideon with him. "We'll stay with you until Dovia is delivered back to her parents," the vampire said without preamble. "The additional reinforcements will allow you both a chance to recuperate."

"Is a guard necessary?" Rand asked.

"Yes," Cai said, at the same time Daegan and Gideon did. "Goddard's an isolationist, but the mountains are the preferred habitat for plenty of Trads. I don't know if there are more in the area, but best not to get careless. She'd be valuable to any of them."

Even more valuable now.

Rand could see that troubling thought reflected in Cai's face and doubly cursed himself for treating the topic carelessly. The vampire's thoughts were weighted with exhaustion, laced with too much pain for Rand's liking. How many times could a vampire get so wounded, replenish himself with blood, and get up, as vibrant with health as if it had never happened?

"We have a cat's nine lives, times a billion," Cai reassured him, and repeated his earlier concern. "You're taking blood from me. That leg doesn't look good."

Cai could be right on the physical end of things, but Rand's question had been directed to Cai's state of mind.

"You first," Rand said.

Even Daegan and Gideon looked concerned about the vampire, though Rand was pleased to see both warriors also looked at Cai with respect. As they damn well should. He'd surprised and impressed the hell out of the wolves, Rand knew.

As for his own feelings...well, it might be foolish, but as soon as he could lay hands on the vampire, he hadn't let go of him or moved more than a few paces away, and it wasn't because of a bad leg.

With a weary half smile, Cai nudged Rand, bringing his attention back to him. "Fine. I'll take a mouthful or two from you, but I'll do it on the way. Let's go see what our rescued princess needs."

CHAPTER SIXTEEN

*R*and was right. Stalker had taken her somewhere pretty. The secluded mountain glade had a deep pool of water fed by a short waterfall from higher ground. The water zigzagged along shiny rocks and fed the pool, which trickled out into the gurgling, continued track of the creek. There were little purple wildflowers and mossy banks. It was cool, and the moonlight filtered in through the interlaced branches of the trees above, providing illumination but not an overbearing amount of light.

She was sitting on the bank by herself. Windrunner and Stalker were close by, but it was clear she'd asked for the space. She was wrapped up in a blanket they'd provided. When Dovia lifted her head at their approach, her gaze went to Rand, but the shifter surprised Cai by directing her attention back to him, to let him say what needed to be said.

"They're dead," Cai said. "All of them."

Her jaw tightened, and she nodded. Her gaze went to Daegan and Gideon, standing on the perimeter of the glade, a discreet distance away. "They helped," Rand added. "They're with the Council. They'll provide a protective escort back to your family."

"You're leaving?" The note of panic cracked through a voice held under tight control.

Rand shook his head. "No. They're for additional protection. Since it's too close to daybreak to drive back tonight, we'll spend the day at my friend Fane's, and you'll go home tomorrow. If you feel up to it then."

She turned haunted eyes to him, and her firm chin quivered. "Can you be..."

She recalled herself and looked toward Cai again. He saw her mental flinch at all the blood, his torn clothes. The sparse amount of blood he'd allowed himself from Rand gave him the ability to stand on his own. For extremely short periods of time. But hell, he likely looked like a demon. He should have hung back with Daegan and Gideon, or stayed out of sight altogether.

"Is it polite to ask your servant to be a wolf and come sit with me?" she asked. "If it won't hurt his leg."

She said it with such formal courtesy, a proper noblewoman, Cai almost had to bite back a smile. He didn't show respect for most people, deserved or not, but he gave her what was due. She really was a remarkable young woman.

Cai looked toward Rand. *Is it better for your leg to be in this form or the other?*

As a wolf, I'd have three legs to help me walk, not just one. No need for crutch.

Cai felt a welcome surge of humor at the practical response. But Rand would also have to remove the splint.

Bones are usually easier for shifter healing ability than organ damage, or blood loss from knife and bullet wounds. Rand's mind sent Cai a flash of how they'd met. *The bone should hold if I shift now. Plus, I have a vampire's healing blood on the way.*

Usually and *should* were the words that caught Cai's attention. He didn't like the idea of Rand risking it, but he could tell the wolf wanted to give Dovia ease, and he knew his own healing abilities better than Cai. Unless Rand was feeding him a load of crap, somehow hiding it under a nice innocent-looking cloud in his brain.

Rand's expression showed a glimmer of humor. *Brain clouds?*

Cai snorted. *Your call. She needs her big bad wolf.*

Rand watched the vampire move away, toward Gideon and Daegan. Whatever Cai murmured had the two fanning out and melting into the trees to keep watch. Most the wolves had headed for their respective homes, their job done, but Fane waited with Windrunner and Stalker. However, after Cai spoke to them in the same low tones, they rose and followed Daegan and Gideon into the trees. After Fane glanced at Rand to be sure he agreed with Cai's opinion. The vampire didn't seem to take offense.

Though he was the only one other than Rand who stayed in sight, Cai backed off as well. Rand suspected the vampire wanted the cleansing touch of that water like he wanted air, but in that odd way of his, he'd cede the honor to Dovia first.

It made Rand think of how pups were allowed to eat from a kill first, no matter the adult pecking order, because their need was greater. Cai took a seat on a rock across the creek, probably figuring the boundary might increase her comfort zone.

Rand came to Dovia first as human, moving with his makeshift crutch. He did expect the leg would heal up better after he had some of the vampire's blood, but there was a fiery ache to the injury different from wounds he'd experienced before. Even when the hunter had shot him in the haunch, it hadn't had this deep throb that seemed to vibrate with the pumping of his heart.

He was fine for now, though. He really wanted Cai to recuperate some more before taking any more of his blood. However, as he sensed the vampire's eyes on him, he expected the stubborn bastard was going to insist before long. Rand knew Cai was worried that his magic had done something irreparable. Rand wasn't worried about that. The most important thing had been accomplished. She was here. Someone had been saved from evil. It was possible. That thought alone dulled pain.

Plus, though today was a victory, there was still much tending to do for others who were wounded...in both body and mind.

Fane had provided him a pair of loose shorts that could be worked over the splint and hung loose over it. While modesty wasn't usually a big concern, they were all sensitive to how Dovia might be feeling about fully grown naked men around her.

She was a slim figure in the blanket, but her back was straight. Her gaze clung to the moving waters as if she wished she could melt into their flow. Rand took a seat next to her, a little surprised when she immediately moved, wrapping her arms around and burrowing against him. He bent his head over hers protectively.

You have that effect on those who need to feel safe.

He glanced toward Cai, but the vampire was also staring at the water. A different look from Dovia's, harder to interpret.

"They killed Petra," she said. "She tried to stop them. Even knowing she had no chance...she tried. She gave her life to protect me. If she hadn't fought so hard, maybe they would have brought her... but she was so fierce."

Rand had to search his memory, but Cai remembered. *Her second mark servant.*

"I'm sorry," Rand murmured. She nodded against his chest.

"I smell bad," Dovia whispered. "I'm sorry."

Shock. It could keep the mind shifting drunkenly from topic to topic, no order to it. He remembered that. Rand rubbed his head along her crown, her temple.

"Thank you for coming for me," she said. "All of you. I...I want to thank Cai, but...he smells like them. Blood and earth. I'm afraid."

"He smells like earth, but not like them. Like me. He belongs to the forest. That's how he and I came together. He saved me. He's not like those others. He's not even like a lot of vampires, I think. He's hard to classify. A long time ago, he belonged to Goddard. Or Goddard thought he did. But Cai got away from him. Yet he came back to help you. Why don't you have him come sit on the other side of you? We'll both keep you warm. And I'll become a wolf, like you wanted."

He felt Cai's attention rise and rest on him as he spoke. *Come closer, vampire. Trust me. She needs you, too.*

"He might smell a little bit bad, too," Rand admitted. "But he usually smells bad."

Uncertain humor passed over her face. "You're not very respectful to your vampire." Her voice, while still low, had gained enough steadiness to reveal an appealing hint of Southern accent.

"The two of us aren't really like the vampires and servants you know." Rand ran a hand down her back. "Do you want to wash off some in the pool? There'll be a hot shower back at the house, but I know Cai wants to rinse off, too. Wash it all away."

After a long moment, she nodded. "Can you..." She was too well-raised to badger or insist, but when she started trembling, he didn't think anyone with a heart could say no to her. Rand squeezed her, and straightened. He removed the splint first, and her gaze cleared, as if she'd just put together how a shift would affect that.

"Oh...you probably shouldn't..."

He made a dismissive gesture. "It will be fine."

Brain cloud aside, Rand hadn't been feeding Cai a load of crap. Not really. The wound where the bone had punched through was knitting, and he could feel a tentative bond happening at the broken part. This probably was going to set him back, but he'd recover the ground. She was more important.

She already looked as if she thought she'd asked too much and was going to argue again, that little set to her chin, but he slid himself across the ground, far enough away to give him the necessary room. Pulling off his clothes, he shifted.

Yeah, it hurt like a son of a bitch, but the wolf's leg bone held, basically in the same state as the human version. Which meant he couldn't put any weight on it, but he could move. When he padded back to her, her arms were already lifting. She pressed against him again. "I'm sorry," she whispered.

He made a whuffing noise and put his head over hers.

Cai. Come. Needs both.

I truly doubt that. But the vampire complied, maybe because he needed them. Not that he'd ever admit such a thing. But Rand suspected it. Felt it. Scented it.

When Cai sat down on the other side of her, he left an inch or two of space, probably expecting that she wouldn't want the same proximity she had with Rand. But Rand saw surprise flash across his face when, after a few moments, she tentatively ventured a hand toward Cai, though she kept her face in Rand's fur. Rand wasn't sure what Cai would do with such a gesture, but fortunately, the vampire wasn't as emotionally clueless as he sometimes pretended to be. He took her hand, closed his fingers carefully over it, and held it on his knee.

She shuddered, but she gripped him harder. Cai adjusted closer, stroked her hair, and she let out a little sigh. They sat that way for some time. The creek sang its rushing song, the moonlight touched them, and the trees rustled in the easy breeze. It was the kind of night when a wolf would run for the joy of running, but Rand was content to be here.

If Cai's mind was as quiet as his, then the vampire felt it when he did, the shift in Dovia's emotions. They were still a tangled mix, but one rose to the top. Resolve.

Straightening up, Dovia rose. She swayed on unsteady legs, the two males watching her closely, ready to catch her. But she let the blanket slip off her shoulders, and she moved toward the water. Her hair was hacked and burned; her body was bruised and dirty. The water would wash it away; blood nourishment would help the bruising fade and the hair grow back. Even so, Rand expected Cai felt the same way Rand did looking at those marks; a lethal desire to kill them all over again.

But Dovia's mind was on something else. Slowly, she turned and looked at Cai. From her solemn look, Rand wondered if she was remembering what he had told her about Cai belonging to Goddard. She extended a quivering hand to the vampire. "Let's go get clean," she said.

Again, Cai surprised Rand, with simple acquiescence. Rising, he stripped off his jeans, and took her hand. Together, they moved to the bank. Though a wolf didn't cry like a human, Rand felt an odd stinging in his eyes, watching them steady each other.

At the edge, she hesitated. His threat of tears became a poignant mental smile as he recognized a typical girl's hesitance about the water temperature—and likely a vampire's regarding the depth, since they had no buoyancy. Rand had learned that during one of the random, idle conversations he and Cai had shared on their hike deeper into the mountains.

"Allow me," Cai said. He jumped into the water with a quiet *sploosh*. When he broke the surface and stood, the water came up to his chest where he was standing. As he stroked closer to her again, it came to his waist. He extended a hand. "It's chilly, but it's not bad. The water held on to the day's heat. It was a pretty hot day."

His lips twitched as his gaze shifted briefly to Rand, reminding him the vampire had had firsthand experience of it.

"My lady?" Cai prompted gently.

The formality helped. Dovia wet her lips, and leaned down to graze his fingertips with her own. He caught her on the jump, easing her down and away from him before she could stiffen at the physical intimacy. Cai stayed close enough though, since he and Rand shared a concern about her strength. Rand would give her more blood soon, for nourishment as much as to heal the wounds.

You're going to get fed first.

She needs it more. So do you.

The vampire scowled his way. He wanted Rand to feed before feeding anyone else, but the plain truth was Dovia wasn't likely to let any other shifter near her yet. Or at least without it making her uncomfortable or nervous, and neither of them wanted to inflict that upon her.

I'm a shifter, and a third marked servant. Both come with accelerated healing abilities. She can have some of my blood without it endangering me. Long as you aren't planning any more fights to the death today.

Cai's scowl deepened. *Fine. But you will get some blood from me before I go to ground tonight, wolf.*

Rand's answer was a noncommittal grunt. Fortunately, Cai's attention was sidetracked when Dovia dropped below the surface. She emerged before either of them could worry she'd collapsed or moved to a section over her head. She'd simply wanted to immerse herself.

She stood, stroking water through her hair, over her skin, removing blood and memory. She was a lovely creature, as all vampires were. Her breasts firm and nipples peaked from the water, her skin pale and soft. With her hair wet, it hinted at the waves of shimmering silk it would be when it grew back to its former length and fullness.

Her delicate chin dipped, her profile pensive. Her hands slid just beneath the water's surface to fold over her stomach. Her gaze lifted and met Cai's. The tension that thrummed between them now had a different weight, but Cai didn't back away from it. He drew closer, stood before her.

"I'm sorry," he said. After taking the blood, he'd become easier to understand, though he still spoke low, in a gravelly rasp. "It was the only way I knew to protect you until we could figure out an escape."

Her head bowed again in that posture of deep thought. "It's an amazing gift," she whispered.

"I didn't think so. Not for a long time, since it was what...it was why they took me when I was a kid. But today...yeah. I was glad to have it. Wish I'd known how to use it to roast that bastard's ass a long time ago. If I hadn't fought it for so long..."

A shudder ran through her and her eyes closed tightly, her face folding in on itself. For the first time since they'd arrived at the water, she looked hunched, defeated. Cai shook his head at himself. Putting the self-flagellation aside, he moved closer and put both hands on her shoulders.

His voice dropped so he spoke even more softly.

"I can take it away."

She stilled and lifted her head, staring at him. Cai held her gaze. Her hand lifted between them, as if she was going to touch his face, but it hovered there, and her body started to shake harder. Cai clasped the hand in his larger one, letting them both rest on his chest, over his heart. The rhythm of it seemed to steady her, though her expressive face was gripped by anguish.

"I just need it gone," she whispered. "I can't feel it grow and know...I see their faces...I can't do it. I know it's...innocent, and there are too few of us, but I can't. If my father knew, if any of them knew... it would be too much. My father, he's already..."

This time it was Cai's chest where she pressed her face, her arms folded against her. She convulsed as if she was in greater danger of breaking now than even before. Cai's arms slowly slid around her. He didn't look toward Rand this time. His expression became harder. Starker.

"There's no shame in it," he said. "No wrong. Me doing it, that was the wrong, even if I couldn't think of anything else. I've never considered it a gift, my lady. It's like on some particularly irresponsible day, a god tipped over a wine cup and splashed the gift of creation into the hands of a court jester, born a halfwit."

His sudden harsh chuckle made Rand tense. He didn't worry that Cai would harm the girl. It was more that he didn't seem to know how to deal with people and sometimes said the absolute wrong thing. Which most people and circumstances could absorb, but Dovia couldn't handle right now.

Cai took a breath, his shoulders lifting. When he spoke against her hair, the gravelly tone had evened out. "It was totally random, Goddard discovering my gift. I was out in a hay field one night with a girl. I wasn't supposed to be with her, but we'd snuck out. I made a plant sprout from a seed in my hand. I did it to impress her. Goddard was watching.

"My guess is he'd planned to make us dinner. He killed her...took me. I was human with them for a while, until one night, Lodell...he turned me. Another Trad. The good kind, and there are some good ones out there. Lodell said he turned me to even the odds, and his money was on me. They chopped off one of his legs below the knee and burned it with his own blood so it wouldn't grow back. To punish him."

Dovia tipped her head back, her mouth tight. *She can't handle this right now*, Rand thought, but then her eyes met the vampire's. In that blink of communication, Rand recognized that there were things the vampire species shared that weren't part of the shifter world. The underlying violent nature of the vampire world, for instance. Dovia understood.

Her slim hands reached up and cupped Cai's jaw. "You risked much, coming back to save me. You'll always have my gratitude. I can't ask any more of you."

"You're not asking anything of me." His much larger hand touched her face, tracing the delicate line of it. "Turn around and lean back against me, little girl."

Warmth and hope filled Rand's vitals when her sad face rearranged into a faintly irritated expression, the kind a young woman might make when a male called her a little girl. But Cai nudged her, and she relented, turning around and putting her back to him. He laid his hands on her shoulders again.

"I'm going to need to press against you. Intimate, but not sexual. I promise. Can you trust me? Or at least trust that if I tried anything inappropriate, Rand would rip off one of my arms?"

That produced a tiny smile. "He's your servant. He'd do no such thing."

"Oh, hell yes he would. He doesn't have a subservient bone in his four-legged body. The two-legged one, either."

Cai folded his arms around her, his hands cupping her belly, over her womb.

Rand worried that Cai didn't have the strength for whatever he was about to do, but the vampire seemed unconcerned about it.

Creation is as easy as breathing, wolf. Part of what makes it so fucking scary.

Rand felt the power building as Cai matched heartbeats with her. Their chests started to rise and fall together when Cai murmured to her to intentionally mimic breathing. An obvious way to center and align their energies.

Sensing movement, Rand saw Daegan appear. He'd arrived silently, despite the dense undergrowth skirting the perimeter of forest. His gaze moved to Rand and Rand shook his head, a reassurance he hoped he didn't have to reinforce by shifting back to human. After all that had happened tonight, it felt far better to be more animal than man right now.

Cai's power floated out over the water, touched Rand like a mist and spread out. Daegan felt it, too, lifting his hand as if to twine it over his fingers. His dark eyes were unfathomable. As Cai had said, the vampire sensed something was up. The question was what he'd do with the knowledge.

With Dovia aware of Cai's creation magic, it was possible a larger audience would know about it soon, anyway. Rand knew Cai would place no obligation upon her, even the holding of his secret. No matter what that might cost him.

Yet after what Rand had seen tonight, and ever since Cai had mentioned his abilities, he had to wonder just how far Cai's creation magic could go if he did pursue it, study it. A question for another time.

Daegan lowered his hand and gave Rand an odd look, but melted back into the woods. A few moments later, Cai's shoulders and lower back shuddered, a ripple of power.

"It's all right," he said. "Open your eyes if you like."

She'd closed them during the process, leaning fully back against him. Now Rand saw her head raise. Cai lifted his hands before her, opening them like a bird's wings. Rand, gripped by a sudden sense of awe, watched the mote of energy roll over his fingers and start to rise. It was tiny, like a shard of light caught in a dewdrop. Cai and Dovia's heads tilted upward in sync, watching the soul rise, and rise. Then it was gone, melted into moonlight.

There was a sculpted, severe beauty to Cai's face, sorrow and heartbreak for once uncontained, exposed. His life, horrific as many parts of it had been, hadn't taken away his wish to bring a damaged spirit what ease he could.

The vampire still knew what compassion was, even if he often pretended otherwise.

The girl's control completely broke. Her sobs came in powerful waves. Cai's arms swept around her again, his body curving over her, head tucked down on top of hers. He spoke so softly to her, that this time even Rand's enhanced hearing didn't pick it up, but his mind and senses did.

You'll be all right. You don't think you will be. But you will, because anything else means they win, and you're too damn strong to let that happen. You'll grow into a formidable woman. When you think of this, you'll think of how it helped make you. You're no victim. A soul can't be broken. A body, sure, like kindling. A heart? Into a million pieces. But not the soul. That goddamn thing is industrial strength energy. It's not letting anything break it apart.

"You can be anything you want to be, love anyone you fucking want." Cai spoke louder. "Don't let them take any of that from you."

Maybe she was hearing it, maybe she wasn't. Rand figured she was mostly benefitting from the comforting, non-threatening strength of his arms, the flow of words. That was fine, because he was pretty sure the words weren't just for her.

He saw the vampire's shoulders tremble from the girl's sobbing. But as Cai's arms constricted around her further and he buried his face in her hair, as if he was winding the two of them into a cocoon, Rand's eyes darkened. For he could tell when his Master's shoulders trembled not just from her tears, but from his own.

Why he should think of him that way right now, Rand wasn't sure. Maybe because *Master* meant something far more complicated to him right now, impossible to explain, but something he innately knew fit. Maybe because he was the only one who had the right to call Cai that, a unique link they shared, a two-way ownership hidden in the word.

It was difficult, but he stayed on the bank, just watching over them, until at last she was quiet in Cai's arms. When Cai brought her to shore, he was carrying her. She'd finally given out, though Rand didn't know how Cai himself had the strength to carry her, because he wasn't much better off. He stumbled on the bank, but Rand was there. He'd shifted to human and wrapped the girl back up in the blanket.

They sat down on the bank together and held her between them. Their arms were overlapping, Cai's shoulder pressed against Rand's side. Cai curled his fingers around Rand's wrist and brought it to his mouth. When he bit him with the one fang, almost gently, it wasn't to drink. Rand stretched out his fingers, rubbing the pads over the single tear track he saw marking Cai's face.

The vampire's gaze lifted to him, held. He took Rand's hand away, and pressed the open vein of his wrist to Dovia's lips. She drank automatically, trusting as a babe, already half asleep. Numb, her consciousness had fled to relief-inspired oblivion and exhaustion. She was safe. Battered, traumatized, but safe.

When Cai finally closed the wound, Dovia muttered "wolf." A smile touched Cai's lips but didn't reach his eyes. Not even close.

If I didn't enjoy plowing your ass so much, I'd never want you to change out of being a wolf, either. You have this nice stillness. No words. We all talk too much, us humanoid types.

The vampire reached over, stroked a casual knuckle down Rand's face. "Shift back. Your wolf body will keep her warm and she likes it."

That an order, vampire?

Rand wasn't sure what made him press that trigger, but the trace of heat that went through Cai's expression, no matter his exhaustion, made him feel he'd done the right thing. Maybe because he'd wanted to do it for his own reasons, too.

If you like.

Cai adjusted Dovia to give Rand room to shift into a wolf. When he drew close to the girl again, Rand felt oddly content as Dovia curled inside the curve of his body, her hands wrapped in his ruff. Even better, Cai leaned in, sandwiching her between them so he could idly stroke and run his fingers through Rand's fur. In silent stillness, they watched the water flow and the moonlight glitter.

It was enough.

In time, Rand's compulsion to tend the other being that needed his care grew too strong for him to deny himself. He didn't care if Cai mocked his nurturing side. The vampire seemed half asleep, most of his weight leaning against Rand behind Dovia, his head tipped downward. He barely lifted it when Rand made a couple of yipping noises.

Fane emerged almost immediately, with Stalker and Windrunner at his side. Daegan and Gideon came from the other side of the creek, verifying they'd coordinated full perimeter coverage. In wolf speak, Rand asked Fane if he would take Dovia to his house. He was relieved that Fane agreed without hesitation, no apparent discomfort about having Daegan and Gideon as escort without Rand's mitigating presence.

Rand suspected it wasn't so much the male had decided vampires were trustworthy, but he'd accepted he could trust this small group of them. That decision was also heavily influenced by Fane's guilt about the two human women. Rand didn't want to take advantage of that, but he was glad not to have to expend energy convincing Fane the vampires wouldn't be a risk to his family.

When Fane shifted to human and explained the plan to Daegan and Gideon, the two males nodded. Gideon stepped forward to take Dovia.

She barely stirred, which gave Rand further comfort, since he'd been concerned she wouldn't allow him or Cai out of her sight. But she needed female care now, and Fane's wife and daughters would handle that end. Suspecting she was experiencing the first real sleep she'd had since she'd been taken, he hoped she wouldn't rouse until the following twilight. Lynn, Sangra and Cilya could handle the more delicate care she might need, cleaning and tending her so she could wake feeling as normal as possible.

Gideon lifted her in his arms in a protective, gentle manner. But before he followed the shifters and his Master out of the clearing, he paused. His lips twisted in a half-smile as his gaze coursed over Rand's wolf form. It reminded Rand of Jacob's initial reaction to seeing him shift. However, as Gideon met Rand's bi-colored gaze, his own dark blue eyes grew more somber.

"Don't know how much of this you get when you're four-legged, but if it was me, I'd want some time to care for my Master one-on-one, too," he said. "You're new to it, but don't let it freak you out. There's no one who can understand him, be in his head, more than you. No one he'll ever be able to trust the same way. That's why they have us. And why we have something inside of us that needs that, just as much."

Daegan had reappeared at the forest edge, his gaze resting on his servant. Though his expression didn't change, there was an energy between him and Gideon that said the two of them would always be visible to one another, in ways that no darkness could ever hide.

Daegan and Gideon disappeared into the woods. Rand's sharp ears detected the formation, the wolves and the vampire falling into position to run point around Gideon and the girl. They'd be all right.

Rand needed the mental reassurance. Despite his reasons for remaining behind, protective instincts kicked back in as soon as Dovia was out of his immediate reach. That urge was tangled up with some quick flashes of his own children, of Sylvan's, and things he really didn't want in his head right now.

Fortunately, another more recent memory took him back in the right direction. Cai, staring up at the mote of light leaving his hand. A baby's soul he'd planted and then plucked, returning it to its Maker.

Cai had roused sometime during the shift of guard duty, but he hadn't said anything. Merely stayed where he was, leaning against Rand. His gaze followed the track of the waterfall, lifting briefly when the wind touched the trees over them. The movement showed Rand a glimpse of his eyes, flickering shadows and moonlight flashes against the irises framed by his thick-lashed eyes.

He liked the vampire's quietness. It seemed an acknowledgement of things they didn't even have to word-think to understand one another's feelings on it. Rand was also starting to understand the rise and retreat of the vampire's emotions when things became too much, enough that he wasn't surprised when Cai abruptly rose.

"You've given a lot of blood tonight," he said. "I'm going to go get you dinner."

You're too tired. Rabbit have to be old, slow. Tough meat.

"Better shot at it than you, crashing through the undergrowth on three legs." Cai tugged one of his ears. Rand nipped at him and the corner of the male's mouth lifted slightly.

If Rand had been in human form, he might have stroked a knuckle down Cai's face, his jaw. Spoken aloud and told him *we're okay.*

"Yeah. We are." The vampire sent him a weary, twisted smile. Turning on his heel, he moved toward the woods. He was steadier on his feet, but not moving with his usual lithe grace. It'd been a rough night on all of them.

Rand knew Cai was looking for space. He should give it to him, no matter how concerned he was about the vampire's state of mind, the weakened state of his body.

So he sat on the bank of the pool for another full minute. He remembered the single tear track he'd traced on Cai's cheek, along the straight line of his nose. How many times had it been broken when he was with the Trads, at the hands of someone like Goddard? Or out in the world, because he refused to bend toward any authority? Actively went out of his way to oppose it, whether sensible or not.

Before he realized he'd made the decision, Rand left the secluded glade and moved into the surrounding forest. He couldn't move fast, but having three legs did help. He and Cai were a dangerous pair right now—if there'd been an impending threat from an army of turtles.

Cai was deep in his head, because for once he didn't seem aware of Rand's approach until Rand was almost upon him. Rand drew his attention by shifting to human. Conveniently, he'd done it next to a tree, so he could brace himself for support if needed.

Cai turned and looked at him. A long, silent, weighted moment. "Come here, vampire," Rand invited.

Cai's firm lips twisted, though his dark eyes became darker. His emotions had all those layers right now, making him harder for Rand to read, but Rand picked up enough to know his presence wasn't unwelcome. Far from it.

"Is that an order?" he responded.

Rand lifted a brow, and repeated the vampire's earlier words. "If you like."

When Cai didn't immediately move, Rand moved a step toward him. One halting, limping step that told him he was going to be on all fours again fast, though it was likely to be palms and knees. Well, in the right mood, Cai might find that convenient.

Cai made a face at him as he closed the distance, putting a bracing hand on Rand's waist as Rand clamped a palm on the vampire's shoulder to steady himself. His bare shoulder.

Yeah, they were both beat to hell, but they were alive.

"Fucking alive," Cai added, that appealing hint of a smile on his mouth, though it was marked by other things that could tear Rand's heart into pieces. They both understood loss far too well, didn't they?

Rand didn't answer with words or thoughts. Just feeling. He shared relief that they'd survived the nightmare, that Dovia had a chance of healing from her emotional scars, the way she would the physical. It didn't matter about his leg or how the rest of him felt; Rand wanted to give Cai blood, wanted to nourish him, give him back his strength.

Body, mind and soul. Maybe not fuel his sharp tongue, but he supposed that was part of the whole package.

Cai gave a half laugh, but it had a note of despair to it. Rand moved his hand to the side of Cai's throat, feeling the pulse. "You were still, by the water," he murmured. "Quiet, inside and out. Keep being that way with me."

No acid sarcasm, no attempt to push him or anyone else away with his inappropriate humor, his endless running monologue of jokes and one-liners. Rand wanted him to lay down those weapons, lay down all weapons, and simply...be still. With him. "You can do that."

Cai's gaze had shuttered, but he hadn't looked away. A muscle was flexing in his jaw and his body was...tense, but not stone-wall tense. More like electric-wire tense, ready to conduct electricity with the right contact.

Taking it as the invitation it was, Rand did as he wished. He dropped his touch to Cai's side, caressing the hard curve of biceps, the shallow valley between every rib. He wasn't emaciated, but there wasn't a spare ounce of soft flesh on him. Touching the bone structure reminded Rand that they were all breakable. Maybe the boon of mortality was that he only had to go through the pain of being broken a certain number of times before the body and soul called it quits. Cai didn't have that luxury.

"Sit down before you fall down," Cai said gruffly, easing them both to the forest floor, using the tree as their backrest. "You're having my fucking blood. No argument. Shut up and drink it."

He'd lifted his wrist, but Rand clasped it, holding it between them. His gaze shifted upward. "Someone told me it's better from the throat."

"Did they? Sounds like a way to try and take advantage of you."

"It worked. Have you ever watched the way wolves approach the alpha in a pack, vampire?"

"No. They're a jumpy bunch. They tend to scatter when they sense me."

"Hmm. Well, you can always tell the alphas in a pack. Tail high, direct gaze, ears up. They just project it."

"Because it's hard to mask it, to pretend to be something they're not?" Cai supplied, recalling their earlier conversations. Rand tightened his grip on his wrist.

"Yeah. But if he doesn't want to fight, an alpha approaching another alpha goes through some of the same rituals as the non-alphas in the pack. I'll show you sometime. When we're both a little less beat all to hell."

"Okay."

Rand smiled a little at the simple response. When he brushed his thumb over Cai's lips, the vampire let his fang score the knuckle. "Let me feed you, wolf. The leg thing is messing with my head."

"You shouldn't let it. Your blood will help. I know it." Rand shrugged. "And if it doesn't heal all the way, it's a small price to pay for getting Dovia back."

"Not a small price. Not if I never get to see you run again, like you did the night you chased that deer."

Rand pressed his lips together, and Cai's hand slid to his nape, drawing him forward. "Take it from wherever you want it," the vampire said.

He wanted the throat, but thinking it over, Rand settled for the wrist. He couldn't say exactly why, except when he bowed his head over the offering and felt Cai stroking his hair, saw his eyes closing in an expression of relief, Rand knew it had been the right choice. Their souls were out and exposed, too raw. Keeping it quiet, gentle, that was what was needed.

He had to bite with human canines, but experience breaking through skin with wolf fangs made it quick. Cai didn't seem bothered by any pain from it.

The blood was nourishing, as potent as ever. And a surprising comfort food. Lord Brian probably had an explanation for that, related to the bond between vampire and fully marked servant. But Rand didn't need to understand the whys right now.

He didn't take as much as Cai wanted him to, but he took enough that, when he eased back, Rand felt steadier, the pain of the leg less bothersome. Still there, but less distracting. He was certain a good day's sleep would help their respective wounds heal, so he squeezed Cai's arm, a silent reassurance when the vampire watched Rand adjust to sit hip to hip with him, still favoring the leg.

"Let's just lie here for a while," Rand suggested.

Cai nodded, but his gaze remained on the leg until Rand eased them down and turned them both on their sides, Rand behind him.

Cai suddenly felt tense again, things bending, but in a stiff, rigid, old-man kind of way. Rand had wrapped an arm around his chest, his mouth against his nape. Touch was so easy for wolves. And not easy as in meaningless. Cai realized every touch Rand offered was sincere, the full weight of his personality behind it so whoever he was touching felt central...and centered. Dovia had gravitated toward it like a toddler toward a teddy bear. Cai had different feelings about it, but no less strong and real.

Rand's knees pressed into the backs of Cai's, his chest against his shoulder blades. Cai swallowed, his eyes closing. A part of him just wanted to go, to pull loose. Perhaps Rand registered his conflict, because his breath was a caress on his neck that matched the light stroke over Cai's chest, both soothing.

"What?" the wolf asked.

"Nothing." But it wasn't nothing. It was a nothing thing to most people that was so far from nothing for Cai, he couldn't bear to face it. He didn't think of these things, hadn't had to think of them. It was easier to ignore what you'd never had when it was never offered to you. But when it was offered, it could open this whole damn empty chest of nothing that could jump out, pin you to the ground and strangle you. Christ, how could he be strangling?

"Hey. Hey, easy." Rand started to move, but Cai grabbed his hand on his chest, kept him there, pushed back into him so he had to stay where he was, as long as he could. Without looking at Cai's face. He couldn't bear looking at anyone right now.

"Okay," the wolf murmured. "It's all right. I'm right here."

"Fucking spooning. I've never...hell." Cai tried to laugh, and it came out in that weird, strangled, hysterical note.

Rand simply kept stroking him. He was rocking him, too, a very subtle motion, but it helped as Cai tried to level out. His heart had a jumpy pace that hurt. Would have hurt more if Rand hadn't fanned out his hand and pressed it there, absorbing it, somehow bringing it back down to normal.

"Rest a few minutes," the shifter urged. "We'll head back in a bit, but it's a nice night. Nice to be out here, just the two of us, like this."

"Yeah." Cai swallowed again, adjusted his head down and back and found Rand's bent arm there waiting, the massive biceps the perfect pillow. Cai closed his eyes and tried to relax his death grip on the guy's other hand. If Rand hadn't been a shifter and a third mark, Cai could have broken the fingers. "We got her. She's safe."

"Yeah. She is. Queen Lyssa might even pin a medal on you. She'll stab you with it first, but you'd have that coming. You did call her a bitch."

Cai snorted, the ground under his mental feet becoming less tentative. "A reward from Council vampires probably isn't a big step up from Trads. 'Hey, adequate job. We won't kill you this time.'"

"Well, what more precious gift could you give someone than their life?"

Cai turned his head enough that he was rubbing himself against the male's face. One of those wolf gestures. Rand made a pleased sound, crowding closer to him. If he'd been in wolf form, Cai thought he'd hear a tail thumping. Big puppy. But the momentary humor faded as he thought of Rand's words, the wolf's memories behind them.

"I'm really sorry, Rand. About your family." His grip on Rand's half-closed hand adjusted to his wrist, his thumb sliding over the scar from that time of dark despair in Rand's life. And Cai didn't question the fierce satisfaction of feeling his third mark overlaying it. "I can't imagine how hard it was to go on after that."

Rand said nothing at first, but he was still holding Cai, so he was okay. Just thinking. "Yeah, you can," he said at last. "Because the same thing happened to you. Just in a different way. Did you ever see them again, your family?"

He'd never spoken of it to anyone, not even Lodell. Hell, what he'd told Lyssa had been rote, the carefully structured bare facts that he could get through without opening deeper things that he always told himself he didn't feel anymore. But Rand saw the locked rooms, knew the lock on it was rusty and could be busted loose with one good kick of memory.

"No. It took me a hundred years to get away, and my parents were dead by then. My brothers and sisters may have had kids, and their kids had kids, et cetera, but I didn't look. Goddard told me if I ever tried to escape, he'd have the males killed and take the females in as potential breeders, regardless of their age. Even after I won my freedom, I couldn't...the idea of putting them at any risk... It didn't make sense, anyway. Not after so many years, you know."

"Yeah." Rand's breath was a caress against his neck. His chest expanded against Cai's back in a sigh. "I'm really sorry about your family, too."

Silence reigned for a while, their minds drifting, touching, moving away. No words exchanged, just images. When Cai saw Rand's children, overlaid with Fane's, his thoughts went in a different direction. He didn't have to voice the thought. Why torture himself? Because he was a damned pro at it, that was why. "So, you want kids again someday, I'll bet. You're great with Fane's."

"Maybe. We'll see. Got all I can handle right now with one annoying vampire. Shut up and let's sleep a bit. Don't know how long I'll have to stay up once we get to the house. Fane may want to crack open a keg and celebrate. Unlike you vamps, we don't have a mandatory bedtime."

"Sure, send me to bed so you can drink all the beer. What an asshole."

Rand chuckled. "Speaking of drinking, while you're holding onto that wrist, you could take some more. I'm feeling stronger, thanks to you. It's nice, that rejuvenation thing. Works fast."

Lyssa had mentioned that back-and-forth blood feeding between vampire and servant could be a surprisingly quick-acting spiral, making strength and healing go in the right direction for both. And the thought of drinking from Rand was a nice one, but it also reminded Cai of that annoying empty gap in his mouth. He wanted to sink two fangs into Rand, even if one was fake. He pushed that aside. There were way more important considerations right now. Like his wolf's well-being.

The leg had been a bad break, yes, and he agreed with Rand a good twelve-hour sleep would help the healing process, but Cai had a bad feeling about what was going on with it. So he went with his gut.

"Since we agreed our rabbit-hunting skills are at an all-time low, we'll go back to Fane's and get you something to eat first. Like another bucket of venison or something. I'll be fine until then."

When Rand's chest expanded again, a hint that he was about to argue, Cai increased his grip and the force of his resolve.

Not until you've eaten.

Rand went quiet, but stayed close. Maybe even adjusted closer. Master and servant. It was having a lot more meanings in Cai's head than it ever had before, which was just opening himself up to getting kicked in the face. But that had been done to him plenty. For now, he'd sit here and let himself marinate in those feelings he couldn't explain, running the words through his head. Master and servant.

They drifted back into that somnolent haze together, but Cai kept his grip on Rand's wrist, thumb sliding across the layered scar and third mark. He held the male to him while the night watched, waiting for two predators to decide what they were going to do next.

Cai wished like hell he knew.

~

When they rose, they took another dip in the creek to wash. Rand donned the shorts again, and they found a change of clothes for Cai on the ATV Fane had left on the nearest accessible deer trail. A pair of jeans and a T-shirt, clothes that Cai expected belonged to one of Fane's family. They were a decent but loose fit. Good thing he could rely on the charity of Rand's friends. He'd been losing a lot of backpacks lately.

He was glad Fane had left the ATV. While on a normal day the running distance wouldn't be much of anything to him or to Rand, it had been a long-assed night, and they would have had to hoof it to get in close to dawn. He could stay out, burrowed in the earth, but they both wanted to check on Dovia, no matter how effective her protection detail.

Rand was still limping, but when he used a sturdy branch Cai found for him, he employed it more like a cane than a crutch. Still, Cai unapologetically searched his mind to find out if Rand was masking pain, acting like he was doing better than he was.

He was.

Muttering a curse, Cai slid himself under Rand's shoulder, told him to shut up when he said he didn't need the help, and lent him extra leverage to get to the ATV. He'd never driven one before. Rand walked him through it while sitting on the back-facing seat, leg stretched out and propped on a short platform. He teased Cai about running them off a cliff or crashing them into a tree, until Cai threatened to do it for real. In time, with careful navigation of the deer trails, they came out behind Fane's home.

He'd seen Fane and Lynn's house through Rand's eyes, but in

person it was even more comfortably chaotic and homey. The Wolf Waltons. Okay, not his best material, so he kept that observation to himself. Mostly. Rand sent him a wry look as Cai helped him up the stairs where Todd and Fane waited. He and Todd examined Rand's leg on the porch.

"It probably would be in better shape if you'd left the split in place," Todd said, a firm rebuke. "Stubborn wolves. But swelling's gone down some."

Yeah, it had. Even Cai could see that. Maybe he was just being impatient, too worried, his head too messed up about today. He needed to shut it off for a while.

Before someone accuses you of acting like a fussy old woman.

Before Cai could retort with some mature response like *takes one to know one*, they were in the kitchen.

Lynn and Darcy provided Rand what Cai would consider the equivalent of a bucket of deer meat. Though the shifter consumed over half of it quickly, the kind of day they had had overtook him. Cai had to save him from falling asleep and doing a face plant in the remains of the meal.

"Good enough. Time to go to bed."

"Dovia first," Rand insisted. Cai didn't disagree.

Lynn went with them, guiding them down the steps to the cellar. Rand held onto the railing, but managed it capably enough. Cai just needed to be patient, give it time.

Patience was so not his strong suit.

You waited decades for the right moment to kill a Trad and free yourself from them, Rand observed. *You have patience. It's just selective.*

Rand's ability to read his emotions aside, Cai knew he should at least try to close his mind to Rand. If for no other reason than to prove he could. Honor the bullshit elitist vampire code. Yeah. That was so him.

But for some reason, he just hadn't felt like it since the whole rescue and magic bonfire thing. Having an open door to Rand in his mind kept Cai from being in there all by himself, weird as that sounded.

Maybe it gave Rand reassurance, too. Cai knew it made him feel better, dipping into the wolf's mind and seeing that Rand sincerely wasn't worried about his leg. And that concern grew even more distant when the shifter had the satisfaction of seeing Dovia in far better surroundings than when they'd seen her last.

Fane's mate and daughters had turned the girl's corner of the cellar as much into a bedroom as they could, transporting a double-sized bed down there, outfitting it with comfortable linens and pillows. A soft, stuffed animal, a bunny with long, velvety ears, was on the pillow next to Dovia's head, mostly submerged under the covers. It reminded Cai of her mother.

Cilya sat on the foot of the bed, her hand resting on Dovia's leg, hidden underneath the same blankets. She was humming a soft, formless tune that was nevertheless soothing, her dark eyes concerned and focused on the sleeping young woman.

Cai had listened in on some of Rand's visit with the family before they approached Goddard's camp, so he knew Cilya worked at a school. Seeing her in person, Cai could easily imagine it. She had the kind of female energy that broadcast firm authority, gentle care and competent experience, things that could figure out what a young, hurting soul most needed. They'd chosen the right one of Fane's children to be sitting with Dovia.

"I know she's probably too old for the rabbit," Lynn whispered to Rand. She stood on the bottom stair, Cai standing behind her, Rand at ground level. All three watching the female vampire sleep. "But when we were cleaning her up, she was a child in need of mothering. Cilya thought it would bring her comfort. She'd bought it for a teacher friend's baby shower. Plenty of time to pick up something different if Dovia wants to keep it."

"Good thought," Rand said. "She's in good hands."

"Cilya and I have been taking turns watching her. Sangra gave her the sedatives in the dosage you instructed, so she's out, but whenever one of us isn't sitting on the bed, she becomes restless." Lynn paused. "She asked for you and Cai last thing before she fell asleep. I made you up a cot down here with the others. I figured you'd want to stay close to her anyway and..." Her gaze strayed briefly to Cai and skittered away. "And him."

"If you think she's better with the two of you, with females, I can bunk down elsewhere," Rand said, concerned.

"No. She asked for you. Sangra says one of the best things she could have around her right now is male energy she trusts." A shadow crossed Lynn's expression, a deep anger on Dovia's behalf. "A reminder that there are good males. If you decide she needs one of us down here, just come get us, but...

Lynn's brow creased, as if the woman was having difficulty comprehending whatever she'd intuited from Dovia, but her words were sincere. "I have a feeling you're what she needs right now."

She patted Rand's arm and said her goodnights. A low word to her daughter had Cilya rising. The younger woman came to the stairs. She didn't speak, but she squeezed Rand's arm before she went up the stairs. Cai adjusted out of the way. She nodded to him, her pensive expression saying having a bunch of vampires in the cellar wasn't her uppermost concern. However, Lynn skirted around him on the way up with an awkward but courteous nod. As the door above closed behind her, Cai raised a brow.

It's safe to say the matriarch of the house will be happy when the vampire guests are gone.

He shifted his attention to the other side of the cellar. Daegan sat on a cot against the wall at watchful attention, but he was in the farthest, shadowed corner, perhaps so he wouldn't be conspicuous to Dovia if she woke.

Lynn had been right. Only a couple moments had passed since Cilya had left her side, but Dovia was already showing signs of distress. Her lips parted as little whimpers escaped her. One arm emerged, fingers fisting on the covers.

Daegan's gaze shifted to Rand. He'd figured it out, too. It wasn't likely a vampire she barely knew could bring her much comfort. Cai might be a passable second, but he suspected Lynn had said Dovia had asked about both of them just to be courteous.

Not likely. You underestimate what the girl feels toward you, vampire. Rand moved toward the bed.

Cai let it lie, but stayed at the stairs, watching him. *Good thing they went with a full-sized bed. You wouldn't fit on a twin by yourself, let alone with her, no matter how petite she is.*

No twin beds in the house, Rand responded. *Shifters rarely sleep alone. Giving wolves from the same litter separate beds while they're growing up is a waste of money.*

Rand slid in behind Dovia. He wore the shorts but nothing else.

She immediately turned toward him, flattening herself against his broad chest, fingers curling in his chest hair.

Cai noted the two cots near Daegan's. Lynn might not be comfortable having him here, but she was a good hostess. However, she might have saved the effort with Daegan, since Cai was pretty sure the Council's pit bull was genetically engineered not to sleep, ever. If he did, it would be long after Cai had to succumb to the pull of the oncoming daylight. Damn age difference. He wondered where Gideon was, and then realized the obvious; the male would be the topside lookout during daylight hours.

He moved toward one of the empty cots, but Rand's thought stopped him.

There's plenty of room over here, if we stay close together. Wolves don't often have nightmares. Another benefit of sleeping together as a pack. I think it works on other species as well.

Cai turned back toward his servant. *Do I look like the type that gets nightmares?*

Stupid thing to say since yes, Rand had seen him have nightmares, but Cai had had a long day.

I think it has been a very long day and night. I would like you to be closer. If you are willing to indulge me.

A clingy and needy wolf. Great.

But as a smile touched Rand's lips, his steady eyes serious and knowing, Cai came to the bed. There *was* enough room for three, if they were as close as Rand and Dovia were now. *I don't want to upset her.*

You won't. You didn't see the two of you enter the water together, or the way she looked at you after you helped return her babe to the heavens. From that moment forward, she knew your heart. She'll recognize it as she rests. The two of us will make sure she can sleep peacefully. Take off your shirt. She'll need the heat.

Cai met Rand's gaze. The wolf was merely stating the truth, but the slight twitch to his lips said he wouldn't mind the view. Cai found that gratifying and arousing, though he squelched the latter since... well, obviously inappropriate timing.

Asshole.

Rand's lips stretched into a deeper grin, but his eyes fell shut. Cai climbed into the bed on the other side and slid in close to Dovia's back. He wondered if they should have told Daegan what they were about. If he thought Cai was taking advantage of her vulnerable state, he'd likely skewer him. But Daegan hadn't moved.

He understands what we're doing and is pleased with how much we care for her welfare.

You can get all that from his scent?

Rand nodded. "Pretty much." He had his arms around Dovia's lower back and shoulders, so Cai draped one of his own over her, resting his hand on Rand's hip, the other tucked under his own head as he considered the male. He thought of how Rand had chased him down in the forest. Then he saw the shifter's expression tighten, the lingering smile gone. He was thinking of Cai wounded again, nearly baked by the sun.

"Hey," Cai said quietly, making the male open his eyes. "You did what you were supposed to do. You got her out of there. And you came back for me. Plus, none of the wolves were hurt."

"Thanks to you and your plan to divert attention. Though we didn't anticipate you'd turn it into a match of honor with your old nemesis." Rand had his hand on Cai's leg. The touch was welcome, though he'd never thought of himself as a touchy-feely person.

Maybe because you've never been able to indulge the pleasure. You may be more of a pack animal than you think, vampire.

If you're going to insult me, I'm going to go sit next to Daegan. Mimic his stoic samurai pose until I irritate the fuck out of him and he goes to sleep.

Or he kills you and we end this night as we expected. Dead.

Cai lifted his gaze to Rand's. Because he wanted to do so and couldn't think of a reason to deny himself, he curled his fingers against the shifter's hip, hooking his thumb in the waistband of the loose shorts. "I couldn't have done it," he admitted quietly.

If our positions were reversed, I couldn't have left you, Rand, knowing what they might do to you. Dovia... I would have given her a head start, told her which way to go, maybe. And we would have both died. Dovia probably, too. You were the smart one.

"Well," Rand said after a long moment. "One of us has to be."

Cai snorted, but he could feel the male's reaction to his words. A big, gushing emotional surge that would have discomfited Cai and made him regret his admission, if Rand hadn't tempered it with the mildly insulting comment. Probably why he'd done it. The wolf got him. A useful thing in a servant, right?

Another silence ensued. Cai had no idea how much Daegan was listening, but the hell with it. He needed to speak aloud before he said more stupid things in his head. "Fane and his pack want you to stay with them, you know."

Rand's eyes had fallen shut again during their pause. They didn't open now. "Sshh. Go to sleep."

"Did you really just *ssh* me?"

The curve to Rand's lips deepened, his lashes fanning his cheeks. "I did. Sleep, vampire. Now's not the time for talking."

He didn't think Rand was wrong, but him setting the terms were kind of annoying. He'd take him to task for that when he woke. Much later.

As Cai closed his eyes and let out a long, relieved breath, Rand's hand moved to rest briefly on his jaw, his fingertips slipping through Cai's hair, a soft stroke, before he returned his palm to Dovia's back, his knuckles resting against Cai's chest.

Yeah, Rand needed a pack. Needed to stay with family who could appreciate that kind of stuff. Because Cai really wasn't a touchy-feely kind of guy. No matter how good Rand's touch felt. Cai didn't take another breath, because the motion only rubbed the jagged edges of the thought against his insides in a way he didn't like. Rand was right. Now wasn't the time for talking, even to one's self.

Maybe especially to one's self.

CHAPTER SEVENTEEN

*H*umans talked about the three a.m. hour being when demons would most likely walk on their grave, wake them with worries. From Cai's struggle with nightmares, Rand had surmised it was between one and two in the afternoon for vampires, when the sun had settled into its peak time.

Dovia was below ground and protected physically, but the hour still had the power to bring unrest to her that even their proximity couldn't keep at bay. Though Cai had said it would be hard to rouse a vampire so young at that hour, no matter how deep below ground she was, obviously terror had the power to yank her from that rest.

She woke fighting, thrashing, hissing, her cries echoing through the cellar. Between them, Cai and Rand brought her fully awake, helped her realize she was safe, and with them. Even so, in those first volatile moments, Rand wouldn't have been surprised if she'd tried to shove them out of the bed or bolted from it herself. He could tell Cai was as ready as he was to give her enough room she wouldn't feel trapped, while doing their best to keep her from accidentally harming herself.

However, she started to calm without exiting the bed. As she relaxed inside the span of his arms, Rand crooned to her, rubbed her back. When she settled, Cai likewise adjusted himself back onto his pillow and folded arm. He ran his hand lightly up and down her arm, over her shoulder and hair.

Lynn and her daughters had trimmed it, evening up the chopped section so it was neat, shoulder length on one side. On the burned side, they'd buzzed it evenly. Rand vaguely recalled the style from a couple of the magazines the women had lying around upstairs. A deliberate close crop buzz over one delicate ear, a straight fall of hair over the other. All she needed was a dainty nose ring or a rose shoulder cap tattoo. Greenwald would love that.

But Rand couldn't argue with the look, which highlighted Dovia's delicate features, yet also underscored the set of her chin, her firm lips, that spoke of resolve. Determination. The ability to survive.

He expected Darcy, Fane and Lynn's fashion-conscious teen daughter, had likely suggested the cut. While Dovia wouldn't be able to see it in the mirror, when she woke, Rand bet money the shifter teenager would be ready to show her the magazine picture.

He remembered paging through one of those magazines the night before they went to rescue Dovia. It had been a culture shock dip into the world he'd been away from for over two years. How fast did vampire hair grow? Not as fast as visible wounds healed, but Rand expected it grew faster than a human's.

Idle thoughts. Normal things like that, they hurt and comforted at once. He remembered Sylvan's boys playing catch, the smell of Sheba's fried chicken...

Cai's eyelids were drooping again and Rand let his eyes half close, figuring their ease would help draw the girl back to the same kind of slumber. It did. She was drifting back into a doze, he could tell, even as she pressed closer, nuzzling her face in his chest.

A half hour later, he returned to a wakeful state. He wasn't exactly sure why, until he realized Dovia's hands were moving over his chest, then down, under his arm. She was...caressing him, her touch drifting around to his back, fingers exploring with obvious sexual intent.

He couldn't have been more startled if she'd turned into a two-headed wolf, right before his eyes. He stiffened when she slid both hands down to cup his ass, and knead. His gaze shot to her face. Her eyes were closed but her lips were slightly parted. Her body moved more urgently against his. She was asleep, mostly. In a half-waking dream state, somewhat conscious but not.

He should speak her name, wake her fully, but he honestly had no clue how to handle the situation. It made no sense to him. After what she'd endured, no female would want... What the hell was happening?

It wasn't manly, but panic rarely was. *Cai? Cai.*

"Cai," he hissed. Lifting his head, Rand realized, with both relief and annoyance, the vampire was awake and watching her progress. Cai lifted a "what?" kind of brow.

"We need to wake her. Now. She couldn't possibly want...this kind of thing." Rand spoke low but aloud. He'd hoped Daegan was asleep, but his wolf senses told him he wasn't, so he wanted to be sure the male with the lethal sword knew he wasn't encouraging this.

Cai's eyes sparked with humor, making Rand's teeth grind. "She's a vampire," Cai answered, just as low. "Remember, vampire libidos are like ten times that of a twenty-something human male's. It's as much a part of us as the need to drink blood, so claiming that for herself, doing it right now? It's a good sign that she's reaching for that. Even if in her sleep."

"But I...I don't..."

"It's okay." Cai put his hand on the young woman's shoulder, sliding his fingers along her arm, down to where it curved over Rand's hip. Cai covered her hand on Rand's backside, closing his grip on her wrist, caressing. As he gently brought her touch away from Rand, he spoke quietly.

"Dovia. Wake up, princess."

He eased her arm into a folded position where her hand was by her shoulder, and dipped his head to kiss her fingertips, an easy gesture. Her head dropped back on his shoulder.

"I'm awake," she murmured.

Rand had been wrong. She *was* awake, and her half-closed eyes were on him, her pupils big and dark, the tips of her fangs showing.

"I want him," she said, with an almost animal note to her voice that startled Rand anew.

She's a fledgling, Cai said, another reminder. *When she wants blood or sex, her impulse control is almost non-existent. Take the stress of the past few days, add it to being safe now and wanting to reinforce that, by feeling in control of something... You're what she wants. A servant.*

She's so young, Rand thought desperately.

She's twenty-two. Remember Giles and Petra? She wouldn't have used them only for blood. Lyssa said born vampires start combining blood and sex in their early to mid-teens.

Rand barely digested the information. His wolf was still struggling with the more immediate issue.

She wants me to have sex with her.

She intends to have sex with you, Cai corrected. *She's a vampire; you're a servant. In this mode, she sees herself as in control. Rand, it's okay. You don't have to do it.*

Cai wasn't sure why the wolf was looking so distressed about it. There were other ways to deal with Dovia's need. Nobody would question him if he denied a fledgling the right to enjoy his servant, since she had no authority or rank over him.

No. Rand's jaw set. *If that's what she needs...to feel better, to feel more in control, I can do it. I just...I don't know how.*

Cai blinked. *It works pretty much the same as it does with a guy. Just a different orifice. Usually. Though she might take that as an option.*

No. Rand shook his head vehemently. *I understand the mechanics. I want it to be pleasurable for her, and I don't...know how to do that.*

The male's ears were turning pink. He was blushing like a damn school boy. Holy fuck. He'd never... Cai lifted both brows.

What about Sheba? You had a litter together.

Yes. We mated as wolves, because that was easier, more instinctive for me, more straightforward for her, not as difficult with her grief for Sylvan still so fresh. Not...man and woman.

"Ah." It struck Cai as ridiculously sweet, the wolf shifter wanting to make sure it was pleasurable for Dovia, do it right. And willing to do it against his own preferences and nature simply because Cai had told him it would help her heal the wounds that were far deeper than the physical.

Rand was strong, but a gentle male, too. With a hell of a tempting service sub streak.

Dovia's moist lips had parted. She slid her hands up Rand's chest to his throat, fingers stroking, digging in. Her nails had been cleaned and trimmed. Even painted, a delicate pink hue. Rand wet his lips and she stretched up to brush her lips over them, her fangs grazing his mouth. His wolf was still figuring things out. Slowing things down, Cai slid an arm over her chest and tightened his grip. It kept her from deepening the kiss and won a small annoyed hiss.

"Don't get petulant," he told her, putting his other arm at her waist, giving Rand some distance. She stiffened, but Cai wouldn't let her get caught up in a waking nightmare.

"See?" he whispered as she curled her fingers over his forearm. "It's like I said. They didn't take a damn thing from you."

It was nowhere near that simple, but Cai knew right now it could be. If it had only been her and him in the bed, she wouldn't have been capable of contemplating, let alone feeling, this kind of sexual hunger. A servant was different. A servant was theirs, completely under their control. Under her control. A way to feel back in control.

Today, Cai understood it, in a way he knew he wouldn't have, only a few days before. He remembered the first few times he'd had sex with his human prey, after leaving Goddard's fold. He'd practically received a contact high from holding the reins, having full control of a human's pleasure during sex. Cai could bring that reaction to the edge of pain, and inspire a thrill-ride kind of fear.

It made him want Rand all over again, to do it even better, harder, edgier. Cai wanted to explore those feelings a hundred ways with him, because it would never be the same with the shifter.

It was the difference between day and night, that desire and how Goddard took and gave nothing back. Hell fucking no. But having the right and ability to control a servant's pleasure? Dovia's naturally Dominant desire for that was feeding her already enormous fledgling hungers.

"I want him," she repeated. "I'm hungry."

"That's up to me, isn't it? He's my servant, and if I say he's off the table, he damn well is. Right?"

She stiffened again, but this time in typical aristocratic offense, making him smile against her delicate ear. "So don't tell me, princess. Ask me."

She released Cai to curl her fingers against Rand's chest once more. Over her head, Cai held his servant's gaze. He could tell what Rand did and didn't want. He was apprehensive, but truly willing to give the girl what she needed. More important to Cai, Rand was willing for the right reasons. Plus, in that intuitive way of his, he'd also picked up what Cai had realized, why it had to be now.

At Dovia's home, she'd only have access to the safe, totally controlled servants she knew. Responding to what had happened to her, they would be almost too compliant, falling short of making her feel like she did in fact have control over this part of herself again.

"I don't want to feel...the others, inside me," she said. "Around me. Please let me...let me immerse myself in him, drink from him, have him inside me."

"All right," Cai said. "That's the right way to ask."

She won't ask me? Rand's expression reflected neutral curiosity, rather than judgment.

No, she won't. Vampires ask other vampires about their servants. Technically, the servant's opinion doesn't count, but that's because it's assumed the servant is on board with what his Master or Mistress wants. But she won't be as high-powered about it as an older vampire. If you're reluctant, she'll likely back off. And if she doesn't, I'll stop it.

I'm not reluctant. As long as you're here...helping me.

Rand's blue eyes flickered. There were a lot of layers to that thought. Layers that made Cai's cock harden, his bloodlust rise and other things knot up in his gut. But he tamped that down. He didn't want Dovia to feel him getting aroused, even if it wasn't directed at her. This was a tightrope walk between what she was trying to grasp and what her fragile, traumatized psyche could handle. Something else he and Rand recognized in a way she didn't.

She was trusting them as strangers thrown together in intense circumstances did. Or like warriors emerging from a blood-soaked field, sharing an aftermath experience uniquely theirs, one that validated their life and worth. Their connection. Something he and Rand would have done in the forest if they hadn't both been beat all to shit.

But the short respite they'd had, and blood they'd exchanged, had equipped them to handle one kid-gloves encounter with a traumatized vampire female.

Rand nodded, an affirmation. Cai squeezed Dovia, warning her of a change in position. He left the bed, circling to the other side as Rand curled his arm around her waist and adjusted the two of them to make room for Cai to get in behind him. Cai first sat on his hip next to him, though, threading his fingers through Rand's hair.

"He's got gorgeous, fucking hair," he murmured. "All over. Enjoy it, princess. Enjoy every inch of him. Don't rush a good meal."

Her eyes glowed. Her fangs were lengthening, curving over her bottom lip. "I'd like for his hands to be out of the way. I want to control him."

The need for that rose in her eyes like a tidal wave, impossible to mistake. If Cai was detecting it, Rand was feeling it full force with his wolf senses.

Cai bent, spoke in Rand's ear. "Put your arms above your head and grab onto that pipe."

There was a water pipe running horizontally above the bed that seemed sturdy. At least Cai hoped it was, or that Rand would stay mindful of his own strength. Sending water spewing over them would be a literal cold shower moment. Plus, if they caused Fane a major plumbing issue, they probably wouldn't be invited back. Not that Lynn was going to add him and Daegan to her Christmas list anytime soon, Cai was sure.

Then his dry humor disappeared, his attention captured by the sheer beauty of his servant. Rand lifted his arms, his back muscles and ass tightening as he curled his large hands around the pipe. A sound escaped Dovia's lips; unmistakable female hunger.

You don't have to do a thing, wolf, except follow her lead. And respond to your Master's touch.

He wanted to call himself Rand's Master right now, particularly with another vampire touching him. Too damn bad if it bothered him, though Cai had a pretty good idea that it wasn't Rand who struggled the most with it. The wolf's arousal had shot up another notch, as soon as Cai spoke that trigger word.

He did a quick check over his shoulder. In the shadows beneath the stairs, Daegan lay stretched out on his cot, his ankles propped on the metal frame. His eyes were closed, arms crossed loosely over his chest—akimbo, not Count Dracula style—but Cai wasn't fooled. Daegan knew everything that was happening over here, but vampires were vampires.

It was as Rand had said earlier. What they were doing wasn't something that would alarm or anger Daegan on behalf of the girl or Lord Greenwald. It would be considered something she'd needed, requested, for her care. To help her take a step toward a semblance of normal. For vampires, it was all about control. Control, sex and blood.

Tell me about it. Rand's nervousness was still there, but his wry response almost made Cai smile.

Dovia's small hands fanned out over Rand's wide chest. When her nails scraped his nipples, he responded, his hips flexing. He immediately froze, as if he thought that was too aggressive. His courtly wolf wanted to make sure he didn't startle her. But him gripping the pipe, purposefully surrendering to her needs and demands, was a powerful statement. Despite Rand's instinctive understanding of dominance and submission in animal form, it might be impossible for the wolf to completely understand how a vampire experienced those feelings. Nothing he did would scare or deter Dovia now. It was far more likely to make her demand even more of him.

Dovia's head dipped, her fangs scraping and lips brushing Rand's heated flesh. Cai had third marked him specifically for their mission, but now he discovered the wonder of being able to stay deep in his wolf's mind, see all that was happening to him. All his responses.

Her touch alone couldn't arouse Rand. Partly because he was too protective of her, seeing her as a female he'd rescued. Partly because of her age, too close to what Sylvan's teenage wolves would have been now. But mostly because he truly was a man's man, a female touch doing little for him. Yet he genuinely wanted to be responsive, to care for her, give her the satisfaction she needed. So he'd asked for Cai's help in that. Cai liked knowing that it was his Master's touch Rand needed, wanted, the most.

Cai scraped back the thick, long hair and wrapped it around his fist. It gave him unimpeded ability to put his mouth on Rand's throat, suckle him hard, tease him with his one fang as he pushed his pelvis firmly against Rand's superior ass. He slid an arm around Rand, loosened the drawstring tie of the shorts, and made short work of the garment, tugging them off, though he was careful of the leg. Despite her blood lust, Dovia seemed to be staying mindful of it, too. Though her feet shifted restlessly, she hadn't hooked her leg over it, since Rand rested on his non-injured leg side. Cai approved of her kindness. It made him like her even more.

She showed less mercy in other ways. He liked that, too.

Rand drew in a breath as Dovia gripped him, her small fingers far stronger than they appeared. She licked her lips, her eyes glowing. Cai enjoyed the multiple feedback readings from Rand's mind. He was registering everything Dovia was doing with her unexpectedly experienced touch—well, unexpected to Rand. Stroking him, cupping his balls, spreading her other hand over his abdomen and learning the shape of every impressive muscle. Tugging on the arrow of hair on his lower belly.

She tasted him; chest, stomach, upper arm, giving him small bites, some of them sharp enough to draw blood. Her hunger was rising, the primal noise constant now, as if she were one of Fane's wolf children. Both species were predators, after all.

Dovia kept her eyes on Rand as she put her hands to the hem of the nightshirt she'd been given. She was riding the tide of her own lust, wanting to feel him, skin to skin. But when she curled her fingers around the cloth and started to lift it, that was when other things interfered. Under Rand's intent male gaze, her own faltered. Cai could almost feel the flashback slam into her. Probably a memory of Goddard and his hell spawn stripping her, staring at her, exposing her in every way.

Before Cai could even think it, Rand lifted his gaze to where he held the pipe.

"You're beautiful," the wolf shifter rumbled. "But I will only look at you if you command me to do so, my lady."

Fuck. Whatever *good* meant, that was Rand. He understood so much.

She wouldn't expect Cai to be submissive as Rand was being, but he wasn't going to disrupt her with a male stare, either. He made sure his attention remained on Rand, though he did sneak enough of a discreet look to verify that Lynn and her daughters had cared well for her, and the blood Rand had given the girl had helped.

Dovia's skin was like unblemished cream, her body a lovely sculpture of sweet curves. It really was on the border of obscene, how fast vampires could heal from things that took much longer to heal on the inside. Rand had acknowledged that, felt it, answered and healed the rawness of that wound when Cai had struggled with it in the forest.

Cai pushed away the darkness that path in his mind could take. He had better things to command his attention. To command, period.

He caressed the shifter's back between his shoulder blades, dipped down to the lower back, that shallow valley that led to the enticing rise of his tight buttocks. He stroked with his knuckles, gave him a hard pinch or two that had Rand muttering an oath as Dovia reclaimed his mouth with scraping fangs, and a needy, moist heat.

Her fingers still gripped his cock as if she intended to lead him around by it, stretching that connection with deliberate discomfort. That thing in Rand that roused when Cai gave him pain and took control, responded. He was getting harder, pressing into her touch as Cai slid his fingers over and dipped into his rim, caressing. The male rocked and shuddered at the dual stimulation. Cai pressed on the opening, enough to awaken nerves, make the sensitive opening twitch under his fingertips.

"How would you like that, wolf? To have me inside you while she fucks you?" Cai whispered it against his ear, his eyes meeting Dovia's lust-filled ones. She had a nice storm of sensation moving through her, helping to obliterate other kinds of thoughts and noise she didn't want. She had closed up the wound on Rand's neck, done with her blood feeding, but she licked the residual from her lips. Cai inhaled the scent, and felt some of the same hunger stir. He might have a taste himself before this was over.

"Yes," she said, her voice breathless. "I would like that."

Cai tossed a feral grin at her. "But I asked him."

"Yes. God, yes," Rand said.

Good. Slide her up your body and suckle her nipples, her neck. Women love that. And it drives vampires fucking over the moon.

Like you. You like it when my mouth is at your throat.

Fuck yeah. But with her, go gentle at first, then be more insistent. Grip and caress her breasts as you do it. Don't just pay attention to the nipples, because that can get uncomfortable. But when she gets more aroused, you can pinch and tug. If you're doing it right, she'll rub her wet little cunt all over those obscenely hard abs of yours.

The male might not know his way around a woman, but he earned high marks for following instruction. There was a brief hesitation as he realized he'd be releasing the pipe she'd commanded him to hold, but Cai sent him an encouraging push in his mind. It was okay. The time was right, and Rand had proven he could follow his instincts about her better even than Cai could.

Despite a half-hearted protest from the female, Rand gripped Dovia beneath the arms and brought her up higher, adjusting his hands to circle her breasts, squeeze them with caressing pressure as he took first one nipple in his mouth, then the other, suckling. Her head dropped back on a gasp. Cai's satisfaction surged as she hooked her leg high over Rand's hip, her calf brushing Cai's, and she rubbed her mound hard against Rand's washboard stomach.

She'd brought the leg into play well above his wound, their considerate princess, and Cai gripped her thigh, additional strength to keep it above the affected area, and offer her support.

Rand made noises as he was suckling her, the right kind that increased her response. And the size of Cai's cock, because it was his servant doing this, bringing pleasure to another vampire. Not his own vampire, so Cai was damn well going to remind him what vampire commanded him. Even though he didn't begrudge Dovia this. He'd given her permission and he was stronger than her, higher on the food chain.

The two different feelings made total sense. No conflict. Just what it was. Right now, there was no question of time limits between him and Rand, or what would change in their relationship when Dovia was back with her family. Rand was Cai's, and he was going to reinforce that claim with the subtlety of a baseball bat.

It didn't help ease that fire and need to see in Rand's mind that he wanted that reminder, craved it. He was getting caught up in the experience of being between the two of them, the worry that he wouldn't be able to please Dovia diminishing.

The only way Rand couldn't be pleasing was if he were a stone-cold corpse. Only if all that character, power and life were leeched away from the physical form. The male had a hell of a body, but it was the charisma and energy that infused it that made him so desirable.

Rand had put one hand behind her head, cradling it, and Dovia turned her mouth to the inside of his forearm. As he continued to suckle at one of her breasts, she struck again, looking for more blood. She wanted to feed again, but for different reasons this time.

Bring her down to your throat, wolf. Give her time to unlatch so she doesn't tear your flesh.

"Kiss me," Rand murmured, and Dovia eagerly disengaged her mouth from his arm to bring blood-tinged lips to his. Rand did a proper job on that, cupping her head again to make the kiss deep and long, a kiss that would melt any woman's knees and liquefy her in all the right places.

Cai saw the wolf imagining the first kiss the two of them had shared. Though Rand kept the present-moment kiss sensual, forceful to the right amount for a young woman, the elements of the near-violence he and Cai had shared were there. Cai got lost in the memory as he pressed his face to the back of Rand's shoulder and stroked his hip, his buttock.

Cai used his saliva to lubricate himself, but it wouldn't be enough. He was too big, too hard. He'd underestimated his response to the horror of everything that had happened. He wanted to take his servant with the primal instinct of a tiger, set free from the soul-shattering prison of a circus. *I am vampire, hear me roar.*

A little tap and thump. The sound of something hitting and tumbling off his hip, behind his ass on the bed. Cai felt for it and came up with a tube of lubricant, the perfect pocket carry size. He lifted his head to glance over at Daegan's bed. The vampire still had his eyes closed, but his hands had changed position.

"Nice aim," Cai muttered. "Thanks."

The vampire's head inclined slightly. Of course Daegan would carry lube. While Cai still had mixed feelings about Gideon, the vampire hunter was undeniably fuckable-looking. If he was Daegan, Cai would be tapping that ass whenever he could.

But he had his own servant who made him feel the same fucking way. Rand was pushing back against him, and he took it for the invitation it was. Cai lubed up fast. Dovia had broken the kiss, Rand directing her to his throat as Cai had suggested. He let the hand that had been holding the back of her head drop, his arm settling around her upper back, stroking. However, he'd returned the other over his head to grasp the pipe again, as she'd originally dictated. When she struck at his carotid, fangs sinking in deep, Cai slid his cock into his backside.

Rand arched into both stimuli, a groan breaking from his lips. Cai slid a hand forward to Dovia's hip, gripped there. The shifter's cock was near the opening of her slick pussy.

Condom...

His wolf, so conscientious.

No need. He could get into why vampires didn't use protection, rare fertility, no STDs and all that, but all he needed was one explanation to allay Rand's concerns. One that underscored why Goddard's no-marks behavior toward his human captives had been purist idiocy.

Vampire-human conception doesn't happen outside a full servant marking. Only I can impregnate you, wolf.

Rand choked on a sound that might have been a laugh, or a lust-filled response to what they were doing to him. Or both.

Cai could smell Dovia's arousal, strong and thick. She was ready, but they both waited, knowing the importance of her being the one to decide when and if. Rand's thighs shuddered as Cai thrust into him again. The shifter's cock slid along her thighs, teasing her clit while she drank from his throat, nourishing herself. And suddenly, her hands clutched his biceps, she adjusted herself over him, and she sank down, down. She did it fast, as if running from demons, and as she took him to the hilt, she made a deep, moving cry against Rand's flesh, an overflow of emotions.

When she lifted her mouth from his throat, Rand sucked gently on her lips to remove the blood. She had her eyes on his, still lowered. He didn't put her in a spotlight. This moment was all hers. There were a couple tear tracks on her face, but it was still suffused with physical desire. She began to move.

Lifting and lowering herself, the strength of Rand's arm helping, adding to the movement. Another cry broke from her lips when male need took over and his grip on her waist tightened, bringing her down more firmly upon him. A reaction to Cai, who'd thrust deep in the very same motion, plowing him. The muttered expletive that escaped Rand's working throat was music to Cai's ears.

"Yeah, we'll both fuck you into oblivion, wolf," he muttered. "Use your cock and your ass until you're worn out, every beautiful inch of you."

Rand choked on a snarl. The two of them were building fast toward a pinnacle. Cai reined himself back, remembering that this was about more than the two of them. "Not until she goes. When she goes over, so can you. She's getting close. You can tell from how she's gripping you, those sweet little sounds she's making..."

Rand nodded, a quick jerk of acknowledgement, but Cai loved feeling his struggle and didn't mind making it even more difficult for him. Bringing his fingers around to grip Rand's base, he played around that hard, thick circumference, made slick by Dovia's juices. Her pussy pushed against Cai's hand, a nice, soft female cushion of heated flesh. He played his fingers over Rand's balls, dug deeper to find the space between them to knead and roll.

"Fuck..."

It was rare he could get the wolf to curse during sex. He took it as a victory. Cai's arms overlapped Dovia's as they held as tight to the large male as they could, their movements becoming close, small, increasing the intensity. *There she goes...*

Dovia's head dropped back, a cry breaking from her lips, body rippling and flushing. Rand caught her skull in his large palm, brought her back to his lips and captured her wails. Cai bit Rand's earlobe as he slammed into his ass a couple more good, grinding times. "Go, wolf. I want to feel you release."

Want you to go first. Rand's mind-voice was blissfully strained, on the edge of breaking.

"Wasn't giving you a fucking choice. Go. Now." Cai teased and stroked, thrust and demanded, with body, voice and heat. Rand succumbed with a groan, his body bucking between the two vampires. Dovia's climax had ebbed, but she held onto him, a generous lover, her lips passing over his cheekbone, his throat, his chest, murmuring to him as Cai did the same, only with far rougher endearments.

When the male's ass tightened down on him like a lemon press, Cai released, pressing his face in his hair, against the side of his throat. He loved the movement of their bodies together, how he could feel every inch of Rand's rippling, writhing response against his heart, his loins, every possible exposed inch of skin.

They'd survived, and this was a hell of a reward. As well as a victory for the young woman whose cheeks were flushed, eyes bright and mouth set in a way that Cai well-recognized.

I'm broken, I'm wounded, but you fuckers did not break what mattered.

He'd always told himself that, over and over, because he was determined to make it true. But holding Rand now, Cai felt it down to his soul. For a second, Cai even believed it.

As the three of them drifted toward sleep, Cai had an alarming thought.

Fuck. He did love the guy.

CHAPTER EIGHTEEN

*V*oltaire's betrayal had been communicated to the Council delegation still camped at Greenwald's. Directly after, Daegan had kindly informed Dovia that, "Your parents are eager to have you home. But they want you to stay here one more day to address additional security measures."

Gideon re-phrased Daegan's message a little less subtly to Cai and Rand when they were alone. "The housekeeping staff needs to mop Voltaire's blood off every-fucking-where. And they need to finish interrogating Chavez and Tyra, make sure no one else was involved."

"Just tell me Greenwald got to do the honors on Voltaire," Rand had said, with a set jaw and flashing eye.

"Even better." Gideon's lip curled with satisfaction. "After Greenwald messed him up so bad he couldn't walk—hard to do when someone's broken every bone with a tire iron—

Leona staked him. Lyssa said this was a no-brainer exception to the servant-killing-vampire death sentence provision."

Rand blinked. "I would hope so."

Dovia had seemed oddly relieved to have more time to recuperate. Or perhaps she was glad that, when she came home, she wouldn't have to see the male who'd been responsible for her kidnapping, and the killing of her second mark.

So that decision made, they all passed a companionable evening with Fane's pack. Rand played video games with the teens on the braided rug in front of the hearth. When the competition turned fierce, it became an excuse for roughhousing. Darcy and Chad tackled Rand like a litter of pups with a favorite uncle. He was saved from complete annihilation—according to Chad—when Lynn announced the homemade ice cream was ready. That brought Fane, Gideon and Stalker in from the porch, where they'd been discussing everything from football to car engines.

Cai sat on the periphery in a far-too-comfortable chair. With no lamp in that corner, it was thankfully flanked by shadows, which allowed him to do more blending and listening than having to engage in conversation. It was a lot of bodies in one space. A lot more noise than he liked.

But he couldn't leave while Rand was playing video games, laughing and teasing with the kids. Or now, when he was eating ice cream.

The night before the rescue, there'd been a lot of underlying tension, but it was gone tonight. This was a side of the shifter he hadn't yet seen. Cai wondered how long it had been since Rand had allowed himself to be this relaxed. He hadn't been among his own kind in over two years, but fitting in with a pack seemed as easy to him as doing magic was for Cai.

It was kind of a magic on its own, because despite the noise and more than a mild case of agoraphobia, Cai stuck. He wondered what it would be like to taste the butter-pecan and hot fudge sauce on Rand's lips. He'd politely declined a bowl for himself, but he took a tumbler of Jack from Fane and clinked glasses companionably with him. See? He could do social.

Now leave me the fuck alone, so I can watch my servant.

Dovia spent most of the evening in a protective circle of female offspring. Cilya engineered that, effectively drawing the young vampire into deliberately light fare conversation, and picking up on Dovia's specific interests that meshed with that of the other females. Soon, they were all chatting about everything from fashion to books, movies and travel experiences.

Not including the current abduction trip, obviously.

Dovia was handling the social interaction with grace and class, until someone let the screen door slam a little too loudly. In a blink, she'd bolted to her feet like a startled animal. She nearly tripped over

Darcy as she escaped to a corner where she had a wall on two sides. Her fists clenched and she was breathing fast, her face two shades paler, except for spots of color high on her cheeks.

Before either Cai or Rand could move, Cilya had stepped forward. Not touching her, but close enough she drew Dovia's attention.

"Boys," Cilya said firmly. "They're like having a bunch of animals in the house."

Dovia steadied, a weak smile on her face. Cilya drew her back toward the other women with an easy palm on her lower back. As Dovia sank down on a cushion, Darcy was looking at her with sober brown eyes. However, at a subtle but meaningful gesture from her older sister, she recovered and picked up a bottle of nail polish and a container of what looked like tiny gemstones. "So, as I was saying, why don't you let me add a couple touches to your manicure? You should have seen the night we painted Chad's toenails while he was all furry. We took pictures. Sangra, where's your phone?"

As Sangra complied and showed Dovia the picture, Chad groused in the background.

"Do you have any brothers and sisters, Dovia?" Lynn asked. She was sitting in a nearby chair with a lapful of newspapers and a steadily growing stack of coupons next to her.

Coupon cutting, thought Cai. Crazy, unsettling stuff.

"Um, no." Dovia shook her head as she let Darcy take her hand. "Vampires, we don't... It's rare for vampires to have any children, and then only one."

Her gaze flicked to Cai, and suddenly there was something stark there. It was gone in a flash, but Cai knew Rand saw it. Felt how Cai reacted to it. The wolf was thinking of extricating himself from the couch to come to him. To do what? Reassure him?

Dovia was still looking at him, though thankfully her expression had changed. He found himself offering her a stiff version of a smile, which he hoped was reassuring. Whatever she saw in his face, he expected it wasn't his smile that helped, because her eyes grew even more serious. She offered him a cryptic, brief nod before she turned her attention to Darcy again.

Daegan was handling the perimeter watch. As uncertain as Lynn was around Cai, Daegan made her jumpy as a cat. Not a comparison a wolf would appreciate, Cai was sure. The older vampire had noted it and was being considerate. Cai decided it was time to join him.

Cai rose, taking his Jack with him. He took the time to alleviate Rand's concerns, though, stopping by him to touch his shoulder where he sat on the sofa. Rand dropped his head back, his temple brushing Cai's forearm.

All right, Cai?

Had he ever called him by his name? He wasn't sure. But Cai nodded. *All good. I'll be back in at dawn. Just going to night owl it with Daegan. He might need backup. You know, in case more than a hundred bad guys show up. I can take a little one or two. Give him a chance for a Gatorade break.*

Rand's lips twisted, but his eyes had some of the same unfathomable look as Dovia's. They all knew what was happening with each of them, an aftermath kind of thing that straddled the thank-god-we're-alive and the how-the-hell-are-we-alive lines. With a healthy dose of what-do-I-do-with-myself-now.

Because the bitch of it was, after something like that, the psyche expected some kind of life-altering, I'm going to go out and be a different kind of person transformation. Or some amazing meaning of the universe revelation.

The truth was, life just went on, as confusing as it always was. Horror and miracle were woven on the same loom, and in the end, each of them was one straight thread, with a beginning, middle and end.

Wow. He could become a life coach with bullshit like that. Or the cheering section for a pro-suicide hotline.

He spent the rest of the evening keeping an eye on the periphery, Daegan agreeably pretending like Cai's reinforcement was necessary. Cai did hang with him long enough to learn from the vampire that Tyra and Chavez had been cleared of any involvement.

"How can they be sure?" Cai asked. "Greenwald's judgment may not be the best."

"The Council handled the interrogation. They're not easily duped, and certainly not by vampires of such younger ages and obvious ambitions." Daegan's gaze held a dangerous gleam. "Ambitious they are, but in the way typical to vampires. They're not so disloyal to their lord they would cause harm to his daughter."

"Well, good. And bad. Would have kind of liked Chavez to be obliterated. Tyra, not so much. Have to appreciate a good-looking woman who can kick my ass. Though she did have the advantage of surprise."

Daegan responded to that with a chuckle that made the vampire surprisingly appealing, but Cai wandered off soon after, taking the opposite side of the house as his watch point. It gave him a good view of the porch and the living room, which was almost like watching TV, thanks to the wall of windows on that side.

After the teens went off to bed, the adults settled into some serious drinking and casual talk on the back porch. Cai had to admire their stamina. The wolves acted like they intended to stay up until the night waned to dawn, and Dovia had to go to bed.

Since the pack run had seemed like an evening ritual, Cai had expected them to do that. At first, he surmised they didn't because of Dovia and the Trads, and maybe it partly was that, but a conversation between Fane and Sangra suggested there was more to it.

When the father and daughter stepped outside and into the yard, far enough away from the rest of the family to have what was apparently a serious discussion, Cai was fortunately down wind and motionless, a part of the forest. Never one to be ashamed of eavesdropping, he tuned in, and not just from idle curiosity. With Sangra being a nurse, he had a pretty good idea who they were discussing.

"It would be best if he stayed here," Sangra said. "You remember Tom, the tech I dated before I met Idris? He could help us get some images of his leg, off book. Give us more information."

"Why?" Fane asked. "He's still limping, but he doesn't need the crutch or splint. The vampire's blood and his own healing abilities are helping."

"They are. But I have a feeling the improvement will plateau." She made a face. "I know you don't like when I mention my 'new age nonsense,' Dad, but when I run my hands over it, the energy...the magic you saw the vampire do, it's like it's in the bone. Stuck there or something. It's not going to let it heal the same way. I think he needs more expertise than I have."

A faint, humorless smile touched her lips. "Someone who has even more skill at that new age nonsense stuff than I do. But a good work-up on it would help us know for sure."

Fane studied his daughter as Cai absorbed the words. Words that confirmed the uneasy feeling he had about Rand's leg.

"He won't let Dovia or Cai leave without him," Fane said at last. "He's determined."

She nodded. "Okay. But maybe when that's done, he'll come back. If you can encourage him, Dad, that would be good."

"I will." Fane put an arm around her shoulders, directing her back toward the double doors that led into the house. "After his promise to deliver the girl home is done, I'm sure he'll realize, as I think the vampire already does, that he belongs with a pack."

Perceptive bastard. Wolves. They saw so much; picked up even more by scent.

The two of them went inside. Cai stared into the night for a few thoughtful moments, but his brain got tired. When he noticed through the windows that the kitchen was momentarily deserted, he did a vampire-quick trip there to snag the half a bottle of Jack left. Then he returned to his needless patrol.

He kept his mind mostly blank through the remaining couple hours of the night. When dawn approached, he didn't go to the cellar. He went to earth on the edge of the property, a good place to stay in contact with any movement around it. If someone came scouting, he'd be able to back up Gideon, who'd taken over Daegan's watch, with a fast alert to Rand. At least until early afternoon, when he'd be so deep asleep he'd be as useful as a turnip.

Daegan and Rand manned the cellar post. Cai tuned in when Rand fed Dovia. Proving that what had happened the previous night had been more about reclaiming herself than sating a vampire's sexual drive, Dovia had only requested Rand's blood for the second night.

Well, that, and an even more shy entreaty. In a quick, off-to-the-side moment earlier in the evening, she'd asked if it was okay for Rand to sleep in the bed with her. Hold her as she slept.

To keep the nightmares at bay. She hadn't said that, but she hadn't needed to do so.

The third mark practically let Cai step into Rand's body, feel him spooned about the girl in her nightshirt. He thought of when Rand had spooned around him. Rand's mind was relaxed, a little anesthetized by alcohol. Had he done it to ease the pain in the leg? Or, like Cai, to stop any pointless thinking?

While Dovia had the stuffed rabbit clasped in her arms, her hands were latched onto Rand's forearm across her chest. If she stayed that way all day, Cai expected Rand wouldn't move, even if his arm fell asleep so soundly he'd have to beat it against a tree to wake it up later. Honorable wolf.

Good night, vampire. Rand's mind touched his. He was looking for a response, so he'd know Cai was all right and close. Cai almost didn't respond, though he couldn't explain why. He told himself not to be an anti-social, dysfunctional bastard. Like that was something he could control.

Night. Don't let me oversleep our ride home.

I'll come dig you up before sunset.

Cai's lips curved despite himself. Rand grew quiet, and soon gave himself to sleep. Cai's mind moved over him like hands, every curve and angle. The rise and fall of his chest, the brow and strong jaw. But for all of Rand's outside beauty, it was what lay within that held Cai. The great heart, the courage. He saw him rush Goddard with the stake gripped in his fist. No fear.

And truth? As he replayed it over and over in his head, Cai saw Rand had matched that son of a bitch and *overpowered* him. Shifters. If they did decide to make themselves known to the vampires, it would change the nonhuman landscape in intriguing ways.

Cai tracked Rand's sleep, and Dovia's through him. As the sun rose, he detected how some of the wolves joined Gideon, taking shifts on patrol, scouting and making sure there was no sign that other Trad enclaves were aware of what had gone down or were connecting any dots to Fane's home. Or getting close enough to scent vampires.

While the protective measures were sound, they fortunately proved unnecessary. When Cai started to rouse at twilight, after having slept only a few fitful hours at the height of daylight, all was quiet. Blissfully uneventful. Either Goddard had kept Dovia's presence tightly under wraps, or leaving the ash of their four bodies and torched camp had sent its own deterring message to any area Trads.

So Fane and his family were safe. A good reassurance for Rand, who Cai knew was worried about that. And Cai? Cai wasn't worried about anything, as usual. Things began and ended. It was the way it worked. Right?

Yeah. That bullshit was getting old, even to him.

~

A limo arrived to retrieve them soon after full dark. Rand, dressed in a pair of dark jeans and muscle defining T-shirt, both of which probably belonged to Stalker, had finished up the enormous meal Lynn made for him. Cai drank coffee, leaning against the counter, listening to the conversations going on around him and occasionally making eye contact with his shifter.

A lot was happening, but not a lot was being said, even in their minds. But when he looked at Rand, Cai thought of him in bed with Dovia. He vividly remembered being pressed up behind him, taking his body, Rand's heart thundering under his palm.

Rand picked up his own coffee cup, sipped, his gaze resting on Cai's face. *Missed you, too, vampire. You could have come to bed.*

"Limo's here," Chad announced, coming in the back door. Cai was saved from replying by the interruption. And Chad, who stopped self-consciously before Cai.

"Rand says you usually carry a knife, but yours got lost or burnt up. I kind of collect them, so thought you might want this one, until you replace yours." The teen proffered a serviceable, good quality pocket knife. At Cai's look, Chad lifted a shoulder.

"You did a lot to make sure none of my family got hurt. Even if you don't see it that way. So thanks. And here." Chad laid it on the counter next to him when Cai didn't put out his hand. Cai could feel Rand's gaze on him. He'd be a prick if he said nothing, right?

Cai eyed the teenager. "Sure you're not just feeling sorry for the handicapped, kid?" He bared the one fang.

Chad started, then smiled, albeit cautiously. "Rand's right. You're pretty cool for an asshole."

Despite standing with a knot of the females in the dining area, Lynn had apparently caught that. She shot a motherly glare their way, but before Chad could get the sharp end of her tongue, Cai lifted a brow. "Were those his exact words?"

"Pretty much," Chad said, shoving his hands in the pockets of his jeans. Either out of fear of his mother's scolding or because he was out of courage, talking one-on-one to the vampire, the teen then made a beeline back to the screen door to the porch. Though Cai noticed the considerate kid caught it before it could bang the way it had last night.

Picking up the knife, Cai looked at it. He did like having one on him. What the hell. He pocketed it, and felt like an idiot when Rand's approving look made him feel good.

Jesus. He was becoming part of one of those "very special episodes" of the Waltons. Rand's look became a grin, the slow kind that made his eyes even bluer and encouraged Cai to kiss him senseless.

Instead, he followed Chad out into the yard before he showed the impulse control of a fledgling.

Seeing the stretch limo, Cai wondered how the vehicle had made it up the windy, twisty roads, all the way to the deep middle of the nowhere of Fane's place. But there it was. Sleek and dark, as incongruous in its mountainous surroundings as a woman in an evening gown.

The driver, an impassive-looking male of Asian Indian descent, was tall, with steady dark eyes that promised he could kick anyone's ass that needed kicking. Cai concluded combat driving training was probably how he'd made it to Fane's front door. He might not be vampire, but he wouldn't run from a fight, either.

The Dovia that emerged with Cilya was dressed in a classy black sheath and wore a string of pearls on her neck, matching earrings on her lobes. Her hair on the shoulder-length side was pulled up, a pretty, shiny auburn-red wing. The other side looked like gleaming peach fuzz and didn't detract from the princess persona. A very mature princess, with serious eyes, soft mouth.

She was still holding the stuffed bunny. She had her arms folded over it, the bunny tucked against her stomach, under her breasts. But when she reluctantly started to let go of it, hand it back, Cilya pressed it into her hands and hugged her. The shifter female rubbed Dovia's back and murmured, "Keep the rabbit. You can give it away to someone who needs it, when you don't anymore."

Cilya thankfully hadn't said "to your own child." She'd picked up the hint from her mother's innocent question last night. Or maybe she thought, in time, Dovia would want to be rid of anything that reminded her of this experience, including an act of kindness. Sometimes it was necessary, to move on. Even an act of kindness could be a tether to something one wished to forget. Lodell flashed through Cai's mind.

"I made up sandwiches for Gideon and Rand," Lynn was saying to him. It snapped his attention to the present, which must have caused an alarming change to his face, for Lynn stepped back a small pace. But she recovered, with the stiff politeness of a determined hostess. "Fane says you sample, so there's enough for, well, sampling."

Cai didn't know what to say to that, to her, to someone obviously so uncomfortable with him. Her gaze continually strayed to Rand, filled with an obvious plea for him to return. To give up the foolishness of being with a vampire as soon as he could manage it.

Rand would be another strong male to help protect the pack, not a threat to it. He was a good friend Fane and Lynn cared about. Fane was also connected to other shifters in the southeast area. In time, another like Rand, who preferred males, might just present himself. A mate would tie him more securely to the pack, adding to its numbers the way Idris's mating with Sangra had. Great. Whoopee.

Rand gave Lynn a warm hug, drawing her attention from Cai, and then hugged each of the children. He embraced Fane and Stalker last, murmuring to each. Cai didn't tune into it. He wandered over to the limo.

Correction. He did know what to say to someone that uncomfortable with him. Usually something that would make them even more uncomfortable. But he wasn't so uncivilized, or ungrateful to the pack for their help, that he would do that here. So he did what the humans taught their young. *If you can't say something nice, don't say anything at all.*

"Hell of a lot of things you can learn from reading children's books," he said to no one in particular. The limo driver glanced at him. Though a badass, he was human, a Council servant, so therefore deferential and attentive, but Cai turned away so he knew he wasn't being addressed. He didn't need a damn thing from a human.

Speak of the devil.

Gideon was leaning against the back of the limo, apparently having left the group, too. Maybe to double check whatever ammo and munitions they were carrying in the trunk, but now he was fishing around in the bag Lynn had offered.

"Hey, Rasheed," he said, calling out to the driver. "Roast beef sandwiches. Lots of extra roast beef."

Rasheed merely lifted a brow, and Gideon grinned. "I know you're going to want one, even if you have to act like you have a stick up your ass." He shifted his glance to Cai. "Good thing about being a servant. You know your vamp won't take the lion's share of your food, even though they have an annoying tendency to steal a couple fries every damn time we hit a McDonald's."

Despite the banter, there was a stillness in the hunter's eyes that told Cai that Gideon was measuring his intent, likely down to having calculated several different ways to counter him—futilely—if thoughts of Lodell propelled him to murder. Which, now that they weren't facing a life-or-death situation, could happen. Except Daegan had made it clear that Cai wouldn't survive a second attempt on his servant. Keeping Rand alive had become important to Cai. It was a bitch of a dilemma.

A lot of things were.

"Rand said Goddard didn't mark the women because of some purist bullshit," Gideon remarked. "Kind of hard to get one pregnant that way."

"What he most wanted was a pregnant female vampire, but he was adamant that legitimate attempts could be made upon human vessels without binding souls." Cai shrugged. "A lot of the Trads, even if they shared his view of humans, realize you can't argue with the science. None of us had ever heard of a born vampire with a human parent who wasn't the fully marked servant of the other vampire parent."

"Guess that was the only good thing about the guy," Gideon said. "The woman who went to the hospital is going to make it."

But how many years would it take her to believe she'd survived? Or want to? Cai pushed away that personal trip down memory lane. He hadn't asked about the woman, but Gideon had volunteered the info as if he wanted to know. And he was still talking. Maybe it would be worth it to get run through again.

"If he'd third marked her, or any of her boys had, she would have followed them into the afterlife," the hunter said.

"According to 'civilized vampire' crazy shit," Cai said.

Gideon's lips twitched, though his eyes became flint-like. "I sure as hell hope there's arbitration on the other side. If there's any truth to it, a person like her shouldn't be bound forever to a vampire like him."

"Unless the tables are turned and he's at her mercy. That'd be justice."

"Fucking A."

Cai didn't want to feel a sense of accord with the servant who'd murdered Lodell, so he settled for a spare nod.

Fortunately, Dovia, Rand and Daegan joined them then. They all got into the car, Rand holding the door for Dovia. Once they were settled, a couple more good-byes said, the family waving at them from the front porch—Christ, just like the Waltons—they were on their way down the mountain.

Done. Cai let out a breath, even as he felt a weird sort of pang that made him want to go back, say something nicer to Lynn. Thank Fane personally. Maybe check out that game box a little closer.

Pushing those unexpected thoughts aside, Cai focused on Dovia. He noticed her hand on the bunny was relaxed, but her other hand was a different matter. Lying on the door handle, at different times it tightened, her body making a little twitch that betrayed a great deal was happening beneath the surface as she stared out into the night. And it didn't seem to be connected to nerves, caused by Rasheed's handling of the limo on hairpin turns.

She'd wanted a window seat. Rand had chosen the seat facing her, his legs stretched out so they bracketed her neatly crossed ankles and folded legs. Cai had taken a position to her right while Gideon and Daegan were in the next row up, near the driver.

Cai shifted closer to her. "You don't have to be this together, you know."

She turned her gaze from the window. He caught the flash, a haunted look, before a polite distance settled into her expression. His kneejerk reaction was to assume the aristocrat was climbing back up on her pedestal, now that she no longer needed the riff-raff who had saved her ass. Rand's mind provided him a different explanation, one that made Cai kick his own ass.

"Yes, I do," she said quietly. "For my father. He won't be able to handle knowing...what happened to me. He'll of course *know* it, but seeing it too blatantly in my behavior...he can't handle that. I don't want to make things worse for him."

"Your mother..."

"She's a servant. You know our world. Or enough of it. There's limited compassion for weakness, so I need to start being strong now. When I get home, I won't allow anyone to think I've become an easy target because of this."

The veneer slipped as Dovia bit her lip and shifted. But she touched Cai's hand where it rested on his knee, a surprising reassurance. "My mother will bring me comfort, and so will my father, in the ways he's still capable of doing. I won't be alone in dealing with what happened to me. You're kind."

"I am *so* not kind," he said, but she just smiled. Her touch became a full grasp of his hand as she turned her gaze back to the window. She also slipped her feet out of her shoes and curled them against the denim covering Rand's calf, a prop.

Neither man broke the contact as she closed her eyes and laid her head on the seat back. In time, she slept a bit, her head shifting to Cai's shoulder. Her hand was small and far too delicate in his.

Cai's attention went to Rand. He was an appealing sight, his hair brushed and tied back, arm resting on the door handle. Those jeans of Stalker's were a distractingly good fit. The T-shirt was tight, not a bad look. His long legs were bent and knees spread, the usual sprawl of a large man in a car that could accommodate his size.

Daegan had his eyes closed in the facing seat one row up, but with his straight stance, he looked like one of those stone statue guardians that meditated on the universe until summoned with one trigger word. Gideon was slouched down next to him, arms crossed over his broad chest, eyes also closed. They'd all been pretty much on guard for the past couple days. In a moving car, they could catch a few winks.

Daegan was the kind of authority figure who normally triggered Cai's smartass switch to full volume, but something about the guy kept it toned down. He and Gideon had helped save their asses, and the relationship between Daegan and Gideon...well, it kind of interested Cai, how they pulled it off.

Vampire-servant relationships weren't what he'd expected them to be, all formal and arms' length, with the servant acting like a stiff butler from an old movie. And these guys were part of the top-of-the-heap vampires. Not on the fringes, where stuff like that would pass unnoticed. Plus, they were both total badasses and fighter types.

They'd also both been exactly what Dovia needed around her. Quiet, courteous, showing sensitivity to her situation but not smothering pity.

Like now. With all of them cognizant she was in an enclosed space surrounded by testosterone, everyone was going out of their way to keep their presence low profile, protective without treating her like glass.

Hard to get pissy toward the other vampire and his vampire-hunter servant when they were being like that.

See, he could be mature. Occasionally.

Rand's gaze lifted, showing amusement, and Cai curled his lip at him. *Nosy wolf.*

"I want to stop here."

Before Rand could reply to that, Dovia spoke up. It surprised Cai, because he'd thought she was dozing. But she'd lifted her head and had her hand on the door. The urgency in her tone suggested she meant right now. Was she sick?

All four men bolted into immediate action, mobilizing to handle the awkward possibility of female illness. Rasheed was already pulling over, responding to Daegan's gesture.

They'd emerged from the cow path road system a while ago, and were now on a winding, still rural but four-lane highway. Though they'd been gaining on and passing the occasional car, for the most part they had it to themselves. Even so, Daegan and Gideon were out of the car first, scoping the area. Proving they knew their job, they didn't allow anyone out until they gave the all clear, Dovia's request notwithstanding. When they did give that go-ahead, Cai exited and offered Dovia a hand out, Rand climbing out behind her.

She brought the stuffed rabbit with her. The girl didn't head for the roadside to get sick, as Cai had suspected. She headed across the two lanes toward the center median. Exchanging a glance with Rand, Cai followed her, the shifter trailing behind at a discreet distance. Gideon and Daegan stayed where they were, by silent accord sharing lookout duty with Rasheed and giving Cai and Rand the personal bodyguard duty.

This stretch of highway participated in the state's wildflower program, and the median was overflowing with a combination of red poppies, yellow lilies and lavender. Dovia went into them, her free hand trailing along the bobbing stems and blooms, her body turning as she looked at the flowers surrounding her.

"It's so beautiful," she said. "I haven't been up this way before. And when they brought me here, they had...I was hooded, and tied."

Cai moved closer to her.

"Can I borrow your knife?" she asked.

"Depends on why you want it."

She held out a palm. Imperious little miss. He stared her down and she sighed. "I want to cut a lock of my hair."

"Oh. Okay, let me do it. Sorry, but I'd feel better not seeing anything classified as a loose weapon near you for the next hundred years."

"And you think you're not kind." But she pulled out the comb holding up her hair. The dark red strands rippled as she grasped one lock about three inches from the end. Given the hack job that had been done on it before, he hesitated, but she met his gaze, telling him it was what she wanted. When he cut the piece for her, using the pocket knife Chad had surprisingly offered him, she took it and sat down on the ground, her knees folded, the bunny on her thighs. It had a satin pale green ribbon around its brown neck, and she untied it, retied it, with her lock of hair in it. Then she positioned the stuffed creature against a clump of the cheerful poppies, the ribbon and hair in its lap.

She knelt there for a few minutes, silent. Her head bowed and Cai thought she might be praying. Unexpected. Not many vampires he'd met were all that religious, though some believed in a higher power. But then she spoke, and he realized, both from the words and the weight of the emotions they were carrying, that she'd been collecting her thoughts.

"I'm sorry I couldn't be your mother," she said quietly. "Please forgive me. I hope my selfishness, my inability to handle being a mother now, doesn't keep me from having the privilege and honor of bringing another life like yours into the world. I know..." Her voice cracked. "You were not of him, nor of me, but a gift from God, and I should be stronger..."

She stopped. Cai dropped to one knee and slid an arm around her shoulders, under her chin. He pressed his lips to the crown of her bowed head. "God—whatever that is or means—understands. That kid, too," he said shortly. "I feel it, you know. When I handle that spark, I can feel what it feels, somewhat. It understood. It knew now wasn't the right time, the right circumstances."

She stilled in his arms. "Truly. You're not lying to me."

"If I am, may I be damned to hell. Or have to wear bright, happy colors, which is the same thing."

A slight smile pulled against his cheek, but she turned her head, meeting his gaze with a piercing look that told him yeah, one day this girl would be a hell of a mother. Or the next Lady Lyssa. "You're telling me the truth."

"I am," he said.

He wasn't. He was lying his ass off. He could feel that spark, yes, but not any thoughts that specific. But he could feel if it was distressed, and he'd felt nothing from it but peace, so it felt like he might be telling the truth.

As good as she was with "the look," he'd had to lie to save his ass for decades. She wasn't even in his league when it came to a believable poker face.

After a long moment, her shoulders slumped with relief. Her face was wet with tears, but she was quiet with it, no sobbing. Her head bowed again and he shifted his hands to her shoulders, backing off some. From dealing with his own shit, he knew sometimes you had to feel stuff to get rid of it, but he wished he knew how to bring a smile to her face, help her feel better. Put something on the scale to balance the overwhelming load of what she was carrying on her shoulders. She was too young to have to deal with this crap.

A rustling noise brought both their heads up. It took several blinks for Cai to process the unlikely sight of a giant black wolf bounding through the flowers like goddamn Bambi, apparently chasing a cadre of moths. The pale yellow winged insects flapped around in a confused vortex as he snapped at them. It made them dance away so he could continue chasing, large body spinning in wide circles, leaping. Practically cavorting.

He was sparing the leg, doing a lot of it on three, which just increased the Bambi bouncing effect. Dovia sat back on her heels,

watching Rand as Cai rose to his feet. That put him in the right position to see a smile bloom on her face, as rare and precious as one of
the flowers around them.

Yeah, flowers were something special. Anyone who saw a flower
break out of a seed pod, push out of the ground and become something as· delicate and beautiful as what it was, despite the inner
strength it took to do all that, knew they were looking at something
precious.

Dovia was up on her feet, chasing after the wolf, trying to catch
the moths with her hands. Years fell away and she was a young girl
playing, not a sexually mature woman. Rand brushed against her, and
her hand dropped to hold onto him. She'd left her shoes behind and
Cai collected the feminine pair of modest heels by the ankle straps,
watching her dance and play. She didn't laugh; he was sure she would
again, but it was too soon for that. But she was smiling, her eyes
possessing a promising light that showed her spark had not been
doused.

She wasn't going to become a cranky, surly, closed off bastard like
him, beyond help or repair. He glanced across the road and confirmed
Gideon and Daegan were still at the car. Gideon was grinning, and he
spoke a few words to Daegan. Cai could have heard some of it if he
tried, but he knew it wasn't important. At his servant's words, Daegan
tilted his head toward Gideon, his serious lips curving.

"I'm ready to go home now."

Dovia was standing in front of him, a chain of flowers in her hair,
Rand at her side. The wolf panted happily, a moth wing stuck in his
teeth. Dovia fastidiously removed it, showing no hesitation at
reaching into that toothy mouth. Rand landed an appreciative lick on
her wrist that had her making a noise damn close to a giggle.

Show off. Flirt. "Okay, shift back into a human so you don't get hair
all over the limo," Cai advised. "Or we'll tie you to the back bumper
and make you run the rest of the way."

"We will not," Dovia said indignantly.

"Not your servant, is he?"

Cai said it more sharply than he'd intended, what the fuck. Rand's
ears pricked up. Cai felt the mental rebuke from the wolf almost
before Cai registered Dovia's instant flinch.

"Sorry," he muttered. "I didn't mean to sound like an ass. I'm just saying...well. Never fucking mind." He pivoted on his heel and strode back to the car, leaving Rand and the girl to follow at their leisure. What did it matter to him?

Cai made sure to keep his mind firmly closed. Yeah, Rand maybe could read his emotions as easily as his head, but he was done letting Rand meander through it like he had the poppy field.

Getting into the limo, Cai found the wet bar and took a nice, burning swallow of what was there. Yeah, vampires couldn't get drunk, but it still felt good going down.

Treat his servant like he was hers. Just because he looked damn good taking care of a young woman, playing with pups, or teasing Fane's mate, helping with dishes and looking as domestic as any spread in *Better Homes and Gardens*, it didn't give her the right.

Didn't give any of them the right to act like he belonged more to them than to Cai. Even if he did.

And even if Cai damn well knew it was better that way.

He acted like all was good when they got back into the car, not wanting there to be any tension for Dovia to handle. She didn't deserve to have to deal with his shit. He felt Rand's questions, the male's blue and gold-flecked eyes searching his face, but he refused to engage, shrugging it off with a slight head shake that said, *Forget it, I'm fine.*

Rand didn't look like he bought that for a second, but that wasn't Cai's problem. Dovia asked Gideon and Daegan some polite questions about Anwyn, typical girl interest in another woman, and the conversation turned in that direction. She looked amused at both men's confusion when she asked them where Anwyn liked to shop in Atlanta. Proving his resourcefulness, Gideon texted his Mistress and provided Dovia some answers, adding, "Anwyn said if you come there, she'll be happy to take you out to the best nighttime shopping spots."

That seemed to please Dovia, but it also exhausted her ability to be polite and social as her obvious upbringing had taught her to be. She subsided, but her tension became a humming wire whose vibration level rose, the closer they came to her home. When they turned onto the long drive, her hand was on the door as if she'd jump out before the car even stopped. Rand had sat next to her for the final leg of the journey. When he ran a soothing hand down her back, she nodded, acknowledging the reassurance, but then Leona and Georg came into sight, standing in the driveway in front of the house.

Tears overflowed Dovia's eyes, her shaking taking over. The young woman who was determined to be impossibly strong was overridden by the traumatized girl who needed her parents' reassurance and love. At least for a few minutes.

Dovia practically sprang out as the car stopped. Her parents' arms folded around her as if they'd let her go in an eternity or two. Maybe. Thankfully, Georg seemed pretty lucid. He held both his women as if he'd protect them from hell itself. Dovia held them as tightly, sobbing, but also telling them she was okay. Cai saw her touch her father's face, hold her mother's waist. "I'm okay, Daddy. I'm all right. It's going to be okay."

No sign of Tyra or Chavez. Not involved with Voltaire's plan, but probably no longer in favor either, Cai supposed. He looked toward Rand, whose concern about Greenwald, about how it would all turn out for her, was obvious. Cai nudged him with his foot, drawing his attention.

No, we can't keep her. Sure, you'll promise to feed and walk her. But I know who'll end up taking care of her.

Rand curled a lip at him, that sneer that made Cai want to do all sorts of things to him, but as the wolf continued to look worried, he sighed.

"She'll be okay. And she knows she can call on us if ever she has need, right?"

Rand nodded. Daegan had emerged from the car with Gideon, and Cai and Rand followed them a few steps away, where they weren't infringing on the family reunion. Rand spoke in a low voice.

"What happens when he...when he can't be overlord anymore?"

"Lady Lyssa and the Council are very mindful of what is happening with Georg," Daegan answered. "Though his illness has been concealed as much as possible, word is spreading. The Council has made it clear that any who act to inappropriately take his title from him will face Lyssa's displeasure. When she transitions him out of the role, the Council will ensure he and his family are well protected."

"Will Leona go with him?" Cai told himself not to ask, not to reveal he was as worried about the girl as Rand was. Overnight, they thought they were a pair of big brothers.

"Yes," Daegan said, exchanging a glance with Gideon as if they'd discussed how much information could safely be risked with Cai and Rand. Cai felt oddly gratified that the decision was in their favor. "She loves her daughter dearly, but he is her Master. She cannot bear to be separated from him, and if she remained in our world, she would have to become bound to another vampire who might or might not have Dovia's best interests at heart. Dovia will become heir to her father's holdings and officially be designated Lyssa's ward, for her protection, until she has the strength to hold those assets on her own."

"From what I've seen of that girl's strength of will, that'll be about a minute or two from now," Cai observed.

Gideon grunted an assent, his eyes glinting. "She's one tough little lady. And look out, she's coming back this way."

"Probably to hug Rand one more time." Cai started to retreat for the car, but Rand curled his fingers around his elbow, holding him. Cai shot him a scowl, but since the alternative was a juvenile wrestling match in front of Daegan and Gideon, he held his ground as if he meant to stay, rather than preferring to bolt like a rabbit.

Sure enough, Dovia hugged Rand, speaking softly in his ear. She had to stretch up on her toes to manage that, even with him bending over to accommodate her. But then she turned to Cai.

For a long moment they studied one another, a couple feet between them. Before he realized he was doing it, he'd run a light fingertip over the peach fuzz on one side of her head. She self-consciously followed the motion with her own hand, brushing his. "My parents wanted to thank you personally, but I knew you'd hate that, so I told them it was best to send a note."

"Yeah. I'll work on that address thing."

"They haven't thought of that yet, so you better make your escape while you can," she said with a faint smile. While tinged with a sad tiredness, it held peace and relief, too. Reaching up, she slid a hand along his face. In involuntary reaction to being touched without his say-so, he gripped her wrist, but he didn't push her away, and she didn't stop stroking his cheek. Her legs trembled some, and suddenly Rand was behind her, steadying her with hands on her shoulders.

She kept her eyes on Cai. "You know what you told me, about not letting them take away my ability to love whomever I want to?"

"I think I said 'fucking want to.'"

That faint smile came again, but it didn't detract from the seriousness of her gaze. "You should take your own advice."

She tossed a meaningful look upward, indicating Rand, without letting the wolf see the look. Then she hugged Cai's stiff body, gave him and Rand one more poignant smile, and returned to her parents, and her world.

CHAPTER NINETEEN

$\mathcal{A}$s they were pulling out of the long drive, Cai's thoughts were turning to where Daegan and Gideon could drop them. Daegan had other ideas.

When he sat back and surveyed Cai from head to toe, it was with an unsmiling look that instantly put Cai on guard.

"Lady Lyssa has requested"—the vampire said it with the type of stress that Cai immediately understood as *required, commanded, get-your-ass-down-here or I'll fuck it up good* —"that you attend her at Council headquarters in Savannah before you depart. Her plane has been made available to us to shorten the trip, and she says once she has spoken to you, commended you on your help in this matter, that you can request any destination of your choosing."

"But we have to see her first before we're free to go."

"She said you had an interest in Lord Graham's status and where-abouts. She has that information."

"She could text me. Or I'm sure I can find him on my own in another hundred years or so. Or he'll be dead. I really don't care if I'm the one who kills him. Dead is dead." Not exactly true, but he wasn't going to be bribed or baited. Or manipulated in any way. This was why getting in bed with Council vampires was like stepping into the mouth of a giant killer shark who promised not to bite.

"Cai," Rand said. He was sitting next to Cai, his warmth and strength near. "You did an amazing thing. Let her say thank you. Let them thank you."

"Having lots of friends and family is important to you. Not to me. I don't need to do this. You can go in my stead like an ambassador or some damn thing. Maybe she's going to give you a key to Vampire City. Don't really care. It won't mean anything. It never does."

He knew their departure from Dovia's had tripped his asshole switch, but he really didn't deal well with good-byes and transitions. He thought of Dovia, standing there with her two parents, so straight and tall, because she couldn't afford to be anything different. No matter how she'd been abused and raped. Then he thought of himself, nearly falling apart the first time Rand had fucking spooned with him.

"I'll tell you what the plan is," he said abruptly to Daegan. "Drop me off here at this convenience store coming up. Let Rand out wherever he wants to go so he can get back to Fane and his family where he belongs, and we all say how nice it was to meet one another, blah, blah, blah. Unless you want to drag my bloody body before her the same way Greenwald did."

Daegan's impassive expression showed no more reaction than if he'd been a brick wall. "She doesn't require that. If you don't wish to accept her gratitude, then I'll do as you prefer. But I think you'll want to hear what she has to say. A vampire can't have too many allies in this world, and your actions in the past few days have won you quite a few."

"You know what allies are? People who sucker you into thinking you can trust them, until they turn on you because something that's better for them but worse for you happens and they don't see the need for the alliance anymore."

Is that how you see our alliance? Rand's voice in his head had a deceptive calm to it, though the blue eyes were glinting ominously. *Our mission together is done, so our bond is no longer necessary?*

Cai had stepped in it, but he wasn't backing down. *No, it's not. Just the simple truth. On second thought, we do need to go to the big fancy Council headquarters. The queen can pat me on the head for a job well done, and Lord Brian can separate us. You can be on your way. Go make a million puppies with Cilya, who looks at you like you're a steak with a box of Milkbones and a squeaky toy on top.*

Because he was. And Cilya and Rand would make beautiful pups. More simple, detestable truth.

Rand stared at Cai, then turned his attention to Daegan. "Will you ask Rasheed to stop the car, please?"

Daegan nodded. Rasheed pulled into the convenience store parking lot, pulling into the back, where there was a small natural area and a copse of trees to provide some privacy.

Ironically, Rand noted it was an area for travelers with pets, where they could take their dogs out to relieve themselves. Oh, he was about to relieve himself all right. The shit was going to hit the fan. A very pain-in-the-ass, one-fanged fan.

He slid out of the limo and bent to look in at Cai. "You wanted to be let out," Rand said pleasantly. "So get out of the fucking car."

Cai's attention snapped to him. Rand slammed the door before he could reach for it, and marched away toward the grassy area.

Inside the limo, Cai's expression darkened. He turned the latch and shoved out, slamming the door with equal force. Fortunately, not a vampire's force, or they would have had to explain why the limo was returned to the Savannah headquarters with a crumpled door that wouldn't open.

Gideon stretched out his long legs and yawned. "That's going to be an ugly conversation."

"Hmm," Daegan said. "First time I've heard the wolf curse like that."

"Yeah, takes a bit to rile him. Reminds me of someone else I know." Gideon moved to the spot the two had vacated. "I'll keep an eye on them in case they need an intervention. Might draw some attention if they get into a fight."

"Good thinking." Daegan braced his shoe against the seat between Gideon's spread knees, one toe under his thigh. Gideon's hand naturally fell on his shin as a resting spot, fingers curled to stroke Daegan over the black slacks he was wearing. "While you do that," the vampire said, "I'll call Anwyn and give her an ETA she can pass on to Jacob."

"Sounds like a plan. Though we might not know what the ETA is, until these two sort this out."

"They'll either stay here or come with us. Should be no more than a fifteen-minute difference either way." Daegan's lips quirked. "As

Anwyn has pointed out, a disagreement between males rarely takes more than five or ten minutes to sort out, since it's usually resolved with a shared beer or one knocking the other unconscious."

"She says that like it's something annoying. Why she thinks women chewing on a conflict for hours is the better way is beyond me. But it's okay. She's so damn hot when she puts her hands on her hips and lectures us on being male and therefore stupid, I'm not filing any complaints."

Daegan smiled, a rare but brilliant gesture that caught Gideon's attention as it always did, tripping his heart up a few notches. The vampire noticed as he always did, his eyes heating and his toe moving to stroke the inseam of Gideon's jeans. It had Gideon thinking that it would be good to get to Lyssa's Savannah estate sooner rather than later.

"Agreed, vampire hunter. While other vampires are less shy about these things, I would prefer to have you and Anwyn to myself when I get you bare-assed and at my mercy."

Amen to that. Gideon assumed indifference, which he knew Daegan could read as a complete lie, but focused out the window, hoping these two got their shit together sooner than later. And didn't knock one another unconscious to do it, but if they did, they could drag the bodies back into the vehicle and be on their way within the fifteen-minute range. Win-win.

Rand strode into the copse of trees, out of sight of the limo occupants. Cai beat him there, stepping in front of him to bring him up short and square off. "What's got your panties in a bunch?" he demanded. "That I told the truth?"

Cai should have seen it coming. He could be in the guy's mind, after all. Instead his head snapped back from a punch that was like being hit by a hammer. He stumbled and landed on his ass, though he was on his feet in a blink and had Rand shoved against a tree, pinned there with an arm on his throat and his one fang bared at him. But Rand's teeth were already showing, his eyes blazing with an unexpected level of fury.

The shifter could have fought back, pit strength against strength, but he went with an even more devastating tactic. He used words, a flood of raw, honest feeling.

"No. You didn't tell the truth. You spout this bullshit until it over-flows on everyone around you. Great way to shove away those who care about you."

"It's like Dr. Phil and Captain Obvious had a baby. Thanks so much for the news flash." Cai thrust away from him and stood back. "If only telling people why they act the way they do would actually change them. It doesn't. People are the same assholes they always are, even when they try to act like enlightened, self-aware assholes. I don't see the need to make the effort."

"That's what you want everyone to believe." Rand snarled it. "So here's a news flash for you. You saved a girl no one else could save. You saved my life, helped me see there are things worth living for again. You've protected me whenever I'm threatened. You've opened your-self up to me when you feel things you don't want others to see."

Rand moved in and clamped a hand on the back of his neck. Cai countered with a grip on his forearm, but Rand tightened his own hold so he'd have to cause harm to dislodge him. "You have trouble with people acknowledging that you can be a decent person, that's fine. But do not, under any fucking circumstances, paint me as a trai-torous backstabber to fortress yourself against betrayal, when you know that wall is already crumbling. I've done nothing to deserve that."

You will, Cai thought desperately. But that was his shit, wasn't it? Rand was right. Just because the male did deserve to be with a wolf family, wasn't something that made him disloyal to Cai. This had never been about a Master-servant relationship, and hell, he didn't even know what that was anyhow, did he? It had all been circum-stances, need, choices limited to what would suit the mission objec-tive. Keeping Rand alive, then getting Dovia back safe. Rand hadn't chosen him, and who would, anyway?

This was his deal, his shit. He needed to step away from it. Appre-ciate the male while he could, and damn well treat him the way he deserved. Cai could do that.

Rand looked poised to fight some more. Cai knuckled the blood off his lip. Hell of a punch. He reached toward Rand's face. The male tensed, as if expecting a wrestling move, but when Cai touched him, his eyes took on a wary, surprised look.

"I'm sorry," Cai said. "I tend to have to say that a lot around you. You've been nothing but a true friend and comrade, Rand. The closest thing I had to that after I got with the Trads was Lodell, and to say that was a dysfunctional relationship doesn't describe the half of it. You're right. That shit spills over, but if you can believe it, I really don't want you to be covered in it. I'm not good at any of this, never will be. But I do think you're one of the best, most honorable males I've ever met. Even if you have a shedding issue I really think you need to address."

Rand's lips tightened. His expression warred with hurt and anger, exasperation, some resignation, and a tenderness Cai didn't think he could bear to see. So he closed the distance between them and kissed the male, pushing him toward the tree until his back hit it. This time, when Rand's hands gripped him like he would take Cai to the ground or back him off, Cai increased the strength of his hold. They could fight about it, or Rand could let him keep him against the tree as long as Cai damn well pleased.

As Cai leaned in, nuzzling Rand's throat, he felt every part of his own body tighten when Rand made his decision. The wolf turned his head, gave him free access. Even pissed, the male responded to him, responded to his needs, and he could feel Rand's wonder at that, a reaction that only added to his own.

"As long as we're laying down ultimatums," Cai said, "if you *ever* talk to me like that in front of other vampires again, I'll fuck you in front of them just to underscore who's got control here. You got me, wolf?"

Cai let him see it in his mind in nice visual detail, adding some lurid touches that proved the threat of discipline very much overlapped with his own personal fantasies involving Rand.

A quiver went through the shifter's muscles. It made it even worse for Cai when he saw that the idea of Cai branding Rand in such a possessive way wasn't entirely displeasing to his servant.

That knowledge also seemed to startle Rand, though. Maybe it was a vampire talent, revealing a servant's deepest, darkest fantasies, and exploiting the hell out of them for mutual benefit. Cai had picked up the hints from Lyssa, but hearing about it and being the direct beneficiary of it...no contest. He wanted to do it right here and now, but he had enough presence of mind to know it was hardly the time or place.

Plus, taking Rand down was a hard, ugly fight with no guarantee of victory, though he might have a slightly increased advantage because of Rand's bum leg. Rand had stayed steady during their toe to toe, but Cai could detect the change in balance, the way he was bracing his weight more on the good leg.

He wouldn't play dirty if he could help it. Fortunately, Rand's hunger, held at bay for the past couple days while they took care of Dovia and put her first, came surging right up when Cai let himself feel the same need.

As he took Rand's mouth, hard and hungry, and pushed against his body, feeling every powerful, equally hungry inch of it, he received a comparable response. He'd told Rand about the vampire libido. Cai hadn't mentioned it could be stoked beyond that ten times ratio to about a hundred, when someone they considered theirs got in their face and challenged that same vampire. As a result, fuck it—he wasn't going to deny himself.

He shoved Rand down onto his hands and knees, though he made sure it wasn't a hard descent. Rand would say he was coddling him, but fuck it twice. Cai wasn't going to do something worse to that leg. But he could unleash his more demanding side other ways.

"Shirt off and get the jeans off your ass, or I'll tear them," he said, sharp and short.

Rand pulled the shirt over his head. He'd barely gotten the zipper down on the jeans before Cai was on him, pulling the pants the rest of the way down to his muscled thighs. No underwear beneath, thank you Jesus.

Dropping to his knees behind him, Cai reached under Rand and captured his cock. A double thank you for the steel heat of it. Cai worked the shifter's shaft with ruthless, stroking intent, giving Rand no time to take a breath, to grab onto anything but what the vampire would let him hold.

"Cai..."

"You come for me, right now. I need something to slick up my cock and I don't want anything out of a damn tube. Only you. That's all I want."

Rand came with hard jerks, his body registering his shock that Cai could command him so swiftly, so ruthlessly. *Yeah, you better believe it, wolf. I can see down into your soul and I know you have this in you. As much as you have the looks outside that make the girls cream their panties. But your cream...that's all mine.*

The words came, no brain cells needed. Catching a generous handful of the male's release, Cai used it, working it over the cock he'd freed from his jeans. He used the residual in that tight opening he wanted enough to kill anyone who tried to stop him. Then he thrust in, hard and fast, giving Rand no option but to do his best to keep up. The male's fingers were digging into the forest floor, his head dropped.

Cai ripped out the tie for Rand's hair, and it spilled gloriously over his bare shoulders. He'd go back into the limo looking used. Cai should have shredded that shirt.

He preferred him naked. The Rand in clothes, riding in a limo, that wasn't Rand. Rand was a wild thing, running through the forest on four legs. Shifting to two and standing aroused and virile, watching Cai stalk him with narrowed eyes that said he'd put up a fight, but if and when Cai took him down, he'd be generous in defeat.

Such that, when all was said and done, it felt like Cai was the one surrendering, the one gifted.

Cai exploded, the release relentless. Hammering, pounding, shot after shot of his come in Rand's ass, until he ran out and was draped over him, hand on the back of his neck. A position of control, but when Cai felt the quiver through Rand's thighs, the mix of emotion coming from him, messed up, he couldn't not respond.

"Sometimes," he murmured, his voice not quite steady, "This is a moment where calling me Master might help. To keep it all straight." He didn't clarify for who, because he wasn't sure how to answer that question.

Rand slightly stiffened, his gaze sliding up to meet Cai's in that position that was so hot, so subjugated, and yet not. Rand wet his lips, eyes sharpening. They pierced Cai through. "Master."

Cai closed his eyes, riding that feeling. Rand let out a groan as one more spurt of seed came from Cai, inciting an extra little push of his hips.

What the hell was he doing? He'd gone from being a vampire who claimed to know nothing about how the whole Master-servant bond worked, because he wanted nothing to do with it...to this. He must have internalized more about vampires and servants than he realized. Or maybe it was just instinct, like blood drinking. The bond between vampire and human servant wasn't learned. Okay, yeah, the marking process needed some guidance—he had an uncomfortable flashback to that major gaffe—but the connection...the soul connection...it guided a vampire like a damn lighthouse to claim full ownership of his servant, hold him, keep him. Need and want him.

Cai remembered a few moments ago, when their bodies had been melded together and the shifter had shuddered, every muscle tightening, his throat working against a cry. He'd been pissed, but he hadn't refused Cai. He'd never refused him, had he? He'd never refused his Master.

Cai drew out, reluctantly. If Daegan and Gideon had any kind of vampire-servant senses at all, they'd know exactly what they were doing, so in a way, he'd done as he'd threatened Rand. It didn't feel bad to either one of them. But the whole thing had taken things up a notch into complicated waters.

Waters hard to describe, but made Cai want to get where they were going, let the dawn come, and fall asleep buried in his servant, arms and legs tangled. He'd order him to keep his damn beautiful ass in the bed with him. That way, if Cai woke any time during the day, he could have him again and again. Rand might just obey.

He'd struck out in anger in the limo, because Rand was a first for him, on so many levels. He'd had plenty of things he wanted in his life. For a hundred years, his batting average in getting any of those things had been zero. So when he'd won his freedom from the Trads, he'd made a practice of not wanting anything beyond what he could completely control. Being alone helped with that.

He'd stayed isolated, even when he'd immersed himself in the human world to stay out of the range of Trads, but that need for isolation had eventually taken him back into unpopulated places, far beyond where anyone could reach him. No connections to vampires there, and choosing to take humans down as full kills, rather than drinking them or entering servant relationships, kept any human connections out of the picture. Except temporary ones, like the kid at the cabin, or the special forces guy who'd never seen Cai.

But Rand was different. Cai wanted Rand, and not just temporarily.

It didn't matter. He could feel it, savor it, even knowing it wouldn't happen. Cai squeezed the male, pressing a kiss between his shoulder blades. "It's okay," he murmured, just as Rand had done for him the other night. He nudged Rand up onto his knees. Since the male seemed dazed in a way that was kind of gratifying yet alarming, Cai handled getting his jeans back over his beautiful ass, tucking in that gorgeous cock, fastening and zipping things again.

"On your feet, wolf." He helped, and when Rand's head turned, rather than meet the gaze, Cai brushed a kiss over his mouth and slid an arm around his waist, steadying him. "It's all right," Cai said again. "You're right and I'm a jerk. What else is new? We'll go let the queen pat me on the head."

But when Rand would have followed his cue back to the limo, a sudden thought struck Cai, making him plant his feet. "I figured it out. What the marks mean."

At Rand's puzzled look, Cai turned to face him and dropped his hold to his wrists, pulling Rand's arms up between them. He cupped the backs of Rand's hands, so they were looking down at Rand's wrists, side by side. The old scars and the new marks over them. The narrow figure eight and the spout of flame.

It's not a figure eight. It's the symbol for infinity, which also represents brothers-in-arms. Cai's gaze slid up to meet Rand's. *The other one, the flame? That's a symbol for hell.*

He gripped Rand's wrists anew, thumbs overlapping those marks.

No matter what happens, where our paths end up, you need me, I'll be there. Whether it's to fight an enemy, or share a fucking beer. He caressed the infinity mark. *That's what this one means.*

Rand's gaze darkened, and he flinched, an emotional response, as Cai dipped his head and bit his other wrist, let him feel the penetration of his one fang next to the flame mark.

This one? If you ever try to take your life again, I'll make your life a living hell, far worse than you can imagine. I'll follow you if necessary into the after-life to make that happen. Count on it.

In this moment, he felt like a fucking Master, all that meant and could mean. When he had to let the shifter go, as he knew he would, Cai was damn well making sure that Rand remembered one thing. That life was worth living. Not for the reasons Cai lived—to send Fate a daily huge fuck you—but for the reasons a guy like Rand should live.

The world was a much better place with him in it.

CHAPTER TWENTY

*T*he small airport was only a few more minutes of driving. The private jet put them in Savannah in short order, and they were back in another limo, headed for the Council's headquarters. Despite never having been in a private plane before, one outfitted like a luxury hotel suite, Rand didn't feel like saying much. Occasionally, Daegan and Gideon conversed about some things and Cai joined in. They attempted to keep Rand included, a courtesy he would have appreciated if his mind wasn't overwhelmed with a lot of other input. Like the faint tingle that lingered on his wrists, the psychological imprint Cai had left by defining what those marks meant.

At length, they'd stopped trying to talk to him, and Rand suspected Cai had given them some type of subtle indication to leave him be, let him deal with what he was dealing with.

After what Cai had done in that small grove of trees, Rand honestly wasn't sure where his mind was. He'd seen Cai vulnerable, had looked into his heart. Rand knew Cai had a ruthless side, a cruel side. But he'd overlooked the Master side. Or rather, he'd acknowledged it here and there as a sexual charge, something to lend extra spice to their fucking. Or even to take it to a deeper level.

But in some way this time it had been different. Their unplanned stop, the fight they'd had, had unleashed that side of Cai in a way Rand hadn't experienced before. Or perhaps, hadn't let himself experience it. Maybe it was the anger, or some emotional fallout from the close call with Goddard, or the whole past several years' accumulation.

Whatever it was, what had set Rand off balance, what had him feeling so pensive, was accepting his own response.

He could hold his own with the vampire. Even Cai knew it now. But Rand had capitulated. Willingly. Cai was every bit as much of a Dominant and Master as the other male vampire in this vehicle, no matter the different shape of it. But unlike Daegan, Rand had looked at Cai as *his* Master.

In a pack, an alpha would give way before a stronger alpha, and it didn't have to get ugly. But it had gotten ugly between him and Cai, and some of that had remained, adding to the confusing mix. Those echoes of conflict remained even now.

Until Cai closed a hand over his, linked fingers. He put his other arm behind Rand's shoulders, curling his fingers in Rand's still loose hair. When he dipped his head, he brushed his mouth and nose against Rand's face. It was more a wolf gesture than a vampire one, something he would do because he knew Rand responded to it, would nuzzle back, open his mouth and nip Cai's cheekbone lightly.

Rand felt the vampire's lips pull in a faint smile when he did. Lifting their linked hands, Cai touched his mouth to the top of Rand's. Turning it over, Cai did the same to the wrist, above the markings, sending questing tendrils into Rand's stomach.

It's okay, wolf. What can I do to make it better?

He didn't know. He didn't know...anything. Not this way. It wasn't like Cai to be gentle, considerate. But he had been, in the aftermath of the rough sex, and now. It felt like there was something driving it, something Rand couldn't put a finger on. Like they were on a sand timer with the sand running out.

Their argument in the limo had started on that subject, but it was Cai's callous treatment of their friendship that had set Rand off, not the knowledge that their time together might be drawing to a close. Cai had always treated the marking as temporary. So as not to make Rand feel trapped. So Cai could protect himself from rejection.

The vampire had noticed how Rand gravitated toward Fane's family. Maybe that was what had triggered what happened in the limo. Cai had decided the best thing was to treat their relationship exactly like a soldier thing. When the combat was done, they'd go their separate ways but still be friends, linked by the intense experience.

And it had pissed him off, his reaction to anything that he didn't want to feel. Cai was damaged. No question. The family dynamics, the emotions that Rand felt and proffered so easily, were a foreign language to Cai. Maybe that was why Cai had switched gears now. Realizing there was no point to being pissed off. It was what it was, and all fighting did was squander the time they had left.

He hadn't given Cai an answer to his question, but the vampire wasn't pressing him. His gaze had turned to Daegan.

"How far are we?" Cai asked the other vampire.

"About five more miles." They were going down a wooded two-lane road, and Cai peered out at it through the darkness. When he pressed a button to roll the window down, he let in the scent of deep forest. Rand lifted his head, nostrils flaring. "The estate surrounded by this, too?" Cai asked.

As Daegan nodded, Cai's fingers tightened on Rand. "Pull over and let him out. He needs to run. He'll meet us there."

Yes. Things loosened in his gut and heart like they'd been freed from a cage. Cai slid a knuckle along his cheek. "Give me your clothes and I'll take them with me."

Rand took off the shirt. He stepped out of the car to remove the rest. He didn't look toward Daegan and Gideon. He only wanted to look at Cai. But he also wanted everything to disappear for a while.

Before he shifted, Cai set the clothes aside and held out his hand. "Other wrist," he ordered.

When Rand complied, he brushed his lips above that scar, closing the circle. "Meet us at the house, wolf. Just follow our mark or track my scent. I want your ass in my bed at dawn, though. Got me?"

Rand should have a smartass remark for him, but he was the more serious one of the two. The one-liners didn't come to him the way they did to Cai.

But as he met Cai's gaze, he didn't see any humor there. The vampire dropped his grip and nodded.

Rand backpedaled and then turned. The forest was calling to him. The wolf, too, humming through his blood. God, he was glad for the freedom to shift and tune it out, run. He glanced back at Cai, but Cai had closed the door. The limo was pulling off. Rand had a weird compulsion to chase after it. He put that aside as some latent canine thing, something no wolf with any pride would indulge.

That wasn't why he wanted to chase after the car. He wanted Cai to run with him. Maybe Cai could hear it in his head. Maybe he wasn't listening. Rand wasn't sure which option made him feel any better.

So he shifted, and let it all go to run.

Soooo… Here they were, in the fucking Council headquarters. Lots of brick and spires, gardens and fountains. According to Gideon, it was similar to Lyssa's primary home in Atlanta. The limo pulled up to the front door, set at the top of ten graduated marble steps. Gargoyles both menacing and majestic flanked either side of the doorway. Cai would have felt more comfortable entering through a side entrance. Garage. Kitchen.

"With it being close to dawn, Lady Lyssa plans on meeting with you at twilight rising," Daegan said. "For now, you'll be shown guest quarters and given what's needed to see to you and your servant's comfort. The only vampires here are the Council delegation you already met, and the servants and house staff whose discretion is assured. With Voltaire dead, you don't have to be concerned about concealing your servant's nature."

"Good enough. Kind of sorry I missed seeing him get his."

"Not alone in that," Gideon grunted. "Think Mason also wished he'd had a shot at him."

Cai hoped they'd made Chavez watch and he'd pissed himself at the warning. But in hindsight, maybe not. Oh, not about the Chavez thing. That would have been tons of fun. But on further reflection, Cai wasn't sure if he was in the mood to see anything killed for a while. Or even imagine someone else watching someone get killed. He turned his mind to better things.

"I'm going to hang out until Rand arrives. Who do we need to see? Once he gets here."

"Him." Gideon pointed to the wide and tall front door, which had opened and revealed a slim boy in early adolescence. Dark skinned and with expressive eyes that reflected keen interest in the new arrivals. Well, not the ones getting out of the vehicle. As his gaze darted over and past them, Cai suppressed a smile. Vampires were old hat around here. It was obvious he was looking for the wolf.

Cai didn't detect a full marking on the kid, but he was at least second marked, under someone's protection. With his superhero nose, Rand could probably tell him who, though Cai could make an educated guess. If the boy was confident enough to be escorting strange vampires to their rooms, then he belonged to Lady Lyssa. No one was going to fuck with a human marked by her.

"Is she aware of child labor laws?" Cai queried.

Gideon chuckled, and even Daegan's eyes sparked. "John's the grandson of her majordomo, Elias Ingram. John works with Lord Brian in the labs a lot, because he's a science geek, but he also likes to help his grandfather out. When he's not at school." Gideon tucked his tongue in his cheek and confirmed what Cai had suspected. "But he's Johnny-on-the-spot today because he heard a rumor that there's a shifter around."

Rand, you might want to come in hot as a wolf. There's a kid here expecting to be mightily impressed.

He didn't know if Rand would answer him. They weren't fighting, not exactly, but there was definitely a strangeness between them right now.

John's mark wasn't considered a sure protection in certain company, apparently, because as the kid came down the steps and they exited the limo, Daegan ambled over to a pretty trellis area. He took a seat on its bench, obviously intending to wait until Rand arrived and ensure that John had no issues getting them to their rooms.

"I just got my ass barbecued to get Dovia away from those assholes," Cai directed bluntly to the male. "You really think I'm going to do something to hurt a kid? And Rand would chew off one of his own feet first."

Daegan lifted a shoulder. "Dovia is a vampire. You follow the Trad preference to kill humans for food. So you assign their right to live no more value than the fisherman does the fish he has snared. While I don't believe you intend to harm him, your lack of regard for his kind means a mistake could be made. John is quite important to all of us."

"I suppose the non-Trad kind of vampire is so much better," Cai said bitingly. "Where humans are important when it suits your purpose. Whether it's for food or fucktoys, or to be a bellboy, they're still being used according to vampire whim, right? Your property."

John's eyes had widened. Maybe Lyssa didn't let vampires use rough language around him. Maintain the illusion that the kid was being raised in some Beaver Cleaver style household.

It stuck in Cai's craw. He didn't like Daegan's even tone. Yeah, nothing he'd said was technically wrong. But Cai felt like the hillbilly vampire who might just decide to eat the help because he didn't "know no better."

Fuck all of them. He'd sleep in the woods and, if he decided to hang around and talk to Lyssa in the evening, he would. Or he'd take off and say forget it.

He'd opened his mouth to spout out just that when he felt Rand's approach. The wolf was coming in according to his suggestion. It distracted him enough that he turned to John, gave him a wink and said, "Look over there, kid."

Rand emerged from the woods on the right side of the house, clearing a log as he did. He appeared to sail into the clearing, landing with powerful grace. Cai wasn't sure what the demo had cost the leg, but he did notice Rand slowed down quite a bit after only a couple loping strides.

But that was before the pack of Irish wolfhounds came around the house at a full run.

There were six of them, one giant male in the lead, his teeth bared and eyes lit. Daegan had realized they were coming even sooner, because he was already on his feet. But for the first time since Cai had met the male, he looked at a loss about what to do. Well, fuck that. Cai knew exactly what to do. He could break a few dogs' necks before they set one tooth into Rand. Rand was bigger and broader than any of them, but it was six to one, and the leader was no pampered poodle. He looked like he knew his way around a fight.

Cai heard John and Gideon shouting, trying to call the dogs back. Standing on the porch steps, they were too far away to affect the dogs' course. They obviously didn't answer to any of the men present.

Rand had spun toward the threat. Even before the male's eyes went full gold, Cai felt the wolf take over. He braced himself, a menacing growl in his throat, lips peeled back.

It served the purpose of slowing the ongoing pack, but only so they could strategize. They split into a circle around him. Cai was already headed that way, vampire speed propelling him, his first target picked out, the tall gray male in charge.

The upper window of the house slammed open and Lyssa leaned out. "Bran!" she snapped, strident as a fish wife who would gut anyone who didn't mind her. "Maggie! Down. Go to John. Go to John *now*."

The pack leader hesitated, territorial aggression warring with something else. Lyssa kept those jade green eyes fixed on him like a laser. The rest of the pack milled, uncertain.

Rand stayed in his impending attack pose, and now Cai knew what he could do. He reached for the human part of Rand. *Shift, Rand. Let them see you're not a wolf. That will confuse the shit out of them and ramp everyone down a few notches.*

Fight...kill...threat.

No. They live here. The dogs are protecting their home. It's okay. Lyssa's dogs. Shift, Rand. Shift for me.

The wolf backed up, moved forward, shaking his head, fighting whatever compulsion he was handling. But Cai kept pushing. Relief swept him as Rand let out a frustrated snarl and his body shimmered with that energy that passed over him before the bones started to stretch and alter. His head bowed and then came back, twisting in the quick, startling way that gave Cai a sympathetic twinge in his own neck. Another couple blinks and Rand stood there. Impressively naked, but very much not a wolf.

The wolfhounds whined, started back. All but that lead dog, the one who still had wolf smell in his nose. Cai guessed he was Bran. He kept his steady gaze fixed on Rand, his posture remaining stiff and combative. With a huff of frustration, Lyssa disappeared. Less than a blink later, she was next to John, pressing a brief hand on his shoulder before she marched down the rest of the steps.

"Males," she was muttering. "Testosterone-driven idiots, the lot of you." Her hair was caught in a tail on her nape and she wore a dress that had dirt on it, suggesting she'd been...gardening? There was a smudge of soil on her nose. Cai wondered if she knew it, but he sure as hell wasn't going to point it out.

She'd reached the dogs and put her hand on Bran, tugging at his collar. Noting the eye contact between them, Cai wondered if she'd marked the wolfhound. Geographical mark would be like microchipping, so that would make sense, but would she have done a second mark on the canine? He'd never heard of a vampire doing that to an animal.

There were rumors that if a vampire second marked a human who didn't speak the same language as the vampire, they might not be able to understand one another when speaking aloud, but the mark translated it into the proper language inside each brain. Did it work that way for animals?

Had hearing Lyssa's thoughts freaked the dog out at first, both getting a glimpse into a language neither one could speak fluently? Cai guessed he was in a position to sort of answer that question, since he and Rand didn't have too much problem figuring one another out, even when Rand retreated fully into the head of his wolf side.

Bran stood down reluctantly. He followed Lyssa's insistent command and imperious finger to plod up the stairs to John, disappointment emanating from every stiff stride. The other dogs followed. When they were assembled around John as she'd required, Lyssa nodded, satisfied. "Kitchen," she said briskly.

Canine eyes that had been filled with menace brightened, tails came up. The pack clattered down the marble stairs and took off around the corner, though Bran cast Rand one more speculative look on his way.

"Well, I did say make a dramatic entrance. Nice of you to arrange for that," Cai said, meeting the shifter halfway to the stairs. Rand rolled his eyes.

"Got my clothes?"

"Yeah. So?"

Rand gave him a searing look. Cai grinned and returned to the limo, pulling them out and tossing them to Rand, who'd followed him. Lyssa sent Rand her appraising look, the very thorough one that tempted Cai to block her view. He managed to quell the embarrassing compulsion. Barely.

"I would have made him leave them off," the queen said. "It's good to have you back safe and sound. All of you." Her gaze encompassed Gideon and Daegan. "Lord Greenwald has already called to express his deepest thanks. Cai, he said if there is anything you ever need, you have won a favor from him."

"Tell him to kill Chavez and stake himself. Then we'll call it even." Cai said it without much malice, though.

"Not Tyra?"

"She had a decent rack. Be a shame to let that go to waste, and she wasn't as much of a sadist. Think she pulled one or two of her punches, and she only kicked me about half as much as the other two."

He could literally feel Rand's wince, and Gideon choked back a snort of laughter. Cai straightened, trying to look like he knew how to behave. Lyssa's eyebrow lifted in dubious acknowledgment.

"I'll let you think that message through before I pass it on," the female vampire said neutrally. She turned her attention to Gideon, who still appeared amused, but no longer about Cai's comment. "What?" she said testily.

To Cai's bemusement, Gideon closed the distance between himself and the Council head before rubbing his thumb over her nose, removing the dirt. Lyssa blinked at it, then smiled.

"I was adding new plants to the pots in the upstairs sun room."

"Don't you have a servant to help with that? Or is he lying on his ass somewhere? Hard to find good help these days."

"Yes, it is. Daegan and I were just talking about that." She nudged him. "Jacob had errands in town, but will be back soon. John, please show Cai and Rand to their rooms. Do not assault Rand with too many questions. Give him and Cai time to rest, and then he may answer some of them for you."

"Yes, ma'am," John said. His calculating expression suggested he was already contemplating creative ways around the mandate. But Lyssa put a firm hand on his shoulder until he met her gaze and repeated his response, this time with honest intent. "I will, my lady. It's just so hard not to ask questions."

"I know. You'll be giving Lord Brian a run for his money before you're in high school." She smiled at him and brushed his cheek with her long-nailed fingers. "Take good care of my guests."

She glanced back down at Cai, encompassing Rand in the look, since the wolf-shifter was dressed and standing at his side. Her gaze was no less appreciative of his form in the snug denim. Cai might not be pleased, but he couldn't argue with it. He wanted to ogle the guy himself, but he forced himself to keep his gaze on the vampire queen.

"I'll look forward to seeing you at our next rising," Lyssa said. "Job well done, all of you." Then she was gone. Not much of a chatter box. He liked that about her. He was starting to like a lot of things about her, despite his strong wish not to do so.

"If you'll follow me, sirs," John said courteously, pushing open the door. A glance around showed Cai that Daegan and Gideon were headed off in a different direction, apparently satisfied that John would come to no harm. Was that a communication from Lyssa, or something else? Regardless, Cai was glad not to have the watchdogging detail.

He ascended the stairs to follow John, Rand at his heels. Rand's hand brushed his hip, probably an inadvertent thing, but he liked the casual intimacy. As he'd suspected, Cai noticed the wolf had paid for that dramatic entrance, because his limp as they moved up the stairs was more pronounced, though Rand shrugged off Cai's offer of a shoulder to grab.

Inside the house, a wide foyer with lots of marble and mahogany led into an almost equally wide hallway. At the end of it, a ten-foot-tall stained-glass window provided the focus feature of an atrium decorated with palm trees and comfortable wicker furniture. Lots of windows for nighttime viewing of the stars. Or for servants to enjoy during the day, maybe.

The slim boy led them down a winding staircase from there to the underground levels. More marble, polished wood, torch lamps set in the wall, and fancy art. But it was warm stuff, not the type of pieces that made Cai wonder why anyone spent loads of money for crap. This was Council headquarters, but from what Cai had gleaned, Lyssa had to spend a lot of time here. She obviously wanted it to be a home, not just a monument to Council power, though he expected there were chambers here that made that part of things clear to anyone stupid enough not to pick up on it.

Though Cai could still see all the ideas bouncing around behind his steady, intelligent brown eyes, John remained obedient to Lyssa's order. He kept his questions relevant to their stay as he escorted them toward the quarters that would be theirs. "It's normally assumed that a visiting vampire wants his servant to be given a separate room in the servants' quarters," he said. "Close, where he can quickly respond to your call. Is that what you wish?"

"If that's the normal thing, why are you asking me?" Cai said.

The boy's dark skin flushed. "Lady Lyssa said you were raised among the Trad and your servant"—his gaze shifted to Rand—"is a wolf shifter, so it didn't seem courteous to assume you'd follow the normal protocol for vampires. I wanted you to be aware of all the options."

The way his attention lingered on Rand showed a boy's eager hope that the male would morph into a wolf again, right before his eyes. Cai could feel Rand's amusement and a tenderness toward the kid that was tempting him to do just that.

Hold off for just a bit. We don't know Lyssa's policy toward animals in this part of the house. And she just talked Bran and his pack out of tearing you apart.

Rand shot him a look as Cai tossed him a grin, then answered the boy. "We'll share a room. He's not entirely housebroken."

"Says the vampire who called Lady Lyssa names and attacked another vampire's servant," Rand said dryly.

John's eyes popped open even wider than they had when Rand shifted. "You called Lady Lyssa names? And who did you attack?"

"Someone who deserved it. Aren't servants supposed to be seen and not heard?" Cai asked John. "I expect you know the protocol better than we do."

He surprised a shy smile out of John. "It depends on the vampire and the servant, sir," he said with deliberate graveness. "Like Lady Lyssa and Jacob. He may not say a lot out loud, but there's plenty of talk going on between them. They don't always agree on things. You can kind of tell because he gets this look—Lady Lyssa calls it his stubborn Irishman look—or her eyes get a bit sharper, like icicles. But he won't have said a word, and she won't say anything to him. Most of the time the disagreements are about stuff to keep her safe. Or him safe. They love each other, see, so they have to fight about that kind of thing."

If the boy had said that Lyssa turned into one of the front porch gargoyles and flew around on full moon nights, he couldn't have startled Cai more. Yeah, he'd already put together that some of the vampire and servant pairings weren't what he'd expected, but to hear it said so matter-of-factly, and by a kid, as if it was no big secret, was another level of WTF. Cai masked his reaction with a tone of forced casualness. "I thought Council vampires were anal about saying that shit out loud."

John looked discomfited, as if he realized he was saying too much, but after reflection, he nodded. "A lot of them are. But she's not. I guess because she's the biggest and strongest of all of them. Nobody's going to say she's wrong."

"Well, strongest maybe. I'm a lot bigger. You're almost taller than her yourself."

John beamed. "Almost. Another inch or two. She measures me against the door of my room and marks it. Says when I'm taller she'll let me do more to help my grand-dad. If he's okay with it."

Picturing Lady Lyssa as a maternal aunt-type, one openly in love with her servant, was kind of freaking Cai out. Especially after the fish wife/gardener routine, calling down her dogs and having dirt smudges. So he wasn't unhappy when John took his leave with a courteous encouragement to use the house phone if they needed anything else.

"Better than a fucking Hilton," Cai muttered, looking around at the posh appointments. Cushioned chairs, deep couch and a wide bed with lots of pillows. Though they were below ground, it didn't feel like any basement he'd ever experienced. Even nicer than at Greenwald's, and that had been pretty nice. There were lots of green plants, kept alive God-knew-how. A wide screen TV was set up to show different views of the outside grounds. Good as having a window.

Rand was moving around, examining the bric-a-brac at the writing desk and night stand. His hair was still loose. It was in need of a brushing, which didn't detract from his good looks in the slightest. It did give Cai an odd desire to brush his hair. He saw one, with a variety of other toiletry items, set out in silver containers on the spacious bathroom counter.

He was fucking losing it. He needed air, but dawn was too close. Fuck it. He and Rand needed the forest. They didn't belong here. He should have gone to run with Rand, the way Rand had wanted him to. Fucking idiocy. All of it.

He noticed a mental wince from Rand and cocked his head.

"What?"

"Nothing."

"Not nothing. When I said fuck it, you winced. You don't agree."

"I do agree. I just wish you wouldn't curse so much."

Cai was able to read his mind, but that was so outside what he'd expect to hear from Rand, he realized he would have overlooked the thought as no more than wind in the trees if the wolf hadn't said anything. "Seriously?"

Rand shrugged. He was standing in front of the mounted flat screen. As he studied a garden view, he lifted his arms, combing his fingers with brisk practicality through his hair. With a distracting display of bunched biceps, he started to braid it. Maybe he'd heard what Cai thought about his hair.

"You talk the way you want to talk. It's okay," Rand added. "The profanity just gets a little heavy for me, sometimes."

"Oh." Cai thought he'd never noticed it, but now, thinking back, he realized that little wince had happened more than once. The Goddard thing had merely pushed it far down the things-to-notice list.

Rand had moved into the bathroom to check it out. After a moment, Cai followed. He laid a hand on Rand's forearm, drawing his attention, and touched the braid. He'd bound it with the tie he'd apparently retrieved at the convenience store and tucked back into his pocket. "You're supposed to brush this before you braid it."

"Women do that," Rand responded.

"Well, yeah. But excess profanity seems to bother women more than men, too."

Cai laughed and fended off Rand's punch, though it took effort and skill. The male never did anything without focus and intent, his finger on the trigger always intended to shoot. Cai pressed him against the sink, arm folded up behind his back, and stared at him in the mirror. The strong face, mildly annoyed eyes, but with a slight curve to his mouth and a touch of heat in his expression. Cai rubbed his hardening groin against his tight ass and felt the surge of answering response go through Rand.

"Take off your clothes. I prefer you naked."

"Yeah? Same goes."

Cai put his mouth to the joining point of broad shoulder and corded neck, and slid his one functional fang along it. "Glad to hear it. But right now, I want you naked for me, while I stand here fully clothed and enjoy...

What's mine.

"...you."

From the look in Rand's gaze, Cai knew the shifter had picked up the meaning. Cai pressed past it, keeping it physical. Just fun and games. Mostly.

"I'm going to have that ass, and that surly mouth," he murmured. "But first I'm going to brush your hair. Take off your clothes."

Okay, hair brushing really didn't fall under fun and games. It brought some confusion into the situation, but Cai couldn't bring himself to take it back. After a brief hesitation, Rand removed his shirt with that appealing upper torso stretch, then toed off his shoes and opened the jeans, working them off his hips.

Cai had stepped back to watch. He savored each inch of skin revealed; lingered on every movement of Rand's body. It was like time had slowed down and he was caught up in some kind of weird romance novel moment, where all of it mattered to him.

He pulled his attention away from Rand's body to the brush. A sturdy wooden back and stiff bristles. "I may have other uses for this, too. Like..." An idea dawned.

"A profanity jar."

~

"What?" When Rand turned his head, he noticed the vampire's eyes had lit up in an unsettling way. "What do you mean?"

Cai twirled the brush. "Whenever you think my cursing is getting too excessive, I'll keep a count of those reproofs. And then," he twirled it again, "I'll paddle your ass with this for that number of strokes."

Before Rand could part his lips to say *what the hell*, Cai gave him a demonstration, hitting his buttock with enough strength and accuracy to damn near elicit a yelp. Rand started to whirl, but Cai caught him, turned him to face the sink again. Rand gripped the sink edge in both hands. He could fight him, knock him back on his ass. But...

"How," Rand said between his teeth, "is that a way to help you with *your* profanity?"

"Don't know if it fucking will. But I think it will change *your* attitude toward it."

"If you think a little spanking is going to change my mind," Rand muttered and then bit back a curse as Cai administered another three thwacks, one perilously close to the joining point of his balls, because Cai knocked his legs out wider with a forceful maneuver that put Rand off balance a second. Mainly because the whole situation had him off balance. While the pain sang through him, it was eliciting another reaction, crazily enough. In a weird way, Rand wanted him to do it again.

"My fucking pleasure," Cai said. "Making your dick hard, isn't it?"

"Would it do the same to you?" Rand retorted, and earned another hard whack.

"Nope. And we won't find out, because I'd rip your fucking head off if you tried. I don't have what you have inside you, Rand. Deep inside. Yeah, you're a pack leader"—two more whacks, and Rand was pretty sure the sensation sang through his bones like a hammer strike —"but you got that thing in you, that if someone can prove they have a bigger dick, it's not so bad to let them win, take control from you."

Some of the amusement had dropped from Cai's voice. What lay beneath it took Rand back to the convenience store, when Cai's nature as a Master had taken them both over.

"Just so you realize I'm letting you win," Rand managed. He could feel the vampire so close. It was erotic, having the male's scent and heat, but not seeing him reflected in the mirror, while Cai was obviously drinking his fill of Rand's reflected image *and* the real thing.

"It's not your nature, not bone deep," the vampire said, "but because of the way you and I come together, you've figured out when you're in that zone, you're not grieving. You're not worrying about the next step. You're just letting your Master use you, and that fucking turns you on. Which is convenient, because seeing your dick get hard because I'm paddling your ass, makes mine get even harder."

"Didn't we just...do this?" Rand didn't know how to address the other part.

"Yeah. Awesome, isn't it? Never ends. This is the easy part."

~

Rand went quiet. Well, one part of his mind did. The other part spiked each time Cai hit him with the brush, making his ass red, the muscles flex and tighten in his buttocks, his shoulders and thighs.

How far could he push his wolf? Cai let go of Rand's nape, trailing his fingers down the slope of his back toward his raised ass. Rand stayed where he was, still as a pack of dynamite about to go off. "Yeah," Cai growled. "Stay just like that."

He hit him three more times, reveling in the meaty smack between wood and flesh, the shudder that went through Rand's body, the arousal Cai could fucking inhale, it was getting so thick and heavy.

He tossed the paddle aside and strode out of the bathroom, stripping off his clothes as he did. Sensing it when Rand straightened and turned, Cai stretched out on that cushy, wide bed. It was framed on a high platform. Even had steps up to it which Cai didn't need, but someone like Dovia would have used.

Lacing his fingers behind his head, he looked, biting back a hungry groan at the sight of Rand standing in the bathroom doorway, cock brushing his belly. All of his muscles were deliciously tight.

He moved to the end of the bed and braced his hands on the foot board. Those wolf eyes narrowed, drinking in Cai's full length just as deeply.

"Time for my servant to get his ass up here and suck me off," Cai said, an unmistakable order. "Or do I need to find a belt and drive the lesson in a little harder?"

Rand showed teeth, but then he moved. Like a wolf.

One leap, and he was over the foot board and poised above Cai, balanced on his heels and tented fingers. He eased forward so he was staring down into Cai's face, the two of them inches apart.

"Bet that hurt the leg."

"Nothing hurts right now."

Cai reached up and curled his hands in the male's hair, tightened hard. "Don't test me," he said gruffly. "Turn your ass around and get to work."

But despite Rand's words, Cai saw the conflicting thoughts and feelings in his wolf's head. Responding to Cai like this was something Rand wanted, but he still didn't quite understand it. So Cai tugged on his hair again, with a different kind of pressure. "Don't think so much. It doesn't have to mean anything." *Even when it feels like it means everything.* "Put your mouth on me, wolf," he murmured. "Trust me."

Then, he took a risk with no calculation, just something he wanted, needed to say. "Trust your Master."

Rand waited another long moment, but he turned, adjusting so his knees were pressed into the bed over either of Cai's shoulders. Cai was rewarded with a close-up view of that fabulous ass, the heavy testicles hanging free between his thighs as Rand bent his elbows and gripped Cai's cock. He fed it into his lips, down, down, all the way to the sensitive base.

Cai was more than willing to just feel that for a few hundred years, but he was greedy enough to want more. He wanted to drive his wolf crazy. He parted his buttocks and lifted his head, using his tongue on Rand's rim, making his servant groan against his cock. Rand had to work to stay focused on going down on him, doing all the necessary things to bring Cai to climax. Cai repeatedly chastised him for losing rhythm as he worked his tongue in him, replaced it with his fingers, gripped and tugged his balls. He threatened to strap them up in rope, hogtie and leash the male to keep him at his mercy.

Which stirred Rand up even more, until he was growling against Cai's cock. All while he was desperately sucking and licking him with an incredible driving need that made Cai lose his own fucking mind.

Cai adjusted so he could put his mouth on Rand's cock, suck it into his mouth. It became a duel then, to see who could get who off first, but he already had a head start. Rand's thighs were trembling under his caressing hands, and when Cai started giving those flexing buttocks an occasional hard slap, leaving a hand print there, or tugging and twisting on his balls to hold him back, he felt that moment when Rand's mind let go and was all his. Everything his Master wanted to do to him, he would follow and succumb, because all of it felt too damn good. And with Cai's mind open to him, he knew how good it felt to Cai, too.

His alpha pack leader, service sub, total badass, beautiful wolf...

Every brushing contact was like fire across Cai's skin, inside his loins, his balls boiling, ready to let go. But he wanted to drive this ride all the way to the end, let Rand feel what he could give him. A complete free fall, with a safety net at the bottom, all of it Cai's doing. Why he wanted to show him that, give him that, he didn't care to analyze, but he was damn ruthless at wanting to prove he could do it.

When Rand started to come with a startled protest, an attempt to tighten up, hold back, Cai was having none of it. *You're mine, and you fucking come when I demand it. Right now.*

The male groaned, a sound that became harsh and close to a howl as his hips worked. He acted as if he would pull away, but Cai wrapped his arms around his hips and held him, pushing him even deeper into his mouth, letting him gush into his throat. Rand's big fists bunched in the comforter, hips pistoning hard against Cai's face as he sucked and nipped, and sucked harder. Rand's howl turned into something close to a hoarse shout as Cai added to it by shoving three slickened fingers into his rectum. The male's power was awe-inspiring. Cai was having to do everything he could to hold onto him. Gloriously strong son of a bitch. All his.

Maybe just for right now, but Cai was determined to make *now* everything.

As Rand rode that climax to the throbbing ebb point, Cai shoved away his own raging need and took care of him, bringing him down slow. Licking, more gentle sucking, kneading his strong buttocks. He did one last hard suck to make Rand flinch before Cai pulled off him and gave his ass a burning smack. "Okay, don't slack off down there. Finish me."

He was pretty sure Rand figured out some kind of half shift to nip him with sharper canines than a human form should have. Cai let out a dark chuckle and responded with a sharp twist to his servant's balls that had those teeth easing and Rand's mouth going back to its proper job. Cai closed his eyes tight, mental fists clenched to hang onto the edge of that precipice. He wanted to savor the incredible sensations before blissful annihilation of all thought.

His movements might be getting more jerky and uncoordinated, but it didn't stop him from caressing Rand's cock, his fine ass, stroking his thighs.

Now. Now, now, now. Rand's thought was a violent demand, a desire. A wish.

Cai thrust up into his mouth and let go with a deep groan, pumping seed down his throat. He was fiercely gratified by the shifter's determined effort to take it all in, swallow him down.

When Rand eased up at last, sensing Cai's completion, Cai traced a finger through the faint smears of blood he'd left on his thighs when he'd nipped him. A vampire couldn't help but bite during love play. "Stay where you are," he said, low.

Rand stilled, and Cai angled his head so he could punch his fang into the femoral, his hand still covering Rand's cock and balls. Fuck, he missed that other fang.

But imagining the picture it made, his servant poised in stillness above him on all fours as he fed, enjoying the powerful pump of Rand's rich blood, took his mind off that. Cai gripped his servant's genitals like his hand was a manacle while he took his fill of both body and blood.

Yeah, his wolf would be staying at his side while he slept. For as long as he could have him, Cai wanted Rand right here with him.

Touching him, holding him, until the sun set and darkness came again.

CHAPTER TWENTY-ONE

*T*hey slept together; woke together. Hands stroking, caressing. Rand's head was on Cai's chest, his big arm lying over Cai's hip. They didn't say a lot until the knock came on the door, a polite wake-up call from one of the house servants, along with a change of clothes.

The quiet didn't mean there was distance. They showered together. No sex, but a lot of touching. Cai did Rand's back; Rand did his. They talked of a couple things, idle, casual stuff. Rand brushed against him plenty as they got dressed. It was a wolf thing, that constant contact. Cai welcomed it regardless.

As they went up to the main floor, they headed for the dining room where the meet with Lyssa was going to happen. As well as some eating, because even Cai's less developed nose could detect some decent eats. About halfway down the corridor, they were joined by Jacob. The male was dressed in slacks and button-down shirt, a more formal attire than what they'd last seen him wearing. Now Cai knew why new clothing had been brought for him and Rand. Dinner was more formal at Council headquarters.

Rand looked hot as hell in fitted black slacks and matching trim black belt. The maroon dress shirt that had silk in the cotton outlined his powerful upper body. They'd given Cai a pair of gray slacks and black dress shirt like Rand's, with a matching gray suit coat. The fit was almost supernaturally good. Whoever had chosen the clothes had an excellent eye for sizes.

When he mentioned as much to Jacob, the servant grinned, his midnight blue eyes dancing. "Thanks. I handled the size guess. Our tailor is a closely guarded secret, for fear one of the other Council members will steal him away."

He gestured, presumably toward their destination. "The same Council members will be present at your meeting with my lady, with one addition. Lady Carola. Lady Lyssa felt that was a properly sized delegation to debrief you on what happened up in the mountains, and honor your efforts."

"I can't speak to the debriefing, but as far as honoring us, a gift certificate to a steak house for Rand and a free ride back to the mountains in that fancy limo would have worked for me. Oh, and these clothes. Can I keep these?"

Rand grimaced and Cai lifted a brow. "What? Like you weren't wondering the same thing."

Jacob's lips twitched, but his expression became serious as he came to a halt, raising a hand to have them pause with him.

"My lady doesn't expect you to be well-versed in protocol minutiae. But she's also not a fool. She understands the difference between acting ignorant and being ignorant, and the former is far more likely to spike her temper. She has a regard for you. She won't compel anything from you that you're not willing to give. Your actions have earned that consideration. But in return, I advise respect."

The look in Jacob's blue eyes shifted, and Cai saw the family resemblance between him and Gideon even more prominently. Particularly if he recalled when Gideon was backing up Daegan in Goddard's camp, ready to take on anyone who posed a threat or slipped under the vampire's guard. Yeah, some more details of that literal fire fight were coming back to him. Wolves, fighting ferociously alongside vampire and servant, all of them kicking ass.

"Which means," Jacob said in the same steady, even tone, "if you decide to call her what you did on your first meeting, I'll do my best to stake you myself."

After that ballsy statement, he stepped back and looked toward Rand. "Your Master can proceed to the ballroom," Jacob said politely. "But if you'll hang back a moment, I'll give you some tips on servant etiquette in the dining area that may help things go more smoothly." He cut a glance to Cai when the vampire started to object. "And more swiftly."

That made Cai hold his tongue. Yeah, getting out of this circus sooner than later was a priority. Nice digs, though. The carpet on the floor felt as deep and soft as a snow drift.

He wondered what "protocols" a servant would observe, and whether he needed to hang back to inform this high-handed ass that Rand wasn't part of that world and could do whatever he wanted, even not show up if he preferred to go roll around in the garden. But Rand sent him a reassuring thought.

Jacob's just protective of his Mistress. And I don't mind being in there with you.

You just want a chance at some of that meat they're cooking.

I'd likely get better scraps in the kitchen.

Especially if he flashed that charming smile at the kitchen staff. Tease. With a snort, Cai left the two and headed for the dining room.

At the open double doors, he got a glimpse of a roomful of vampires, their combined age and power resulting in a sudden and entirely unexpected wave of dizziness. He stepped back. What the hell...

It was like a ball of anxiety suddenly appeared in his stomach and shot up into his chest. Along with the vivid reminder that every time he was around a group of vampires much older and stronger than him, he got the shit beat out of him. Or, in the case of the Trads, enslaved for a century. The longing for the forest was so immediate and strong, he had to fight the urge to bolt for it like Rand.

He was so not having some weird delayed PTSD thing. He was two hundred fucking years old. A totally stompable age, by everyone in that far too small room, even if it was the size of a ballroom.

At Greenwald's, at least things had been diffused by the mission, Lord Georg's Ennui, and everyone's agitation at Dovia's kidnapping. Now the power of the gathered vampires spread out to every corner, filled it up. It would surround anyone who entered like a heated cloak. Smothering. He stood at the threshold, holding an indifferent mask in place, while things in his stomach flipflopped and he couldn't make his feet move.

This is different, fuck it all. You know it is. You're a vampire. You don't do flashback bullshit trigger stuff. You're decades past all that. Never mind that he'd just been in the thick of it with a very live and real part of that past only a couple days ago. Who was now dead as a fucking...darn doornail.

Rand stepped to his side and laid a hand on his shoulder. "You're trying," he said, a pleased note in his voice.

Fuck off.

That just seemed to make the shifter smile more, but there was a serious look in his eyes, and the grip of his hand increased. He didn't think something reassuring that would have made Cai feel more like an idiot. Instead, Rand let Cai see him thinking about where they were only an hour ago. Coming awake together, limbs tangled, the room so quiet. Everything so quiet, just breathing together.

Yeah. That worked. Okay. Though he kept his gaze high level, not focusing on any particular thing, Cai was able to test his reaction by looking into the room. No squeezing tightness in his chest. He was all right. Cai moved his gaze back to Rand's, held there and gave him a nod.

Rand dropped the hand and adjusted so he was at Cai's shoulder, one measured step back. *It goes easier if you follow the protocols. Don't be a smartass about it,* his wolf advised.

He was about to ask Rand what the deal was about the change in position, but then Cai took closer note of the arrangement of vampires and servants in the room.

Helga, Mason and the vampire he assumed was Carola were seated at the table. Carola spoke with an accent that suggested she was of German descent, like Helga. But where Helga was blond and buxom, Carola had a short dark bob around distinct cheekbones and mink-lashed gray eyes, a feminine, foxlike face. An array of sampler-sized food selections and a bevy of wine choices were laid out on fine china settings. The vampires' servants stood behind their chairs or, more exactly, a few feet back, against the wall. They were standing at respectful, silent attention, except when one was summoned by their Master and Mistress, as Torrence currently was. He was leaning over Helga while she spoke quietly to him. Her fingertips slid inside his shirt to caress his chest, tug on the hair there, before he nodded and she released him to step back again.

Apparently, no one had noticed Cai's crazy moment. Standing at the head of the table, Lyssa was involved in conversation with Mason. At Lord Greenwald's, Cai had been distracted by having the shit kicked out of him. Taking a closer look at the male vampire now, he realized Mason wasn't passing as human by anyone's standards. He had that fixed stillness the really old ones did, and his amber-colored eyes had the focus of a hunting tiger. He wasn't a vampire Cai would meet at the mall anytime soon. His sleek copper hair, tied back with an elegant pewter clip, was like rippling silk over his shoulder. Different from the thick mane of his wolf shifter, but Cai still liked Rand's more.

This was all good. He could handle it.

Stop being a chickenshit, Cai told himself, and stepped fully into the room, no matter that he was a little too relieved to have Rand at his back. Lyssa looked up, her reserved smile crossing her face.

"Thank you for joining us, Mordecai. If you will take the empty seat, the house servants will pour you a drink. You can add your servant's blood to it, if you prefer."

He noticed each setting came with a sharp curved knife, probably for that purpose. Cai wondered if that was a standard inclusion in flat-ware for vampires. *Ooh, I want the military grade knife with rose print handle, so it matches the rest of my china pattern.*

He thought of Jacob's warning. He wasn't usually the type to heed warnings, but just this once, maybe he would. Maybe he was mellowing. Or anticipating that he should save it up for when someone deliberately did something to piss him off, which would likely be soon in this group.

Any group. You're not really a people person.

Aren't you supposed to be standing against the wall, looking meek and subservient?

Which was a joke, on a couple levels. First, Rand couldn't look meek and subservient if his life depended on it. Second, every servant in here looked as if he or she could throw down with a ninja and come out on top.

Jacob headed that list. However, as he entered the room and moved to his Mistress, Cai was reminded of what John had said. Their eyes locked and a million things passed between them, the humming energy of a connection with so many threads, it was a rope that would never break. Jacob came to Lyssa, his hand grazing her lower back before he pulled out her chair for her. After she was seated, he caressed a strand of her hair, letting it slide between his fingertips before he stepped back to the wall. A position not of meekness nor subservience, but reflecting what was between them.

It was Mistress and servant, but the brand of power exchange between them said it was also love. Too obvious for even a cynic like him to deny.

"Cai, have you ever attended a social gathering like this?" Lyssa's question was posed with pleasant courtesy, so he tried not to feel self-conscious. She'd mostly focused on the don't-rip-your-servant's-soul-apart stuff in their pre-Goddard heart-to-heart; not so much on what to do at formal occasions. Probably didn't figure there was any point to giving him that lecture unless he survived. He appreciated her pragmatism, though now he wished he had eavesdropped on Jacob's impromptu instruction course with Rand.

Regardless, honesty seemed to be the best course, so Cai quelled the "do I look like a vampire you'd find at a social gathering" vein of sarcastic commentary and shook his head.

Wise. And you actually look pretty hot.

Yeah, him and his one fang. But the amused comment from his servant helped him relax a little. *Same goes. They should change the arrangement so servants are* across *from their vampires. That way I could look at you.*

"Dinner is a sampling of things for us, along with wine and discussion," Lyssa said smoothly. "Servants eat a full meal of the same later in the kitchen, but you're welcome to offer your servant food by hand if that gives you pleasure. After we eat, there are often entertainments with our servants. It's fortunate yours is male, because we are down one male servant tonight. Lady Carola has both a male and female full servant, but she left Wilhelm at home. Shondra is attending her on this visit."

With a sudden uneasiness, Cai noticed Carola and Helga perusing his wolf with sexual avarice. *Boy, ladies, are you barking up the wrong tree.* But Torrence was eyeing him with equally intrigued speculation. Shondra was an Indian-African beauty, and she was also measuring up the new servant in the room with dark, kohl-rimmed eyes.

Jessica, Lord Mason's servant, had a different expression. More neutral and kind. Perhaps she understood how unsettling this kind of thing could be for people new to it. Which suggested it was still recent enough for her that she could remember how it had felt at first. Now that Cai had more time to get an impression of her, he saw she was a lovely, fragile-looking thing with lots of silky brown hair and a light scattering of freckles across her fair skin. However, noting the set of her jaw and tilt of her head, the sharp, intelligent gray gaze, Cai expected that fragility, while real, covered a core of steel. She looked as ninja-capable as any of them.

Picking up a whiff of danger, he shifted his gaze toward it and met Lord Mason's tiger-like stare. A clear warning lay in the amber depths. *Look but don't touch, and if you look too hard, I may stab out your eyeballs with my fork.*

Cai had made a neutral sound at the information Lyssa provided, so she smoothly moved on to another topic. "Daegan has covered a great deal of what happened in the mountains, but can you give us your accounting, in case there are relevant details that happened before he arrived on scene?"

He wasn't sure how much she wanted, but he needn't have worried. As he hit the high spots, the Council asked him questions, a lot of them focused on the capabilities of the Trads, how they lived, what their resources were. It made sense, so they were better prepared for any future female vampire snatchings, but Cai still felt a little unsettled by the depth of the inquiry. The Council members weren't just a bunch of figureheads.

"Very well," Lyssa said at last, sweeping her gaze over the table to ensure no other questions remained. "If we're done, let's enjoy our dinner now, and we can take our dessert out into the garden."

There were plenty of things Cai knew he didn't excel at. Small talk headed that list. Fortunately, with him being the "junior" vampire, no one thought it all that odd for him to stay mostly quiet unless addressed. He was perfectly cool with that and focused on the food. Rand was interested in the meatball things. The rare cooked beef had tomato and spices in them.

Do not throw one of those over your shoulder for me to catch in my mouth like a trick poodle.

Spoilsport. Cai scowled, because he'd thought about doing just that. He was becoming too predictable.

You could kneel at my side and I could handfeed you, he retorted. *The meatballs are really good.*

His servant's interest stirred, which provided Cai a hidden smile. Rand couldn't completely squelch those wolf instincts.

Then Carola spoke, and Cai knew his temporary respite from unwelcome attention was about to end.

"I'm curious about your servant, Mordecai," she said, as Shondra replenished her Mistress's wine herself, taking it from the hand of the house servant. "Have you ever enjoyed him in wolf form?"

Before Cai could stiffen in shock, thinking the Council vampires were going in the same direction Goddard had, Helga spoke.

"Like making excellent use of that long tongue?" She purred it with an impish smile. "Perhaps he'll show us after dinner. I'd be happy to be the first volunteer."

Fuck, how had he missed that? He'd been so focused on the whole "debrief and honor" bullshit, Cai hadn't connected the dots, realizing that this would also be considered "that" kind of vampire gathering. But Rand...

What did Jacob tell you about these dinners?

They eat, talk politics, and often indulge in sexual entertainments using their servants.

So why the hell did you follow me in here? Cai demanded. *Never mind.* He knew the answer to that.

He ignored Rand's half insulted, half confused response. The only thing that mattered was knowing tension had increased in Rand's mind as soon as Helga made the nature of her interest known, and Cai was going to deal with it.

Keeping his focus on his meal, Cai responded to Helga with an indifference he didn't feel.

"That's very generous of you, my lady, but when he's a wolf, he's a wolf. Which means he does what any animal does with his mouth. Licks his ass, eats raw meat, has no dental hygiene. His breath in that form could knock down bowling pins. If you want that near your delicate parts, it's your business." He waved a forked meatball at the house servant who was refilling Mason's wine glass. "These are good. Can I have a few more?"

The house servant darted a look at Lyssa, but then bowed her head and disappeared, he supposed to comply. He tried to ignore the weighted silence and focused on his plate. *Go back to talking to each other. Ignore me, ignore us...*

He didn't get his wish.

"I assume it's because you're a made vampire that your digestive tract can handle greater quantities of food," Carola observed.

The born vampire condescension was evident as a wart would be on her pert nose, but Cai expected nothing less. He ignored the anxiety growing legs inside his stomach, an echo of what he'd felt at the doorway. If he succumbed to that pansy-assed behavior in front of them, he'd stake himself.

"Hell, no. I just throw it up later. That's the key. Eating's only problematic if you eat too much and wait for it to digest. That's a train that's not coming for us vamps, right? I once ate a whole shepherd's pie because I was missing the damn things so much. That's how I figured it out."

Mason was regarding him with fascination. Cai saw his female servant hide a smile. Cai liked her more for that.

Lyssa had an unreadable expression, while Helga and Carola looked less than friendly. Yeah, Jacob had warned him. He needed to tone it down.

You think?

Ssh. Be a good servant. Stay. Play statue.

Rand had such an interesting way of thinking *Fuck off* at him without actually saying the words. It was more of a feeling, a push.

"Um, thanks," he told the house servant when she returned and rolled another half dozen of the meat balls onto his plate. She was a neat little bland thing in a white apron and beige-colored dress. Ducking her head quickly in acknowledgement, she disappeared.

"It's a miracle you survived the Trads as many years as you did," Lady Helga observed, her voice flat. "Perhaps, Lady Lyssa, we could conclude our business with this male so that he may take his plate of food and go eat in the kitchen, where his lack of manners would be far less disruptive."

The surge of feeling that flooded him propelled Cai's head up. His gaze lasered across the table to lock upon the female vampire's. Even if he'd wanted to, he wasn't sure he could have pushed down or muted his expression. Suddenly things were a lot more still in the dining room.

It had been a hell of a week, and he had zero experience in political fencing. He shouldn't have ever come here, and he saw the regret in Rand's mind for pushing him to do so. But it wasn't the wolf's fault. Rand hadn't been able to answer why he followed Cai in here, knowing what might happen. But Cai did know why. It was that instinctive loyalty and protectiveness, which he totally did not deserve from the wolf. But Rand deserved it from him.

Yeah, Cai didn't think a lot before he spoke. The truth had never required much thinking over. With deceptive casualness, he ate another meatball, holding Helga's gaze an extra second before he shifted his attention to Lyssa.

"My lady, do you consider yourselves Trads?"

The flash in Jacob's gaze was a clear, "Were you even listening?" reproof. However, at the end of the day, Jacob was a human and a servant, and Cai didn't answer to him. He didn't answer to fucking anyone.

"I'm sure you know we do not," Lyssa said coolly. "Though we are all vampires."

"Okay. Well, Trads, they take what they want when they want it. The only thing that stops them is someone stronger beating the shit out of them until they realize they can't have it, or the cost will be too great. I said I hadn't been to a vampire social gathering. But you told me the high-level version about them, when I third marked Rand. And I've heard about them. Hell, all the Trads have."

He swept his gaze around the table, over the assembly of attractive servants. "It's the Trad version of Penthouse letters, swapping blown up accounts of what happens at dinners for the 'civilized' vampires. My dick sure got hard, hearing about it. And some of it sounded real intriguing to me; can't deny it."

Cai broke open a piece of bread, so soft it could be used as a pillow, and put butter on it. When he met Helga's gaze, she was now wearing a downright hostile look. Yeah, he wasn't making any headway, but he was just going to say it like it was.

"Rand's not human. He became my servant to help me extract Dovia. I'm not one of you and I'm not a Trad. If I'm okay with him participating in something tonight, and he thinks he can handle it and wants to do it for the right reasons, then yeah, he will. But under no circumstances will that involve his wolf. Period. He's not a goddamn circus act. Whatever parts of him I command when he's human, it doesn't extend to the wolf. The wolf belongs entirely to him."

Feeling Rand's sudden stillness behind him, Cai put more words into that space. *You told me. It's a sanctuary, isn't it? Everyone should have a sanctuary. It's the most goddamn precious thing anyone can have.*

Cai took a breath. Every vampire here *could* annihilate him without breaking a sweat. Didn't matter. "If someone tries to take that away from him, those choices, then they'll end up just like that bastard Goddard. Or you'll kill me, and that will be the end of it, too. Same difference. But just as a point of 'etiquette,' if this is how you treat somebody who brought home one of your special 'born' vampires, then good luck finding someone to do it next time."

In the next ticking-bomb silence, Cai felt something he rarely felt from Rand. Speechless shock. And it wasn't the reproving, can't-believe-you-shot-your-mouth-off-like-that kind.

Lady Helga's eyes flashed with anger, but Lyssa raised a hand. "Enough," she said quietly.

All eyes turned toward her, telling Cai who was the head bitch in charge. As if there'd ever been any doubt.

"He's being rude and deliberately insolent," Helga pointed out.

"Yes. He is." Lady Lyssa considered him. Since Cai had just told everyone at the table off, he did his best not to squirm, but hell, she made it hard. "He has never lived among us," she said slowly. "Never internalized our ways. Nor does he have a desire to do so. Though that in itself does not exonerate his behavior, or give him leave to live outside our society, other factors must be considered."

Her attention moved to Rand. Cai recognized then the difference between her earlier appraisal of him versus that of Carola and Helga. Cai's possessiveness had made him want to shield Rand from her view. His need to protect was what provoked the desire with Helga and Carola.

Lyssa meant his wolf no harm. She *saw* him.

"We were unaware shifters truly exist, and now we know they do," she observed. "Rand helped bring back one of our own, and, according to Cai, saved his life."

She leaned forward, folding her hands on the table. Her back straight, chin up, eyes fixed on his shifter. "We are aware of the dangers of pushing our servants' minds too far beyond what they can handle," she said. "We've recently discussed putting in place measures to protect them from vampires who would destroy their minds simply because they can. Unfortunately, we still have doubts if it is enforceable before the damage is done, since how much a human servant can and wants to take from their Master or Mistress is often a very subjective matter."

Cai thought of the things he and Rand had faced together, shared together, and knew it for truth.

Lyssa shifted her gaze to Cai. "If it would be a serious breach of Rand's mental state to explore his sexuality in his wolf form, I feel that must be honored, even if he is a third marked servant. We are learning respect is a two-way street with other species, are we not? Our communications with the Fae over recent months have taught us that."

The Fae? News to him, but pretty interesting news. Lyssa continued. "Lord Keldwyn, our Fae liaison, would say so, as would Lord Uthe, who is involved in other Council business tonight and could not be here."

"Which explains why Keldwyn is not," Carola put in, in a more amused tone. She apparently wasn't as uptight as Helga. "He can't do without his weekly chess matches with your right hand, Lady Lyssa."

Lyssa acknowledged that with a faint smile. "The two of them make a formidable diplomatic team, so I expect Keldwyn's presence will be helpful to Uthe, much as he might deny it."

She shifted the subject back toward the topic at hand. "I think we have far more important things to discuss with Mordecai. Up until now, we have had a tolerance toward the Trads, a respect for a different culture and structure existing among those who are still part of our species. However, recent events may very well change that."

Her green eyes grew colder, and they fixed upon Cai. "As you know, our recent intel has suggested stealing our young females for breeding purposes isn't just an isolated goal of one or two fringe members. As a result, we're close to declaring the Trads enemies, and cleaning out their nests. I expect you know where a great many of them are."

Shit. A servant had brought in a new platter of God-knew-what fancy foods, though the cheese things looked okay. Cai quelled the immediate urge to fork a few on his plate. Having his mouth full would seriously undermine the second line in the sand he was about to draw.

Winning friends and influencing people, that was him.

"I know the general proximity of some of them, yeah," he said. "But as much as I hate Trads, my lady, I'm not a vengeful and pissed-off kid any more. Most Trads aren't like Goddard. They're like deep mountain people, preferring to live rough and in secluded places. They just want to be left the hell alone, as far from human settlements or 'civilized vampires' as possible. They won't stop killing humans for food just because you tell them not to do so. Treating them as deer instead of milk cows is part of who they are. And I can't say they won't try to snatch female vampires or humans, but that's because they're genuinely desperate about the numbers issue. Just like you are. Fertility is a problem for them, just like it is for you all."

He set down his fork. "So maybe the answer isn't trying to force me to be a snitch, but getting a message to them. There's a rumor going around, that vampires who have a strong relationship with their human servant are more likely to conceive."

At her unreadable look, he lifted a shoulder. "Doesn't matter how many leaks you try to shut off, water's going to find a way to flow out a dam. The sudden poker faces around the table tell me it may be more than rumor. If so, maybe the Trads need to hear that. Maybe it would make them look a little differently at humans if they see them, not as food or objects, but a legitimate pathway to an increase in their birth rate. They're not all idiots about that, like Goddard was."

"An emissary of sorts." Lyssa pursed her lips thoughtfully. "Not a bad idea. Would you be willing to be that emissary, Cai? This latest incident won't help reduce tensions between our two peoples. While I won't shy away from war if that's where it goes, we'd all prefer a different outcome. Well, most of us." Her lips twitched. "Lord Belizar is not here to voice his opinion, but he far prefers battle to diplomacy."

"You think *I* would be a good diplomat?" Cai tried not to scoff. For one thing, he'd just eaten a cheese thing and was afraid he might accidentally spit some of the crumbs in the queen's direction.

Lyssa's lips twitched. "You've said they're a rough group, with no patience for civilized vampire polish. I think you'd be exactly the right person. It's not a decision to make tonight. But if you do decide to serve in that role, your interactions with vampires in our world will necessarily increase."

She glanced around the room. "Our social-gathering etiquette is in place for a reason. It allows all of us a place to safely exercise the more savage parts of ourselves, in ways that don't result in bloodshed. It's also a way to explore our natures and that of our servants. You yourself indicated you might warm to it. Even if you don't feel you have the right to command your servant's choice, if he agrees to take that step with you, you might find it brings both of you pleasure and a deeper understanding of your bond."

She's encouraging you to go ahead with the dinner stuff, if I'm okay with it. Rand spoke in his head.

Really? She painted it on the wall in big red letters. I missed that. Rand ignored the sarcasm. *I can do this.*

Do you have any clue what they want you to do?

No, but I expect I'm about to find out.

You don't have to. I'm not going to be some bullshit emissary. I'm going to get the hell out of here and leave this area for a good long while so they can't irritate me. Go to the desert, like I said.

The obvious place for a sun-averse species, Rand observed. *Cai, I can handle this.*

No. He said it decisively.

Rand's mind voice was puzzled, even a little hurt. *With Dovia, I was able to...*

I won't allow it. Cai brought his palm down on the table with a sharp impact that shuddered through the wood. He didn't care.

Before the vampires could react, he answered Lyssa. "I might be willing to talk to some Trads, get some kind of dialogue going between you so you could meet," he said. "But once I did that, then I'd be done. I'm not interested in being a formal emissary to you or to the Trads. Neither one of you is part of my world."

Older vampires really did have extraordinary eyes, the jade green of hers like a spiral, taking him deeper, holding him. No one spoke, which probably meant bad things for him and Rand, worse than him being sent from the table. Unavoidable consequences usually called for him to say something snarky, and he had a million possibilities on the tip of his tongue.

But as he looked at the vampire queen, he saw her in bare feet, calling back her dogs. Or reaching out to lay her hand on Georg Greenwald's arm, steadying him. Most importantly, he thought of every look and touch she'd shared with Jacob. Her servant. Maybe he was crazy to talk to a thousand-year-old-plus Council vampire like this, but something entirely unplanned came out of his mouth. Straight from the heart.

"I didn't feel like I belonged to or with anybody...for a long time," he said. "But the worst part was remembering when I did. I was a kid. A kid with a family, some ideas about what I'd do with my life. I'd probably have ended up working the land like my father did, at his side, until I found some village girl to marry, have a bunch of babies with, and keep the cycle going. There'd be sunrises and sunsets, early dawns and hard work, where I'd wish for just a few more minutes of sleep. I'd look forward to harvest festivals where I could dance with girls with flowers in their hair."

He was aware of a change in the scrutiny toward him, but he kept his attention on her. Except for her and Rand, there was no one else in the room. "I remember a couple times I noticed the muscles of farm boys as much as the soft tits of farm girls, but I pushed that away. Wasn't any context for having those thoughts in that world. But other than that....it was a life. The life I thought I'd been given."

He picked up his fork, put it back down. "Goddard took that away, and then he and his Trads took everything, every bit of who I was. I thought about dying, a million times, and then one particularly awful night, I decided I'd had enough. I killed myself. Or I thought I did. Instead, Lodell found me before I was all the way dead, and he turned me."

He felt Rand's gaze boring into the back of his head, but he didn't look toward him. Didn't need to. Those threads between Lyssa and Jacob? He and the wolf had their own version of those, particularly in a moment like this.

Cai shook his head, barked a harsh half laugh. "Said he wasn't going to let me give up on life. That I was too damn tough of a little bastard, and I was going to figure it out, figure out how to live life on my own terms. Fuck, I hated him for that. Hated him for a good ten years, until I realized he was the best and only friend I'd ever have in the Trads."

Rand had moved, because he rested a hand on Cai's shoulder. It was a ballsy decision in this crowd, but Cai took it, accepted it. He felt the understanding in Rand's mind. He'd sense it, see it, but Cai still opened his mind wide to him, so Rand could see the more complicated layers of what Cai couldn't express, even in formed thought.

It wasn't that Cai didn't think Rand could handle a fun orgy with some hot-looking human servants. Cai couldn't handle it. Something he hadn't realized until just now.

Lyssa's eyes were assessing, measuring, but they weren't unkind or cruel. He didn't take stock of what else was happening at the table, but he'd probably ruined the mood for the after-dinner fuckfest. *Yeah, don't invite that guy again. What a killjoy.*

"I've been around enough to know what being a vampire's about. I don't know your world well, but I get some of the whole vampire-servant thing and why it's so fucking fabulous to have this person who belongs entirely to you. Maybe in time, if I hung around with you all long enough, in your world, I'd start to feel more comfortable with it, and so would Rand. Then we'd all enjoy it a lot more, right? Because the big difference between you and the Trads is the servants. Your servants are with you willingly and, for some of you, that bond...it's a strong, indescribable thing."

His gaze shifted meaningfully between her and Jacob. "The Trads destroyed who I was, remade me. Am I a Trad? Maybe I am. I'm broken, I know it. I've killed plenty of humans for blood needs; haven't thought a damn thing about it and probably never will. I don't dream about their faces or who they were to their families. They were food, pure and simple."

Now it was harder to feel Rand's gaze upon him. But he pressed on. "Rand reminded me of what it was to notice. Of why it makes sense to take what you need without taking a life, when it's possible. He reminded me how bloody awful killing and taking away free will is. He took me back to the beginning, and has stood at my side, seen what I am and still stood at my side. Just like he's doing now. We haven't known each other long, but it feels like a lot longer."

He saw understanding, not only in Lyssa's eyes, but in Jacob's, who had also shifted closer to his lady. Cai could cover both their expressions in one glance. Fortunately, Jacob's looked a lot less like *You are so fucking up.*

Rand's fingers tightened on him. "I'm still not sure if that's a gift or curse," Cai continued. "But it makes me sure of one thing. I'm asking you, respectfully as I know how. Don't push him into the world where I had to live for too long. Don't do that to him."

He set his jaw. "If you try, I'll finish what Lodell interrupted and take us both out. My pathetic life is totally worth protecting him from that treatment, ten times over."

Cai pushed away from the table, causing Rand to step back, but he did it to rise and face Rand. "And if the only way to free Rand from your demands, now and going forward, is to remove our marking, then I request that."

He couldn't believe how hard it was to push the next words out, but he did it. They were for Rand alone. "Probably the best thing. You know my mouth is going to get me killed, and you don't want to die because I'm an incurable smartass."

Rand's blue and gold eyes were fixed on his with an intent look. When the wolf spoke in his head, the words lodged in Cai's chest, like a thrown spear.

Gotta die of something.

Cai swallowed. He offered a bare nod of acknowledgment and turned to face Lyssa, though he executed a credible bow to all of them. Pretty well, if the surprise on Helga's face was any indication.

"I'm sorry if I was rude to anyone here. I'm willing to help improve relations between you and the Trads, the way I described it. I'll hang around tonight if you want to talk about that with me, but I'll be gone before dawn. Back to the world where I belong." He straightened. "Though if we could have a doggy bag of those meatball things, Rand would appreciate it. So...um. Good night."

He'd almost made it to the door when Lyssa spoke, bringing him to a halt.

"Mordecai."

Hell, he'd known it wasn't going to be that easy. He turned, subtly —or maybe blatantly—positioning himself in front of Rand. When the wolf began to move, intending to stand shoulder-to-shoulder, Cai warned him against it.

Protocol, remember? You don't stand next to or in front of your vampire. Jacob said so.

Rand stayed where he was, but it was a tenuous leash that might snap at the least provocation from the table. It was what Sheba had known, and Cai did, too. Rand was a pack leader. No one was threatening his pack, and Cai...Cai was his pack. Thanks to Cai's big mouth, Rand was obviously feeling that even more strongly now.

But it was sloppy seconds, falling so short of the kind of pack Rand should be leading. One that would want to be led, for one thing, rather than one constantly doing his own thing and dragging Rand into this kind of trouble.

Lyssa rose and came to stand before Cai. She had a graceful, gliding kind of movement that Cai expected spawned the lore about vampires floating just above the ground rather than striding like a human.

"This Council and I are deeply grateful for what you and your servant did for Dovia and Lord Greenwald," she said with quiet formality, though her gaze said a lot more. "You have our leave to depart whenever you wish, but you have friends on the Council now. Please do not hesitate to come to us if you have need of that friendship. If you are willing to approach Trad colonies you think would be amicable to meeting with a delegation from this Council, to discuss ways to resolve some of our deeper conflicts, then see Ingram before you leave. He'll provide you my contact information."

Her gaze shifted to Rand. "Just as we are learning more about the Fae culture, thanks to the liaison role of Lord Keldwyn with our Council, I think it would be beneficial to learn more of your kind, Rand. I understand you are a private people, and you may not wish this. We'll leave it to you and them to decide if you wish to initiate those dialogues.

"If you do, then Cai will have the contact information so you may seek informal or formal audience with me about it. Vampires are learning, slowly, painfully, that we benefit more from friendships than conflict or isolationism. I know trust of our kind has not always been warranted, but we are working on that."

Isolationism is a hell of a lot easier than that other stuff, Cai observed to Rand. *And you don't have to dress up for dinner.*

Cai...

Rand's warning kept the words inside, but Cai was just yanking the wolf's chain. He gave Lyssa a slight bow.

"Thank you, my lady. I would also ask...what you promised, or implied you'd do, earlier. Can you not speak of what Rand is outside this room? As I said, water finds a way past a dam, but no reason to help it." A tight smile touched his lips. "Sometimes it's better for some things to remain a fantasy."

Lyssa looked to the others, meeting each vampire's eyes in turn, finishing with Mason. Whatever was communicated between them had her offering Cai a nod.

"If the time comes when the rest of the Council must know, I will speak of it, but as long as there is no pressing issue related to shifters, I see no reason for the information to go further than the Council in this room and the staff here, whom you may trust to keep the information to themselves."

"Thank you." And he meant it. Which felt awkward. "In return, I'll never reveal to any vampire I was here, or what we did for you. Even if I meet one of those absent Council members. Wouldn't want it to get around that you guys owe a favor to a bastard like me."

Her eyes glinted with amusement. Beneath that was something more serious, unsettling. "I think there are far worse favors to owe. Before you go, see Lord Brian. He has something for you. It will please you. Also, Rand may visit the kitchen and request any leftovers either of you desires."

She'd let him off the hook. Her lips twitched, acknowledging his barely masked relief and Rand's doggy bag needs, before she turned away, a clear dismissal.

Cai didn't need to be told twice.

Cai didn't slow his strides until he was deep into one of the gardens, where the forest was only a few hundred feet away. Tempting. Way too tempting. He was under an archway of a big vine thing that formed a cave. He'd told Rand to go to the kitchen and get some food. Had insisted on it, making it clear he needed some alone time. The wolf complied, especially when Cai shut down any mind communication and ignored Rand's silent questions.

He stayed in the garden for a while, trying to sort through his thoughts. Removing the third mark... Yeah, he should deal with that. He didn't really care what Brian had for him, but maybe the servant's vampire had to sanction the separation in person, or there were forms to sign. Who the fuck knew.

He thought of being with Rand without the bond the mark provided. He didn't like it, but it wasn't about what he liked or disliked. It was what made the most sense. Which was why he was sitting in the middle of a Council-vampire garden, brooding over it. Shit.

He tried not to think of anything. Trying not to think of what was behind all of it, and what had been reinforced with a big highlighter tonight, after seeing Rand around the Council vampires. A huge, Grand Canyon contrast to him being with Fane's family.

Shit and double shit. Cai rose and wandered into a different section of the garden. It was then that another scent came to him, one that a vampire found hard to resist. Especially a vampire looking for a much-needed distraction.

Following the path with quiet stealth, Cai discovered exactly why those "servant entertainments" had sounded so intriguing. And why wouldn't they be, with so many hot looking servants close to hand?

The Council delegation had retired to a large open pavilion to enjoy after dinner coffee and the tableau currently on display before them.

Jessica, Mason's servant, was stretched out in pale, silky nudity upon a patch of soft green grass, populated by lavender flowers. Shondra, a lovely woman with hazelnut skin and a million dark ringlets of soft cottony hair, had her mouth buried between Jessica's legs. Mason's servant was writhing, her arms stretched out to either side, mouth open and neck arched back, so close to release. But it seemed Carola kept Shondra curbing her pace, so she took Jessica up and up, then brought her back from the edge, intensifying the experience.

"Master..." Jessica's self-restraint broke with the plea. Mason had pulled his chair close enough to her that her fingers coiled and uncoiled on the hem of his slacks. His gaze remained fixed upon her, his mouth set in a stern, waiting line, though his eyes had fire in them. Before the night was over, Cai expected his servant would be fucked past the ability to walk. Mason looked like he put the D in Dominant. Whenever his servant was touched by another, even a woman, he was probably quick to reinforce his own claim on her. Repeatedly.

Cai thought of Rand and Dovia. Yeah, he got that.

He imagined Rand in the same position, the female servant working him in her mouth. Rand would be blindfolded, so he wouldn't know if the mouth was male or female, except by guessing. Since a cock could care less when it came to the tactile stuff, it would be ramrod straight, the knob slick and gleaming as she sucked and polished, went all the way down, earning a strangled groan from him.

Would the words come from his lips the way they did Jessica's now, a whispered supplication?

"Master...let me please you."

Jessica was blindfolded, too, so her Master's gaze was on her mouth, her parted lips, tongue touching them. Did the movement show that she wanted her Master's cock, even more than she wanted the orgasm she was so perilously close to experiencing? Cai expected it did. What Master could resist that?

Lyssa sat quietly in a basket swing, her feet swaying an inch or two above the ground. Jacob stood behind her. Close, because she had her hand behind her back. From the rhythmic movement of her arm, Cai was pretty sure she had threaded her hand through the open spaces of the swing and was working him with a healthy grip. Jacob had his palm molded on the top of the swing, the fingers of his other hand curled in a near fist around the chain holding it.

That fist said he wanted to touch her, to take her down. When Lyssa tipped her head back to look at him, his hot eyes said the same. His mind was probably being even more insistent about it.

Yeah, having an alpha servant was like a constant drug.

Cai hadn't intended to linger, but he rested on his heels in his hidden position, all his vampire carnality on full, appreciative alert. He was sure the others were aware of him, but it was apparently okay to watch.

He really might get into this, in time. And Rand? Rand was a guy like any other. He'd said it himself. He wanted to please Cai. It turned him on, which was the key to all of this, wasn't it? It was the lack of choice which had caused Cai a problem, but if they both were into it, it might be all right. Cai just didn't want anyone telling him what to do, with his servant or anything else.

Torrence joined the action now. After unwrapping the kilt he wore, he shrugged out of the shirt. He looked as virile and powerful as Rand, which Cai sure as hell could appreciate. Reaching down, he grasped Shondra's hips and pulled her up into a near head stand. Flexible minx, because her mouth remained on Jessica's cunt, though a cry broke from her lips as Torrence shoved his cock inside her obviously slippery pussy. Her bent knees pressed against his forearms, pointed toes past his elbows, swaying as Torrence thrust into her, pushing her face deeper into Jessica's core.

Penthouse letters had nothing on this. Cai put his hand on his cock and idly stroked it over his slacks. He wanted Rand here, fiercely, but he kept that thought to himself. Let the guy eat, hang out in the kitchen, do normal things.

Mason rose. He squatted above Jessica's head and put two fingers in between her lips, hooking there to hold her head tipped back. He removed the blindfold so her eyes could be upon him, as his thumb stroked her full bottom lip. "Now," he said.

Jessica's body shuddered violently, and she screamed against his hand as the climax grabbed her. Her head arched back further, her neck offered to her Master. Her skin flushed like a rose in the garden.

The command to come had likewise been given to the other two, so Cai had the pleasure of seeing that accrued energy surge into an explosive release. Shondra's nails raked Jessica's thighs. Torrence's head fell back on his shoulders, animal grunts coming from his throat. His ass and thighs flexed as he pounded into Shondra.

The circle was complete. The vampires had commanded their servants to satisfy them with a riveting erotic choreography that held Cai. But that wasn't the end of it.

Torrence lifted Shondra in his arms and returned her to her Mistress, sitting her on Carola's lap. Shondra's vampire mistress cuddled her like a child. Except her legs parted so that Carola could slide two fingers into her to play, make her whimper with need. Torrence returned to kneel at Helga's feet, lay his head on her thighs. His face was turned toward her, as if his Mistress was rewarding him with the scent of her pussy. Letting him know how much he'd aroused her, and what she might let him taste before too much longer.

And Mason and Jessica... As the young woman finished her climax, she lifted a trembling arm to his face, curling her fingers in the thick tail of hair that had fallen forward over his broad shoulder. He cradled her under her shoulders, brought her up to him so their mouths met, and then she dropped her head back again, so he could sink his fangs into her throat.

This was the vampire form of a pack, Cai realized. That total, immutable bond between Master and servant.

Something deeper and harder than Cai's cock was being affected by the scene. It was...intimate. He thought of the time he'd woken from his daylight sleep and Rand had been curled up on top of the mounded earth. Guarding him. Watching over him. Or maybe simply staying close.

Fuck. Cai adjusted his unthinking dick into a more comfortable position, blanked his mind and exited the gardens. He cornered the first house servant he encountered, and figured out where Lord Brian was.

It was a brief, cursory visit, where he annoyed the vampire by cutting off most his questions about shifters, but he was older than Brian, so screw him. Rand could handle his Q&A.

Brian gave him the item that Lyssa had mentioned. His new fang. Brian had put it in a small, flat box, but when he offered to open it, do a fitting, Cai offered a short thanks and pocketed it without looking at it. Instead, he asked Brian to tell him about the separation process between Master and servant. After Brian complied, Cai donated the blood needed to make it happen, and took off. He'd kept it as short as possible, but by the time he left the scientist's lab, just that short conversation about breaking the bond had something about to explode in his chest.

He stopped in the hallway, staring sightlessly at the wall. Why had he done all that without Rand? But even as he asked himself the question, he knew why, with a sinking feeling attended by the same spiraling anxiety as his earlier near panic attack. Which he refused to call a panic attack.

Some part of him had intended to go back to their rooms, wait for Rand. They'd leave together, maybe find the nearest quiet stretch of woods and fuck. Even before seeing that little display of the Council servants, Cai had wanted his wolf. Hell, he felt that way all the time.

They'd go to the desert, or just go back to West Virginia, hang for a while. That'd be the easy way, wouldn't it? Let it run its course, and Cai could enjoy it as long as it lasted. No decisions.

But maybe for the first time in his life, he needed to be an asshole for the right reasons. Rand cared about him, considered him part of "his pack," because that was how wolves were wired and they'd been through life-and-death shit together. He'd seen inside Cai's soul, knew he was fucked up. He needed Rand, and Rand had picked up on it.

But Cai had more perspective on this. About a couple centuries of it. Just because Cai needed the shifter didn't mean he should have him. Or that Rand should be sentenced to him. And the longer they stayed together, the more chances he could fuck up Rand's head over it so the shifter would end up back in that desolate, isolated space. There was nothing desolate or isolated about Fane's family, the pack of warm and loving shifters. Cai didn't even think it caustically. Family was what every soul not damaged beyond repair longed to have.

Time to shit or get off the pot. It was abrupt and rude, but he had to go. Go now. It might be chickenshit, but he'd leave Rand a note. Not because Cai wanted to be cruel, but because...in person, he wouldn't have the courage to do it. He was glad Rand couldn't put together his feeling-thought stuff when Cai out of his sight. At least that was what he told himself.

Just as Rand had given Cai a different way of seeing things again, Cai knew—though mostly by luck rather than intent—he'd helped Rand find his way to a better place in his head. A place that would want to be part of a pack again. Without Cai, Rand would go back to Fane and his family. Rebuild his life with them. Find a home.

Cai would go back to his forest haunts, though right now it was the desert calling to him. He didn't want to be on forest trails where he could imagine wolves padding along in the dark of night, blue-gold eyes glowing...

He'd learned a long time ago that when something crappy had to be done, he made the decision and did it, no thinking further about it.

So he procured paper and pen from yet another oh-so-helpful servant, and scribbled out what he needed to say. Didn't think about it, make it mushy or sentimental or any of that shit. Leastwise, he tried to do it that way. The more he wrote, the harder it got to draw a breath.

Why was it vampires didn't need to breathe except when they were feeling shit, and then it was like they were strangling? Just like that night Rand freaking spooned with him. How many times had Cai had that gorgeous ass, and yet *that* was what stuck in his head now? It was messed up.

Cai finished the note, handed it off to the same servant and told her where to deliver it. This was Council headquarters. If a vampire told a human to do something, it would be done. Just in case, he gave her a hard look, squeezed her hand holding the note. Her startled expression and proportionate increase in deference, which had already been gratingly excessive, said Rand would get the note.

That was that. He had the clothes on his back. He could have requested a new pack of basics from the house staff, he was sure, but he'd rather just pick up his own stuff. He even left the jeans and shirt Fane's family had provided, so Rand could return those. But he did keep the pocket knife.

Cai headed out of the mansion. As he reached the forest edge, those feelings started to grow stronger again. Lust, need, loneliness, regret, guilt...Rand. Just Rand. Rand was a bunch of feelings, all wrapped up in one word.

Fuck it. Cai abandoned his cool, nonchalant stride and took off, running for the shelter the trees and darkness provided. And kept running.

Long past when he thought he'd slow down, something in him said no. He'd just run and run and run, until he was too tired to do otherwise. Or until the sun broke over the horizon and the earth called him into its embrace.

CHAPTER TWENTY-TWO

Two Weeks Later

*R*and paused, scenting the wind. He looked down the slope of the hill, to where the younger wolves were currently pulling apart and devouring the deer that he, Fane and Stalker had brought down. They had a second one, untouched, they'd bring home, to store the meat the way a human would. Another of the many ways they smoothly straddled two different worlds.

They had a good setup here. A good life.

He was miserable.

He shouldn't be, damn it. Cai's note had been clear. They were friends, brothers-in-arms, if ever he had need of him, he'd be there for him. It was similar to what Cai had said when he'd figured out the infinity mark on Rand's wrist. He'd even drawn a simple replica at the top of the note, a reminder to Rand.

The vampire had finished up the note with some stuff like how maybe their paths would cross again soon. Blah blah blah. If all that was true, the bastard would have told him that in person, clapped him on the back, indulged one more intense fuck and been on his way. He'd literally fled after that dinner. A dinner where the guy who was as emotionally repressed as a brick wall had put everything out there for all to see. For Rand.

Rand had wanted to go after him, soon as he received the note, but he'd thought it through and hadn't. Because everything Cai had said, whether it was bullshit on his side of things or not, could very likely be true for Rand.

These were his people. No question. The ache over Sheba and Dylef and the pups would never be gone. It would hit him hard when he least expected it, and those nightmares would come and go, forcing him to relive it. But during his time with Cai, it had lessened enough that his self-destructive urges couldn't take the upper hand, and he could feel good things about life again. Thanks to Cai, Rand could be part of a pack again.

His leg was still giving him trouble. Which meant him hunting in a pack wasn't a bad thing, since he doubted he could have caught the deer on his own over open ground. Fane and Stalker had handled the running and directing. Rand had trailed behind—just behind, but still behind—until the kill point, and then Rand had jumped in.

He'd agreed to the X-rays Sangra recommended and meeting with her alternative healing contacts, but he'd anticipated the outcome. None of them had direct experience with what they diagnosed as the problem. An injury infected with strong magic needed to be healed by a magical healer who understood that specific kind of magic

The limp wasn't bad, and he managed to pull his weight just fine in the pack, so he asked Sangra to let it be, for now. Even with the handicap, he was considered the next beta in line behind Stalker. At full strength, he would have stepped into the role of Fane's top beta with no objections from Fane's son. They all knew he was really an alpha being a polite pack member.

But this worked. He had no problem deferring to Fane or Stalker. He trusted their judgment. Rand didn't have to be chief, but he could be if needed, his injury notwithstanding. That knowledge brought Fane peace. Though they'd crafted a pretty safe world here, and were growing a strong pack, Fane only had to look as far as Rand's experience to know it was important to be prepared for the worst to happen.

With Rand present, Fane's pack now had backup if something happened to Fane, and Stalker needed the mature guidance of an older male. Or even during the times that were more mundane, like Fane being gone on temporary trips with Chad, who worked together with him on his lucrative carpentry business.

But in his heart, Rand knew he was padding. Overall, their world was decently secure, well connected to the human one where those threads were needed. Stalker was almost equal to Fane in strength. Todd, Cilya and Sangra more than pulled their weight, and the teenagers were only a few years out from being able to contribute in their own way to the pack's overall strength.

But function wasn't all that a pack was about. It was also about family, and wolves loved a big family. He was accepted with no qualms. They knew girls weren't his thing and no one commented on it. Not ignored, like they didn't want to talk about it. It simply was, and nothing needed to be said.

He wasn't a monk. He would need male company in time, but he could drive to the nearest town, where there were plenty of opportunities for hook-ups.

An idea which made him nauseous. He needed that male company now, but he didn't want "male company." He wanted one particular male. One excessively foul-mouthed, cynical, sarcastic, strangely honorable, foolishly brave and touchingly vulnerable at unexpected moments, male. A male whose commanding touch he craved, even as he felt the desire to hunt him down to stay close, protect him from his worst enemy—himself. They had that in common, didn't they? They both needed the occasional reminder to pull their heads out of their asses.

Ever since Cai had left, Rand had to tamp down an anxious pulling in his gut, like Rand wasn't where he needed to be, with the person he needed to be with.

That could easily be explained by biology. In his note, Cai had told him he'd left Brian what was needed to end the marking. After Rand read the note, he sat there for a while, quelling the desire to search the grounds—as Cai might say—like Lassie frantically trying to figure out where Timmy had fallen down the well. After a time, he'd left his room with its smell of Cai in the bed linens, and gone to find Lord Brian.

Rand's mind went back to that last night at the mansion, to that conversation and his decision. Which would have been unexpected, except...it really wasn't, was it?

~

"We still don't have many of these requests, but it must be requested by the vampire," Lord Brian said. He frowned. "Cai left direction that it would be done, if it was *your* wish. That he was indifferent to the decision. Which is rather unorthodox and suggests the exact opposite to me. While the nature of that lies between the two of you, a bond remaining between a separated vampire and servant can be problematic, especially where the servant's memory of the bond is not going to be blocked. It requires Council approval. I spoke to Lady Lyssa."

That caused a spurt of uneasiness in Rand, especially when Brian paused, as if considering what was appropriate to say to a servant.

"She told me that due to Cai's youth and his relative unimportance, requiring the separation is not as critical to the Council as it would be normally." Brian shook his head as Rand scowled. "I'm not insulting your Master. She meant he isn't a highly placed overlord or one whose servant's unsupervised connection could make the vampire world more vulnerable. The memory block is not required for you because you're not human. You understand the gravity of revealing the nature of beings that humans convince themselves don't exist."

Translation: If you rat on us, we rat on you. It wasn't said that explicitly or unkindly. More a sensible practicality Rand understood. Unwittingly, Brian had also confirmed that they didn't suspect Cai's magical abilities. If they had known about that, particularly the fertility angle, Rand expected Cai's political importance would have skyrocketed.

"So the decision remains with you," Brian continued. "There are complications, if you're not having the mark removed and you and your Master won't be together. The mark creates a magnetism, if you will, between the vampire and servant. When separated, you'll experience an anxiety, in greater or lesser amounts, depending on your personality or environmental stressors. Over time, you can learn to manage it, but it will be uncomfortable at first."

Rand considered. "Does he experience it?"

Brian hesitated. Debra's head lifted from her microscope at the question, her gaze on her Master unfathomable. "Vampires experience it to a lesser degree, for the most part," Brian said. "Particularly if they view the bond as more functional. But if they have grown attached to their servant, yes, they will experience it."

Rand frowned. "How can you tell what's from the marking, and what's simply missing each other?"

Debra suppressed a smile. Brian cast her a wry but fond look and lifted a shoulder. "I deal in science. The realm of the heart is a powerful but completely unquantifiable measurement. I leave that answer to your own speculation. But thank you for the reminder that science can never cover all the variables."

"One day, with the right brilliant mind, it just might," Debra pointed out, letting her smile show. Brian snorted.

"Time will tell," he said. "But if I had to guess which scientist here would figure out the universal equation, I would have to defer to my servant's intelligence...and female intuition. It has often progressed our work in ways I didn't expect."

Debra flushed and shook her head at him before returning to what she was doing. Brian looked at Rand. "So, do you wish the mark removed?" He lifted a generous vial of blood. "Cai left this to facilitate things. We've made improvements to the process recently where we create a profile from his blood and your physiology to determine how to tailor the separation serum more closely to your bond. I just need to know if you want us to begin, since that procedure is fairly labor-intensive."

Rand knew the smart thing to do. What did it matter? Cai could always mark him again, right? If their paths crossed in the future, and things were different, and they both wanted... Though that time it would stay permanent, because it was clear this procedure was a rare and by Council-approval type thing. They didn't do it like returns at Walmart.

He'd thought about it ever since reading Cai's note. Waffled on the way here. Thought about all the variables, even during Brian's explanation. But when it came down to it, Rand trusted his wolf more than he trusted his human side. So he asked that part of his heart, and the wolf's answer came without hesitation.

"Thanks," he said. "But I want to keep the marks. Um...can I have the blood, if you're not going to use it?"

With a neutral look, Brian handed it over. "Thanks." Rand nodded. "I'll be leaving shortly. Is there anything...do I need to sign out?"

Brian's lips twitched. "No. If your Master has already departed, then your business here is concluded. Do you have transportation to where you're going?"

"Yes." He'd probably take the offered limo ride to get back to the national park in West Virginia. Convenience and all. If he didn't decide to track Cai down, damn it all. "Thanks."

Rand held out a hand, before he realized that vampires and servants might not shake hands. But Brian took his hand in an easy, strong grip.

"Good luck, Rand. And thank you for answering my earlier questions about shifters. I have plenty more, so if you ever feel like it, I'd like the opportunity to continue our discussion."

He'd answered some of Brian's high-level questions, but hadn't gone more in-depth. Until he'd shown up, vampires had thought wolf-shifters were myth. Lyssa had mentioned an improvement in Fae relations. There were Fae, deep forest dwellers, who walked between earth and their own world and knew of the small enclaves of shifters. But knowing the suspicion and dislike the Fae had felt toward vampires until apparently recently, Rand doubted they'd be volunteering that awareness. Maybe it was best to keep it that way for now. He didn't feel comfortable taking it upon himself to enlighten the vampire race about his own.

"Okay." Rand nodded courteously to Debra and headed for the door. However, he paused at the threshold. "If it's okay to ask, what did you have for him? Lyssa said you needed to give Cai something."

"The prosthetic fang," Brian responded. "It had a permanent adhesive to hold it in place, almost as securely as a rooted fang. I offered to install it, since it's easier to have someone else do it, but he declined. He took it with him, however."

"The fang was designed by a dentist who works with our kind," Debra said, an intriguing twinkle in her eyes. "He's an artist, of sorts. Kibler personalized the fang with an emblem very appropriate to your Master's...personality."

"There's a skull-and-crossbones etching on the widest part," Brian offered.

Despite the heavy weight in his chest and gut that hadn't abated, Rand felt a slow smile cross his face. "Cai will like that. I'm sure he appreciated the fang...even if he didn't say so."

Brian's expression sobered, his intelligent gaze suggesting he understood a lot more about the situation Rand was facing than he was saying. Debra's even more so, and with enough sympathy to tell

Rand he needed to take off before he embarrassed himself. He gave them one more nod and took his leave.

His intent was to get back to the room, collect his small bundle of belongings and go...somewhere. He wanted to go after Cai, wanted to make the hard pounding in his heart, head and loins stop. But every word of Cai's note had been as subtle as a sledgehammer on a railroad spike.

Rand needed to think, even if his wolf didn't want to think at all. Just wanted to track. He'd find where Cai had gone to earth, because they weren't too far off from dawn. He'd lay on top of that mound of earth, until...

Back in their room, Rand sighed and laid down on the bed, on Cai's spot. There was no one to see, anyway, and he couldn't feel Cai in his mind. Which didn't mean he wasn't, but he knew Cai well enough to believe the vampire had closed himself off, at least for now. Emotionally suppressed asshole.

Rand uncapped the vial and closed his eyes at the scent of the blood. Until Cai, blood had been what he associated with prey. But Cai's blood was different. It was an offering, a reminder of the bond between them. Rand put it to his lips and downed the few meager swallows. His fist clutched the vial as he savored the taste.

Cai had said it before. They really hadn't known one another long, and there was a hell of a lot of things they still didn't know about one another. But for wolves, relationships were built differently. Non-shifter wolves only lived ten to fifteen years in the wild, on average. So when they mated, that connection had to happen far more immediately than was required by a longer expected lifespan.

While shifters lived to a human old age, they had that same trait. Usually the first impression was all that was needed to figure out the shape of another's heart and soul. From what he'd learned during his short time at Fane's, Sangra and Idris had been married within a month of meeting one another. Todd had known upon his first meet with Zelda, though Zelda, being human, had needed longer to make up her mind. He and Dylef, Sheba and Sylvan, Lynn and Fane...they all had similar courtship stories.

Rand had had a lot of his own shit to deal with when he and Cai met. It had interfered with what he really thought of the vampire, that first key scent-and-soul impression, but his instincts had won out.

Every time his human side had suggested he needed to get rid of the vampire's company as soon as possible, his wolf had stuck. Even followed him into hell.

So why wasn't he following him now? Rand turned his face into the pillow, inhaling deep. Maybe because he couldn't give straight answers to the questions Cai's note raised. Even if he had bonded with Cai, could Rand handle being without other shifters, not part of their pack and what they gave to his soul?

He sighed. Time to go. He'd figure out the answers along the way.

As he put the nice clothes Jacob had said he could keep in a backpack Lyssa's servant had provided, Rand's gaze kept returning to the pillow. Maybe Cai had been a bad influence on him, but the hell with it. Rand stripped the case, folded it up and tucked it into the pack with the rest of his clothes. He had the secondhand jeans and shirt Cai had worn but left behind. However, Fane's scent was too strong upon them, interfering with Cai's.

The actual pillow would hold Cai's scent even longer, but Rand couldn't fit that in the pack, and he was pretty sure walking out with it might be frowned upon. *Add that pillow to Mr. Rand's bill...did we get a credit card from him at check-in? No? Just take a few extra pints from him as payment, then.*

His weak sense of humor was even picking up Cai's cadence. It made the aching worse.

Rand read the letter again, then slid it into the folds of the pillow case. He dialed command central for the house servants, wherever that was, and learned the limo and driver were standing by and could be ready to go in a few minutes. Good. And bad. It was too much like a sign.

Shouldering the pack, Rand looked around the room, took one last deep breath and left it. He nodded courteously to the few staff members he encountered as he reached the top of the stairs and moved through the house. He stopped himself from assigning meaning to their speculative looks. A servant whose vampire had left without him...

But he had that third mark bond. He was keeping it, God knew why. Maybe he'd regret it in a few days, but he had plenty of regrets. He had room for one more.

As he stepped out the front door, he saw Jacob leaning against the limo, a large brown paper sack sitting next to him on the back trunk. Bran, the Irish wolfhound, lay nearby. At the sight of Rand, his lip curled, but Jacob spoke a word and he subsided, his head thumping down on his paws in belligerent acquiescence.

Rand came down the steps. Jacob handed him the bag.

"Some food for the road. From the weight of it, you made quite an impression on the house staff. You're welcome to reach out to us again if you have need of us." Jacob's eyes showed amusement as he glanced toward Bran. "You'll be welcomed by my Mistress, even if the dogs don't agree. As you probably picked up last night, good relations between different species has recently become a higher priority to the Council."

With dwindling numbers, their allies were few in a dangerous world. Rand got that. Having a pack brought a sense of safety, of balance.

"My brother respects you and would feel the same, if you cross paths again," Jacob added. "I know he's sorry he killed Cai's friend. Things have changed a lot for him since he bonded with Daegan and Anwyn."

Life was like that. Made up of love and loss, and wisdom often so hard-earned it rode hand-in-hand with guilt, regret and nightmares.

"Rand." Jacob had put a hand on his shoulder. The contact was welcome. Too welcome.

"He just left. Left me a goddamn note."

Rand bit back the words too late. But the servant merely nodded, more understanding in his face than Rand could handle. Just like Debra.

"Vampires aren't different from any other humanoid species when it comes to relationships. They think they're above it all, but they aren't. They're just blessed with an overabundance of the control freak gene. Which means when they care, they're not only overprotective. They think they know every damn thing that's best for you. You have to push back sometime. And push back hard."

The personal note of resolve in Jacob's voice told Rand he'd had to do that with his own Mistress. A formidable challenge Rand was sure had been volatile and intriguing to watch.

"I'm not sure if that's what was driving him." Rand sighed. "And he may be right about some of it. I have to think."

"Did you keep the mark?"

Rand nodded. "I did."

Satisfaction flared in Jacob's gaze. "I was pretty sure you would. So go think. You'll be able to find him if you want him. But if you need help, my brother and Daegan won't mind taking a break to track his ass down. They're the best trackers there are."

Rand felt an easing in his chest. It didn't eliminate all the stuff churning in him, but it did give him some breathing room.

"Not the best trackers," he corrected. "But decent for a vampire and a human servant."

Jacob grinned and opened the limo door for him. Rand got in, taking the food and his pack.

When the driver pulled out, Rand dropped his head back on the seat and closed his eyes. He didn't want to think about how every mile passing under the wheels was taking him farther from Cai.

You'll be able to find him if you want him.

Want wasn't the problem. All the emptiness inside of him was filled with raw, aching want.

～

Returning to the present, Rand glanced over his shoulder as Fane joined him. The male was back in human form, which was curious, since they often didn't do that until they were close to the house. Fane took a seat next to him, joining Rand in watching the younger shifters feed.

"What do you think you're waiting for?" Fane asked at last.

Rand shot him a surprised look, and Fane shook his head. "Losing Sheba, Dylef and your children that way, it hurt something deep inside. Broke it. No wolf stays alone as long as you did when the hurt isn't grievous. You're a noble male, a strong leader. I don't claim to understand your attachment to the vampire, but maybe...there are so few wolves like you, preferring your same gender..."

Fane shifted uncomfortably. Rand offered a panting grin and sidled closer to him. Fane snorted and shoved at him. "Yeah, yeah. Make fun of the straight guy awkwardness. Have pity." He sobered. "What I'm saying is maybe the two of you were meant to be. You seem to fit together, in some hard-to-explain way. I think...he needs you."

Fane firmed his lips and nodded to himself, reflecting his certainty that he'd chosen the right words. "And you need him. You said he left without saying good-bye in person. That's what someone does when saying good-bye is going to be too hard. Doesn't sound like a guy who doesn't want to be with you, does it?"

Rand huffed a sigh and laid down, putting his head on Fane's thigh. Fane stroked his ruff, wrapping his arms over him and giving him a light bite on the nape. "We are brothers always. Go and find him. No bullshit about him being gone. You're blood-linked, which I know you told me he can shut down to make it harder to find him, but you're not human. You've got a nose and you're the best tracker I've ever met."

Rand said nothing and Fane heaved a sigh. "Fine. Cilya networks with pretty much every female shifter, coast to coast. You wait much longer to deal with this, I'll tell her to send out a blast that you're on the market. With pictures. They'll arrive in droves, bringing their best meat pies and fried chicken. I won't have to worry about feeding my own brood for weeks. Plus, I get to watch you squirm under their attentions and try to be polite."

Fane laughed when Rand wriggled free and tackled him. As they rolled, Fane shifted back to his gray and brown wolf. Rand pinned him then jumped back, letting Fane spring up and pounce, with an impressively ferocious sound that was all show. They continued to wrestle, tumbling down the hill toward the younglings. Having finished their meal, they were more than ready to join in the fun when they saw it happening.

Rand participated in the play, but Fane's thoughts had watered what was already well on its way to being a firmly planted tree. Or, since it was caused by Cai, a weed-like, invasive species. Rand felt a spurt of wry humor.

Either way...Fane was right. And because Rand realized that, the urgency that Brian said could be chemical, and Debra's smile said could be something else, seemed to triple inside of him. It wasn't long before Rand broke off from the play and headed back to the house at a lope. It was time to go find his other pack.

~

He gathered some things together, hiked back out to civilization, and hitched a ride on the rural highway. It would lead to one of the towns where he kept a cache of human necessities in a storage facility. Riding in the back of the rattling pickup truck gave him time to think about the best strategy for finding Cai.

He'd kept the vial, even after he'd emptied it, so he had that scent. He also still had the pillow case. Slept with it under his own pillow. Since Lynn could ferret out any hidden laundry, Rand had had to tell her to leave it unwashed, and suffer the unmanly flush summoned by her knowing look.

Did Cai know he slept with it? He'd wondered how much of his mind Cai had tapped. Unlike Rand, who could only wonder what the vampire was doing, Cai could check in anytime, until he was a few thousand miles away.

Rand had a bad moment, thinking of that possibility. For two weeks, there'd been nothing but silence in his head. He'd expected Cai to eventually speak to him, just a deceptively casual reaching out, but nothing. Not even a random flash of emotion. Cai had done the vampire equivalent of shutting off his cell phone.

Rand had attempted more than once to reach out himself.

I want to come see you, talk to you.

You promised me a trip to the desert.

Where are you? Are you really going to make me track you?

If you really meant that "we can still be friends" bullshit, you wouldn't be acting like this.

Asshole.

Nothing.

Cai would know Rand hadn't had the mark removed. What had he thought of that?

Yeah, Rand could track him. It would take time. There were about a million acres of forestland where he might be. Like Rand, Cai preferred the wild spaces. Or maybe Cai had planted himself in the middle of a human population somewhere, the way he'd distanced himself from the Trads when he left their ranks. It irritated Rand to think that Cai would use the same tactics to avoid him he'd used to avoid Goddard.

But there were other reasons Cai would do it. He would need human blood. He might go with the camper or hiker routine, but Rand had a feeling—hopefully not wishful thinking—that Cai might not revert to killing on a routine basis again, particularly if he was staying in more populated areas. Which meant he'd need wider and more frequent access to humans, to secure that "milk cow" approach to feeding.

He'd said his compulsion skills weren't highly developed, but with his looks, he wouldn't need magic to attract prey. That thought brought a snarl to Rand's lips, unfortunately timed, since at that point he was in a mini-mart and startled the clerk.

But that was when another idea hit him. Which would work, as long as Cai truly wasn't out of range. A good hunter knew when to track prey, and when to bait a trap. Thinking of all the things he knew about vampires in general, and this specific vampire, one sprang to mind in front of all the others.

Cai had vulnerable moments when he'd let Rand take the upper hand. But his core was vampire, which could make itself known in sudden, dangerous and pleasing ways. Dominance was an integral part of him. Possessiveness. And Rand *was* his servant. No matter that Cai had presumably let him go, Rand thought the emotions provoked by that bond weren't easily set aside.

A gay bar for a casual-hook up wouldn't be enough. He knew exactly where he was going to go. To a BDSM club. And not just any club. He would head for Atlanta. If he let his mind drift into some interesting areas, revealing some of his plans, though not the underlying strategy... If he could keep his thoughts high level and somewhat vampire proof, he maybe could draw Cai to him. Even if Cai was geographically far off, maybe that would get him headed in Rand's direction. So Rand wouldn't actually have to go all the way through with the plan he was concocting.

But if he had to, he would.

After the mini-mart stop for gas, the driver of his hitched ride dropped Rand off near the storage units where Rand kept clothing, a small box of personal memorabilia, and an old Honda motorcycle in running condition. When Rand swung his leg over it and started it up, he liked the humming vibration it sent through his whole body, as if he were a live wire.

It was what he felt like, the whole time he rode to Atlanta. Once close enough to the city, he checked into a hotel that backed up to a forest and used the room phone to call Club Atlantis.

Despite his short stay at the Council's Savannah headquarters, there'd been time to pick up some interesting tidbits of servant talk. Like how Anwyn ran a BDSM club, and that was where she and Gideon lived. Daegan as well, Rand assumed, when he wasn't traveling on Council business.

"May I speak to Anwyn? Yes, ma'am. My name is Rand. She met me recently."

It only took a moment for the phone to transfer and Anwyn to answer. He remembered her sultry voice, the Mistress quality sending a shiver down his spine. Not because he wanted a Mistress, but because it reminded him of Cai when he was in that Dominant mode.

"Rand?" she said, her tone torn between frost and courtesy. His vampire had tried to kill her servant, and though she knew Rand was a different animal—no pun intended—it would still make her wary. "Why are you calling?"

No friendly chitchat. He could handle that. "Yes, ma'am. I have a problem, and I thought you could help me. You heard that we uh, took care of the problem with the girl?"

"I did." Her voice warmed slightly. "Gideon told me that you and Cai worked well with him and Daegan...when it mattered. Which means I should forgive him. I might, sometime in the next several centuries. Is he with you? Can I interest him in a forced demonstration of an anal probe?"

Rand choked on a chuckle, feeling a little more at ease. She was feisty, like Sheba.

"Uh, he's not. But that's why I need help. I...um, I'm new to all this, but here's what I'm trying to do. First, I need some expert advice to know if it's a crazy idea. Second, some more advice, to know how to pull it off."

He explained the details, more than a little relieved that he could do it over the phone rather than face to face.

He wasn't sure how to interpret the long pause until she spoke. "Oh, hell yeah," she said mildly. "He might not be listening in, but if he really didn't want to give up the connection, I'd bet good money he stays tied in to your state of mind. If you go down the road you're laying out, you'll get his attention. But are you willing to take this all the way?"

"I want to take it as far as I need to get an answer, one way or another. So, if I get nothing...I guess I'll have my answer." His gut tightened unpleasantly at the thought. "I can handle seeing it through if that happens. Hell, it won't really matter then, will it? It'll just be sex with a stranger, which is what I'd eventually do anyway, if he's really done with us."

"Men are such idiots." She sighed. "If he'd left you a cell phone number, this wouldn't be necessary."

"Well, doing it this way is kind of like a rom-com," Rand said. "With a bondage twist."

He was channeling Cai again. Anwyn chuckled. "All right. Let's set up a night and time, and I'll put the details in place. I just need to ask you a few more questions..."

She'd asked him a lot more questions, many of which had him blushing even harder than he had with Lynn and his pillow case. Anwyn's Mistress side came through more strongly during the interrogation. It ran even deeper than the vampire part of her, if that was possible. But since she owned and operated a BDSM club, and had apparently identified as a Domme well before she was turned, he guessed that made sense.

The date and time set, he turned to the other things on his to-do list. Over the next couple days, he went out and splurged some of his carefully saved money. He bought a new pair of jeans and a good after-shave. A better quality razor.

The night he was going to go to the club, he donned the silk and cotton maroon shirt he'd worn for the Council meeting. The fabric lay like a thin, soft fur against his flesh. His stressed jeans had the right kind of fit on his lower body. He had the frayed cuffs pulled down over his motorcycle boots.

When he was human, he pretty much always had stubble, even if he shaved twice a day, so he shaved a third time. He'd visited the barber, so his long hair was brushed and trimmed.

It lay in waves on his shoulders, though the wolf in him still gave the texture some coarseness. He didn't want to be taken for a model in one of those girly shiny hair commercials. But looking in the mirror, he admitted it looked thick, touchable, and Cai really liked tangling his fingers in it. That was what mattered.

He took a cab to the club, so he wouldn't mess it up with a motor-cycle helmet. He was amused that he had an army of frogs in combat boots marching through his stomach. Thank God Anwyn had handled his follow-up vetting with another phone call last night, bypassing all the orientation stuff. Rand knew what to expect, mostly, and what was expected of him.

As he recalled parts of the conversation, his slightly damp palms curled on his splayed knees.

~

"When you get to the club, you'll be on the guest list. Go to the bar, order a nonalcoholic drink and hydrate well. You'll know the Dom I've assigned to you when you see him. I decided the best way to do this is with one of my staff."

Her cryptic tone gave him a spurt of anxiety, but not necessarily the bad kind. "Did you tell him I'm trying to bait a vampire?" Rand asked wryly.

She chuckled. "There's only one human staff member here, other than Gideon, who knows what I am, and that's my security head, James. He's second marked. But Wolf..." She paused. "I've told him you want to be pushed kind of hard, that's your thing. But if you say 'sunset,' he's to immediately stop what he's doing, and call off the session."

"Wolf?"

"That's his scene name. Worked out well, didn't it? Gideon appre-ciated the coincidence." She sounded amused. "And my safe word choice. But seriously, though Wolf's only been with us a short time, he's already one of my best. And if Cai *is* listening in, Wolf is exactly the kind of red flag you're seeking."

Another little spike, especially since she sounded a little too satis-fied with that thought. Rand cleared his throat. "What happens if I don't call off the session?"

"You'll get the workout of your life, and be very pleasurably and thoroughly spent. Wolf's not doing this as a staff member, so though he'll stay as conscious of your intentions as I'd expect him to do with a client, you'll be interacting as member and guest. If you don't call it off, he'll fuck your brains out. He's a plow horse and thoroughbred, all in one."

Rand felt his loins tighten and pushed that down. Damn third mark libido. Or maybe it was too many nights, missing and thinking of Cai. "Why would Wolf do this for nothing? Did he owe you a favor?"

She chuckled. "Not hardly. Even when they're on the clock, they go with their preferences. None of them fake it for money."

Her voice dropped to a purr. "Nothing gets Wolf going like the challenge of an alpha male. So when I told him no holds barred, and primal play accepted, he was all over that. And totally good with it being on his own time."

More dry throat, more clearing. "Great. I don't expect Cai to show in person, because he's probably not anywhere near Atlanta. But my hope is he'll open up in my head."

"Which accomplishes what you want."

"Hope so." Envisioning Cai appearing at the exact right moment was right in line with that rom-com illusion Rand had half-joked about, but the reality was a different matter. Having Cai show up was too much to want. It filled Rand up too hard.

They hadn't been apart more than a couple weeks, so it shouldn't seem so dramatic. However, if Cai came to Rand because of this, it would be a game-changer neither one could deny.

"Okay, unless you have any other questions, I'll see you tomorrow night," Anwyn finished. Rand hoped he hadn't missed something important, caught up in his own head.

"I'm good. But..." Rand paused. "I know Cai will probably never say he's sorry, but I wanted to say it for him. I think he understands why Gideon did the things he did to vampires. It's just...Lodell was his friend."

"I know. Gideon is my servant, and one half of my heart. Daegan is the other. It doesn't beat without either one of them." Her voice had an intriguing way of being warm, and yet resonating with authority. "So Cai and I will remain amicable enemies for a time. It doesn't mean I don't understand, or support your desire to reunite with your Master. You can trust me."

"I do. I just felt badly about how things were left."

"Ah." He could almost see her dismissive wave. "Vampires. We're never an easy bunch. Throw the Dom factor in with the egos and insane need for control, and a few bumps in the road happen. Don't worry over it, Rand." Her voice softened. "And don't be nervous about this. Wolf will take very good care of you. Or I'll put his superlative ass in a meat grinder."

So here he was. Rand paid the cab driver and entered the club. From the outside, Club Atlantis looked like many of the buildings in an industrial area. Big, box style, painted brick. Only a few scattered windows at the upper corners, all dark tinted glass. But the silver sign over the arched doorway, Club Atlantis, was classy and expensive-looking, and there was a glassed-in viewing room perched on the very top of the multi-storied building. Rand suspected it was a fancy pool area, something rentable for parties. Or maybe it was part of the private residence he assumed was below ground, since Anwyn and possibly Daegan lived on the premises.

Once inside, he was greeted by James, head of security for the club, instead of a hostess. The strong-looking male with short hair and steady eyes had the look of former special-ops or Secret Service. After James gave him a close once-over, he provided him a basic layout to the club and directions to the bar.

As Rand moved deeper into the club, a world of shadows, glitter, and people absorbed by one another in a variety of distracting ways, he had to block a lot of the input. He'd overlooked his lack of fondness for crowded human venues. It wasn't really crowded here, the layout one that provided plenty of opportunities for intimacy, even in the public spaces, but the scent feedback was overwhelming. He focused on the bar, pointing his feet there.

It was possible that Cai was keeping enough emotional distance to have only a peripheral sense of Rand's feelings. He might not even have an actual view of what Rand was doing. Now that he was here, Rand wasn't sure he could take it all the way. It wasn't just cold feet. If the Dom he was supposed to meet wanted to do a public scene, he wasn't sure how he'd handle that. He'd told Anwyn whatever it took... had he lost his mind?

He ordered a soda and consumed a bracing swallow. Using his one free hand, he rubbed his leg, an absent massage to ease the twinging the cramped cab ride had caused it. The thing kept flaring up at inopportune times, but Rand hoped tonight wasn't one of them.

Turning from the bar, he surveyed the lounge.

You'll know the Dom I've assigned to you when you see him. She might have missed on that one. There were a lot of males in here with the Dom vibe happening, and...

There he was. The male he was immediately, instantly sure was Wolf.

And suddenly, Rand wasn't sure of anything.

Aching for and craving Cai's touch for two weeks, remembering every single thing the male had done to him and made him do, had led to a lot of very uncomfortable nights and days, and a lot of jacking off. So much that Rand had reached that empty point where he hadn't had the heart to do it anymore. Even though his cock stayed in a semi-alert state, as if waiting to spring to full life at Cai's command.

Well, it was wide awake now.

Wolf was as big as Rand. He had polished charcoal skin, and muscles that rippled like an onyx statue, liquefied and come to life. His eyes were light-colored, almost silver when he turned his head and they caught the room's illumination. The firm line of his mouth enhanced the sternness of his carved, granite features.

But there was one quality that overrode all the others, became the ice cream substance to the sundae, while all the rest was chocolate sauce, whip cream and cherry.

Wolf was a vampire.

It made sense, so much damn sense. Anwyn's cryptic answers hadn't been evasive in the wrong way. Well, okay, there had been that note of female satisfaction underscoring the words *Wolf is exactly the kind of red flag you're seeking.*

But Rand had to hand it to her as a Domme—she'd apparently known holding back that vital tidbit of info would result in this flood of feeling inside him, strong enough to be like a beacon to another vampire, wherever he was.

She also knew that if Rand had interacted with a mere human, someone he wouldn't view on the same level as another shifter or a vampire, he couldn't let himself go as much. That wasn't going to be a problem now.

The wolf in Rand sat up and was ready to fight, the type of fighting that would mean blood, yes, and some pain, but that would all be part of the pleasure. He almost bared his teeth, feeling his beast surge to the forefront when Wolf locked gazes with him.

The male wore a pair of dark, shiny pants and boots. Nothing else. The pants were a second skin that were going to get a hell of a workout when he moved. The waistband was low, below his hipbones, so every abdominal muscle showed. Since the pants tucked into the boots, Rand saw the crop stuck in one of them. This Dom could do exactly what Anwyn had suggested. Fuck a sub's ever-loving brains out.

Wolf lifted a hand, crooked a finger at him and pointed to the floor at his feet. The light in his eyes said he knew exactly how Rand would respond to that. Rand didn't disappoint. Sitting down the drink, he presented his middle finger. Then he silently spoke two words, mouthed in best Cai-fashion.

Fuck. You.

CHAPTER TWENTY-THREE

*W*olf grinned like a lion about to tear apart his dinner. He jerked his head in the direction of the private rooms, turned and strode away. Rand was right. Those pants were getting a hell of a workout. His own cock was hard against his jeans, his muscles twitching with adrenaline. *Let's do this.*

If Cai didn't reach out, if Rand had to absorb the hurt, face the truth that he was facing loneliness again, then this would be a hell of a balm for it.

At least for tonight. Because as Rand well knew, good sex only lasted that long when it didn't offer anything to the heart. But he'd take it. Hell, Rand better get used to it, if Cai decided not to tune in ever again.

Warring with mixed emotions, he crossed the floor, and went into the room where Wolf had left the door standing open.

Spartan. Not much in there but a wrestling mat, some manacles on the wood floor, the attached chains draped from the ceiling. A padded bench was anchored close to them.

"Before the night is over," Wolf said, in a voice so deep the vibration resonated inside Rand's chest and—holy hell— made his nipples tighten, "I'll have your ass over that bench and be fucking you until you bleed."

Rand bared his teeth again. He bent and took off his boots, then surprised the male when he began to unbutton his shirt, shrugged out of it, and opened his jeans to remove them. He was way too aware of Wolf's scrutiny as he stripped himself to the skin.

"I fight better this way," Rand said, straightening, pleased his voice sounded just as steady. "How about you? Can you even breathe in those pants?"

Wolf knew the warrior code. Evenly matched, evenly weaponed. Though when he set aside the crop, removed his own boots and took off the pants, Rand rethought that. Holy mother of God. Cai would have said holy fucking mother of fucking God, fuck it all.

If Rand did get plowed with that thing, he hoped one of the items Wolf had close to hand was enough lube to grease a truck through a key hole. Wolf's white teeth flashed at his expression.

"Want to give up now, whelp?"

Wow. Anwyn might have prepared Wolf for Rand being "other," since obviously some vampires could pick up traces of what was humanoid but not human, but she wouldn't have let slip exactly what Rand was. Therefore, he had to conclude Wolf's choice of male insult was fortuitous chance. He also had to remind himself of something very important about the fight that was about to happen.

He had to lose.

Must. Lose. Must. Lose.

Rand snorted at Wolf's insult. "I think the weight of that thing might unbalance you. Want to tie it to your leg before we get started?"

Wolf chuckled, and he was in motion. Rand met him, barely remembering not to shift as he would in a fight with another shifter or creature who lived in a world where shifters, vampires and Fae were realities. But it was hard, because the wolf wanted badly to come to the top and take over.

He learned a couple things fast. Wolf was more than just an intimidating Dom and a big bastard. He was combat-trained. Rand was a good fighter himself, and had some training, but he relied a lot on experience and his strength. Wolf had matching strength but superior skill, and quickly gauged Rand's weaknesses. He started whittling away at them, taking over the fight. That was when the gloves really came off.

Rand's next punch brought blood, and the two males landed against the bench, nearly tearing it free from the floor. Rand briefly wondered what it would take for anyone to interfere with what was happening in here. He suspected only if Anwyn thought the property damage was tallying up too high. Since the bench was the only thing breakable, beyond the walls themselves, Rand figured all was good.

Wolf flung him back toward the mat. Rand rolled away, flipped and went in low, bowling the guy over at the legs.

Anwyn's wisdom increased Rand's debt to her. A human Dom might have had Wolf's combat training and a decent level of strength, but there was a difference between a man trained to be a predator and a male who actually was one. When his own instincts kicked in, Rand didn't have to rein it back the way he would have if Wolf was human. Rand could let all of it come out. The frustration, the need, the giant ball of emotions he'd been sitting on for weeks.

He did note that, no matter how dirty the fight was getting, the one thing Wolf wasn't taking advantage of was Rand's leg. Anwyn had pried that one out of him on her follow up call, when she'd insisted on knowing if he had any physical issues that should be considered. Since third marks were considered pretty invincible, he had to conclude Daegan or Gideon had given her the heads up about it.

Wolf wasn't holding back in any other way, so Rand didn't feel coddled. But he wanted to make damn sure of it.

He wrenched the guy's arm on the twist a little too enthusiastically and got a solid slam in the face with Wolf's elbow that had him seeing stars. Wolf flipped him in that split second of disorientation and had one of the manacles locked around his wrist. Rand whipped the free chain at him, but Wolf dodged, swept his legs and secured another manacle on his opposite leg. Then he was at the wall, drawing up the chains, limiting his mobility.

Rand yanked against the bonds hard enough to send a sprinkling of dust off the ceiling. Wolf's gaze swept over his taut body, all Rand's bunched muscles. "Fucking beautiful," the Dom murmured.

Stay human, stay human... But so much in Rand's head was wolf right now, calculating, studying. Except the erection that was big enough to split skin. It was all human.

Wolf closed in on him again. Though Rand put up a hell of a fight, he was now working with one free arm and leg, the other two limbs restricted by the shortness of the chains.

The vampire ducked under a blow, spun him toward the bench. With that incredible burst of speed that vampires had, he had Rand over the bench and his other arm and leg locked in manacles, but he wasn't done yet.

To hold him in place, Wolf tossed another crisscrossing of chains over his back and locked Rand's torso to the padded surface. In a couple more expert moves, he had Rand's arms spread out, pulled forward and down, the chains hooked to rings in the floor. Then he bound Rand's ankles to more bolts in the floor on the other side of the bench, keeping his thighs spread.

Wild animal panic speared through Rand, a reaction to being so quickly and securely restrained. He could fight the chains, break a couple. Or he could use the safe word he'd been given by Anwyn.

If he did, it would be over.

His human side might chicken out and do it, but the wolf wouldn't. The wolf didn't even know what a safe word was. To guarantee that he would see this through, Rand needed to let more of his mind go to the wolf.

The problem with letting his mind go to his wolf was his wolf didn't play the denial games with his head that his human side did. The wolf knew what he really wanted, and it wasn't in this room. Empty need and lust curled around something a lot more painful.

Which was aggravating, since Wolf was basically 100% fantasy material.

Well, hell, that was the point, right? Give himself to the fantasy, let every physical and emotional reaction loose, let it emanate from him like sonar waves. But if he did, his heart might crack in the process, those waves going flat before they reached anyone's radar. One particular person's radar.

"All right there?" Wolf murmured. The hand he had on the back of Rand's neck was suddenly a little less hard. He was in control. It had been primal play, Rand told himself. He didn't know all this stuff, but Anwyn had given him a BDSM 101 kind of thing. Primal play was a rough and violent—within certain limits—form of tussling. The way animals did it.

Proving that they were still working within a structure, Wolf had picked up on Rand's distress and checking in with him, helping him out. But not too much, because as Rand managed a jerky nod, Wolf gave him that diabolical grin again.

"Good. Because I *am* going to fuck your ass until you scream."

Reaction clutched inside of Rand when Wolf moved between his spread thighs, that giant dick making not-so-incidental contact with the inside of one. Up high.

"And I'm going to use your pretty, pretty mouth to lube me up," the Dom continued. "So you better do a very good job, else this will get a might uncomfortable. You'll be walking up on your toes for a week."

As he spoke, his hand trailed down Rand's back to his buttocks, and between his thighs to caress his balls. He did a brief side trip, running down Rand's injured leg, gauging the tension there. It was fine. Rand didn't want him focusing on that.

Wolf didn't concede the point until he seemed satisfied the binding wasn't causing the leg the wrong kind of distress. Then one finger played at Rand's rim with clever skill, making Rand writhe, his cock leak pre-come. *Get lost in the physical. Let it happen.*

"Look at all those fucking gorgeous muscles. Thought you about had me there, whelp. You're a hell of a fighter. With a little more training, you could have kicked my ass and our positions would be reversed. A little punishment for that first, I think. You're trapped in your head, aren't you? I can help you with that."

Moving back into Rand's view, Wolf sauntered over to another set of controls that rolled back a screen, revealing a wall full of very adult toys. The male pulled an Indiana Jones style whip from the offerings. In the same instant hard-on inspiring motion, he snapped his wrist and five feet of braided rawhide slithered and cracked, with a noise loud enough Rand felt it in his balls.

Can't do this. Will do this. Can't not do this...

Wolf moved in front of Rand and stroked a hand over his hair. Gathered it up only to release it, letting it spill forward over Rand's shoulders. Cai liked doing that, too. Rand closed his eyes, but then they snapped back open when Wolf took a handful of his hair and yanked his head up. His monstrous dick was only inches from Rand's flashing gaze. Before he could stop himself, Rand had licked his lips.

"Yeah, you can't help yourself," Wolf said in that ball-tightening voice. "But what gets me off is seeing how pissed you are, how much you'd like to be free and fighting me, at the exact same moment you're imagining sucking me off."

In one menacing note, Rand telegraphed the most creative curses

Cai could have dreamed up. Wolf's lips split in a dangerous smile. "Let's see how much more pissed off I can make you, whelp."

He coiled up the whip and left it lying in the small of Rand's back as he moved behind him. Footsteps, and the sound of another screen rolling back before Wolf returned, standing between Rand's knees.

Rand sucked in a breath as the male gripped his cock and balls with the confidence of long practice. He cinched them into some kind of tight harness. Really tight. Rand grunted as Wolf pulled it in another hole.

"Going to turn that bad boy blue. You aren't coming until I get my rocks off three times with you, at least." Retrieving the single tail and positioning himself in front of Rand, Wolf cocked his head, crossing his arms across his massive chest. "If you want me slick before I fuck your ass, you'll do two things. You'll use your mouth, as I said, and get me good and slippery. Do it well, and I'll be kind, add a nice spicy warming lube to your efforts that'll ease my way but keep the burn."

He held up two fingers. "Second, you'll ask me for the privilege, addressing me properly. "Let me suck your big dick. Master.""

Rand had another Cai-ism to answer that. Wolf's gaze lighted and he caressed the single tail he'd wrapped around his wrist and forearm and was clasping in his other big fist. "Just the answer I was hoping to get."

He circled behind Rand, and went to work. Cai had paddled him with a brush, used his bare hand on him. This was a burning sting that built in intensity, making Rand jerk and dance in his bonds, roar when the popper hit his balls, his tender inner thighs. The stinging sensation spread, making his skin more sensitive, so when Wolf started to cover the same area again, everything went to flame.

Rand's cock was screaming in agony in the harness because he was so damn hard. It was that thing that Cai had discovered in him, that the pain and the animal could be brought to the top, arouse Rand even as he suffered. That's what he wanted to do for Cai, with Cai. Sometimes to Cai. Wouldn't that be a hell of a fight?

Wolf traded the whip out for a metal paddle that was the hairbrush on steroids. It had raised edges from the holes drilled into it. And they cut skin. Bloodletting had been a key part of this scenario when Rand discussed it with Anwyn, though Rand's mind was in such a chaos of lust, rage and helpless emotion, their conversation was a long time ago and far away.

He strangled on his cries. When Wolf paused an eternity later to reach beneath him, let the harness out a hole and caress his balls, Rand almost groaned in relief.

"See, whelp?" Wolf whispered. "I can be your demon or your Daddy. All you have to do is call me Master."

Twice more Rand refused. The punishments became more severe. At one point, Wolf brought that cock close to his face, teased him with it, put it to his lips. He let Rand lick the tip, taste the thick fluid at the top. Then Wolf went around back and rubbed that tip against his rim. Rand couldn't help but lift his ass, strain for it, even as it felt like his chest was going to explode. His body wanted all of this...and his heart was breaking, just as he'd feared.

If Cai wasn't feeling him, hearing him, or reaching out to him, he might shatter. He was going to shatter. Rand had thought he could go all the way with this, to deal with the silence. But he didn't know if he could.

"Ready to be fucked?" Wolf said once more. Now he'd picked up a violet wand and was testing it on a metal spatula, the crackle sending up blue sparks. "No, don't call me Master yet. I know you were about to. Wait until I put this spatula against your balls and add the wand to it. Nice little jolt. Don't want you ruining all my fun."

He came back to Rand's face, but he squatted, touching his jaw, his thumb sliding along Rand's lips. Wolf became more serious, his deep voice even lower. "It's okay to give it up, baby," he murmured. "You're a tough bastard, but if he's not smart enough to claim your ass, I can give you what you need. All it takes is one little word."

Master. All he had to do was call him Master. Anwyn was right about Wolf being one of her best. He'd figured out it was Rand's trigger. Each time Cai had used the word, or Rand had spoken it, it had held such special significance on both sides. But his cock was impossibly hard, his body was aching, his heart was going to explode. He couldn't take anymore. Didn't matter if the rest of him was screaming *no*, there wasn't going to be anything better than this waiting for him if Wolf let him loose. Might as well get an amazing fuck from a guy straight out of a firefighter beefcake calendar, so the night wouldn't be a total loss.

He might not be able to look at himself in the mirror later, but he'd be headed back to West Virginia in the morning. Back to Fane and the second-best choice of lives he'd been offered.

He wet his lips.

You call that fucking bastard Master, you come for him, and he will not live to see fucking sunrise. And I'll fuck you over his fucking beautiful corpse.

It was amazing, how hearing the voice of the person he'd most wanted to hear for over two weeks could be as powerful as a stroke of his cock right on the edge of a universe-shattering climax. Rand almost lost it right there, but he managed to call it back, to save Wolf's life.

Cai's tone said he meant it. He'd do it. The vampire really needed to work on his humanitarian side.

"Sunset," Rand said. His safe word.

Wolf was gratifyingly disappointed, but Rand suspected Anwyn had prepped him for what might happen, because he took it all with good grace. Or his Dom side was professional enough to override his vampire take-what-I-want impulses, something Rand had to guess was pretty unique.

He immediately removed Rand's bonds, helped ease him back to the mat, and treated the cuts he'd inflicted on Rand's skin. Underscoring that impulse control, Wolf didn't seem to get distracted by Rand's blood, though Rand noticed Wolf did that clean up more swiftly than the rest of his aftercare, but all without stealing a taste.

Then the Dom gave him a massage that made Rand want to hump the mat and let go right then. Wolf knew it, offering a velvet chuckle and a friendly ass slap before he clasped Rand's hand and helped him to his feet, tossing him his clothes.

A staff worker brought in a change for Wolf, so he hitched on parachute fabric cargo pants over snug boxers, and shrugged into an open white shirt made of some type of gauzy linen. He looked like he should be stretched out on a lounger on some Bahama beach. He made sure Rand drank some more water and sat with him. Engaged him in casual chitchat that Rand realized the Dom was using to gauge the sharpness of his mind, make sure that he was a hundred percent.

Cai had said only one other thing.

Two hours.

Rand couldn't say what Cai's terse command meant in terms of things going forward, but it meant one thing for sure. Cai was coming. He wasn't here yet, but he'd be here soon. He hadn't been thousands of miles away, out of range of their mind-link. Rand took that as a hopeful sign.

No matter the irrationality of it, he wanted to put on his clothes and head out right away, but Wolf wouldn't let him go until he felt right about his physical and emotional state.

"Don't test me, whelp," the Dom had said, half-seriously. "If I have to put you on the ground and sit on you for thirty minutes, I will. My dick alone is heavy enough to pin you to the ground."

Rand had snorted, but he pushed down his anxiety and reasoned he'd probably go crazy if he had two hours with nothing but his own speculation for company. So he sat with Wolf on a couch in a quiet corner of the bar area for about a half hour and admittedly enjoyed the male's version of "after" aftercare.

Though he was sure Wolf was aware that Rand knew he was a vampire, Rand decided to leave that alone. Opening that door meant quid pro quo, and he didn't know Wolf well enough to give him clues as to what Rand's "otherness" was. But he liked the guy. His cock really liked him, but Rand suspected there wasn't a gay male or straight woman on the planet who wouldn't agree with that assessment.

So they talked about Atlanta, the club. Rand asked some more questions about BDSM stuff, increasing his knowledge base. Wolf didn't react like Rand was a clueless idiot, though Rand was sure his questions proved just how virgin-new he was to a lot of this stuff.

Wolf confirmed he had combat training and had served in the military, which told Rand he was a made vampire. He hadn't seen anyone hovering too near the male, so Rand surmised Wolf didn't have a servant yet. Lucky bastard, whoever it turned out to be. Or female, because, like a lot of vampires, Wolf seemed to radiate equal sexual warmth toward the male and female staff members who stopped by to speak briefly to him, when it was clear he was in a social conversation, not a session. Apparently, he was part of management, reinforcing Anwyn's high opinion of him.

But as good as the company was, the need to move, to run, grew too much. "I think I'm good," Rand said, rising. Wolf's gaze swept him, assessing, but he must have passed, for he rose, extending a hand.

"If ever you need to reach an important decision like that again, I hope I'll be at the front of the line to help with it. You're tough, man. I loved it. Would have loved it more if I could see it through." Wolf winked. "Keep me in mind."

"I will. And if ever I need to invade a small country and need a one-man battering ram, you'll be at the top of that list, too."

"Done my time in those war zones. Prefer this kind. But for the right cause, I'll always be there. That's the code."

"Yeah." Rand had never served, but in protecting his family, he knew exactly what Wolf meant. He clasped the man's hand, enjoyed the strong handshake, and parted ways with him.

Anwyn was in the building somewhere, but occupied, so Rand scrawled out a quick note to her, leaving it with James. Maybe he'd come back and take her to dinner in a couple days. She could bring Gideon along and they could hope that Cai wouldn't try to stab the former vampire hunter with a fork.

As he stepped out of Club Atlantis and lifted his head, Rand closed his eyes, opened all his senses. Both that of the wolf and the third marked servant. He and Wolf had been able to discuss some shared favorite parts of Atlanta, because Rand had been here a weekend or two with Dylef. They'd come to see Cirque du Soleil, stayed in a fancy hotel downtown. Just a weekend away from the farm, the kids, Sheba waving them off and teasing them about needing their "guy time."

In an urban center, a shifter always knew the area parks. He visualized Stone Mountain for Cai now, where the Confederate generals Lee and Jackson, as well as Jefferson Davis, were impressively carved into the mountain's face in a three-acre bas-relief. He made it clear the park was where he was going, where he'd be. Where he hoped Cai would come. Then Rand ducked into the cab he'd requested the hostess call for him, returned to his hotel, picked up his motorcycle and headed for that destination.

The acceleration and roar of the engine matched what was going on inside him. Two hours. If Cai was punctual—lesser miracles had probably been known to happen—that wasn't long from now.

If the vampire wasn't feeling contrary, that is. In which case, Cai might stop at a Starbuck's for a cup of coffee. Finding a secluded area near the park's campground, Rand parked the motorcycle and stripped down, putting the clothes in the saddle bags. Then he shifted.

God, it felt good. He needed to hunt, to take the edge off. Because he was hungry, he flushed and caught a rabbit for dinner. While he hadn't agreed to pursue more in-depth healing things, he had listened to some of the physical therapy stuff Sangra's friends had recommended. It had kept him limber enough to catch small game, if he used stealth in place of speed.

But he could still run, thank God, even if he couldn't run as fast. After eating, Rand explored, avoiding the attraction areas and sticking to the forest trails. He found his way up the mountain and trotted along the top edge above the carved generals. He paused there to howl at the moon, his wolf a silhouette against its light. He received no answer, except from a couple of dogs. No wolves in this part of the world.

But there are things that will hunt with you.

Cai's voice. It set off a ripple through Rand's every nerve, his heart and gut. Then the vampire did what Rand had hoped he would do. For the first time since Savannah, Cai opened the connection between their minds, a binding that filled Rand, making him realize exactly how empty he'd felt without it.

It was also something a servant could follow like a scent trail straight home.

Rand plunged back into the forest. Over bushes, through them, over and between rocks. An edgy need took hold, the predator and hungry male coming together. He needed, wanted. He'd had blood taken from his flesh but not consumed, his cock worked out with no release, and been told only one Master could have that from him. And guess what? That was the male he wanted to give that. The only one to whom he would offer his throat, his capitulation.

Was a hell of a way of showing it.

As Rand crossed a clearing in several powerful leaps, he was hit in the side and rolled. He snapped, but no matter how charged up he was, Cai for once had the clear advantage. The vampire wasn't in the mood for mercy or conversation.

Shift, goddamn you.

Rand was already in the process, so that when they came to a skidding stop on the forest floor, his body was a hundred percent human.

Cai attacked his mouth, with hard, single-minded purpose. A tumultuous mix of possessive, desire-driven fury. The tempting hints of this side of the vampire, revealed in greater or lesser amounts so many times, had led Rand to take this gamble. That he could drive it up a few more notches, with the right provocation.

He'd unleashed a beast.

Rand groaned against the wave of relentless demand, a blazing hellfire. The vampire had him on his back, body pinning him down, hand clamped over one wrist. No give and take. Only taking. But Rand had his own needs, and he'd fight for them. When Cai broke the kiss to stare down at Rand, Rand curled a lip at him.

You wanted to bust my ass for letting Wolf have it. It's here and waiting, vampire. If you have the balls to take everything I'm offering.

Cai's gaze had that predatory glitter that was terrifying if you were his food, and impossible to resist if you were simply his. As he bared his fangs, Rand saw the new one, with the tiny skull and crossbones etched on it. Cai's tongue flicked behind it, resulting in an almost unnoticeable click...but a very noticeable extension of the fang, that matched the natural lengthening of the real one.

It was totally badass, and Rand hardened further, imagining both fangs sinking into his throat. He wanted the vampire to feed from him.

Cai's gaze heated further. "Lift your chin," he demanded.

Rand complied. Cai dropped his head. At the first touch of his mouth, Rand closed his eyes and shuddered, pure relief and desire combined. He curled the fingers of his free hand in Cai's side, in the stuff of his shirt. When the vampire bit into the artery, Rand's fingers convulsed, and the shirt tore. He didn't hesitate to take advantage of it, touch sliding along bare skin, the firm flesh over Cai's ribs and down to his lean waist. The solid angle of hip bone, accessible below the loose-enough waistband of his jeans.

Cai reached between them and seized Rand's bare cock, tugging on it, nearly lifting his hips off the ground. Rand groaned.

"Whose is this?" the vampire demanded.

"Whose do you want it to be?" Rand said, just as fierce. Cai's grip tightened and Rand let out an oath.

"I can fuck you. That's it," the vampire said.

"Lot of talk. Haven't done it yet."

Cai's eyes sparked. He stood up, looming over Rand, one foot planted between his spread legs, the other on the outside, his thick-tread shoe pressed against Rand's thigh.

"I want to fuck, not fight." Cai fished lube out of his jeans pocket and dropped it on Rand's stomach. "Get me ready for your ass."

He pulled off the torn shirt in a mouthwatering motion, and opened the jeans with impatience, freeing a cock as thick and hard as Rand's own was.

Rand sat up. He was aware of how Cai looked at him, the dangerous avarice suggesting the vampire might not stop with blood; he might devour Rand whole. Despite Rand's combative attitude, he wasn't immune to that level of need. He just wanted to make damn sure Cai knew that Rand wanted—and could take—whatever he brought.

"We'll see when I'm reaming your ass for the tenth time tonight."

Rand saved his retort. He had better things to do. Fisting Cai's cock, getting it all glistening with the oil, made a bunch of things in his own loins and lower regions tighten up with a hunger so bad there was only one way to express it.

Cai felt it, too. His Master rocked into his touch, his hand landing on Rand's head to tangle in his hair, grip and pull. Like Wolf had done, only this felt so much better...God, so much.

Cai did it hard enough to jerk Rand's head back, bare his throat. Rand drew in a surprised gasp as Cai struck, bending fast to take the hard bite. The other wound was closed now, but this was about marking, not feeding. When Cai pulled away, Rand thought there'd be an abrasion there he'd feel below the skin for days, no matter his healing ability.

Cai shoved him back down onto his ass and used one foot against Rand's thigh to widen the spread of his knees. Rand showed teeth, but Cai put his hiking shoe against Rand's cock and balls and applied pressure.

"You've pushed me as far as you'll get away with tonight, wolf," he said softly.

Rand could have countered that threat, but Cai wasn't waiting. In a swift move, he'd pushed the jeans off his hips and dropped to his knees between Rand's spread legs. Hooking Rand's leg over his elbow, Cai lodged the head of his cock where he wanted it. "Now," he said. "You give me the word he wanted."

"He had to beat me to make me even consider it," Rand countered. God, he was dying. His cock had never felt so aching hard.

Cai bared his fangs again. There was still a trace of Rand's blood on one, adding to the impact and menace. "You ask, or I jack off on top of you, watching you suffer."

Rand wet his lips. Their eyes were so close. "Cai..."

"Shut up. Say it. Now."

Rand's whole body screamed with need, and Cai would hold there until the end of time. Rand said it.

"Master."

Cai moved forward what seemed like a bare millimeter, stretching the opening enough to rock Rand with an explosive burst of feeling. "Again," he demanded softly.

"Master."

Slow, steady, a millimeter at a time, their eyes locked the whole time. Rand said it again. And again. And again.

Despite all the violence in the air, the unresolved crap beneath it, it felt like coming home, fulfillment. Everything.

Cai's eyes flickered, but he didn't respond to the impulsive thought. "So could he do...this?" Cai asked, pushing in deep, hitting the right note so Rand's feet curled and his body arched to Cai's.

"Didn't get...that far. And he was hung like a fucking moose." Rand let out another half snarl, half moan, as the taunt had Cai shoving harder into him. The vampire was no lightweight himself.

"You just have a tight, virgin ass." Cai grunted. "Every time. Fucking love taking it."

Rand couldn't keep up. Cai let him hold onto nothing. His eyes lingered on Rand's face, sweeping over his body, down to Rand's cock, beating a tattoo on his lower belly with Cai's strokes. "Grip it," the vampire said. "Try to work it while I'm inside you."

Rand did his best, but the vampire was too good at this stuff. Cai gripped his hand, the two of them double fisting Rand's cock between the friction of their bodies. Rand grew more savage and mindless. They both did, rutting on the forest floor, with groans, and gasps, pleas and demands that intertwined and swapped until it was hard to know where one of them ended and the other began.

Rand freed his wrist from Cai's manacle grip so their fingers were a tight knot on the ground together. He wasn't going over the edge without that connection. Cai's hand convulsed in his, but he didn't pull away.

"Come for me, wolf."

Rand was so close he started to come as Cai said it, his seed shooting out over his chest. Yet even as he gasped through it, Rand spoke in the vampire's head.

You come for me, too. Master.

The two of them were like a pair of combatants, locked together in the darkness of the void. But fuck, nothing had ever felt so good as that climax, seizing Rand hard and taking him over. Except Cai releasing with him, both of them riding together, over wave after wave of sensation.

Cai spilled hard and deep. It took a long time for them to stop moving together in that endlessly pleasurable rhythm, well past when they were spent. But Cai finally let his arms bend, bringing their upper bodies closer.

The forest noises resumed, and they were a quiet part of it. Rand inhaled Cai's scent and realized that unique identifier could make his brain simply stop. It was that way, when a wolf bonded with another.

Rand started to slide his arms around the vampire to draw him all the way down, let him rest. He wanted to feel their hearts thudding together.

Cai stiffened and drew back, pulling out. They'd been done, their cocks ready for a break, but it still left an empty feeling high in Rand's chest.

Much as Rand wanted it to be, he'd known this wall wouldn't be breached the way wolves would do it, with a simple exchange of feeling. But that was okay. Cai was here. They'd figure it out.

Cai didn't act like he'd heard that. He sure as hell didn't act like he had the same level of confidence in that as Rand did. He sat back on his heels, running a hand over his face. Abruptly, he stood and tugged up his jeans. Picking up his shirt, he yanked it onto his shoulders, though he left it open.

Rand sat up, studying the male as he prowled around the clearing. Even after the violent coupling, aggressive energy was spilling off him.

"Would you have done it?" Cai said. "If I hadn't spoken?"

Rand had known the question was coming, the answer Cai would demand to know.

"Yeah."

Cai pivoted to face him. "You were going to have a meaningless, stupendously pleasurable fuck. Just to say piss off to me for giving you the silent treatment."

"No. So I could put off for a little longer the way it was going to feel, knowing you didn't want to be with me."

Something flashed through Cai's blue eyes, then shuttered. "I never said that."

"Your letter said that. Brothers-in-arms. Buddies. Let's be friends." Rand growled it. He rose, careless of his nudity. Other parts of him were warring between the want and need. "Next time, just write *fuck you* on the mirror and be done with it."

"What you want from me makes no sense."

"Then why are you here?" Rand demanded. Fuck it. He'd let temper take the lead. Two weeks of stewing over that note didn't sound bad, but wanting this male and not having him for that long was a lifetime.

Cai scoffed. "Figured it was obvious. I wanted to mark every inch that bastard touched. Be inside you. Inside your ass and your mouth. I want to jack off over your body, so you never go down that road again. Another shifter, fine. Human, whatever. Not a fucking vampire."

A quiver went through Rand at the words. Buck ass naked, there was no way he could conceal his reaction to them, and damn if the third mark libido didn't have his cock twitching, despite releasing a handful of minutes ago.

Rand could handle the vampire being an asshole. What he wouldn't tolerate was him lying. And he was lying his ass off.

Rand offered a short, curt nod. "Fine then." Holding Cai's gaze, he closed the distance between them. Dropped to his knees in front of the vampire. "Why don't you start with my mouth? I'll get you started again."

Cai stared at him. "You can't pretend you don't need more. You don't want this. I'm not what you need. You need a family."

Rand rose, coming toe-to-toe with him. "What the *fuck* do you think you and I are?"

~

The vehemence struck Cai in the chest, opened a window he didn't want to look through. The view was murky to him, but Rand could apparently see through it clearly. Which meant the wolf was delusional.

Two and a half fucking weeks. Cai had lasted two fucking weeks before he couldn't stand it any longer. Admittedly, Rand had probably accelerated the timeline with his stunt tonight, but who was Cai kidding? He could have held out maybe another week. Tops. And Rand was continuing to talk, saying things that were so terrifying, Cai should be running.

"You may not have sought that, but I don't believe you don't want it. I'm offering it to you, freely, willingly, to figure out where it will take us. You're the bravest and stupidest male I've ever met, because you back down from nothing." Rand's gaze flashed. "After all the things you've faced, I can't believe you'll back down from this."

Cai gripped Rand's shoulder, digging in. Part reproof, part warning, but the second he made the contact, it became about more than that. He didn't want to fucking let go. They were standing so close, barely two feet between them. His wolf was as immodestly naked as he often was, but Cai was the one who felt stripped.

"Doesn't matter," Cai said. "I don't know how to love someone."

"Bullshit." Rand said it evenly, without malice. "You took off because you wanted what was best for me. You were willing to give up your own happiness for it."

"Well, happiness is a strong word," Cai pointed out. "And I abandoned you at a vampire stronghold and left you to find your way home."

"I did. I just had to come to Atlanta to bring home back to me."

Too much. Way too much. Cai should have kept it on the footing of him busting Rand's ass in all sorts of obscene, unspeakably delicious ways for being at Club Atlantis. Not allowing the conversation to go in this direction. He had no idea where to go from here with it. He was going to get hot and hard again soon, which meant he'd say stupid things. Even now, he wanted the wolf under him, but there were other things causing problems. Like that strangling thing, and apparently shrapnel had exploded inside his chest.

"Don't talk anymore," Cai said. He moved away. Not a retreat, but to deliberately establish distance. Rand ignored his words and followed him. There was a big-ass rock in front of Cai and a big-ass wolf behind him. One who would not shut up.

"You took care of me," Rand continued. "Helped me want to live again. Yes, because that was what you wanted, but later on more was driving it than that. Because it bothered me, you even stopped cursing as much, for a second or two. Though you took it out on me in other ways. Swear jar, my ass. Literally."

Cai huffed a chuckle, but he stared at the rock, wondering what it would be like to achieve his lifelong dream of becoming stone, incapable of feeling anything, so nothing would ever hurt. So something, anything, would finally stop fucking hurting.

Can't fight what you can't change. Hurts. Just want to stop...hurting.

Cai suddenly recalled his wolf's thought, all that time ago. In the same heartbeat, he knew the truth. The meaning of those words to Cai, as much as the wolf's fine ass, was why Cai had refused to let him die.

Cai. Rand closed the distance between them. Didn't touch, but was so close. So fucking close.

"If you leave them to stay with me," Cai said bitterly, "it will always be because you settled, gave up the family idea. I'll be less. I'll feel that. Fucking pathetic, but there it is."

A sudden heavy silence. Cai wished he hadn't said it. He could feel the wolf's eyes upon him and, as usual, they would be seeing too much. He should just turn around, deliver on his threat. Fuck Rand a dozen more times, until the wolf would be crawling away from him, barely able to walk, finally understanding just how much Cai wanted and could take from him, without giving enough back.

Cai stiffened when Rand placed his mouth on the sun-like scar beside his shoulder blade. He tasted flesh with tongue and caressing lips as his hands slid down Cai's back. Fanning them out to grip Cai's waist, Rand dipped his thumbs inside the waistband of the jeans, caressing the upper rise of Cai's buttocks.

"I thought the last two weeks at Fane's were hard on me," Rand murmured. "Every day hurt more and more. The nights; they were pure torture. But it was worse for you. You were alone. I didn't think about that."

Cai tried to jerk away from the contact. Rand moved with him, earning a hiss and answering it with a growl.

"It's no different between vampire and servant than it is in a pack," the wolf said. "I give up my choices to my alpha, because I trust that he'll care for me. Isn't that what a servant does with his Master?"

Cai turned his head, startled, and Rand met him, eye to intense eye. "You remember me saying I'd tell you sometime, how an alpha wolf approaches another alpha?"

"Yeah. I remember."

Rand nudged Cai forward so he was closer to the large rock. Then the shifter put a palm against it by Cai's shoulder, leaning forward so he could bring his mouth to the vampire's collar bone from behind. Rand tilted his head, nudging at Cai's jaw until he lifted it.

"The alpha adopts some of the same submissive body language as other wolves," Rand said in a husky voice. "So the other alpha knows he's not interested in a fight. He nips at his chin and throat."

Rand continued the demonstration, using teeth, mouth and tongue to arouse. "And to make the point, the wolf might go down on his belly and avert his gaze."

"Why do I expect you wouldn't do the averting gaze part?" Cai managed.

Rand half-chuckled. "It's not a capitulation. Just an acknowledgment of what I'm willing to give."

Cai's pulse accelerated as Rand's capable hands slid over his ass and thighs when he dropped to a kneeling position behind Cai. The shifter was too close for Cai to turn, unless Cai swung a leg over his head. He would have done that, but Rand had reached around him and slipped the button of his jeans, taking them back down off his ass.

"You're right. A vampire's body can take a hell of a lot of punishment and still be beautiful," Rand said. "But in this case, I think that's because of the male inside."

~

Cai's fingers dug into the rock, a harsh noise breaking from his throat when Rand parted his buttocks and licked his rim, reaching beneath him to caress his testicles.

The vampire could try to change their position. But Rand made sure it felt too damn good for Cai to work on the thought. *Let me please you, Master.*

Cai stilled at the mental address, his breath rasping. "I'm still going to fuck you through a wall," he promised, a hoarse threat.

Okay. Rand continued to play with his ass with a heated, wet tongue. Cai's hips flexed, his cock pressing in a humping rhythm against the rock as that oh-too-fucking-good-to-describe feeling rocketed through him. He opened his mind further, let Rand have the gift of knowing what he was doing to him. In return, Rand's heart cracked open.

I want to be inside you, Master. Let me fill you. Let me fill up everything.

Yeah, he hadn't won the war, but Cai was here, and he'd finally said by implication what Rand had suspected was true. Cai had never asked for a family, for a pack, but he wanted, needed one. Everything that Rand had learned about Cai over the past few weeks, and everything that Cai knew about him, had tangled up into a big knotted ball that would likely never get unknotted. Rand was okay with that. They'd continue to fight it out, and that might take a couple decades. Or longer, if Rand stayed with him, as his servant.

Cai went even more still, a clue he was listening in. Good. But Rand didn't want things to go wrong if Cai got stuck on that, so he renewed his efforts, closing his hand around Cai's cock to pump it. Hadn't they just done this, a matter of minutes before? Didn't seem to matter. The vampire was already stiffening. The same response gripped Rand when Cai lifted his hips, grinding his muscular ass in Rand's face, wanting more of his tongue. Cai left furrows on the stone with his fingernails.

"Fuck, hell...fuck me, wolf."

Rand still had the lube within reach, and he one-handed it on himself while he kept after Cai's ass, using the long fingers of his other hand to keep the vampire open to him.

When Rand rose to his feet and pressed against the vampire's back, he savored their bodies straining, tight against one another. Cai's head tilted. His eyes were closed.

"Just drill it. Fuck, it can hurt. I just want you all the way in."

That last part was exactly what Rand wanted, but he took his time, wanting his Master to feel it the way he did, all the way to the root. Not just the root of his cock. The third marking linked the soul of vampire and servant. Rand wanted that bond. What's more, he wanted to know the path to the very center of a vampire's soul. This vampire.

Cai had thought the absence of a finish line meant he could never quit. Whereas Rand had tried to draw his own before it was time. For the first time, he realized he was glad that he'd failed. And that the vampire had never given up.

Rand could feel Cai intertwined with his thoughts, listening, feeling. Having his own reaction, and it wasn't a bad one.

Rand wrapped his arm around Cai's chest as he thrust inside him, setting a slow, easy rhythm that gave them an excruciating stroke on each forward and retreat motion. Cai had adjusted his hips toward Rand to make the angle work. While one hand was braced against the rock, the other gripped Rand's forearm as the feelings built. Rand closed his eyes. He wondered if the vampire realized how much of himself he was giving. Rand didn't need access to his mind. He could feel, scent, taste and simply know, deep inside, what was happening in the roller coaster of Cai's emotions and physical response.

Then Cai's mind opened even more to Rand, so wide he felt like he did when he was running full out in the forest, leaping and twisting through endless passages, open and closed spaces.

Hell, I might as well let you all the way in. You're already there. Know more about my thoughts than my mind could ever tell you.

Rand smiled against his shoulder, brushing his lips against the flexing muscle. He didn't stop with that, rubbing his cheek there to enhance the contact, the marking.

Marking could be an act of dominance, of connecting, of recognition. Of ownership. Rand felt some of all of that, and the vampire didn't seem inclined to argue. At least at this second. That was miracle enough from the contrary male.

"Fuck you," Cai muttered. Rand slid his palm down Cai's chest, over the taut bud of his nipple. Along the sectioned stomach muscles, to the iron evidence of his arousal. Curling his fingers around it, Rand began to stroke it in rhythm with his thrusts, his fingers playing, caressing, nails digging in at unexpected moments, thumb rubbing over the slit and spreading the thick fluid gathering there.

Cai groaned at the sensation. They moved together, Cai's hand slamming against the rock, sending a vibration through them both. Then the vampire was coming, body jerking, beautiful, animal-like sounds breaking from his lips.

Come for me, wolf.

Rand was already hovering on that precipice. His movements became stronger, more forceful, a growl meeting Cai's snarl as he thrust deeper, harder, into his ass. He let his release fill the vampire, wet heat. His teeth were set to Cai's shoulder, fingers digging into his chest as he took them to the end of it.

Or to the beginning.

❧

As they finished, they slowly slid down so they were kneeling together. When Rand pulled out, they were nested hip to hip, shoulder to shoulder. So much of the wolf was with Rand, even in human form. Rand proved it when he slid an arm across Cai's chest and laid his cheek in between his shoulder blades. It was a sheltering, protective move that also drew comfort. A balance. Rand was good at balance. Cai wasn't.

Even so, Cai turned his head to meet the shifter's mouth with his own. The annoyance and anger about Rand's stunt, his irritability and confusion about the things he didn't understand, had receded. The kiss wasn't edgy and angry. It was soft, tender, long and heart-altering. When Cai finally raised his head, he realized he'd turned, was framing the shifter's face to hold him still and savor his mouth. Rand was gripping his forearms.

Rand had called him Master. More than once. Cai liked that, way too much.

"Don't get used to it," Rand said, in a voice laden with that sexy, post-coital thickness. "Asshole fits you a lot better."

480

Cai tried for a smile, failed. He couldn't get used to it, because he still hadn't agreed to this. And Rand damn well knew it, even if he was pretending otherwise. "How about the kid thing?"

At Rand's bland expression, Cai shot him a don't-bullshit-me look. "I know you want them."

"There's a lot of ways to do that. If we decide to expand our pack, we can."

Before Cai could point out just having a servant was freaking him out, Rand pushed onward. "Dovia's father is ill and the wrong kind of wolves are circling the door, right? Leona is a servant. Brian thinks Greenwald has less than a couple more years to live, because he's having less success controlling his disease. When he dies, so will Leona. Before Dovia is thirty years old, a fledgling among born vampires, she'll be alone."

Cai narrowed his gaze at Rand. "When did you have this discussion with Brian?"

"When I met with him to discuss the marking, I also asked him about that." Rand's eyes sparked with a pointed complaint about Cai's note and taking off, but he continued, leaving that alone. "Sounds like she'll need a vampire willing to mentor her, protect her. Why not us? You live a long time and, as your servant, I'll be around quite a while. I bet Lyssa would support that, because unlike Tyra and Chavez, we don't have any designs on Dovia's wealth."

Cai drew back and sat down, rubbing his forehead. "You have us adopting a vampire and taking on the cadre of opportunistic sycophants around her. Even before we pick out curtains."

A slight smile touched Rand's firm mouth. "I don't have us doing anything. I'm just pointing out the possibility. We can be a big or small family, but it starts here, you and me, the two pillars holding up whatever we decide to put under its roof."

He curled his hand around Cai's forearm. Cai had drawn up his knees and linked his arms around them. Rand was totally missing that this conversation had turned Cai into a vertical fetal ball.

Noticing it, vampire. Just not mentioning it, to spare an insult to your manhood.

Cai coughed over a half laugh. That explosion in his chest still hurt, but it was hurting less. He found that even scarier, because it meant he was listening to Rand.

"We have time to decide," the wolf said. "We'll go to the desert a few months, think it through. Hell, I'm still working through shit, too. This whole vampire-servant thing, it messes up my head sometimes. You've seen it."

Rand took a breath. For the first time, his gaze skittered away from Cai's, which sharpened Cai's attention on him. "When I was there at Fane's, late at night, and then here in Atlanta, the few days in the hotel... That despair...the grief. When I realized you might be gone for good, and that feeling came back, I knew—"

Cai was out of his curl in a blink. He had Rand by the throat and on his back, his body pressed to him and fuck, he felt so good. But Cai didn't let that detract from the red haze covering his vision. "Never," Cai snarled. "You got it? I don't care whether we're a family or not. That thought's never crossing your mind again. If it does, I will put a flagpole up your ass to give you something else to think about."

Rand blinked up at him, and slowly a smile tugged his lips in a sensuous curve. "There's my Master," he said.

"Fuck. Fudge. Darn." Cai sat back on his heels and rubbed his hand across his face once more.

"If you'd let me finish before you had your caveman moment," Rand said, earning that narrow look again, "I was going to say I realized those feelings wouldn't ever push me down that road again. And that's because of you."

Rand sat up and touched his arm, but his face remained resolute. "I'm more than capable of deciding where I want to be, and who with. You told the Council not to take that from me. You don't get to do it, either. You don't want me, I'm gone. But you'll have to make me believe it."

"Fuck me." Cai sighed. "Well, in those touchy-feely animal movies, they do it by throwing rocks at the wild creature and screaming, 'Go! I don't want you anymore!' And the wolf or deer or water buffalo or whatever goes away, looking back like he's really hurt. Though he usually comes back at just the right moment to save the day."

"You tried that tactic once before. Not falling for it again. And you throw a rock at me, I'll feed it to you," Rand promised.

"I throw a rock at you, and you'll be knocked unconscious. Or have a great big through-and-through hole through your head."

Rand adjusted so they were sitting shoulder to shoulder. "Have you watched any TV since Lassie?"

"That kind of scene has been in plenty of dog movies," Cai said defensively. "And Lassie's been in syndication forever. Some of the people I've taken...I've stayed at their houses a few days. Watched their TV, that kind of thing."

"Oh." Rand sobered, making Cai wish he hadn't brought it up. But then Rand nudged him. "Did you mean it, about not killing humans anymore?"

"I'm considering some changes in my diet. You know, only criminal assholes from here forward. Got to expend my rage against life somewhere."

At Rand's look, Cai sighed again. "You wondered why I didn't razz you about not knowing how to arouse a woman. I was told I could have sex with a human before I killed them. I thought that meant rape, and I had no stomach for that."

He shook his head. "Lodell pointed out that if I could make it pleasurable, make them think something else was about to happen, then they wouldn't suffer. And since I still killed my prey, the Trads would feel I was being ruthless like I was supposed to be. That's why I learned how to pleasure a woman. As a way to make her death more humane. I actually envy you your innocence, because it's for the right reasons."

He didn't look toward Rand. He didn't need to do so, the feeling from the shifter complicated and painful. Cai didn't want to unravel that to see what was inside. "So, see? On top of not knowing how to be a family, I'm not a good man, Rand."

"I think you want to be. You've just never had anyone who appreciated the effort before, who could tell you that it matters. Every step you take back toward who you want to be matters, no matter how slow, or if you get knocked back some."

"Very inspirational."

"Shut up." Rand sighed and touched Cai's face, bringing his eyes to him. "For once, just shut up, and feel. Feel what I believe about you. Feel what I feel for you."

Cai immediately wanted to take off, but Rand had his arm curled around his thigh, his other hand around his nape. "Climb inside my head, vampire, and stay there. Stay as long as you like, until you figure it out. Drop down all the way to my soul, and you'll find a lot of things there. Dylef, Fane, Sheba, the pups. But you'll also find you. Solid, permanent and big as life right in the middle of them. A part I want to keep there, and right here. Figure it out, and I'll work on doing the same."

Cai made a frustrated noise and pushed away, but only to flop down on his back. "You are such a pain in my ass."

But Rand followed him down, amusing Cai in a despairing sort of way by putting his head on Cai's chest, his arm loosely around Cai's waist. Cai realized if he imagined Rand as a wolf, this was how he'd laid upon Cai days ago, only Cai had been on his stomach and the wolf's head had been resting above his hips.

Cai ran a hand over the strong back that was pleasantly accessible to him in this position. "How can you be so sure of this shit?"

Rand's lips pulled in a smile. "I'm not sure about any of it. But I'm willing to take it on faith, figure it out as we go. You remember that T-shirt Jacob was wearing in Savannah? *If you love something, set it free. If it doesn't come back, hunt it down and kill it.* That's a very wolf sentiment, you know."

Cai snorted. "Not too far off from vampires, either." He went still, though. The night seemed to close in, become colder. Despite the words and feelings shared, the shadows of the past were never very far away, the darkness too close. Maybe what he feared most was losing his willingness to be lonely. Knowing it, that darkness would rise to take him, and take Rand down with it.

For decades, a fifteen-year-old kid had lurked in his subconscious. Whether he'd experienced a bloodcurdling victory or deep despair, or anywhere in between, the question was always the same.

Am I lost or found?

Rand held him even closer, speaking in Cai's ear as he brushed it with his lips. "Perhaps both. And that's okay, too."

~

They lay together a long time. Murmured, stroked. Listened to the night. Cai never said yes, not with his lips. But Rand didn't listen to his words. *Take it on faith.* The wolf saw something in Cai he couldn't see for himself. And somewhere in the past two weeks, the past few minutes, that faith had set up a small camp inside of Cai. When he realized it, the significance of it hit him hard.

He had a permanent servant. A family. Rand considered him his pack.

Lust had brought Cai back here to chase Rand down. That's what he told himself. But Rand had brought heart and soul into it, and here they were.

Cai swept his gaze over his servant. His servant. Hell, he was going to be like a girl with an engagement ring, captivated by the sparkle of the two words.

All that furred, tanned, muscled chest, bare flexing haunch. His servant's cock was looking decidedly interested in something again...

Or someone. Rand sat up and stretched, cracking his back and tilting his head to gaze down at Cai. His brown hair slipped over one broad shoulder. Cai reached up and tangled his fingers in it.

"You thinking about that big-dick Dom at Club Atlantis?" Cai asked. "That why you're getting hard again? Can't blame you. Let's go back. I'll put him down hard and we'll both fuck him."

Rand's lips curved, his eyes showing a feral light. "I don't want you anywhere near him. You'll decide to keep him."

"Sorry, I've got all the family I can handle now. And it's a lot more trouble than it's worth."

Rand's blue eyes warmed, and damn if it didn't tilt Cai's heart over, just a little. He found his own lips curving.

"I'm worth it, vampire," Rand responded. "So are you. Catch me if you can."

Rand was off at a run, one long stride, two strides. In a bound of motion, full of sinuous power, he shifted in mid-air and hit the ground as a wolf, running full out.

Show off.

Cai waited all of three heartbeats, maybe two. Then he was after him. He caught up fast, but they didn't lock in sensual combat, not yet. He melded with Rand's mind, immersed himself in the wolf's love of running with a pack, of play, the nipping at heels or flanks or ruff as they ran. He bumped Cai's shoulder once and almost sent him tumbling over a log. He huffed a snort and caught up to tug the wolf's tail, sending him in a comical spin to nip at Cai's hand, before they were off again. Just running for the joy of it.

Eventually, he'd grab him, send him tumbling, hold that warm, furry body close. He'd whisper in his mind, tell him to shift so Cai could take him again, take it deep, have Rand at every physical and mental level, because that was what a servant could offer. Cai would also *really* kick his ass over the Atlantis Dom thing and enjoy every damn minute of it. There'd be restraints, blunt objects. Cai's fist was going to be up his ass and bring Rand to a climax, so Rand would know the true knife edge between arousal and not necessarily unbearable pain, but a wise anxiety about the limits of his anatomy.

But for now, they ran together. Running toward whatever challenges they'd face, toward the demons they still had left to fight in their hearts and souls. He'd noted Rand was still having problems with that leg, favoring it as he ran. Which was probably why Cai had caught up with him. Not that Cai would admit that.

They'd talk to his friend in Syria about it, the sorceress with healing skills.

Because that was the way Rand had said it could work from now on. Neither one would be in the fight alone, and that would give life a lot more meaning. One day, Cai hoped he would believe that. If anyone could help him get there, he expected it would be Rand. And he'd try his damn level best to do the same for his wolf.

Be his family, his pack, his alpha.

His Master.

* * *

WANT MORE OF THE VAMPIRE QUEEN SERIES? It's 1941, and Nina is with the Australian Army Nurses Service in Singapore. What happens to her when the city falls to the Japanese will shatter Nina's soul. But life seems determined to give her more than she can bear. When her sister dies in a car crash, Nina is informed that she must take her place as an Inherited Servant, a human bound to the vampire world. She will be given to Lord Alistair, a vampire who sees Nina as his property, to do with as he pleases.

Even as she fights the decision, the ways in which Alistair commands her surrender leads her to a terrifyingly different understanding of her will and her dreams. By binding herself to him, can she become whole again, but in a way she never expected?

**CLICK HERE TO READ NOW
VAMPIRE'S EMBRACE**

Reading this in print format?
Look for it at your favorite book vendor!

ABOUT THE AUTHOR

Having penned over fifty acclaimed BDSM contemporary and paranormal titles, which includes six award-winning series, *Joey W. Hill* has been awarded the RT Book Reviews Career Achievement Award for Erotic Romance. A submissive herself, Hill brings authenticity to her intensely emotional love stories.

She is grateful for the support of a wonderful and enthusiastic readership, which allows her to live on her beloved Carolina coast with her even more beloved husband and menagerie of animals.

- On the Web: https://storywitch.com
- Twitter: https://twitter.com/JoeyWHill
- Facebook: https://facebook.com/JoeyWHillAuthor
- Facebook Fan Forum: https://facebook.com/groups/JWHMembersOnly
- MeWe: https://mewe.com/i/joeywhill
- GoodReads: https://www.goodreads.com/author/show/103359.Joey_W_Hill
- BookBub: https://bookbub.com/authors/joey-w-hill
- Amazon: https://amazon.com/Joey-W-Hill/e/B00IJSCIW0

ALSO BY JOEY W. HILL

Mirror of My Soul

Mistress of Redemption

Rough Canvas

Branded Sanctuary

Divine Solace

Worth The Wait

Truly Helpless

In His Arms

Ignition Sequence

Naughty Bits Series

Naughty Bits

Naughty Wishes

Vampire Queen Series

Vampire Queen's Servant

Mark of the Vampire Queen

Vampire's Claim

Beloved Vampire

Vampire Mistress *(VQS: Club Atlantis)*

Vampire Trinity *(VQS: Club Atlantis)*

Vampire Instinct

Bound by the Vampire Queen

Taken by a Vampire

The Scientific Method

Nightfall

Elusive Hero

Night's Templar

Vampire's Soul

Vampire's Embrace

Vampire Master *(VQS: Club Atlantis)*

Vampire Guardian *(VQS: Club Atlantis)*

Vampire's Choice

www.ingramcontent.com/pod-product-compliance
Lightning Source LLC
Chambersburg PA
CBHW051936020726
47501CB00001B/145